PENGUIN BOOKS

# MORE STORIES FROM THRUSH GREEN

Miss Read, or in real life Mrs Dora Saint, is a teacher by profession who started writing after the Second World War, beginning with light essays written for *Punch* and other journals. She has written on educational and country matters, and worked as a script-writer for the BBC. Miss Read is married to a retired schoolmaster and they have one daughter. They live in a tiny Berkshire hamlet. She is a local magistrate and her hobbies are theatre-going, listening to music and reading.

Miss Read is the author of numerous books, which have gained immense popularity for their humorous and honest depictions of English rural life, including, most recently, *The Year at Thrush Green* and *A Peaceful Retirement*. Many of her books are published by Penguin, together with seven omnibus editions. She has also written several books for children, including the Red Bus series for the very young (published in one volume by Puffin as *The Little Red Bus and Other Stories*), a cookery book, *Miss Read's Country Cooking*, and two autobiographical works, *A Fortunate Grandchild* and *Time Remembered*, published together in one volume as *Early Days*, with a new foreword by the author.

D1153839

'*Miss Read*'

# More Stories
# from
# Thrush Green

*Illustrated by*

*J. S. Goodall*

**PENGUIN BOOKS**

## PENGUIN BOOKS

Published by the Penguin Group
Penguin Books Ltd, 27 Wrights Lane, London W8 5TZ, England
Penguin Books USA Inc., 375 Hudson Street, New York, New York 10014, USA
Penguin Books Australia Ltd, Ringwood, Victoria, Australia
Penguin Books Canada Ltd, 10 Alcorn Avenue, Toronto, Ontario, Canada M4V 3B2
Penguin Books (NZ) Ltd, 182–190 Wairau Road, Auckland 10, New Zealand

Penguin Books Ltd, Registered Offices: Harmondsworth, Middlesex, England

*Battles at Thrush Green* first published by Michael Joseph Ltd 1975
Published in Penguin Books 1978
Copyright © Miss Read, 1975

*Return to Thrush Green* first published by Michael Joseph Ltd 1978
Published in Penguin Books 1980
Copyright © Miss Read, 1978

*Gossip from Thrush Green* first published by Michael Joseph Ltd 1981
Published in Penguin Books 1983
Copyright © Miss Read, 1981

Published in one volume as *More Stories from Thrush Green* 1985
9  10  8
All rights reserved

Printed in England by Clays Ltd, St Ives plc
Typeset in Monophoto Plantin

# Battles at Thrush Green

*To Norah*

*for times remembered*

*with love*

# Contents

# Part One

# Alarms and Excursions

## 1. Albert Piggott is Overworked

At a quarter to eight one fine September morning, Harold Shoosmith leant from his bedroom window and surveyed the shining face of Thrush Green.

The rising sun threw grotesquely elongated shadows across the grass. The statue of Nathaniel Patten cast one a dozen times its own length, with the head and shoulders at right angles to the rest, where it was thrown against the white palings next door to The Two Pheasants.

The shabby iron railings round the churchyard made cross-hatchings on the green, and the avenue of chestnut trees, directly in front of Harold's window, formed a shady tunnel with a striped floor of sunshine and shadow.

The view filled Harold Shoosmith with deep contentment. This was the place for retirement! After years in Africa, moving from one post to another, each hotter and more humid than the last, he had come home to roost at Thrush Green, the birthplace of Nathaniel Patten, whose missionary work he had so much admired, and whose memorial he had been instrumental in establishing.

But no living figures were apparent on this bright morning, with the exception of the Youngs' old spaniel Flo, who was ambling about examining the trees in the avenue in a perfunctory fashion. Nevertheless, the sound of distant whistling alerted Harold.

Someone in the wings was about to enter the empty stage, and very soon the stout figure of Willie Bond, one of Thrush Green's postmen, emerged from the lane, which leads to Nod and Nidden, and propped his bicycle against the hedge.

Tightening the belt of his dressing gown, Harold Shoosmith descended the stairs to greet his first caller.

'You gotter mushroom as big as a 'nouse in your 'edge,' announced Willie, handing in half a dozen letters.

'Let's see,' said Harold, following him down the path. Sure enough, at the foot of his hawthorn hedge, stood a splendid specimen, as big as a saucer, but young and beautiful. Two or three fine pieces of grass criss-crossed its satin tip where it had pushed its way into the world and, underneath, the gills were rosy pink and unbroken.

'Do fine for your breakfast,' said Willie, putting one foot on the pedal of his bicycle.

'Too much for me,' said Harold. 'Why don't you take it? After all, you found it.'

Willie shook his head.

'Never touches 'em. Them old things are funny. My auntie, down the mill, she died after havin' a dish of them for breakfast.'

'Surely she must have eaten toadstools by mistake?'

'Maybe. But she died anyway.'

He mounted his machine and began to weave away.

'Mind you,' he called back, 'she'd had dropsy for five years, but we always reckon it was the mushrooms what done for her in the end.'

Harold bent and retrieved the mushroom. The fragrance, as it left the ground, made him wonder, for one brief moment, if he could bother to cook some of it with a couple of rashers for his breakfast, as Willie had advised.

But he decided against it and, returning to the kitchen, set about making his usual coffee-and-toast repast, using the upturned mushroom as a decoration for the breakfast table.

His morning mail was unremarkable. Two bills, one receipt, a bulky and unsolicited package from *Reader's Digest* which must have cost a pretty penny to produce and was destined for the wastepaper basket unread, and a postcard from his old friend and neighbour Frank Hurst and his wife Phil, posted in Italy two weeks before, and extolling the beauties of the scenery.

It was while he was sipping his second cup of coffee, and wondering idly why literary men always seemed to write such a vile hand, that the door burst open to reveal Betty Bell, his exuberant domestic help. As always, she was breathless and smiling. She might just have galloped up the steep hill from Lulling non-stop, but in fact, as Harold well knew, she had simply wheeled her bicycle from the village school next door where she had been 'putting things to rights' for the past half-hour.

'How's tricks then?' inquired Betty, struggling out of her coat. 'All fine and dandy? Wantcher study done first or the bed? Laundry comes today, you know.'

Harold did his best to look alert and to switch to the faster tempo of activity which Betty's arrival always occasioned.

'Study, I think. I've still to dress and shave. I'm rather behind this morning.'

'Well, time's your own, now you're retired.'

Her eye lit upon the mushroom.

'What a whopper! Where'd you find that?'

'Willie Bond found it. It was growing just the other side of the hedge. Would you like it?'

Betty Bell gave a shudder.

'I wouldn't touch it if it was the last thing on earth to eat. Not safe, them things. Why, my old auntie died of eating mushrooms. Honest, she did!'

Betty's eyes grew round with awe.

'What an extraordinary thing,' exclaimed Harold. 'So did Willie's aunt!'

'Nothing extraordinary about it,' replied Betty, rummaging in the dresser drawer for a clean duster. 'She was my auntie too. Me and Willie Bond's cousins.'

She swept from the room like a mighty rushing wind, leaving Harold to ponder on the ever-enthralling complications of village life.


Some time later, Harold emerged from his front door bearing the mushroom in a paper bag. Behind him the house throbbed with the sound of the vacuum cleaner and Betty Bell's robust contralto uplifted in song.

It was good to be away from the noise. The air was fresh. A light breeze shook a shower of lemon-coloured leaves from the lime trees, and ruffled Harold's silver hair, as he set off across the grass to the rectory. He had remembered that the Reverend Charles Henstock and his wife Dimity were both fond of mushrooms.

On his way he encountered the sexton of St Andrew's. The church stood at the south-western corner of Thrush Green, and Albert Piggott's house was placed exactly opposite it and next door to The Two Pheasants. Albert divided his time, unequally, between the two buildings.

The sunshine and serenity of the morning were not reflected in Albert's gloomy face. Hands in pockets, he was mooching about among the tombstones, kicking at a tussock of grass now and again and muttering to himself.

'Good morning, Piggott,' called Harold.

'A good morning for some, maybe,' said Albert sourly, approaching the railings. 'But not for them as 'as this sort of mess to clear up.'

Harold leant over the railings and surveyed the graveyard. Certainly there were a few pieces of paper about, but to his eye it all looked much as usual.

'I suppose people throw down cigarette boxes and so on when they come out of the pub,' he remarked, 'and they blow over here. Too bad when there's a litter box provided.'

'It's not the paper as worries me,' replied Albert. 'It's this 'ere grass. Since my operation, I can't do what I used to do.'

'No, no. Of course not,' said Harold, assuming an expression of extreme gravity in deference to Albert's operation. Thrush Green was learning to live with Albert Piggott's traumatic experience, as related by him daily, but was finding it a trifle exhausting.

'Take a look at it,' urged Albert. 'Take a proper look! What chance is there of pushin' a mower up these 'ere paths with the graves all going which-way? One time I used to scythe it, but Doctor Lovell said that was out of the question. "Out of the question, Piggott," he said to me, same as I'm saying to you now. "Out of the question." His very words.'

'Quite,' said Harold.

'And take these railings,' went on Albert, warming to his theme. 'When was they put up, eh? You tell me that. When was they put 'ere?'

'A good while ago,' hazarded Harold.

'For Queen Victoria's Golden Jubilee, that's when,' said Albert triumphantly. 'Not 'er Diamond one, but 'er *Golden* one! That takes you back a bit, don't it? Won't be long afore these railings is a 'undred years old. Stands to reason they're rusted. 'Alf of 'em busted, and the other 'alf ought to be pulled out. There was always this nice little stub wall of dry stone. That won't wear too bad, but these 'ere railings 'as 'ad it!'

Harold looked, with more attention, at Albert Piggott's territory. To be sure, he had some grounds for grumbling. Tall rank weeds grew inside the stub wall, nettles, the rusty spires of docks, cow-parsley with skeleton umbels turning papery as the summer waned, with convolvulus entwining all and thrusting its tentacles along the railings.

The tombstones stood among hillocks of grass which had grown beyond a mower's powers, as Albert had said. Here and there, a few grassy mounds, neatly shorn, paid tribute to the loving hands of relatives who did their best to honour the resting places of their dead. But these islands of tidiness only served to throw the neglected whole into sharp contrast.

Albert was right about the railings too, Harold observed. Several had splintered with rust and would be dangerous to handle.

'Is there any need for the railings, I wonder?' said Harold, musing aloud.

'There's need all right,' responded Albert. 'That's why they was set 'ere. In the old days there used to be cows and that, grazing on the green, and they could get over this liddle ol' wall easy as kiss your 'and. And the kids too. You gotter keep people and animals out of a churchyard, stands to reason.'

'You won't keep people out for ever,' pointed out Harold, preparing to go on his way. 'We'll all be in there together before long.'

'Some sooner than others,' retorted Albert, with a morose sniff, as Harold departed.

The rectory, some hundred yards from St Andrew's, was a high Victorian monstrosity, facing north, and perched on a small mound the better to catch the chilly winds of the Cotswold country.

It was, thought Harold, as he waited on the doorstep, the most gloomy house in Thrush Green. Unlike its neighbours, which were built of local stone, the rectory had been encased in grey stucco early in its life. The ravages of time had caused pieces to break away here and there, so that newer patches of different grey made the whole affair appear shabbier than ever.

Large sash windows and a tall narrow front door were all in need of paint, but there was little money to spare, as Harold knew too well. In any case, Charles Henstock cared little for creature comforts, and had lived for several years alone, in appalling conditions of cold and discomfort, until his marriage to Dimity Dean a few years before had brought companionship and a slight mitigation of the hardship of his surroundings.

Dimity opened the door to him and greeted him with cries of welcome.

'What a day you've brought with you! I'm in the kitchen, and the sun is just streaming in.'

She led the way, still chattering, down the long dark corridor which acted as a wind tunnel, and kept the rectory in a state of refrigeration during the winter months. Harold's feet echoed on the shabby linoleum, and he thought guiltily of his own carpeted home across the green. It was shameful to think how appallingly some of the clergy were housed. Charles's stipend was barely enough to keep body and soul together, as

Harold well knew. Not that he or Dimity ever complained. Their hearts were thankful, their concern for others governed all their thoughts. They were two of the happiest people Harold had ever met. But he grieved for their poverty secretly, whilst marvelling at their shining goodness.

The kitchen was certainly the most cheerful place in the house. It was the only downstairs room which faced south, and the comfortable smell of cooking added to the warmth of its welcome after the bleakness of the rest of the house.

'Charles is writing letters in the study,' said Dimity. 'I'll let him know that you're here. Do find a seat.'

'Don't bother him,' said Harold, but she had gone already, fluttering up the dark passage, still uttering little cries of pleasure at his visit.

Harold sat down by the kitchen table, first removing a pile of parish magazines from the seat. He observed Dimity's cooking paraphernalia with interest.

A pudding basin stood close to him, and a piece of pastry was in the process of being rolled out. A floury rolling pin lay dangerously near the table's edge, and Harold moved it prudently to a more central position. Something was sizzling gently in a frying pan, and Harold hoped that Dimity would return before it needed attention. His own culinary skills were enough for self-preservation, but he did not feel equal to attending to other people's creations.

A large tabby cat was curled up on the sunny window sill. Harold had known it since it was a kitten. It was one of a litter born to Dotty Harmer's cat, and it was sheer luck that Harold did not own a cat himself from that household. The eccentric Miss Harmer, animal-lover and amateur herbalist, was a power to be reckoned with when she had a litter of kittens needing homes. The Henstocks' cat, Tabitha, seemed to have struck lucky, thought Harold, looking at the array of saucers set down for it by the sink.

Dimity and Charles entered.

'I'm sorry to have interrupted the letter writing,' said Harold.

Charles Henstock's plump face was creased with a smile.

'I can always set aside letter writing,' he assured his friend. 'It's a task I abhor, especially when there are a score of complaints to answer.'

'Such as?'

'Why is the church so cold? Why didn't I see the kneeler that mother gave in 1892, when I visited the church recently? Why is Uncle Thomas's grave so neglected?'

'Poor Charles!' murmured Dimity. 'It's really too bad of people to worry him so.'

She turned her attention to the piece of dough.

'Do you mind if I finish this? It's going to be a steak and kidney pudding, and it should have been on an hour ago.'

'I'm not going to stop,' said Harold, rising. 'But I thought you might like this.'

He handed over the paper bag.

'It couldn't have come at a better time,' cried Dimity. 'I shall put half in the pudding and keep the other half to fry with the breakfast bacon tomorrow morning.'

'Don't go yet,' said Charles. 'Come into the study, out of Dimity's way, and perhaps she would make us some coffee when the pudding's in.'

'Of course, of course,' she exclaimed, her eyes still on the massive mushroom. 'I'll call you the minute it's ready.'

Reluctantly, Harold followed his friend to the study. It was a lofty room, with dark green walls and an inadequate strip of thin carpeting lying in front of the great desk which dominated the room. A crucifix hung on the wall behind the rector's head, flanked by several fading photographs from college days.

From his chair, Harold could see, through the window, the thatched cottage across the way where Dimity had lived before her marriage. She had shared it with Ella Bembridge, another of Thrush Green's redoubtable spinsters, who still lived there, coming over to see her old friend at least once a day.

If anything, Harold was rather more afraid of the ruthless Ella than he was of scatter-brained Dotty Harmer. The latter he could dodge. Ella never gave up. How Dimity could have survived such a partnership for so many years, he just did not know. Another instance of her selflessness, he supposed, although he was ready to admit that Ella's gruffness no doubt hid a warm heart. At least, that's what people told him at Thrush Green, and he was only too willing to believe them.

Certainly, her cottage, glimpsed through the rectory window, looked as snug as a cat sunning itself. Its thatch gleamed. A row of hollyhocks swayed in the breeze, and Ella's open bedroom window flashed dazzling lights as it reflected the sunshine. Did Dimity ever regret leaving that haven, he wondered?

He looked at Charles, turning the papers on his desk. It had been no sacrifice for Dimity, Harold decided, when she gave up her home across the road. There was no finer man than the rector of Thrush Green.

'Do you get many letters of complaint?' he asked.

'A few each week. I try and keep one morning a week for answering them. I don't quite know what I am expected to do. Some are most unreasonable – this kneeler one, for instance. But of course people are distressed and I must do my best to explain things, and perhaps to comfort them.'

'We might do something about the churchyard between us,' said Harold diffidently. 'I saw Piggott as I came across, and of course he's past keeping the place as it should be.'

'I've done my utmost to get another man,' replied Charles, 'but no one seems to want the work.'

'We might organize a working party,' suggested Harold. 'We could take down the railings, for instance. They're getting downright dangerous.'

'They are in a bad way,' agreed the rector, 'but I think we should probably have to get a faculty to remove them. I must go into it.'

A cry from the kitchen told them that coffee was ready.

'Of course,' went on the rector, following his friend down the passage, 'Piggott never makes the best of anything. No one could accuse him of looking on the bright side of life. However, I will go and see what can be done during the week. Thrush Green must have a tidy churchyard.'

'Yes indeed,' echoed Dimity, passing steaming cups. 'Thrush Green must have a tidy churchyard.'

Had they known it, on that serene September morning, those simple words were to become a battle cry. The resting place of Thrush Green's dead was soon to become a field of conflict.

## 2. Miss Fogerty is Upset

Thrush Green, which is roughly triangular, is bordered by two highways which converge at the southern end in Lulling. A fine avenue of chestnut trees lines the third side at the northern end, joining the two roads.

Harold Shoosmith's house stands on the smaller road which leads northward to the villages of Nod and Nidden. Next door stands the village school, one or two cottages, including Albert Piggott's, and The Two Pheasants.

The other road is larger and busier, leading northward to other Cotswold towns, and finally to the Midlands. It is on this road, facing across the green to the village school and public house, that some of Thrush Green's most attractive houses stand, although the finest of all, everyone agrees, are the three magnificent dwellings whose frontages lie along the chestnut avenue.

Ella Bembridge's cottage, at the head of the steep hill which drops down to Lulling High Street, is one of the pretty houses on the main road and Dr and Mrs Bailey live in another, a solid Cotswold stone house weathered to a perfect blend of grey and gold.

Next door to the Baileys' stands a small square house, of the same age, called Tullivers, and to this house, some time ago, came a young woman and her little son Jeremy. Thrush Green, of course, was avidly interested in the newcomer and speculated about the non-appearance of her husband.

But speculation turned to sympathy when Thrush Green heard that he had been killed in a car crash in France, and sympathy turned to rejoicing when she married again later. Frank and Phyllida Hurst were popular members of the Thrush Green community, and young Jeremy one of the star pupils at the village school.

On this sparkling September morning, as the rector, his wife and their visitor sipped their coffee, Phil Hurst was cutting roses in the garden of Tullivers. This second flowering was infinitely better than the first, she decided, snipping busily. Just as second thoughts usually were – or second marriages, perhaps?

She straightened up and stood, silent, lost in her thoughts. Across the green the schoolchildren shouted in the playground. From a garden nearby came the sound of a lawn mower, and swallows, strung along the telegraph wire like beads on a thread, chattered together. But Phil heard nothing.

The old tag: 'Comparisons are odious' came into her mind. It was true in this case. This second marriage was wonderfully, strongly happy despite the difference in their ages. But no one could say that it was better than the first – simply different. Marriage with John had been a gay affair, exciting and exacting, two young people learning to live together – until the last unhappy months when he had left her for a French woman.

Marriage with Frank was happiness in a different way. It had a quieter, more companionable quality. It was Frank who gave comfort, whereas it was she who had comforted John. There was a solid strength about the older man which John had lacked, but which she had never realized until now.

And then he was so good with Jeremy! How heartwarming that was, to see the affection between them! It would have been understandable if a man of Frank's age had shown some irritation now and again in the presence of a vociferous little boy. After all, Robert, his only son by his first marriage, who was now a farmer in Wales, had four children of his own, and Frank's youngest grandchild was much the same age as Jeremy.

She moved thoughtfully towards the house where a Golden Shower rose flaunted its lemon flowers against the stone wall. At the moment there was one flaw in their otherwise perfect relationship. Frank dearly wanted Jeremy to go away to school, positive that it brought out the best in any child. Phil hated the idea, at least until he was considerably older. He loved his present school. He loved Tullivers and the simple life of Thrush Green. He had lost his father, and had had to adapt to another man taking his father's place. Phil felt sure that it was best to let him stay as he was for some time.

There was a good day school in Lulling which Paul Young attended, and he was going on from there to his father's public school. Phil thought that this was the ideal plan, and decided that she must speak to her friend Joan Young, who lived in one of the three splendid houses in the chestnut avenue, to elicit her help if a battle with Frank became unavoidable. It was the one thing, she told herself, snipping ferociously, for which she would fight. After all, Jeremy was her child – hers and John's – and she was determined to do the right thing by him.

A woman's voice broke upon her militant thoughts, and she turned to see her neighbour Winnie Bailey at the gate.

'And how is the doctor this morning?' inquired Phil, going towards her.

'Not too good today. He's up and down, as you know, and had a trying night. He's asleep now, and I thought I would slip down to Lulling for some meat while he's resting.'

'Shall I look in?'

'No, no, many thanks. Jenny's there till twelve, and I shan't be long. Anything I can fetch for you?'

'Nothing, thank you. Frank's at the office today and won't be back until tomorrow. He's dining with an American editor and hoping to do a deal.'

'Good luck to him! So I suppose you and Jeremy are having boiled eggs?'

'Absolutely right! I'll start cooking again tomorrow.'

'Well, I must be off,' said Winnie, casting an anxious look at the doctor's bedroom window. 'He likes me to be there when he first wakes.'

She hurried away, and for the first time Phil thought how old and frail she looked. What a burden of anxiety she carried constantly! It put her own trivial worries into perspective, she thought.

And what a daily battle was being fought by the gallant doctor next door! It was a long and valiant campaign waged against the grimmest of all adversaries.

Sadly, as Phil and all Thrush Green knew, victory would have to be conceded to the enemy before long.

Playtime was over, and in the infants' room at the village school little Miss Fogerty sat at her desk with a small group of children gathered about her.

The rest of the class was engaged in various activities. Some of the childen were copying sentences from the blackboard, others were reading at their tables, and the usual hard core of juvenile delinquents was making itself objectionable to the more law-abiding of its neighbours.

The group clustered by Miss Fogerty consisted of those who found reading difficult. In her young days, they would have been known as 'backward'. Halfway through her career, the term was changed to 'less able'. Now that she was nearing retirement, she believed such a group was called 'remedial'. The name might change, thought Miss Fogerty – the children did not. They provided her with the hardest session of her teaching day.

By dint of using every reading method known, she battled on day after day. Some, she knew, would never read, and would rely on television, radio, and the age-old practical methods of personal demonstration to acquire knowledge.

Others would gain enough mechanical skill to make out the headlines or to puzzle out where to sign a form. A very few would catch up with the rest of the class, and on these Miss Fogerty relied for any encouragement.

Grubby forefingers were descending the long cards made by Miss Fogerty years before.

'Per – in' they chanted, gazing at the picture beside the first word.

'Ter – in' they went on.

'Fer – in.' Really, thought Miss Fogerty, with pride, that fish was very well executed!

'Grer – in.' And that smile too! The cards had worn extremely well.

She stood up suddenly, and looked over the heads of her pupils to the back row of the classroom.

'Any more of that pinching, Johnny Dodd, and you will stay in after school.'

She sat down abruptly. The drone continued without interruption.

'Cher – in.'

She allowed her thoughts to wander. Miss Fogerty disliked change.

She and Miss Watson, her headmistress, had held sway at Thrush Green School for many years, and were firm friends. But now, after all this time, a third teacher had been appointed, and although the term was yet young, Miss Fogerty could see signs that disturbed her.

For one thing, the girl was only just in her twenties, and though Miss Fogerty was fair-minded enough to see that this could not be helped – after all, the time of one's birth was beyond one's control – she realized that Miss Potter's view of teaching was quite different from her own and Miss Watson's.

And then she dressed in such a peculiar way, pondered Miss Fogerty, automatically replacing a wavering forefinger upon the reading card. If she were headmistress she would never allow a teacher in her school to wear a trouser suit. Most unbecoming. Most unladylike.

'But very practical, dear,' Miss Watson had said, in answer to Miss Fogerty's expressed doubts.'And will keep the girl warm in that rather draughty new building.'

The new building, called colloquially 'the terrapin' was a purely functional classroom which had been erected at the farther end of the playground to house the young juniors. It was termed a temporary building, but Miss Fogerty and Miss Watson, with years of experience behind them, faced the fact that the terrapin would still be there long after they had retired.

The new housing estate, built along the road to Nod and Nidden, supplied most of the extra pupils at Thrush Green School. For generations the village school had accommodated about fifty or sixty children in its two rooms, but now that the number on roll had risen to over eighty, the third classroom had been deemed a positive necessity.

Miss Fogerty would dearly have loved to have the terrapin as her classroom. As soon as the building began, she put forward excellent reasons why the room should be put at the infants' disposal.

'You know how much noise they make,' she pointed out to Miss Watson. 'We shouldn't disturb anyone over there. And the cloakrooms and lavatories are all built in – so convenient for small children. You know how they bang the lobby door every time they need to go across the yard.'

'The room is far more suited to the needs of the juniors,' said her headmistress firmly.

'And then it's so sunny,' pleaded Miss Fogerty, 'and will bring on the mustard and cress and bean seeds and bulbs so beautifully. As well as being healthier for the babies.'

'All that applies to the junior class too,' pointed out Miss Watson obdurately. She used her trump card.

'Besides, Agnes,' she said, more gently, 'I should miss you. I like to think of you at my right hand.'

There was no answer to this, and Miss Fogerty gave way with her usual docility.

But the decision rankled. She would have liked a change. Hadn't she spent the best years of her life in the infants' room which faced north east and was decidedly shabby and dark? The fact that its main window overlooked Thrush Green, and thus afforded an interesting view of the comings and goings of its inhabitants, was a point in the classroom's favour, but even that could pall. It would have been lovely to have a new view looking acros the little valley to Lulling Woods, and to have the sun streaming through that beautiful low window, so infinitely preferable to the high Gothic one which the Victorian architect had considered right and proper for the original building.

And although it was uncommonly nice of dear Miss Watson to say that she would miss her, pondered Miss Fogerty, would it not have been even nicer if she had taken her old friend's wishes into consideration? After all, she had loyally served Miss Watson and Thrush Green School through thick and thin, and had rarely asked for a favour. It would have been gratifying to think that those long years had been recognized and rewarded with a willingness to meet her request.

It would be easier to bear, Miss Fogerty considered, if Miss Potter had appreciated the new classroom, but there had been a great many grumbles from the newcomer about draughts, and glaring sunlight, and doors which stuck, and even about noisy lavatory cisterns, which Miss Fogerty thought privately it was indelicate to mention.

No, Miss Potter was not an asset to the staff, that was plain. Certainly, it was early days to judge, and maybe she would improve on acquaintance, and mellow a little in the company of two older and wiser women.

Nevertheless, that old tag about two being company and three none, had some horse sense. Things could never be quite the same between dear Miss Watson and herself with a third member of staff to consider.

A thought struck her. Of course if Miss Potter continued to be disgruntled about the terrapin, then she might prefer to take over her own room. And if that didn't suit, then the girl might apply for a post elsewhere. Heaven alone knew, a good teacher would be snapped up anywhere.

Miss Fogerty's spirits rose at the thought. She smiled upon her labouring readers.

'Very good,' she told them warmly. 'You've all tried hard this morning. Rose, collect the cards, and then take round the sweet tin. I am very pleased with you.'

## 3. *Dotty Harmer's Legacy*

True to his word, the Reverend Charles Henstock made a point of examining the churchyard of St Andrew's, with particular care, within the week.

He was not a man who responded to his surroundings with any great degree of sensitivity. On the whole, he was unobservant, and perhaps this was a blessing when one surveyed the gloomy setting of the rectory, and the cold and undistinguished interior of his church. Someone, a century earlier, had removed, with a heavy Victorian hand, any little prettinesses which St Andrew's once enjoyed, and put in a truly appalling reredos at much the same time as the iron railings had been erected upon the low Cotswold stone wall which Thrush Green had once thought adequate as a boundary.

There was no doubt about it, thought the rector, pacing the uneven paths between tilting tombstones, the place *was* neglected. He looked over the railings across the green, noticing for once how spruce it looked, how fine was the chestnut avenue in the morning sunlight, as the leaves began to turn from green to gold. The hedges and gardens were tidy. The hanging baskets, outside The Two Pheasants, were still ablaze with geraniums and lobelia plants. Only here, in this corner of Thrush Green, was there something shabby. The most hallowed spot of all, thought the rector, turning to survey it again, was the most shameful. Something would have to be done.

But what? He was debating the advisability of calling at Albert Piggott's cottage, when the sexton emerged from the vestry door. No doubt he had been checking the boiler fuel. Very soon it would be needed, and what an expense! Charles Henstock sighed as he approached Albert.

'Another lovely day, Albert.'

'Need some rain.'

'Surely not.'

'Runner beans is drying out.'

Albert passed on the information with morose relish. Albert hated optimists.

'I've been thinking about this churchyard, Albert. Do you happen to have heard of anyone to give you a hand?'

'Not a living soul. What about that bit you put in the paper? Any takers?'

'I fear not. It seems that no one wants this sort of work.'

'Can't blame 'em,' said Albert laconically. 'They gets more standing by some bit of machinery doin' dam' all.'

The rector decided to let the oath pass.

'Well, we must do something ourselves, I suppose. Mr Shoosmith suggested a working party to help you.'

Albert flushed an ugly red. If there was anything he hated more than optimists, it was newcomers putting their oar in where they wasn't needed. Cheek, coming into his churchyard!

'And what does this 'ere *working party* intend to do, may I ask?' he inquired, with heavy sarcasm.

The rector, who was no coward, spoke out.

'To cut the grass, straighten some of these tombstones, and get rid of that dreadful mess of weeds which has been an eyesore for months. That would be a start, anyway.'

Albert's anger now became tinged with self-pity. There was a decided whine in his tone when he replied.

'Well, that's all very fine and large, but a bit of tem'pry help don't go far. Since my operation I'm a sick man, as well you knows. It ain't that I'm not willing, but the flesh is weak, hacked about as I was by that ol' butcher Pedder-Bennett down the hospital.'

'You were extremely lucky,' said the rector severely, 'to have such a distinguished surgeon to operate on you. You might not have been here at all, if the Lulling Hospital staff had not worked so swiftly and so well.'

Albert did not reply, but turned to spit neatly behind the angel erected in pious memory of one Hepzibah Armstrong by her sorrowing husband. The rector, with Christian fortitude, restrained his temper.

'But that is exactly the point, Piggott,' he continued. 'We must rely on volunteer help. What else is there to do?'

'They used to have a few sheep in here in my Dad's time, to crop the grass. Be less bother than a lot of amachoors stamping about breaking things when I wasn't looking.'

The rector sighed.

'Well, we must think of every possible method, but the aim is plain and clear. We simply cannot have God's acre neglected like this. It is a disgrace to Thrush Green and an affront to all decent men, dead and alive. In the meantime, you must do the best you can, Piggott, and accept any help that we can muster.'

He strode to the gate, leaving Albert to digest this unpalatable morsel of news.

Working parties! Interfering old busybodies! Best cut across to The Two Pheasants for half a pint, he decided, setting off in the direction of that hostelry with more energy than he had shown that morning.

The rector had just reached his front door, when a high-pitched hallooing caused him to turn.

There, at the gate, was Dotty Harmer, Thrush Green's most famous eccentric. She was scrabbling helplessly at the latch of the gate, pulling it, as always, when it needed to be pushed, and becoming more and more breathless with her exertions.

'Let me, Dotty,' called the rector, hurrying to her aid. Two magazines slipped from her grasp to the ground, and as she bent to retrieve them her hat fell off. To the rector's surprise, he saw that it had a piece of elastic attached to it, but he could not recall Dotty ever having such a thing under her chin, as his sisters used to have as children. A less polite man might have tried to satisfy his curiosity with a blunt question, but Charles refrained.

'Thank you, thank you, Charles dear,' babbled Dotty, preceding her host up the path. As usual, Dotty's stockings were in concertinas round her skinny legs. Although Charles was a married man, he was hazy about the mechanics of keeping stockings at the correct tension. Dimity, he believed, had some sort of thing called a suspender belt, but surely these days ladies wore thin pantaloons – 'tights' did they call them? – which must be much simpler than tethering one's leg coverings. Perhaps Dimity could have a word with Dotty about these delicate matters? It really must be most uncomfortable for Dotty to go about like this.

By now they had entered the hall, but almost immediately Dotty turned, voicing protests, and practically capsizing the rector.

'No, I didn't mean to come in! I won't come in!'

'But you *are* in,' pointed out Charles patiently. 'Come through to see Dimity.'

'Well, I mustn't stay,' said Dotty, turning round again, and resuming her progress with much agitation. 'I've so much to do before I go away.'

'Go away?' echoed Dimity, appearing at the kitchen door. 'What's all this about?'

'Oh, I'm not going for a day or two. As soon as it suits Connie, I shall be off.'

'I don't think I know Connie,' began Dimity.

'Connie? My Connie? You *must* know her! That niece of mine with the red hair. Used to lisp as a child, but grew out of it, I'm thankful to say.'

'And you are going to stay with her?' inquired the rector. 'Do sit down, Dotty.'

Dotty's agitation doubled.

'No, no! I really must go,' she said, remaining rooted to the spot.

'But I should very much like to sit down,' replied Charles patiently, 'but I can't if you won't.'

'I don't see why not,' said Dotty, hitching up one of the cascading stockings. 'Your joints are all in order, I take it?'

'I was brought up to stand whilst ladies were standing,' smiled Charles, 'and somehow I still do so. So please sit down.'

Dotty thumped down into a kitchen chair, and the rector and his wife followed suit.

'Satisfied?' said Dotty.

'Thank you, yes,' said Charles, sighing with relief. 'I've been talking to Piggott, and I must say it is an exhausting activity.'

'That churchyard's a disgrace,' pronounced Dotty.

'I know. That's what I was discussing with Piggott. He tells me that a few sheep used to graze there years ago.'

Dimity looked alarmed.

'I shouldn't think the relatives of the dead there would care to have sheep roaming about.'

'Why on earth not?' demanded Dotty. 'Very sensible arrangement, I should say. But why sheep? Why not let my two goats have the run of the graveyard? They'd keep it down beautifully.'

It was now the rector's turn to look alarmed. Dotty in pursuit of an aim was a force to be reckoned with. As the daughter of a long-dead local headmaster, whose discipline was still spoken of with shuddering, Dotty's spirit was militant and tenacious.

'I could take them up each morning,' continued Dotty, waxing enthusiastic, 'and bring them back for afternoon milking time. Or even milk them there, of course. Ella could slip across for her daily pint much more conveniently.'

'But Dotty –' began Charles.

He was swept aside. Dotty in full spate had the same overwhelming force as the River Niger in that condition.

'Mind you, you'd have to remove those round metal grid things with everlasting flowers stuck in them. The dear girls would be bound to try and eat them, and even goats would find those indigestible. Marble chippings couldn't do much harm, I imagine. Simply provide roughage. But we'd better take away the plastic vases.'

'*I could not countenance goats in the churchyard*,' trumpeted Charles fortissimo.

Dotty looked flabbergasted.

'Then why countenance sheep?'

'I have not said that I would countenance *sheep*,' replied Charles, in his usual dulcet tones. 'All I said was that *once* – many years ago – sheep, so Piggott assured me, and he may well be wrong, knowing Piggott, were allowed to crop the grass.'

'It's nothing short of racial discrimination!' exclaimed Dotty. Her face was becoming very flushed.

Dimity hastily changed the subject.

'Tell me about Connie, dear. I think I remember her now.'

Dotty allowed herself to be side-tracked, but Charles had the uncomfortable feeling that she would return to the attack shortly.

'My brother's child. David, you remember? Died last spring?'

'Indeed I do.'

'Well, at last the lawyers have sorted things out – though why they take so long remains a mystery. David left a perfectly straightforward will. One or two small bequests to relatives and friends and the rest to Connie. A child of seven could have settled it during an afternoon, but here we are – months later – only just about to take possession. I'm going down to fetch my car.'

'Your car?'

'Yes, yes,' Dotty said testily.

She rose from the chair, dropping the magazines which she had been clutching the while.

'Thought I'd hand these in before I forgot them. Such a lot to do before setting off.'

'But can you drive?' asked Charles.

'Of course I can drive! I had a licence on my seventeenth birthday and I've always kept it up. Luckily, I shan't need to take a test.'

'But, Dotty dear,' said Dimity, 'I've never seen you driving, and I've known you for quite twenty years.'

'Maybe, but it's all in order, and the car is taxed and insured. I quite look forward to the drive back.'

Charles and Dimity exchanged looks of horror behind their departing guest's back.

Charles spoke with some authority.

'Dotty, do I understand that you propose to make the return journey alone?'

'Naturally. Go down by coach, back in the car. Simplicity itself.'

'Can't you get a garage to deliver it for you? Or Connie? You see, things have altered since your driving days. The traffic, for one thing. And then, cars are quite different now. You might not be able to control it.'

Dotty's face became quite puce with indignation.

'Not able to control it?' she echoed. 'If I could manage Father's Studebaker and my dear little bull-nosed Morris, which tended to be temperamental, I don't mind admitting, then I can certainly drive David's car. Don't forget, I often sat in it when I was staying. It was very easy to drive. David always said so.'

'Nevertheless,' said Charles, 'I think you should have someone with you. If need be, I will accompany you myself.'

'Rubbish! Stuff and nonsense!' exclaimed Dotty, making for the door. 'I never heard such a lot of fuss about nothing. I wish I hadn't told you about my little legacy.'

She began to storm along the corridor to the front door, Dimity following her.

'Don't be upset, Dotty dear, and do think over Charles's offer. And, by the way, what is Connie's address, just in case we want to get in touch while you're away?'

'The Limes, Friarscombe, will find me,' said Dotty, struggling with the front door.

'And perhaps we'd better have the telephone number,' continued Dimity, opening the door. 'Just in case the goats come to any harm, you know.'

Dotty, for a brief moment, remained motionless, as the full horror of this possibility burst upon her.

'Sensible, Dimity. Friarscombe Two One Three. I'll see you about, probably, before I go.'

She set off down the path without so much as one backward look. Her stockings, Charles noticed, were in a highly dangerous state of decline.

Dimity returned to the kitchen, looking determined.

'Charles, we must get in touch with Connie and see that Dotty is kept from driving that car alone.'

'I quite agree. She really wouldn't be safe.'

'And nor would anyone in her path,' added Dimity.


'Heard about Miss Harmer's car?' inquired Betty Bell of her employer the next morning.

'No,' said Harold, removing a glass ash tray, in the nick of time, from the path of Betty's onslaught with a duster.

'She told me yesterday while I was giving her kitchen a going over. And did it need it? She's got a great cardboard box standing on that dresser of hers – why, it's been there ever since I started doing for her, and that's how long?'

She stood transfixed, frowning with concentration. Harold took advantage of the lull to rescue *The Times* hoping to find a more peaceful spot in which to peruse it.

'Must be all of eight years,' announced Betty, coming to life again and attacking the mantelpiece.

'And this box is absolutely chocker with bits she's cut out of newspapers. One of 'em was over twenty years old! Think of that! I'm telling you!'

'I know you are,' said Harold patiently.

'Well, at last I got her to let me sort it out, only we didn't get far. Know why?'

'No.'

'There was a mouse's nest down the bottom.'

'Good heavens!' exclaimed Harold.

'Not a *modern* one,' said Betty comfortingly. 'A proper broken down old thing it was – no babies or that! But still, a nest, and all made of chewed up paper. Quite pretty really. Miss Harmer was all for taking it into the village school for the children to see but I said not. I could just see Miss Watson's face if Miss Harmer took that thing out and sprinkled mouse confetti all over the floor. Besides, it's me that has to clear it up.'

'What's this got to do with the car?'

'Only that she told me while we made a bonfire of all the kitchen muck. Her brother's left her his car and she's going to get it on Friday.'

'I didn't know she drove.'

'She don't. At least, she hasn't for donkey's years. We all used to rush up into the hedge when we was kids if old Dot – I mean Miss Harmer – was coming.'

'I expect someone will drive her back,' said Harold, anxious to get to grips with *The Times* crossword. A swift glance had shown him that 'dairy cats' could easily be turned into 'caryatids' at 6 across.

'Rather them than me!' replied his help. 'Not that there'll be any need. She's driving it herself.'

'Good Lord!' exclaimed Harold, suitably shaken, and made his escape.

By the time night fell upon Thrush Green, Dotty's news was common knowledge, and consternation was rife.

Doctor Lovell, Doctor Bailey's young assistant, told his wife Ruth about the projected trip by one of his more difficult patients.

'But she's a perfect menace!' cried Ruth. 'She once took Joan and me to a fête, and I wonder we ever got back alive. How father and mother ever came to give her permission, I can't think. We were about ten and eight, I suppose. I had nightmares for weeks afterwards.'

'She certainly hasn't driven since I came here,' said her husband. 'Do you think you could offer to drive the car back?'

'With Dotty in it? Panting to get her hands on the wheel? You don't know what you're asking,' cried Ruth with spirit. 'And the answer is a resounding "No!"'

Doctor Bailey shook his tired old head when Winnie told him about Dotty's car.

'The same angel that guards drunkards will guard Dotty,' he told her, smiling.

'It's other people I'm thinking of,' retorted Winnie.'

At the rectory, Charles had telephoned to Connie at Friarscombe and put forward the fears of all at Thrush Green. The reply was not very satisfactory.

'I'll do my best,' said the distant voice, 'but you know Aunt Dot.'

Sadly, the rector agreed that he did indeed.

He put down the telephone and turned to his wife.

'One last hope – Ella,' he said. 'She drives, and she can sometimes persuade Dotty to do things when other people have failed.'

'I'll go over tomorrow morning,' promised Dimity.

She found her old friend in the garden. Ella was picking runner beans, and successfully trampling upon a row of carrots next in line.

'They'll survive,' was her answer to Dimity's protests. 'Want some beans? Enough here to feed an army. All or nothing with runners, isn't it?'

'I'd love some. I'll pick them.'

'No, you won't. There's ample in the basket.'

She led the way back to the path, stepping from carrot fronds to shallots and then on to the onion row. Dimity, wincing, picked her way after her.

Ella sat down heavily on the wooden seat by the back door, and began to remove her muddy shoes. Dimity sat beside her. The sun was already warm and she thought, yet again, what a wonderfully pleasant place the old cottage garden was. There was no such sheltered spot across at the rectory. She chided herself for disloyalty, and turned to Ella.

Her friend had produced the battered tobacco tin so familiar from times past. Ella began to roll one of her disreputable cigaretes.

'Well, what brings you over?' she asked, licking the edge of the paper.

'Dotty,' said Dimity. 'She's been left a car –'

'I know,' replied Ella, fumbling for matches.

'And she really can't drive, you know, and we're all so worried. Charles and I wondered if you could have a word with her, and persuade her to let you go with her –'

A cloud of pungent smoke polluted the morning air before Ella replied.

'You're too late, Dim my girl,' she said, slapping Dimity's thin thigh painfully. 'I saw her going down to catch the nine-thirty coach, case in hand.'

'But she said Friday!' cried Dimity, appalled. 'And today's Thursday!'

'I expect she got wind of all the fuss,' said Ella, 'and decided to get away while the going was good.'

She struggled to her feet and retrieved the basket.

'Can't say I blame her,' she puffed, her grizzled head now wreathed in blue smoke. 'Dotty knows her way around for all her scatter-brained ways.'

She began to lead the way to the kitchen.

'You mark my words,' said Ella, 'she'll arrive back at Thrush Green safe and sound. They say the devil looks after his own, don't they?'

Later, beans in hand, and Ella's dire words ringing in her head, Dimity returned to the rectory to break the news to Charles.

She refrained from quoting Ella exactly. At times, she felt, her old friend expressed herself rather too forcefully. The rector's comment was typical.

'We can only hope that Connie will be given strength to prevail. It will need great courage to oppose Dotty.'

'It will need more to drive with her!' retorted his wife with spirit.

# 4. Driving Trouble

The matter of St Andrew's churchyard continued to perplex the rector and the parochial church council.

At an emergency meeting it was decided to put up one or two notices in public spots asking for volunteers to help to tidy the graveyard. The rector also drafted a paragraph for inclusion in the parish magazine.

Reaction was varied, and mainly negative.

'What's old Piggott get paid for then?' queried one belligerently.

'He's past it,' said another, more kindly disposed.

'Then he should pack it in, and let someone else get the money,' retorted the first speaker.

'I reckons the council ought to keep it tidy. What do we pay rates for?' demanded another, reading the notice which Harold Shoosmith had pinned up in the bar of The Two Pheasants.

'Don't talk daft!' begged a stout-drinker. 'It's got nothing to do with the council!'

'Well, I've been a Wesleyan all my life. I don't see why I should clean up for the C. of Es.'

'You'll be put in there, won't you?' demanded another. 'Whatever you be, you'll end up there. Why your old ma and pa are up agin the wall already! Don't matter what church or chapel we goes to, that's the common burial ground. I reckons we all ought to lend a hand.'

But not many agreed with the last speaker, and as he was a shepherd, bent and weatherbeaten, and now in his eighty-fifth year, he was not in a position to engage personally in the project.

The rector, experienced in the ways of men, was not surprised at the lack of response, although he was disappointed.

'It seems sad,' he said to Harold Shoosmith, 'that none of the younger men has offered. In fact, the only people willing to do anything are you, and Percy Hodge, the farmer, and myself.'

'I really thought we might get some volunteers from the new housing estate at Nod,' replied Harold. 'Plenty of able-bodied chaps up there.'

'They have their new gardens to see to,' said Charles charitably. 'And most of them do over-time, you know, to make ends meet. They are rather hard-pressed. It's quite understandable.'

'You're a good deal more forgiving than I am,' said Harold. 'Young Doctor Lovell told me he could offer an evening a week, and if he can, then why can't others?'

'Better one willing fighter than ten men press-ganged into the battle,' replied the rector philosophically.

'I suppose you're right. We muster at the church gate next Wednesday then?'

'At six, my dear fellow. What a blessing the evenings are still light! Piggott will be there to help.'

And to make sure we know our place, thought Harold, watching his friend's receding figure.


'Coffee up!' shouted Betty Bell, as he re-entered his house.'Want it here or on your own?' Sometimes, when Betty gave him just such a comradely salute, he found himself thinking of the obsequious native boys who had waited upon him for so many years, with deference and respect. Or had they perhaps, simply acted a part? In any case, it was no good harking back. Times had changed.

'I'll have it with you,' said Harold, entering the kitchen. Two cups steamed on a tray, and a plate held some dark sticky gingerbread.

'Have a bit,' said Betty, pushing the plate towards him. 'It's a present for you.'

'Very kind,' said Harold, looking at it doubtfully.

Betty broke into a peal of laughter.

'You're thinking Miss Harmer sent it! Well, she didn't. I made it myself.'

'Then I should love a piece, Betty,' said Harold, smiling.

'You don't think I'd let you eat anything *she'd* made, do you? No disrespect, mark you – Miss Harmer's a real lady, I always say – but that kitchen of hers is a right old muddle, and you'd as likely get bird seed or Karswood powder in your cake as not.'

'It's delicious,' nodded Harold.

'Seen her car yet?'

'No. She drove it back herself, after all, I suppose?'

'Between you and me, that's what she wants Thrush Green to think, but actually that niece of hers drove most of the way. They came back that night, and her Connie got Reg Bull's taxi from Lulling to take her back, as soon as she'd had a bite.'

'But why the secrecy? And why didn't the young lady stay the night?'

'Miss Harmer's proud, see. Didn't like to let on that she'd never driven herself home, after all she'd said. And that Connie's like her auntie. She's got all manner of animals to look after, so she had to get back.'

'I see.'

'Besides,' went on Betty, beginning to stack the china swiftly, 'would you want to stay the night with Miss Harmer?'

Harold assumed that this was a rhetorical question, and forebore to answer.

'You'd never know what was in your bed,' said Betty. 'I've known the time the cat had kittens there, under the eiderdown, and Miss Harmer wouldn't hear of them being moved for days. Some people don't like that sort of thing, you know. We haven't all got Miss Harmer's funny ways.'

Harold nodded agreement.

'But what about the car? No one has seen her in it yet.'

'She's been out in it all right. Got some petrol from Reg Bull's, 'cos my nephew served her, but she's only took it round the lanes, testing it a bit, I reckon.'

'It sounds as though she is being very sensible,' said Harold, rising. 'She's bound to feel that she needs a little practice after such a long time without a car.'

'It isn't *practice* she wants,' said Betty downrightly. 'It's a chauffeur.'

She deposited the china in the washing-up bowl, and Harold escaped.

It so happened that Harold was vouchsafed the vision of Dotty Harmer at the wheel, the very next afternoon. He was standing outside his front gate, contemplating some dwarf marigolds. Should he pull them up in readiness for planting the wallflowers, or should he enjoy their colour for another week or two?

Since his return to England, some few years earlier, he found that such problems occurred regularly. Was it his imagination, or did the Spring in his boyhood start earlier, and finish, in a tidy fashion, in good time to put in the summer bedding plants? Now, it seemed, it remained cold in June, and everything was proportionately later. These dwarf marigolds, for instance, had only come into flower a few weeks ago, he told himself, and yet, if he wanted to get the beds dug over and the wallflowers established, then they really should be removed now.

He had just decided to grant them a reprieve for a week or two, facing the fact that by that time continuous rain, no doubt, would frustrate any gardening whatsoever, when he became conscious of a cacophony of horn-blowing coming from the steep hill which led from Thrush Green to Lulling.

Harold strode over to the green, and stood by the statue of his hero, Nathaniel Patten, the better to see the cause of the fuss. The main road, leading northward to the midlands, appeared to be free from traffic.

Whatever the obstruction was, which was causing such irritation to so many drivers, was out of sight.

Harold continued to wait. The children from the village school, just let out to play, crowded against the railings behind him like so many inquisitive monkeys.

Albert Piggott appeared on his doorstep. Joan Young, girt in her gardening apron, came across the chestnut avenue, trowel in hand, to join Harold, and at least a dozen twitching curtains told of more sightseers.

'Do you think there's been an accident?' asked Joan. 'Perhaps we should run over.'

Even as she spoke, a small car, jerking spasmodically, came into view. It was impossible to see, at that distance, who held the wheel, but Harold guessed, correctly, who it might be.

'Dotty!' cried Harold and Joan in unison, setting off across the grass at a brisk pace.

The car had come to another stop, by the time they arrived, just outside Ella Bembridge's house. Behind it stretched a long queue, the end of it out of sight in the main street of Lulling. Immediately behind Dotty's small vehicle was a Land-Rover towing a horse-box.

'Get the bloody thing off the road!' shouted the driver. His face was scarlet with wrath, as he leant out of the side window. 'Dam' women drivers! No business to have a licence!'

Further protestations came from those behind, and the additional music of car horns rent the air.

Dotty, peering agitatedly at the car pedals, was pink herself, and very cross indeed.

'Here,' said Harold, wrenching open the door, 'hop out, Miss Harmer, and I'll park her in the side road.'

'Why should I get out?' demanded Dotty. 'And what right have you to order me out of my own carriage, may I ask?'

'Pull the old besom out,' begged the Land-Rover driver. He began to open his door, and Harold feared that battle would be joined.

'*Please*,' he pleaded. 'You see, there is such a long queue, and this road is far too narrow here to overtake safely. I'm afraid that the police will be along to see what's happening.'

'*You* may be afraid of the police,' said Dotty sharply,'but I am *not*. Now kindly take your hand from the door.'

'But –' began Harold, but could not continue, as, by some miracle of combustion the engine had started again into spasmodic life and Dotty moved slowly, in a succession of convulsive jerks, into the side road leading to the church. There was a mild explosion, a puff of smoke, the car stopped, and Dotty put forth her deplorably-stockinged legs and got out.

'Stick to your bike, lady!' shouted the Land-Rover man rudely, as he quickened his pace along the main road. A few imprecations, some shaken fists and vulgar gestures were directed towards Dotty as cars passed, but most of the drivers contented themselves with resigned glances as they glimpsed the scarecrow figure of the one who was responsible for their delay.

The three waited until the last of the queue vanished northwards, before speaking.

'Would you allow me to have a look at the car?' asked Harold.

'Of course, of course,' said Dotty airily, as if washing her hands of the whole affair.

At this moment, Ella appeared and crossed the road.

'What on earth have you been up to, Dotty? Never heard such a racket since just before D-day when we had all those tanks rumbling through.'

'I simply drove quietly from West Street up the hill here. Just because I do not care to *scorch* along, this queue formed behind me. I had some difficulty in changing gear at the bottom, I must admit, but there was no need for the vulgar demonstration of impatience which you have just witnessed. No manners anywhere these days! A pity some of these men weren't taught by my father. He wouldn't have spared the strap, I can tell you!'

Harold climbed out of the car and came towards them.

'It's quite a simple problem,' he said. 'The petrol's run out.'

'The *petrol*?' echoed Dotty. 'But we only filled it when we brought the car from Connie's, not ten days ago!'

'Nevertheless, it's empty now.'

'But how can you tell?' demanded Dotty. 'You didn't put in your dip stick.'

'There's a little gauge on the dashboard,' explained Harold patiently. 'Perhaps you would allow me to show you?'

'Don't trouble,' said Dotty, setting off towards the car. 'I'll just push her round, if you'll give me a hand, and coast down the hill to Reg Bull's for some fuel.'

'But it's not allowed!' cried Joan.

'You'll stop half way along the High Street, Dot.'

Dotty looked coldly at her old friend.

'I suppose there are still plenty of people capable of *pushing* me along to Reg Bull's,' she said witheringly. 'It's little enough to ask.'

Harold took command. Years of administration in far-flung corners of the world stood him in good stead.

'I have a spare gallon of petrol in my garage, and I shall put it into your tank, Miss Harmer. That should get you home safely, and then you can fill up next time you are out.'

'And while Harold's doing that,' said Ella, 'you can come and see my parsley. You know you said you wanted a root to take you through the winter.'

'Very well, very well,' muttered Dotty, allowing herself to be led away.

Joan Young accompanied Harold back across the green. Her expression was troubled.

'You know, she really shouldn't be allowed to drive that car.'

'I absolutely agree,' said Harold, 'but what's to be done?'

'I don't know, but I feel sure there's going to be some awful accident if Dotty is going to drive around these parts.'

'That might be a blessing in disguise,' said Harold, opening his gate. 'If she had to go to court she might be taken off the road for a while.'

'Let's hope it doesn't come to that,' exclaimed Joan.

'There was a lot to to be said,' remarked Harold reflectively, 'for a man with a red flag going ahead of a car in the early days of motoring.'

'Dotty could do with one,' laughed Joan, 'but I wouldn't volunteer for the job if I were you.'

'No fear!' said Harold, making for the garage.


## 5. *Skirmishes at the Village School*


The serenity of September gave way to a blustery October, and Thrush Green was spattered with dead leaves.

The chestnut avenue shed its massive leaves, brown and crisp as cornflakes, and the children of Thrush Green School spent every available minute scuffling about happily, looking for conkers brought down by the wind. It was as much as their life was worth to throw sticks up into the branches to bring down the coveted nuts, for Miss Watson and Miss Fogerty, not to mention the occupants of the three houses which faced the avenue, kept a sharp eye on offenders and delivered swift punishment. Legend had it that a long-dead gardener, by the name of Dobb, had once clouted a young malefactor caught in the act of stick-throwing, with such severity, that he had been taken to Lulling Hospital with mild concussion. In such a rough and ready way had the beauty of Thrush Green's avenue been maintained over the years by those who loved it.

One tempestuous morning, the three teachers of Thrush Green School were sipping their tea in the infants' room and watching the school at play in the windswept playground.

It was young Miss Potter's turn for playground duty, but she continued to stand in Miss Fogerty's room, out of the weather, and enjoy her tea in comparative peace.

Miss Fogerty found this irritating for two reasons. In the first place, the girl's duty was to patrol the playground, no matter how inclement the weather, and to keep an eye on her charges.

Secondly, this was one of the few occasions when she could have had Miss Watson's attention, without the unwelcome presence of this newcomer. There were one or two little matters, such as the disappearance of the emergency knickers from the lower shelf of the infants' cupboard, which she needed to discuss with her headmistress. Miss Fogerty did not care to embark on the subject of knickers – even infants' knickers – with Miss Potter present. There was a coarse streak in the girl, Miss Fogerty feared, which might lead to some ribaldry – a thing which Miss Fogerty detested.

'Could I have some more coloured tissue paper from the stock cupboard?' asked Miss Potter.

'Of course, my dear,' replied Miss Watson. 'If I give you the key, you can help yourself.'

Miss Fogerty drew in her breath sharply. To be given a free hand in that holy of holies was something which she herself had never been granted, and which she would certainly never have expected.

Miss Watson, rummaging in her large handbag, produced a bunch of keys, indicated one, and handed over the bunch.

'Thanks,' said Miss Potter perfunctorily. 'I'll bob along now, I think.'

At that moment a piercing wail from outside the window called attention to some infant misdemeanour.

Miss Watson looked hastily at the wall clock, and remembered her responsibilities.

'You should be in the playground,' she said, 'Get the paper afterwards.'

'OK,' said Miss Potter, moving languidly towards the door. Miss Fogerty felt her cheeks flushing with anger. OK indeed! And to her own headmistress!

'Really!' she exclaimed as Miss Potter vanished, 'I don't know what the world is coming to!'

Miss Watson smiled indulgently.

'Times change, Agnes dear, and you must remember that not all teachers had the advantage of your excellent upbringing.'

Miss Fogerty, who had been looking, for all the world, like a little ruffled sparrow, allowed her feathers to be smoothed.

Head teachers, if they are worth their salt, are past masters of such diplomacy.

The wailing, it transpired, came from young Jeremy Prior, the son of Phil Hurst by her first marriage.

Miss Potter led the child into the lobby, glad to be once again out of the bitter wind. Her charge, still weeping, bled profusely from his right knee, and studied two scratched palms through his tears.

'It will soon be better,' said Miss Potter. 'We'll just wash you clean.'

'I will do the washing,' said a stern voice.

Miss Fogerty had entered the lobby, and now advanced upon the pair.

'Your place,' she said firmly, 'is in the playground. I will look after Jeremy. After all, he is in my class. You'd better hurry outside again before there are any more accidents!'

Miss Potter tossed her unkempt head and sniffed contemptuously. Interfering old busybody! Always got her knife into me! Her gestures communicated her feelings as plainly as if she had spoken, but little Miss Fogerty remained unmoved.

She fetched the first-aid box, and sat down by the tearful boy on the shoe lockers. She had never seen Jeremy crying before. He was a tough, cheerful child, who got on well with his classmates.

'How did it happen?' she asked, dabbing gently at the grazed knee with wet cotton wool.

'Johnny Dodd tripped me up,' said Jeremy, trying not to wince.

'Then I shall have something to say to Johnny Dodd,' replied Miss Fogerty.

The dabbing continued. A weak solution of antiseptic liquid was applied, and finally Miss Fogerty began to cut lint and unroll bandages.

Jeremy, whose tears had now ceased, watched with some alarm.

'Will it stick?' he asked tremulously.

'Hardly at all,' said Miss Fogerty, combining comfort with honesty. She remembered, all too clearly, her own broken knees in childhood, and the horror of soaking off bandages made of old clean linen sheeting. She felt great sympathy for the little boy. He had endeared himself to her from the first, and she wondered now if it might not be a good thing to take him to his home across the green, for the rest of the morning.

Permission, of course, must be obtained from Miss Watson.

'Is mummy at home?' she inquired, rolling the bandage deftly round the quivering leg.

'Yes. She waved to me when I was playing just now.'

Miss Fogerty slit the end of the bandage and made a neat bow.

'Go into the classroom and keep warm. I'll be back in a minute.'

She found Miss Watson in her room, and told her what had occurred.

Miss Watson's face began to assume a stern expression. Miss Fogerty knew, from long experience, that her headmistress was in one of her 'What-will-the-office-think?' moods.

She moved swiftly to the attack.

'I think it's one of those occasions when you can afford to be lenient,' said Miss Fogerty, with unwonted determination. 'After all, if you can stretch a point about fetching our own stock from the cupboard, I should think Jeremy could be sent home to get over the shock for a couple of hours. He will be back this afternoon, I have no doubt.'

Miss Watson gazed sharply at her assistant. Her glance took in the militant gleam in Miss Fogerty's normally mild eye.

She answered with due deference.

'As you think best, Agnes dear. You know I have every confidence in your judgement.'

She watched the little figure wheel about and march towards her own classroom.

Miss Watson sighed, and turned to face her reflection in the dusky glass of 'The Light of the World', behind her desk, which served as a somewhat unsatisfactory mirror.

She patted her hair into place in readiness for the return of her class.

'I must walk warily with dear Agnes,' she told herself. 'Even worms will turn!'


Mrs Hurst, thought Miss Fogerty, behaved perfectly when she presented her with her wounded son a few minutes later.

'Hello, then,' she said, in some surprise. 'You've been in the wars, I see.'

She bent to give him a swift kiss and led him and his teacher indoors out of the wind.

'How very kind of you to bring him,' she said to Miss Fogerty. 'Do sit down.'

'I really mustn't stop,' said Miss Fogerty, glancing around her at the chintz covers, the table littered with papers and the typewriter open and in use. A log fire burnt in the grate, and a cat was stretched before it warming its stomach blissfully. How snug it all looked!

She explained about the accident and how it had seemed best to let Jeremy come home at once.

'He was very brave,' she said.

Jeremy's answering smile touched her heart.

'I cried a bit,' he told his mother.

'Hardly at all,' said Miss Fogerty stoutly. 'A very brave boy.'

She turned towards the door.

'And now I must hurry back. My class has some work to do, but I don't want Miss Watson to have to keep an eye on the children for too long. She has enough to do with her own class.'

Phil accompanied her to the door, repeating her thanks.

'He'll be quite fit to come this afternoon, I feel sure,' she said.

'I *must* go,' said Jeremy.'It's my day to fill in the weather-chart.'

'Then that settles it,' agreed his mother, exchanging glances with his teacher.

'Then I'll see you at two o'clock,' said Miss Fogerty, as Phil opened the front door.

They both started back. For there, about to ring the bell, was Winifred Bailey, the doctor's wife from next door, and there were tears on her cheeks.

Miss Fogerty was the first to collect herself. She acknowledged the doctor's wife, made swift farewells and set off briskly across the green.

'Not Donald?' queried Phil.

'I'm afraid so, and my telephone's out of order. I must get young Lovell immediately. He's in a very poor way.'

'Shall I go into him while you ring?'

'No, no, my dear. Jenny's there, and I'll go straight back.'

Phil left her by the telephone, and took the child into the kitchen, so that Winifred might have a little privacy.

'What's the matter with the doctor?' asked Jeremy, in far too loud a voice for his mother's liking.

'We don't know. That's why Doctor Lovell's coming.'

'But if he's a doctor,' began Jeremy.

'Hush, hush, for pity's sake,' pleaded his mother. 'Come and change your shoes, and help me to make an omelette for lunch.'

She was beating eggs when Winifred came into the kitchen. The older woman looked less strained.

'Thank you, Phil. He's coming immediately. I'll let you know how he gets on.'

Phil followed her to the door.

'*Please*,' she begged, 'let me do anything to help. I could take a turn at watching him or –'

Winifred put her hand on the girl's arm.

'You would be the first person I should turn to,' she assured her, before hurrying down the path.

Little Miss Fogerty, returning briskly to her duties across the wet grass of Thrush Green, was both excited and saddened by the scene which she had just witnessed.

It is always exhilarating to be the first to know of something of note, particularly in a small community, and Miss Fogerty's quiet life held little excitement.

On the other hand her grief for Doctor Bailey's condition was overwhelming. He had attended her for many years, and she remembered, with gratitude, his concern for her annual bouts of laryngitis which were, fortunately, about the only troubles for which she had to consult him.

His most valuable quality, Miss Fogerty considered, was his way of making one feel that there was always plenty of time, and that he truly wished to hear about his patient's fears and perplexities. It was this quality, above all others, which had so endeared the good doctor to Thrush Green and its environs. He had always been prepared to give – of his time, of his knowledge, and of his humour. His reward had been outstanding loyalty and affection.

Miss Fogerty pushed open the school door to be confronted by Miss Potter. Her arms were full of sheets of tissue paper in various colours, and her expression was unbearably smug, to Miss Fogerty's eyes.

She held the door open for the girl to pass. Miss Potter, without a word of thanks, allowed the older woman to shut it behind her, and made her way across the playground to the terrapin.

Miss Fogerty seethed with a mixture of emotions, but remained outwardly calm as she returned to her classroom.

The children were virtuously quiet. The door between the two rooms was propped open with a waste paper basket, and Miss Fogerty put her head into the neighbouring room to express her thanks and to report back on duty.

Miss Watson gave her a friendly smile and said that the children had been no trouble at all.

Miss Fogerty, bursting with the news she had so recently acquired, would have liked to tell Miss Watson all. In the old days, there would have been no hesitation. Out it would have come with a rush, and Miss Watson would have nodded gravely, as became a headmistress, and advised secrecy until the tidings were confirmed elsewhere, and both ladies would have felt pleasantly important, and with a strong bond of self-imposed propriety uniting them.

But the memory of Miss Potter, laden with goodies from the stock cupboard, checked Miss Fogerty's natural loquacity. She did not feel inclined to share this delicious tit-bit with her headmistress. She still smarted from the favours shown to that detestable Miss Potter. Let Miss Watson find out for herself, and then, when she told her assistant the news, Miss Fogerty would have the exquisite pleasure of saying, in as off-hand a manner as she could produce, that she had known for some time.

She sat down at her own desk and surveyed the orderly rows of tables with unseeing eyes.

Her heart was troubled. How *could* she, Agnes Fogerty, respected teacher at Thrush Green School for over thirty years, behave in such a despicable way! What would dear Mr Henstock say if he could read her mind at the moment? And were her thoughts worthy of the high ideals which had always directed the conduct of poor Doctor Bailey, now so near his end?

It was a terrible thing to find that one could become so mean and so petty. And so unhappy too, thought poor Miss Fogerty.

But, unhappy as she was, and torn with remorse and self-disgust, she knew that it was impossible to feel for Miss Watson that warm respect and friendliness which had meant so much to her for so long.

If only Miss Potter had never come to Thrush Green! If only Miss Potter were not here! If only Miss Potter would go!

The clock hands stood at twelve o'clock. Sighing, little Miss Fogerty stood for grace, and thanked God for blessings received, with a heavy heart.

On the way into the lobby, Johnny Dodd, arch-malefactor of the infants' class, whispered to his neighbour:

'We was quiet all that time and she never give us so much as a pear drop out of the sweet-tin!'

Injustice rankles at any age.

# 6. Doctor Bailey's Last Battle

Before nightfall, the news that Doctor Bailey was sinking was common knowledge at Thrush Green.

There was general sadness. Even Albert Piggott had a good word to say for the dying man, as he drank his half-pint of bitter at The Two Pheasants.

'Well, we shan't see his like again,' he commented morosely. 'He done us proud, the old gentleman. I s'pose now we has to put up with young Doctor Lovell dashing in and out again before you can tell him what ails you.'

'There's the new chap,' said the landlord. 'Seems a nice enough young fellow.'

'Him?' squeaked Albert. 'Nothing but a beardless boy! I wouldn't trust my peptic ulcer to him, that I wouldn't. No, I'll put me trust in strong peppermints while I can, and hope Doctor Lovell can spare a couple of minutes when I'm real hard-pressed. You mark my words, we're all going to miss the old doctor at Thrush Green.'

It was the older people who were the saddest. Doctor Bailey had brought their children into the world, and knew the family histories intimately. He had not been active in the partnership for some years now, so that the younger inhabitants were more familiar with Doctor Lovell, who had married a Thrush Green girl, and was accepted as a comparatively worthy successor to Doctor Bailey.

But it was the old friends and neighbours, the Youngs, the Henstocks, Ella Bembridge, Dotty Harmer, the Hursts next door and the comparative newcomer, Harold Shoosmith, who were going to miss Donald Bailey most keenly. Most of them had visited the invalid often, during the past few months, marvelling at his gallant spirit and his unfailing good temper.

Now, as the day waned, their thoughts turned to that quiet grey house across the green. The rector had called during the afternoon and found Winnie Bailey sitting by her husband's bedside.

He was asleep, his frail hands folded on the white sheet. A downstairs room, once his study, had been turned into a bedroom for the last few months, and his bed faced the french windows leading into the garden he loved so well. Propped up on his pillows, he had enjoyed a view of the flower beds and the comings and goings at the bird-table all through the summer.

His particular joy was the fine copper beech tree which dominated the scene. He had watched it in early May, as the tiny breaking leaves spread a pinkish haze over the magnificent skeleton. He had rejoiced in its glossy purplish midsummer beauty which had sheltered the gentle ring-doves that cooed among its branches. And now, in these last few days, he had watched its golden leaves fluttering down to form a glowing carpet at its foot, as the autumn winds tossed the great boughs this way and that.

For once, the boisterous wind was lulled. Wisps of high grey cloud scarcely moved behind the copper beech. The garden was very still, the bird-table empty, the room where the dying man lay as quiet and tranquil as the grave to which so soon he would be departing.

Charles Henstock sat beside his old friend for a short time, his lips moving in prayer. After a little he rose, and Winnie went with him into the sitting-room. She was calm and dry-eyed, and Charles admired her control.

'He's very much in our thoughts and prayers, as you know,' said Charles. 'I know that Ella and Dimity – everyone in fact – will want to know how he is and would like to call, but they don't wish to intrude at a time like this. Shall I tell them the latest news? Or would you like one of us to sit with you?'

Winnie smiled.

'You tell them, please. Doctor Lovell says it is only a matter of hours now. I shall stay by him. He has a few lucid moments every now and again. Why, he's even doing the crossword, bit by bit, but I think visitors would tire him too much. I know that they will understand.'

Charles nodded.

'Jenny is with me,' continued Winnie. 'She insisted on staying today, and I'm grateful to have someone here to answer the door. I will keep in touch, Charles dear, and I'll tell Donald you called.'

The sun was setting as the rector set off homeward. Long shadows stretched across the grass from the chestnut avenue and the houses round the green. Above The Two Pheasants a curl of blue smoke hung in the still air. The bar fire had been lit ready for the customers.

Willie Bond, the postman, was pushing his bicycle along the road to Nidden, at the end of his last delivery, and in the distance the rector could see Ella vanishing down the alley that led to Lulling Woods and Dotty Harmer's house. No doubt, she was off to collect her daily pint of goat's milk.

Sad though he felt, there was a touch of comfort in these manifestations of life going on as usual. Donald Bailey, he knew, would agree with him. He remembered his philosophy so clearly. We are born, we live our little lives, we die. Our lives are cut to the same pattern, touching here, overlapping there, and thus forming rich convolutions of colour and shape. But at the end, we are alone, and only in the lives and memories of our children, our friends and our work can we hope to be remembered.

Charles Henstock, whose belief in an after-life was absolute, had never been able to persuade his old friend to share his convictions, and he had once told Donald, after an amicable exchange of views on the subject, that he considered the doctor to be the finest unbeliever he had been privileged to meet.

In some ways, thought the rector, observing the cock on St Andrew's spire gilded with the setting sun, one could have no better epitaph.

A few minutes later, Harold Shoosmith walked through the chestnut avenue to post his letters at the box on the corner.

At the same time, Frank Hurst's car came up the hill and turned into the drive of Tullivers, next door to Doctor Bailey's.

He got out of the car and hailed his old friend. Harold thrust his letters in the box, and turned to meet Frank who was hobbling towards him.

'Rheumatism, Frank?'

'No, just stiff with driving. The traffic gets worse. I've been over two hours getting home.'

'You want to retire.'

'I will as soon as I can. Come in and have a drink. Phil would love to see you.'

They walked up the path, Harold glancing at the next house, but there was no movement there, except for the thread of smoke which hung above the chimney.

'Phil!' called Frank. 'I've brought Harold in for a drink.'

His wife came hurrying from the kitchen. Harold thought that she looked prettier than ever, and envied Frank the welcoming kiss. Once, for a short time, he himself had wondered if he might ask Phil to marry him, but it had come to naught, and looking at their happiness now, he felt glad for them, and relieved for himself that he still had his bachelor independence.

'What news of the doctor?' asked Frank. 'Any improvement since yesterday?'

Phil told him of Winnie's visit.

'I'm afraid he's on his way out,' said Harold. 'Thrush Green won't be the same without him.'

'I only hope that Winnie decides to stay,' said Phil. 'She has a sister somewhere in Cornwall who wants her to join forces with her, I know. They get on quite well, but . . .'

Her voice trailed away.

'As you say,' agreed Harold, holding up his sherry to admire its glow in the dying rays of the sun. 'People will make decisions when they are still in a state of shock. Not that I think Winnie will do anything so foolish. She's the most level-headed female I've ever met.'

At this moment Jeremy entered bearing a saucer.

'Hello, young man. Are you bringing us nuts or crisps?' asked Frank.

'Can't find them, so I've brought you some of my jelly babies,' said Jeremy, offering them to Harold.

'That's extremely generous of you,' said Harold politely. 'May I have a red one?'

'Not for me, thanks,' said his stepfather hastily.

'Not even a head? I'll eat the rest.'

'Not just now, my boy.'

His eye fell upon the bandage round the child's knee.

'Hello, what's this? A hospital job?'

'I fell over in the playground,' explained Jeremy. He deemed it wiser not to mention the infidelity of Johnny Dodd. He had been ticked off once before for telling tales.

'And Miss Fogerty brought me home,' continued the child, 'and I missed the last lesson at school this morning.'

Frank gave a quick enquiring look at his wife, Harold observed.

'Oh, nothing serious – just a graze. I think Miss Fogerty was glad to have him looked after for that half-hour. It bled quite a bit, you know.'

'You're a lucky chap,' said Frank. 'You won't be spoiled like this when you go off to boarding school.'

'Well, we won't talk about that just now,' said Phil hastily, and Harold thought that she had become rather pink. This was obviously a sore point at the moment.

He drained his glass, and heaved himself out of the armchair.

'Well, I must be getting back. Many thanks for the restorative. By the way, Charles is going to let us know how things go next door, so he told me. Shall I ring you?'

'Please do,' said Phil. 'I think he left there a few minutes ago.'

Harold made his farewells, and returned across the darkening green.

'I wonder who will win that particular skirmish?' he thought, remembering the faces of Frank and his wife, whilst Jeremy looked from one to the other.

At the gate, he turned and looked once more at the Baileys' house. A soft light in the doctor's downstairs bedroom made a golden square in the dusky stone of the house.

There was, alas, no doubt who would win the battle there.


The same subject was the topic of conversation between Ella Bembridge and Dotty Harmer, in the latter's cluttered kitchen near Lulling Woods.

'Jolly sad,' boomed Ella, 'snuffing it like that. The end of everything, I suppose.'

Dotty, scrabbling for change in a jar which, long ago, had held Gentlemen's Relish, gave a snort.

'If you were a true Christian, Ella, you would look upon it as a new beginning.'

'But who's to know?' Ella's voice was almost a wail.

Dotty looked at her friend sharply.

'Well, I, for one, know! If my dear father believed in the hereafter, and all the good and intelligent clergymen we have met in our lives do so too, then I am *quite confident*.'

'But what do you think happens, Dotty?'

'We are simply translated,' said Dotty briskly. She looked at the coins in her hand.

'Are you giving me five pence or five Ps for the milk? I quite forget.'

'It started at sixpence, if you remember, but now things have got so out of hand I thought you ought to have five Ps.'

'But isn't that a shilling? That's far too much.'

'The milkman charges more than that for his homogenized muck, so take the bob, Dotty dear, and we'll all be content.'

'It's more than generous. And I shan't have to bother with change, shall I?'

'No. And now, how do you mean *translated*? Drift off into other new babies, d'you mean, or daffodils, or wire-worms? Some other form of life, as it were?'

Dotty grew scarlet with impatience.

'Of course not. I've no time for all that wishy-washy muddled thinking! When you die you simply leave your worn-out body behind, and your spirit takes off. Don't you ever pay attention to the teachings of the Church?'

'But takes off to *where*, Dotty?'

'To heaven, of course,' said Dotty tartly, seizing an enormous wooden spoon and advancing upon an iron saucepan which had been rumbling and grumbling to itself throughout the conversation.

'And don't fuss any more about such things,' said Dotty. 'I really haven't time to explain it all when the chickens are waiting to be fed.'

'Quite,' agreed Ella, taking up the goat's milk. 'It makes me sad, though, to think that we shan't see Donald Bailey again.'

'Speak for yourself,' replied Dotty, stirring furiously. 'I have every expectation of seeing the dear man again, in a better world.'

'That must be a comfort,' rejoined Ella, as she shut the kitchen door behind her.

'But not for me,' she added sadly to herself, setting off homeward through the twilight.

Donald Bailey stirred, and opened his eyes.

'Hello, my dear,' he said to Winnie. 'What's the time?'

'Six o'clock.'

'Good heavens! I must have slept most of the afternoon.'

He began to struggle to sit up, and Winnie helped him into a more upright position against the pillows.

'I feel all the better for the doze,' he said. 'Let's have another look at the crossword. It's almost done.'

She put the paper on his knees, and the pen in his hand.

'Only my specs,' he said, smiling. 'I'm worse than a baby. Poor Winnie! What a lot of work I make for you!'

'Rubbish,' said his wife. 'Would you like a drink?'

'Nothing, thanks. But have you eaten?'

'I haven't felt hungry.'

'But you must, my dear. I prescribe a light repast for you immediately, and eaten here where I can watch you.'

Winnie laughed.

'Well, I might make some coffee. Will you be all right for a minute or two?'

'Of course,' said the doctor, with a contented sigh. 'Just look at the top of the beech tree! Absolutely on fire in the setting sun. What a perfect sight!'

She left him marvelling at it.

As she hurried to the kitchen, it was Jenny's welfare that was engaging her attention at the moment. Had she helped herself to food? She doubted it.

Jenny had worked for the Baileys for several years. She came two or three mornings a week, from the other end of Lulling, on a decrepit bicycle. Her home was in a maze of alleyways in one of the most ancient and dilapidated quarters of the town. She looked after her aged foster-parents, Becky and Bill Fuller, who had taken her in as a little girl of ten.

They had been strict, honest and hard-working. The child had been pitied by neighbours for having 'a lean time of it'. But Jenny never complained. She was grateful to the couple for a home, and now that they were old she was glad to repay their goodness.

They had put their names down on the council's list for a small home for old people, and Jenny hoped that they would get it, although what would happen to her then, she was not sure. In any case, she told herself, as long as she could work she would be all right. And Jenny was prepared to die in harness.

'No,' she confessed, in response to Winnie's enquiry.

'But, Jenny dear, just because I didn't need anything –'

'I didn't either,' said Jenny, 'but I'll make us both some coffee. How is he?'

'Sitting up and looking better. Did I hear the telephone ring about half an hour ago?'

'Only the exchange people, testing. There was a fault. It's all right again now.'

'That's a blessing,' said Winnie. 'Now as soon as you've had this, Jenny, you must go home.'

'I'll willingly stay. Ma and Pa know how things are here.'

Winnie shook her head.

'You've done more than enough. I don't know how I should have managed without you.'

'Let me know if you want me, Mrs Bailey. I can come back any time.'

'We'll be all right, Jenny, and I'll see you in the morning, anyway.'

She took her cup, and made her way to the door.

'I'll say goodbye now, Jenny. Don't bother to call in before you go.'

'I won't. It might disturb the doctor,' said Jenny.


But when Winnie re-entered the room, she saw that nothing would disturb the doctor again.

He lay back on the pillows, his eyes closed, and his spectacles awry.

The room was very still. Winnie put down the coffee cup noiselessly upon the mantelpiece, and went to look at her husband.

She was surprised to find how calm she felt – as calm as the figure before her. The fear, the panic, the overwhelming sense of loss, which she had so often envisaged, were simply not there, at this moment.

She took the spectacles and folded them neatly, and removed the pen which was still lodged between the thin fingers. She automatically put the fast-cooling hands beneath the bedclothes, and smoothed the rumpled coverlet.

As she did so, she heard the sound of Jenny's bicycle being wheeled to the gate, and was glad to be left alone and in privacy.

She picked up the newspaper which had slipped to the floor. Still dry-eyed, as if in a trance, Winnie looked at the last entry, and remembered her husband reading out the clue. It was 'Bravery! Many lead the twentieth century', and Donald had filled it in, at the point of death. 'COURAGE' he had written, in faint capitals.

Winnie looked, with unseeing eyes, into the darkening garden.

He had possessed that all his life, and he had fostered it in others, inspiring and strengthening them when most in need.

And now, this one word, his last, might almost be considered as his final message to her.

She sat down by the bedside, and began her silent vigil, as night fell upon Thrush Green.

# Part Two
# Fighting Breaks Out

## 7. The Rector is Inspired

On the day after the funeral of the good doctor, Winnie Bailey accompanied her sister when she returned to Cornwall.

The inhabitants of Thrush Green voiced their approval. It was best to get right away for a time, they told each other. The house would be full of memories. Even more distressing, the mound of flowers above the doctor's last resting-place could be clearly seen from the upstairs windows. A very good thing that poor Mrs Bailey should be spared such pain.

The house looked blind and forlorn with all its windows shut. Only the surgery, built at the side, showed signs of life twice a day, when young Doctor Lovell, or his still younger assistant, opened the place from nine till ten-thirty and from six to seven-thirty in the evening.

What would happen to the house now, people wondered? It was a big place for one woman to live in. On the other hand, she had lived there almost all her married life, and she would not want to part with all the loved things around her which she and Donald had shared for so long. It was generally hoped that Winnie would return to Thrush Green, and that the sister would not be able to persuade her to stay in foreign parts.

The quiet weather, which had started on the night of Donald Bailey's death, continued to wrap the countryside in still greyness.

The sky remained overcast, the air humid. The hedges and trees were beaded with drops, and the turf of Thrush Green was spongy with moisture.

Gardeners, anxious to get their autumn digging done, found the heavy Cotswold soil too wet to turn. Lawns waited for their final cutting. Sodden roses, rusty with the damp, awaited pruning, and a general air of lethargy enveloped man and beast.

Tidying the churchyard still went on in a desultory way. The evenings now were too dark to allow much work to be done, but one Saturday afternoon found the rector, Harold Shoosmith and the oldest boy Cooke, from Nidden, busy with bill hooks and shears.

Albert Piggott hovered about ostensibly straightening the vases on various graves, but really watching the intruders on his preserves. That dopey Bobby Cooke, he told himself sourly, didn't know a hawk from a handsaw, let alone a dock from a privet bush. He guessed, correctly as it happened, that his mother had shooed him out of her way. How many was it she'd got? Seven or eight? And she'd been a nice looking girl when they had been at the village school together years ago.

'How's yer mum?' asked Albert, suddenly affable.

'Eh?' said the boy. He wiped a wet nose on the back of his hand.

'How's yer ma?' repeated Albert.

'What?' said the boy. He began to look hunted.

'Lord love old Ireland!' snapped Albert, his brief store of affability vanishing. 'You wants to wash out yer ear-'oles! I asked how yer ma was, that's all.'

'Me ma?' echoed the boy, looking dazed. 'My mum, d'you mean?'

'*Mum, ma, mummy, mother!*' shouted Albert in exasperation. 'Her what bore you – more's the pity! I simply asked – civil – how she was.'

'Oh!' said the boy, and turned back to the hedge again.

Albert, near to gibbering, wrenched at the boy's shoulder.

'Well, answer me then, you dope,' screamed Albert. '*How's yer ma?*'

'All right,' said the boy, looking faintly surprised. He stood there open-mouthed, watching Albert hobble away to a distant vase, muttering the while.

'Loopy!' said the boy aloud, taking a leisurely swing at a lilac bush.


At the further end of the graveyard, Harold and Charles sat on the stub wall and puffed in unison. Their knees were wet and muddied, for they had been crawling along the perimeter path trimming the tussocks of grass which no mower could hope to cut.

'Good of Bobby Cooke to turn up,' commented the rector, putting a hand to his aching back.

'Is it Bobby? I thought that one was Cyril.'

'To be honest,' said the rector, 'I muddle them myself. There are so many Cookes. She used to clean the village school you know, before Nelly Tilling – I mean, Mrs Piggott – did it.'

'Any chance of Mrs P. returning?'

'None, I should say, and in any case I doubt if Miss Watson would want her back at the cleaning – excellent though I believe she was! Your Betty Bell is so satisfactory, I gather.'

'She's a good girl,' agreed Harold.

He caught sight of the eldest Cooke boy slashing at the lilac bush, and hurried to the rescue. The rector rose painfully from his resting place before resuming his task. Certainly the path looked neater, but for how long? And would it be possible to restore the graveyard to its earlier neatness, without at least two men working full-time?

'Sometimes,' he said sadly to his friend, when Harold returned, 'I think we'll have to have those sheep back. Something drastic must be done. We're only nibbling at it, you know. What we want is a clean sweep.'

Harold nodded.

'Are you free on Monday? I'm running down to Stroud to pick up some rush mats for the kitchen, and I'd like you to come with me, if you can spare the time. There's a graveyard on the way which might give us some ideas.'

'I should like that immensely,' said the rector.

'Right,' said Harold, 'and now back to work. Only another thirty yards to go!'

'Thank God!' said the rector from his heart, sinking to his knees.


Monday was another still grey day, but the mists had lifted, and the distant views showed the autumn fields a patchwork of green, brown and gold.

It was a treat for Charles Henstock to have a day out. His parish duties occupied his time, and as a neighbouring parson was on the sick list, he had been particularly busy helping with his services for the past month.

Harold's car was large and comfortable. What was more, it had an efficient heater which the rector's did not have.

'You should get Reg Bull to look at it,' said Harold, when Charles told him.

'But he has. He services it regularly, you know, and I always mention the heater. I suppose it's beyond human aid.'

'Rubbish!' said Harold robustly. 'Tell Bull you won't pay the bill until the heater's put right. That'll make him move.'

'I really don't think I'm equal to that,' replied the good rector unhappily.

'Then you'll have a cold car. And what's more, so will poor Dimity.'

This was a shrewd thrust, and Charles moved restlessly in his agitation.

'Yes, of course. You are quite right. I must think of Dimity. She's not strong, you know, and with the winter coming on, I suppose I must put some pressure on Reg Bull.'

'Good! You make sure you do. He won't trouble, if you don't.'

Harold navigated a bend in a village street, and drew up by a grass verge. To their left stood a square-towered church of golden stone, set in a large graveyard.

The two men got out and went to the wall which bordered the verge. It was a little more than waist-high, and sprinkled with dots of green moss and orange and grey lichens.

The two rested their arms on the top and gazed before them. Around the other three sides stood tombstones, placed upright just inside the wall. Some were of weathered local stone, some of marble, some of slate or granite, with here and there an iron cross of the late Victorian era.

They made a dignified array, in their muted colours and varied shapes, set so lovingly around the noble church which sheltered them.

The churchyard was a completely flat close-cut lawn. The stripes of a fresh cutting showed how easily a mower could keep the large expanse in order. Only one or two cypress trees, and a cedar of great age, broke the level of the grass, and the whole effect was of space and tranquillity.

'Beautiful!' whispered the rector. 'Simple, peaceful, reverent –'

'And dead easy to keep tidy,' broke in Harold practically. 'We could do the same at Thrush Green.'

'I wonder,' pondered Charles. 'You notice, Harold, that there are no modern graves here. I take it that there is a new burial ground somewhere else in the village?'

'I suppose there is. But I don't see that that should pose a problem. After all, the new addition to Thrush Green's churchyard is quite separate. When was that piece purchased?'

'Just before the war, I believe. They intended to plant a hedge between the old and new graveyards, but war interfered with the work, and in any case, the feeling was that it should all be thrown into one.'

'Would it matter?'

The rector stroked his chin thoughtfully.

'We should have to get a faculty, of course, and I've a feeling that it would be simpler if we only had the old graveyard to deal with as, obviously, they have had here. But I must go into it. I shall find out all I can as soon as we return.'

'So you like the idea?'

'Like it?' cried Charles, his face pink with enthusiasm. 'Like it? Why, I can't wait to get started!'

He threw his arms wide, as though he would embrace the whole beautiful scene before him.

'It's an inspiration, Harold. It's exactly what I needed to give me hope. If it can be done here, then it can be done at Thrush Green. I shall start things moving as soon as I can.'

Harold began to feel some qualms in the face of this precipitate zeal.

'We can't rush things, Charles. We must have some consultations with the village as a whole.'

'Naturally, naturally,' agreed Charles. 'But surely there can be no opposition to such a scheme?'

'I think there's every possibility of opposition.'

The rector's mouth dropped open.

'But if that is so, then I think we must bring the doubters to see this wonderful place. We could hire a coach, couldn't we? It might make a most inspiring outing –'

Harold broke in upon the rector's outpourings.

'Don't go so fast, Charles. We must sound out the parochial church council first. I must confess that I didn't think you would wax quite so enthusiastic, when I suggested this trip.'

'But why not? It's the obvious answer to our troubles. Even Piggott could keep the grass cut once the graves were levelled. A boy could! Why, even young Cooke could manage that! And we could get rid of those appalling railings at the same time as we put the stones against the wall. It's really all so simple.'

'It may seem so to you, Charles, but I think you may find quite a few battles ahead before you attain a churchyard as peaceful as this.'

Charles turned his back reluctantly upon the scene, and the two men returned to the car.

'You really must have more faith,' scolded the rector gently. 'I can't think of anyone who could have a sound reason for opposing the change.'

'Dotty Harmer might,' said Harold, letting in the clutch. 'And her hungry goats.'

'Oh, Dotty!' exclaimed Charles dismissively. 'Why bring her up?'

'Why indeed?' agreed Harold. 'Keep a look out for a decent pub.'

At that very moment, Dotty Harmer was driving into Lulling High Street.

She was marshalling her thoughts – no easy job at the best of times – but doubly difficult whilst driving. She had a parcel to post and stamps to buy. The corn merchant must be called upon to request that seven pounds of oats and the same of bran be delivered within the next week. And it might be as well to call at the ladies' outfitters to see if their plaited lisle stockings had arrived.

After that, she was free to keep her luncheon engagement with the Misses Lovelock, three silver-haired old sisters whose lavender-and-old-lace exteriors hid unplumbed depths of venom and avarice. Their Georgian house fronted the main street, which gave them an excellent vantage point for noting the activities of the Lulling inhabitants. Any one of the Lovelock sisters could inform you, without hesitation, of any peccadilloes extant in the neighbourhood. Dotty looked forward to her visit.

Halfway along the High Street Dotty stopped, as she had so often done, outside the draper's, and prepared to alight. A short procession of vehicles, which had accumulated behind her slower-moving one, swerved out to pass her, the drivers muttering blasphemies under their breath. Dotty was blissfully unconscious of her unpopularity, and was about to open the door into the pathway of an unwary lorry driver, when a young policeman appeared.

'Can't stop here, ma'am,' he said politely.

'Why not?' demanded Dotty. 'I have before. Besides, I have to call at the draper's.'

'Sorry, ma'am. Double yellow lines.'

'And what, pray, do they signify?'

The young policeman drew in his breath sharply, but otherwise remained unmoved. He had had a spell of duty in the city of Oxford, and dealt daily there with eccentric academics of both sexes. He recognized Dotty as one of the same ilk.

'No parking allowed.'

'Well, it's a great nuisance. I have a luncheon engagement at that house over there.'

'Sorry, ma'am. No waiting here at all. Try the car park behind the Corn Exchange. You can leave it there safely for two or three hours.'

'Very well, very well! I suppose I must do as you say, officer. What's your name?'

'John Darwin. Four-two-four-six-nine-police-constable-stationed-at-Lulling, ma'am.'

'Darwin? Interesting. Any relation to the great Charles?'

'Not so far as I know, ma'am. No Charles'es in our lot.'

He beckoned on a line of traffic, and then bent to address Dotty once more.

'This is just a caution, ma'am. Don't park by yellow lines. Take the car straight to the car park. You'll find it's simpler for everyone.'

'Thank you, Mr Darwin. As a law-abiding citizen I shall obey you without any further delay.'

She let in the clutch, bounded forward, and vanished in a series of jerks and minor explosions round the bend to the car park.

'One born every minute,' said P.C. Darwin to himself.

The luncheon party was a great success. Bertha, Ada and Violet owned many beautiful things, some inherited, some acquired by years of genteel begging from those not well-acquainted with the predatory ladies of Lulling, and a few – a very few – bought over the years.

The meal was served on a fine drum table. The four chairs drawn up to it were of Hepplewhite design with shield backs. The silver gleamed, the linen and lace cloth was like some gigantic snowflake. Nothing could be faulted, except the food. What little there was, was passable. The sad fact was that the parsimonious Misses Lovelock never supplied enough.

Four wafer-thin slices of ham were flanked by four small sausage rolls. The sprig of parsley decorating this dish was delightfully fresh. The salad, which accompanied the meat dish, consisted of a few wisps of mustard and cress, one tomato cut into four, and half a hard-boiled egg chopped small.

For the gluttonous, there was provided another small dish, of exquisite Meissen, which bore four slices of cold beetroot and four pickled onions.

The paucity of the food did not dismay Dotty in the least. Used as she was to standing in her kitchen with an apple in her hand at lunchtime, the present spread seemed positively lavish.

Ada helped her guest to one slice of ham, one sausage roll and the sprig of parsley, and invited her to help herself from the remaining bounty. Bertha proffered the salad, and Dotty, chatting brightly, helped herself liberally to mustard and cress and two pieces of tomato. Meaning glances flashed between the three sisters, but Dotty was blissfully unaware of any contretemps.

'No, no beetroot or onion, thank you,' she said, waving away the Meissen dish. There was an audible sigh of relief from Bertha.

The ladies, who only boasted five molars between them, ate daintily with their front teeth like four well-bred rabbits, and exchanged snippets of news, mainly of a scurrilous nature.

'I saw the dear vicar and Mr Shoosmith pass along the street this morning. And where were they bound, I wonder? And what was dear Dimity doing?'

'The washing, I should think,' said Dotty, eminently practical. 'And I can't tell you what the men were up to. Parish work, no doubt.'

'Let's hope so,' said Violet in a tone which belied her words. 'But I *thought* I saw a picnic basket on the back seat, with a *bottle* in it.'

'Of course, it's racing today at Cheltenham,' said Ada pensively.

The conversation drifted to the death of Donald Bailey, and even the Misses Lovelock were hard put to it to find any criticism of that dear man. But Winnie's future, of course, occasioned a great deal of pleasurable conjecture, ranging from her leaving Thrush Green to making a second marriage. 'Given the chance!' added Violet.

The second course consisted of what Bertha termed 'a cold shape', made with cornflour, watered milk and not enough sugar. As it had no vestige of colour or flavour, 'a cold shape' seemed a fairly accurate description. Some cold bottled gooseberries, inadequately topped and tailed, accompanied this inspiring dish, of which Dotty ate heartily.

'Never bother with a pudding myself,' she prattled happily, wiping her mouth on a snowy scrap of ancient linen. 'Enjoy it all the more when I'm given it,' she added.

The Misses Lovelock murmured their gratification, and they moved to the drawing-room where the Cona coffee apparatus was beginning to bubble.

What with one thing and another, it was almost a quarter to four before Dotty became conscious of the time.

She leapt to her feet like a startled hare, grabbing her handbag, spectacle case, scarf and gloves which she had strewn about her en route from one room to another.

'I must get home before dark. The chickens, you know, and Ella will be calling for her milk, and Dulcie gets entangled so easily in her chain.'

The ladies made soothing noises as she babbled on, and inserted her skinny arms into the deplorable jacket which Lulling had known for so many years.

Hasty kisses were planted on papery old cheeks, thanks cascaded from Dotty as she struggled with the front door, and descended the four steps to Lulling's pavement.

The three frail figures, waving and smiling, clustered in their doorway watching the figure of their old friend hurrying towards the car park.

'What sweet old things!' commented a woman passing in her car. 'Like something out of *Cranford*.'

Needless to say, she was a stranger to Lulling.

The overcast sky was beginning to darken as Dotty backed cautiously out of the car park and set the nose of the car towards Thrush Green.

The High Street was busier than usual. Housewives were rushing about doing their last-minute shopping. Mothers were meeting young children from school, and older children, yelling with delight at being let out of the classroom, tore up and down the pavements.

Some of them poured from the school gateway as Dotty chugged along. Several were on bicycles. They swerved in and out, turning perilously to shout ribaldries to their friends similarly mounted.

Dotty, still agitated at the thought of so much to do before nightfall, was only partly conscious of the dangers around her. She kept to her usual thirty miles an hour, and held her course steadily.

Unfortunately, one of the young cyclists did not. Heady with freedom, he tacked along on a bicycle too big for him, weaving an erratic course a few yards ahead of Dotty's car.

The inevitable happened. Dotty's nearside wing caught the boy's back wheel. He crashed to the ground, striking the back of his head on the edge of the kerb whilst Dotty drove inexorably over the bicycle.

She stopped more rapidly than she had ever done in her life, and hurried back to the scene. A small crowd had collected in those few seconds, expressing dismay and exchanging advice on the best way to deal with the injured child.

'You take 'is legs. I'll 'old 'is 'ead!' shouted one.

'You'll bust 'is spine,' warned another. 'Leave 'im be.'

'Anyone sent for the ambulance?'

'Where's the police?'

Amidst the hubbub stood the rock-like figure of a stout American boy, known vaguely to Dotty. His face was impassive. His jaws worked rhythmically upon his chewing gum.

He was the first to address Dotty as she arrived, breathless and appalled.

'He's dead, ma!' he said laconically, and then stood back to allow *P.C.* John Darwin 42469, stationed unfortunately – for him – at Lulling, to take charge.

## 8. Dotty Causes Concern

Ella Bembridge was in her kitchen, her arms immersed in the sink.

She was soaking cane. It had occurred to her, during the week, that she had a large bundle of this material in her shed, and with Christmas not far off she had decided to set to and make a few sturdy articles as a change from the usual ties she manufactured for presents.

This sudden decision had been made whilst examining some flimsy containers in the local craft shop in Lulling High Street. Ella picked up waste-paper baskets, roll baskets, gimcrack bottle holders and the like and was more and more appalled at the standard of work as she took her far from silent perambulation about the display.

'Some are made in Hong Kong,' explained the arty lady in charge, in answer to Ella's protestations.

'So what? As far as I can see, the things from there compare very favourably with this other rubbish.'

The arty lady fingered her long necklace and looked pained.

'There's nothing here that would stand up to a week's use,' proclaimed Ella forthrightly. 'Look at this object! What is it, anyway?'

'It's a hair tidy,' quavered the arty lady.

'A *hair-tidy*?' boomed Ella, much as Lady Bracknell declaimed: '*A handbag?*'

'Who the hell ever uses a *hair tidy*?' demanded Ella. But her victim had fluttered away to attend a less difficult customer choosing joss-sticks, and Ella made her way home determined to look out the cane and fashion something really worthwhile.

The light was fading fast as Ella struggled to immerse the cane completely. She was about to leave it to its own acrobatic writhings and fill the kettle for a cup of tea, when Dimity burst through the back door, wild-eyed.

'Oh, thank goodness you're here!'

'Well, where d'you expect me to be? What's up, Dim?'

'It's Dotty. She's at the police station.'

'That doesn't surprise me. That confounded car, I suppose?'

'Yes, but . . . Oh, Ella, it's really serious this time. She's knocked down a boy and he's had to be taken to hospital.'

'That's done it! How badly hurt is he?'

'Someone said he was dying.'

Dimity's eyes filled with tears. Ella, used to her old friend's ways, spoke robustly.

'You know *people*. Some of 'em love a bit of drama. Bet he's only had a bump on the head. Probably been sent home again by now.'

'I hope so. Anyway, Dotty rang up, really to speak to Charles, I think, but he's still out with Harold. She's worried about the animals. They seem to be asking her rather a lot of questions at the police station.'

'Then I hope to goodness she's got her solicitor with her,' said Ella.

'I didn't ask. The thing is, Ella, I'm expecting the men back for tea any minute, and I wondered if you could see to Dotty's chickens and things, before it gets dark?'

'Of course, of course. I'll go straightaway.'

She began to tug at a disreputable anorak hanging on the kitchen door.

'I'll get my milk at the same time. I suppose Dotty'll be back in time to milk Dulcie? That's one job I won't tackle.'

The two friends left the cottage and crossed the road to the green. As they parted, Harold Shoosmith's car drew up, and Ella heard his cheerful greeting as she hurried off through the dusk to Dotty's hungry family.

The grapevines of Lulling and Thrush Green were at work within minutes of Dotty's accident. She had been born in the little town, and was known to almost everyone in the neighbourhood. The victim too was soon named. He happened to be the third son of Mrs Cooke's large family at Nidden, and he was named Cyril. He was in his first year at Lulling School, having left Miss Watson's care – much to her secret relief – that summer.

Within the hour it was variously known, in Lulling and its environs, that Cyril Cooke was dead, dying, on the danger list, suffering from a fractured skull, conscussion, two broken legs, one broken leg, one broken arm, multiple fractures of the pelvis and internal injuries. A few, however, were of the opinion that Cyril Cooke was shamming, and only had slight bruising.

Conjectures about Dotty were equally confused. Some said she would be charged with dangerous driving, careless driving or simply with having no lights. Others said she would face a charge of manslaughter, if Cyril Cooke succumbed to his injuries. There was a certain amount of sympathy for Dotty, but undoubtedly there was also a feeling of 'it-was-only-to-be-expected', laced with considerable excitement at this dramatic turn of events.

It was at Thrush Green that consternation was at its most acute. The good rector was much agitated, torn with anxiety for Dotty and sympathy for Mrs Cooke, whom he proposed to visit at once.

'Who is Dotty's solicitor?' inquired Harold Shoosmith.

'Justin Venables,' answered Dimity. 'Her family has always dealt with that firm. There was a case once against Dotty's father after he had caned a boy. I've an idea Justin handled that case as a young man. Mr Harmer got off, I remember.'

Harold Shoosmith forbore to comment, but was secretly dismayed. He had only met Mr Venables once or twice at social gatherings, and found him a charming old man, silver-haired and gentle. He was also, in Harold's opinion, a good twenty years too old to be practising with efficiency.

'I do so hope that she's had the sense to send for him,' said Charles. 'He's such a wise fellow, and so experienced. This could be a very nasty case, and I wouldn't put it past Dotty to insist on making her own defence. It could be disastrous.'

Harold nodded.

'I take it that one of the junior partners might take it on?'

Charles looked surprised.

'I suppose they might be asked, but I doubt if Justin would let such an old client down. Besides, they're mere boys, mere boys.'

Harold was aware that 'the mere boys' were all around the age of forty, but managed to keep silent. It seemed quite obvious that Dotty would be supported by the aged Mr Venables unless she decided to defend herself. Either course, thought Harold, seemed fraught with danger.

He made his farewells to the Henstocks and set off across the green. It was a pity that such a fruitful day had had to end so disastrously. They had both enjoyed their trip, and certainly Charles now had plenty to think about when planning improvements to Thrush Green's churchyard. Perhaps it was as well, thought Harold philosophically, that he had something else to think of at the moment. His enormous enthusiasm for levelling the graves had quite startled Harold who disliked undertaking anything too precipitately, particularly a project which must certainly face some opposition. By morning, dear old Charles should be seeing matters in perspective, he hoped.

He was shutting his gate, when Joan Young, who was exercising her dog, called across to him.

'You've heard about Dotty's accident, I suppose?'

Harold said that he had.

'Any news of the boy?' he asked.

'Yes. As luck would have it, Ruth's husband was at the hospital, so he examined him. Too early to say yet, the doctor said, but it's mainly head injuries. He's in the intensive care unit.'

'That sounds bad.'

'I feel sorry for that poor Mrs Cooke. She's at the hospital now, I believe.'

'Charles was going to call on her.'

'I'll give him a ring. He can telephone the hospital, and see if she's there. It's poor old Dotty who will need help.'

'I agree.'

'She should never have had that wretched car. We should have seen that she didn't drive it.'

Harold laughed.

'Can you see *anything* we said being considered by Dotty? She's a strong-willed woman – not to say positively pigheaded.'

'True enough,' conceded Joan, and broke into a run as her dog caught sight of Albert Piggott's cat and gave chase.

The morning dawned with a beauty rare in autumn. Fluffy pink clouds reflected the rising sun, and Thrush Green was bathed in rosy light.

After the spell of grey weather it was wonderfully cheering to see the sun again, and prudent housewives made sudden decisions to wash woollies, and gardeners determined to get on with the digging.

At the village school Miss Watson chose: 'Those roseate hues of early dawn have waked me from my sleep,' for the morning hymn, thus confusing several infants, still unable to read, who misheard the opening line and later argued fiercely with Miss Fogerty about 'the rose ate shoes' which needed a lengthy explanation just when Miss Fogerty was trying to fathom the problem of the still-missing emergency knickers. However, infants' teachers are used to coping with such difficulties, and Miss Fogerty was no exception.

The fine weather meant that the children could play outside in comfort, and Miss Watson had time to remark on the sad affair of Miss Harmer's accident.

'I'm afraid I foresaw this sort of thing happening,' she confided to her assistant. There was an element of self-satisfaction in her tone that nettled little Miss Fogerty.

'No one can help an accident,' she responded. 'And you know what boys are on bicycles.'

'My boyfriend,' announced Miss Potter, who should have been on playground duty, but was loitering as usual, 'says that *everyone* should take a test, no matter how long they've had a licence.'

'Has he taken one?' inquired Miss Fogerty, unusually tart.

'Yes, five times,' replied Miss Potter, drifting towards the door.

'That may account for his dictum,' said Miss Fogerty, to the girl's retreating back.

'Have a biscuit, Agnes dear,' said her headmistress hastily. Really, Agnes was getting quite waspish!

'Thank you,' said Miss Fogerty, accepting an Osborne biscuit. 'It ill behoves any of us,' she pronounced in a milder tone, 'to lay blame at *anybody's* door in a matter like this. I'm sure Miss Harmer and Cyril Cooke both deserve sympathy – not censure.'

'Yes, indeed, Agnes,' agreed Miss Watson, with unaccustomed meekness.

'Bad luck about Miss Harmer, isn't it?' cried Betty Bell when she reported for her morning duties at Harold's. 'I called in to see her on my way up. She don't say much, but she looks a bit shook up.'

'She's bound to be upset,' said Harold diplomatically, watching Betty unwind the cord of the Hoover from the intricate figure of eight which she employed for its resting hours.

Harold had asked her, on many occasions, to wind it straightforwardly up and down, because of breaking the covering of the cord, but he might just as well have addressed the moon on the subject, and was now resigned to the habit.

'She's a funny old party,' announced Betty, dropping the plug with a crack on the kitchen tiles. Harold winced, but remained silent.

'I know she feels bad about that Cooke kid, but she won't say so. Says it was all the child's fault. He wasn't looking where he was going, and she was, and all that. Let's hope she's got some people as'll back her up.'

'There must have been plenty of witnesses at that time of day.'

'Ah, *witnesses*!' agreed Betty knowingly. 'But who's going to *be* a witness? As soon as a policeman comes, they all scarpers, don't they? Don't want to know. Might have to spend a day up the court having questions fired at 'em. You can understand it really.'

'It's a duty, Betty, which every citizen must accept.'

'Well, you try telling that to some of them Lulling lot! The only person I've heard of so far is the butcher. He saw it all evidently. Anyway, Mr Venables'll nobble him, I expect, to speak for old Dot – Miss Harmer, I mean.'

Harold was relieved to hear that the redoubtable Dotty had seen fit to call in help, even if it was in the ageing form of Justin Venables. However, he did not pursue the subject with Betty.

'Thought I'd make a start in the bathroom,' shouted his help, heaving the Hoover towards the stairs. 'You finished up there? Shaving, and that?'

'Yes, thank you,' said Harold. For a moment he felt as he had done at the age of six, when a particularly strict nurse had had charge of him, and demanded to know the most intimate details of his morning sojourn in the bathroom. It was only his advanced age, Harold felt, that kept Betty from just such an inquisition.

Halfway up the stairs she paused and put her face over the banisters.

'Know what I told her? I said them Cookes needed more'n a crack on the head to knock them out. And what's more, it was no good worrying about going to court.

'"If it comes, it comes," I told her. "It's no good fretting about right or wrong, or what really happened. It's the chap who lies best wins the case."'

She resumed her ascent, leaving Harold to muse on the layman's view of the legal profession.


Surmise and conjecture were thick in the air at Thrush Green all that day, but nobody saw Dotty.

The sun shone warmly, and the inhabitants revelled in this brief span of brightness. Even Dotty's sad affairs could not seem entirely hopeless amidst such sunshine.

The early sunset was as spectacular as the dawn, but in tones of amethyst rather than rose, with a hint of mist rising along the river valley and veiling the ancient Cotswold bridges.

Just before dark fell, a new sign upon Thrush Green deflected interest from Dotty and focused it upon Dr Bailey's house.

For, against the darkening sky, a plume of smoke rose from Winnie Bailey's sitting-room fire. A few minutes later, Jenny was observed wheeling her bicycle out of the gate on her way home.

Winnie Bailey, the watchers on Thrush Green thought, with immense satisfaction, was coming back!


# 9. Objections

It was dark when Winnie Bailey arrived alone at her door. She had come from Lulling Station, some two miles away, in the local taxi.

It had seemed odd to travel along the dark High Street. It was months, she realized suddenly, since she had seen Lulling after dark, and its empty streets presented an alien air.

Lights shone from the windows at Thrush Green, and Winnie breathed a sigh of relief as she paid the man. Now, fumbling for her latch key, she heard the sound of the taxi dying away as it ran down the steep hill from Thrush Green.

Inside, the house was so dark that she felt a quiver of fright, instantly suppressed. From now on she must face things alone. Plenty of women came home daily to a dark empty house. She must get used to the idea, she told herself.

She pressed the light switch and made her way to the kitchen. Everything was tidy. Jenny's hand was apparent everywhere – in the dusters drying above the stove, the saucepan with soup in it awaiting heat, the set tray carefully covered with a snowy tea cloth.

Dear Jenny, thought Winnie, warmed by the welcome. She carried her case upstairs, and began to unpack it. A late rose stood on her dressing table. The bed was turned down, and upon investigation, Winnie found a hot water bottle in its midst.

Well, it wasn't so bad coming home after all, thought Winnie, washing her hands. She had been longing to come back for several days, but had dreaded secretly the loss of Donald's presence in the home they had shared for so long. Jenny's ministrations had softened the blow wonderfully. She could never thank her fully, she realized.

She went downstairs and opened the sitting-room door. Joy flooded through her as she saw the fire. This she had not expected, and the sight of the flames, and the logs stacked in the hearth, made her home-coming suddenly complete.

She paused by the fire, sniffing the scent of woodsmoke, and another indefinable smell which she could not place for a moment, but which disturbed her strangely.

Suddenly, she realized what it was. It was the mingled smell of the eau-de-cologne which Donald always used after shaving, and the faint smell of tobacco. She looked across at the pipe rack where six much-loved stalwarts stood – the cherry wood, the one with the amber stem, the silver banded beauty, and all the others he had loved so well.

The room shimmered through the tears which welled in Winnie's eyes. She had been undone, in one swift moment, by the agonizing poignancy of small familiar things.

She sat down by the fire and let the tears fall. Afterwards, she felt better, and went to the kitchen to prepare her simple meal.

From now on, she told herself as she rubbed her eyes with her damp handkerchief, she would have to put a brave front on things. She was glad to have been alone when grief had overtaken her so completely.

But she was determined that it should not happen again.

She carried her tray to the fireside, breathed in the mingled scents of home, and took up her spoon thankfully.


The sky was clear the next morning when Winnie awoke, much refreshed. To her surprise and relief, she had slept soundly from eleven until eight, and felt stronger for it.

By daylight, the house seemed its usual friendly self, and the dreadful loss of Donald's presence was more bearable. There were a number of things to attend to. She had a few clothes to wash, some shopping to see to, some telephone calls to make and letters to answer.

She intended to busy herself throughout the day, gradually accustoming herself to the quiet house, without a companion. But as soon as she had finished breakfast she went into the garden.

There were still a few late flowers. One or two roses, their outer petals rusted but still vivid, clung to the bare thorny branches. A few pinks and pansies still bloomed bravely, and the winter jasmine was already putting out its bright yellow stars.

In the shelter of the wall which divided her garden from Tullivers', the Christmas roses were in bud, and Winnie realized, with a shock, that she had made no preparations at all for that festival.

'Hello! Nice to have you back,' said a voice hard by. And there was Phil Hurst smiling at her from the next garden.

'Nice to be back,' responded Winnie. 'Nothing quite like your own home.'

'Are you busy today? Would you like to take your chance and have lunch here? Frank's home for the day.'

'I'd love to. I've got all sorts of things I'm supposed to be doing, but it would be lovely to leave them in the middle and see you both.'

'Right. Do you mind an early meal? Jeremy gets home soon after twelve. Say half past?'

'Perfect,' said Winnie, watching her neighbour speed back into the house where the telephone had started ringing.

She went about her morning tasks, warmed by the encounter, and presented herself at twelve-thirty promptly. A Golden Shower rose nodded about the Hursts' porch, its pale yellow blossoms enhanced by the blue sky beyond. The November sun was warm upon her back, and a sleek robin bobbed and whistled from the laburnum tree by the gate. Despite the gnawing sorrow which now seemed part of her, Winnie's spirits rose. It was good to be in Thrush Green, good to feel the comfort of sunshine, flowers and birds. Better still, it was good to realize that, no matter how dark the day, 'cheerfulness breaks in'.

She was smiling when the door opened, and Phil greeted her with a hug.

'Hullo! Hullo! Hullo! Hullo!' cried Jeremy, bounding up the hall, and Frank appeared, bottle in hand, to add his welcome.

'I can't tell you how desolate we've felt with the house next door shut up,' said Frank as they lunched. 'Don't ever go away for so long again, Winnie.'

'Somehow,' she said slowly, 'I don't think I shall. You know, Peg was wonderful to me, and her cottage is lovely. We've always been close, right from babyhood, and she's the first person I turn to in trouble. But we couldn't live under the same roof for long. She invited me to, and meant it, but she has so many things to do there – all sorts of clubs and things she helps at, and so many friends – it would have taken years for me to settle there, and I'm sure I should have been in the way sometimes.'

'I doubt it,' said Frank, topping up her glass.

'It's true,' continued Winnie. 'And it's the same with me. My life is here, at Thrush Green. And besides, I couldn't possibly part with three-quarters of my home. Everything in it has some meaning for me – is part of Donald's and my life – it would be like pulling a snail out of its shell.'

'Then it would be a slug,' said Jeremy, passing his plate for more fish in parsley sauce.

'And I don't intend to be one,' replied Winnie, laughing. 'No, we shall visit each other more than we did, and probably spend a few holidays in each other's company, but we each keep our own home.'

'That's good news,' said Phil.

'And now tell me what's been happening while I've been away.'

'The most hair-raising event is Dotty's accident,' said Frank, and went on to tell her what was known.

'And there's also some talk of levelling the churchyard,' said Phil, when Dotty's affairs had been discussed. 'At least, so I gather from Harold.'

'That won't please everybody,' Winnie said. She watched Frank helping to clear the table, and thought what a perfect family scene was here. This was a marriage which had turned out well. The three of them had fallen neatly into place, it seemed with the minimum of adjustment.

When she remembered the girl's unhappy first marriage and the tragedy of her husband's death, she rejoiced that this second venture was turning out so well.

'Time to go back, Jeremy,' said Phil before long. 'Run upstairs and wash. We'll take our coffee into the sitting-room.'

'I wish I could have coffee,' said Jeremy, lingering at the door. 'It's handwork this afternoon and I hate my raffia mat.'

'You shall have a chocolate mint to give you strength,' promised Frank, 'but only when you've washed.'

And the child vanished.

A week or so later, a meeting of the parochial church council took place in the rector's dining-room.

The evening was so cold and windy that even Charles Henstock became conscious that the icy room was not very welcoming, and suggested to Dimity that they should light a fire.

The meeting was at seven-thirty (thus successfully interfering with most people's meal arrangements) and the fire was alight by six. Even so, the lofty room was barely warm, despite Dimity's efforts, for the fire had smoked when first lit, and the windows had had to be opened for a time.

Nevertheless, it looked quite cheerful to see a fire in the grate, and when the curtains were drawn and some chrysanthemums set centrally on the table, Dimity was pleased with the result.

If only they could afford some really thick curtains, she thought, fingering the dull green rep ones which she had found at the windows when she came as a bride. These were almost threadbare, badly faded, and completely uninspiring. The carpet too was equally shabby, but there was no possibility of replacing either curtains or carpet on Charles's modest stipend. Dimity thrust away self-pity, reminded herself of those in worse plight, and went to open the door to the first of the visitors.

It was Percy Hodge from Nidden, who farmed a large acreage north of Thrush Green. His family had been staunch Wesleyans until the present generation, when Percy had fallen out with one of the ministers – for what reason no one could really tell – and had transferred his presence to St Andrew's. As he was very much the head of his household, he was accompanied by his dutiful wife and children, and the presence of the Hodge family at Mattins and Evensong helped to mitigate the sparseness of the congregation.

With him was Mrs Cleary, the widow of James Cleary whose family had run the corn merchants' business in Lulling from time immemorial. Hard on their heels came Harold Shoosmith and Miss Watson. She had emerged from the school house just as Harold set off, and they had walked across the green together.

They all exclaimed with pleasure at the sight of the fire, and Harold thought how much more cheerful the room looked than it usually did. The whole house could do with a fire in every room was his personal opinion, and a sound central heating system as well, but one would need at least twice as much as Charles's salary to afford that, he surmised.

Charles hurried in to greet his friends, and busied himself in setting them round the dining-room table. They left the fire, with some reluctance, as the rest of the council arrived.

'Well now,' began Charles, when they had worked through the usual preliminaries, 'we come to the next item on our agenda: "The Future of the Churchyard". I have a little proposition to put forward.'

He began to expound it with clarity and enthusiasm. The difficulties of its present maintenance and the sadness which the community felt at its dilapidated condition were put forward admirably, and there were murmurs of agreement as the rector made his points.

When he reached the proposal, however, the murmurs grew less noticeable, and Harold Shoosmith saw signs of restlessness among one or two members.

Oblivious of the drop in the temperature of the meeting, Charles described the visit to the churchyard in the west which had done so much to arouse his ambitions for their own.

'The place is an inspiration,' declared the rector. 'And I feel sure that Mr Shoosmith will bear me out.'

Harold nodded.

'It can be done here,' he went on, 'and I don't think there would be any difficulty in getting a faculty.'

He paused and looked hopefully at the faces round the table.

Percy Hodge was the first to speak.

'Mr Chairman, sir, I don't altogether like the idea. This tampering with graves will upset people. It does me, for that matter.'

'Me too,' said Mrs Cleary, with some indignation. 'My husband and I spent a lot on that cross and kerb for his mother, and now his name is engraved under hers, and I just don't want the stones shifted. Our nearest and dearest are there, in that spot – I may say, that *hallowed* spot – and to have the memorial stones put elsewhere is downright misleading, not to say sacrilegious!'

She was quite pink in the face after this outburst, and poor Charles gazed at her in dismay.

'But they would not be *disturbed*, my dear Mrs Cleary, simply removed to the perimeter of the churchyard. It would all be most reverently done, I assure you. The graves themselves would not be touched.'

'I still think it's wrong,' said Mrs Cleary forcefully, slapping her gloves on the table.

'I must say that I agree,' said Percy Hodge. 'All my family are there from 1796 onward, as near the yew tree as they can cluster, and I'm only sorry there's no room for me, except in the new part. I shall definitely oppose any move to shift the headstones, kerbs and any other memorials.'

Charles's chubby face began to pucker like a hurt child's, and Harold hastily intervened.

'Mr Chairman, I think this is a very natural reaction to the suggestion, and one with which we can sympathize. I'm sure that other parishes who have faced this problem have also had to overcome some misgivings. There is the other proposition, you remember, about the sheep.'

'*Sheep?*' squeaked Miss Watson.

'I can remember sheep in the churchyard,' quavered her elderly neighbour, one of the churchwardens.

'Thank you, thank you,' said Charles. 'It was suggested by someone that if the churchyard stayed as it is now, then a few sheep might graze there and help to keep it tidy.

'That's even worse!' exclaimed Mrs Cleary. 'Sheep indeed!'

'Wouldn't be practical with all the yew there is there now,' said Percy Hodge. 'Fencing alone would cost a small fortune.'

'What about Miss Harmer's goats?' suggested someone, half-jokingly.

Harold saw that Charles was beginning to get distressed as well as dismayed.

'Not goats,' said the rector. 'I don't think either sheep or goats are a good idea myself.'

At this point, Miss Watson spoke up bravely.

'I think the rector's first suggestion is a good one, and we ought to consider it. Those railings are a downright danger, and the state of the churchyard is a positive disgrace. What's the use of my telling the children to keep the place tidy, with that muddle facing them every time they go out on the green?'

'Quite right,' said Harold.

'And to my mind,' continued Miss Watson, 'it's far more irreligious to neglect the dead as we are doing at the moment, than to rearrange things so that the place can be a fitting memorial to those who have gone before us.'

There were murmurs of assent for this point of view, and Charles began to look a little happier.

'That is exactly my feeling,' he said. 'It is quite impossible to get help, either paid or voluntary, to keep the churchyard as it should be. We can put several matters on the one faculty when we apply. The railings should certainly go. The headstones – er, rearranged – and the turf levelled so that a mower can keep the whole space beautifully cut. I do urge you to visit the church which I mentioned. It would be inspiring, I assure you.'

'Know it well,' said Mrs Cleary. 'Looks like a children's playground.'

'I really think,' piped the very old churchwarden tremulously, 'that Miss Watson's point, about the churchyard's untidiness being a bad example for her pupils, is one of the most telling. I should like to see this other place. To my mind, the idea is sound.'

There was general discussion, some against, but more for, the proposal, and the hideous black marble clock on the black marble mantelpiece struck nine before the rector could restore order.

'It seems to me that we should take a vote on this project,' he said at last. 'Those for?'

Eight hands were raised.

'And against?'

Three hands went up.

The rector sighed.

'Later on there will be a notice on the church door. Any objections, I believe, must be sent to the Diocese. Meanwhile, I will find out more about applying for a faculty.

'Thank you, my dear people, a most interesting meeting.'

Mr Hodge and Mrs Cleary were two of the last to leave. Their faces were stern as they shook the rector's proffered hand at the front door.

'You'll see my name among the objectors, sir, I'm afraid,' said Percy.

'And mine *most certainly*,' said Mrs Cleary, sweeping out.

Harold and Charles watched them depart beneath the starry sky.

'Dear, oh dear!' cried the rector. 'Would you have thought it?'

'Yes,' said Harold simply, and began to laugh.

## 10. Problems at Thrush Green

News of the St Andrew's project soon ousted Dotty's accident as the prime subject of debate at Thrush Green.

As is so often the case, those most vociferous were the people who had the least to do with the church. Several stalwart chapel-goers, whose parents and friends lay peacefully beneath the tussocky grass of the graveyard, were among the first to put their names on the list of objectors to the scheme. Percy Hodge's name, of course, was there, in company with Mrs Cleary's.

'I've been tending the graves of my old grandpa and grandma since I was big enough to hold shears,' Percy said fiercely to Joan Young who had been unfortunate enough to meet him on Thrush Green.

'And then my dad's and mum's. Four graves I've seen to every other week, and four nice green vases I've paid for and put up respectful.'

'It isn't such people as you,' said Joan, in a placatory manner, 'that the changes are being made for. It's dozens of graves that are neglected that make the place such an eyesore.'

'Maybe, maybe! Nevertheless, there's some as adds to the ugliness simply by tending the graves without real taste. Take that one next door to old Mrs Curdle now. I'm not mentioning names –'

Joan Young knew it was a relation of the Cooke family whose grave was under discussion, but let the old man continue.

'– but that woman has put five jam jars along her husband. *Five jam jars*, mark you, and everyone full of dead asters for month after month, not to mention stinking water. Now, there *is* an eyesore! With what she spends in cigarettes she could well afford a nice green vase like mine.'

At The Two Pheasants the debate went on night after night. Albert Piggott, with proprietorial rights, as it were, over the plot in question, found his opinion sought in the most flattering way, and very often a half-pint of beer put into his welcoming hand as well. He had not been so happy since his wife Nelly left him to share life with the oil man.

He adopted a heavily impartial attitude to the subject. He found he did better in the way of *pourboires* by seeing both sides of the question. He saw himself as a mixture of the-Man-on-the-Spot, Guardian-of-Sacred-Ground and One-Still-Longing-to-Work but regretfully laid low by Mr Pedder-Bennet's surgical knife.

'No one who ain't done it,' he maintained, 'can guess how back-breaking that ol' churchyard can be! If I 'ad my strength, I'd be out there now, digging, hoeing, mowing, pruning.'

'Ah! That you would, Piggy-boy,' said one old crone, and the other made appreciative noises of agreement, although every man-jack of them knew that Albert Piggott had skrim-shanked all his life, and that the churchyard had never been kept in such a slovenly fashion until it fell into his hands.

'Well, I call it desecration,' said the landlord, twirling a cloth inside a glass. 'Plain desecration! What, flatten all them mounds containing the bones of our forefathers? It's desecration, that's my opinion. Desecration!'

'I'm with you,' said a small man with a big tankard. 'And not only bones! Take a newish grave now, say, old Bob Bright's, for instance. Why, he hasn't even got to the bones stage! He must –'

Someone broke in.

'Them mounds don't have bones or anything else in 'em!'

'What are they then?'

'Earth, of course. What the coffins displaced. The body has to be a proper depth. That's right, ain't it, Albert?'

Albert drained his glass quickly and put it in a noticeable position on the counter.

'That's right. So many feet, it's all laid down proper, or there'd be trouble. And hard work it is too. Specially in this 'ere clay. But that's what them mounds are, as Tom 'ere says. Simply earth.'

'Another half, Albie?' queried Tom, gratified at being supported by authority.

'I could manage a pint,' said Albert swiftly.

'Right. A pint,' agreed Tom.

'I don't agree about the desecration,' said a large young man with a red and white bobble-hat. 'It's more of a desecration to see it full of weeds and beer cans, to my mind. I'm all for straightening it up. It's the living we've got to think of, not the dead.'

'That's sense!' said the small man who had feared more than bones in the mounds.

'Ah!' agreed Albert. 'It's the living what has to keep it tidy, and the living what passes by and has to look at it.'

He took a long swig at the freshly-drawn pint.

'I'm backing the rector,' said bobble-hat. 'He wouldn't do anything what wasn't right, and I reckon his idea's the best one.'

'A good man, Mr Henstock,' said Albert, wagging his head solemnly. 'Wants to do right by the dead and the living.'

'Well, he's not flattening my Auntie May without a struggle,' announced the landlord, still twirling the glass cloth madly.

'We all respect your feelings,' said bobble-hat, 'but they're misplaced, mate.'

Albert put his empty glass on the counter. It rang hollowly.

'You gotter thoughtful mind,' he said to bobble-hat, with a slight hiccup. 'A thoughtful mind what thinks. I can see that. I'm a thinking man myself, and I recognize a man as thinks. A man as has thoughts, I mean. You understand me?'

'Yes,' said the thoughtful one. 'Want another?'

'Thanks,' said Albert simply.


The lack of harmony among his parishioners affected Charles Henstock deeply. His own enthusiasm for transforming the churchyard had made him unusually blind to the possible reactions of the community.

The fact that there was dissension grieved him sorely. He was essentially a man of peace. Charles had never been called upon to be a militant Christian. Anxious not to hurt people's feelings, uncommonly sweet-tempered and unselfish, it was not surprising that he was generally beloved and, to a large extent, protected from trouble by his well-wishers.

He was quite sure, in his own mind, that it was right to apply for a faculty to alter the lay-out of the churchyard. It was the strife which this decision had aroused which shocked him.

There were other, more practical, worries. The fee for the faculty, if all went smoothly, would be modest enough – a few pounds evidently. But if there were serious opposition, and if legal advice had to be sought, heaven alone knew how much money would be needed! If matters became really desperate, then the whole affair might have to go before a Consistory Court to be fought out. No wonder poor Charles Henstock began to feel that he had put his foot into a hornet's nest. After his initial enthusiasm for the scheme, this fierce opposition from some of his parishioners was doubly shocking.

Dimity watched his unhappiness with much concern. For the first time in their married life he seemed unable to discuss a problem freely with her. It showed, in some measure, how grievously he was hurt by the situation. But to be powerless to help him caused Dimity untold misery.

Thrush Green's rectory, bleak enough at the best of times, seemed more cheerless than ever as the storm winds blew around it.


Storm winds blew in plenty, as it happened, for November gave way to a particularly boisterous December.

Thrush Green, perched on its little hill, caught the full force of the gales which roared across the Cotswolds. A large branch was wrenched from an ancient plum tree in Winnie Bailey's garden. A stone tile was flung from the roof of the Young's house into their greenhouse, and at the village school the lobby door kept up a deafening banging as the infants took their many trips across the playground, and forgot to secure the door as they came and went. If only her class had been housed in the new terrapin, thought Miss Fogerty! If the whole school were disturbed by this endless coming-and-going, well – she was sorry, of course, but it must be expected.

As usual, boisterous weather was matched by boisterous spirits, and the children were restless. Windows rattled, vases blew over, papers were whirled to the floor. Miss Fogerty had difficulty in making herself heard above the din, and the tortoise stove took to belching forth smoke. It was small wonder that the three members of staff were unusually short with each other when they met. The final straw came when Miss Potter, after three days of noisy nose-blowing and sneezing, took to her bed with laryngitis, and her class had to be divided between the remaining two staff. It was at times like these that poor Miss Fogerty counted the years to her retirement, and sometimes doubted if she would ever achieve that longed-for state.

Among the trees at Lulling Woods the wind roared and raged. The last few of the leaves were snatched away, branch clashed against branch, and trunks groaned as they were wrenched this way and that by the elements. And, hard by, at Dotty Harmer's, that indomitable spinster battened down the roof of her hen house, tried in vain to persuade the goats to take shelter, and kept all the animals, wild and domestic, protected from the weather as far as lay in her power.

She was glad to have some extra physical work to do. It saved her from dwelling unduly on the possible outcome of that wretched car accident.

Several weeks had passed since the incident, and still neither Dotty nor Justin Venables yet knew if the police were going to prosecute. Not that Dotty cared unduly if the case did go to court. She had never feared authority – except, perhaps, that exerted by her formidable father – and was quite prepared to face prosecutors, the public of Lulling and the local press, with her usual outspokenness.

No, it was not the publicity which disturbed Dotty. It was the warring factions in her own mind.

On the one hand, she was genuinely distressed to have injured the boy, and his continuing presence in hospital was a constant worry to her. She rang the hospital daily for news of the child, careful not to give her name, for she had a feeling that Justin Venables might not approve of her actions.

On the other hand, she was quite sure that the accident was entirely due to the boy swerving in front of her. Her speed was no more than the thirty miles an hour allowed in Lulling High Street. She had maintained a steady course, and felt entirely innocent of blame.

But would she be believed? Dotty was fully aware that her eccentricities amused Lulling. Not that she cared a fig what people thought, in the normal way, but when it came to finding witnesses one needed reliable people to back one. Where were they? Among the throng who had gathered round Cyril Cooke and his mangled bicycle that wretched afternoon who, if any, would speak for her?

It was at times like this, thought Dotty, that one could do with a husband, or a really close friend, with whom one could discuss one's fears and doubts. To Ella and Dimity, Winnie Bailey and all the other good friends at Thrush Green, Dotty displayed a calm exterior which belied her inner agitation. Her apparent insouciance worried her friends.

'If that Cooke boy croaks,' said Ella darkly to Dimity, 'I suppose our Dotty could face a charge of manslaughter.'

'Surely not!' cried Dimity, horrified. 'Anyway, wouldn't it be a charge of causing death by dangerous driving?'

'Cooke boys don't croak,' said Winnie Bailey. 'They recover from all the slings and arrows of outrageous fortune. At least, so Donald said.'

'He should know,' agreed Ella. 'He brought most of them into the world.'

'Do you think it would be a good thing to talk to Dotty about it?'

'She evades any mention of it,' said Dimity. 'Charles has tried, and she deliberately turned the conversation.'

'Justin Venables should do that anyway,' pointed out Ella. 'I'm not going to worry poor old Dotty. To my mind, she has some uncomfortable moments despite the good face she's putting on things. With any luck, the police will let the matter drop.'

The only person who truly gauged Dotty's anxiety was Betty Bell, who was rather more perceptive than most of those who dealt with her. She expressed herself on the subject to Harold Shoosmith when she arrived one morning, wind-blown and weather-beaten, to 'have a good bash at the oven'.

Her entry into the kitchen set the hall door vibrating, an upstairs window crashing and a laundry bill, insecurely anchored to the kitchen table, floating floorward.

'Lor!' puffed Betty. 'Knocks all the stuffin' out of you, this wind. Any damage?'

'Only in the garden,' said Harold. 'What about you?'

'It tore my boy's shirt on the line, and I can't find a pair of socks. Blown into Lulling Woods, I shouldn't wonder, and the shed door's bust its top hinge and won't shut. Otherwise we're all right. But I had to give Miss

Harmer a hand with the felt on the goats' shed. All flapping loose and them animals eating it as though it's licorice strips.'

'Won't it harm them?'

'Shouldn't think so. They managed an oven cloth and a hank of binder twine last week, and seemed to enjoy them. Funny things, goats.'

'And how is Miss Harmer?'

Betty stood stock still, kitchen knife in hand, and spoke more soberly.

'Worried. Poor old lady! She don't say much, but she's upset about that Cyril Cooke, but won't admit it. She's proud, see. Like she was about driving that car herself. Won't admit she's wrong, ever. I like her for it. Plenty of spunk, old Dot – Miss Harmer, I mean – always had. Stood up to her old father, I've been told, and the only one who could too. He was a Tartar.'

She flung open the oven door and sank to her knees, the better to examine the interior.

'What you been letting boil over then?'

'Stewed apple, I expect,' replied Harold. 'It seemed to spread itself.'

'I'll sort it out,' said Betty, flinging herself to the attack with the kitchen knife. 'And while I'm at it,' she yelled above the din, 'you'd better nip up and shut that banging window before it blows off and down to Lulling.'

Later that morning, leaving Harold's stove spotless and the kitchen in immaculate condition, Betty Bell set off on her bicycle against the strong head wind to return to her home at Lulling Woods.

Outside 'The Two Pheasants' she saw Mrs Cooke waiting for the bus. Two toddlers stood to leeward of their mother, who was looking unusually tearful.

'How's Cyril?' called Betty, dismounting.

'They've sent word to say he's took worse,' said Mrs Cooke, her eyes filling. 'I'm just off to see him. Running a high temperature, so they say. They don't seem to know why.'

'They wouldn't tell you anyway,' said Betty. 'You'll know more when you get there, I expect. You'll feel better when you've seen him,' she added comfortingly. 'Ah! Here comes the bus. Give poor young Cyril my love.'

She watched the three scramble aboard, before turning down the narrow lane which led homeward.

'Poor young Cyril,' she echoed. 'And poor old Dotty too! She's the one I feel sorry for, and that's a fact!'

# 11. *Winnie Bailey's Private Fears*

As the end of the Christmas term approached, Thrush Green village school became embroiled in its usual festive arrangements.

Miss Watson's earlier years of teaching had been spent in various large town schools where dramatic talent was fostered by those members of staff who had experience and natural aptitude for the job. Moreover, those schools were equipped with large halls and stages, so that Christmas plays and concerts could be given in comparative ease.

In such sophisticated circumstances had the young Miss Watson developed her enthusiasm for junior drama. It was an enthusiasm which grew with the years, and even led her to the adaptation of children's stories into simple plays, some successful, others decidedly not.

For what Miss Watson seemed incapable of understanding was the simple fact that a crowded classroom, with no raised dais for the actors, no wings in which to wait, no curtains, and certainly no adequate ventilation, is not the place to perform even the most elementary dramatic work.

Consequently, as soon as December appeared on the calendar, poor little Miss Fogerty awaited the spate of suggestions for 'our Christmas fun', knowing full well that all Miss Watson's ideas would be quite impossible to put into operation in the limited confines of Thrush Green school, and quite beyond the comprehension of the unbookish and inarticulate children who formed the main bulk of the pupils.

'I thought a nativity play would make a nice change this year,' said Miss Watson one morning. 'I wrote a little thing when I was at Aberconway Avenue, and it went down amazingly well, I remember. And only six changes of scenery.'

'But we haven't *got* any scenery,' wailed Miss Fogerty.

'Oh, we can run up something,' murmured Miss Watson vaguely. There was a dreamy stage-struck look in her eyes which turned her assistant quite cold with foreboding.

'I believe the Lulling Operatic Society did "The Desert Song" last season,' went on Miss Watson. 'I should think we might borrow some of their clothes, the head-dresses, and so on, for the three wise kings. And palm trees, perhaps, for the desert scene.'

'There won't be room for the children, let alone palm trees,' said Miss Fogerty tartly, but she was ignored. Miss Watson, when caught in the fever of drama production, became temporarily deaf and blind, as Miss Fogerty was acutely aware.

'My new blue dressing-gown will do splendidly for Mary,' said Miss Watson, 'and I thought I would ask the manager at the Co-op butcher's if we could borrow those two plaster lambs that stand in his windows. They would look very attractive by the manger.'

'There weren't any lambs in the stable,' pointed out Miss Fogerty. 'Only the beasts of the stall, if you remember. Any lambs would be outside, with the shepherds.'

If this crack-brained scheme were to go forward, she thought mutinously, at least let the circumstances be as accurate as possible.

'Then they could stand up-stage in the shepherds' scene,' replied Miss Watson, undaunted. 'I can visualize them, silhouetted against the back-cloth as the dawn slowly rises, turning from black to grey, and then through strengthening shades of pink and gold.'

'We should need to engage a trained lighting team for effects like that,' said Miss Fogerty. 'I doubt if the school fund, which now stands at one pound seventy-five – as I well know, as I did the accounts last weekend – could face the bill.'

At that moment Miss Potter appeared.

'I was just discussing the possibility of a nativity play this Christmas,' began her headmistress.

'But we haven't got a stage,' said the young teacher, coming with admirable economy, thought Miss Fogerty, to the nub of the matter.

'We've managed *many times* before,' said Miss Watson, with a touch of frost in her tone. 'And that was when we were less fortunate with space.'

'And where,' asked the girl, 'would this play take place?'

'In your terrapin, dear. The perfect spot!'

And before either teacher could reply, she had drifted back to her own room. Miss Watson had learnt to make her exit at the right moment, if nothing else.


While the rumblings of war were growing ominously in Thrush Green school, Winnie Bailey was engaged in a much more private skirmish in coming to terms with her changed circumstances.

She was lucky, she realized, that her financial situation remained much as it was in Donald's life-time. For many widows, the sudden drop in income was the greatest worry they had to face, and that she was spared, although steeply rising costs, in fuel and rates alone, meant that the old house would be expensive to run. Repairs, too, would be another hazard to face, but the structure was sturdily built and had always been well maintained. With any luck, it should not need much doing to it over the next few years.

The thing was, of course, that it was really too big for one woman. Winnie felt guilty, sometimes, when she read of people crowded into tenements, and thought of her own empty bedrooms.

On the other hand, she loved the house, and could not bear to leave it. Its sheltering walls had enclosed their happy life together. The furniture, the pictures, the loved knick-knacks, all told their story of a lifetime spent together in this small community where both had played useful parts.

No, the house was not the main problem. She intended to stay there, and was willing to retrench in other ways so that she could continue to live in Thrush Green among her friends, and also have room to entertain more distant friends who would be invited to stay.

The worry which most perturbed Winnie, was one of which she was deeply ashamed. She had found, since her return to the house, that she was horribly nervous of being alone in it at night.

She tried to reason with herself about this. After all, she argued, poor Donald could not have protected either of them if burglars had broken in. They never had been so unfortunate as to have intruders, and were unlikely to start now. What would there be, of any value, for a thief to find? There were far more profitable houses to burgle within a stone's throw of her own modest establishment.

But such sweet reasoning did not comfort her. As soon as nightfall arrived, she found herself locking doors, shutting windows, and finding strange solace in being barred and bolted.

She made up her mind never to open the doors after dark to people knocking. Stupid though it might appear, she went upstairs and spoke to them from an upper window. There were far too many accounts in the papers of unsuspecting women who opened doors and were hideously attacked by those waiting. As far as lay in her power, Winnie took precautions against violence.

Nevertheless, her feelings worried her. She tried to analyse them as she took an afternoon walk along the road to Nidden one winter's day. The wind was fresh, and although there was no rain, there were puddles along the length of the chestnut avenue, and water lay in the furrows of the ploughed fields. A pair of partridges whirred across the road in front of her, and Winnie remembered that she had read somewhere that they mated for life. What happened, she wondered, to the survivor of such a devoted couple? Was she too as bereft as she now was?

Things were not too bad during the day. There were so many little jobs to do, and trips into Lulling for shopping when she met friends and had company.

And Jenny, of course, was a constant comfort. She grew to look forward to Jenny's mornings more and more. She was deft and quiet, with the rare gift of speaking only when something needed to be said, but her friendliness warmed the house for Winnie, and the knowledge that Jenny would do anything, at any time, to help her, was wonderfully comforting.

She supposed that she must face the fact that she was run down after the years of nursing and the final shock of Donald's death. She refused to look upon herself as an invalid, but it might be sensible to take a tonic, say, during the coming winter months, and to catch up with the loss of sleep she had so cheerfully endured. With returning strength these unnatural fears might vanish.

It was natural too, she told herself, to feel vulnerable now that Donald had gone. For years now, she had been the protector, taking decisions, fending off unwelcome visitors, sparing Donald all unnecessary cares. It was understandable that there should be some reaction.

She had reached the new housing estate by now, which stretched away to the left, and covered the fields she so well remembered that overlooked Lulling Woods.

The houses were neat and not unpleasing in design, though to Winnie's eyes they appeared to be built far too close together, and the low wire fences gave no privacy. Washing blew on most garden lines, and a number of toddlers played together in the road, jumping in a big puddle to the detriment of their clothes and their obvious delight.

Winnie smiled at them and walked on.

'Who's that old lady?' asked one of the neighbours, in a shrill treble that carried clearly through the winter air.

Old lady, thought Winnie, with sudden shock! Well, she supposed she was. But how surprising! An old lady, like that ancient crone who lived in the cottage she had just passed, who had a hairy mole on her chin and squinted hideously. Or like Jenny's mother, whose grey head trembled constantly, so that she reminded Winnie of a nodding Chinese doll she had owned as a child.

An old lady, an old lady! The houses were behind her now, and the lane stretched ahead bounded by high bare hedges. On her right stood an empty cottage, fast becoming derelict. She stopped to lean on the stone wall and rest.

The house stood forlorn and shabby, shadowed by a gnarled plum tree.

Ivy was growing up its trunk and the recent gales had wrenched some of it from the bark. It waved in the wind, bristly as a centipede's legs.

The garden was overgrown, but the shape of submerged flower beds could still be seen, and the minute spears upthrusting by the house wall showed where there remained a clump of snowdrops.

Behind the house, a rotting clothes line stretched, a forked hazel bough still holding it aloft. Bird droppings whitened a window sill, and from the bottom of the broken front door Winnie saw a mouse scurry for cover in the dead grass by the door step. Neglected, unloved, slowly disintegrating, the house still sheltered life, thought Winnie.

Although no children played, no parent called, no human being closed and shut the door, yet other creatures lived there. Spiders, beetles, mice and rats, many birds, and bats, no doubt, found refuge here from the cruelty of wind and weather.

It was, she supposed, simply a change of ownership.

She looked kindly upon the old quiet cottage. An old cottage! An old lady! She smiled at the remembrance.

Well, in many ways they were alike. They had once been cherished, had known warmth and love. Now they were lonely and lost. But the house was still of use, still gave comfort and shelter. There was a lesson to be learnt here.

She must look about her again, and try to be useful too. There were so many ways in which she could help, and by doing so she might mitigate the fears which crowded upon her when dusk fell.

It was growing colder. The wintry sun was sinking. The sky was silver-gilt, against which the black trees threw their lacy patterns.

She turned and made her way homeward, feeling much refreshed.


One December morning, Betty Bell set off for her duties at the village school and then at Harold Shoosmith's next door.

The weather had changed, much to everyone's relief. The gales had blown themselves out, and a clear sky had brought frost in the night. Underfoot the grass was crisp with rime, and the remaining puddles were frozen hard.

Betty Bell welcomed the improvement in the weather, and hummed cheerfully as she pedalled along the path to Thrush Green. In front of her, in the bicycle basket, was lodged a large pudding basin which she intended to return to Dotty Harmer as she passed.

Dotty was in the habit of buying enormous lumps of suet for the birds. The trees in her garden were festooned with it throughout the winter months, and a goodly amount was rendered down into fat. Some of this she mixed with stale bread, oatmeal, currants and chicken corn into a concoction which she called 'my bird-cake', and which was thrust into various receptacles nearer the house for the birds' attention.

Usually there was so much fat that Dotty poured it into a basin, and the resultant dripping went to Betty, who was very glad to have it. It was last week's dripping bowl which was now being returned, with a small jar of tomato chutney of Betty's making, as a little return for the dripping.

She was propping her bicycle against Dotty's hedge when Willie Bond arrived with the post.

'Wotcher, Will. How's auntie?' she inquired.

'All right, but for her back.'

'Shall I take that in for you?'

'Not this time, gal, thanks. It's recorded delivery, see. Got to get her signature.'

'Oh well, you'd best go in first,' said Betty, collecting her bowl, and following her cousin up the path. She went, as she always did, round the house to the back door, as Willie knocked at the front.

She heard them talking, and waited, looking at the chickens who clustered hopefully round her feet, their heads cocked, uttering little hoarse cries of expectation.

Willie's whistling faded away as he went back to his bicycle and Betty rapped on the back door. Dotty, looking even more bemused than ever, opened it.

'Come in. Is it your day, Betty? I must have forgotten.'

'No, it's not,' said Betty. 'I only called in to return the basin. Lovely dripping this time. Must have been beef suet.'

She stopped suddenly. Miss Harmer was looking decidedly queer.

'Here,' said Betty, suddenly solicitous. 'You come and sit down. You look poorly. Had bad news?'

Dotty allowed herself to be propelled towards a kitchen chair. A bad sign, indeed, thought Betty. The letter was still gripped in her hand.

'Had your breakfast yet?' asked Betty.

'No, no. I don't want any.'

'I'll make you a cup of coffee then,' said the girl, pushing the kettle on to the ring. 'I've got a minute or two to spare, and I'll wash up these odds and ends while I'm waiting. This 'ere frying pan can do with a clean. It's all cagged up with grease.'

She set about the job briskly, one eye on the older woman who continued to read the letter.

'Listen to this,' said Dotty, in a stunned manner. ' "Dorothy Amelia Russell Harmer drove a motor vehicle on a road called High Street, Lulling, without due care and attention, contrary to Section 3 of the Road Traffic Act 1972." What do you think of that?'

'Nothing!' said Betty stoutly. 'I shouldn't let that put me off my breakfast. You take that letter and all them forms straight up to your nice Mr Venables and he'll look after you.'

The kettle began to rattle its lid, and Betty spooned some instant coffee into the largest cup she could find. She then poured the top of the milk into the steaming brew, and brought it to the table.

'Betty,' said Dotty, 'you've given me the cream, and I always keep that for Mrs Curdle.'

'The cat can go without for once,' replied Betty, unrepentant. 'Your need's greater than hers this morning. Now, I must be off. Soon as you've drunk that, you go up and see Mr Venables at the office.'

Dotty sipped the coffee gratefully.

'It really is delicious with the cream in it,' she admitted.

'You want to take it more often,' advised Betty. 'That cat'll get fatty heart if she has it, and you're not likely to get that – with the little bit you eat.'

She hung up the clean frying pan, stacked the crockery, spread the tea towel to dry, and then made for the door.

'See you tomorrow,' she cried, 'and keep your pecker up.'

She left Dotty folding the grim missive and returning it to its envelope. Pedalling swiftly towards the school, she was seriously concerned about Miss Harmer. Say what you like, it was a shock getting a summons, although it must have been expected. And to think her own cousin Willie brought it to the door!

Poor old Dotty! What with this and Cyril Cooke still on the danger list, the outlook for her was certainly black. Let's hope, she thought, that Mr Venables could help, though, when you came to think of it, he was pretty well as doddery as Dotty. Two for a pair, you might say.

Pushing her bicycle across the playground, Betty gave a rare sigh of despair. Life could be a proper turn-up for the book at times.

## *12. The Summons*

Throughout Lulling and Thrush Green, preparations were in full swing for Christmas.

At Ella Bembridge's cottage, a stack of serviceable waste paper baskets was stacked, flanked by half a dozen stout shopping baskets. Ella was proud of her industry and there was no doubt that the recipients would be pleasantly surprised, being already resigned to appearing delighted with lumpy handwoven ties.

Dimity had washed the figures for the crib in St Andrew's church in preparation for their arrangement. Winnie Bailey was nurturing her Christmas roses ready for the great day, and in all the houses around the green, cakes were being iced, and parcels prepared.

The shops in Lulling High Street were decked with cotton wool, tinsel and bright baubles, and the window of 'The Fuchsia Bush' had a cardboard model of a church, with stained glass windows, illuminated by an electric light bulb in its interior. Flanked, a trifle incongruously, by a lardy cake on one side and a chocolate Christmas log on the other, it still commanded widespread admiration.

The Misses Lovelock, practically next door to the café, were busy sorting out all the unwanted presents, which they had frugally stored away since last Christmas and during the year, for redistribution.

The operation was rather more fraught with anxiety than usual this year, as the list of donors which was scrupulously kept, lest the giver received her own gift back, had been mislaid, and the three ladies were obliged to rely on their failing memories. Acrimony prevailed, as Bertha tried to recall who had presented her with a crinoline-lady tea-cosy, Violet racked her memory in vain for the kind person who had supplied a bottle of 'Dusky Allure', and Ada complicated matters by appropriating anything under discussion for her own pile.

In the dining-room at Tullivers, young Jeremy and his friend Paul Young were busy making Christmas cards. The table was littered with coloured gummed squares destined to be hacked into rough represen-tations of Christmas trees or angels, and a roll of white cartridge paper which put up a vicious fight every time the boys attempted to hold it flat for cutting.

Progress was slow, but their spirits were high and the noise consider-able. Half a dozen lop-sided cards, already completed, were propped up on the mantelpiece, destined for mothers, fathers, aunts and uncles.

'And I shall do one for Miss Fogerty,' said Jeremy, snatching up the scissors. 'She'd better have an angel.'

'I shan't waste paper on my teachers,' said Paul roundly.

'Well, I like Miss Fogerty, and she's been sad lately too.'

'Perhaps she's ill,' suggested Paul.

'Having a baby, d'you think?' inquired Jeremy, scissors poised.

Paul, with two years' superiority on the subject, pooh-poohed the idea. 'How can she? You have to be married.'

Jeremy pondered the point.

'Sawny Sam's sister wasn't,' he said, naming the local half-wit. 'She had twins, and she wasn't married.'

'Oh, well,' shrugged Paul, 'twins are different.' He changed the subject swiftly. 'You doing cards for Miss Watson and the new one?'

'No,' replied Jeremy. 'Just Miss Fogerty. I like her best. I hope I don't have to go up next year to Miss Watson's.'

'I heard my mum saying you might come to my school with me,' volunteered Paul, folding paper with a grubby forefinger.

'Your school?' Jeremy went pink with excitement. 'When? Next term?'

Paul began to wonder if he had let the cat out of the bag.

'Well, it wouldn't be next term, I shouldn't think. Prob'ly next September. That's when the school year starts. Didn't you know you might come?'

'Dad wants me to go away,' replied Jeremy. 'I don't want to, and I don't think mummy does either, but I suppose she has to do what he says. At least, sometimes.'

Paul nodded.

'It's not too bad,' he conceded at last. 'Better than being sent away. You can come home each night and play with your own things. I'd fight for staying here, if I were you.'

'Don't worry,' said his friend, licking a gummed angel and thumping it heavily on the waiting card. 'I'll fight all right, but I want to stay with Miss Fogerty as long as possible.'

He held up the latest card and gazed at it with immense satisfaction.

'Think she'll like it?'

'Smashing!' said Paul.

They continued their labours.

The same subject was being debated by the grown-ups in the next room.

'I can't see any harm,' Frank was saying, 'in going down to look at the place. It doesn't commit us, but if he's due to start next September we'll have to get him entered. Actually, I don't suppose they'll have him until the following year, but we ought to get moving.'

'But Frank, he's so young,' protested Phil. 'And you know how I feel about it. He's getting on perfectly well at the village school, and he has the fun of living at home. What's more, I can see that he is properly fed, and happy. And he is! That's the whole point! Why snatch him from here?'

Frank smiled and shook his head.

'That's partly why. I can see your point, my darling, but don't you see that the very fact that you and Jeremy are so close means that it may not be good for him to stay that way for too long? He's an only child – and likely to be so. You've had to be father and mother to him for most of his life, and he needs the rough and tumble of school to toughen him.'

'He gets the rough and tumble of the village school. He has friends, like Paul next door. Above all, he has a decent home. I can't see why he should be taken away from all that he enjoys, especially after the loss of his father.'

'That's just another reason for getting away to school – away from the unhappy memories he must have when you were left alone. He doesn't say much, but he understands a lot. I think a fresh start, away from Thrush Green, would be an excellent thing for the boy.'

'Well, I don't,' said Phil mutinously. 'And I don't see any point in going to visit your old prep school if I feel that the whole thing is wrong for Jeremy. I hate to say it, Frank, but he is *my* child – mine and John's – and I intend to do what I think is right for him.'

Frank shrugged his shoulders, and walked to the window in silence. Phil realized that she had hurt him deeply and was sorry. Nevertheless, she intended to stick to her guns. She did not mind making sacrifices herself for peace and quiet; but to sacrifice Jeremy's happiness was unthinkable.

'There's no sense in prolonging the argument,' said Frank at last. 'I can see you're adamant, at the moment, anyway. But there's just one last thing I want to tell you.

'If I thought there were any doubt about the school, I'd give way, but I truthfully was extraordinarily happy there, and so was Robert. The head was a splendid chap – a real inspiration, and he had a fine staff. I know there's been a new head for these last few years, but from all accounts he carries on the good work. Tom, at the office, has both his boys there and they seem to do well. Think about it, my dear. I've Jeremy's welfare as much at heart as you have, and perhaps in a more detached manner.'

At that moment, the telephone rang and he hurried from the room to answer it. It looked, thought Phil, as though he had had the last word on this vexed question, but she knew, only too well, that he had not.

*

Dotty Harmer had taken Betty 's advice on that dark morning when the summons had arrived, and proceeded in her car down the hill to Lulling and up the High Street to the market square where Justin Venables had his office.

She drove with unusual caution, so that the procession of vehicles which she led was of some length, and friends on the pavement had plenty of time to exchange witticisms about Dotty's driving.

Anxious not to offend against the traffic laws in any way, Dotty drove straight to the car park behind the Corn Exchange, as previously advised by P.C. Darwin, and backed carefully between a van labelled 'Lulling Rodent Control' and another bearing the inscription 'Vacuum Chimney Cleansers'.

'And what's wrong with Rat-catcher and Sweep?' muttered Dotty crossly to herself, locking the car.

She then realized that the important envelope was inside on the back seat, unlocked the door, rescued the documents, relocked the door, and decided she should have her umbrella, which necessitated putting the package on the car roof, unlocking the door again, fetching out the umbrella, relocking the door, and setting off. That she had forgotten the package on the roof will surprise no one who has to do these manoeuvres, but luckily Dotty remembered before she had gone far, and only needed to return to collect it before it blew away into oblivion.

Twitter and Venables' office had changed little during the years. Mr Basil Twitter and Mr Harvey Venables, Justin's father, had set up their plate as young men just before the outbreak of World War One, taking over the practice from an eighty-year-old solicitor, and returned to their office at the cessation of hostilities, with honourable war records which rightly impressed the good folk of Lulling and district.

The practice flourished, and with the growth of motor traffic more people needed litigation. A third partner, called Treadgold, was taken on, but was soon discovered to be what Mr Twitter called 'flighty', and when he ran away with the wife of a wealthy land-owner, thus justifying Basil Twitter's misgivings, his name was erased from the board, and Twitter and Venables reigned supreme.

In the twenties, young Justin joined his father in the firm, amidst general approval. 'Very solid chap. Very solid,' was the comment one heard most, and when Basil Twitter succumbed to pneumonia in the wicked winter of 1947, and Harvey Venables to sunstroke in Spain five years later, Justin became senior partner and still so remained.

There were three junior partners, now men in their forties and fifties, but still looked upon, as the rector of Thrush Green had said, as 'mere boys'. The older generation always asked for Justin to attend to their business and were sometimes hurt and suspicious when one of the younger men was assigned to them. Dotty Harmer counted herself lucky to be represented by the senior man at Twitter and Venables.

Justin's office was on the ground floor for the very sensible reasons that, firstly, it always had been, and secondly, the younger men could manage the stairs better.

It was somewhat dark, for across the lower half of the sash window was black gauze bearing the wording 'Twitter and Venables Solicitors' in gold letters, forming a tasteful crescent. The walls were lined with the ginger-coloured match-boarding beloved by the Victorians, and rows of shelves carrying black tin boxes added to the general gloom.

Justin Venables sat behind a massive desk which had once been covered in red leather which had now darkened to brown. Upon it were piles of papers, some tied with pink tape, which Dotty supposed, correctly, to be 'the red tape' one hears so much about. A hideous cast iron ash tray, bearing the legend 'Long Live Victoria 1837–97' stood at one corner, for the benefit of clients, as Justin did not smoke himself.

A heavy oblong glass inkstand held two cut-glass ink bottles, one containing blue, and the other red, ink. Each was topped by an apple-sized silver lid, and the stand itself was embellished with an engraved silver plate testifying to the fact that it had been presented to Harvey Venables on the happy occasion of his silver wedding. Dotty, not normally observant, could not help thinking that it could do with a polish.

They sat on hard wooden chairs facing each other across the assorted objects on the desk top while Justin read the documents, nodding solemnly.

'You see that you are asked to state if you will be pleading "Guilty" or "Not Guilty".'

'I am *not* guilty,' said Dotty hotly, 'as you well know.'

'Quite, quite,' murmured Justin soothingly. 'A simple clarification at the outset. I think we can fill in these forms together.'

They bent to their task. Justin's beautiful unhurried copperplate filled the appropriate places, while Dotty answered relevant questions and admired progress.

'Well, now,' said Justin, leaning back and looking at his client over his half-glasses. 'We must turn our attention to witnesses. Mr Levy is being most public-spirited, and will add great weight to our defence. It's a good thing his butcher's shop has such a clear view of the scene of the accident.'

'I'm pretty sure,' said Dotty, 'that there was a school teacher near the playground gate. He might help.'

Justin made a note on a little pad.

'And some boys, of course,' added Dotty.

'Boys are sometimes unreliable,' said Justin weightily.

'Perhaps some of the other shopkeepers might have seen something,' said Dotty hopefully.

'Maybe, maybe,' agreed Justin. He leant back again and put the tips of his fingers together. He blew thoughtfully upon them for a minute.

Outside, Dotty could hear a dog barking, and the raucous squabbling of the starlings which lived in the eaves of Twitter and Venables' property. Two women talked and laughed together, and Dotty thought how lucky they were to be there in the normal bustle of the street, and not cloistered in this fusty room with all the cares of Christendom which she was bearing.

She sighed involuntarily, and Justin put on his professional air of modified hope.

'Now, don't be cast down, Miss Harmer. We have a very good case, you know. I have every confidence that we shall be successful. I shall make it my business to get in touch with Mr Levy at once, and no doubt he will know other reliable witnesses. It is a pity, of course, that you were alone in the car. A passenger could have been of vital importance. Vital!'

'I don't propose to carry a passenger in my car in the expectation of an accident,' said Dotty bridling.

'Quite, quite,' said Justin. He patted the papers together, and stood up. 'I really think that is all that we can do at the moment, but I shall be in touch, naturally, at every step. I see we have a month before we need to appear at court. Much may happen, I assure you, Miss Harmer. We must live in hope, live in hope.'

He accompanied her to the front door, and watched her cross the market square. The hem of her coat had become unstitched, he noticed, and her stockings were in wrinkles round her skinny ankles. Really, she dressed in a deplorable manner.

It was a great pity, he thought, returning to the office, that he could not ask her to dress decently for her court appearance. It could make all the difference.

But there it was. One must take the rough with the smooth in this life!

He rang his bell, and Miss Giles, who had been with the firm for almost as long as Justin had, appeared at the door with a cup of coffee.

'Mr Baxter from the car dealer's is waiting, Mr Justin,' she said.

The rough with the smooth, thought Justin! After Dotty, Mr Baxter would be very smooth indeed.

'Show him in,' said Justin, 'and bring another cup, if you please.'

## 13. A Question of Schools

When Dotty heard from the sister in charge that Cyril Cooke 'had had a slight set-back', she found herself trembling as she replaced the receiver.

'A slight setback!' Unspecified, of course, but it could mean anything from bed sores to a serious relapse. All that she had elicited so far had been such euphemisms as: 'Comfortable' or 'Making progress' or 'Getting on quite nicely' which, though vague in the extreme, were mildly reassuring. 'A slight setback' sounded ominous.

She muddled about her domestic affairs in her usual haphazard way, her mind much agitated. After lunch, taken standing, with a stalk of celery in one hand and a lump of cheese in the other, she could bear it no longer, and decided to call on Mrs Cooke.

That lady was taking some dilapidated tea cloths from the line when Dotty arrived, and took her visitor to the shelter of the back porch, but did not invite her inside. To Dotty this appeared a bad sign.

She had called on Mrs Cooke once or twice since the accident, and although somewhat truculent, Cyril's mother had not been actively hostile. This afternoon, however, she looked decidedly grim.

'I came for news of Cyril,' said Dotty coming straight to the point. 'The hospital people said that he had had a slight set-back.'

'You can say that again,' said Mrs Cooke menacingly. 'I saw that poor child, after they'd sent word he was bad – and bad he is! High temperature, tossin' and turnin', and can't swallow nothin'.'

'I am very sorry to hear it,' said Dotty.

An ugly flush crept up Mrs Cooke's grimy neck and over her face.

'Yes, you should be too. See where your rotten driving's landed my poor boy! If he passes on, his death'll be laid at your door. And rightly too.'

Dotty, inwardly shaken, nevertheless held her ground. She had faced worse than this in her father's time.

'I am not going to argue with you, Mrs Cooke, about a matter which must be decided in court. I simply came to see if there was any practical way in which I could help, and to find out the latest news of the boy.'

Mrs Cooke suddenly lost control.

'You clear off! Go on, clear off! I've enough to put up with, worrying about my boy what you've near enough done in! You old maids don't know what us mothers suffer!'

She advanced upon Dotty with upraised fist. A lesser woman would have fled in the face of such threats. Dotty stood stock still. Her steady gaze was fixed upon Mrs Cooke's inflamed countenance.

Despite her raggle-taggle appearance, there was dignity in Dotty's demeanour, her back straight as a ramrod, her face expressing cold disdain.

Mrs Cooke stopped in her tracks, and let the intimidating arm fall to her side.

'I can sympathize with your concern,' said Dotty, 'but I deplore your insulting behaviour. I shall bid you good day.'

She turned and strode towards the gate, watched by Mrs Cooke. It might have been her father all over again, thought that lady, and everyone knew what he was!

'Murderess!' she shouted after her.

Dotty returned in good order outwardly, but was seriously upset by the turn of events. Her anxiety for the boy's condition was now tempered with concern for her own position if the child succumbed. This possibility had never really occurred to her, and Mrs Cooke's final dreadful word rang in her head.

Of course, it could never be construed as murder! There would have to be intent, surely, plotting or passion or some true evil, thought Dotty, clinging to those principles with which she was familiar. But it could well be a charge of causing death by dangerous driving, she supposed. Should she call on Justin Venables and find out? What an appalling thing!

Dotty was not normally imaginative, but anxiety thrust a hundred horrid scenes into her agitated mind. She could see herself in one of those dreadful cells, at Holloway, wasn't it? The window always appeared to be hermetically sealed, in the pictures she had seen of the place, and the very thought produced acute claustrophobia. And to hear a key being turned in the lock, and to know that one could not possibly get out! Naturally, prisons had to be secure, that was sensible, but it did not lessen their terror.

Then the food, she had heard, was so starchy, most unhealthy, and the company would, at best, be suspect. Dear, oh dear, what a prospect! And for how long, she wondered?

And who, she thought with sudden shock, would look after the animals while she 'did time', if that was the right expression? This last terrible thought stabbed her to the quick. Would Ella, perhaps, of her charity, see that they were fed and cared for? It was a lot to ask, and one could not really expect such kindness if one were a common criminal.

A common criminal! Something about the cold phrase acted like a splash of icy water upon the fever of her imaginings.

She was *not* a common criminal. She was an unhappy woman who had, by sheer accident, knocked down a boy who had crossed her path. She was in the right. She must hang on to that basic fact. Dear Justin had been hopeful, and she would be too. For had not her upright father said many times that if one spoke the truth and shamed the Devil then right must prevail?

She turned into her gate slightly comforted, and set about preparing the animals' last meal of the day.

That the goats received the chicken's mash, and the chickens received the goats' cabbages was some small indication of Dotty's inner turmoil. Not that they complained. Dotty's charges soon learnt to be adaptable, and to be grateful for favours received.

One winter evening, Charles Henstock paid a call upon his friend Harold Shoosmith.

It was clear and cold. The stars were already pricking the sky, and frost was in the air.

Charles was glad to settle by Harold's log fire, and to accept a small whisky and water.

He looked about the room appreciatively. There was a fine cyclamen on the side table, leather-bound books on the shelves, and a well-filled tantalus on the sideboard. Everywhere the hand of Betty Bell was apparent in the glossy furniture, the plump cushions, the shining glass.

'You manage to make things so very comfortable,' commented Charles. There was a wondering note in his voice. 'Somehow the rectory never achieves such snugness.'

Harold could hardly point out that good curtains and carpets were one of the basic requirements for soft living, and an ample income another, to supply other amenities, including first-rate domestic help.

'I have the advantage of lower ceilings, for one thing,' said Harold, 'and not such an exposed position. Those Victorian Gothic buildings never were designed for cosiness.'

'Dimity does wonders,' went on Charles, nursing his glass. 'When I think how bleak the house was when I lived there alone, I never cease to be thankful for her presence. Do you remember Mrs Butler who kept house for me?'

'I shall never forget her,' said Harold firmly. 'I have never, in all my travels, met a meaner, tighter-fisted old harridan.'

Charles looked shocked.

'Oh, I wouldn't say that,' he protested.

'Of course you wouldn't. But it's true. I remember the disgraceful way she allowed you to be neglected when you had flu, only bringing up a water biscuit or two when she deigned to climb the stairs! You were sorely put upon, you know that, Charles. Saints often are.'

'She was rather *frugal*,' admitted the rector. 'But why I mentioned her was that I heard by chance that she has married again.'

'Poor devil,' said Harold. 'I hope he belongs to a good club.'

'I really came,' said Charles, changing the subject tactfully, 'to have a word with you about this matter of the faculty. So far there are eight names on the list of objectors, but I fear that there may be some who object in their hearts but have not the courage to state so publicly.'

'In that case,' said Harold reasonably, 'they shouldn't worry you. I suppose you still want to go ahead and apply?'

'I do indeed. And so, of course, do most of the parochial church council members, as you know.'

'I believe we could get the churchyard taken over by the parish council, if that body were willing. It has been done elsewhere, and then of course the upkeep comes out of public funds.'

The rector put down his glass with a quick gesture of repugnance.

'I shouldn't dream of it,' he said sharply. 'Would you?'

'No, indeed. I think it is the church's business and should remain its responsibility.'

'Absolutely! Absolutely!'

'I only mentioned it as a way of solving our problem. Somehow, I didn't think you would jump at the idea.'

'My chief worry is two-fold,' said Charles. 'The village must agree about the matter, so that there are no grievances, and secondly, we must consider expense.'

'The faculty shouldn't run us into much more than ten pounds or so,' said Harold. 'The church funds can stand that all right.'

'I'm aware of that. What disturbs me is the possibility of a real battle in the village. If those eight objectors are truly all we have to contend with, then there's hope. But if, suddenly, more join the fight, we may even need to call in lawyers, and you know what that means!'

'It won't come to that.'

'Who can tell? I was talking to the vicar of my old parish at the Diocesan Synod last week, and their affair went to a hearing in the Consistory Court. The expense was astronomical. It depressed me very much.'

Harold took his friend's glass to the sideboard to replenish it.

'I still say, it won't come to that. We'll fight our own battle here at Thrush Green. I feel sure that we can talk to the objectors on their home ground, and get them – or some of them, anyway – to see things as we do.'

'You won't get Percy Hodge to,' said Charles, accepting the glass. 'He hasn't appeared in church since the meeting, and I fear that he is deeply hurt. The graves of his forefathers mean a great deal to him. It makes me very unhappy to see such bitterness.'

The rector sighed.

'Ah well, Harold. It does me good to talk over things with you. Somehow, they are never quite so bad after a gossip in this cheerful room.'

He prodded a log with the toe of a shabby shoe.

'Do you pay much for logs?' he inquired.

Harold told him.

'And how much is coal?'

Harold told him that too.

Charles looked thoughtful.

'Perhaps that's why we so seldom have a *big* fire,' he said, quite without self-pity. 'Dimity deals with the bills to save me trouble, and so I hadn't quite realized how much a *big* fire costs.'

He stood up and smiled radiantly.

'But how lovely it is,' he cried. 'I can quite understand people practising fire worship. I'm a little that way myself, I believe!'

The night air was sharp as he crossed the green. Already the grass was becoming crisp with frost. Two miles away, at Lulling Station, a train hooted, and from Lulling Woods, in the valley on his right, an owl quavered and was answered by another.

His tall house loomed over him as he unlocked the front door. It looked gaunt and inhospitable, he realized. His thoughts turned on the conversation he had just had with Harold.

He found Dimity in the sitting-room, close to the fire. It was half the size of the one he had just left, he noticed, unusually observant. One could see the edges of the iron basket which held the fire. The coals were burning only in the centre of the container.

He looked aloft at the distant ceiling, and at the expanse of sparsely curtained window space. Although the night was still, some wayward draught stirred the light drapings.

The lamp by which Dimity was seated had a plain white shade which threw a cold light upon the knitting in her hands. Harold's shades, he remembered, were red, and made a cheerful glow.

'My dear,' he said abruptly. 'Are you cold?'

Dimity looked surprised. She put down her knitting, the better to study her husband.

'Why no! But you must be. Come by the fire.'

He threw off his coat and took the armchair opposite her, spreading his hands to the meagre warmth.

'I don't mean just now, my dear. Do you find the house cold? Habitually, I mean? Do you find it colder, say, than Ella's?'

'Much colder,' agreed Dimity, still looking puzzled. 'But naturally it would be. It faces north, and it's twice the size.'

'And we don't heat it as well, I fear,' said Charles.

'Ella always liked more heat than I did.'

'I've just come from Harold's. His fire seems enormous. I'm beginning to think we must give a very chilly welcome to visitors here. But my main concern is for you. You know that you tend to be bronchial. We really must keep a better fire, or see if we can put in some central heating of some sort.'

'Charles dear,' said Dimity, 'it simply can't be done. Do you know how much coal costs?'

'Harold told me. I couldn't help thinking that he must have made a mistake. Why, as a boy, I remember coal carts coming to the house with a large ticket displayed, saying two-and-six a hundredweight.'

'And that,' pointed out Dimity, 'was over half a century ago! Times have changed, and I'm sorry to say that Harold's figure is the correct one.'

'There must be many ways of making this place snugger,' argued Charles, looking about him with fresh eyes. 'What about a red lamp shade, like Harold's?'

'We could do that,' said Dimity, nodding.

'And a screen? My mother had a screen. She said it kept off draughts. And a sausage filled with sand at the bottom of the door. That would help.'

Dimity suddenly burst into laughter.

'Oh Charles! To see you as a domestic adviser is so funny! And such a change! What this house really wants is doubleglazing, central heating, thick curtains and carpets, cellars stuffed with coal, and a log shed filled with nice dry logs. But we should need to find a crock of gold, my dear, to provide ourselves with all that.'

'But the shade,' pleaded Charles. 'And the screen?'

'We'll manage that, I think,' smiled Dimity. 'And I'll make the door sausage before the week is out. By the way, its proper name is a draught-excluder.'

'Let's hope it lives up to it,' said Charles, recklessly putting two lumps of coal on the fire.


The subject still occupied Charles's mind later that night. Beside him, Dimity slept peacefully, but the rector could not rest.

There was no doubt about it, he was failing as a husband if he could not provide such basic things as warmth and shelter for his wife. It was not fair to expect Dimity to put up with such discomfort. He was used to it. He hardly noticed it, unless it was drawn to his attention, as it had been that evening, by the contrast between Harold's circumstances and their own.

Well, he supposed that he could look out for another, better-paid, living; but the thought appalled him. He loved Thrush Green, and now that he had embarked on the churchyard venture it would seem cowardly to run away from it and all its many problems.

Then there was the possibility of part-time teaching at the prep school in Lulling which Paul Young attended. Charles was friendly with the headmaster, and he recalled now that only a week or two earlier he was saying that he was looking out for someone to take Religious Instruction. No doubt, he had been sounding him out, thought Charles, but at the time he had not realized that, in his innocence.

But would it bring in any reasonable sum? And how much of that would be taken away in tax? And had he really the time to pay three or four visits a week to the school? His parish was an extensive one, and he took sick-visiting seriously. It was one of the qualities which endeared him to his flock.

The poor rector tossed unhappily. Something must be done. He had certainly been failing in his duty towards Dimity. Because she was so uncomplaining, he had let things slide.

'Sins of omission!' sighed Charles, thumping his pillow. 'Sins of omission! They must be rectified.'

He fell asleep soon after three o'clock, and dreamt that he was stuffing a red draught-excluder with sausage meat.

# 14. Dotty's Despair

As the end of term approached, the preparations for the nativity play made uneasy progress.

Miss Watson turned a blind eye and a deaf ear to the protests of her truculent staff, but some points had to be conceded.

For one thing, Miss Fogerty refused point blank to try to train the infants in speaking parts. They were too young for it. They would be unreliable and let the others down. They could sing the carols at the end of the performance and she was quite willing for them to take non-speaking parts, such as oxen and asses and so forth, which were well within their capabilities, but the speaking cast must come from the junior school.

When little Miss Fogerty adopted this militant attitude, Miss Watson knew that she must give way. Dear Agnes was usually so cooperative, but there was no doubt about it, she had not been her usual tranquil self this term, and it would be as well to humour her.

Consequently, the long desk at the side of the infants' room was piled high with animal masks of extraordinary variety. The most life-like was one made by an artistic young mother who had adapted an oblong box, which had once held sticks of chalk, into a splendid muzzle for a cow. With a head-dress of magnificent horns, her daughter was the envy of the class.

There were several donkeys, recognizable mainly from their long ears, although most of them drooped so pathetically that Miss Fogerty privately thought that they looked more like the Flopsy Bunnies. However, the mothers would form the most important section of the audience, and the eyes of these beholders would see only beauty and delight.

To Miss Watson's secret dismay, Miss Porter was being extremely awkward about using the terrapin hut for the performance. She ignored her headmistress's requests to take down models, remove sand trays, dismantle the nature table and generally clear away such obstacles which would impede rehearsals. She also refused point-blank to attempt to make scenery of any sort. Miss Watson was nonplussed by this rebellious attitude.

'No one has scenery now,' the girl assured her. 'If we must have this play which, frankly, I think far too ambitious for these children, then the audience must imagine the settings. We were always taught at college that it was better training for the children to leave the stage clear for their own interpretations. Besides, where could we store the stuff? And who's to assemble it and take it down?'

There was much good sense in these remarks, but Miss Watson could not get over the fact that they had been expressed by a very junior member of staff to her headmistress. To give up the idea of the play was out of the question. Nevertheless, if it were to be done at all, it would have to be done, as Miss Potter said, without scenery.

'We've always managed before,' Miss Watson told her frostily, 'but there's no harm, of course, in making the experiment. Let no one say that I set my face against progress! We'll try it without scenery. It will certainly simplify matters.'

Miss Potter's partial victory, however, did not seem to sweeten her attitude to the project. Her children were slow to learn their lines, their costumes were slipshod, their movements ungainly. Miss Watson's and Miss Fogerty's classes were well-trained and showed up the deficiencies of the younger juniors. Miss Watson found it all very vexing. In the old days she could have discussed the difficulties with Miss Fogerty, but that lady's distant manner did not encourage confidences.

It was a wretched time for all concerned, and when the great day came, Miss Watson was obliged to go into the terrapin herself to take down pictures, diagrams and wall charts which she had expressly asked Miss Potter to remove. One would have thought the girl would have realized that the Three Wise Men would not look right against a background of 'Wild Birds of Britain' and 'Have You Learnt Your Kerb Drill?' Or was she being deliberately obstructive?

Torrential rain persisted throughout the day, so that the cast were obliged to wear wellingtons under their Eastern costumes, and the dark powder ran in rivulets down their faces as they splashed from the school to the terrapin. Matters were not improved by Miss Potter asking audibly what could you expect without a green room at the terrapin?

By the time the mothers and their young children arrived, the play-ground was awash, and still the rain fell. The lobbies were cluttered with dripping prams and umbrellas, and steam rose from the audience when at last they had paddled through the floods to their uncomfortable seats. Miss Potter and Miss Fogerty wore looks as black as the clouds above whilst trying to keep their flocks in order.

It says much for Miss Watson's self-control that she was able to welcome her packed audience with smiles, and to assure them of 'a lovely performance'.

Before the clapping had died down, one of the Flopsy Bunnies was led on by Joseph, horribly impeded by a blanket which had slipped from his shoulder, and followed by Mary in Miss Watson's blue dressing-gown which, she was sorry to see, was trailing along the wet floor, much to its detriment.

There was a painful silence, broken ony by the thumping of Joseph's walking stick on the boards and the impatient prompting by Miss Potter from her seat on the side radiator.

At last Joseph gave tongue and Thrush Green's ill-fated nativity play stumbled into life.

Apart from one disastrous incident in the shepherds' scene, when young Richard Wright found himself pinned to the floor by the heavy foot of a Flopsy Bunny, and was unable to rise after his obeisances, and consequently uttered a terrible word which should have been unknown to, let alone uttered by, one of such tender years, all went well.

Miss Watson and Miss Fogerty turned pink. Miss Potter shrugged her shoulders. The mothers tried to suppress their giggles, and the play continued. But no one could pretend that it was a success, and when at last the children bowed, Miss Watson had the uneasy feeling that the applause was of relief rather than rapture.

When the last of the mothers and children had splashed homeward, Miss Watson surveyed the general chaos of chairs, muddy floor, and discarded costumes.

'Well,' she said, with forced brightness, 'it went better than I expected.'

Miss Fogerty preserved an ominous silence.

'I thought it was a disaster,' said Miss Potter shortly. She took her coat from the peg on the door, and set off for home, with never a backward look at her ruined classroom.

Winnie Bailey observed the exodus of mothers and children from her bedroom window. She had gone upstairs to put on her coat, ready to make a dash through the rain to St Andrew's church.

How dark it was! How wet and gloomy! But there, she told herself, it would be the shortest day very soon, so what could you expect? She had been kept in by the appalling weather, all that day, and felt that she must have a breath of air before settling by the fire for the evening.

She had promised to be responsible for the Christmas roses on the altar on Christmas day. Were there any pin holders in the vestry cupboard, she wondered? It was a good excuse for an airing. Tying a scarf over her head, Winnie set out.

Rain lashed her umbrella, and the onslaught took her breath away. She was glad to gain the shelter of the church porch. Across the road, she saw Albert Piggott's morose countenance pressed against the window pane. He was keeping a sharp eye on his property evidently, thought Winnie, shaking her umbrella free from drops.

She pushed open the door, and was met by that indefinable smell of damp stone, hymn books and brass polish which greets so many church-goers. She made her way to the vestry, which stood below the belfry, and began to rummage in the cupboard which held vases, crumpled chicken wire, balls of plasticine and other aids to flower arranging. At the very back of the bottom shelf she found four pin holders, heavy and prickly. Should she take them home for safety, or should she leave them here and trust that none of the other flower ladies appropriated them?

She had just decided to take two and to leave two, when she heard a faint noise. Tip-toeing to the door of the vestry she gazed down the length of the aisle. A small figure was kneeling in one of the front pews.

It was so dark by now that Winnie could not recognize the person, although she guessed it was a woman. She hoped that her movements had not disturbed whoever-it-was at her devotions.

She tip-toed back to the cupboard and replaced two of the pin holders. The remaining two she thrust into her handbag.

Very quietly she emerged from the vestry and began to tip-toe to the door. At that moment, a loud sniff shattered the silence. The little figure stumbled from the pew and hastened up the aisle towards Winnie, who saw, with astonishment, that it was Dotty Harmer, and that she had been weeping.

Winnie did not speak until they were both in the porch. She retrieved her umbrella.

'I'm going back, Dotty dear, to make myself some tea. Come and join me.'

Dotty nodded.

Winnie put up the umbrella, and linked Dotty's frail arm into her own. The lights were beginning to glow from the windows at Thrush Green.

'Not fit to be out,' shouted Winnie above the noise of the wind and rain. A faint pressure on her arm showed that Dotty had heard, but she said nothing. Winnie began to find this unusual silence unnerving, and was glad when they reached her home and she could busy herself with the latch key.

'Come by the fire, Dotty, while I put on the kettle. Here, let me take your mackintosh. It can drip in the kitchen.'

She drew a chair close to the blaze and settled the woebegone figure in it. There were no tears now, but Dotty looked white and exhausted. What could be the matter?

When she returned with the tea tray and a plate of homemade short-bread, she found Dotty leaning back with her eyes closed, but to her relief she sat up when Winnie began to pour the tea, and drank the liquid as though she had not had food for hours.

'That *was* good, Winnie dear,' she said thankfully, replacing her empty cup. 'I don't usually bother with tea.'

'Did you bother with lunch today?' asked Winnie, emboldened by the improvement in her guest's condition.

'Well, no. To tell the truth, I was a little upset yesterday, and didn't sleep last night.'

She stopped, took off her glasses and began to polish them with the hem of her petticoat. Without her spectacles, Winnie noticed, her face seemed very small and vulnerable. A short-sighted child might look like that, bewildered and questioning.

Winnie said nothing. She was determined not to pry into Dotty's troubles. She knew about the impending court case and suspected that this breakdown might have something to do with it. But somehow, it was not in keeping with Dotty's habitual chirpiness. She had given no sign, over the last few weeks, of caring deeply about the affair. It was odd that she should collapse now.

Dotty accepted her second cup of tea and stirred it slowly, her eyes on the dancing flames.

'I went to see Mrs Cooke yesterday,' she began. 'At Nidden, you know. The mother of the child who swerved in front of my car.'

'I know,' said Winnie.

Dotty put down her cup, and began to tell Winnie the whole appalling tale. The anxiety, the daily bulletins, the horror of the child's relapse, the possibility of the boy dying, of taking another's life – it all poured out, until the dreadful climax was reached of Mrs Cooke's blood-chilling cry of 'Murderess!' which had haunted poor Dotty ever since.

'And so you see why I was in church, Winnie. I simply had to tell someone. Someone I could trust. Living alone does tend to make one exaggerate one's fears and I couldn't stay in the house a moment longer.'

'You did the right thing,' Winnie assured her. Dotty's fingers were pulling her handkerchief this way and that in her agitation.

'And now I've burdened you with it,' cried Dotty distractedly. 'You won't ever tell anyone, will you, Winnie dear? I couldn't bear Thrush Green to get wind of my shameful fears.'

'No one will learn anything from me,' Winnie promised. 'And you know, Dotty, we all have fears, and I'm beginning to realize that we must accept them and not feel ashamed of them.'

She went on to tell Dotty about her own nervousness at night-time in the house, and how difficult it seemed to overcome it. As she spoke, she noticed that the handkerchief was put away, that Dotty was nodding agreement, and drinking the second cup of tea, engrossed in someone else's troubles now.

'Perhaps I could come and sleep here,' said Dotty eventually, 'at least for a bit, until you feel better about things.'

'I shouldn't dream of allowing you to,' said Winnie. 'If you can cope alone, down at Lulling Woods, which is far more remote than this place, then I can too. I shall get used to it in time, but what I'm trying to say, Dotty, is that it does no good to torture oneself with guilt and shame simply because one has fears. We're *right* to have fears about some things; evil, for instance, and violence and lying, and I'm not going to add to my misery by feeling ashamed of my loneliness. I am lonely now, but it will pass. You are desolated now by what might occur, but that will pass too.'

Dotty sighed.

'What a comfort you are, Winnie.'

'I don't know about that, but you've certainly cheered me by giving me your company.'

Dotty stood up and began her usual disjointed quest for her belongings.

'Must you go so soon?'

'I really must. I feel so much better for the tea and sympathy. Where's my raincoat? And did I have a scarf?'

Winnie piloted her old friend into the hall, and helped her into her raincoat.

'Would you like me to walk back with you?'

'Not in this rain, Winnie dear. I promise you that I shall be quite all right now.'

'Then you must borrow the umbrella. No hurry for its return. It's an old one of Donald's that lives in the porch here for just such a downpour.'

Dotty accepted the umbrella, but before putting it up, she gave Winnie a rare kiss.

With something of her usual jauntiness she set off down the path. Beneath the great umbrella her thin legs in their wrinkled stockings splashed purposefully through the puddles.

Winnie watched until she vanished from sight across the darkening green, and then closed the front door and began to bolt and bar ready for the long night.

Twenty miles away, in the children's ward of the county hospital, the doctor on duty sat on Cyril Cooke's bed.

The boy was sitting up. His flushed face was between the doctor's two cold hands. They strayed over the cheeks, behind the tousled hair, and massaged the glands behind the ears and down the neck.

The child winced.

'Ever had mumps?' inquired the doctor.

Cyril, never a garrulous boy, was even less articulate in his present pain. He shook his head.

'Positive?'

He nodded, and emitted a squeak of agony.

The doctor stood up.

'Well, son, you've got 'em now,' he said laconically. 'See to him, nurse.'

# Part Three

# The Outcome of Hostilities

## *15. The Sad Affair of the Bedjacket*

The cold dry weather continued. Most nights there was frost, blackening the few remaining dahlias and stripping the last of the leaves from the trees.

'Do you think we might get a white Christmas?' asked Charles Henstock of Harold.

'No good asking me, my dear chap. Most of my Christmases were spent with the air conditioner going full blast, and the sweat still running down my back.'

'It does seem extraordinary,' ruminated the rector, 'how mild the winters are these days. I haven't been skating for years.'

'Skating?' Harold looked at his friend with new respect. 'Can you really skate?'

'Good heavens, yes! Most of us older folk can, you know. I learnt on Grantchester Meadows. A splendid chap from Durham taught me. He was up at Cambridge with me. I often wonder what became of him. He took part in an arctic expedition – that I do know – because he used to practise paddling his kayak on the Cam, mostly upside down. He loved it.'

'Paddling upside down, or skating?'

'Both really. He loved life – a great capacity for enjoyment. I think of him often, especially in cold weather.'

'And you think we might get some at Christmas?'

The rector sighed.

'I suppose not. It will be mild and muggy, I expect, and everyone will tell me the weather will make a full churchyard.'

He stopped. His chubby face began to pucker with concern.

'And that reminds me. I really came to tell you that there is a special meeting of the parochial church council at the rectory on the twenty-second. Can you manage it?'

'Of course,' said Harold.

'Seven-thirty, as usual.'

'I was afraid so,' replied Harold. 'I'll have an egg to my tea, as they say up north.'

'And a very sensible idea too,' responded Charles. 'I shall suggest it to Dimity. An empty stomach produces a lack of concentration, I find.'

'In me,' said Harold, 'it produces the most extraordinary noises.'

'You don't think,' said Charles, 'that this business is likely to go on for years? I really want to get things started. I read only the other day of a similar affair concerning a churchyard in East Anglia where controversy has continued for eighteen years.'

The rector turned troubled blue eyes upon his friend.

'*Eighteen years!*' he repeated. 'Can you bear to think of it, Harold? Why, I shall no doubt be among the blessed dead myself, if we take that time.'

'At least you wouldn't be worrying about it,' pointed out Harold reasonably.

On the last day of term, little Miss Fogerty carried her attaché case with extra care to school.

It contained two presents. One for Miss Watson, and a smaller one for the detestable Miss Potter.

Miss Fogerty had had mixed feelings about the presents, and was ashamed that she had harboured them. Never before had she felt anything but unalloyed pleasure at giving dear Miss Watson a Christmas present. This year, she had begun to wonder if she would give her one at all after the pain she had caused her during this most unpleasant term.

But the knitted bedjacket had been started last summer, long before Miss Potter arrived on the scene. The pattern was intricate, involving sixteen rows to each feather-and-shell design. Executed in pale pink three-ply wool it had taken Miss Fogerty many hours of fiddling work – and some of unpicking – to complete the garment, and even now she had her doubts about the scalloped edges to the collar and the width of the much-too-expensive satin ribbon which ensured modesty.

It should have been a labour of love. It started that way. It was in November, when the first sleeve was begun, that Miss Fogerty started to wonder if Miss Watson really deserved such efforts. She told herself that such thoughts were unworthy of a practising Christian, and continued to knit. But the thoughts intruded many times before the bedjacket was pressed and wrapped in Christmas paper.

However, she told herself as she hurried along to school, this was the season of goodwill, and Miss Watson would really appreciate her handiwork. It gave her a comfortable glow to think of her headmistress sitting up in bed reading, snugly embraced by the pink woolly.

As for Miss Potter, well – at Christmas one must be generous. A box of good linen handkerchiefs, bought at the church bazaar, accompanied the bedjacket, wrapped in similar Christmas paper but with a slightly smaller tag and a slightly more formal message. Privately, Miss Fogerty thought, the girl was very lucky.

Miss Fogerty put her attaché case on her desk and lifted out the two parcels. She carefully opened one end of Miss Watson's parcel to assure herself that the bow was uncrumpled. At that moment, Miss Potter entered.

'Brought your spencer?' she giggled, peering over Miss Fogerty's shoulder, in the rudest fashion.

Miss Fogerty closed the parcel swiftly.

'I fail to see anything funny about spencers,' she responded. 'But for your information I have not had occasion to wear mine as the weather has been so mild.'

Miss Potter had the grace to look slightly abashed. To tell the truth, she had been under the impression that such garments went out with Queen Victoria. That they were still winter wear at Thrush Green only confirmed her view that her present abode was abysmally behind the times.

Miss Fogerty produced the box of handkerchiefs and a creditable smile, and wished her young colleague a merry Christmas.

'Crumbs!' ejaculated that lady. 'Do we do all this present-giving? I haven't done anything about you or Miss Watson. But thank you very much,' she added hastily. 'I'll keep it till Christmas Day. We put all our presents round the tree, you know.'

The clanging of the hand bell announced that Miss Watson was in charge of the playground that day, and the two teachers hurried out to marshal their charges.

What with one thing and another, Miss Fogerty did not get the chance to give her headmistress the present until school was over. For one thing, Miss Watson was in the playground most of the time. Then the children were unusually boisterous, and there had been two infant puddles caused by pre-Christmas excitement (and *still* no sign of the emergency knickers, an unsolved mystery!), with the added complication of Albert Piggott's cat which had taken it into its head to explore the premises during the reading of 'The Tale of Mrs Tiggywinkle', thus distracting the children's already wayward attention.

Recognizing defeat, Miss Fogerty had allowed the children to give it half a bottle of school milk in the saucer lately occupied by mustard and cress, which the poor animal lapped so ravenously that, as she suspected, it was obvious that Piggott neglected it. Only when it had consumed half a digestive biscuit, the end of a ham sandwich, and a piece of chocolate pressed upon it by its doting hosts, did the animal settle to sleep by the tortoise stove and allow Miss Fogerty to resume her reading. Even then, she was exhorted to: 'Read soft, miss!' in case she disturbed the intruder.

The children had streamed home. Albert Piggott's cat, carefully wrapped in someone's scarf, was accompanied by a dozen well-wishers although, as Miss Fogerty had pointed out, the cat knew its own way home and would probably prefer to make the fifty-yard journey on foot.

Miss Potter put her head round the door and called: 'See you next term! Happy Christmas!' in a perfunctory manner, and promptly vanished, and Miss Fogerty and Miss Watson were, at last, alone in the building.

Miss Fogerty, back to her usual warm-hearted self in these familiar circumstances, put the parcel on Miss Watson's desk and stood back, smiling.

'Oh, Agnes dear, how *very* kind!' exclaimed the headmistress. 'And what pretty paper! You are always so clever about finding something that little bit different.'

Her eyes were sparkling. Miss Fogerty's hard thoughts had long ago vanished. The spirit of Christmas warmed her.

'Can I open it now, Agnes? I can never bear to wait until Christmas Day. I'm sure it's something wonderful.'

She began to undo the paper, Miss Fogerty watching indulgently. Just like a child, she thought, the same excitement, the same lovable impatience! Dear Miss Watson!

By now the parcel was opened and Miss Watson began to lift up the creation.

'Another bedjacket,' she cried with delight.

'*Another?*' quavered Miss Fogerty faintly.

'And what a beauty!' gabbled Miss Watson, struggling valiantly to cover her slip. 'Did you do all this wonderful work yourself, Agnes dear?'

But Miss Fogerty was still stunned by the blow.

'You've had *another* bedjacket?' she queried, bemused. 'This Christmas? *Another* one?'

'Just a little thing from my brother,' said Miss Watson, torn painfully between Truthfulness and Kindness-to-Others, and attempting to sound airy at the same time. It was just such a situation, she thought desperately, that could bring on a stroke.

'It could never mean to me what this *perfect* present does, Agnes, I assure you! To think that you did every stitch – with your own hands!'

Not that she would have done every stitch with anybody else's hands, of course, thought poor distracted Miss Watson, but really, what could one say for comfort? Agnes looked positively shattered.

'How long did it take you?' she pressed, stroking the satin bow.

'I began it in June,' replied Miss Fogerty. She still sounded dazed.

'Come and have a cup of tea,' urged Miss Watson, 'before you go home. I'm afraid I haven't wrapped your present yet, Agnes dear. End of term, you know.'

'I must go,' said Miss Fogerty, as though in a trance, 'I too have a lot to do. I go away tomorrow.'

'Then I shall walk round this evening, if I may,' said Miss Watson. 'I shan't be leaving here until Christmas Eve. There is a Meeting Extraordinary of the Parochial Church Council on the twenty-second,' she continued importantly, 'so I shall stay to see that through.'

Little Miss Fogerty did not appear to hear her. She went blindly to her room, picked up her case and handbag, and walked out of the school door.

Behind her, sorely upset, Miss Watson set about wrapping the bedjacket with shaking hands.

Cold with shock, Miss Fogerty scuttled home through the dusk to her lodgings. She should never have said it! Never! Not even if she had received ten, twenty – nay, a *hundred* – bedjackets, she should never have uttered that dreadful, cruel, unforgivable word 'ANOTHER!'

To think of the hours, the weeks, the months of constant love – well, *almost* constant love, conceded Miss Fogerty honestly –which had gone into that bedjacket! And how had it been greeted? With admiration? With gratitude? Not a bit of it. It was 'Just Another Bedjacket'!

She could imagine the brother's 'little thing', of course. Some splendid quilted article, no doubt, of pure silk, possibly trimmed with swansdown, and costing as many guineas as she earned in a month's teaching. Oh, it was easy to give something splendid if one had a great deal of money, as she knew Miss Watson's brother had, but how much more worthwhile was her own hand-knitted beauty? Or so most people would think, Miss Fogerty told herself, putting her key in the lock. But not Miss Watson evidently! The pink bedjacket might be used for second-best, when the brother's superior article was at the cleaner's possibly, but that's what Miss Watson would think of it. Second best! *Another bedjacket!*

'Don't bother with a meal for me, Mrs White,' she called to her landlady. 'I'm catching the evening train after all.'

Equally unhappy, Miss Watson wandered about her school house suffering bitter remorse. Unable to face even her usual cup of tea, she watched the clock, determined to call at eight upon Agnes. By then she should have finished her meal and perhaps be feeling less upset.

Dear, oh dear, thought Miss Watson, struggling into her coat, what a trial life was! She picked up the parcel which she had just wrapped. To the original present of Yardley's lavender water she had felt the need to add a box of Yardley's lavender bath cubes, providentially given to her by her cousin. There was something to be said for undoing one's Christmas presents as they arrived, she thought, as she smoothed the wrapping paper.

She walked through the darkness, across Thrush Green, still in a severe state of self-flagellation.

Why on earth had she said such a stupid thing? Why couldn't she simply have said: 'A bedjacket'? Why '*Another* bedjacket'? Why let slip that perfectly idiotic unnecessary, *wounding* word? Really, it made one wonder if the devil were still at large, popping such monstrous words into one's mouth! And how to explain? How to comfort poor Agnes? How to comfort herself? It was the sort of ghastly thing which would haunt her on sleepless nights; another to be added to those gaffes over the years which had power to torment her even though they had been committed over twenty years earlier.

Mrs White answered her knock.

'May I see Miss Fogerty, please?'

'Oh dear, you've just missed her,' cried the landlady. 'She left for the station half an hour ago.'

'But I thought –' began poor Miss Watson.

'So did I. But she said her friend would be pleased to see her tonight.'

'Have you got the friend's address?'

'I'm afraid not.'

Miss Watson shifted the parcel from one hand to the other in her agitation.

'Did she mention the name? Ida, or Elsie? She must have said something.'

Miss Watson's voice grew higher and higher. A lesser woman might have sat on the doorstep and drummed her heels in wild hysteria. But

Miss Watson was a headmistress and, although goaded almost beyond her limits, maintained some dignity.

'To tell you the truth,' said Mrs White, 'she seemed a bit upset. Not herself, as you might say.'

Miss Watson drew a deep breath.

'I can quite understand it,' she said. 'I will look forward to seeing her when she returns.'

'Would you want to leave the parcel?' inquired Mrs White. To her mind, Miss Watson looked a bit upset too. What could be the matter?

'Would you like to come in?' she asked. 'Sit down or anything?'

'No, thank you,' replied Miss Watson. 'I must go home. As for the parcel, I will give it to her myself later. There are one or two things to explain.'

She nodded politely, and set off in the darkness.

'She's aged a lot,' said Mrs White to her husband when she had closed the door.

'It's end of term,' replied Mr White sagely.

## 16. Getting Justice Done

The members of the parochial church council met in the dining-room at the rectory, and tried gallantly to look warm in that bleak apartment. The more prudent of them had added cardigans or waistcoats to their attire before setting out, and the aged churchwarden flatly refused to remove anything but his hat, with a courage which his fellow members secretly admired.

There were two vacant chairs, and the rector explained the matter at the outset.

'This meeting has been called, in the first place, because I have received the resignations of Mrs Cleary and Mr Hodge. I very much hope that they can be persuaded to change their minds, and we are here to discuss ways and means of meeting the views of the objectors.'

'I suppose it was to be expected,' said Miss Watson. She looked pale and dejected, thought Harold Shoosmith sitting opposite her. Glad to have a break from those children, he supposed. He'd sooner be in a trade than teaching, that was sure!

'It grieves me very much,' said the rector, 'to have this split among our good people.'

'You can't call eight a split,' broke in Harold.

'A disagreement then,' amended the rector. 'I wondered if you would think it a good idea if one of us met the objectors, or invited them to meet us, as a body, to see if we couldn't come to some amicable arrangement?'

'Sound 'em out, you mean?' said someone. 'Who are they anyway?'

The rector consulted the list while various voices recited names around the table.

'Besides Mr Hodge and his wife, and Mrs Cleary, there are Mr and Mrs Jones from The Two Pheasants and John and James Howard, and Martin Brewer.'

'You may not have noticed,' quavered the aged churchwarden, 'that John and James Howard work for Mr Hodge, and live in one of his tied cottages.'

'Surely,' said Miss Watson, 'he wouldn't interfere in their religious convictions?'

'No, I'm not saying that. But they'd do as he told 'em.'

'And Martin Brewer,' pointed out someone else, 'works at Mrs Cleary's shop.'

'I thought he had a job as a van driver for the laundry,' said the rector, looking bewildered. 'I'm sure he calls here. A very pleasant young fellow, and understands all about decimal coins.'

'He doesn't drive now,' said Harold. 'He was disqualified for twelve months after an accident.'

'Deserved it too,' said the churchwarden.'Doing seventy round the new estate. Dreadful!'

'Only according to the radar trap,' said another. 'I don't hold with those things. It isn't British, catching people when they're not looking.'

A heated debate might well have broken out, but the rector, familiar with the signs, banged the table and restored order.

'So Mrs Cleary gave him a job?'

'That's right. He's weighing up corn and grit and that, and loading the van for her.'

'I like oyster shell best,' said someone conversationally. 'My hens won't touch anything else, though my old dad used to sweep up the grit from the road, I remember, and our chickens at home seemed to thrive on it.'

'*And you think,*' said the rector, regaining control with some effort, 'that Martin might have signed because he felt grateful to her, or some such thing?'

'Could well be,' said Harold. 'Who does that leave?'

'Mr and Mrs Jones. I know he has been very forceful about it.'

'Only because of his Auntie May,' said the churchwarden. 'He thought the world of her. She's buried up near the yew tree. Nice bit of pink sandstone, she's got over her.'

'It occurs to me,' said Harold suddenly, 'that Mrs Cleary's family grave, and the Hodge graves are all close to the yew tree, and if the Jones's Auntie May is there too, we may be able to leave that small area undisturbed and still go ahead with levelling the rest.'

There was a respectful silence as the council digested this.

'What a happy thought!' said the rector.

'And Mrs Jones's Auntie May,' said the churchwarden, 'was a Hodge, of course. That's why she's there.'

'A Hodge?'

'Yes. May Hodge. Pretty girl, she was. Married Jones's uncle, and brought up Jones when his mother died. Now, she *was* a one! Proper harum-scarum! D'you remember that time she climbed up the rookery, George?'

He turned to a contemporary, wheezing with ancient laughter.

'*We are most grateful,*' cried the rector above the asthmatic noises, 'for bringing this to our attention. And how do you feel about Mr Shoosmith's suggestion that the area near the yew tree could be left?'

There were general murmurs of approval.

'That part,' said Miss Watson, suddenly coming to life, 'is so close to the new graveyard, which I think we agreed would remain as it is, that surely some beds with shrubs could make an attractive corner by the Hodge and Cleary graves, and at the same time provide a partial screen for the new graveyard.'

'It was supposed to be a privet hedge,' said the churchwarden. 'I well remember the row about green or golden, but the war came, you know, and we never got round to it.'

'I'm sure Miss Watson's idea could form the basis of an excellent scheme,' said Harold. 'But first things first. What about our eight objectors?'

'May I propose,' said Miss Watson, 'that some of us – or the rector himself, better still – approach them and see how they react?'

'Get 'em to withdraw their resignations,' growled George. 'Silly lot of nonsense! Old Percy Hodge is a useful chap and Mrs Cleary's all right when she's not on her high horse. I say, let the rector talk to 'em. The others will follow.'

'I should be only too happy to do what I can,' said Charles. 'This estrangement has been a great grief to me. And, of course, the sooner we get unity, then the sooner the faculty may be granted. If the objectors remain adamant, we must face considerable delays and considerable expense, as we are well aware. Nothing would please me more than to be able to resolve our differences here, at Thrush Green, without the unhappiness of going to court.'

'Then I propose that the rector sounds them out,' said Miss Watson.

'I'll second that,' said George.

'And what about some rough plan of the graves' area?' said Harold. 'Wouldn't it be a good thing to have something to show our objectors? They might be able to suggest further improvements.'

'Perhaps Miss Watson would help?' said Charles. 'It was her idea.'

'And Mr Shoosmith,' suggested another. 'He knows his onions when it comes to gardening.'

Thus it was left. Miss Watson and Harold would draft a rough plan for the rector to show the objectors, and it was left to him to see if some compromise could be arranged.

The meeting dispersed. Harold and Miss Watson walked together across the moonlit green.

'I go away tomorrow,' she told him, 'but I'll think about shrubs and so on which follow each other through the year, and perhaps we can meet when I get back in a few days' time.'

'I don't suppose Charles will have much time before that to do his visiting,' agreed Harold. 'Christmas keeps him pretty busy. No holiday for clergymen!'

They reached the school house gate.

'I hope you enjoy your break,' said Harold politely.

'Thank you,' replied Miss Watson. 'For once, I shall be glad to leave Thrush Green.'


As the rector had forecast, Christmas was mild and damp, and four of his parishioners told him to expect a spate of funerals within the next few weeks. It seemed to give them some satisfaction to impart the knowledge, which the good rector accepted with mingled resignation and fortitude.

Winnie Bailey spent the day with the Young family, in their handsome house so near her own. Ella and Dotty joined the Henstocks for tea, and the Hursts had gone to Frank's son in Wales for Christmas, leaving Tullivers and the cat in the care of Winnie Bailey.

In the week that followed, the inhabitants of Thrush Green turned, with some relief, to their usual way of life. Apart from dozens of Christmas cards blowing to the floor in every passing breeze and generally holding up the daily dusting, the main problem was to find a new way of presenting the remains of the turkey.

'I think curried turkey is the best way of finishing it up,' said Dimity one morning, when she was taking coffee at her former abode with Ella and Winnie.

'Not bad,' agreed Ella, 'but I prefer it with mushrooms and white sauce. Easy to do too. Or shepherd's pie, of course.'

'The fact is,' said Dimity, 'that *any* turkey dish, after five days of it, tends to pall. I'm *longing* for a steak and kidney pie!'

'I didn't buy a turkey this year,' said Winnie.

'Then you're extremely lucky,' her friends told her.

'And now we've January to look forward to,' sighed Ella. 'Talk about the January blues! What with the bills, and the general damp and gloom, and so long to wait for spring – it does get one down!'

'I cheer myself up,' said Dimity, 'by tidying a cupboard. It makes me feel so virtuous and efficient.'

'I buy a new pair of shoes,' said Winnie.

'A packet of bourbon biscuits peps me up,' said Ella. 'Or putting out a new tablet of soap. Very therapeutic, putting out a new tablet of soap, I find.'

'As good as a day in the garden?' asked Winnie.

'Far better, in January,' replied Ella emphatically. 'Have some more coffee? I asked Dotty to come up, but she doesn't seem to want to be sociable these days. Worrying about that confounded court appearance, I suppose. One thing, the Cooke boy is home again, I hear, and getting over the mumps. That must ease poor old Dotty's conscience.'

Winnie said nothing. Dotty's confidences would never be disclosed, but she knew that she would never forget the depths of misery in which she had found her old friend on that dark afternoon.

'Well, a court case *is* worrying,' said Dimity. 'I think we're all worried for her. It will be a good thing when it comes up in a fortnight or so, and we can all forget the wretched business.'

There was one person who was more worried than most about Dotty's case, and that was the clerk to the Lulling magistrates. A comparative newcomer to the area – he had moved from a busy London court a mere ten years earlier – he could not be expected to know the ramifications of relatives, employers and employed, and other complications of rural communities.

To give him his due, he readily discovered the difficulties within a few months of taking up his appointment. He tackled his job with outstanding ability and good humour, and was readily accepted by a community which normally took some time to acknowledge a newcomer as 'one of us'.

He was used to the occasional 'sitting back' of a magistrate in cases where the defendant was known to, related to or employed by that particular justice. The case of Dotty Harmer was creating even more trouble.

Six of the twelve Lulling magistrates stated roundly that they could not possibly sit in judgement upon Dotty. Not only had all six been instructed – painfully, sometimes – by Dotty's notable father at the local grammar school, which would not have mattered greatly, but all knew Dotty from childhood days.

'Used to play tennis with her, didn't we, Bob?' said one farmer to his fellow magistrate. 'She never did get round to serving over-arm, but she was deadly at the net.'

The fishmonger cried off because Miss Harmer was one of his best customers 'owning all those cats'.

Another justice was her builder. Another had been employed by her family for a time. Another claimed that he was 'a sort of cousin' and poor Mr Pearson, the clerk, could see it was going to be hell's delight to find three justices willing to hear the case.

Urgent telephone calls to the remaining six justices brought little help. One was waiting to go into hospital, and a third, the youngest newly-appointed matron, confessed that she had just discovered that she was to have a baby. At that moment, Mr Pearson's coffee arrived, and he suspended operations to fortify himself.

Really, he thought, stirring pensively, it was all very fine for Lord Chancellors to urge the appointment of young females to the bench, but it did complicate things! He stopped stirring as a thought struck him. If she had only just discovered her condition, then it was reasonable to suppose that her confinement was some months distant. Consequently, there seemed to be no reason why she should not attend court on the day of Dotty's case. He resolved to try the last three justices, and to ring back to Mrs Fothergill if he could not gather three together.

He finished his coffee and tried again. This time he was lucky. Mr Jardine could come. His wife, he believed, knew Miss Harmer at the Field Club, but he had only met her once. No, he had no objection to sitting. Dam' it all, if one were to sit back every time someone slightly known appeared before one, it would be impossible to conduct a court at all!

Mr Pearson agreed heartily, thanked Mr Jardine sincerely, and set about the ensnaring of Lady Winter.

That lady said she had a great many engagements on at the time of Dotty's case. When was it? One moment, she would consult her diary. It was not very convenient as she was organizing a Charity Ball that evening and would be getting her hair done. Would Mr Pearson care to come? The tickets were five pounds each and she was personally making the punch.

Mr Pearson, with his usual diplomacy, turned down the invitation, and then threw himself into urgent pleading, explaining the terrible predicament he was in. Lady Winter, who had a soft spot for the clerk, allowed herself to be persuaded, and agreed to make her appointment in the late afternoon instead of the morning. No, she had not the pleasure of knowing Miss Harmer, although she had heard of her father. Who hadn't?

'One to go!' murmured Mr Pearson, twirling the dial with a pencil.

Mrs Lucy answered the call. She was sorry but Edgar was out, should he ring when he came in?

Mr Pearson gave her the date of the hearing and said he would try Mrs Fothergill, and let the Lucys know the outcome.

'I must tell you,' said Mrs Lucy, 'we are in the most awful muddle at the moment. Edgar's father has been taken ill, and we are setting off to see him later today.'

His father was in Huddersfield, added Mrs Lucy, but, from what the doctor said, would be leaving for Higher Things before long. Edgar, as the only son, would have everything to clear up.

Mr Pearson condoled, promised to ring again, and returned to Mrs Fothergill. The clock told him that he had spent an hour in his searchings, and a pile of papers awaited his attention.

Mrs Fothergill said she could come *easily*. Mr Pearson sighed with relief.

'And you don't know Miss Harmer?'

'I once helped to push her car into a side street, but I was one of about six others. She doesn't know me, and I've never met her otherwise.'

'Good,' said the clerk. 'That's three of you rounded up.'

'I've heard of her father, of course,' said Mrs Fothergill.

'Who hasn't?' agreed Mr Pearson. After mutual felicitations, they rang off.

'Just the Lucys once more,' said Mr Pearson, strong again.

Humming blithely, he dialled for the last time.

On the same morning as the clerk to the justices was engaged in telephoning, Charles Henstock set out from the rectory to pay his appointed call on Percy Hodge.

He approached his task with some trepidation. Rumour had it that Percy Hodge, when crossed, could be a formidable adversary. Charles did not doubt it. The removal of himself and his family from church, the wording of his resignation and the obstinate set of Percy's mouth all told of a stubborn character. He might prove impossible to move.

But the rector, despite his misgivings, went steadfastly upon his way. If Percy could be persuaded to fall in with these new suggestions, then he felt sure that the other objectors would follow suit.

He had debated with himself about the advisability of calling upon Percy first. Dimity had suggested that it would be politer to visit Mrs Cleary, on the 'ladies-first' principle.

Charles had wondered about the Joneses. He had a feeling that, despite his blusterings, Jones might give way more readily, especially when he had seen the suggested plans, so neatly executed by Harold.

But, after much cogitation, the rector had decided to crack the toughest nut first. For one thing, Percy would resent being put after anyone else. If the others had agreed, it would make him doubly adamant about resisting. The rector, innocent in so many things, was wise in discerning the motives which stirred human passions.

He came to the farmhouse gate and, like all good countrymen, went to the back door of the house to knock for admission.

Percy himself answered the door.

'Come in,' he said. 'I've been expecting you!'

With pleasure or anger, wondered the rector? He stepped bravely into the lion's den.

## 17. *The Rector in Action*

'Sorry I'm a bit late,' cried Betty Bell. 'Been trying to get that new floor to rights next door, and forgot the time.'

'Don't worry,' said Harold. 'I didn't realize you had to call in at the school during the holidays.'

'Lord love you,' responded Betty, 'that's my busiest time! I mean, termtime it gets a lick and a promise, as you might say, except for Friday nights. But I gives the whole place a thorough scrub through during the holidays.'

'I should have known.'

'I don't see why you should. Selling things was your line. Floors is mine. But you never saw such a pig's breakfast as that new floor. That young teacher lets 'em do as they like, from what I can see. There's glue and paint and plasticine and ground-up crayon, and enough bubble-gum to keep you going for a month.'

'Not me,' said Harold, shuddering.

'Well, you know what I mean. Now, Miss Fogerty's room is a treat to do. Everything left tidy, chairs on desks ready for me to sweep, nice bit of paper lining the waste basket so there's no pencil shavings and that dropping through. She's even got a little brush to sweep up the coke bits! Takes me half the time to do her room.'

'Bully for Miss Fogerty!' said Harold, making for the refuge of his study. It was plain that Betty was in full spate today.

'Well, that's as it should be. Children wants training. I know my mum never let us leave things about. If we did, they was thrown in the pit, up the end of our garden. We never had no dustbins in those days. I can remember rescuing an old dolly of mine, in the pouring rain. She never looked the same after a night in the pit, but it learnt me a lesson, all the same.'

'I had a nurse,' replied Harold, halted in his tracks, 'who threw my things on the back of the fire. I can remember watching a lead soldier – a cavalry officer, too – melting away. It broke my heart.'

'That was downright cruel!' cried Betty indignantly. 'I hope she got the sack!'

'She did, as soon as my father realized she was sampling his brandy,' said Harold, and made his escape.

At much the same time, across the green, Jenny arrived at Winnie Bailey's. Jenny very rarely spoke unless she had something worthwhile to say, but this morning she looked unusually animated.

'Had good news, Jenny?' asked her mistress.

'Yes. Willie Bond brought a letter for the old folks. They've got a new house at last. One of those old people's homes the council built.'

Jenny's honest plain face glowed with pleasure.

'How wonderful! Just what they've always wanted. And when can they move in?'

'About a month's time. There's got to be an inspection or something, to make sure everything works. As soon as that's done they can go in.'

'And what about your present house, Jenny?'

'Well, that'll come down. All our row will, and a good thing too. It's been condemned for years now. We knew it would happen one day.'

'So what will you do?'

'I'll face that when the time comes,' said Jenny cheerfully. 'I'll find a room somewhere I expect. Might even go nursing – I did a bit once – and I could live in the hostel.'

'Would you want to do that?'

'Not really,' said Jenny. 'Besides, I'm a bit old. I don't know if they'd have me. But I shall find something all right. Just get the old folks settled, and I'll start thinking.'

She went humming upstairs to clean the bathroom, while Winnie turned over in her mind a plan which had been lurking there for some time.

It continued to engage her thoughts as she sat knitting that afternoon. Her dislike of being alone after dark had certainly diminished as the weeks went by, but she could not honestly say that she was completely carefree. She had wondered if it would be sensible to let two rooms upstairs. She would still have a spare bedroom, quite enough for the modest entertaining she proposed to do in her widowed state.

The two rooms adjoined. Both had wash-basins, one of which could be changed to a kitchen sink. There would be plenty of room for an electric stove and for cupboards, and it would convert easily into a comfortable kitchen.

The room next door was larger and would make an attractive bed-sitting room. Both rooms overlooked the green and were light and sunny.

The difficulty was, who would be acceptable? Winnie did not want a married couple, and such a minute flat would not be suitable for people with babies or pets. A single man might be useful for attacking the marauders that Winnie feared, but then he might expect his washing and ironing to be done, and his socks darned, and Winnie was beginning to feel rather too old for such mothering.

No, a pleasant single woman was the answer! One with a job during the day, who enjoyed looking after her small domain, and who did not demand too much attention from her landlady. The financial side was something of a problem to Winnie, who had not the faintest idea what should be charged. Nor did she know if there should be some legal document setting out the terms upon which landladies and lodgers agreed.

And then, supposing they did not get on? It was common knowledge that one really had to live with people before one knew them properly.

Look at that terrible Brides-in-the-Bath man! No, thought Winnie, don't look at him, with dusk already beginning to fall!

She rose to draw the curtains and to switch on the lamp. Across the green, she saw the rector marching purposefully toward The Two Pheasants. Unusual, thought Winnie. Perhaps he was calling on his sexton, Albert Piggott, or on Harold Shoosmith nearby.

But the rector was opening the wicket gate at the side of the public house, and vanished from sight.

Winnie resumed her seat and her knitting. Over the past few weeks she had come to the conclusion that the person she would most like to share her home was quiet, devoted Jenny. That is, of course, if she would come.

And now, with this morning's news, it looked as though there were a chance. She would await her opportunity, and put the proposition before Jenny. How lovely, thought Winnie, letting her knitting fall and looking at the leaping flames, if she agreed! The bogey of loneliness would be banished, and the tiresome business of trying to find out what would be a fair rent would also be solved, for Jenny would live there rent-free.

Winnie allowed herself to indulge in happy daydreams for some five minutes, and then pulled herself together sharply. It was no good getting too hopeful. Jenny might well have other plans, besides the vagues ones she had mentioned, and in any case, a shared home at Thrush Green might be abhorrent to her.

Well, time would show. Winnie picked up her knitting again, determined to remain cool-headed over the whole affair. But hope warmed her throughout the evening.

Charles Henstock, whom Winnie had glimpsed from her window, was making the second of his visits that day on the vexed question of the graveyard.

Percy Hodge had greeted him somewhat grimly, but had ushered him into the parlour, in deference, presumably, to his cloth.

Frankly, Charles would have preferred the kitchen, where the life of the farmhouse revolved. For one thing, it was warm and cheerful, a great room dominated by an immense scrubbed table, and an Aga cooker which dispensed heat and a delicious smell of baking bread.

The parlour was neither warm nor cheerful. Percy switched on the electric fire as he entered, but the rector might just as well have been in his own study for all the comfort it gave.

Two enormous pictures of stags standing in water, against a background of Highland mountains, dominated the walls, and a vast three-piece suite, upholstered in drab moquette, filled most of the floor space. The linoleum, meant to represent, not very convincingly, a traditional Turkish carpet in crimson and blue, gleamed icily.

'Take a seat,' said Percy. 'I take it you've come about me not coming to church.'

Percy was nothing if not direct, thought Charles.

'Not quite that, although we've all missed you and the family at our services. You are still opposed, no doubt, to the churchyard scheme?'

'Of course I am,' said Percy forcefully. 'It beats me why more people didn't sign. You hear enough about it in the village, but people are afraid to put their names down.'

'Are you sure? I shouldn't like to think that was so.'

'Well, maybe they talk that way when I'm there. I don't know. Folk will try to run with the hare and hounds, and to my mind you can't do both. You know my feelings on the subject. I'm against the thing.'

'Tell me your strongest objection.'

'My strongest objection is having the resting place of my forefathers disturbed.'

'And if it were to remain undisturbed, would you then approve the project?'

'How d'you mean?'

Percy looked suspicious. Charles spread his hands towards the meagre heat from the electric stove, and began to outline the suggested proposals. He explained things gently and patiently, his brow furrowed with concern, and towards the end of the explanation, he took the sketch map from his pocket.

Percy's expression grew grimmer at he listened.

'Trying to buy me off, are you?' he said at last.

For the first time in Percy's life, he saw a flash of anger cross the rector's face.

'I should never have imagined that you would stoop to such a remark,' he said. 'It does you no credit, and is insulting to me. There is conflict in my parish which I am trying to stop. No one can ever know the grief which it is causing me.'

He rose as if to go.

'Sit down, sir, sit down,' urged Percy, looking uncomfortable. 'I shouldn't have said that. I'm sorry. I know you well enough to know you're dead straight. Sit down, and tell me more.'

The rector resumed his seat.

'When I was a schoolboy,' he said, more calmly, 'we had a prayer about being careful not to mistake bluntness for frankness, and obstinacy, I think it was, for constancy. You know, Percy, I have always respected your principles, but you must face the fact that we all have to make compromises in this life, if we are to live amicably together. All I am doing is to show you how willing we are to settle things for the best. Even hares and hounds have to shake down in the same world.'

'Let's have a look at the plan,' said Percy, holding out his hand for Harold's rough sketch. He studied it in silence, while the rector observed him. A whirring noise from the wall clock behind him caused him to turn. A wooden cuckoo burst from its lair and shouted three times. In the distance the cows lowed. It would soon be milking time.

'What happens,' said Percy, returning the sketch, 'if we don't change our minds?'

The rector told him of delays, expense, the possibility of a consistory court, and the usual procedure in such a case.

Percy listened attentively.

'Well, I'm not going to say now one way or the other, but I'll think things over, and let you know. I'm not an unreasonable man, I hope, but I want to do what's right.'

'I'm sure of that.'

'And I'll tell my two men what you've told me,' went on Percy. 'They'll do as I do, of course.'

Charles felt a tremor of dismay.

'I shouldn't want them to go against their consciences. You know that, I feel sure. They must weigh things up, just as you are going to do.'

'I'll see to them,' said Percy, and with this somewhat ambiguous remark, he saw the rector to the door.

It was not much, thought Charles Henstock, as he walked home to Thrush Green, but at least he had not had the door slammed in his face. He bitterly regretted his own flash of anger, but Percy's remark had cut him cruelly. Perhaps, however, his own outburst had cleared the air. Certainly, Percy seemed more reasonable after it.

He went into the long corridor leading to the kitchen, expecting to find Dimity, but remembered that she had proposed to go shopping in Lulling. The kettle purred on the stove, and he wondered whether to make tea.

It was now half-past three. This would be a good time to call on the Joneses'. Lunch would be over, and the pub would be closed until six.

Heartened by the glimmer of hope given him by Percy, he decided to try his luck, and set off.

Mr Jones was alone and showed the rector into a sitting-room which was the very opposite of Percy Hodge's.

'The wife's gone shopping,' explained Mr Jones. 'We don't get much time for that sort of thing. Very tied with a pub, you know, but it suits me.'

He indicated an armchair and Charles sank down into depths so soft that he wondered if he would ever be able to rise again. There were flowers everywhere. The covers were ablaze with roses, the walls with wistaria hanging on trellis. On the mantelpiece, above the roaring fire, was an arrangement of plastic flowers and fern, where tulips, delphiniums, crocuses and chrysanthemums rioted together in defiance of the seasons.

Even the kettle-holder, hanging on a hook by the fireside, had a posy of forget-me-nots on it, and the spaniel which lay at their feet, Charles remembered, was called Blossom.

He began to feel guilty, a worm in the bud, a serpent in this bower of flowers.

'What can I get you, padre?' asked his host. 'Whisky? Drop of rum to keep out the cold?'

'No, nothing, thank you. I shall be having some tea very soon. How snug you are in here!'

'We need somewhere comfortable when we're on our own,' said the landlord. 'Our job means you've got to be among a crowd most of the time. And standing too. It's good to sink down in here when we can.'

'I've just come from Percy Hodge's,' said the rector, coming straight to the point.

Mr Jones began to look wary.

'About the churchyard? What's Perce say?'

The rector told him the gist of their conversation, and handed over the sketch map.

'Could look rather nice,' said the landlord slowly. Charles's spirits rose. He remembered that Mr Jones was a great gardener.

'If it did come about,' he said cautiously, 'we should need some advice about planting and so on. At the moment, Miss Watson and Mr Shoosmith are thinking about shrubs.'

Perhaps Charles had gone too far and too fast. The landlord's face tightened, and he handed back the piece of paper.

'What happens if we still object?' he said. Charles was reminded that Percy and this man were related.

He told him. Mr Jones nodded.

'You don't want to get mixed up with lawyers,' he said, at last. 'You'll have Thrush Green in debt for years if you take this matter to some court or other. I'm not saying yes or no, but I can see your point, and I reckon we ought to settle this business here in the village ourselves.'

'Exactly my feelings,' said the rector.

'What did Perce say?' he repeated.

'He said much the same as you are saying, that he wanted time to think about it.'

'And what, padre, do *you* think? As man to man, I mean?'

'I want the churchyard to look beautiful, a fitting place for the loved dead here. But I want harmony among the living. If we give and take – all of us – I think we can resolve our difficulties. That's why I'm approaching all the objectors.'

'Well, you've got some pluck, that I will say, and I promise to think it over. Mind you, I've shot my mouth off about it pretty strong in the bar here, but I'm not above changing my mind if it's the right thing to do.'

'It isn't a sign of weakness,' said the rector, attempting to struggle from the chair, 'rather the contrary.'

'Here,' said Mr Jones, proffering a hand, 'let's give you a haul up.'

The two men stood on the hearthrug smiling at each other. A smell of singeing made the rector move suddenly from such unaccustomed heat.

'Well, I'll be off, and leave you to your rest,' said Charles. He turned at the door.

'You'll let me know your decision, won't you?' he pleaded. 'I care very much about the outcome.'

'You shall know before the week's out,' promised the landlord.

At Tullivers, that evening, Frank Hurst broached again the thorny subject of Jeremy's schooling. Little had been said about it since their earlier difference of opinion, but Phyllida remained determined to keep the boy at home for a few more years, and Frank was equally desirous of the child going to his own old prep school, which he remembered happily.

'Tom's taking his youngest down to Ribblesworth next week,' he announced, when Phil returned from putting Jeremy to bed. 'He's sitting the entrance exam.'

'Is he?' said Phil guardedly.

'Do just come and have a look at the place,' persuaded Frank. 'I know how you feel at the moment, but indulge me, and pay a visit with me. You may change your mind. I could ring the head, and make an appointment.

Phil hesitated. It seemed a complete waste of time to her. She was against the principle of wresting young boys from their homes, particularly in

Jeremy's case where the child had had some tough knocks in his short life and was getting over them well in his present happy circumstances.

On the other hand, she could see Frank's point, and it would be unkind to ignore his wishes.

'Very well,' she agreed. 'But it will have to be a positive paradise to convince me. You know that well enough.'

Frank laughed.

'I'll take the risk. Here, sit down, and I'll bring you a glass of sherry.'

## 18. A Cold Spell

Little Miss Fogerty returned from her Christmas holiday two days before term began.

She had not intended staying so long with her friend Isobel, but had been persuaded to extend her visit. Isobel, recently widowed, said that she would be grateful for her company, and Miss Fogerty, touched and flattered that she should be needed, readily agreed to stay.

'Besides,' added Isobel, 'you don't look as fit as you usually do. I expect you have been over-working.'

'It has been a trying term,' admitted Miss Fogerty, but wild horses would not have dragged from her the true miseries which had caused the shadows under her eyes, and the wretchedly disturbed nights.

She certainly began to feel better after a week or so with dear Isobel. The house was large and warm. The spare room had a bed which was plump and soft, and a bathroom of its own, which Miss Fogerty considered the height of luxury. The bath sheet alone gave Miss Fogerty an exquisite sense of being cossetted. It was pale blue, and so large and fluffy that it could wrap her small frame twice round, and then have a generous wrap-over. Mrs White's bath towels were less than half the size, and made of some harsher striped towelling which simply pushed the water from one part of one's body to another without doing its proper job of absorption.

It was delightful too to be taken everywhere by car. Not that Miss Fogerty was lazy, nor that she underestimated the well-being which results from healthy exercise, but in the depths of winter the taking of a brisk walk so often meant cold fingers and toes. It was true too, as Isobel said, that she was not feeling as well as she normally did, and to lean back in a comfortable car seat and watch the wintry world roll by, without any effort, was exceedingly pleasant.

When the time came to depart she felt all the better for her rest, and tried to tell her friend how much the break had meant to her.

'I've loved having you,' Isobel said, gazing up at the carriage window which framed Miss Fogerty's small face topped by a neat beige felt hat. 'Now, do as I say, and take a tonic while the winter lasts.'

The train began to move.

'And wrap up warmly,' cried Isobel more loudly. 'We're going to get a cold snap.'

The two friends waved until a curve in the line separated them. Miss Fogerty pulled up the window, and sank back into her seat. She took out a handkerchief and blew her nose. Emotion was one cause of this operation, but a piercing east wind was a greater one.

Two hours later, as she trudged from the station through Lulling High Street, she shivered in the icy blast which swept that thoroughfare. It seemed colder still at Thrush Green at the top of the hill.

She looked across at the school house. A light shone from the sitting-room window. No doubt Miss Watson was reading, or perhaps enjoying her tea by the fire. On other occasions, Miss Fogerty might have been tempted to tap on the door, but not now.

She put down her case and rammed on the sensible felt hat more firmly. Only another few yards and she would be home again!

She picked up her case and set off once more. With any luck, Mrs White would have a tea tray ready for her in her room. She could have the kettle boiling on the ring in less than five minutes.

With a pang, Miss Fogerty recalled the log fire, the plump cushions, and the silver tea pot which had graced the tea time hour at Isobel's.

Ah well! It would not do to become too fond of soft living, she told herself firmly, and after all, this was her home and all her dear familiar things would be there to welcome her.

The first fat white snowflake, drifting as easily as a windblown feather, fluttered to the ground as she opened the gate. By the time the kettle boiled, the sky was awhirl with flakes, spinning past the window, veiling the garden, tumbling dizzily, helter-skelter, as though some gigantic feather bed had burst in the dark leaden sky above.

Isobel was right, thought Miss Fogerty, sipping her tea gratefully. Wintry weather indeed, and from the look of things, more to come!'

Thrush Green awoke to a white world. The Cotswold stone walls were covered in snow four or five inches deep. The gateposts wore white tamo-shanters, and Nathaniel Patten held out his snow-covered book and gazed upon his birth-place from under a crown of snow.

The green itself was a vast unsullied expanse. The wind had blown a great drift against the railings of St Andrew's church, so that only the spikes were visible. Their black zig-zag, and the dark trunks of the chestnut avenue, served to accentuate the dazzling whiteness of the scene.

It was still snowing when the rector arose and went downstairs to make tea. His breath billowed before him in the chill of the house, and he was glad to gain the comparative warmth of the kitchen.

The cat stretched, mewed, and leapt upon the table asking to be let out of the window. The rector gazed up at the whirling flakes. They fluttered against his face like icy moths. One fell into his open mouth, and he remembered suddenly how he used to rush about in the snow, as a child, catching the snow flakes on his tongue, and then how he had seized a handful from a wall and had crammed it into his mouth, spluttering excitedly, and crying: 'You can *eat* it! You can *eat* it!'

How beautiful it was! He closed the window, and watched two sparrows alight on the roof of Dimity's bird tray. Their tiny claws formed hiero-glyphics in the snow, like foreign letters printed on the virgin page.

Beautiful indeed, thought the rector, fetching the teapot, but how cold! Perhaps he needed a thicker dressing-gown. His present one had been given to him long ago by his dear first wife. No doubt twenty years of wear had worn it rather threadbare. The cuffs were certainly quite frayed, and he seemed to remember that the whole surface had once been fluffy. Now it was smooth, and almost worn through at the elbows. Well, it would probably last another few years, thought Charles cheerfully, advancing upon the boiling kettle.

He was about to pick up the tray when the cat returned to the window sill demanding entry. Its coat was flecked with snowflakes, its eyes wild at finding itself in this unaccustomed element.

It shot in, and ran to the stove, shaking itself spasmodically, and uttering little cries of dismay. Outside the snow hissed sibilantly against the window pane, and a great cushion of it fell with a flurry from an overloaded branch nearby.

Hitching up his dilapidated dressing-gown, the rector lifted his tray and made for the stairs.

The snow was still thick on the ground when term began. Miss Fogerty wore her wellington boots and some extra thick ribbed woollen stockings. She also wore her spencer underneath her sensible brown twin-set, for she knew, only too well, how draughty Thrush Green School could be when the wind was in the north east.

She had hoped that Miss Watson might call, but no doubt she was busy with preparations for the term, she thought charitably. In any case, the weather had not been very tempting, and most people had been glad to stay by the fireside.

Although the memory of the bedjacket still had power to cause Miss Fogerty some unhappiness, the balm of Isobel's hospitality had taken some of the sting from the wound. It was no good dwelling on the affair, she told herself, as she trotted through the snow to school that first morning. We have to work together. We are two grown women, and we must treat the incident as closed.

Nevertheless, she could not quite overcome her uneasiness at meeting Miss Watson again. Their last meeting, after all, had been so dreadfully painful. She listened for her headmistress's footsteps as she hung up her coat and removed her wet wellingtons. Her little black-shoes hung in their cretonne bag, inside the map cupboard, where she had placed them on that last disastrous day.

She was buttoning the straps when Miss Watson entered. The headmistress held out a parcel wrapped in Christmas paper.

'Much too late, Agnes dear, I'm afraid,' she said, smiling. 'I did call to give it to you, but I just missed you, so Mrs White told me. Had a good holiday?'

Miss Fogerty was relieved to see the smile, and to realize that they were back – or nearly so – to their normal friendly relationship. It was a mercy not to have an emotional scene, and yet Miss Fogerty could not help thinking that it might have been even better if Miss Watson had shown some remorse for that unfeeling remark which had caused her assistant such misery. It would have been nice if Miss Watson had begged for forgiveness, and had recognized her own culpability. Not that she wanted her headmistress to *grovel*, but after all, it would have been truly heroic if she could have brought herself to apologize or to explain.

However, thought Miss Fogerty, undoing the parcel with little cries of gratitude, perhaps 'Least said, soonest mended' was Miss Watson's motto, and a very sensible one too.

'My favourite perfume!' cried Miss Fogerty. 'You couldn't have given me anything more welcome.'

'Well, it isn't anywhere near as splendid a present as yours to me, Agnes, but I'm glad you like it.'

The bell clanged outside.

'Miss Potter's on time for once,' commented Miss Watson, and the two teachers hurried to greet their pupils in the lobby.

Nothing more was said about the bedjacket, and Miss Fogerty resolutely put aside any little feelings of rancour as being quite unworthy of a sensible middle-aged schoolteacher.

It was during this wintry spell that Frank and Phil Hurst went to visit the prep school at which Frank had been so happy.

Phil resolved to enjoy the outing and to try and bring an open mind to the question of Jeremy's boarding. The sun came through now and again, lighting the snow into unbelievable beauty and casting blue shadows under the trees.

They lunched on the way and drove up the long road to the school about two o'clock. A group of little boys in very large boots rushed about frenziedly between two sets of rugby posts, urged on by a hefty young man girt about with striped scarves.

The boys, to Phil's pitying gaze, looked blue with cold and grossly underclad and underfed. But she was prudent enough to make no comment as they drove to the front door.

A homely touch, which cheered her, was the sight of a splendid snowman on the lawn, also wearing a striped scarf, a dilapidated mortarboard, and a clay pipe. Some wag had thrust a stick, where his arm might be, to represent a cane.

A pasty-faced maid, very short of breath, answered the door, and led the way, puffing, through a maze of corridors to the head's study at the back of the building.

'Used to lead off the front hall,' observed Frank to his wife. 'Can't think why they take us all round this way.'

'The old study's a staff room now,' volunteered the maid wheezily.

She stopped at a door and knocked.

'Come in,' came a shout.

'Mr and Mrs Never-Caught-Your-Name,' announced the maid.

The head welcomed them boisterously.

'Frank Hurst,' said Frank, 'and my wife. I'm an old boy. We rang some time ago, you remember.'

'Indeed, yes. Indeed, yes. So delighted you could come. My wife, unfortunately, has had to go to a meeting. Now, let me see ...'

He began to shuffle papers on a very untidy desk. Phil sat back and looked around her. The passages which they had traversed had been somewhat grubby, she had noticed. This study was not much cleaner, and the head himself, though handsome once, no doubt, now looked in need of tidying up, she thought.

His tie was greasy, his coat spotted, and his suede shoes needed brushing. Not a very good example to the boys! The only feature which brightened his appearance was a gold tooth, which dominated the conversation to such an extent, that Phil found herself making a strong effort to direct her gaze well above it into the head's eyes.

After a few reminiscences Frank turned to the subject of Jeremy, entrance examinations, further schooling and present attainments.

'And now you must come and see how we live and work,' said the head. 'Mothers always like to see the kitchens and dormitories.'

They followed him back through the labyrinth of corridors until they came to a fine oak staircase. It was badly splintered on the treads, and the banister felt sticky. Phil thought how sad it was to see such a splendid stairway so unloved. Once, it must have been a family's pride, suitably furnished with a fine carpet, and cared for with brush and dustpan and polish by a generation or so of devoted housemaids.

They were shown into several dormitories. Bare boarded, apart from a single strip of thin carpet between the two rows of beds, and curtainless, they appeared to Phil unbelievably bleak. Red blankets did little to mitigate the cheerlessness and the sight of battered teddy bears and other much-loved toys on the beds only added to the poignancy of the scene.

'And this is matron's abode,' said the head leading the way through an elementary surgery-cum-bathroom to an inner sitting-room. Here an auburn-haired young woman hastily rose, and stubbed out a cigarette before greeting them.

'Marjorie,' said the head, 'Mr and Mrs Hurst. Their boy David may be coming here.'

'Jeremy,' said Phil automatically.

The head laughed heartily, the gold tooth glinting.

'Jeremy! Jeremy, of course.'

'He'll love it here,' volunteered matron. 'They are all ever so happy, aren't they, Peter?'

'I think we can say so,' agreed the head, 'I think we can say so.'

Did he say everything twice, wondered Phil? What a perfect person for rude little boys to mimic!

'Might have a day or two feeling a bit homesick at first,' admitted matron, stroking her well-filled mauve jumper while the head eyed her approvingly. 'but we soon jolly them out of that.'

'That's true. That's very true,' agreed the head.

They were led on their tour. The classrooms were large and shabby. The desks were well-carved, the easels splintered, the blackboards needed resurfacing and over all hung the indefinable smell of boy – a fatty, sweaty, chalky smell.

They went out into the snowy wastes to look at the workshop, the gym, the swimmimg-pool and the new half-built pavilion. The little boys had finished their games session and now ran past them, tumbling about together like puppies, sniffing with the cold, hitting each other playfully.

'Sir!' they shouted, when they saw the head, as they passed. Their breath blew around their heads in silver clouds. One or two smiled at Phil, some so young that their front milk teeth had gone. Their gappy smiles made her think of Jeremy, with a sharp pang.

They returned to the car.

'You'll have some tea?' invited the head, but Phil said that they had such a long journey that she felt they had better not stay longer.

'The playroom?' said Frank suddenly. 'What's happened to the play-room?'

'We use it as a science lab. now,' said the head. 'Needed the space, you know.'

They made their farewells, the head's gold tooth flashing in the winter sunlight, and drove homeward.

'Gone to seed a bit,' said Frank thoughtfully.

Phil did not reply. She had found the whole visit thoroughly depressing. It only strengthened her conviction that Jeremy would be better off at home.

They drove in silence for a mile or two.

'Of course, we saw it at its worst,' continued Frank. 'Always looks grim – a school in winter.'

They drove through a small town. The snow had been swept into two grubby mountain ranges, one each side of the main street.

'Didn't take to the head particularly,' went on Frank. 'But there, no one would come up to our old man! Rough luck having to follow him, really. Mustn't make comparisons.'

Dear Frank! Phil was suddenly amused at this display of mingled honesty, generosity and fair-mindedness.

After all, wasn't it for just such qualities that she had married him? She began to feel more hopeful about Jeremy's future. Frank was obviously having second thoughts.

## 19. Dotty in Court

Mr Jones, the landlord of The Two Pheasants, was as good as his word. Soon after six one evening, within a week of Charles Henstock's visit, he rang the bell at the rectory.

Charles opened the door and found himself facing not only the landlord, but also Percy Hodge.

'Come in, gentlemen,' said Charles, leading the way to his study.

'Take a seat, and let me get you some refreshment.'

'Not for me, thanks,' said Mr Jones.

'Nor me,' said Mr Hodge.

The rector's heart sank a little. Had he further antagonized them by calling upon them earlier?

'We've come about the graveyard business,' said Mr Jones, coming straight to the point. 'I promised to turn it over in my mind.'

'Indeed, yes. And what is your decision?'

'I thought I'd have a word with Perce here,' said the landlord, refusing to be hurried.

'Very sensible.'

'And Perce and I had a good sit-down talk about it, didn't we?'

'That we did,' said Percy. 'We fairly thrashed it out.'

'And in the end,' continued Mr Jones, 'we decided that the place is a proper eyesore as it is.'

'Disrespectful too,' added Percy.

They sat back with an air of finality, and the rector's heart sank still further.

'It is indeed,' he agreed. 'That's why we felt something should be done.'

'Yes. We saw that,' said Percy. 'I said to Bill here: "That's a fair eyesore, that graveyard, and something's got to be done about it." Didn't I?'

'You did, Perce.'

'Good,' said the rector faintly. He was beginning to feel slightly dizzy.

'So we came to the conclusion that *provided* our family graves were left alone we'd agree to the levelling and general tidying-up, like you said.'

Charles Henstock gave a great sigh of relief. To his surprise and shame, he felt tears pricking his eyes. He had not realized how deeply he felt about the matter until now.

'My dear Mr Jones, I can't tell you how grateful I am!'

He turned to Percy Hodge.

'And to you too, Mr Hodge. This is a most generous and public-spirited gesture. I shall certainly see that the graves in that corner remain as they are.'

'What about Mrs Cleary's?' asked Percy.

'She is away at the moment,' said Charles, 'but I propose to call on her within the next day or two, as soon as she is back.'

He remembered something suddenly.

'And what about your two men?'

'They're agreeable,' said Percy shortly. The rector decided not to press the matter now, but to have a word in private with Percy's employees later.

Mr Jones stood up.

'Well, sir, I'm glad you're pleased. We didn't want to be awkward, and now we know our people won't be disturbed, we're quite content. I must be off now. I've left the wife in charge of the bar, and we'll be getting busy soon.'

The rector shook hands with his two parishioners, and took them to the door.

The night was still and icy-cold. The widespread pall of snow reflected a little light.

'I'll be at church next Sunday,' said Percy gruffly, ramming on his cap.

'I am thankful,' said Charles sincerely, raising a hand in farewell.


Later that evening, the rector crunched across the snow to tell Harold Shoosmith the good news. The moon was rising, a splendid golden full one, glinting on the snow and throwing the dark trees into sharp relief.

'It's a beautiful night,' said Harold in greeting.

'In more ways than one,' agreed Charles, settling by the fire. He told Harold the good news.

'And now I have only Mrs Cleary to see and Martin Brewer who works for her,' went on the rector. 'And I really should have a private word with the Howard brothers. I'm not too sure if they really agree with Percy Hodge. It would be a bad thing if they have been coerced.'

'I don't think there will be much opposition from them, or from Mrs Cleary and young Martin Brewer. I must say, Charles, you have handled the thing very diplomatically.'

'I don't think that I can lay claim to diplomacy, Harold. Let's say that Thrush Green preferred to remain united when it came to it. The very thought of courts and lawyers was enough to bring out the good solid British quality of independence.'

'Talking of courts,' said Harold, 'isn't it tomorrow that Dotty's case is heard? Are you going?'

'Yes, I thought I would stand by her.'

'Unfortunately, I have to go to London to settle some business affairs, otherwise I'd join you. Poor woman! I hope that Justin gets her off.'

'I have every confidence in him,' said the rector firmly. Harold refrained from voicing his own doubts.

'Did I tell you,' said Charles, 'that we have copied your example and bought a red shade for our sitting-room lamp? It makes such a warm glow.'

'I'm flattered.'

'And Dimity has made a long draught excluder for the bottom of the door. Most efficient.'

'A sausage? Why, we used to have one of those, I remember,' said Harold. 'What a good idea! The rectory tends to be a little draughty, I know,' he said, making the understatement of a life-time.

'Well, it all looks much more snug,' said Charles, 'inspired by this room. I thought credit should be given where credit's due.'

He rose to his feet.

'Must be off. Court starts at ten in the morning, so I want to get ahead with my correspondence. I thought of calling on Dotty tonight, but it may be kinder not to. She may be washing her hair or something,' he added vaguely.

Harold doubted it, but kept silent, and showed his kind-hearted friend out into the black and silver world.

At Lulling Woods, Dotty Harmer leant on her gate and surveyed the peaceful landscape. The air was very still. The full moon, turned from gold to silver in its majestic ascent, lit the snowy scene with a gentle radiance. To Dotty's left, the bulk of Lulling Woods showed navy-blue against the starry sky, with one warm red spot where the wood cutters had made a bonfire that afternoon.

Dotty had watched the blue smoke spiralling aloft in the quiet air. Now only the embers glowed, the aftermath of the two men's energetic work with the axe and electric saw. In that black and white world, it added a touch of colour, of warmth and, Dotty thought, of hope.

A mood of resignation enfolded her. What would be, would be! She had worried herself into a state of suspended animation, unable to think clearly, or to care very much what the outcome of tomorrow's hearing would be.

She was content now to drink in the tranquillity of the view before her. There was something strangely comforting in being along with elemental things, the moon, the snow, the distant fire. A mere summons to court seemed ephemeral in their presence. Guilty or not guilty, the moon would rise again tomorrow, the snow would remain, the fire would be rekindled.

Dotty took a deep breath, and realized how bitterly cold she felt. She turned her back upon the scene of her comfort, much fortified, and made her way to bed.

It was clear and bright again next morning when Charles Henstock called for Dotty, as he had arranged to do some days earlier.

'I am going in any case,' he replied, when she demurred, 'and parking is always difficult near the court house. Besides, you will have enough to worry you without the bother of driving.'

And so Dotty entered the rector's car looking surprisingly well-dressed for once. It was true that her stockings were in folds, and that her hair escaped in wisps from underneath a formidable black hat which must once have been her mother's, Charles surmised. But she wore a fur coat, which Charles had never seen before, and her black suede gloves were impeccable.

'Allow me to say how nice you look, Dotty,' said the rector.

'Thank you, Charles. I hope I know what's fitting to the dignity of a court of law. You didn't imagine I'd be in my gardening outfit?'

To tell the truth, Charles would not have been surprised to find his eccentric friend in just such a garb, but changed the subject.

'Dimity insists that you come back to our house for a meal, whatever the time.'

'That is kind of her. I should love to.'

They drove slowly up Lulling High Street, passing the three Miss Lovelocks in snow boots, scarves and Sunday hats, all making for the same destination.

'Vultures,' said Dotty mildly.

'I beg your pardon?' Charles sounded startled.

'Nothing. I was thinking aloud.'

They entered the market place. The court house flanked one side of the square, an ornate Victorian building comprising various municipal departments as well as the court on the ground floor.

Justin Venables was waiting for his client in the doorway. Charles dropped his passenger, watched the two meet, and then drove round to find a parking place.

The court room, when he entered it, was less than half full. It was Charles's first visit to Lulling Magistrates' Court, and he looked about him with interest.

It was a lofty pseudo-gothic building, with all the woodwork varnished to a sticky brown. Like a treacle-well, thought Charles, who was a devotee of *Alice in Wonderland*.

The public benches were rather uncomfortable, and he wondered if the benches set high on the dais in front for the justices were any more comfortable. If not, he was sincerely sorry for those magistrates who were obliged to spend the day there.

The dock stood on his left, a sturdy structure of carved, well varnished wood and brass, and at the front of the court, on the right, were the jurymen's benches, facing the witness box.

The benches where counsel and solicitors were seated were directly ahead of him, and he could see Justin Venables, silver head bent in conversation with another local solicitor. There were two more people there, one, Charles guessed, the prosecutor for the police. If he were the six-footer with the massive shoulders of a rugby forward, and a jutting jaw, then Charles trembled for Dotty. His appearance alone was enough to strike terror into any heart.

At that moment, the gowned usher stood up at the side of the court and spoke in a tremendous roar.

'The court will be upstanding!'

They all rose obediently, and watched the three magistates file in, followed by Mr Pearson who went to his desk below the dais and stood facing their worships.

Lady Winter led the way, wearing a grey flannel suit, a blue silk blouse, four rows of pearls and a fur hat.

Mrs Fothergill followed in a dashing brown and white dog-tooth check, a gold brooch and no hat, while Mr Jardine decorous in navy-blue pin stripe stood in front of the large chair in the middle beneath the royal arms.

Polite bows were exchanged. The magistrates, clerk and everyone else took their seats, and proceedings began with the granting of occasional licences to various local publicans, and other everyday business.

It was during this part of the proceedings that the door opened to admit six venerable gentlemen from the neighbouring almshouse. Charles had heard that they enjoyed a morning session at court, and were consequently something of experts on British justice. Certainly, their forecasts of the verdicts found by the bench after long and weighty discussion by that august body were usually the same. If anything, they were inclined to be a little stiffer in their sentences when the victims were elderly, and on the whole disliked probation for anyone over the age of twenty. Some in Lulling maintained that they would prefer to face the men from the almshouse, who saw things perhaps more clearly than magistrates who had had their brains addled by a lot of case-reading and attending conferences.

The old men settled wheezily into the bench behind Charles, arranging sticks, undoing scarves and having recourse to their handkerchiefs after the cold air outside.

'Started on time for once,' said one to his neighbour.

'I see Pendle's prosecuting. Ought to be done by dinner time. He don't waste words.'

'But Mr Jardine's a rare one for retiring. Wants a drag, I daresay. Proper chain-smoker.'

The usher gave a stern glance towards the whisperers, who subsided slightly.

'Old Tom thinks hisself God Almighty, in that there gown,' muttered one softly, just behind Charles. 'He forgets we can remember him sitting on the kerb with his bottom through his breeches.'

Two youths appeared in the dock flanked by a policeman. They faced charges of stealing from Puddocks', the stationers at the corner of the market-square, and of assaulting a policeman in the execution of his duty.

They pleaded guilty, through their solicitor who was sitting beside Justin Venables, and grinned sheepishly at each other when told to sit down.

Mr Jardine, who had served in the army in his youth, always did his best to overcome the natural repugnance he felt for long unwashed hair, dirty blue jeans, and sweat shirts bearing such legends as: 'I am the Greatest', 'I love Everyone' or simply 'Tottenham Hotspurs'. But he drew the line at giggling in court, and chewing gum, in which the present offenders were indulging.

'Take that stuff out of your mouth,' he directed sharply, 'and behave yourselves.'

Meekly, they removed the offending gum, gazing at their fingers in bewilderment.

'Give it 'ere,' said the policeman, producing an envelope. The matter was placed within, and the usher put it ceremoniously in the waste paper basket.

'Your worships,' began the six-foot prosecutor, 'the facts of this case are as follows. At three-twenty on the afternoon of Thursday, December 8th, in answer to a telephone call from the manager, Police Constable Carter proceeded to Puddocks', the stationers, where these two young men had been detained.'

Charles found his attention wandering. He looked discreetly about him. Two young men from the local newspaper were scribbling busily at a side table. Would this case make headlines? No doubt an assault on a policeman would. And quite right too, thought Charles. Policemen had enough dirty work to do without being attacked into the bargain. He began to muse about one of his godsons who was now a police sergeant in Leeds.

A change of voice brought his attention back to the court. The youths' solicitor was now making an impassioned plea for leniency, emphasizing that this was only their second time in court, they had no homes and had been out of work and sleeping rough at the time of the theft and assault. He did the job so well, that Charles would not have been surprised to see tears in the eyes of the justices, but they appeared impervious.

When the solicitor had taken his seat, the chairman conferred briefly with his colleagues.

'The bench will retire to consider this case,' he announced, and stood back for the ladies to precede him into the magistrates' retiring room.

'Court will be upstanding!' shouted the usher, and it was.

'Havin' their coffee now,' said one of the old men. 'They always retire just after eleven. You going to try a cup out of that new machine?'

'I'm durned if I'm putting a bob into that contraption to get a lousy cardboard cup of wishy-washy chicken soup I don't want, when I'd put me money in for coffee,' said his neighbour stoutly. 'It's a ruddy swindle.'

'He's right,' agreed another.

There was a general relaxation in the courtroom, people moving across to speak to friends, and the solicitors standing up to consult each other. Charles waved to the Misses Lovelock and was embarrassed to receive a blown kiss from Miss Bertha, which he acknowledged with a formal bow.

The clerk, who had gone out later to join the magistrates, now returned, and the court room became rather more seemly. Three minutes later their worships returned.

'You will be remanded in custody for three weeks for reports,' said the chairman.'We need to know more about you before we pass sentence.'

The youths followed the policeman from the dock.

'Back to the bloody glasshouse,' muttered one, as he passed Charles.

'Told you they was off for coffee,' said the old man behind him. 'They could've done that without retiring, and saved a lot of time.'

'Call Dorothy Amelia Russell Harmer,' said Mr Pearson. The usher departed into the lobby.

'Dorothy Amelia Russell Harmer,' echoed round the building.

Justin Venables stood up awaiting his client. She entered briskly, pointing to the dock.

'Do I go in there?' she inquired of the usher.

'No, no,' said Mr Venables hastily. 'Come and take your place by me.'

Dotty's case had begun.

'You are Dorothy Amelia Russell Harmer of Woodside, Lulling?' asked Mr Pearson.

'I am,' said Dotty politely.

'I appear for Miss Harmer,' said Justin to the bench.

'The charge against you is that on 20 October of last year, you drove a motor vehicle on a road, namely Lulling High Street, without due care and attention, contrary to Section 3 of the Road Traffic Act 1972. How do you plead?'

'Well, naturally –' began Dotty, looking nettled.

'*Please,*' said Justin hastily. 'My client pleads "Not Guilty" to the charge.'

'Sit down, please,' said Mr Jardine.

The prosecuting solicitor rose to his full six feet, and gave the facts of the case concisely.

'And I shall be calling three witnesses,' he added. 'The first is P.C. Darwin.'

That officer carried a well-thumbed notebook in case his memory needed refreshing. Hardly surprising, thought Charles, when you heard how long it took to bring a case before the court! He himself would be hard put to it to tell anyone what he had done the day before, let alone four months earlier!

He gave his evidence clearly and agreed with Justin Venables, in cross examination, that Miss Harmer had given every possible assistance after the accident. He then made way for Mr Giles, the second witness.

Mr Giles kept a music shop in Lulling High Street almost opposite Mr Levy's butcher's shop. He was a frail elderly man, white-haired and wearing glasses. He took the oath in a quavering voice.

Yes, he had witnessed the accident, he told the bench. He had heard the crash and said to his assistant –

'You mustn't tell us what you said,' Mr Jardine told him.

'Well, *he* said –'

'Nor what *he* said,' replied Mr Jardine firmly.'It is hearsay, you see, Mr Giles.'

'No, I don't see,' said the old man, with a flash of temper. 'How am I to tell the truth, the whole truth and nothing but the truth, if you won't let me?'

'As a result of what you heard,' said Mr Pearson, coming to the rescue,'what did you do?'

Things then proceeded more smoothly.

Justin Venables made a shrewd point by asking about Mr Giles' spectacles. Was he short-sighted or long-sighted?

He was short-sighted.

Was he wearing his spectacles when he saw the accident?

'Probably,' said Mr Giles, now a trifle rattled.

'If you were *not* wearing them you would be unable to see clearly what was happening at a distance of some thirty yards?'

'I could see quite a bit,' said Mr Giles.

'But you can't say positively that you *were* wearing your spectacles.'

'Not on oath, no.'

Mr Venables sat down looking smug.

The third witness was a woman shopper who had been on the pavement at the time of the collision. She answered the prosecutor's questions clearly, but added little to the evidence. Justin did not cross-examine her.

'I will call my client,' he said, when the prosecutor sat down.

Dotty entered the witness box and picked up the New Testament.

'Please remove your gloves,' said the usher.

'As you wish,' said Dotty, tugging at the splendid suede pair.

She took the oath firmly.

'Now, Miss Harmer, will you direct your answers to the bench,' said Justin, 'although I am asking the questions?'

Dotty turned obediently, recognized Mrs Fothergill as an acquaintance, and wished her 'Good morning' affably.

Mrs Fothergill gave a sickly smile, but forbore to reply. Lady Winter and the chairman ignored Dotty's civility, and remained impassive.

'You are Dorothy Amelia Russell Harmer, residing at Woodside, Lulling?' said Justin, in dulcet tones.

'You know I am!' responded Dotty, astonished.

'A formality,' murmured Justin. Good heavens, was she going to be in one of her prickly moods?

He led her, with exquisite caution, through her narrative. It soon became clear that despite her odd appearance and a certain impatience with some of the questions, Dotty was transparently honest about the whole affair. She was not in the least put out by some fairly searching questions by the prosecution, and even congratulated the police in having such a pleasant young fellow as Mr Darwin in the force, before Justin could quell her.

Mr Levy, enjoying every moment of his public appearance, was equally hard to restrain.

'You saw the boy riding before the accident?' asked Justin.

'If you can call it riding,' said Mr Levy. 'He was on a bike far too big for him – sawing away he was, wobbling all whichways, and yelling to his mates. He swerved straight into Miss Harmer. She was well into the middle of the road. I'll take my oath on it –'

'You have,' put in Mr Pearson drily.

'And I've known Miss Harmer since she was a little girl, and she's as straight as a die! She'd say if she'd been at fault. It was that ruddy boy – begging your worships' pardon – as crashed across her path.'

'Miss Harmer's integrity is not in question,' said Justin austerely. 'Just let us take your account of the boy's movements, point by point.'

With some difficulty he led his ebullient witness through his story. The prosecutor had no questions to ask. Nor had the bench.

Justin's last witness was one of the teaching staff who had been in the playground when the accident occurred. He was a nervous young man, but Justin soon put him at ease, and he agreed that the boys were rather noisy and excited when they left school, and did not take as much care as they should about traffic conditions. He agreed with Mr Levy that Cyril Cooke's bicycle was in a poor state and much too big for him. He himself had told Mrs Cooke so, and suggested that the boy walked to school. She had not been co-operative.

By now it was almost one o'clock, and Charles was beginning to get hungry. The almhouse men had shuffled away some half-hour earlier, but the rest of the spectators were obviously waiting to hear this case completed.

Justin Venables gave a brief but well-expressed summing up on behalf of his client, pointing out that she had held a licence for almost half a century, and that she had no previous convictions. To his mind, the prosecution had failed to prove the charge and he suggested, with all due respect, that it should be dismissed.

'Bench will retire,' growled Mr Jardine, and Mrs Fothergill led out the three.

Charles remained standing to ease his aching back. Whoever designed the public seats at Lulling Court deserved to be sentenced to sitting in them for twenty-four hours non-stop, he decided.

The Misses Lovelock, aflutter with scarves and gloves, came up to speak to him.

'Didn't Dotty do splendidly?' quavered Miss Violet.

'Surely she will be found not guilty?' said Miss Bertha.

'I always knew she was a cautious driver,' said Miss Ada. 'I hope that horrid boy gets sent to a penal institution.'

Charles did not feel equal to explaining that the boy was not being charged, only Dotty, and was spared further conversation by the return of the justices.

Dotty remained standing by Justin Venables. Suddenly pale, she looked incredibly old and tired. Charles felt shaken with anxiety for her. What an ordeal! He would be glad to get her into his car and back to the haven of the rectory and Dimity's ministrations.

Mr Jardine cleared his throat with peremptory honkings.

'We find you not guilty of the offence with which you have been charged.'

Dotty looked with bewilderment towards Justin Venables, who was smiling and bowing.

'The case,' explained Mr Jardine, looking directly at Dotty 'is dismissed.'

Dotty inclined her head graciously, and murmured thanks.

'The court will adjourn until two o'clock,' said Mr Jardine.

Everyone stood as the bench retired. The door to the magistrates' room had scarcely closed when Dotty's clear voice was heard.

'Could you, by any chance, lend me a handkerchief, Mr Venables?'

Head up, back like a ramrod, Dotty faced her solicitor. Tears were coursing down her papery old cheeks and splashing unchecked upon the fur coat.

But, through the tears, Dotty's expression was one of utter triumph.

## 20. Peace Returns

News of the outcome of the court case soon swept Thrush Green and Lulling. Approval was general, although Albert Piggott, and one or two other curmudgeons, expressed the view that it was a pity Dotty would still be able to terrorize the neighbourhood with her driving.

Mrs Cooke, when told of the verdict, executed a complete *volte-face* and said she had told her Cyril, times without number, to give over riding his dad's old bike, and now look where it had led him. She prophesied a piece of his dad's tongue for getting in Miss Harmer's way, and causing everyone a mint of trouble.

Dotty herself, after her brief spell of emotion occasioned by relief, appeared to forget all about the incident, and returned to her many chores in the cottage and garden. It was noticed, however, that the car rarely came out of the garage in the weeks that followed.

The snow was a long time in clearing, but gradually the grass showed again on Thrush Green, and the first early crocuses began to spear the ground.

The rector rang Mrs Cleary, a day or two after Dotty's case, to see if he might call on her to talk about the graveyard. To his amazement, that lady seemed anxious to settle the matter there and then.

'I heard that Mr Hodge and Mr Jones have climbed down,' said the imperious voice at the rector's ear. 'In which case, I think it pointless to continue with my objections.'

The rector rallied from the shock.

'There are one or two points I should like to discuss, nevertheless,' he said. 'We have a sketch map showing our plans for that part of the churchyard where your own family are buried. I should like to show you that.'

'I take it none of my family would be disturbed?'

'None, Mrs Cleary. Simply, their surroundings would be much beautified.'

There was a silence for a while.

'Very well. I'm content that you should go ahead, if the others have agreed. I'll vouch for Martin Brewer too.'

Really, thought the rector, anyone would think Lulling were ruled by despotism – one could only hope it was a benevolent one.

'I shall have a word with young Brewer myself,' said Charles firmly.

He broached his second point.

'Would you consider withdrawing your resignation from the parochial church council? I have persuaded Mr Hodge to serve again, now that this little difference has been sorted out, and we should all be glad if you would return to us.'

'I will think about it,' said the lady graciously. She sounded mollified, thought Charles thankfully, as he replaced the receiver.

During the next week he managed to buttonhole the two Howard brothers, as well as Martin Brewer, and was shaken to find how little they really cared about the matter of the churchyard.

'Mr Hodge is boss. We does as he says. We lives in his cottages, see,' explained one of the brothers, as though that made the whole thing completely understandable.

Martin Brewer's attitude was much the same, but tempered with gratitude for Mrs Cleary's generosity in providing a job while he was without a driving licence.

'They don't seem to have any minds of their own,' said Charles despairingly to Dimity.

'They do, dear. But they know which side their bread is buttered.'

The rector still looked pensive.

'Cheer up,' said his wife, 'now you can sit down and apply for the faculty with a clear conscience, and leave it all in the laps of the gods.'

'In the lap of the Chancellor,' amended Charles, smiling at last.


Cyril Cooke was not the only person to suffer from mumps that winter. At the village school the number of sufferers gradually grew from three in January to fourteen in the first week of February.

It meant that work was very much easier, with fewer children in the class, and Miss Fogerty was grateful. The first term of the New Year was always a trial, with bad weather, poor light, and innumerable complaints and epidemics. Added to this general depression was the continuing estrangement from Miss Watson, despite surface civilities.

But one afternoon, when she had seen her depleted class buttoned and shod properly against their homeward journeys through the melting snow, she was surprised to be invited to the school house for a cup of tea.

Miss Watson appeared much agitated as she busied herself with spoons and biscuits, and her hand trembled as she passed Miss Fogerty her cup.

'I hardly know how to begin,' she said. 'Miss Potter has just told me she is leaving at the end of term.'

Miss Fogerty's heart leapt with joy, but she managed to look suitably concerned.

'But why? She seems to have settled down quite well. And heaven knows,' said Miss Fogerty, unable to resist a slight dig, 'she has been given everything she has asked for.'

'I am sorry to say, there is a baby coming,' said Miss Watson. Her face was stern.

'A baby? But she's not married!' cried Miss Fogerty, dropping her spoon.

'It has been known to happen,' pointed out Miss Watson.

'Oh, I know, I know,' agreed Miss Fogerty wisely. 'But how on earth did the silly girl get so involved?'

'She told me, *quite calmly*, that she went away with that young man of hers last summer, and there we are. She was rather nonchalant about the whole thing, which made me cross. She's arranging to marry him in the Easter holidays.'

'What a good thing for the baby,' said Miss Fogerty sincerely.

'But not for *us*,' said Miss Watson with asperity. 'We shall have to be three-in-a-desk all next term, unless we get that dreadful Mrs Spears in as supply, and you know what *that* means!'

Miss Fogerty nodded. Mrs Spears was the only supply teacher in Lulling, a vast noisy creature, reputed to carry a flask of gin among her school books, and much given to teaching the children mid-European folk dances involving a lot of clapping and stamping. The last time she had spent a fortnight at Thrush Green School, she had broken one easel, three tea cups and a child's finger. Miss Watson and Miss Fogerty had suffered from splitting headaches throughout her stay, and had watched her departure with relief.

'You'll put in an advertisement for the post, I suppose?' said Miss Fogerty.

'Oh, I shall see that it goes in immediately, but I don't suppose there's any hope until the girls come out of college in July.'

She replenished Miss Fogerty's cup and sighed.

'Oh, Agnes dear, what a comfort it is to have you to confide in! I can't tell you how I've missed our little chats since Christmas. Nor how *dreadful* I've felt about that bedjacket! To have upset you so grieved me terribly, as I'm sure you know, Agnes. I hope I'm forgiven. I wouldn't have had it happen for the world.'

Miss Fogerty felt suddenly warm. The vision of a little brook which had remained frozen for weeks near her house but, only this week, had thawed and started to run merrily again, flashed across her mind.

So too did she feel. The ice had melted, the bonds were broken, and joy flowed again.

'It is all forgotten and forgiven long ago,' said Miss Fogerty.

'Ah, Agnes,' sighed Miss Watson. 'Teachers may come and teachers may go, but you and I go on for ever it seems.'

Miss Fogerty decided it was time to change the subject.

'And what about a wedding present?'

'We might club together and buy a cradle,' rejoined Miss Watson, with rare tartness.

Across the green, at Tullivers, one of the mumps' victims sat up in bed. Jeremy was a woebegone figure, his face and neck so grotesquely swollen that even his mother might have had difficulty in recognizing him if she had met him away from home.

Charles Henstock had called in to see the patient, and to deliver a box of coloured pencils and a drawing book thoughtfully provided by Dimity.

Conversation was limited to expressions of sympathy on Charles's side and sad, inarticulate little cries on Jeremy's. Before long, Charles left the sickroom and accompanied Phil downstairs.

'At least he's in a comfortable bedroom,' said Charles, 'with a kind nurse to look after him. I had mumps at my prep school, and the san. was full, of course. A horrible place – bitterly cold, with lumpy flock mattresses to lie on. And nurse was run off her feet, naturally, and let us know it.'

'Poor Charles!' said Phil. 'I can imagine the misery.'

'The worst thing was being dished out with doorsteps of leathery toast when one could hardly open one's jaws. What is there about boarding schools?'

'I assume that that is a rhetorical question,' said Phil, with a laugh. 'We went to see Frank's the other day, and I was most depressed at the sight.'

'Does Frank still want Jeremy to go away?'

'Let's say he's thinking twice since seeing his old school, but in principle I think he likes the idea of boarding, if only we can find a good place. As you know, I want Jeremy to go with Paul Young in September to Lulling, until he's twelve or thirteen.'

'Well, I'm sure you'll both do the best thing for the boy, as you are at the moment.'

He rose and made for the door.

'Sorry to miss Frank. You know the application for the faculty has gone in? We can only wait and hope now.'

'How soon shall we know?'

'Whenever the Chancellor has time to attend to it. He's a busy man, but very meticulous about his correspondence I know. Maybe within a month.'

'How lovely! And when will the work begin?'

Charles laughed, and held up two crossed fingers.

'Don't go too fast, my dear,' he said.

He had been gone less than ten minutes when Frank arrived home from the office.

'How's Jeremy? Can I go up?'

'Yes, he's awake. Charles has just been to see him.'

She followed her husband up the stairs. Frank, startled at the boy's appearance, stood stock-still in the doorway.

'My goodness! You're twice the boy I left behind me this morning!' he cried.

Jeremy lowered his eyes.

'Not funny,' he muttered.

Frank was instantly contrite.

'You're quite right. It's not funny, and I'm sorry. Got all you want?'

'Yes, thanks,' said the child, looking more cheerful, 'except a drink.'

Phil refilled his glass and sat on the bed watching him take the liquid in painful sips.

Frank surveyed the scene thoughtfully.

'I should have a nap,' advised Phil, at last.

'I think I will,' said the invalid, sliding down the bed. 'My eyes won't stay open.'

Downstairs, Frank turned to Phil.

'He looks pretty snug up there. I had mumps at school. It was ghastly.'

'So did Charles,' said Phil. 'He told me the grisly details of a boarding school illness.'

'I've something extraordinary to tell you,' said Frank, helping himself to a drink. 'About Ribblesworth. Tom had the news this morning at the office.'

'Burnt down?' asked Phil hopefully.

Frank laughed.

'Worse, really. That headmaster's run off –'

'With the matron,' interrupted Phil.

Frank looked at her in astonishment.

'How did you know?'

'She was exactly the sort of person who would be run off with.'

'You must have second sight! That's exactly what's happened. I never took to that chap. And what a scandal for the school!'

'I daresay it's happened before.'

'Not to Ribblesworth,' said Frank loyally.

He put down his drink and began to pace the room.

'What with going to see it, and remembering mumps at school, and now this business,' said Frank, 'I'm coming round to your way of thinking. Let the boy have a few more years at home as a day boy. Agreed?'

'You know I've never wavered in my feeling on the subject,' said Phil,'but I think it's downright noble of you to change your mind so generously.'

'Let's go and see the head at Lulling, and get him entered for next September if there's a place, shall we?'

'An excellent idea,' said Jeremy's mother.


Next door, at Doctor Bailey's house, a bridge session had just finished, and Winnie, Dotty, Ella and Dimity sat round the fire with the debris of the tea trolley pushed to one side.

The ladies had discussed their hopes for the faculty being granted.

'Charles thinks of nothing else at the moment,' said Dimity. 'He's like a child waiting for Christmas.'

'Is Albert Piggott going to be in charge when the churchyard is altered?' asked Ella.

'I suppose so,' said Dimity.

'It's a great pity,' announced Dotty, searching in her knicker leg for a handkerchief, 'that my goats weren't allowed to keep the place tidy while we were waiting.'

After further scrabbling she produced a crumpled piece of linen and blew her nose with a resounding trumpeting. Only Dotty, thought Winnie, would keep her handkerchief in the leg of her knickers, thus needing to expose wrinkled stockings and bony shanks whenever it was needed.

'Thrush Green's going to see some changes,' said Dimity.

'One is going to happen in this house,' said Winnie, who had managed to keep her domestic plans secret, but now felt that things were advanced far enough to tell her friends. They looked suitably eager.

'Come on, Winnie,' commanded Ella, beginning to roll an untidy cigarette. 'Tell all.'

Winnie explained about the two upstairs rooms, without going too deeply into her own fears at night.

'And Jenny told me yesterday that the old people move next week.'

'How marvellous! And she comes then?'

'No, not for a month or two. There are several things to be done. My nephew Richard is spending a week here soon, putting in cupboards and so on, and the plumber has to fit a sink in the kitchen-to-be. She can stay in her present home for some months if she likes, I gather. Demolition doesn't start until the autumn, so she can take her time.'

'So you'll have someone in the house before long,' said Dotty, remembering that dark afternoon when she and Winnie had exchanged confidences. 'It will be company for you, especially welcome next winter.'

'Lucky Jenny!' exclaimed Dimity.

'Lucky me!' responded Winnie, rising. 'Come upstairs and see what I'm planning to do.'


When Dimity returned to the rectory, she was bubbling over with Winnie's good news and all the plans for Jenny's new flat.

The rector was standing with his back to the small sitting-room fire. In his hand was a letter.

Before she could tell him the news, Charles spoke.

'My dear, I have had a letter from the Bishop.'

'Oh Charles,' cried Dimity, remembering, with sudden fear, being summoned to her headmistress's study years before. 'What *have* you done?'

'Why, nothing –' began Charles in bewilderment.

'Or is it about the faculty?'

'That is the Chancellor's affair, my dear. This is from the Bishop himself.'

Dimity sat down abruptly.

'Well, tell me quickly. Is there some trouble?'

'Just the opposite. He has been kind enough to make me a Rural Dean.'

Dimity gazed at him open-mouthed.

'A Rural Dean,' she echoed, and then the full glory of the promotion burst upon her, and she leapt to her feet to put her arms round him.

'My darling, how wonderful! And you deserve it too. I'm so glad the Bishop has recognized all your hard work.'

'Others work harder, I expect,' said Charles. 'But I am truly grateful. I must write to him this evening and try to express my appreciation of the honour.'

'Do you know,' said Dimity, sitting down again, 'I feel quite faint. It must be the excitement. The room is swinging about.'

Charles looked alarmed.

'Stay there! I'll find a little brandy.'

'No, no,' protested Dimity. 'I shall soon be all right. I really mustn't start getting a taste for brandy. It's so expensive.'

'Are you sure? Some water then?'

'No, really,' said Dimity, sitting up straight. 'It has passed now. It was simply pure joy! It's heady stuff, isn't it?'

The rector was looking at his letter again.

'It is indeed. Now, Dimity, help me to compose a meet and proper answer to His Lordship for honours joyfully received.'

Later that evening, Charles was in his study, writing a fair copy of his letter to the Bishop, when the telephone rang.

Dimity, by the fire in the sitting-room, wondered at the length of the conversation. Someone in sore trouble again, she supposed. But when Charles entered the room he was smiling.

'That was Bruce Fairfax from the prep school. He asked me to take Religious Instruction twice a week and I have agreed. He is glad of help and we shall be glad of some extra money.'

Involuntarily, Dimity glanced towards the tall, draughty windows.

'Yes, my dear,' said Charles. 'I think you can safely order some new curtains.'

One blue and white March morning Willie Marchant, one of the postmen at Thrush Green, tacked purposefully up the hill from Lulling, causing alarm to various drivers going about their lawful occasions on the right side of the road.

Willie ignored their shouted protestations, as usual, and dismounted at the rectory. A stub of cigarette exuded pungent fumes, killing temporarily the fragrance wafting from a clump of early narcissi.

He opened the door of the rectory and collected half a dozen letters left there, and put the one he was carrying in their place.

'Only one this morning,' called Dimity, when she went to collect the post. Charles was coming down the stairs.

'But it is the one we've been waiting for,' said the new Rural Dean.

He opened it hastily, and his pink face creased into a beam.

'It's granted!' he said, with a gusty sigh of relief. 'The precious faculty itself . . . to be deposited in the Church Chest. Now, at last after all our battles, we can go ahead!'

On the last day of term, Miss Potter was presented with a set of silver coffee spoons (not a cradle) by Miss Watson and Miss Fogerty, and was given every felicitation for her future happiness.

They were to live in Scarborough, said Miss Potter, and she hoped that they would call if they were ever in that neighbourhood. As the ladies were positive that they would never go so far afield, they were in a position to thank her effusively for the invitation, and Miss Potter departed in a cloud of cordial farewells.

'Well,' said Miss Watson, turning into her classroom, 'I must spend half an hour tidying up here. I suppose you will be going over to your new domain, Agnes?'

'I thought I would take the bulk of my things across,' agreed Miss Fogerty.

'Come back when you've done,' said Miss Watson, 'and have tea with me. I've made a chocolate sponge to celebrate the end of term.'

Miss Fogerty thanked her, and went into her old classroom to collect a large case of infant handwork which was to be transferred to the terrapin across the playground.

The sun was hot on her head as she made her triumphal progress to the promised land. She dumped the case, and stood by the beautiful low window which would do so much to bring on the mustard and cress, the bean seeds and the bulbs, in the happy days ahead.

The little valley leading to Lulling Woods shimmered in the spring sunshine. Somewhere a lark was singing, and in some distant field lambs bleated.

Miss Fogerty sighed with happiness. Here she was – where she had longed to be. After all the struggles of the winter, peace had come with the spring.


Miss Watson was tapping the school barometer when Miss Fogerty returned. It was a handsome mahogany piece left her by an aged uncle, and as it was too large for the school house it had taken up its abode in her classroom.

'I must say,' said Miss Watson, peering at the instrument, 'it's pleasant to see the needle at "Fair" after "Stormy" and "Rain" and "Change" and all the other unsettled conditions we've had lately. Do you think Thrush Green will remain at "Set Fair" for a time, Agnes?'

'I have no doubt about it,' said Little Miss Fogerty.

# Return to Thrush Green

*To*

*Sir Robert Lusty*

*whose early encouragement*

*began it all*

# Contents

## Part One   Travelling Hopefully

## Part Two   Change at Thrush Green

## Part Three   Safe Arrival

## Epilogue

# Part One
# Travelling Hopefully

## 1. Spring Afternoon

The finest house at Thrush Green, everyone agreed, was that occupied by Joan and Edward Young. Built of honey-coloured Cotswold stone, some hundred or so years ago, it had a beautiful matching tiled roof, mottled with a patina of lichen and moss. It looked southward, across the length of the green, to the little market town of Lulling hidden in the valley half a mile away.

The house had been built by a mill owner who had made a comfortable fortune at the woollen mill which straddled the river Pleshey a mile or two west of Lulling. It was large enough to house his family of six, and three resident maids. A range of stone-built stables, a coach house and tack room, stood a little way from the house, and at right angles to it. Above the stable was the bothy, where the groom-cum-coachman slept, and immediately above the bedroom was the stable clock.

The Youngs often wondered how on earth people managed without such storage space. Nowadays, the buildings were filled with furniture awaiting repair, lawn-mowers, deck-chairs, tea-chests full of bottling equipment or archaic kitchen utensils which 'might come in useful one day', two deep freezers, a decrepit work bench and an assortment of outgrown toys, such as a tricycle and a rocking horse, the property of Paul Young, their only child. Everything needing a temporary home found its way into the stable and then became a permanency. Sagging wicker garden chairs, shabby trunks, cat baskets, camping stoves, old tennis racquets, fishing waders, and Paul's pram, unused for nine years, were housed here, jostling each other, and coated with dust, bird droppings and the débris from ancient nests in the beams above.

'If ever we had to move,' said Edward to Joan one sunny afternoon, 'I can't think how we'd begin to sort out this lot.'

He was looking for space in which to dump two sacks of garden fertilizer.

'Those new flats in Lulling,' he went on, 'have exactly three cupboards in each. People seem to cope all right. How do we get so much clobber?'

'It's a law of nature,' Joan replied. 'Abhorring a vacuum and all that. However much space you have, you fill it.'

She pushed an unsteady pile of old copies of *Country Life* nearer to a mildewed camp bed.

'I suppose we could set a match to it,' suggested Edward, dragging the first sack to a resting place beside some croquet mallets. There was a rustling sound and a squeak.

'That was a mouse!' said Joan, retreating hastily.

'Rats, more like,' commented Edward, heaving along the second sack. 'Come on, my dear. Let's leave them to it. I'm supposed to be meeting Bodger at two-thirty and it's two o'clock already.'

Together they made their way back towards the house.

When her husband had gone, Joan sat on the garden seat to enjoy the spring sunshine. Cold winds had delayed the opening of many flowers. Certainly no daffodils had 'come before the swallow dared to take the winds of March with beauty'.

Here we are, thought Joan, surveying the garden through half-closed eyes, in mid-April, and the daffodils and narcissi are only just in their prime. Would the primroses be starring the banks along the lane to Nidden, she wondered? As children, she and her sister Ruth had reckoned the first outing to pick primroses as the true herald of spring.

How lucky they had been to have grandparents living at Thrush Green, thought Joan, looking back to those happy days with affection. She and Ruth lived most of the year in Ealing, where their father owned a furniture shop. They lived comfortably in a house built in King Edward's reign. The garden was large for a town house. The common was nearby, and Kew Gardens a bus ride away. But to the little girls, such amenities were definitely second-best.

'It's not *the country*!' they protested. 'Why can't we live in *the country*? Why don't we go to Thrush Green for good?'

'Because my living's here,' said Mr Bassett, smiling. 'There are four of us to keep, and the house and garden to care for, and your schooling to be paid. If I don't work, then we have nothing. You must think yourselves lucky to be able to go to Thrush Green as often as you do.'

He too adored Thrush Green, and when his parents died, it became his. Barely fifty, he intended to continue to live and work in Ealing. By this time, Joan had married Edward Young, an architect in Lulling known to the Bassetts since childhood, and the young couple had lived in the house ever since.

'But the day I retire,' Mr Bassett had said, 'I'll be down to take over, you know!'

'I'll build a house in readiness,' promised Edward. That was over ten years ago, thought Joan, stretching out her legs into the sunshine, and we still have not built it. Perhaps we should think about it, instead of drifting on from day to day. Father must be in his sixties now, and had not been well this winter. The time must come when he decided to retire, and only right that he should come to Thrush Green to enjoy his heritage. They had been wonderfully blessed to have had so long in this lovely place.

The telephone bell broke in upon her musing, and she left the sunshine to answer it.

Some two hundred yards away, the children of Thrush Green Village School were enjoying the first really warm and sunny playtime of the year.

Squealing and skipping, jostling and jumping, they celebrated the return of spring with youthful exuberance. Little Miss Fogerty, teacup in hand, watched their activities with fond indulgence. She had coped with playground duty now for over thirty years. The mothers and fathers of some of these screaming infants had once cavorted here under her kindly eye. She lifted her wrinkled face to the sun, and watched the rooks flying to the tall trees on the road to Nidden. Two of them carried twigs in their beaks. It was good to see them refurbishing their nests, she thought, and better still to note that they were building high this year. A sure sign, old countrymen said, of a fine summer to come. Well, it could not be too hot for her old bones, thought Miss Fogerty. She must think about looking out her cotton dresses. What a blessing she had decided not to shorten them last year! Hems were definitely mid-calf this season, and very becoming too after those dreadful mini-skirts which were downright improper, and must have given many a fast young man ideas of the worst sort.

A windswept child pranced up to her.

'Finished, miss? Give us yer cup then!'

Miss Fogerty held her cup and saucer well above the child's head, and looked sternly at his flushed face.

' "May I take your cup, *Miss Fogerty*," is the way to ask, Frederick,' she said reprovingly. 'Just repeat it, please.'

'May I take your cup, Miss Fogerty?' repeated Frederick meekly. 'And I never meant no harm, miss.'

Miss Fogerty smiled and put the empty cup and saucer into his hands.

'I'm quite sure of that, Frederick dear, but there is a right and wrong way of doing everything, and you chose the wrong way first.'

'Yes, miss,' agreed Frederick, holding the china against his jersey, and setting off across the playground to the lobby where the washing up was done.

Miss Fogerty glanced at her wrist watch. Only three minutes more and she must blow her whistle.

There would be nice time for *The Tailor of Gloucester* before the end of the afternoon. She thought, with pleasure, of the scores of children she had introduced to Beatrix Potter. How many times, she wondered, had she carried the little picture showing the embroidered waistcoat round the room, watching each child's face rapt with wonder at the smallness of the stitches and beauty of the design.

And her new classroom was so pleasant! For years she had worked in the infants' room to the right of the lobby in the original village school building. Now the new classroom at the rear of the school was hers alone, complete with its own wash-basins and lavatories, so that there was no need for any of the babies to brave the weather when crossing the playground, as in the old days.

The new room was a constant delight to her. The big windows faced southwest across the valley towards Lulling Woods. Bean and pea seeds, as well as mustard and cress growing on flannel in saucers, flourished on the sunny windowsill, and it was delightful to stand, back against the glass, and feel the hot sun warming one's shoulder blades through one's cardigan.

It had been good of Miss Watson, her headmistress, to let her have the room. She could so easily have appropriated it for her own class had she wished. But there, thought loyal little Miss Fogerty, Miss Watson would never do a thing like that! There could not be a better headmistress in the whole of the United Kingdom! It was a privilege to be on her staff.

Miss Fogerty fished up the whistle from the recesses of her twin-set and blew a loud blast. Three-quarters of the playground pandemonium ceased. Miss Fogerty's grey eyes, turning like twin lighthouse beams, round her territory, quenched the last few decibels of noise.

'You may lead in, children,' she called. 'My class last this time.'

And as the school filed indoors, she followed the youngest children across the playground to the beautiful new terrapin building where *The Tailor of Gloucester* was waiting on her desk.

From her bedroom window across the green, Winnie Bailey watched Miss Fogerty at her duties. Since her husband's death, she had found herself observing other people with an interest which she had not had time to indulge during the years of the doctor's last illness.

She missed him more than she could say. The fact that their last few months together had involved her in nursing Donald day and night, made their home seem even more lonely now that he had gone.

The tributes she had received at his death, and still received daily from those who had known him, gave Winnie Bailey much needed comfort. He had been a dear man all his life, and a very handsome one when young, but it was his complete dedication to the task of healing which had endeared him to the people of Lulling and Thrush Green. Every day, Sundays included, Donald Bailey had visited Lulling Cottage Hospital, until infirmity had overtaken him. His young partner Doctor Lovell, married to Ruth, Joan Young's sister, knew how lucky he was to have watched and learnt from such a splendid man as his senior partner.

'Never appear to be in a hurry,' the old man had said to him. 'Listen to their tales, no matter how irrelevant they may seem at the time. You'll learn more that way about your patient than any number of tests at the clinic. Mind and matter are interwoven to an extent that none of us truly appreciates. If you are going to expect exactly the same reaction to the same treatment in every case, then you might just as well become a mechanic.'

Doctor Lovell's car backed cautiously away from the surgery into the road. He looked up and saw Winnie at the window, and waved cheerfully. He had probably called for medicines, thought Winnie, and was off to pay a few afternoon calls before evening surgery.

A bent figure was hurrying across Thrush Green from the church. It was Albert Piggott, sexton and so-called caretaker of St Andrew's, and he was obviously intent upon waylaying the unsuspecting doctor.

His cracked voice floated up to Winnie at the window.

'Doctor! Doctor! You got somethin' for me choobs? They've gone again!'

Doctor Lovell wound down the car window and said something which Winnie could not hear. She moved away hastily, not wishing to appear inquisitive, and made her way downstairs, where Jenny, her maid and friend for many years, was getting the tea-tray ready.

I am a lucky woman, thought Winnie, to be able to continue to live at Thrush Green among old friends, to have Jenny with me for company, and to see Donald's work carried on so conscientiously by John Lovell and his new young assistant. How pleased Donald would have been!

Albert Piggott, returning from his foray upon the doctor's car, looked upon the closed door of The Two Pheasants and thought sadly how far distant opening time was. They did things better abroad, he believed. Opened all day, so he'd heard. Now we were all in this Common Market perhaps we'd follow the foreigners' good example.

At that moment, the landlord of The Two Pheasants struggled through the wicket gate at the side of the public house, bearing two hanging baskets.

'Well, Albert,' said Mr Jones, depositing the baskets at his feet, 'how's tricks?'

'Chest's bad,' said Albert flatly.

'Always is, ain't it? Time you was used to it.'

'That's right,' growled Albert. 'Show plenty of sympathy!'

He surveyed the two baskets.

'You being fool enough to put them geraniums out already?' he continued. 'I s'pose you know we're due for plenty more frost.'

'They won't hurt under the eaves,' said the landlord. 'Got some shelter see?'

'Might well get one tonight,' went on Albert, with every appearance of satisfaction. 'My choobs have been playin' up somethin' cruel. Went to see the doctor about 'em.'

'Ah! I saw you,' said Mr Jones. 'Holding up the poor chap when he was just off to see them as is really ill.'

Albert did not reply, but commented by spitting a flashing arc towards the churchyard wall.

The landlord pulled out the wooden bench and began to mount upon it.

'Wouldn't want to give me a hand-up with the baskets, I suppose?'

Albert looked at him sourly.

'You supposes right,' he said. 'I've got work of me own to do, thank you.'

He shuffled off towards his cottage which stood next door.

'Miserable old faggot,' said Mr Jones dismounting, and making towards the baskets. He made the comment quietly, but just loud enough to carry to Albert's ears as he opened his front door.


After the fresh air of Thrush Green, even Albert noticed that his kitchen seemed stuffy.

The general opinion of his neighbours was that Albert's home was absolutely filthy and smelt accordingly. No one had ever seen a window open, and the door was only opened long enough to allow the entry or exit of its master's unwashed body.

Albert say down heavily in the greasy armchair, and began to unlace his boots. He removed them with a sigh of relief, and lay back, his gaze resting upon a pile of dirty crockery which littered the draining-board. He supposed he would have to tackle that sometime, he thought morosely. And get himself a bite to eat.

He became conscious of his hunger, and thought of Nelly, his wife, who had left him over a year ago to share life with the oil man somewhere further south.

'Nothin' but a common trollop!' muttered Albert aloud. 'But, golly, she could cook!'

He thought of the succulent steak and kidney pies which had emerged steaming from the now cold and dusty kitchen range. She made a fine stew too, remembered Albert, his gastric juices working strongly, and liver and bacon pudding with haricot beans. As for her treacle tarts, and rice puddings with a nice brown crinkly skin of butter and nutmeg on top, they were real works of art.

She had a way with mashed potatoes too, beating an egg into them so that the saucepan was full of light fluff, slightly creamy in colour and texture. He could do with a plateful of Nelly's cooking at the moment, he thought wistfully.

He rose from the chair and went to the cupboard where he found a piece of bread. He spread it with a dollop of dripping from a stone jamjar, and began to munch disconsolately. It wasn't right that a man had to find his own vittles, especially one who was delicate. One with ailing tubes, like himself, for instance.

Still, cooking wasn't everything, Albert told himself, wiping his hands down his trousers. She might be a good cook, his Nelly, he would be the first to give you that, but what a Tartar too! What a temper! And sly with it! Look at the way she'd been carrying on with that blighted oil man behind his back! He wished him joy of her, the wicked hussy. He hoped he'd had a lashing from her tongue by now, so that he'd see what he'd taken on, and what her lawful wedded husband had had to put up with.

He filled the kettle and put it on to boil. By the time he'd washed up, and had a snooze, it would be near enough time to go and lock up the church and see that all was straight for the night.

And after that, thought Albert, The Two Pheasants would be open!

Life suddenly became warmer and sunnier as Albert advanced bravely upon the sticky horrors piled in the sink.

## 2. Doctor's Prescription

While the children of Miss Fogerty's class listened to the story of *The Tailor of Gloucester*, and Albert Piggott awaited opening time, Joan Young was busy preparing a salad.

As she washed lettuce and cut tomatoes her thoughts turned time and time again to her parents and her old home in Ealing. She was vaguely puzzled by this. She had an uncomfortable feeling that perhaps something was wrong, and tried to persuade herself that the fact that she had been thinking of her father's heritage, after Edward's return to work that afternoon, simply accounted for this present preoccupation.

But somehow she was not convinced. She was the last person to be telepathic, or to believe in such nebulous things as thought-transference.

Nevertheless, the malaise continued, and for two pins she would have left her salad-making and rung her parents there and then.

'What nonsense!' she told herself. 'They would think I'd gone mad. I should have heard soon enough if anything were wrong!'

She began to slice cucumber with swift efficient strokes.

Some sixty miles away, Joan's father, Robert Bassett, listened to some very unwelcome truths spoken by his doctor.

'These X-rays show that that chest of yours needs a lot of care. And I'm not happy about your heart. I'm not suggesting that you should consider yourself an invalid, but frankly it's time you gave up work.'

'But it's quite impossible –' began his patient, and was interrupted by a violent spell of coughing.

The doctor watched gravely until the attack had passed. He said nothing, but continued to look steadily at the older man.

'Dammit all,' wheezed Robert, 'it's only this confounded cough that makes me so tired! I'm fine otherwise. Look here, I've a business to run, you know.'

'Someone else will have to run it anyway in a few months,' said the doctor soberly.

He rose from the bedside and went to look out of the window at the neat suburban garden. Robert Bassett, shocked by the last few words, addressed the doctor's straight back.

'You don't mean that?'

The doctor swung round.

'I do indeed. All the tests we have done, these X-rays, and my knowledge of you over the last six years show that you are running yourself into the ground at an alarming rate. You need rest, cleaner air and more quiet than Ealing can give you, and a complete removal from sight and sound of your work. If you refuse to take my advice, I don't give you twelve months. It may sound brutal, my old friend, but that's the position.'

There was a short silence. Somewhere in the distance, a train hooted, and nearer at hand a lorry changed gear and ground away up the hill outside.

'I just can't take it in,' whispered the sick man.

'You own a house somewhere in the west, don't you? Can you go and stay there for a time?'

'Now do you mean?'

'Not immediately. You're going to have a week or two in that bed, with a daily visit from me. It will give you time to get used to the idea of moving, and to put things straight this end.'

'But what about my business?'

'Surely, there's someone there who can take over?'

'I suppose so,' said Robert slowly. 'It's just that I've never really considered the matter.'

The doctor patted his patient's hand, and rose to go.

'Well, consider it now, and cheer up. You'd like to go to this country house of yours, I take it?'

'Of course I would,' said Robert. 'I've always promised myself a retirement at Thrush Green.'

'Good, good! That's grand news.'

He picked up his case, and smiled at his patient.

'What's more,' said Robert, 'I've a son-in-law who is the doctor there.'

'Better still! I'll be in touch with him, no doubt, when the time comes. Meanwhile, you stay here and get some sleep. I'll be in tomorrow.'

He closed the door behind him, leaving his patient in mental turmoil.

'Sleep!' muttered Robert crossly. 'What a hope! I must get Milly to ring the office straight away and get young Frank to come over.'

He sat up suddenly, and was reminded of his weakness by a severe pain in the chest.

Rubbing it ruefully, he thought of further arrangements to be made.

'We'd better warn Joan and Edward, poor dears, that they may have a convalescent father on their hands in the near future.'

Nevertheless, the thought of Thrush Green in spring sunshine, gave comfort to the invalid in the midst of his trials.

In Miss Fogerty's classroom *The Tailor of Gloucester* had been returned to the shelf, the children had stacked their diminutive chairs upon the table, leaving the floor clear for the cleaner's ministrations later, and now stood, hands together and eyes closed, waiting for their teacher to give the note for grace.

> Now the day is over,
> Night is drawing nigh,
> Shadows of the evening
> Steal across the sky.
> Now the darkness gathers
> Stars begin to peep,
> Birds and beasts and flowers
> Soon will be asleep.
> Amen

They sang much too loudly for Miss Fogerty's peace of mind. It sounded irreverent, she felt, but she had not the heart to reprove them, knowing how eagerly they were looking forward to running home through the first of the really warm days of spring.

She thought, not for the first time, that this particular closing hymn was not one of her favourites. That line 'Stars begin to peep', for instance, was a little premature at three-thirty, except in December perhaps, and in any case the word 'peep' seemed a trifle coy. But there, Miss Watson wanted the children to use that hymn, and she must fall in with her wishes in these little matters.

'Hands away! Good afternoon, children!' said Miss Fogerty briskly. 'Straight home now, and no shouting near the school windows. The big girls and boys are still working, remember.'

They streamed from the room comparatively quietly, and across the playground towards Thrush Green. Daisies starred the greensward, and the sticky buds of the chestnut trees were beginning to break into miniature fans of grey-green. The children raced happily to meet all the glory of a spring afternoon.

All except Timmy Thomas, always a rebel, who saw fit to stand beneath Miss Watson's window, put two fingers into his mouth and produce an ear-splitting whistle.

He was gratified to see his headmistress's face appear at the window. She shook her head at him sternly and pointed towards the gate. Miss Fogerty had emerged from her classroom, and also exhorted him to depart immediately.

Grinning, he went.

'That boy,' said Miss Watson later, 'will become a very unpleasant leader of students, or some such, as far as I can see!'

'He might make a happy marriage,' observed Miss Fogerty, more charitably, 'and settle down.'

'It seems a long time to wait,' commented her headmistress tartly.


One of the first of Miss Fogerty's pupils to reach home, was young Jeremy Prior who lived just across Thrush Green at Tullivers, a house as venerable as the Youngs', although not quite so imposing.

Jeremy enjoyed life at Thrush Green. His mother Phil had married for the second time, and his stepfather, Frank Hurst, was a man whose company he enjoyed. His own father had been killed in a car crash, but before that had happened he had left home to live in France with another woman, so that the child's memories of him were dim. Frank had given him the affection and care which he needed in his early years, and Jeremy flourished in the happy atmosphere surrounding him at Thrush Green.

Now, as he opened the gate, he was conscious of his mother talking to friends in the garden.

One was Winnie Bailey, their next-door-neighbour. The other was Ruth Lovell, the doctor's wife, and clutching her hand was Mary, her two-year-old daughter.

As soon as the toddler saw Jeremy she broke away from her mother and charged over the flower beds to greet the boy, babbling incoherently, fat arms outstretched.

'*Mary!*' shouted Ruth. '*Not* over the garden!'

But she was ignored. Her daughter by now had Jeremy's legs in a rapturous embrace which nearly brought him to the ground.

'Is it as late as that?' exclaimed Winnie. 'I must get back. Jenny has gone down to Lulling, and I'm supposed to be keeping an eye on a fruit cake in the oven.'

She hurried away and they heard the click of the next-door gate as she returned to her duties.

'How are things working out there?' asked Ruth.

'Very well, I gather,' said Phil. 'It was a marvellous idea to invite Jenny to live with her. At one stage I was afraid that Winnie might think of moving into a smaller house, perhaps near her sister. We should have missed her horribly, and I think she would have been lost without Thrush Green.'

'I'm sure of it. We're lucky to live here. Joan and I always thought it was the best place on earth when we were children. I can't say that my opinion has changed much.'

She walked towards her daughter who was rolling over and over on the grass, being helped by Jeremy.

'Come along, Mary. We're off to see Aunt Joan.'

'No! Stay here,' said Mary, stopping abruptly, her frock under her armpits and an expanse of fat stomach exposed to view. Her expression was mutinous.

'No nonsense now! We've got to collect the magazines.'

'Why not let her stop here while you see Joan?' suggested Phil, in a low tone. 'Jeremy would love to play with her for a while.'

'That's so kind. I won't be more than a few minutes.'

She turned towards the gate.

'Do you mind, Jeremy?' she called.

'I'll show her my new fort,' said Jeremy enthusiastically. 'It's got Crusaders and Saracens, and lots of flags and horses and swords.'

'Mind she doesn't swallow them,' advised Ruth. 'You don't want to lose any.'

She waved to the potential sword-swallower and made her way across the green to her sister's.

Joan Young was sitting in the hall when Ruth arrived. She was listening intently to the telephone, her face grave.

Ruth was about to tiptoe away, but Joan covered the mouthpiece with her hand, and motioned her sister to take a seat.

'It's mother. Tell you in a minute.'

Ruth perched on the oak settle, and fell to admiring the black and white tiles of the floor, and the elegant staircase, which always gave her pleasure.

'Do you want a word with Ruth? She's just dropped in.'

Silence reigned while Joan listened again.

'No, no. All right, darling. I'll tell her, and you know we'll look forward to seeing you both. Yes, *any time*! Give him our love.'

She replaced the receiver and looked at Ruth.

'Poor Dad, he's pretty weak evidently. Bed for a week or two, and then his doctor wants him to come here for a rest.'

She stood up abruptly.

'Come in the garden, Ruth. I've left a cookery book on the seat, and I probably shan't remember it until it pours with rain in the middle of the night.'

'How bad is he?' asked Ruth, following her.

'Mother was calm about it, but sounded anxious. It seems he's had this bronchial trouble most of the winter, but wouldn't give up. I'll be glad to get him here. Mother must need a rest too. Dash it all, they're both around seventy.'

They sat down on the garden seat, and Joan nursed the cookery book.

'Shall we go up tomorrow to see him?' said Ruth.

'Mother says not to. He's not in any danger, but the doctor wants him to be kept quiet.'

She began to laugh.

'Poor Mum, trying to stop him working! As it is, she's had to ring Frank to give all sorts of messages about the office.'

'It's time he retired,' agreed her sister. 'Perhaps this will make him think about it.'

'Funnily enough,' said Joan, 'they've been in my mind a lot today. Probably because Edward said something about moving. It's about time we built a house of our own. We may have to now. Heaven knows we've been lucky to stay here so long.'

'Dad won't let you move,' said Ruth shrewdly. At times she saw more clearly than her older sister, who usually led the way.

'But he'll have to!' replied Joan, beginning to look slightly agitated. 'If he's to have a quiet life from now on, then it's only right that he should come back to his own home.'

'Maybe,' agreed Ruth. 'He'll be willing to come to Thrush Green, I have no doubt, but he won't let you give up your home, you'll see.'

'But where else is there for him? We've always known that they would retire here.'

'Don't forget that Dad hasn't yet said he will retire. So far, he's simply having a short convalescence here. I shouldn't take too many leaps ahead, Joan. Things will work out, you'll see.'

She rose to her feet.

'I came for the magazines really, and then I must collect Mary before she drives Jeremy Prior mad. Noble boy, he's showing her his fort. I tremble to think how much of it is broken already.'

They made their way back to the house, and collected the pile of magazines from the hall table. A dozen or so inhabitants of Thrush Green had begun this communal magazine effort during the war, each contributing one journal and passing the collection from one to the other, and the custom had continued.

'I'll walk across the green with you,' said Joan. 'It's marvellous to feel the sun really warm again after months of shivering.'

They paused at the roadside and Joan gazed across the grass towards the church.

'Do you realize that we shall have the Curdles' fair here again on May the first? Only another week or so. Won't it be lovely to see Ben and Molly Curdle again? I still miss her.'

'The only comfort is that she's a lot happier with her Ben than she was with that ghastly father of hers, Albert Piggott. Isn't that him over there in the churchyard?'

'Looks like it. Waiting for The Two Pheasants to open no doubt.'

'Mary is going to the fair this year,' said Ruth. 'Perhaps we could make up a party with Jeremy and Paul?'

'Yes, let's. Though I may have the parents here by then, of course.'

They exchanged troubled glances.

'I shall ring Mother later on this evening,' said Ruth, 'and we'll keep in touch about developments.'

A yell from across the road drew her attention to her daughter who was struggling to climb over the Hursts' gate.

'I must be off,' she said hastily, and dashed to the rescue.


Joan returned thoughtfully to the garden. Of course, as Ruth said, the parents were only coming for a short stay. But this was a reminder that the future must be faced.

When Edward came home they must have a serious talk about plans. They really must think of the years ahead.

The family cat met her at the door, and rubbed round her legs, mewing vociferously.

'Poor old puss! I've forgotton your lunch and tea,' said Joan remorsefully. 'It's all this thinking ahead that's done it.'

The cat led the way purposefully towards the kitchen. As far as he was concerned, the next meal was as far ahead as he was prepared to consider.

## 3. Prospective Lodgers

If the Youngs' house was acknowledged to be the most beautiful at Thrush Green, the rectory, it was admitted ruefully, was the ugliest.

Unlike its neighbours, its Cotswold stone walls had been clad by some Victorian vandal in grey stucco. It was tall and bleak. It faced east rather than south, and the front door opened upon a long dark corridor which ran straight to the back door, thus creating a wind tunnel which worked so successfully that the unlucky dwellers there needed a fortune to keep the house warm.

Despite the fuel bills, the present inhabitants of the rectory were not unhappy. The Reverend Charles Henstock and his wife Dimity, considered themselves exceptionally lucky in their marriage, and in their work at Thrush Green. Material matters did not affect them greatly, and the fact that their home was cold, shabby, dark, and difficult to clean bothered Charles not at all, and Dimity only occasionally, and then mainly on her husband's behalf.

For years she had lived only some fifty yards from her present home, at a snug thatched cottage on the other side of the road. Her companion then had been a stalwart friend, called Ella Bembridge, who still lived there, and spent her spare time in creating textile designs, which she sometimes sold, and a great variety of handicrafts which she did not.

Not that these products were wasted. Ella's cupboards and drawers were stuffed with handwoven ties, raffia mats, cane basketwork, mirrors decorated with barbola work, wobbly teapot stands, and a number of unidentifiable objects, all of which were destined for Christmas presents or given to charitable institutions, preferably those concerned with animals. Ella rated the animal race rather more deserving than the human one, and who can blame her?

The cottage had been warm, Dimity was the first to admit. It faced south, and was sheltered by the hill which rose steeply from Lulling to Thrush Green. Furthermore, Ella enjoyed a fire, and never returned from her walks without some firewood or fir cones with which to create a cheerful blaze in the evenings. It was not until Dimity had spent her first winter at the rectory that she realized quite how bleak was her present abode.

'The trouble with this barn of a place,' said Ella one morning towards the end of April, 'is that it faces the wrong way. You get no sunshine at all, except in the kitchen. Frankly, I'd live in there.'

She thrust a bunch of daffodils at Dimity.

'Here, these should cheer things up a bit. They're some you planted years ago near the gooseberry bushes.'

'Thank you, dear. They are simply lovely. I shall put some on Charles's desk. The study does tend to be a little dark. Have some coffee?'

'Yes, please. I tried some jasmine tea yesterday that I'd dried myself, but can't say it's really palatable. Probably be better as potpourri. Pity to waste it.'

'You've heard about Mr Bassett, I suppose?' said Dimity, setting out cups upon a tray.

'No? Dead, is he?'

'No, no, Ella! I know he's been far from well, but he's nowhere near dead yet.'

'Sorry, sorry. What's the news then?'

'He's coming down for a rest after a rather nasty illness. Mrs Bassett too, of course.'

'Good. A nice pair. Might get a game of bridge. I miss dear old Donald Bailey for that.'

'I miss him for a lot of things,' replied Dimity. 'And so does Charles.'

At that moment, her husband entered, advanced upon Ella as though about to kiss her, remembered she did not like to be kissed, hastily stood up again, and contented himself with energetic hand-rubbing.

'Yes, they're due next week, I gather,' said Charles. 'But I'm afraid they'll miss the fair. A pity really. I always enjoy the Curdles' fair.'

'Not the same without the old lady,' said Ella, taking out a battered tin and beginning to roll one of the noisome cigarettes for which she was renowned. 'I like young Ben, but I shouldn't be a bit surprised if he didn't give up the job one day.'

'But he can't!' cried Dimity. 'Why, it's a sacred trust!'

'Not *sacred*, my dear,' corrected the rector mildly. 'He may have a *loyalty* to the business and to the memory of his grandmother, but that's not quite the same thing.'

'Well, I can't imagine May the first at Thrush Green without the Curdles' fair blaring and gyrating for hours,' said Ella, putting a match to the ragged end of the very thin cigarette which drooped from her lips. 'But, come to think of it, why on earth should Ben Curdle want to give up a perfectly good living?'

'I very much doubt,' said Charles, pushing an ashtray towards his friend, 'if the fair really does bring in much these days. People demand rather more sophisticated pleasures than our forbears did. And of course there's television to contend with.'

At this moment, the milk rose with a joyous rush to the brim of the saucepan and was about to drench the stove, when Ella, with remarkable speed for one so bulky, leapt towards it, removed it from the heat, and blew heavily across its surface. The milk sank back obediently, and Dimity expressed her gratitude.

She did so with some inner misgivings. She could not feel that Ella's smoke-laden breath could be truly hygienic in contact with milk, but common civility forbade her from pouring it down the sink and starting again. Putting aside her qualms, she poured coffee for the three of them at the kitchen table.

'That smells good!' said Ella, sniffing greedily. 'I'm rationing myself with coffee since it's become so expensive. I did try ground acorns which Dotty said were almost as good, but I found them revolting.'

'Does Dotty really use ground acorns?' asked Charles. 'She hasn't offered me acorn coffee yet. At least, I don't think she has. I must admit that Dotty's coffee always tastes a little – well – er, peculiar.'

'Dear old Dotty is the prize eccentric of all time,' said Ella, 'and I love her dearly, but I try not to eat or drink anything of her making ever since I was laid up for three days with Dotty's Collywobbles after drinking her confounded elderberry wine. D'you remember, Dim?'

'Indeed I do. It stained the kitchen sink a deep purple, I remember. One of Dotty's more potent brews.'

'To come upon Dotty at her cooking,' went on Ella, 'is rather like looking in on the three witches in Macbeth. You know, 'tongue of bat and leg of frog', or whatever it is. I certainly saw her fish a fat spider out of the milk jug before making a rice pudding. It's a wonder she doesn't suffer from her own creations.'

'Hardened to it, no doubt,' said Dimity.

'You are not being very charitable,' reproved the rector. 'Whatever her funny little ways, she has a heart of gold. I hear she has taken on a poor dog which some callous brute abandoned at the side of the main road.'

'Good for Dotty!' cried Ella, 'but how will she manage? That place of hers is crammed with animals already. It must cost her a fortune in food for them. It beats me how she copes. I find it hard enough. In fact, I'm thinking of getting a lodger to help out.'

Her friends looked at her in amazement.

'Are you serious?'

'Well, nothing's definite yet, but there's your old room empty, Dimity, and it seems a shocking waste when the Third World is being rammed down your throat whenever you switch on the television. Besides, a few pounds a week would certainly help with the food bills. I haven't quite got to Dotty's stage of searching the hedgerows for my lunch.'

'Don't do anything too hastily,' warned Dimity. 'I mean, you might get a dreadful man who turned out to be violent or dishonest –'

'Or a drunkard,' put in the rector, retrieving the ashtray, which had not been touched, and putting it resignedly on the windowsill again. Ella's saucer was holding the stub of the pungent cigarette, and ash sprinkled the table.

'Or simply someone with *designs* on you,' went on Dimity earnestly. 'There really are some terribly wicked men about. He might even make suggestions.'

'That'll be the day,' said Ella robustly. She stood up and dusted the rest of the ash to the floor.

'Don't worry. It may never come to pass, and in any case I don't want to be cluttered up with a man as a lodger. He'd want too much done – socks mended, shirts ironed, and all that razmatazz. No, a nice quiet woman is what I had in mind. Do for herself, and be no bother.'

'Well, just don't *rush* into anything,' pleaded Dimity. 'It's better to be poor and happily solitary, than rich with unpleasant company.'

Ella patted her friend's thin shoulder.

'I promise not to be rash. And now I must get back to the garden. You can't see my lettuce seedlings for groundsel.'

She vanished down the dark passage to the front door, and crossed the road to her own snug abode opposite.

Dotty Harmer lived about half a mile from Thrush Green, in a cottage which stood beside the track leading to Lulling Woods.

For years Dotty had kept house for her martinet of a father, a local schoolmaster, feared by generations of Thrush Green and Lulling boys for his iron discipline. On his death, Dotty had sold the house in Lulling and bought this secluded cottage where she lived very happily, quite alone, but for a varied menagerie ranging from goats to kittens.

Whilst Ella, Dimity and Charles were imbibing coffee Dotty was sitting on a fraying string stool in her hall, telephoning the local police station. At her feet lay a golden cocker spaniel, its eyes fixed trustingly upon her.

'Yes, yes,' Dotty was saying testily, 'I am quite aware that I gave you full particulars when I telephoned two days ago. The purpose of this call is to find out if there have been any more inquiries.'

There was the sound of rustling paper.

'Well, ma'am, there doesn't seem to be any message about a lost dog. A golden cocker, you said?'

He remembered that Dotty was unmarried, elderly and perhaps rather prim. He broached his next question with some delicacy.

'Would it be a lady or a gentleman?'

'It's a *bitch*, officer,' said Dotty, who spoke plain English. 'A bitch of about six months old, I should say. Rather thin, and with sore feet – obviously had travelled some way along the main road to Caxley. No collar, of course, but a very nice little dog.'

'Would you want us to take it – her, I mean – to the kennels for you, ma'am?'

'No, indeed. Excellent though I'm sure they are. No, the little thing has settled in very well since Friday, and I am quite prepared to adopt her if she is not claimed.'

'Thank you, ma'am. In that case, I'll make a note to that effect.'

'But, of course, you will telephone immediately if the owner comes forward? I should not wish to deprive anyone of their own animal, although I have the strongest suspicion that this one was purposely abandoned, in the most callous fashion. You are perhaps studying that side of this affair?'

'We're doing everything possible,' said the constable earnestly, eyeing a mug of tea which had been placed at this elbow by a fellow policeman. 'We'll let you know if anything comes of our inquiries.'

'Very well, officer. I shall let you return to your duties. I know how hard-pressed the force is.'

'Thank you, ma'am,' said the constable, replacing the receiver with a sigh, and picking up the mug.

'Chuck over the paper, Ted,' he called to his colleague. 'Haven't had a minute to look at the headlines yet. All go, innit?'

Dotty replaced her receiver, and surveyed her new charge with affection.

'Good little Floss,' she said kindly. 'Good little dog.'

She was rewarded with a frantic lashing of Floss's fine plumy tail.

'It might be a good idea,' continued Dotty, rising from the disreputable stool, 'to give you a little walk today. On the grass, of course, with those tender feet. Perhaps a gentle stroll up to the green? We could take Ella's goat's milk to her, and save her a trip.'

She made her way into the kitchen, closely followed by the dog. A vast iron saucepan bubbled on the stove, cooking the hen's supper. Floss looked at it hopefully, and barked.

'I think not, dear,' said Dotty, 'but I have a bone for you in the larder. Take it under the plum tree while I get ready.'

The bone was located under an old-fashioned gauze cover in the pantry. On the slate shelf beside it were a number of receptacles holding food suitable for Dotty's varied family – corn, bran mash, chopped lettuce leaves, crusts of bread, tinned cat food and the like. The provisions for Dotty seemed non-existent.

Dotty watched Floss gnawing the bone in the shady garden. A fine little animal! Very intelligent too, and very nice to have another Flossie after so many years.

She had been eight years old when she had been given the first Flossie as a birthday present. That little bitch had been another cocker spaniel, but black with mournful eyes, and a sweet and saintly expression which quite belied its destructive nature. Rugs, slippers, upholstery, and Dotty's beloved dolls all fell prey to those sharp teeth, but still the whole family forgave her, including Dotty's stern father.

She was named after a great aunt of Dotty's. Aunt Floss had been christened Florence, after the famous Florence Nightingale, but she lacked her namesake's vigour, and retired to her red plush sofa when she was a little over forty.

Dotty could remember being taken to see her on the family's visits to London. Aunt Flossie's house was in the Bayswater Road, a dark gloomy establishment, and the drawing-room where she lay in majesty seemed to be the most depressing room of all.

The heavy chenille curtains were always half drawn. They were edged with woollen bobbles, looking like the seed pods which dangled from the plane trees on the other side of the window.

Aunt Floss's legs were always covered by a tartan rug. Not that Aunt Floss ever used the word *legs*. 'My *extremities*,' she would say plaintively, 'are very susceptible to draughts.'

A bamboo table stood beside the sofa, laden with medicine bottles and pill boxes, a carafe of water and the latest novel from the lending library. The room reeked of camphor, and to the young Dotty, used to the Cotswold air of Lulling, the stuffiness of this apartment was unendurable.

Aunt Flossie had a long sad face, and wore her hair parted in the middle, and gathered into bunches of ringlets, rather in the style of Elizabeth Barrett Browning. She certainly had a spaniel-like appearance, and when Dotty's father, in a rare mood of frivolity, suggested 'Flossie' for the name of her birthday puppy, the family agreed with much hilarity. Aunt Flossie, of course, never met her namesake, and would have thought the whole thing most indecorous had she ever heard about it.

Armed with an old-fashioned metal milk can with a secure lid, and with Floss-the-second on a long lead, Dotty emerged into the sunshine, and into the meadow at the end of her garden.

The footpath lay across rich grass, used for grazing cattle most of the year. At the moment, the fields were empty, starred with daisies and a few early buttercups. Soon there would be sheets of golden flowers, thought Dotty happily, all ready to

> Gild gloriously the bare feet
> That run to bathe . . .

Rupert Brooke, thought Dotty, might be out of fashion at the moment, but he had supplied her with many felicitous phrases which had given her joy throughout her life. She remained grateful to him.

Floss padded ahead at the end of the lead, keeping to the grass, and pausing now and then to sniff at some particularly fascinating scent. In ten minutes they had reached Thrush Green, and Dotty sat down upon a bench, in order to change the milk can from one hand to the other, and to admire the glory of spring flowers in the gardens.

The hanging baskets outside The Two Pheasants won her approval, and the bright mats of purple aubretia and golden alyssum hanging from the low stone walls. Through the gate of the Youngs' house she could see a mass of daffodils and narcissi under the trees, and a particularly beautiful copper-coloured japonica was in full bloom against Harold Shoosmith's house. Even Albert Piggott's cottage had a few bedraggled wallflowers close to his doorstep.

'A time of hope,' commented Dotty to Floss who was busy licking a paw. 'We must remember that, Flossie dear. Let's trust that it augurs well for us too.'

Refreshed by her brief rest, she collected the milk can and dog again, and made her way to see her old friend Ella Bembridge.

## 4. April Rain

Meanwhile, at Ealing, Robert Bassett's mood changed from stunned shock to querulous fury, and finally to philosophic resignation. Milly, his wife, bore all with patience.

'The firm won't automatically crumble, my dear, just because you are away from the office,' she told him. 'Frank knows the ropes as well as you do, and has always coped during the holidays perfectly well. That old saying about no one being indispensable is absolutely true, so just stop worrying.'

Frank Martell had been with the firm all his working life, starting as office boy at a wage of twenty shillings a week, and soon promoted to thirty shillings a week when Robert Bassett had seen the boy's capabilities. He was now a man in his mid-forties, quiet, conscientious and absolutely trustworthy. To Robert he was still 'young Frank' despite the sprinkling of grey hairs round his ears, and Robert found it difficult to have to face the fact that he would have to give him full responsibility for the business during his own absence.

He felt better about the whole affair after Frank had spent an afternoon by the bedside going through a file of letters and orders. His grasp of affairs surprised Robert. Frank had never said much, and Robert had always been too busy to realize quite how much Frank knew of the running of the firm. His quiet confidence reassured the invalid, and when Milly returned to the bedroom, after seeing Frank out, she found her husband breathing more easily and looking very much more relaxed.

'He's done you good,' she commented. 'You'll sleep better tonight.'

'I believe I shall,' agreed Robert.


Milly brought him an omelette at half-past seven, and for the first time since the onset of his illness he emptied his plate.

When she had gone, he lay back upon the pillows contentedly. The door was propped ajar, and darkness was beginning to fall. He felt as he had as a child, secure and cosseted, with the door left open for greater comfort, and access to grown-ups in case of emergency.

His gaze roamed over the shadowy room. How little, over the past years, he had noticed the familiar objects around him!

He looked now, with renewed awareness, at these old inanimate friends. There, on the dressing-table, stood the shabby oval leather box containing the two splendid hair-brushes which his father had given him on his twenty-first birthday. They were still in daily use, but had far less hair to cope with these days.

Nearby stood the photograph of Milly as he first saw her, hair parted demurely in the middle, eyes upraised soulfully, and never a hint of a double chin. To his mind, she was better looking now, plump and white-haired, her complexion as peach-like as when they first met, and the tranquillity, which had first attracted him, as constant as ever. He had been lucky in his marriage, and lucky to have two beautiful daughters.

On the wall opposite the bed hung a fine print of the Duomo of Florence. They had spent their honeymoon in that city, staying at a quiet hotel which had once been an ancient family home, not far from the cathedral. They had always promised themselves a return visit to that golden city, but somehow it had never happened.

'If I get over this,' said Robert aloud, 'I'm damned if we don't do it. That's the worst of life. One is everlastingly putting things off until it's too late.'

He smoothed the patchwork bedspread. Here was another reminder of the past, for Milly and the two girls had made it together, before marriage had taken them away from home to Thrush Green. Robert had teased them, he remembered, about ever finishing it. They must have spent three winters on the thing, he thought, now tracing the bright hexagons of silk with a finger.

Most of the furniture had come from his own shop, but the bedside table had stood beside his parents' bed. He remembered it well, at the side of his widowed mother during her last long illness, laden with medicine bottles, books and letters, much as it looked now, he thought, with a mild feeling of shock. Well, it had served the generations loyally, and no doubt would continue to be used by his children and grandchildren. There was something very comforting in this quality of permanence. It put into perspective the brief frailty of man compared with the solid works of his hands.

Yes, here, all around him stood the silent witnesses of his life. He was glad to have had this enforced breathing space to acknowledge his debt to faithful old friends.

He slid farther down the bed, sighing happily. When his wife came with hot milk at ten o'clock, she found him in a deep sleep, and crept away again, with a thankful heart.

The last few days of April brought torrential rain to Thrush Green. It drummed on the tarmac of the roads and the school playground, with relentless ferocity, so that it seemed as though a thousand silver coins spun upon the ground.

It cascaded down the steep Cotswold roofs, gurgled down the gutters, and a miniature river tossed and tumbled its way down the steep hill into Lulling High Street.

At the village school, rows of wellington boots lined the lobby, and mackintoshes dripped from the pegs. Playtimes were taken indoors. Dog-eared comics, incomplete and ancient jigsaw puzzles, and shabby packs of cards were in daily use, much to the children's disgust. They longed to be outside, yelling, running, leaping, fighting, and generally letting off steam, and would willingly have rushed there, despite the puddles and the downpour, if only their teachers had said the word.

Miss Fogerty, rearranging wet and steaming garments on the radiators, was thankful yet again for the comfort of her new classroom. At least her charges were able to pay their frequent visits to the lavatories under the same roof. In the old building it had been necessary to thread a child's arms into its mackintosh sleeves (invariably needing two or more attempts) before allowing it to cross the playground during a deluge. Really, thought Miss Fogerty, life was now very much simpler.

Next door to the village school, Harold Shoosmith, a middle-aged bachelor, struggled to locate a leak which had appeared in the back bedroom. He stood on a ladder, his head in the loft and a torch in his hand, while Betty Bell, his indefatigable daily help, stood below and offered advice.

'You watch out for bats, Mr Shoosmith! They was always partial to that loft. I remember as a girl the old lady as lived here then used to burn sulphur candles to get rid of them. Can you see any?'

'No,' came the muffled reply.

'You want a bucket for the drips?'

'No. I can't see a dam' thing.'

'You want another light? A candle, say?'

There was no answer, but Harold's trunk, then his thighs, and lastly his well-burnished brogues vanished through the trap-door, and thumps and shuffles proclaimed that the master of the house was surveying the highest point of his domain.

Betty Bell transferred her gaze from the gaping hole above her to the view from the streaming window. Rain slanted across the little valley at the back of the house, where Dotty Harmer's cottage glistened in the downpour. The distant Lulling Woods were veiled by rain, and the grey clouds, barely skimming the trees, told of more to come. She was going to have a wet ride home on her bike, that was sure.

'Found it!' came a triumphant call from above. 'It's running down one of the rafters. Get a thick towel, Betty, and a bucket, and I'll fix up a makeshift arrangement.'

'Right!' yelled Betty, 'and I'll put on your dinner. You'll need something hot after mucking about up there.'

She descended the stairs and caught a glimpse of a very wet Thrush Green through the fanlight of the front door.

Across the expanse of puddles Winnie Bailey was battling her way towards Lulling with her umbrella already dripping.

'Never ought to be out,' thought Betty. 'At her age, in this weather! She'll catch her death.'

But Winnie was quite enjoying herself. There was something very pleasant in splashing along under the shelter of Donald's old umbrella. It was very old, but a beautiful affair of heavy silk and whalebone, and a wide band of solid gold encircled the base of the handle. It was certainly far more protection from the rain than her own elegant umbrella, which was smaller and flatter, and which she resolved to keep for ornament rather than use in future.

There were very few people about, she noticed, as she descended the hill to Lulling. Hardly surprising, in this weather, but what a lot they were missing! The stream of surface water gushed and gurgled at her side. Silver drops splashed from trees and shrubs, and a fresh breeze whipped the colour into her cheeks. It was an exhilarating morning, and she remembered how much she had loved a boisterous day when she was a child, running with arms thrown wide, mouth open, revelling in the buffeting of a rousing wind.

She was on her way now to visit three old friends, the Misses Lovelock, who lived in a fine house in the High Street. They were making plans for one of Lulling's many coffee mornings, and although Winnie tried to dodge as many of these occasions as she could, the proposed effort was for a cause very dear to her heart, and that of her late husband's, the protection of birds.

If the three sisters had been on the telephone, Winnie might have been tempted to ring up and excuse herself on such a wet morning, but she was glad that the Lovelocks considered a telephone in the house a gross extravagance. She would have missed this lovely walk, she told herself, as she approached their door.

The sisters were, in fact, very comfortably off, but they thoroughly enjoyed playing the part of poverty-stricken gentlewomen. Their house was full of furniture, porcelain and silver objects which would have made the gentlemen at Sotheby's and Christie's pink with excitement. A great many of these exquisite items had been begged for by the mercenary old ladies who had brought the art of acquiring other people's property, for nothing or almost nothing, to perfection. They were a byword in Lulling, and newcomers were warned in advance, by those luckless people who had succumbed in a weak moment to the sisters' barefaced blandishments.

Winnie had been invited to coffee, and was quite prepared for the watery brew and the one Marie biscuit which would be presented to her on a Georgian silver tray.

She was divested of her streaming mackintosh and umbrella in the hall, the Misses Lovelock emitting cries of horror at her condition.

'So brave of you, Winnie dear, but *reckless*. You really shouldn't have set out.'

'You must come into the drawing-room at once. We have *one bar* on, so you will dry very nicely.'

Miss Bertha stroked the wet umbrella appreciatively as she deposited it in a superb China vase which did duty as an umbrella stand in the hall. There was a predatory gleam in her eye which did not escape Winnie.

'What a magnificent umbrella, Winnie dear! Would that be *gold*, that exquisite band? I don't recall seeing you with it before.'

'It was Donald's. It was so wet this morning I thought it would protect my shoulders better than my own modern thing. As you can guess, I treasure it very much.'

'Of course, of course,' murmured Bertha, removing her hand reluctantly from the rich folds. 'Dear Donald! How we all miss him.'

The ritual of weak coffee and Marie biscuit over, the silver tray and Sèvres porcelain were removed and the ladies took out notebooks and pencils to make their plans.

'We thought a Bring and Buy stall would be best for raising money,' exclaimed Violet. 'We can use the dining-room, and Bertha took a lot of geranium and fuchsia cuttings last autumn which should sell well, and Ada has made scores of lavender bags from a very pretty organdie blouse which was our dear mother's.'

'Splendid,' said Winnie, stifling the unworthy thought that these offerings would not have cost her old friends a penny.

'And Violet,' chirped Ada proudly, 'has made dozens of shopping lists and jotters from old scraps of paper and last year's Christmas cards. They really are *most* artistic.'

Violet smiled modestly at this sisterly tribute.

'And we thought we might ask Ella for some of her craft work. She has managed to collect a variety of things, I know, over the years. Would you like to ask her to contribute? It would save us calling in.'

'Of course,' said Winnie, 'and Jenny and I will supply all the home-made biscuits to go with the coffee, if that suits you.'

The Misses Lovelock set up a chorus of delight. Pencils moved swiftly over home-made notebooks and all was joy, and comparative warmth, within, as the rain continued to pelt down outside.

Albert Piggott, standing in the church porch with a sack draped, cowl-wise over his head, gazed at the slanting rain with venom.

He took the downpour as a personal affront. Here he was, an aging man with a delicate chest, obliged to make his way through that deluge to his own door opposite. And he had a hole in the sole of his shoe.

When Nelly had looked after him, he thought, she had always kept an eye on such things. She'd washed his shirts, brushed the mud off his trouser legs, darned his socks, sewn on all them dratted buttons that burst off a chap's clothes, and took his shoes down to Lulling to be mended when the time came.

No doubt about it, Nelly had had her uses, hussy though she turned out to be.

'I bet that oil man's found out his mistake by now,' said Albert to a spider dangling from a poster exhorting parishioners of Thrush Green to remember their less fortunate fellows in darkest Africa.

He hitched the sack more firmly round his shoulders, and made a bolt across the road. Which should it be? Home, or The Two Pheasants? The latter, of course, won.

'Lord, Albert, you're fair sopped!' cried the landlord. 'Been digging up the graves or something?'

Albert ignored the facetious remark, and the titters of the regulars.

'Half a pint of the usual,' he grunted, 'and I wouldn't mind a look at the fire, if it ain't asking too much of you gentlemen.'

The little knot of customers, steaming comfortably by the blaze, moved a short distance away, allowing Albert to enter the circle.

'Terrible weather,' said one, trying to make amends for any offence given.

Albert maintained a glum silence.

'Bashing down the daffodils,' said another. 'Pity really.'

Albert took a swig at his beer. He might have been an aging carthorse taking a drink at the village pond for all the noise he made. The customers avoided each other's eyes.

'You getting your own dinner, Albert, or d'you want a hot pie here?' asked the landlord.

'How much?'

'Same as usual. And as good as your Nelly ever made, I'm telling you.'

Albert cast him a sharp look.

'There's no call to bring my wife into it. But I'll have a pie all the same, daylight robbery though it is, you chargin' that amount!'

'*Daisy,*' shouted the landlord through an inner door. 'Hot pie for Albert, toot-der-sweet.'

Uneasy silence fell upon all as Albert waited, mug in hand. A sudden gust of wind shook the door, and a little trickle of rainwater began to seep below it and run down the step into the bar.

'Blimey!' said one of the men, 'we're goin' to be flooded out.'

'Can't go on much longer,' said his companion, retrieving the doormat before it became soaked. 'Rain this heavy never lasts long.'

'It's been on for two days,' remarked Albert, accepting his hot pie, 'don't see no sign of it letting up either.'

The landlord bustled forward with a mop and bucket.

'Here, stand away and I'll clear up.'

He began to attack the rivulet.

'Let's hope it stops before the month's out,' he puffed, wielding the mop energetically. 'Be a pity if Curdle's Fair gets this sort of weather.'

'Always gets a change afore the beginning of May,' announced one aged regular in the corner.

'You mark my words now.' He raised a trembling forefinger. 'I never knowed old Mrs Curdle have a wet day at Thrush Green. We'll get a fine day for the fair, that I knows. You just mark my words!'

'S'pose he's forgot the old lady died years ago,' whispered one customer to his neighbour.

'No, I ain't forgot!' rapped out the old man. 'And I ain't forgot as young Ben runs it now, and pretty near as good as his grandma.'

The landlord shouldered his mop and picked up the bucket.

'Shan't see you in here next week for hot pies then, Albert. I suppose your young Molly will be cooking your dinner for you while the fair's here?'

Albert thrust the last of his pie into his mouth, and turned towards the door.

'Ever heard of mindin' your own business?' he asked sourly. 'First me wife, and now me daughter. You talks too much, that's your trouble.'

He opened the door, and a spatter of rain blew into the room. The newly dammed river gushed joyfully over the step again, and Albert departed.

'That miserable old devil was *grinni~?!*' said the landlord, and went into action once more, sighing heavily.

## 5. The Coming of Curdle's Fair

The rain was still lashing down on the last day of April, as Ben Curdle and his wife Molly, *née* Piggott, approached Thrush Green with the fair.

They were a cheerful young couple, happy in their marriage, and proud of their little boy George, who was now four years of age.

The child sat between them as they towed their caravan at a sedate pace through the streaming countryside. Molly's spirits were high for she was returning home, and although Albert Piggott was never a particularly welcoming father, yet she looked forward to seeing him and the cottage where she had been born.

She was well aware that she would have to set to and do a great deal of scrubbing and general cleaning before the little house was fit for them all to live in for their few days' stay, but she was young and energetic and had never feared hard work.

She was looking forward too, to seeing the Youngs again. She had worked in their beautiful house for several years, before going to the Drovers' Arms where Ben Curdle had come a-courting. Joan Young had been a great influence and a good friend to the motherless young girl, and had taken pleasure in training such a bright and willing pupil in the ways of housewifery.

Molly had also acted as nursemaid to Paul Young when he was a baby, and had treasured the postcards and letters which the boy, now at school, sent from time to time. The happiest of her memories of Thrush Green were centred on that house, and working for the Youngs had been the highlight of her life. They had provided a haven from the dismal cottage across the green, and from the continuous complaining of her sour old father.

Ben Curdle's spirits were not quite so high. For one thing, he disliked his father-in-law, and resented the fact that his wife would have to work so hard in getting the neglected house together. But he was a sensible young fellow, and kept his feelings to himself. It was good to see Molly so happy, and he was wise enough to make sure that she remained so.

But he had another cause for worry. The fair was bringing in far less than when his redoubtable old grandmother had run it. Now that petrol and diesel oil had supplanted the shaggy-hoofed horses of her day, the cost of moving the fair from one place to the next was considerable. Takings too were down.

It was not only the counter-attraction of television in almost every home. That was one factor, of course, and who could blame people for staying comfortably under their own roofs, especially when the weather was as foul as it was today? No, it went deeper than that, Ben realized.

The fact was that most people wanted more sophisticated entertainment. The children still flocked to the fair, accompanied by adults. But the number of people who came without children was dwindling fast. In his grandmother's time, everyone virtually attended the great Mrs Curdle's Fair. It was something to which farmers, shop-keepers, school teachers, as well as their pupils, looked forward from one Mayday to the next. Those grown-ups came no more, unless it was to bring their children or grandchildren for an hour's frolic.

And then, his fair was so small, and likely to get smaller as the machinery wore out, for replacements were becoming prohibitively expensive. Ben himself was a good mechanic, and conscientious about keeping everything in apple-pie order, but as parts became worn and more and more difficult and costly to replace, he saw clearly that some of the attractions would have to be withdrawn. As it was, the famous switchback, which had delighted so many generations at Thrush Green, would not be erected on this Mayday. It was altogether too shaky, and Ben was not the sort of man to take chances.

The thing was, what should he do? He was used to travelling the country and sometimes wondered if he could ever settle down in one place, even if he should be fortunate enough to find a congenial job.

And then, he was devoted to the fair and had never known any other way of living. His grandmother he had adored. She had brought him up from early childhood, for his father had been killed and his mother had married again. The old lady's upright and staunch principles had been instilled into this much-loved grandchild, and Ben had repaid her care with loyalty and respect. Not a day passed but he remembered some word of advice or some cheerful tag of his grandmother's, and to give up the fair, which she had built up so laboriously, smacked of treachery to the young man.

But there it was. Something would have to be done, and soon. He turned his mind to an offer which had been made to him some weeks earlier, by the owner of a much larger concern.

This man had three large fairs touring the country. Over the years he had bought up many a small business, such as Ben's, and combined them into a highly-efficient organization. He was astute, and could foresee possibilities which a slower man would not. He was not liked, for there was a strain of ruthlessness in him without which he could not have succeeded, but there was grudging respect for his ability, and it was agreed that he treated fairly those whom he employed, as long as they worked well.

Ben felt pretty sure that he would be offered a job if he decided to sell. But would he like working for a master after being his own for so long? And what about his fellow workers? He had little respect for some who had sold up and gone to work for Dick Hasler, and he had heard of some underhand transactions which disgusted him. No, if he had to make the break, it would be a clean one, and he would have a complete change. Surely, there must be something he could do to earn a living. His old grandmother always said he had the most useful pair of hands in the business. What honest living could he earn with them? Perhaps a job in a garage somewhere? He brooded silently, as windscreen wipers flashed to and fro hardly keeping pace with the torrent.

'Soon be there,' cried Molly. 'Look out for the river, Georgie! Once we're over that we're nearly home.'

Ben watched their excitement with a smile. So far he had said very little about the fair's diminishing profits, but Molly must have some inkling, and the time would soon come when they would be obliged to have a straight talk about the future.

The steep hill to Thrush Green was just ahead. Ben sighed, and changed gear. Slowly they came abreast of St Andrew's church, and drew to a halt outside Albert Piggott's cottage. From the joy which lit Molly's face, you might think it was Buckingham Palace, thought Ben wryly.

'Here we are,' she cried, 'home again!'


Ella Bembridge saw the Curdles arrive from her bedroom window. She had gone upstairs to rummage through drawers and cupboards to find some contributions to the Lovelocks' Bring and Buy stall, and Dimity was with her.

'They'll have to look slippy if they want the fair to be ready by the morning,' commented Ella. 'Don't envy them that job in this weather.'

'What about this cushion cover?' inquired Dimity, holding up a square of hessian embroidered in thick wool.

'It's a peg bag,' said Ella. 'Rather fine, isn't it? Bold, you know. Plenty of pure bright colour.'

She looked at the enormous flowers of scarlet and gold with affection.

'Too good for a Bring and Buy. Put it back, Dim. It'll do for a Christmas present.'

'What are they, dear?' Dimity was studying the blossoms, with some distaste. 'Zinnia? Red hot pokers? I can't quite recognize them.'

Ella gave her booming laugh.

'They're no known species. I just made 'em up as I went along. You know, three threads up, four down, and all that. Effective, isn't it?'

'Very,' said Dimity, folding the object carefully and returning it to the drawer.

'Here, they can have this magnolia talcum powder. I'll never use that. Can't think who thought I'd relish magnolia scent. Do I *look* like magnolia?'

'Well, no, Ella. Not really.'

'And this useless handkerchief sachet, and this idiotic comb case. Here they come.'

Ella was now ferreting in the drawer like some eager fox terrier in a rabbit hole. Objects flew from her towards the bed, and Dimity did her best to sort them out.

'But Winnie said they wanted things you'd made,' she pointed out, fielding a crocheted bobble cap rather neatly.

'They can have these as well,' replied Ella, head well down. A long string of plastic beads, pretending to be jet, swung through the air, Dimity added it to the motley collection.

'Right,' said Ella, slamming the drawer back. 'Now let's look in the cupboard.'

One turn of the handle burst open the door. Out from the depths sprang a snarl of cane and raffia, and a few objects made from similar material. Ella bent to retrieve them.

'Two waste paper baskets, and three bread roll holders! What about that?'

'Lovely,' said Dimity faintly.

Ella looked at her handiwork approvingly.

'I was thinking of decorating them with raffia flowers,' she mused. 'But what d'you think?'

'They are just right as they are,' replied Dimity firmly. 'No need to gild the lily, you know.'

'Yes, you're right. Somewhere at the back there are some teapot stands. Push over the chair, Dim, and I'll have a look.'

She clambered up with surprising agility for one of her bulk, and began to scrabble at the back of a high shelf. Dimity drifted to the window and looked out at rain-washed Thrush Green.

Ben Curdle was carrying a large suitcase into Albert Piggott's cottage, and young George was capering beside him, glorying in the puddles.

'Got 'em!' came Ella's triumphant call. 'Catch!'

Dimity caught about half a dozen wooden teapot stands, edged with cane and beadwork, wrapped in a polythene bag, and added them to the pile.

'There!' said Ella, stepping down heavily. 'That's a pretty good haul, isn't it? Do them a good turn, and me too, come to think of it. If I ever take a lodger I shall have to clear out all the shelves and drawers in this room. Made a start anyway.'

'So you're still thinking about it?' said Dimity, following her old friend downstairs.

'Oh, I honestly don't know,' replied Ella, settling in a chair and fishing in her pocket for the battered tobacco tin which contained her cigarette factory. She began to roll one of her deplorable cigarettes. She looked pensive.

'It's like this,' she began, blowing out a cloud of acrid smoke. 'I can do with the money and I've got plenty of spare room, but I'm wondering if I should find a lodger congenial.'

'Anyone in mind?'

'Not really, although I believe Winnie Bailey's nephew Richard is looking for somewhere to stay, but no doubt Winnie would put him up.'

'Are you going to advertise?'

'I think not. I've decided to see if I hear of anyone – personal recommendation, that sort of thing. I don't want a stream of folk banging at the door.'

'Well, I must say I'm relieved to know you are not doing anything too hastily. I know Charles has mentioned it in his prayers.'

Ella patted Dimity's thin arm gratefully.

'You're a good pair. It's plain to see your religion is the mainspring of your lives. Lucky old you!'

'It could be yours too.'

Ella shook her head sadly.

'You know me, Dim. Full of honest doubts. Whenever I read "Thanks to St Jude" in the personal column I think: "How do they know St Jude reads this paper?" It's no good, I'm afraid. What I can't see I can't believe in. I suppose you find that pathetic?'

'Not at all. Someone as honest as you are is never pathetic. But I grieve for all you are missing. If you are a believer then you have so much to look forward to.'

'Bully for you,' said Ella cheerfully, 'but time alone will tell. Here, let's brew a cup of something, and let the future look after itself.'

Within an hour of his arrival, Ben and his workmates were hard at it erecting the various attractions of Curdle's Fair. A knot of interested spectators had assembled, and at playtime the railings of the village school were thick with pupils eager to see what was afoot.

Little Miss Fogerty, patrolling the wet playground, but thankful for a clearing sky at last, determined to make 'The Fair' a subject for the afternoon session, and only hoped that she had enough paper to supply the class with adequate artistic material.

Joan Young, making up beds in the room intended for her parents, noted the preparations outside with approval. Still more encouraging were the patches of blue sky which were appearing over Lulling Woods, and the gentle movement of low clouds moving away to the east, and giving way to high ones from the west. It certainly looked as though the fair would have its usual fine weather.

She smoothed the bedspreads and then went to the window. Leaning out she felt the soft breeze lift her hair. The avenue of chestnut trees still shed an occasional drop into the puddles below, and their stout trunks were striped with little rivulets of water, but there was a warmth in the air which spoke of better weather to come.

The daffodils and narcissi, which had taken such a battering in the last few days, were beginning to lift their heads again, and the wallflowers, their velvety faces still wet, were giving out a heady fragrance.

Tight buds beaded the cherry tree nearby, and soon would burst into dangling snow, and the lilac bushes, massed with pyramids of buds, would soon be adding their perfume.

Tomorrow was May. Ever since she could remember, May the first had meant the coming of Curdle's Fair and the real beginning of summer. Her spirits always rose with the advent of May, 'loveliest of months', as the poet truly said.

Even now, she thought, with a great many problems ahead, her heart leapt to greet the fair, the flowers, the coming of summer, and the knowledge that Thrush Green would soon be gilded with sunshine, and aflutter with birds and butterflies.

It was good to know that her father would be with them at the most beautiful time of the year. Thrush Green could not fail to restore him to health. Of that she felt positive, as she ran downstairs full of hope.

By the time the children ran home from school, a watery sun was shining, sparkling upon the drying roofs and the wet grass of Thrush Green.

The air was filled with the clashing of hammers on metal, and the thump of mallets on wood, as the massive equipment of the fair was assembled.

Ben walked purposefully from one site to the next, followed by the diminutive figure of young George clad in duffle coat and wellingtons. He was a sensible child, and obedient to his father's directions. He knew that if he did not do as he was told, and keep out of harm's way, then he would be dispatched back to his mother without further ado.

Back at the cottage, Molly was making a cup of tea for Albert. She had scrubbed the kitchen table, the draining-board and the cupboard tops, and thrown away several revolting remnants of food in various crocks and saucepans.

After the teabreak she resolved that she would get her father to depart across the road to his church duties, while she had an energetic session with soap, hot water and the scrubbing-brush on the filthy kitchen floor.

There was no doubt about it, Albert Piggott's standards of cleanliness grew lower and lower as the years passed.

She looked across at him now, as he sat sipping his tea noisily. It was not just the house which he neglected. The man himself looked half-starved, sickly and dirty. Molly's kind heart was stirred. He had never been a good father, but after all, blood was thicker than water, and she wanted to see him in better shape than this.

It was a pity that Nelly, her stepmother, had ever left him, although she could not blame her. Admittedly, Nelly was avaricious, flighty and coarse. Nevertheless, she was warm-hearted and lively, and the little cottage had never been so clean and wholesome as when Nelly had cared for it. And Albert had always looked spruce and well-fed, his linen spotless, his shoes polished. He looked now, thought Molly, as if he needed a thorough scrubbing and a completely new set of clothing from top to toe.

'I'd best take me tablets with me tea,' said Albert, rising to run a hand along the mantelpiece. The movement triggered off a vicious bout of coughing.

Molly watched with alarm as the old man rested his forehead on the shelf, his thin frame racked with the cough. It ended at last, and Albert sat down again, medicine phial in hand, and drew great noisy breaths.

'You didn't ought to be about, Dad,' said Molly earnestly, 'with that chest of yours. What about havin' a day in bed? I could ask Doctor Lovell to come and see you.'

'He's seen me,' retorted Albert, 'and a fat lot of good that be! If I takes these tablets it do seem to help a bit.'

He rammed one in his mouth, and sent it down his throat with a mouthful of tea.

'What you want,' went on Molly, 'is a good hot bath. The steam'd do them tubes good, you know. Then a day or two resting in bed. You're properly knocked up, and I don't believe you ever feed yourself, do you?'

'I gets a hot pie next door when I'm clemmed,' muttered Albert.

'And plenty of drink to go with it, I don't doubt,' remarked Molly with spirit. 'And that don't do you a ha'porth of good. You could do with a regular dosing of Nelly's cooking.'

'And you could do with minding your own business,' said Albert nastily. 'I manages all right, and I won't have that trollop crossing my doorstep again.'

He rose shakily, and took down his deplorable jacket and cap from the peg on the door.

'Best see to the church, I suppose, while I've got me strength.'

He slammed the door behind him. Molly shook her head sadly and filled the kettle again, ready for her onslaught on the kitchen floor.

It was all very well for him to tell her to mind her own business. As a daughter, his welfare *was* her business. If he went on as he was at present, he would very soon find himself back in hospital, or in one of Lulling's almshouses. The thought of either filled Molly's mind with horror.

She was half inclined to try to get in touch with Nelly. After all, legally she was his wife, even if she had left him for the charms of the oil man.

On the other hand, Albert had every right to refuse to have her back. It was his house. She had treated him shabbily, and no doubt the two would fight like cat and dog, if they were ever brought together again.

Lord, what a to-do it all was, thought Molly! She would have to see what Ben could do about it.

Perhaps he could persuade her father to have at least one decent meal a day. Someone might come in to cook it, or The Two Pheasants might provide it regularly. They could leave the landlord some money in advance.

Meanwhile, she determined that her father was going to be got into a bath, by hook or by crook, and she would burn those filthy clothes herself, and face the storm afterwards.

Much refreshed by these brave plans, she attacked the kitchen floor, and rejoiced in the shadowy pattern on the linoleum which gradually reappeared as the result of her energy.

## 6. The First of May

May the first fell on a Thursday, and it was Ben's intention to stay at Thrush Green until the middle of the following week. Most of his takings would come on Friday night and Saturday. He might pick up enough to cover expenses early in the following week, if the weather held, but he was not due at his next stand for a full week, and he wanted Molly to have time to see all her Thrush Green friends and to get her father's domestic arrangements straightened out.

Not that they could do anything to satisfy that curmudgeonly old fellow, Ben realized. He was a real problem, and likely to become worse as the years passed. He disliked the idea of living near the old man, and yet he had begun to wonder if that might have to be, as his father-in-law's health failed. Of one thing he was positive – he would never live under the same roof with him. It was bad enough to watch Molly wearing herself out, once or twice a year. To see her slaving for that old tyrant, day in and day out, would be impossible, and he was not going to stand for that, whatever the future held.

The day of the fair dawned with a respite from the rain, but no one could truthfully call it 'Mrs Curdle's weather'. The old lady had always seemed to bring sunshine and cloudless skies, but this particular morning was overcast, with only a few shreds of blue sky among the grey mass to give hope of better things to come.

During the day, Ben completed the preparations to his satisfaction, and gave the men an hour or two off. The fair would open at four o'clock, and most of the trade would come from mothers with young children, for the first two or three hours.

After that, with any luck, a good crowd of adults would arrive, willing to spend and out to enjoy some boisterous fun. At ten-thirty the fair must close, so that Ben earnestly hoped that the rain would hold off for the next few days, and particularly during those few vital hours each day when he hoped to recoup some of his outlay.

He was determined to try and get Molly alone for an hour during the afternoon, out of earshot of her father, and to tell her a little about his fears for the future of the fair. Not that she was completely ignorant of its diminishing returns. It was she who kept the rudimentary accounts, and she who helped at one of the stalls whenever she could. It did not need a vast intelligence to see that the crowds were thinner than before, and that takings were down, but Ben feared that she did not realize how dangerously low their resources were. She knew nothing of the offer made by Dick Hasler, and Ben wanted to know how she felt about it.

A fine brown steak and kidney pie dominated the table at midday, and they all did justice to Molly's cooking. Even the old man, Ben noticed, tucked in, and grunted his appreciation in a grudging fashion.

'Now, you go and have a lay down, Dad,' said kindly Molly, 'while we wash up. Do you good to have a nap, and I'll wake you in time to go over to the church.'

Albert departed aloft and the young couple went to the sink. George was busy with his bricks at the table before going for his own brief rest. Now, thought Ben, was the time to broach the delicate subject. But Molly forestalled him.

'How d'you think dad seems?'

'Not too bad. Ate two platefuls of pie, so he can't be at death's door yet. You worry overmuch about him, and he plays up to you.'

'That's not wholly true. His breathing's that rattly it scares me. He'll be back in hospital if he don't take care, and he's no more likely to do that than young George there.'

'He's a grown man. You can't expect to do everything for him.'

'And that ain't all,' went on Molly. 'His underclothes is in rags. I've torn up most of 'em for dusters as I've washed 'em, and I've taken a set of yours for him to keep the old fellow going until I can get down to Lulling to set him up.'

'Thanks,' said Ben laconically. 'And who pays for the new clobber?'

'Well, he will. I'll see to that. He's got a bit put by in the Post Office, and it's time he took some out for a few decent warm clothes. He don't know yet, but I had a bonfire of some of the worst this morning.'

Ben looked startled, and nearly dropped the pie-dish he was wiping.

'Watch it, girl!' he cried. 'He can be real nasty when he's roused. Lord knows the sparks'll fly when he finds out.'

'Then they must fly,' said Molly flatly, tipping away the washing-up water. 'I'm going to sort him out before we move on next week. And what's more, he's going to be given a good hot bath tonight, come what may!'

'Well, you can face that fight while I'm over the fair,' said Ben. 'And good luck to you!'

He watched her militant face as she shepherded George upstairs for his rest. This was not the time, he thought sadly, to introduce the subject of their own troubles.

That would have to wait.

Harold Shoosmith was busy weeding among the wallflowers by his front gate.

He viewed the fair with mixed feelings. A peace-loving man who had retired to Thrush Green because of its tranquillity, he personally loathed the noise which Curdle's Fair generated, and for that reason would rejoice when the great trailers and caravans departed, leaving the green to recover from the scars.

On the other hand, he was amused and impressed by the ardour with which almost all the older inhabitants greeted May the first. The rites of spring had nothing on it, thought Harold, removing a worm which had become entangled in his shoe-lace. He dropped it nearby, and was roundly scolded by a robin who had been looking forward to snapping up this delectable morsel, but did not dare to come too close.

It was natural that the children should be excited, but surprising to find Joan Young and her sister Ruth Lovell so exhilarated at the thought of going on the swingboats and roundabouts as though they were still about ten years old. Even dear old Charles Henstock had rubbed his hands gleefully, and had said how good it was to see the fair again.

He straightened his creaking back and observed Phyllida Hurst coming out of her gate, across the green, letter in hand.

He waved to her and she waved back, and after putting the envelope in the pillar box at the corner of the green, she walked over to talk to him.

She grew prettier than ever, thought Harold. There had been a time when he had fancied himself in love with this attractive young widow, but she had married his good friend Frank and, on the whole, he was relieved to find himself still a bachelor. But now and again he had a twinge of regret. It must be very comforting to come home to find a pretty woman there, to have someone to talk to, to laugh with, and to share one's problems.

'That's exactly what I should be doing,' observed Phil, pointing a toe at the bucket of weeds, 'but I had a horrible story to alter this morning, and it's put me back in the day's programme.'

'How's the writing going?'

'Oh, slowly. I've about four or five magazines who take stuff regularly, but I'm thankful to say I don't have to worry so dreadfully about making money.'

'I'm very glad to hear it,' said Harold. 'You've quite enough to keep you happily occupied, and that's what matters.'

'Are you going to the fair?'

Harold noticed that the girl's eyes were sparkling as brightly as Joan's and Ruth's.

'Well, no! I'm a bit long in the tooth for all that whizzing round.'

'Rubbish!' said Phil. 'It does your liver a world of good! I'm taking Jeremy as soon as he comes out of school, and if Frank gets home in time, I hope I can persuade him to come too later on.'

'You'll manage that,' Harold told her with conviction.

She laughed, and moved away.

'Change your mind,' she called. 'Do come if you can. It's tremendous fun.'

He smiled, but made no reply. He had no intention of getting mixed up with a noisy, shouting throng of people, of being deafened with the brazen notes from those dreadful hurdy-gurdys, and of tripping over coils of cable on the wet grass of Thrush Green.

But how easy it would have been to say 'Yes' to that invitation.

Lucky Frank, thought Harold, turning again to his digging.


Promptly at four o'clock the strident music of Curdle's Fair rent the air. Outside the booths stood the showmen, shouting their wares. The swingboats began their delectable movement up and down, and the galloping horses moved steadily round and round and up and down, their barley-sugar brass supports gleaming like gold.

Most of the patrons were the children from the village school, with a few mothers. Jeremy, in company with some schoolfellows and his mother, Phil, was astride the horses and ostriches within five minutes of the fair's

opening. If all his customers were as thrilled as this small boy, thought Ben, then this year's visit to Thrush Green might be well worth while.

His thoughts flew back to his wonderful old grandmother whose grave was behind him in the churchyard. She had always looked upon Thrush Green as her true home, the one place where she felt that she could rest, largely because of the affection she felt for Dr Bailey, who had looked after her, so many years ago, at her confinement with George, her son, father to Ben.

Ben too had this feeling of affinity with Thrush Green, partly because of his grandmother's loyalty to the place, partly because she now rested there for ever, and partly, of course, because he had found his dear Molly here, and heard about it from her almost daily, wherever they happened to be.

Yes, he supposed Thrush Green would be the obvious place to settle if the fair had to go. He sighed at the thought. What would the old lady have said?

Guilt flooded him, but within a minute it had given way to a comforting thought. Mrs Curdle had always been a realist. If one stall did not pay its way, she was quite ruthless in scrapping it.

When she had discovered her nephew Sam stealing the takings, she had not hesitated to banish him from the fair. If now she had been alive and had to face the sad fact that the business was not thriving, she would do as Ben was thinking of doing, cut her losses and start afresh, with courage and a stout heart.

It was a warming thought, and Ben felt better as he watched the spinning roundabout and the gaudy booths. She would have understood, and so would Molly when he broke the news.

'Roll up! Roll up!' he shouted with vigour, hoisting a four-year-old into a swingboat, and setting it into movement with a cheerful shove.

Some hours later, Winnie Bailey surveyed the scene from her bedroom window. By now it was dark. A few stars pricked the clearing sky, but it was difficult to see them against the blaze of light from Curdle's Fair.

'It's even better at night,' Winnie murmured to herself, watching the moving figures silhouetted against the glare of the bright lamps. She had a great affection for the fair. The bond between Mrs Curdle, of hallowed memory, and Donald and herself had endured for decades. Every year the old lady had made a magnificent bouquet of artificial flowers for her Thrush Green friends. If she had kept them all, thought Winnie, she must have had several dozen.

They were glowing gaudy blossoms, made of finely-pared wood, and dyed in bright shades of orange, pink and red. Winnie still had one of these offerings in a vase on the landing, a constant reminder of a faithful friend.

'A fine family,' commented Winnie, closing the window.

Tomorrow she would seek out Ben and Molly, and hear all their news. The girl must enjoy coming home again and seeing Albert.

As it happened, at that very moment, Molly was confronting her incensed father across a zinc bath half full of steaming water.

The kitchen was snug and steamy. The kitchen range was alight, and on its gleaming top stood a large kettle and the biggest saucepan the cottage could boast.

'Never!' shouted Albert, his face suffused with wrath. 'I ain't gettin' in there, and that's flat.'

'You are,' replied Molly. 'You're plain filthy. You smell somethin' chronic, and you can get them rags off your back for me to wash, or burn maybe, and get soaping. I'll be upstairs, sorting George's things out, so nobody's going to stare at you.'

'Never!' shouted Albert again. 'Never 'eard such cheek!'

Molly looked at him grimly.

'D'you want me to get the *District Nurse*?'

Albert's bravado cracked a little.

'You wouldn't dare! Besides, it's not decent. That young woman? Why, she ain't even married!'

'She's coming tomorrow, if you don't do as I says, then we'll both get you into the tub. So take your choice.'

Slowly the old man fumbled with the greasy scarf about his scrawny neck. He was muttering crossly to himself.

'That's right,' said Molly, reaching for the kettle. 'I'll just top up the water, and you can have a good soak in front of the fire. See here, I'll spread the towel over the back of the chair. Warm it nice, that will, and keep the draught off of you.'

Her ministrations done, she mounted aloft, leaving the staircase door ajar in order to hear that the old man attended properly to his ablutions. Once he was in, she intended to return to scrub his neglected back, modesty or not. Heaven alone knew when Albert's body had last seen soap and water! Not since his last trip to hospital, Molly suspected.

Albert stepped out of the last of his dilapidated underwear. He put one toe reluctantly into the steaming water.

'Women!' muttered Albert, and braced himself for semi-immersion.

## 7. New Hopes

As Miss Fogerty was on her way to school on Monday morning, she espied Willie Bond, the postman, pedalling towards her.

She waited at the end of the chestnut avenue. Willie was fat, and never hurried. However, Miss Fogerty was in good time, as usual, and observed while she waited, the fine sticky buds of the chestnut trees which were beginning to put forth little green fans of leaves.

'Morning, miss,' puffed Willie, dismounting. He studied a handful of letters and handed over two, much to Miss Fogerty's delight. She did not expect to get more than one or two in a whole week. Two in one day was quite an excitement.

She thanked Willie, and turned right between the trees, opening her first letter. It was a printed message from Messrs Ames and Barlow who, so their heading said, were Drapers, Milliners and Mantle Makers of 82 Lulling High Street, established 1862. They thanked Miss Fogerty for her esteemed order, and begged to inform her that the goods awaited collection at her earliest convenience, and they remained her obedient servants.

Miss Fogerty felt a little glow of pleasure. Her new light-weight mackintosh, ordered at Easter, would be a very welcome addition to her modest wardrobe. She might need to withdraw some money from her Post Office account, but it was a comfort to think that she could face the expense.

The other letter was from her dear friend Isobel, and she resolved to read it at her leisure when she arrived at school. She and Isobel had first met at college, many years ago. Isobel was so pretty and clever, and rather better dressed than the majority of girls. It had always surprised young Agnes Fogerty that they had become such firm friends. It had begun when the two discovered that they both came from the Cotswolds. Isobel's father was a bank manager at Stow-on-the-Wold, while Agnes's father was a shoemaker in Lulling.

Visits had been exchanged in the holidays, and Agnes had attended Isobel's splendid wedding. Marriage had taken her to Sussex where her husband owned several shops dealing in antique furniture.

The two girls kept in touch, although distance and Isobel's young children meant that they saw each other rarely. But whenever Isobel paid a visit to her parents at Stow she called to see Agnes, and the two picked up the threads of their friendship immediately.

When Isobel's husband died, Agnes had persuaded her to stay a few days at Thrush Green. Mrs White, her landlady, had a spare room then, and was glad to put it at the disposal of Agnes's old friend in her trouble.

Since then Agnes had spent several spells at Isobel's comfortable Sussex home. The children were now out in the world, and Isobel seemed glad of company. This letter, Miss Fogerty surmised, studying the envelope, might well contain another kind invitation to stay. In which case, it was a good thing that the new mackintosh 'awaited collection at her earliest convenience'. Isobel was always so beautifully dressed, and although she could never aspire to such elegance, at least she could look *respectable*.

She decided to enjoy reading the letter later and tucked the blue envelope into her handbag, and crossed the playground, nodding and smiling at the early arrivals who rushed to greet her. The asphalt, she noticed with her experienced teacher's eye, was quite dry again.

Thank heaven, the children would be able to play outside! She entered her splendid new classroom in good spirits.

Albert Piggott, on that Monday morning, was certainly not in good spirits. He had woken with a sharp pain in his chest and a severe headache.

He had no doubt about the cause of these symptoms. It was that dratted bath that his fool of a daughter had bullied him into – and he told her so.

'Don't talk soft, Dad,' Molly said tartly at breakfast, but secretly she felt a little guilty. Could he have caught a chill? In any case, it was absolutely necessary for him to be cleaned up, and she did not regret burning his disgusting garments.

'Well, wrap up when you go out,' said Molly. 'And I'll get you some cough mixture when I go down to Lulling.'

The old man continued to grumble throughout the day, and certainly by tea time, was flushed in the face and breathing heavily. Molly, trying to hide her alarm, persuaded him to go to bed early.

'He's not right,' she told Ben. 'I'm going to get the doctor to him if he's no better in the morning. Sometimes I wonder if we oughtn't to settle here. He needs looking after, and there's no one but me, now Nelly's gone. And another thing, we'll have to be thinking of George's schooling soon. It's not fair to send him here, there, and everywhere, for a week or so at a time, as we move around. He won't learn nothing that way.'

Ben nodded understandingly.

'I've been thinking too. I reckon we've got to face staying put, and if you want that place to be Thrush Green, then that suits me. But not in this house, love, and not until we can get a place of our own.'

'But when will that be?' cried Molly, in despair. 'All we've got is the fair, and would you ever want to give it up?'

'It looks as though I might have to,' said Ben slowly, and began to tell her the problems and plans which had been plaguing him for the last few months.

She listened in silence, and then put her hand on his.

'You did right to tell me. You shouldn't have kept all this to yourself, Ben. We'll put our heads together and work out what's best to be done, and find out more from Dick Hasler too. You see, something'll turn up.'

A heavy thumping came from the bedroom above them.

'That's Dad,' said Molly. 'I promised him a cup of tea, and clean forgot it.'

She crossed to the sink.

'You go and earn some honest pennies over the fair there,' she smiled at Ben. 'We're going to need 'em in the future.'

Some sixty miles away, Robert and Milly Bassett were rejoicing in the doctor's verdict that a journey to Thrush Green could be undertaken at any time.

'But watch it!' he warned. 'Keep those tablets in your pocket, and don't ignore any warning signs. I· have been in touch with your son-in-law, Doctor Lovell, and I know you will be well looked after.'

'And I intend to do the driving,' said Milly. 'Not on the motorway though. We'll take the old road, and stop at our old haunts on the way.'

'Good idea. But he's quite fit to drive, you know, as long as he stops if he feels the least bit tired.'

'I shall ring Joan tonight,' said Milly, when the doctor had gone. 'Won't it be lovely to see Thrush Green again?'

'I can't get there fast enough,' confessed Robert. 'Now that I know the business is safe in Frank's hands I have just given up worrying about it completely. It's wonderful to look forward to something. That's been half the trouble, I realize now, thinking about what one has done, or ought to have done, instead of looking ahead with hope. Thrush Green is going to set me up, and I'm not going to be such a fool as to jeopardize my health again. Life's too good to waste.'

'Come on Friday,' Joan said, when her mother telephoned.

'Everything's waiting, and everyone here wants to see you. Don't be surprised if all the flags are out!'

As it happened, Isobel's letter was not opened until after dinner time, for when Miss Fogerty entered her classroom she found that the fish tank had sprung a leak, and that the three goldfish (named Freeman, Hardy and Willis by the adoring class), were gasping in a bare inch of water.

Miss Fogerty rushed for a bucket of water, and the net to catch the luckless fish, and spent a busy ten minutes on this errand of mercy and mopping up the floor and cupboard.

The children were entranced at the mess and added to the confusion by trying to help with their handkerchiefs, hastily removed socks, and any other unsuitable piece of material which they could press into service. The amount of water which had come from one small tank was prodigious, and seemed to spread right across the room as well as flooding the cupboard below it. Naturally, it was the cupboard holding piles of new exercise books, the term's supply of coloured gummed squares, now living up to their name, tissue-paper, drawing paper, and thick paper used for painting. It was all most vexatious, and Miss Watson would not be pleased when she had to beg for more supplies, thought poor Agnes, wringing out the floor-cloth.

She took her class across the playground, to the main building for morning prayers, and was obliged to postpone her account of the disaster until after assembly. Usually, she and Miss Watson had a minute or two together before Miss Fogerty seated herself at the ancient upright piano. Neither Miss Watson, nor any other member of the staff over the past ten years, seemed to have learned to play the piano, so that Miss Fogerty was obliged to face the music every morning.

Today Miss Watson was called to the telephone, and arrived a few minutes late. However, she faced the children with her usual calm smile, and prayers began.

Miss Fogerty noted that the hymn was not one of her favourites.

> Raindrops are our diamonds
> And the morning dew,
> While for shining sapphires
> We've the speedwell blue.

What was more, the thing was in four flats, a key which Miss Fogerty detested. However, she did her best, noticing yet again how sharp the older children's voices became towards the end of the hymn.

As the children were led away to their classrooms, Agnes told her headmistress of her misfortune.

'How tiresome,' said Miss Watson, 'and it would be dreadfully wasteful to have to throw away so much good material! I think you had better spread out the sheets separately, Agnes dear, and dry them as best you can. We simply can't waste things.'

And easier said than done, thought Agnes rebelliously, as she crossed the playground. There were mighty few places to spread hundreds of sheets of wet paper in her classroom, and every time the door opened they would blow to the floor, and the children would rush to collect them, as well Miss Watson knew. There had been a chiding note too in her headmistress's voice, which annoyed her usually submissive assistant. Did she think that she had purposely damaged the fish tank? Good heavens, surely she wasn't being accused of wilful damage, or even of neglect? It was simply an act of God, well, perhaps not of God, thought Agnes hurriedly. He cared for all creatures after all, and must grieve for those poor fish who had been almost literally at their last gasp. No, it was a Complete Accident, she told herself firmly, and the only thing to do was to borrow another tank immediately for the poor things, and to endeavour to get her excited children into a calmer state of mind, ready for a good morning's work.

Consequently, it was not until cold mutton with jacket potatoes, followed by pink blancmange, had been dispatched that Miss Fogerty was at liberty to take out Isobel's letter in the peace of her empty classroom and read the news.

It gave her much food for thought, and distracted her attention for a while from her damp surroundings.

She was contemplating a move, Isobel wrote. Now that she was alone it seemed silly to keep up such a large house. The fuel bills alone were horrifying. The garden was far too big, and dear old Bates, who had come twice a week for more years than she cared to remember, had just told her that he must give up.

She would like to return to the Cotswolds, and proposed to look out for a small house, preferably in the Thrush Green area. Not that she was going to *rush* things. If possible, could kind Mrs White put her up for, say, a week while she got in touch with local estate agents? She would much prefer to stay there, in Agnes's company, than put up at the Fleece in Lulling. Hotel life was rather noisy at night, and the Fleece had no really quiet lounge during the day. Also it was a good distance from

Agnes's house, and it was she that Isobel wanted to see, of course. But perhaps Agnes could find out if Mrs White would be agreeable?

Little Miss Fogerty shook her head sadly when she read that paragraph. Mrs White, she knew, would not be able to accommodate her old friend, for an ailing aunt now occupied the spare bedroom and looked like remaining there for some time to come.

The main news, of course, was wonderfully exciting. To think that Isobel might one day be her neighbour! It would be lovely to have her so close. She knew several people in Thrush Green and Lulling, and it was not very far from the Stow area where some of her relations still lived. How she hoped that Isobel would soon find somewhere suitable! She would help her with the move, of course. Perhaps next summer holidays?

Agnes's mind ran ahead happily, anticipating the joys to come. The only snag was this visit in the near future.

Where could she lodge? Mentally, Agnes reviewed the accommodation available near at hand. The Two Pheasants would never do. If Isobel thought the Fleece noisy, she would find The Two Pheasants insupportable, and there had been occasions when men had emerged *drunk* at closing time. Miss Watson, who lived so close to it, had told her so, and said how disagreeable it was.

She toyed with the idea of asking Miss Watson if she could put up her friend for a week. The two ladies had met, and enjoyed each other's company. But Agnes was not at all sure that Miss Watson deserved to have the honour of having Isobel as a paying guest, after her heartless handling of this morning's mishap.

Besides, Miss Watson had a brother who occasionally called unexpectedly, and the room might be needed for him.

And then little Miss Fogerty had a brainwave. She would call on the dear rector and see if he knew of likely lodgings. He and Dimity knew Isobel quite well, and had invited her to tea and bridge on several occasions. They would know the sort of place which would suit her. Somewhere in the parish there must be someone who would like to let a room to a charming, considerate lady like dear Isobel.

Out in the playground a whistle shrilled, and the children's roaring, whilst not actually stilled, was certainly diminished in volume.

Miss Fogerty put away her letter and her private problems, and went out to meet her class.


By mid-week, Albert Piggott was considerably worse, and was confined to his bed.

Doctor Lovell said that it would be wise for him to stay indoors for the rest of the week. His breathing was giving him pain, and he was seriously under weight, the legacy of a year or so's catering, or rather non-catering, for himself.

The wind had veered to the north-east, and Albert himself had forecast that it would stay in that quarter until Whitsun.

'You mark my words, gal,' he wheezed. 'We shan't have no more rain for a bit, but just this pesky dryin' wind to keep the buds from openin'. Won't get no bees venturing out in this cold weather.'

'Nor you, Dad,' said Molly, tucking in the bed clothes. 'You stay there, and I'll do my best to feed you up, like Doctor Lovell said.'

'It's no good,' she told Ben later. 'I'll have to stop here at least until the end of the week. You'll have to go on to Banbury alone. He's not fit to be left yet.'

Ben was philosophical about it. This had happened before, and was likely to happen again. It brought home to both of them the necessity to find a house and a job somewhere near the old man.

'One thing, our George isn't at school yet. Won't hurt him to stay here a few days. He's better off with you in the warm, than following me around in this wind.'

Albert Piggott was not a good patient. He never ceased to remind poor Molly that it was the unnecessary bathing which had reduced him to his present plight.

He toyed with the food which Molly so carefully prepared, pouring contumely upon such dainties as steamed fish and egg custard which he dismissed as 'dam' slops'. Molly had to stand over him to make sure that he took his medicine every four hours. He took to throwing off the bedclothes, complaining of heat, and occasionally hung out of the window in his flimsy pyjamas 'to get a breath of air'.

Molly was sometimes in despair. Only the threat of calling in the district nurse or, worse still, getting the old man into Lulling Cottage Hospital, kept her irascible patient in some sort of submission.

The fair was due to go on the Thursday. She spent the time washing and ironing Ben's clothes and packing the caravan with groceries and homemade pies and cakes.

'Lord!' commented Ben. 'How long am I supposed to be alone? I'll be back for you and George next Monday, I reckon. I'll never get through that lot in a month of Sundays.'

'You never know,' said Molly. 'You give me a ring Monday morning at the Two Pheasants. I've fixed it with Bob. Then we can see how things are.'

That afternoon she remembered, with shame, that she had not called to see the Youngs where she had worked so happily. She left her father asleep, took George by the hand, and walked across the green to the lovely old house.

The buds of May were being violently assaulted by the rough wind. Dry leaves of last autumn were flying pell-mell across the grass, and a great roaring came from the branches of the chestnut trees. Little eddies of dust whirled like miniature sand storms in the road, and the smoke from the bonfire in Harold Shoosmith's garden blew in a rapidly moving cloud towards the distant Lulling Woods.

It was a thoroughly unpleasant afternoon, and Molly was glad to gain the shelter of the walled garden. She made her way to the back door, and rang the bell. Joan opened it and enveloped her in a warm hug.

'Wonderful to see you. I meant to call, but heard Albert wasn't well, and thought you might be rather busy. Tell me the news.'

The two sat at the kitchen table where Joan had been ironing and gossiped happily. Molly looked with affection at her old place of work. Nothing much had changed, and she commented on it with pleasure.

Joan told her about her parent's visit. Molly, in turn, told her about their hopes to find a settled job one day.

'I'll keep my ears open,' Joan promised her. 'I know how clever Ben is with his hands. It shouldn't be difficult to find a job. The house business will be more difficult, I suspect, but I won't forget, and if I hear of anything I shall get in touch.'

Molly left a forwarding address before she went, and promised to look in before Ben claimed her again.

'No, I best not stay for a cup of tea, thank you,' she said, in answer to Joan's invitation. 'Dad's medicine's got to be down him within half an hour, and that'll take some doing.'

She made her farewells, and set off again to face the biting wind. The children were streaming out of school, followed by Miss Fogerty.

To Molly's surprise, the little figure did not take a homeward path through the avenue, but struck across Thrush Green towards the rectory. Going to collect the parish magazine? Offering to help Miss Dimity with a bazaar or some such? Taking a message from Miss Watson about the hymns? Such surmises are part of the pleasures of country living.

But this time Molly had guessed wrongly, for Miss Fogerty's errand concerned dear Isobel, a lady whom Molly had never met.

Still wondering, she opened the door of Albert's cottage and went to collect the medicine.

# 8. *More News of Lodgers*

Dotty Harmer's new lodger, Flossie, had settled in very well, and the fact that nothing had been heard from her last owner was a great relief to Dotty, who had grown much attached to the young spaniel.

The dog followed her everywhere, as if, having been abandoned once, she feared that it might happen again. Dotty was moved by this affection, and returned it tenfold. The two grew very close and the sight of Dotty, shadowed by the faithful golden cocker, became a familiar sight in Lulling and Thrush Green.

One windy afternoon the two descended the hill to Lulling High Street. Dotty carried a basket in each hand, with Flossie's lead intricately entangled with one of them. They made steady progress against the biting east wind, which reddened Dotty's nose and sent Flossie's ears streaming behind her.

Their destination was the Misses Lovelock's house. Dotty was bearing a collection of contributions for the bazaar, and was glowing with the comfortable feeling of doing good.

'Why, Dotty dear, how kind!' cried Bertha, on opening the door. 'Do bring them in. We'll put them straight on the table. Everything's in the dining-room.'

That gloomy apartment was certainly transfigured. The mahogany table had been covered by an enormous white damask cloth, a relic of some Victorian linen cupboard, and upon it there jostled an odd collection of objects.

Dominating all were Ella's colourful contributions. Dimity had supplied a dozen or so dried flower-and-grass arrangements which the Misses Lovelock wondered if they could sell, as everyone in the district was addicted to making such things, and the market might well be saturated. However, they had been accepted with cries of delight, and one could only wait and see.

More normal contributions, such as soap, handkerchiefs, pots of jam and other preserves were among the rest, and would obviously be snapped up, and Dotty began to put her contributions among them.

'Four pots of preserved boletus, the *edible* kind, naturally,' gabbled Dotty, placing four sinister looking jars on the table. Through the murky fluid, could be seen some toadstools of venomous appearance. Ada's jaw dropped, but she remained silent, with commendable control.

'And six pots of hedgerow jelly,' continued Dotty, diving into her basket. 'It's a mixture, you know, of sloes, blackberries, rosehips, elderberries and any other nourishing berries I could find. I thought "Hedgerow Jelly" on the label, would cover it nicely.'

'Yes, indeed,' said Ada faintly, noting the sediment at the bottom of the jars, and the hint of mildew on the top.

'Not much room to write all the ingredients on the label, you see,' said Dotty, standing back to admire the imposing array. 'But I'm sure people will understand.'

'I'm sure they will,' agreed Violet bravely. But whether they would actually *buy* a jar of something which looked certain to give the consumer 'Dotty's Collywobbles' – a disease known to all Dotty's friends – was another matter.

'You are so generous, Dotty dear,' quavered Bertha, averting her gaze from the jars. 'And now you must stay and have some tea. Ada has made some delicious scones with wholemeal flour which we ground ourselves in father's old pestle and mortar.'

'Exactly the sort of thing I love,' said Dotty. 'And Flossie too, if she may have a crumb or two?'

The old ladies made their way to the drawing-room for this modest repast and a great deal of genteel gossip in which a number of Lulling residents' characters would be shredded finely, in the most ladylike fashion.

That same afternoon, Dimity had crossed the road to her old home to broach a subject which she and Charles had discussed thoroughly since Miss Fogerty's visit.

Charles had been wholly in favour of suggesting that Isobel Fletcher should spend the proposed week's visit with Ella.

'They both get on very well,' he said. 'Much the same age. And then Thrush Green is so central for the little trips she may wish to make for viewing places. I'm sure she would be perfectly happy.'

Dimity had some private doubts.

Everyone liked Isobel. She was kind, charming, and elegant. Ella had always spoken warmly of her, and admired her quick brain.

But Isobel was used to comfort. Her husband had been a prosperous man, and his wife was provided with a beautiful home and everything she could possibly desire. Could she stand the rough-and-ready hospitality which Ella would provide? And what about that all-pervading tobacco smoke? And the lack of punctuality in producing meals?

The meals themselves gave Dimity no fears. Ella had a surprisingly good way with food, and was meticulous about its preparation. The house might be a little dusty and untidy, but Ella's cooking arrangements could not be faulted. The snag was that she might well decide to make a chicken terrine at eleven in the morning, and hope to have it cold, with salad, at one o'clock. Ella never seemed to have mastered the time factor in all her activities.

However, she was now on her way to put the proposition to her old friend. She found her sitting by the window doing the crossword puzzle.

'Funny minds these chaps must have,' said Ella, putting aside the paper. 'This clue "Makes waterproof" is "*Caulks*", and the next one is "Sea travel" which is "*Cruise*", so that makes "Corkscrews", d'you see?'

'No, I don't, dear, but I've something to tell you, and I must get back to take the cat's supper out of the oven, so I mustn't linger.'

'And what is that spoilt animal having this evening?'

'Just a little rabbit. Nothing very special.'

'Lucky old cat! Well, come on, what's bothering you?'

Dimity launched into the account of Isobel Fletcher's need of lodgings for a week while she consulted agents about the possibility of buying a house in the neighbourhood. She explained Miss Fogerty's dilemma. Mrs White would not be able to put her up, as she had done. She *could*, of course, stay at the Fleece, but if Ella were willing . . . ? The question hung in mid-air among the blue smoke from Ella's cigarette.

'Of course I'm willing,' replied Ella. 'I'm very fond of Isobel, and should be delighted to have her here. The only thing is, would she be comfortable?'

Trust dear Ella to come directly to the point, thought Dimity, with some relief.

'I'm sure she will be,' said Dimity bravely. 'If you like, I'll come over and help you make up the spare bed, and empty the cupboards, and so on.'

And give an expert eye to Isobel's comfort, she thought privately.

'When will it be? Any idea?'

'None, I'm afraid, but fairly soon, I imagine. Shall I let Agnes Fogerty know, or will you? I know she wants to write very soon.'

'I'll catch her after school,' said Ella. 'One thing though, I'm not letting Isobel pay me. It'll be a pleasure to have her here.'

'Well, you must sort that out between you,' said Dimity rising to go. 'It will be so nice to see her again, and I do so hope she finds somewhere to live nearby.'

'Unless she gets snapped up by somebody in Sussex before that,' said Ella shrewdly. 'She's eminently marriageable, from all viewpoints.'

'Oh, I don't think that will happen,' replied Dimity, slightly shocked. 'She's still grieving for her husband, you know. They were quite devoted.'

She opened the door to see a few children straggling across the green from the village school.

'Out already?' cried Ella. 'Here, I'll cut across now and see Agnes. No time like the present, and she can catch the afternoon post, if she looks slippy!'

Ben Curdle had departed on his way to Banbury, and Molly was left to cope with George and Albert as best she could.

The old man's temper did not improve. The doctor forbade his going outside in the bitter wind, which still prevailed, and Albert worried about the church and the way in which it was being looked after.

The rector had asked one of the Cooke boys to take on Albert's duties temporarily. The Cooke family was numerous and rather slap-dash, but there was no one else free to lend a hand and Jimmy Cooke had agreed to 'keep an eye on things'.

'And that's about all he will do,' growled Albert. 'And I won't be surprised to find me tools missing. Light-fingered lot them Cookes. Always on the look-out for somethin' to pinch.'

Molly tried to turn a deaf ear to the old man's constant complaining. How right Ben was to insist that they did not live with her father! Whatever the future held, that was certain. Look after him she would, as best she could, but to see dear Ben and young George suffering the gloomy and insulting behaviour of the miserable old fellow, was more than she could bear.

'If that's what old age brings you to,' thought Molly, attacking some ironing, 'I hopes as I dies young!'

Not that all old people were as trying as her father, she had to admit. Dear old Dr Bailey, for instance, had always been a happy man, even in his last long illness, and Mr Bassett, who would be arriving for his holiday that very afternoon, always had a cheerful word for everyone.

Perhaps education helped? Molly pondered on this as she ironed a pillowslip. If your mind was full of knowledge, then perhaps you did not worry overmuch about your body and its ills? It brought her again to the question of George's future. A sound schooling he was going to have, come what may, and he could not do better than start at Thrush Green School with Miss Watson and Miss Fogerty. He was going to have a better start in life than his father. Poor Ben, she remembered, had been unable to read and write, with any competence, when they first met, and she herself had acted as teacher. She had certainly had a willing – even amorous – pupil, and within a month or so he had mastered his difficulties. But he had never forgotten the humiliation of having to confess his ignorance for so many years, and he was as determined as Molly that George should never suffer in the same way.

Well, the next step was to look out for a suitable job for Ben. Once the Bassetts were settled in, she would have another talk with Joan Young, and perhaps walk down to that new Job Centre in Lulling to see if there were any openings for a hard-working man like her dear Ben.

Whoever employed him, thought Molly loyally, would be lucky. There was no one – simply no one – like her Ben.

There was a splendid sunset as Molly finished her ironing. Bands of gold, scarlet and violet clouds transfigured the western sky, and the dark mass of Lulling Woods was silhouetted against the blaze of glory.

The rooks were flapping homeward, their black satin feathers catching the light. Albert Piggott's cat sat on the sun-warmed wall of the Two Pheasants and enjoyed the last of the daylight.

Betty Bell, who was cleaning Miss Fogerty's schoolroom, stopped her ministrations to admire the spectacle. Just like a jumper she'd knitted once! All different bands of colour, she remembered, and no end of trouble with the vee neck. But what a gorgeous sight!

Miss Harmer would have a good view from her cottage, and Mr Shoosmith, next door to the school, would see that sunset even better from the bedroom she had done out that morning. Did you a power of good to see something pretty like that, thought Betty, returning to her desk polishing, much refreshed.

A car drew up outside the Youngs' gate, and before the doors were opened, Joan ran out to set the gates open.

Slowly the car drew into the drive. Out stepped Milly Bassett, to be enveloped in her daughter's embrace, and then, rather more slowly, Robert emerged.

He looked pale and rather shaky, but he stood erect and took in great breaths of fragrant air. His face was alight with pleasure.

'Just what I've been longing for,' he told Joan, holding out his arms. 'To come home again!'

# Part Two

# Change at Thrush Green

## 9. Visitors to Thrush Green

There now began for Robert Bassett a period of intense joy.

It was as if all his senses had been sharpened by the shock of his recent illness. He saw, with fresh awareness, the small beauties around him, and marvelled that he had not enjoyed them before.

The lilac was beginning to break in the garden, each fragrant plume composed of hundreds of exquisite flowerets. Grape hyacinths spread a carpet of vivid blue beneath the burgundy-red stems of the dogwood bushes.

He came across a thrush's nest, cleverly hidden in the crutch of the hawthorn hedge, and admired the smooth mud lining, as beautifully rounded as the speckled breast of the bird that sat so patiently upon the four turquoise blue eggs.

Everything delighted him. He ventured from the garden to Thrush Green, observing the pattern of blue smoke from cottage chimneys which matched the distant blur of Lulling Woods. He sat on the seat near the statue of Nathaniel Patten and gloried in the warmth of the sun upon his face, the droplets spangling a spider's web, the timid advances of Albert Piggott's cat whose curiosity had overcome her fear, and the rough comfort of the blackthorn walking stick in his hand.

How right W. H. Davies had been, thought Robert, when he wrote:

> What is this life
> If full of care
> We have no time
> To stand and stare?

This was the first time, in a long life, that he had savoured to the full the pleasures of his senses. He remembered the extraordinary sensations he had felt, when bedbound, on his sudden awareness of the inanimate objects in the bedroom. That had been the beginning of his new response to his surroundings, although weakness then had blurred some of the pleasure.

Now, with ever-growing strength, he gave thanks for the miracles around him, and his ability to recognize them.

Sickness, reflected Robert, changed a man. He thought of the invalids he had known. How often he had dismissed their querulousness and complaints as the outcome of self-pity! He knew better now.

It was not only with themselves and their pain that the sick were concerned. They worried for others. They grieved for the work they were causing, for the disruption of other people's lives, the sapping of their energy, the tensions within a family, and the awful possibility of increasing helplessness.

He had been lucky, he thought soberly. Lucky to have had his darling Milly as constant support, a doctor he trusted, and a loving family. Lucky too, to have realized this further truth, that the sick are sad, not only for themselves, but for those they love. He would never forget it.

And luckiest of all, thought Robert, gazing around him, to be at peace in Thrush Green on a bright May morning.


Albert Piggott had thrived under Molly's care, and Doctor Lovell assured the girl that her father could cope perfectly well without her presence.

'I'll keep an eye on him,' he promised her. 'I gather from Bob Jones that you've arranged for a midday meal for him at The Two Pheasants. He should do well now that the weather's warmer.'

Molly told him of her fears that he would need more care as the years passed, and of their plans to settle within easy distance of the old man.

'Well, it happens to us all,' agreed the doctor. 'But don't completely upset your lives for Albert. He's by way of being a bit of a fraud, you know.'

He laughed to soften his words, and Molly smiled too.

'Oh, we knows him well enough, Doctor! But it don't alter the fact that he's gettin' an old man. I wish his Nelly hadn't left him. She took good care of him.'

'They weren't exactly turtle-doves,' commented the doctor. 'It was plain that it couldn't last.'

'I know she was a right trollop in her ways,' agreed Molly earnestly, 'but she kept that house spotless, and her cooking was just beautiful. Dad was lucky to get her. After all, you can't expect *everything* in marriage.'

Doctor Lovell tried to hide his amusement as he drove off on his rounds.

There was something very refreshing about Molly's attitude to the wedded state. Obviously, good housewifery was rated rather more highly than fidelity in Molly's scale of reckoning. Her own marriage, he knew, was an outstanding success. So, he thought, was his own to Ruth. They were both lucky to have found the right partners. It did not look as if Albert would find another to give him companionship in his old age.

Ah well! What could he expect? He was a thoroughly selfish old man, and he only hoped that Molly would not put her marriage in jeopardy by trying to live with Albert Piggott.

Not that it was likely, thought Doctor Lovell, turning his car into the village of Nidden. Ben would see to that.

The early days of May followed each other with increasing warmth and fragrance. Spring-cleaning was finished in a spurt of energy. Blankets blew upon clothes-lines, carpets were beaten, curtains and bedspreads washed, and good housewives congratulated themselves upon the amount of work which could be accomplished, given bright sunshine and fair winds.

Dimity had kept her word and helped Ella to prepare for Isobel's arrival. The spare-room awaited her, with cupboards and drawers emptied and relined with clean paper, furniture glossy with polish, and a vase of pheasant-eye narcissi on the bedside table.

'D'you think she'll be comfortable?' asked Ella, unusually anxious.

'Of course,' replied Dimity reassuringly.

'I'm not sure just when she'll arrive,' went on Ella, 'so I thought I'd whip up an omelette for this evening. There's plenty of salad. I wonder if that will be enough?'

'Isobel was always a small eater,' said Dimity. 'And no doubt you've plenty of fruit, and cheese.'

'Dotty brought me some goat's cheese this morning,' said Ella, 'but I'm not putting *that* on the cheese board. Don't want the poor girl struck down with Dotty's Collywobbles while she's here.'

'No, indeed,' agreed Dimity. 'Now, I must get back to Charles. He has a diocesan meeting at six, miles away, and I want to make sure that he has a good tea.'

She hurried across the road to the bleak rectory, leaving Ella to survey her preparations with a critical eye.

'Ah well,' she said at last. 'Can't do any more now. Time I had a cigarette before dear old Isobel arrives.'

She settled down on the window seat, and began to roll a pungent cigarette. But before she had a chance to light it, a small pale-blue glossy car stopped at the gate, and Isobel emerged.

Throwing the cigarette into the battered tobacco tin, Ella hurried to open the gate, enfolding Isobel in a great bear-hug on the way.

'Wonderful to see you,' she boomed. 'Had a good trip? My word, this looks a handsome vehicle!'

She surveyed the car with much admiration.

'It's an Alfa Romeo,' said Isobel, 'and it certainly got me here in record time today. Traffic was amazingly light, and I know my way so well, of course, there was no need to stop for map-reading or asking people.'

'All "strangers in these parts" anyway, I find,' said Ella, helping with Isobel's case which was as sleek and elegant as the car. 'I'm going to put on the kettle. It can boil while I show you your room. That is, if you'd like a cup of tea?'

'More than anything in the world,' said Isobel, following her hostess.

The arrival of the beautiful Alfa Romeo had been noted by Harold Shoosmith who was walking across the green to call upon Charles Henstock.

Harold loved cars, and was beginning to think that it was high time that he parted with the ancient Daimler which had served him so well for years. But what to buy in its place?

All through his life he had bought cars made in Britain. In the long years abroad, his succession of British cars had been a precious link with home, and a source of admiration to friends overseas. Now he found himself looking in vain for the sort of small, distinguished and well-finished vehicle which he wanted.

Parking in Lulling High Street was no easy task with the gallant old Daimler. Its petrol consumption grew as the years passed. The time had come, Harold knew, with sadness, when he must part with it. There were several foreign cars on the market which attracted him, but loyalty to British makers made him hesitant to look at overseas models.

But Isobel's pale blue beauty was certainly an eye-catcher. He looked it over, from a distance, as he waited for someone to come to the rectory door.

Charles greeted him and took him into his study.

'Dimity's gone to take some magazines to Dotty Harmer,' he told his friend. 'Do sit down.'

'I won't keep you long,' replied Harold. He was thinking how dark and cold this room always seemed. Today, with the warm May sunshine flooding the world with golden light, it seemed incredible that this bleak study remained untouched by its ambience.

'I came for the sweep's address,' said Harold. 'Betty Bell tells me that we should have had the chimneys done a month ago. She can't remember the new chap's name, and neither can I, of course.'

'Surely, you have Potter from Lulling?'

'He died last year, I'm told.'

The rector looked shocked.

'I'm truly grieved to hear that. He was not one of my parishioners, of course, but I should like to have called on him during his last illness.'

'He didn't really have one, according to Betty,' answered Harold. 'Dropped down on someone's hearth with the flue brush still in his hand, so she says. "A lovely way to go," was her comment, "but made a terrible mess of the carpet." I'm sorry to have brought bad news.'

'Not at all. Not at all,' replied the rector, pulling himself together. 'But about this new man. I'm sure we are as nonplussed as you are, as we always had poor Potter. Have you any clues?'

'Betty tells me that he lives at the other side of Lulling Woods. He clears cesspits and farm drains, does a bit of poaching, has had three wives and rears ferrets.'

'John Boston, without a doubt,' said the rector immediately. 'Rather a rough diamond, but a very useful member of the community, when he's not in prison. I have a soft spot for John, I must admit. I'm sure he'll do your chimneys beautifully.'

He reached for a piece of paper, and wrote down the address.

'It might be best to call on him, Harold. I doubt if he can read very well.'

He handed over the slip of paper.

'Many thanks, Charles. I'll do that. Now, tell me, whose is that dazzling little car outside Ella's?'

'It must belong to Isobel Fletcher,' responded the rector. 'I know she was expected today, but I imagined she would arrive later than this. A charming woman. Have you met her?'

'No, I'm afraid not.'

'Then you must,' said the rector firmly, accompanying his visitor into the sunshine of Thrush Green. 'She's here for a week, I know, and may settle here permanently if she finds a suitable house.'

He looked about him with some surprise.

'Why, it's quite warm out here! I think I shall leave my paperwork and do a little gardening instead.'

'A very sound idea,' agreed his friend.

Albert Piggott, partially restored to health, was doing a little light gardening himself in the churchyard, Harold noticed, as he returned to his own home.

These days, the churchyard was very much easier to maintain than it had been when Harold first came to Thrush Green some years earlier.

It had been his idea to clear the whole area, to put the gravestones round the low wall which surrounded the plot, and to level the ground so that a motor mower could be used.

There had been some opposition to this scheme, but there was considerable pride in the improved tidiness of Albert's domain, and certainly the little church of St Andrew's was more attractive now in its very spacious setting.

Albert Piggott was the last person to admit that his labours had been rendered considerably lighter by the new layout. From the first, he had refused to touch the motor mower, and the Cooke boy, who had been acting as locum during Albert's illness, had taken on the mowing from the start, and proved remarkably reliable.

Albert's job consisted of a certain amount of hoeing and weeding, the upkeep of the gravel path round the church, and the pruning of the shrubs.

On this particular afternoon he was plucking groundsel from the gravel. It was about the easiest job he could find outside in the sunshine. Also he was in full view of the rectory, should the rector wish to see him at work, and very handy for The Two Pheasants.

He had demolished a helping of steak and kidney pie, with mashed potatoes and tinned peas, at that hostelry, some two hours earlier, paid for by Ben and Molly in advance.

'Not a patch on Nelly's cooking,' he had grumbled to the landlord, who affected deafness. If he took note of all Albert's whinings, he told himself, he'd be in the local loony bin in next to no time. Best to ignore the old misery!

Now, with bending, Albert was suffering from indigestion, and feeling more than usually sorry for himself. Visions of Nelly's pies and roast joints floated before his eyes. No doubt about it, you never got a ha'p'orth of heartburn after Nelly's cooking!

He collected a few more handfuls of groundsel, threw them on to the compost heap, hidden in a remote corner of the churchyard, and wandered across the road to his cottage.

He rummaged in a jam jar which served as his medicine chest, discovered an indigestion tablet, and sat sucking it morosely as he surveyed the kitchen.

Nothing had been done to it since Molly left, apart from a little desultory washing of crockery and cutlery. The stove was dingy. The floor was dirty. The windows were misty with grime, and dust lay everywhere. It needed a woman's hand, thought Albert sentimentally. Here he was, an invalid, with no one to look after him, deserted by his wife and daughter, left to fend for himself in his old age. It was enough to bring tears to your eyes, that it was!

His thoughts turned again to Nelly. She wasn't everybody's choice, of course. For one thing, she must have turned the scales at sixteen stone, and she had a laugh that fairly made your head throb. Then she was a stickler for cutting down on the drink – a bad thing for a man who enjoyed the occasional glass. She was a nagger too, when the spirit moved her. No, she had been lucky to have found someone like himself to put up with her ways, decided Albert.

But there – she was a real stunner of a cook, and could be very loving when she wanted anything. Money, for instance. She wasn't above taking a pound note out of his wallet on the sly, if he didn't pass it over when requested.

And then that flirting with the oil man! That was enough to turn anyone's stomach, remembered Albert. And finally, to leave a good husband and home to live with the fellow! It was unforgivable.

Albert's indigestion grew worse at the very thought of Nelly's infidelity. What if she was a wonderful cook, and a superb housewife? Her morals were no better than an alley cat's. Come to think of it, an alley cat probably behaved more circumspectly than his wife, he decided, rubbing the pain in his diaphragm.

He was better off without her, dirt, indigestion and all. He stumbled across to the sink, and filled the kettle. A cup of tea might settle his tempestuous inside. Nothing like a cup of tea for comfort!

Sniffing slightly with self-pity, Albert fumbled among the dirty dishes on the draining-board and found himself a relatively clean cup.

The golden May day ended in a blazing sunset. The rooks flew home to Lulling Woods, and children pleaded to stay up to play.

The bronze statue of Nathaniel Patten on Thrush Green caught the last of the light, glinting like gold. Lilac, narcissi and early stocks breathed out a heady fragrance, and all was at peace.

Two miles away, a train drew out of Lulling Station. Only one passenger had alighted, and the ticket collector tried to hide his amazement as he took the ticket in his hand.

No words were exchanged, but he watched the traveller out of sight with the greatest excitement.

Purposefully, the large figure waddled towards the town. In one hand it carried a case. In the other, a handbag and a bag of groceries.

For better or for worse, Nelly Piggott was returning to Thrush Green.

## *10. Ella's Party*

For little Miss Fogerty, the arrival of her friend Isobel spelt happy excitement.

Modest and retiring by nature, the very fact that she was immured in the classroom all day, and that her lodgings were a little way from the centre of Thrush Green, meant that she had made few friends in the neighbourhood.

> Be civil to all,
> But familiar with few,

was a precept hung upon the shop wall of her father, the shoemaker. It certainly summed up his attitude to his customers and to his chapel acquaintances. There was little entertaining done. It was not only that money was short. It was an inherent timidity which restrained the shoemaker from giving cause for comment or ridicule. He was a great one for 'keeping himself to himself', and Agnes took after him.

The inhabitants of Thrush Green were fond of her. Many of them remembered her from their schooldays, and always with affection and respect. But Agnes Fogerty was not the sort of person in whom one could confide – or, for that matter, in whom one could arouse laughter or rage. Always kind, always ladylike, shiningly honest and conscientious, these very attributes seemed to surround her with an invisible guard which no one had completely penetrated.

Except Isobel. Perhaps it was because they had first met when they were both young and vulnerable, thrown together in the alien world of college, and grateful for the common memories of their Cotswold background. This friendship had survived the years, the changes of fortune and the many miles between them.

To Isobel it was a source of comfort and quiet pleasure. To Agnes it was much more. She never ceased to wonder that Isobel, so much cleverer, so much more beautiful, so much more prosperous, could still enjoy her own, limited company. Their friendship was an inspiration to the quiet school teacher, and did much to mitigate the fact that she had so few friends at Thrush Green.

Of course, she counted her headmistress, Miss Watson, as a friend, and was glad to hear her confidences and hopes. In times of stress, Agnes knew that she had been of real help, and the thought warmed her. But that inherent timidity, inculcated by her father, made her careful of overstepping the bounds of propriety.

Miss Watson was *The Head*. She was *An Assistant*. Nothing could alter those two facts, and Agnes was careful to keep a certain distance between them, as was only right and proper. Although, sometimes, she had a pang of regret.

It seemed so silly that two grown women, both single, both lonely at times, should not become closer in friendship. And yet, any overtures must, of course, come from Miss Watson. It would look *pushing* if she herself made the running.

Miss Fogerty remembered how much she had enjoyed being of use to Miss Watson on one or two occasions when accident or ill-health had indisposed her headmistress. She was always so grateful for any little kindnesses done, thought Agnes, and for this generosity of spirit it was worth ignoring the minor pinpricks which daily companionship sometimes brought, such as the wounding words on the recent occasion of the leaking fish tank. Perhaps she was over-sensitive about these things? Or perhaps she was getting prickly in her old age?

Well, whatever the cause, the fact that Isobel was in Thrush Green for a week, wiped out any unhappy feelings. For the next few days she intended to see her old friend as often as her duties would allow.

The May sunshine which warmed Thrush Green only increased the inner glow of little Miss Fogerty's heart. An invitation to drinks from Ella was 'accepted with the greatest pleasure' and, in this case, with perfect truth.


Robert Bassett's returning strength was noted with much relief at Thrush Green. Already he had spent an evening playing bridge at Winnie Bailey's in the company of his wife, the Hursts who lived next door at Tullivers, and Charles and Dimity Henstock.

His daily walk grew a little longer, and he began to plan a walk downhill to Lulling in the near future.

Joan and Ruth and his son-in-law Doctor Lovell were begining to congratulate themselves upon the patient's well-being when something happened to jog them out of their complacency.

Robert had gone out on his own along the quiet lane to Nod and Nidden. Milly was going to catch him up, but a phone call delayed her, and it was some ten minutes later that she left the house.

To her horror, she discovered her husband flat on his face, his head upon the grass verge, and his legs in the road. His breathing was laboured, his lips blue, and his hands were cold.

She whipped off her jacket and flung it over the prostrate form, and luckily, at that moment, Willie Bond the postman, came along on his bicycle.

'Lor!' was his comment. 'Has he croaked?'

'Of course not!' retorted Milly, with understandable asperity. 'Could you run to the Youngs' and get help, Willie?'

'Ah! That I will,' responded Willie, throwing a fat leg over the saddle with maddening slowness.

He pedalled off, and Milly felt in her husband's waistcoat pocket for the magic tablets which Doctor Lovell had prescribed. She could not find them, and had to content herself with chafing the cold hands, and putting a scarf under her husband's head.

A minute later, Joan arrived, flushed with anxiety.

'John's on his way with the car,' she said. 'Luckily, he was still in the surgery.'

Robert's eyelids began to flicker, and he attempted to lift his head.

'I'm all right,' he murmured. 'I'm all right. I'm all right. I'm all right.'

But the two anxious women knew that he was not, and saw with relief that Doctor Lovell's car was approaching.

Within twenty minutes Robert Bassett was back in bed, and the hopes of all had plummeted.


The inhabitants of Thrush Green were united in their sadness when the news broke. But prognostications of what might happen differed, of course.

Betty Bell told Harold Shoosmith that her uncle went just the same way. First time, recovered. Second, snuffed out!

Albert Piggott was of the opinion that a new heart put in might be the answer. Why, that chap in South Africa – Christine Someone, wasn't it? – had put a whole hatful of hearts in dozens of poor souls like Mr Bassett. To his mind, it was worth trying. He only wished this Doctor Christine did lungs as well. Pity he lived such a long way off.

Dotty Harmer told Dimity Henstock that she feared that Robert Bassett had eaten far too much animal fat during his life, and this was the consequence.

'I tried, time and time again, to wean him on to a vegetable diet, but with no success,' sighed Dotty. 'Men are very obstinate.'

Naturally, it was a subject of general interest at Ella's small party.

Miss Fogerty had dressed with care. As chief visitor's friend she felt that she owed it to Isobel to appear in her best. She wore a brown silk frock with a small ivory-coloured lace modesty vest let into the front, and her mother's cornelian brooch. She had spent some time trying to decide if her seed pearls could be worn as well, but a horror of being overdressed decided her against them. The brooch was quite enough.

As the weather was so dry and warm it was unnecessary to wear a coat, but Miss Fogerty folded an Indian shawl and put it prudently in her brown leather handbag. It might be chilly later.

She set out from her lodgings in innocent excitement. Outings were rare occasions, and to be the acknowledged close friend of dear Isobel, among her Thrush Green neighbours, meant a great deal to Agnes.

The Henstocks, Winnie Bailey and the Hursts were already there when she knocked timidly at Ella's front door. Isobel came forward to kiss her, and the assembled company greeted her warmly.

'Now, what's it to be?' inquired Ella. She was dispensing drinks with her usual forthright confidence. Some women would have delegated the job to one of the men, but not Ella.

'Tio Pepe? Or a sweet sherry? Gin and lime? Gin and tonic? Dubonnet? Or I've tomato juice and pineapple juice if you like the soft stuff.'

'The dry sherry, please,' said Miss Fogerty. Her dear father had approved of a little dry sherry, she remembered, and despised those who preferred a fruitier variety. Not that sherry had placed much part in the shoemaker's house. At Christmas time there might be a bottle of sherry in the cupboard, but it was certainly looked upon as a luxury.

'Can't think what's happened to Dotty,' said Ella. 'Anyone seen her?'

'She was picking greenstuff for the rabbits,' said Winnie. 'I noticed her when I called to see if I could do anything for the Bassetts.'

'Hope she hasn't forgotten,' said Ella. 'And how was poor old Robert?'

'In bed, resting. I didn't go up. He seems to be sleeping quite a bit.'

'It's too bad, after the marvellous progress he was making,' said Dimity. 'I do hope he won't try to get back to that business of his. Time he retired.'

'I agree,' said Charles. 'I take it that the Youngs won't be coming here this evening?'

'No, they cried off,' said Ella.

'Coo-ee!' called a voice.

'Dotty!' exclaimed Ella, hurrying to the door.

They heard voices and footsteps, and in came Dotty, accompanied by Harold Shoosmith.

'We thought you might have forgotten,' said Dimity.

'Good heavens, no!' replied Dotty. 'Why, I went up to change a full hour ago.'

'My fault entirely,' broke in Harold. 'I waylaid her, and took her to see my tulips. Just showing off really.'

'Well, come and meet Isobel Fletcher,' said Ella, leading him across the room.

Harold found himself standing in front of an extremely pretty woman. There was a gentle serenity and poise about her which immediately appealed to him.

'How do you do?' said Isobel holding out her hand, and as Harold held it, he was suddenly reminded of something which he had read recently. Ellen Terry, if he remembered aright, had talked of 'a holy palmer's kiss, a sympathy of the skin', when some hands met in a clasp. For the first time, he was conscious of it, and was strangely stirred.

They talked of Thrush Green, and of her efforts to find a home nearby.

'I used Williams and Frobisher,' Harold told her, 'when I was seeking a house here. I'd tried four or five other estate agents, but they would keep sending me details of derelict oasthouses and windmills, or manor houses with twenty-two bedrooms and no bath, until I was nearly driven insane. I must say Williams and Frobisher were much more practical.'

'I'll try them tomorrow,' promised Isobel. 'And now I see Ella beckoning to me, so you must excuse me.'

She made her way towards her hostess, and Charles Henstock took her place at Harold's side. If his old friend appeared slightly bemused, the good rector was not conscious of it.

'An excellent party. Ella is so good at this sort of thing, and I always enjoy coming to this house. Something very snug about a low ceiling. The rectory could do with the ceilings lowered by a yard or so. But how would one begin?'

'That's beyond me,' confessed Harold. 'Tell me, how long is Miss Fletcher staying?'

'*Mrs* Fletcher, Harold.'

'Oh, I'm afraid I didn't catch that when we were introduced.'

'I never catch *anyone's* name,' admitted the rector. 'It is a great disability, particularly if one is a parson.'

Harold was looking thoughtful.

'Are you feeling all right?' asked the rector. 'Not finding the room too warm?'

'No, no!' said Harold. 'I'm quite well. An excellent party, as you say. Is Mrs Fletcher's husband here somewhere?'

The rector's chubby face grew sad.

'I am sorry to say that he died last year. A great blow for dear Isobel. They were a devoted couple. It's one of the reasons for the move, I gather. Her present house is really too big now.'

Despite the melancholy news of Isobel's husband's demise, Harold's spirits appeared to revive at once.

'More sherry?' asked Ella, swimming into their ken.

'Thank you, thank you,' said Harold heartily, proferring his glass.

Across the green, as dusk fell, and the lights began to shine from cottage windows, Joan Young and her husband were looking ahead.

Upstairs, Robert Bassett slept fitfully, with Milly sitting in an armchair beside him. Her hands were busy with knitting, her mind busy with plans for the future.

John Lovell, her doctor son-in-law, knew her good sense and had answered her questions honestly. It would be best to face retirement now, to wind up the business, and to find an easily run place near the family at Thrush Green, he had said.

'Would you want to come back to this house?' he asked. 'It's lovely, I know, and it's Robert's, but you'd need resident help, wouldn't you? Have you and Robert ever discussed it?'

'Only very lightly,' admitted Milly. 'We've always had the idea of coming back here to end our days –'

Her mouth quivered suddenly, and she looked down quickly.

John patted her shoulder.

'Don't upset yourself. He's got a good few years yet, you know, if he takes care. We'll work out something together.'

Downstairs, Edward was putting forward a suggestion or two.

'I've been thinking about this for some time. Ever since we had a good look at the stables the other day. They would convert into a beautiful little house of one or two floors, ideal for the parents.'

'But this house is theirs!' protested Joan. 'We're the ones who should move out!'

'I agree absolutely,' said Edward, 'but it would have to be altered. The ground floor would make a splendid flat for them, and we could move up to the first floor and open up the attics for bedrooms, if that would suit everyone better than the stable plan.'

'Would it cost the earth?'

'Well, the architect's fees won't need to be found,' said Edward, smiling, 'and I'm sure we could get a loan for this work. After all, we're thinking of providing homes for two families, aren't we?'

Joan looked at him with affection.

'You've been thinking about this for a long time, haven't you?'

'For years,' confessed Edward. 'I've been longing to convert the stables for some time now, and this seems to be the moment to have a go.'

'We can't do anything until Father's over this attack,' said Joan. 'But we'll have a word with Mother in a day or two, just to prepare the ground. I must say, I should be much happier if they were under our eye. They've been so good to us always.'

'Well, it's their choice, of course. All this is theirs, and, if need be, we must go house-hunting ourselves.'

'Somehow,' said Joan, 'I don't think it will come to that.'


Agnes Fogerty had been invited to supper after the guests had gone, and very enjoyable she had found this meal.

Afterwards, the three women washed up and between them achieved a degree of unusual tidiness in Ella's kitchen.

That done, Isobel accompanied Miss Fogerty along the road to her home. The air was soft and balmy, auguring well for another beautiful spring day on the morrow.

'No, I won't come in,' Isobel replied in answer to Agnes's invitation. 'I know you've things to get ready for school tomorrow, and I must get back to Ella's.'

They parted affectionately at Agnes's gate, and Isobel retraced her steps.

How snug it all looked at Thrush Green, she thought! The houses sat as comfortably as cats before a fire. If only she were lucky enough to find one before long!

Well, tomorrow she would go to see Williams and Frobisher, as recommended by that nice sensible man who lived across the green.

She looked at his house now, a secure bulk dimly visible against the night sky. In a downstairs window, a reading lamp was alight. It looked as though he might be happily settled in there.

She only hoped that she might be as lucky with Williams and Frobisher as he had been, Isobel thought, as she opened Ella's gate.

## *11. Village Gossip*

As Nelly Piggott (*née* Tilling) plodded along Lulling High Street from the station, she looked ahead, with some trepidation, to the kind of welcome she might expect from her husband, Albert.

She had parted from him after a fierce quarrel, but this was only the culmination of weeks of disgust with Albert. He was mean, he was dirty, he was bad-tempered. He drank, he grumbled, he swore. Why she had ever married him, Nelly wondered, shifting her case to the other hand, heaven alone knew.

Well, to be honest, she admitted to herself, she did know. She needed a home. Her own cottage had been sold by the owner, and she had turned down those on offer at the time. Ted and Bessie Allen at The Drovers' Arms at Lulling Woods, had put her up for a few weeks, and she had enjoyed scrubbing out the bar for them.

But a woman needs a place of her own, and Lulling Woods was too quiet for Nelly's taste. Thrush Green seemed just the right setting for a woman of Nelly's sociable habits. The fact that the village school needed a cleaner, just at that time, was another advantage.

And then there was Albert Piggott. Or rather, Albert Piggott's cottage. It was handy for the school, and the bus to Lulling, and looked out on the green where there was always something going on.

Moreover, the cottage was filthy, and Nelly longed to get at it with plenty of hot water, soap and a stout scrubbing-brush. It was a challenge. Dirt was always a challenge to Nelly, and she responded to this one with energy and courage. Within a week the place was transformed, and looking back upon those early days Nelly realized she had been happy, not because of Albert, but because of the satisfaction of cleaning his house.

Not that he was unappreciative. He was particularly grateful for the magnificent meals she cooked, and the fact that she was obliged to curb her art when the doctor told Albert to eat less rich food, was one of the reasons for Nelly's growing resentment. It had culminated in Albert's throwing his helping of Christmas pudding at the wall.

Another factor, of course, was the oil man. He was not every woman's idea of an attractive man, but his sleek black hair and dark beard appealed to Nelly. He had a glib tongue too, and was adept at flattery. It did not need much to woo Nelly away from her husband, and she went to join him with every confidence.

She saw now that his charms were superficial. She had never been so short of money in her life, and she strongly suspected that there were several other women in his life.

Things had gone from bad to worse, and one solitary evening, as she ironed her companion's shirts, she worked out just how little he gave her for housekeeping, and how much she had been obliged to subtract from her Post Office account during her stay. The results frightened her.

Here she was, getting on, not likely to get a job easily, and no future with Charlie as far as she could see. He was a bad bargain. The best thing to do was to cut her losses, return to Thrush Green, where she was more likely to get a job, and to throw herself on Albert's mercy – at least for a time. After all, she was his lawful wedded wife, and plenty of husbands had to turn a blind eye to their wives' little weaknesses, Nelly told herself.

Nelly was a realist. She finished the ironing, and went upstairs to pack. The next day she left a note for Charlie, collected some useful groceries from the larder, including a couple of chops which would do nicely for Albert's supper, and made her way to the station.

'Once I've got Albert sweet,' she thought to herself, as she faced the steep hill to Thrush Green, 'I'll pop along to Miss Watson and see if my old job's still open. If not, she'll know someone who could do with a bit of cleaning, I don't doubt.'

Puffing heavily, Nelly Piggott returned to Thrush Green.

On the morning after Ella's party, Winnie Bailey, the doctor's widow, made her way next door to Tullivers.

The May sunshine gilded the green. Daisies spangled the grass, and a lark's song fell from the blue, as clear and pure as a cascade of mountain water. How Donald loved a day like this, thought Winnie, tapping at the door. But there was no point in grieving. It was the last thing he would have wanted, and since his death she had learnt to savour each day as it came, to count her many blessings, and to try to put sadness behind her.

Phyllida and Frank Hurst had helped enormously, she thought. What a comfort good neighbours could be!

Phil's head appeared at a bedroom window above her.

'Oh, do just walk in, Winnie dear. I'm coming down now.'

'I promised you some pansy plants,' said Winnie. 'I haven't brought them in case it's a busy time for you, but they're all ready next door whenever you need them.'

'Lovely!' said Phil. 'Come in and sit down, or shall we sit in the garden?'

'The garden,' said Winnie. 'It's much too gorgeous to stay indoors.'

They sat on the garden seat, facing the sun. A border of pinks nearby was beginning to break into flower, and the roses were in bud.

'You are going to have a fine show this summer,' commented Winnie.

'I know. The sad thing is that we shall miss most of it this year.'

'Not leaving Thrush Green?'

'Good heavens, no! But we only heard this morning that Jeremy and I can go with Frank to America in June.'

'The lecture tour you told me about?'

'That's right. It was all arranged, as you know, last autumn for Frank, but getting accommodation for Jeremy and me was the difficulty. Now we've heard that a publishing friend in Boston can put us up for the whole three months, if need be, or part of that time. I didn't think it right to drag Jeremy from place to place, but this arrangement will be perfect. Isn't it marvellous news?'

'It is indeed. And don't forget that I shall look forward to keeping an eye on the place for you.'

'You are kind. And Harold has offered to keep the garden in trim, so we feel that we can go with an easy conscience.'

'I hope you'll let me look after the cat too. She'll be much happier staying at Tullivers, I'm sure, and anyway she knows she is welcome next door if she feels lonely.'

'I *was* going to ask you about that,' admitted Phil. 'As a matter of fact, she virtually lives in the garden in the summer, so that she shouldn't be too much of a bother.'

Winnie rose to go.

'Now I must do some telephoning. Ella first. What a good party that was! I do hope Isobel finds a house soon. She'll be a great asset to Thrush Green, won't she?'

'Indeed she will. I heard her say that she intended to see if Williams and Frobisher have anything on their books. They're pretty reliable. What about her present house? Is it the sort that will sell easily?'

'I gather so. An ideal family house in a nice part of Sussex, and with a good train service to London. It should find plenty of buyers.'

'Well, I wish her joy of moving,' said Phil. 'It nearly killed me looking at houses and trying to sell the old one, all at the same time. It's usually so horribly *urgent*. People dying to get in before you are ready to get out, while you are waiting to see the colour of their money, and wondering if you can possibly afford all the alterations you will need in the new place. Heavens, what a terrible undertaking! I'm *never* going to move again!'

'And I'm delighted to hear it!' replied Winnie as she took her leave.

Betty Bell, Harold Shoosmith's voluble daily help, found her employer remarkably vague in manner that morning. She began to wonder if he had heard all the titbits of news which she enjoyed imparting.

'I was saying,' she repeated loudly, flicking a feather duster over Harold's treasured Coalport cottages, 'as Miss Fogerty's a different person now her friend's here. They was always close, you know, ever since they was young girls, and Mrs Fletcher don't act no different now she's rich, to what she did before.'

Harold, now listening, felt some impatience. Why must gossip fly as soon as a newcomer appeared? It had been just the same when Phil Hurst had arrived.

'Why should she?' he commented shortly.

'Well, some does, you must allow,' replied Betty, glad to have his attention at last. 'And that Mrs Fletcher did do well for herself after all. Pots of money, and a husband as worshipped her –'

'I wish you wouldn't tittle-tattle so, Betty,' snapped Harold. 'No one's safe from gossips' tongues, it seems, at Thrush Green. I can well remember what poor Mrs Hurst had to endure when she first appeared here.'

Betty Bell's mouth dropped open in surprise, but she soon rallied, flicking the duster with alarming bravado.

'If you lives in a village, as you should know by now, new people gets talked about because they're *interesting*. Why, when you first come here I heard you'd been growing cocoa from Miss Ella, and coffee from Miss Dotty, and tea from Miss Dimity. And how many wives you'd had was nobody's business.'

'Good Lord!' exclaimed Harold, reeling from the attack.

'And what you'd *done* with them all kept everyone on tenterhooks, I can tell you,' went on Betty. 'So it's no good you trying to muzzle people in a village. They *likes* guessing about other people. It's better than a story in a book, or on the telly.'

'Yes, I do understand that, Betty, but I still think it insufferable to pry into other people's affairs. Particularly unprotected people, like Mrs Fletcher who is still grieving for her husband.'

'She won't need to grieve for long,' said Betty shrewdly. 'She'll be snapped up by some man who's got eyes in his head and some sense too.'

She opened the door.

'Liver and bacon suit you? And a couple of tomatoes?'

'Lovely,' said Harold mechanically. It was funny, but his appetite seemed to have gone.

With Betty's departure to the kitchen, Harold set himself to the task of finishing the letters he had been writing before her arrival.

It was almost noon before he walked across Thrush Green to the post-box, his eyes straying towards Ella's house at the head of the hill.

He felt strangely disturbed by Betty's remarks about Isobel's probable remarriage. The damnable thing was that she was probably right in her forecast. She *was* an attractive women, there was no doubt about it. The effect that handshake had had upon him was quite extraordinary. And yet she was completely without guile and those flirtatious ways which he so much detested in older women.

No, it would be no surprise to hear one day that she was going to marry. A very good thing, of course.

He dropped his letters in the box thoughtfully.

So why did he mind so much? He had only just met the woman, and yet she filled his mind. Did she remind him of earlier loves?

He thought of Daphne, fair and calm. And Lucy, who was a flirt and had married a fighter pilot who was killed. Then that red-haired minx, whose name he couldn't remember for the life of him, and her friend, who jolly nearly proposed to him when he wasn't on his guard.

At that moment, a car hooted, and there was the beautiful Alfa Romeo emerging from Ella's gate. Isobel saw him and waved.

With his heart pounding ('Like some fool boy of sixteen,' thought Harold crossly), he hurried along the road to greet her.

She held up a sheaf of papers.

'Williams and Frobisher are doing their stuff,' she told him. 'I picked these up this morning, and John Williams is taking me to see two houses south of Lulling.'

'Well done,' said Harold happily. The sun seemed extra warm and bright, the flowers twice as fragrant, and Isobel prettier than ever.

He patted the car.

'When you've time, would you tell me how you find this particular model? I think I shall have to change my car soon, and this looks as though it would suit me very well. How does it hold the road?'

'Very well indeed. I haven't had it long, but I tell you what. Why don't you drive it yourself? I want to look at another place somewhere between Minster Lovell and Burford tomorrow afternoon, and if you are free I should love to be driven, if you like the idea?'

'Like the idea! You adorable woman!' sang Harold's heart, but he heard himself thanking her politely and saying how very much he would like to try the car, and tomorrow afternoon was absolutely free, and he was entirely at her service.

'Then shall we say two o'clock tomorrow?' said Isobel, giving him a smile which affected his heart in the most peculiar but delightful way. 'I'll hoot outside your gate.'

She waved, and drove off down the hill to Lulling, leaving Harold to cross the green on legs which had suddenly weakened.

'Here I am,' he said to himself in wonderment, 'in my sixties, a confirmed bachelor, and dammit, I'm in danger of falling in love!'

It was a disturbing thought. Another, even more disturbing, followed it.

'She'll hoot outside my gate at two o'clock! That'll make Thrush Green talk!'

He suddenly felt intensely happy, and went home, whistling.

The children at the village school were just emerging into the play-ground, after demolishing school dinner consisting of cold lamb and salad, pink blancmange and red jelly. They were, as always, in tearing high spirits and rushed about yelling happily, making such a fearful din that Miss Watson, who was on playground duty, only just heard the telephone ringing.

Agnes of course was in her new classroom across the playground, busy cutting up paper ready for her painting lesson that afternoon. The third teacher, a young probationer, would never dare to answer the telephone while her headmistress was at hand, so Miss Watson herself hurried round the side of the building to the lobby door.

Here stood a gigantic metal door-scraper which coped admirably in winter with the sticky Cotswold clay which the children brought along on their boots. In the summer, of course, it was scarcely needed, and Miss Watson had often thought that it should be taken up and stored somewhere during the fine months. It certainly constituted a hazard, and many a child had sustained a grazed knee by tripping over the thing.

On the other hand, where could it be stored? Like most old-fashioned village schools, Thrush Green's was short of outhouses and storage space in general. Such a large, rigid intractable object was impossible to store. Consequently, it remained *in situ* all the year.

In her haste, the telephone bell shrilling its urgency, poor Miss Watson caught her sensibly-shod foot against the edge of the scraper and fell sprawling into the lobby.

A few children hastened to her aid, and Miss Watson began to attempt to regain her feet and her dignity, but realized immediately that something was seriously amiss. It was going to be impossible to stand up. She began to feel faint.

'Get Miss Fogerty,' she told the children, as the playground whirled round and round amidst increasing darkness. The children fled towards the new classroom, and the young teacher appeared.

'Oh dear,' she cried. 'Here, let me help you up.'

She put strong arms about Miss Watson's shoulders and began to heave.

'No, no!' screamed poor Miss Watson. 'Don't move me, please.'

At that moment Agnes Fogerty arrived and took command, marshalling her memories of First Aid, learnt only last winter at Lulling.

'She's quite right,' she said. 'We mustn't move her. But quickly get her coat and a cushion, and then run across to Doctor Lovell.'

The girl fled, and Agnes knelt beside her headmistress.

'Poor Dorothy,' she said, all thoughts of protocol vanishing in her anxiety. 'We're getting help. We'll soon have you more comfortable.'

She took the coat and cushion from her fellow teacher, covered the prone form and tucked the cushion gently under Miss Watson's head. Her face was very pale and her eyes were closed, but she managed to smile her thanks.

Fortunately, Doctor Lovell was still at his surgery, and hurried across. Within minutes he had rung for an ambulance, put the patient into a more comfortable position, and complimented Agnes on her grasp of the situation.

'They'll have to take her to Dickie's,' he said, using the local term for St Richard's Hospital in the county town. 'They've got all the right equipment there, X-rays and so on. It's the hip joint all right. One thing, they've some marvellous chaps there to put it right.'

Miss Fogerty would have liked to have accompanied her old friend to the hospital, but she knew where her duty lay.

'I'll come and see you as soon as possible,' she promised, as the stretcher was put into the ambulance, and Miss Watson nodded wanly.

'Mind the school,' she managed to whisper, as the doors shut.

Agnes watched the ambulance until it vanished down the hill and turned back, shaken in body, but resolute in spirit, to carry out her headmistress's last command.

## 12. House-Hunting

When Nelly Piggott finally arrived at her own doorstep, she dropped her heavy case and grocery carrier and paused to take breath.

The brass door handle, she noticed, was badly tarnished, the step itself, thick with footmarks. Behind the sparse wallflowers was lodged a collection of crisp bags, ice-lolly sticks and cigarette cartons which had blown there from the public house next door, and which Albert had failed to remove.

Time I was home, thought Nelly to herself, and opened the door.

'What's going on?' growled Albert thickly. 'Who's that, eh? Get on off!'

There was the sound of a chair being shifted, and Albert still muttering, approached. Nelly swiftly heaved her luggage inside and followed it nimbly, shutting the door behind her.

Albert confronted her. His eyes and mouth were round Os of astonishment, but he soon found his voice.

'None of that, my girl! You're not comin' back here, I'm tellin' you. Clear orf! Go on, you baggage, clear orf, I say!'

He began to advance upon her, one threatening fist upraised, but Nelly took hold of his thin shoulders, and guided him swiftly backwards towards the chair. He sat down with a grunt, and was immediately overtaken by a prolonged fit of coughing.

Nelly stood over him, watching until the paroxysm spent itself.

'Yes, well, you see what happens when you lose your temper,' she said calmly. There was a hint of triumph in her voice which enraged Albert. He struggled to rise, but Nelly put him down again with one hand.

'Just you be reasonable, Albert Piggott.'

'*Reasonable*!' choked Albert. 'You walks out! You comes back! You expects me to welcome you, as though nothink 'as 'appened? You can go back to that so-and-so. Or 'as he chucked you out?'

'Certainly not,' said Nelly, putting the carrier bag on the table, and feeling for the chops. 'I came of my own accord.'

'Oh, did you? Well, you can dam' well go back of your own accord.'

Nelly changed her tactics.

'You may not like it, Albert Piggott, but you'll have to lump it. Here I am, and here I stay, at least for the night, and you can thank your stars as I've brought you some nice chops for your supper. From the look of you, you can do with a square meal.'

Albert lay back. Exhaustion kept him from answering, but the thought of a return to Nelly's cooking, however brief, was a pleasant one.

Nelly began to busy herself about the kitchen, and Albert watched her through half-closed eyes.

'And when did this place last get a scrub up?'

'Molly done it lovely,' whispered Albert, defending his family.

'And not been touched since,' said Nelly tartly, filling the kettle. 'This frying-pan wants a good going over before it's fit for use.'

She whisked about, unpacking the chops, and some tomatoes and onions. For all his fury, Albert could not help feeling some slight pleasure at the sight of her at her old familiar ploys. He roused himself.

'Seein' as you've pushed yourself in, you'd best stay the night, I suppose. But it'll have to be the spare bed. You ain't comin' in with me.'

'Don't flatter yourself,' said Nelly shortly, investigating dripping in a stone jam jar.

She scoured the pan, and then set the food into it. Once the cooking had begun to her satisfaction, she took up the heavy case and began to mount the stairs.

Albert heard her thumping about above. The fragrant smells of frying onion and chops wreathed about the kitchen, and Albert settled back in his chair with a happy sigh.

As Harold Shoosmith had foreseen, a number of interested spectators focused their attention on the Alfa Romeo at his gate on the afternoon in question. He felt more amusement than embarrassment as Isobel emerged elegantly from the driver's seat, and let him take her place.

They drove slowly along the chestnut avenue in front of the Young's house and then turned right to descend the hill. The sun was warm and the flowering cherries were beginning to break into a froth of pink in the gardens which faced south.

They headed westward through the outskirts of the town and were soon on the windy heights. On their right lay the valley of the Windrush, its meandering course marked by willow trees already showing tender leaves of greenish gold.

'Heavenly afternoon,' commented Isobel. Harold agreed. It was not only the balmy spring weather which made it heavenly for him. Isobel's presence was the main source of his contentment, but he had to admit that the smooth performance of the little car also contributed to his pleasure.

'Can we spare time to drop down to Minster Lovell?' he asked. 'If the Swan still does teas we could call on our way back, if you'd like that?'

'Very much, thank you. But I think we'll be lucky to find anywhere that provides teas these days. Isn't it sad? Tea's such a nice meal.'

'My favourite. After breakfast,' smiled Harold.

They took a turning to the right, and ran down the hill to Minster Lovell. Harold stopped the car outside the beautiful old pub, and got out to speak to a woman who was cleaning the windows.

'No, dear,' she said. 'No call for teas much. And it's getting staff as is difficult. Besides, people don't want tea these days.'

'We do,' said Harold.

'Ah well, dear, "Want must be your master", as my old gran used to say. You going near Burford? You'd get some there, no doubt. You see, there's coaches and that, pulling up there, and there's more call for teas then.'

Harold thanked her, and returned to the car.

'I think,' said Isobel dreamily, 'that is one of the loveliest villages in England. How I long to get back here! Sussex is beautiful, but it's here I belong.'

'Then we'd better push on to see this house,' said Harold practically, letting in the clutch.

It was not easy to find. The little blue car nosed its way through narrow lanes, between steep banks starred with late primroses and early stitchwort. They passed sign posts to Burford, to Astall Leigh, to Swinbrook, to Witney, and were beginning to wonder if the house really existed when they saw the 'For Sale' sign.

The house was built on the side of a hill, and a steep path went from the lane to the front door. It was a substantial dwelling of honey-gold Cotswold stone, and a scarlet japonica covered the side wall.

'Would you like to come in?' asked Isobel.

'I won't, many thanks,' said Harold. 'It's easier for you to ask questions, and take in what the owners tell you, if you are on your own. I'll wait a little farther down the road, where it is wider.'

'Fine,' said Isobel, collecting her bag and papers. Obviously she was expected, for at that moment the front door opened, and a woman peered out.

Harold watched the two meet, and then drove to the arranged parking place. Here he got out, leant upon a conveniently sited five-barred gate, and surveyed the pleasant scene spread out below him.

He could well understand Isobel's longing to return. His own affection for the area grew with every year that passed. He had never regretted, for one instant, his decision to settle at Thrush Green. He had made many new friends, not an easy thing to accomplish when one was a middle-aged newcomer to a small community, and the countryside was a constant delight.

His own domestic arrangements were also satisfying, although of late he had begun to wonder if the years ahead would prove lonely. He had never regretted his bachelor state. After all, it was of his own choosing, and very contented he had been with it. But observing the happiness of the rector, Charles Henstock, in his second marriage, had given Harold cause for thought.

Not that one should contemplate matrimony solely for the betterment of one's lot. Such selfishness would be a sure way to disaster. A true marriage, to Harold's mind, should be a joyous partnership, and if it were not to be so then it were better to remain single.

He had a healthy distrust of strong emotions, and viewed his own present disturbance with mingled amusement, pleasure and caution. But he recognized a deeper feeling towards Isobel which he felt that time would confirm. He hoped that she would soon be living nearby, and that time would prove him right as he grew to know her.

He walked down the lane between the hawthorn hedges shining with new leaf. The sun was warm, some lambs gambolled in the water meadow below, and a thrush sang as it bounced on a flowering spray of blackthorn above him.

When he returned, Isobel was waiting in the car.

'Any luck?' he asked, as he climbed into the driver's seat.

Isobel shook her head.

'Too much needs to be done. It would cost a fortune. And it's dark, and faces north-east. A pity, because the rooms were nice, and my stuff would have looked well there.

Harold patted her hand.

'Never mind, there'll be others.'

'But I haven't much time. Only two more days. I think I must try and come again later on, when I've sorted things out at home.'

'Must you go this week?'

'I'm afraid so. There are various bits of business to attend to in the next two or three weeks, and I certainly hope to have a few offers for my house to consider.'

Harold nodded. At least it was some comfort to know that she planned to return in the near future.

'Will you stay with Ella again?'

'No, I think not. It's not really fair to her. There's the Fleece, though I'm not keen on staying at hotels. The evenings drag so. But don't let's bother about all that now. Who knows what the next two days may bring? And anyway, what about that cup of tea?'

'Burford may be crowded. What about having tea with me? I can offer you Earl Grey, or Lapsang Souchong, or plain Indian.'

'The last will suit me beautifully,' replied Isobel, with a smile which turned Harold's heart somersaulting.

'Thrush Green it is then,' he replied, letting in the clutch. And the conversation on their homeward way consisted exclusively of the merits, or otherwise, of the Alfa Romeo.


Dotty Harmer, with Flossie in tow, had just delivered the goat's milk to Ella, when they both noticed Isobel's car outside Harold's gate.

'They must be back,' said Ella, stating the obvious. 'I wonder if she's had any luck today?'

'But why is she at Harold's?'

'Search me,' said Ella carelessly. 'Popped in to borrow a map or a book, I daresay. She may be staying with me for a week, Dotty dear, but that doesn't mean she's not free to visit whenever and whoever she pleases.'

Dotty ruminated, her hand stroking Flossie's satin head.

'But why *Harold*?'

'He was trying out her car, that's why. And now, Dotty, to business. I've been paying you five peas for years now. I'm sure the milk should be more. That hogwash from the dairy – so-called – has gone up about six times since we fixed things. What about eight peas?'

'Is that more than a shilling?'

'Lord, yes! More like one and six.'

'Then I refuse to take it. One shilling is ample, Ella. I really wish this pea business had never started. There are so many things I find that muddle me today. Metres and litres and grammes. So bewildering. And what's all this voluntary aided tax I keep finding on my bills?'

'*Taxes*,' replied Ella severely, 'are neither voluntary nor aided, as you should well know! V A T stands for *value added tax*.'

Dotty considered the information, her eyes fixed unseeingly on the distant Alfa Romeo.

'If anything,' she remarked at last, 'it sounds sillier.'

Ella rummaged in her purse and handed Dotty a silver fivepenny piece.

'It's not enough, Dotty, but if that's how you want it –'

'It is indeed. I put all the goat's milk money is a special tobacco tin, and it's surprising how it mounts up. I bought a large bag of dog biscuits with it last time, for dear old Floss.'

'Well, she looks pretty fit on it,' agreed Ella, opening the gate for her departing friend.

Dotty hurried away across the green, her stockings in wrinkles as usual and the hem of her petticoat showing a good two inches below her skirt.

Ella watched her go with affection, and turned to carry in the milk. Her eye was caught by Isobel's car again.

'Quite old enough to know what she's doing,' thought Ella, 'and anyway, none of my business.'

Not all the Thrush Green residents were as tolerant.

Bob Jones, landlord of The Two Pheasants, noticed that the dashing blue car was over an hour outside Harold's house, and to his mind, 'it looked bad'. What if Mr Shoosmith and Mrs Fletcher were both middle-aged? Also, they were both unattached, and it was indiscreet, to say the least, to lay themselves open to comment.

Winnie Bailey's faithful maid Jenny also noticed the car and, although she said nothing, she pursed her mouth primly as she set about some ironing in her top flat. Winnie herself was incapable of distinguishing Isobel's car from the milkman's delivery van, and so remained unperturbed by the private tea party.

Albert Piggott was probably the most censorious, but since Nelly's return he was in such a state of turmoil, and his indigestion seemed so much worse, now that he was tempted by Nelly's rich food, that it was not surprising.

'No better than she should be,' he told Nelly. 'I could see she be a proper flighty one as soon as I set eyes on that flashy car of hers.'

'Well, I don't know the lady,' said Nelly roundly, 'but I knows Thrush Green and the tongues as wags round it. I'll bet my bottom dollar she's as innocent as I am.'

'As you are!' echoed Albert derisively. 'Some innocent! And talking of that, when are you gettin' back to that Charlie you're so fond of?'

Nelly folded a tea towel with care.

'See here, Albert. Let's jog on a bit longer, shall we? I've said I'm sorry for that last little upset and you know you needs a woman in this place. What about me stoppin' on and gettin' my old job back? I thought I might call on Miss Watson this evening.'

Albert snorted.

'Then you'll have a long way to go, my gal. She's in Dickie's with a broken leg or summat. It'll be Miss Fogerty in charge now, and for all I knows Betty Bell's doin' the cleanin', and makin' a good job of it too.'

Nelly did her best to look unconcerned at this unwelcome piece of news.

'No harm in asking anyway,' she said, tossing her head. 'Maybe Miss Fogerty'd prefer me to Betty Bell. I always done my best at the school before, and Miss Watson told me so. "Never seen it so clean," was her very words.'

'Go your own way,' growled Albert. 'You will anyway, but don't come grizzling to me when you find there ain't no job there for you, my gal.'

He hobbled to the door, took down his greasy cap from the peg, and began his journey across to the church.

The Alfa Romeo gleamed in the afternoon sunshine, and Albert saw Isobel emerge from Harold's front door closely followed by her host. They both looked extremely happy.

'The baggage!' muttered Albert.

He picked up a clod of earth from the church porch.

'Women!' he added viciously.

He threw the clod spitefully towards an adjacent tomb stone, and was mollified to see that it bespattered one 'Alice, Dutiful Wife and Mother, An Example of Pious Womanhood'.

'Women!' repeated Albert, opening the church door. 'All the same! Dead or living. All the same!'

## 13. Miss Fogerty Carries On

Miss Fogerty rang the hospital in the early evening expecting to hear that her headmistress was either 'comfortable', which no one could be in Miss Watson's condition, or 'as well as could be expected', which was one of those ominous expressions guaranteed to set one choosing hymns for the funeral.

But to her surprise a remarkably kind sister answered the telephone and assured Miss Fogerty that the patient had stood the operation well, and that, although she had not yet come round, she would be certain to enjoy a visit the next evening.

'Can you tell me,' asked Miss Fogerty diffidently, 'I mean, are you *allowed* to tell me, exactly what was wrong?'

One did not wish such a nice woman to break the oath of Hippocrates, if, of course, she had ever had to take one, but one really must know more.

'A dislocated hip joint, with some damage,' said the sister. 'These days it's quite simple to pop it back.'

She made it sound as easy as returning a cork to a bottle top, but Miss Fogerty shuddered sympathetically in the telephone box.

'Thank you for telling me,' she said sincerely. 'Please give her my love. Just say "Agnes rang". And I will call tomorrow evening.'

While she was there, she telephoned to Miss Watson's brother and left a message with his wife. She seemed an emotional woman, and her voice came wailing down the line.

'Oh dear, what a catastrophe! What will Ray say? I'll tell him the minute he gets in. He's so devoted to Dorothy. I expect he'll want her to come here as soon as she's out of hospital, and I really can't see –'

The wailing died away.

'That's looking rather far ahead,' said little Miss Fogerty. 'But let me give you the hospital's number, and then you can keep in touch.'

That done, she rang off, and went across to the schoolhouse to make sure that all was locked up safely.

It did not look as though poor Dorothy would have her convalescence with her brother.

'And probably all for the best,' thought Miss Fogerty. 'She'll be better off in her own home.'


Ella Bembridge said goodbye to Isobel after breakfast one sunny morning.

She watched the little blue car descend the hill, gave one last wave, and turned back to the empty house.

'I'm going to miss her,' thought Ella, fumbling for the tobacco tin which housed the materials for making cigarettes.

She sat on the window seat and surveyed the view across Thrush Green, as she rolled herself a cigarette.

The house was very quiet. A frond of young honeysuckle tapped against the window, moved rhythmically by the light breeze. Ella drew in a satisfying lungful of tobacco smoke, and exhaled luxuriously.

'Quiet, but nice,' she said aloud. 'After all, it's what I'm used to. Nothing like a bit of solitude now and again.'

The sound of a door shutting made her swivel round. Dimity was coming across from the rectory, and Ella stumped to the front door to welcome her.

'Don't say she's gone!' exclaimed Dimity, surveying the empty drive. 'I thought Isobel said "after lunch".'

'After *breakfast*,' replied Ella.

'What a pity! I'd brought her a pot of my bramble jelly.'

'Well, ten chances to one she'll be back again in a few weeks.'

'Staying here?'

'I'd like her to, but from one or two things she said, I think she'll put up at the Fleece. Seems to think it's *imposing* on me, or some such nonsense.'

'She's a very considerate person,' said Dimity. 'We're going to miss her.'

Betty Bell echoed these sentiments as she attacked Harold's kitchen sink.

'I see Mrs Fletcher's gone home. Miss Fogerty will miss her, though no doubt she's got enough to do with that school on her hands. Pretty woman, isn't she?'

'Who?' asked Harold, purposely obtuse.

'Why, Mrs Fletcher! Mind you, it's partly her clothes. Always dressed nice, she did. That's what money does, of course. It's nice for her to have a bit put by, even if she does marry again.'

Harold snorted, and made for the door. This everlasting tittle-tattle was too irritating to bear. As he gained the peace of his hall, he saw the rector at the door, and gladly invited him in.

'I've just come from Ella's,' said Charles, 'and she's given me Isobel's address. She thought you might want it.'

Harold was taken aback.

'Isobel's address?'

'In case you heard of a house, I think Ella said. I know she's got the estate agent working here, but really bush telegraph sometimes works so much more swiftly, and who knows? You *may* hear of something.'

'Of course, of course,' replied Harold, collecting himself. 'Ella will miss her, I expect.'

'A truly *womanly* woman,' commented the rector. 'Who was it said: "I like a manly man, and a womanly woman, but I can't bear a boily boy"?'

'No idea,' said Harold. 'Have a drink?'

'No, no, my dear fellow. I have a confirmation class this evening, and must go and prepare a few notes. And there's poor Jacob Bly's funeral at two, and Dimity wants me to help sort out the boots and shoes for the jumble sale.'

Harold was instantly reminded of another parson, James Woodforde, who had written in his diary, two hundred years earlier, of just such an incongruous collection of activities in one day. The duties of a parson, it seemed, embraced many interests as well as the care of the living and the dead, no matter in which century he lived.

'Then I won't keep you,' said Harold. 'Thank you for the address, and if I hear of anything I shall get in touch with Isobel, of course, although I think that the chances are slight.'

Little did he realize that he would be invited to write to the address in his hand, within a few days.

Agnes Fogerty was indeed too busy to miss dear Isobel as sorely as she might have done.

She was now Acting Headmistress, a role which filled her with more misgiving than pride.

Apart from the day to day responsibilties, there was a profusion of forms from the office which had to be completed and returned, 'without delay' as the headings stated with severity. Agnes, conscious of her duties, spent many an evening struggling with them in her bed-sitting room.

Then there was the supply teacher sent by the office to help during Miss Watson's absence.

Miss Fogerty found her unnerving, and her discipline non-existent. It worried Agnes to see the children talking when they should have been working. She disliked the way Miss Enderby's charges wandered freely about the classroom, in theory collecting their next piece of work, in practice giving a sly clout to anyone in their path. Either Miss Enderby did not see what was going on, which was reprehensible, or she *did* see and condoned it, which was worse. Eventually, Agnes spoke of the matter and had great chunks of some dreadful report or other quoted to her. To Agnes, the report seemed quite irrelevant to the matter in hand, but Miss Enderby seemed to cling so fiercely to the findings of whatever-committee-it-was responsible for this half-inch thick treatise that Agnes decided to retire temporarily from the field of battle. No doubt there would be other occasions when a word of advice could be offered.

There were. There were many occasions, and brave little Miss Fogerty did her best to put things politely but firmly. She found Miss Enderby's attitude quite mystifying. Throughout her teaching career, Miss Fogerty had worked on the principle that children did as they were told. One did not ask them to do anything *impossible*, of course, or *wrong*, or *beyond their powers*. But open defiance, or the complete ignoring of orders given, had never been countenanced in Agnes's classroom, and all had gone on swimmingly.

What was the good, Agnes asked herself, in reading all those papers and reports with terrible titles like: 'The Disruptive Child and Its Place In Society' or 'Where Have Teachers Gone Wrong?' if at the end of it one still could not *teach*? It was quite apparent that the class now under Miss Enderby's care (one could not say 'control') had learned practically nothing since her advent. That it was dear Miss Watson's class made it even worse.

Miss Enderby, it was clear, was a theorist, but one quite incapable of putting theories into practice. The children would not allow it. They were having a field day enjoying themselves without stricture. In a rare flash of insight, Agnes Fogerty saw that her unsatisfactory supply teacher clung to the theories which she so avidly imbibed, and quoted, because they were all that she had to get her through each day's teaching.

Agnes prayed nightly for her headmistress's return to health and Thrush Green School. She was to come home from the hospital after a fortnight, and Agnes had offered, very diffidently, to stay at the schoolhouse if it would help.

'It is more than kind of you, Agnes dear,' Dorothy had said, 'but I expect Ray will want me to convalesce with them. I shall see him one evening this week.'

Agnes had murmured something non-committal, and repeated her willingness to help in any way, but Dorothy seemed to be quite sure that she would be looked after by her brother and his wife.

'I wonder,' thought Agnes, hurrying through driving rain to the bus stop. 'Poor dear Dorothy! I wonder!'


Robert Bassett made slow but steady progress after his second attack, but it was quite apparent that his confidence was shaken.

'He's suddenly become an old man,' said Joan sadly. 'I hate to see it. He doesn't look ahead as he always did. All the *spunk* seems to have gone out of the poor old boy.'

She was talking to her brother-in-law, John Lovell, after one of his visits to the patient.

'It's nature's way of making him rest. You'll see, he'll pick up before long. Meanwhile, there's one good thing to emerge from this setback.'

'And what's that?'

'He's quite given up the idea of going back to the business, and that's as it should be. In a way, I think he's glad that this blow has settled things for him. He's now coming to terms with the idea.'

'He said as much to mother, I know, but he hasn't said anything very definite to us. I believe he worries in case we feel that he wants his own house back!'

'If I were you,' said John, 'I should broach the subject yourselves. Tell him Edward's plans for the conversion, and let him toy with the idea. I believe it will do him good to have something to look forward to and to occupy his mind.'

After this conversation, Joan and Edward took John's advice, and spoke frankly about their plans to the parents. Milly had known what was afoot for some days, but to Robert it came as a complete surprise.

To the Youngs' delight, he seemed excited and pleased at the ideas put forward, and studied Edward's rough sketches with enthusiasm.

'Leave them with me, dear boy,' he said. 'Milly and I will have a proper look at them, and we may even make one or two suggestions. I can see that you two have been hatching up this little plot for some time, and I am really very touched.'

He smiled a little tremulously, and Joan rose swiftly to put him at his ease.

'I'm off to find us something to eat. Come and give me a hand, Edward,' she said, making for the door.

'Bless his old heart,' said Edward, when they reached the kitchen. 'He's as pleased as Punch! How I like satisfied clients!'

'Don't speak too soon,' warned Joan, busy at the stove. 'He may not be satisfied. Besides, he's every right to turn us out, you know.'

'He won't,' said Edward, dropping a basket of bread rolls on the floor, and bending to retrieve them. 'He's the most unselfish soul alive.'

He picked up the rolls, dusted each down the side of his trousers, and put them carefully in the basket again.

Her husband, thought Joan, might be a talented architect, but his grasp of culinary hygiene was nil.


In the Piggott's household an uneasy truce was being carried on.

Nelly was content to live from day to day, gradually cleaning the cottage until it satisfied her own high standards, and cooking succulent meals which Albert secretly enjoyed. Wild horses would not have dragged thanks from him, under the circumstances, and the frequent bouts of indigestion which attacked him kept him as morose as usual.

There was no doubt about it, thought Nelly, as she attacked the filthy cooker one afternoon with plenty of hot soda water, Albert did not improve with age. As soon as she could get a job, she would be off again. But jobs, it seemed, were hard to find.

She had called on her old friends at The Drover's Arms, but they were already well-staffed, and in any case, were not inclined to do anything to upset Albert. She had come back of her own accord, they felt, and it was up to her to do what she could to look after the old man, curmudgeonly though he might be. Work at The Drovers' Arms meant that Nelly would be away from home for a considerable part of the day.

Undeterred by the news that Betty Bell now cleaned the school, Nelly called one evening at Miss Fogerty's lodgings.

Mrs White, Miss Fogerty's landlady, opened the door, and was somewhat taken aback by the flamboyant figure on the doorstep. She knew quite well who the visitor was, but as she strongly disapproved of Nelly, and her morals, she feigned ignorance.

'Someone to see you, Miss Fogerty,' she called up the stairs. 'If you would like to go up?' she said to Nelly, standing back against the flowery wallpaper.

Miss Fogerty looked even more alarmed than her landlady had been at first sight of Nelly puffing up the stairs. She showed her into her bed-sitting room, and closed the door.

Nelly, seating herself in the only comfortable armchair, looked about her. She noticed the faded carpet, the thin curtains, and the bedspread which was not quite large enough to cover the divan bed. But she noticed too, in that first swift glance, that everything was clean – beautifully clean.

The furniture was well polished, the shabby paintwork and the mottled tiles of the hearth were spotless. Miss Fogerty's small array of toilet things stood in a tidy row on a glass shelf over the corner wash-basin. Her books stood neatly, row by row in the bedside bookcase. Only a pile of exercise books, in the process of being marked, gave any clue to the present activity in Miss Fogerty's modest abode.

On the mantel shelf stood two shining brass candlesticks, one at each end. A china cat stood by one, and a china spaniel by the other. A small travelling clock stood dead centre, and on each side stood a photograph.

One showed Miss Fogerty's shoemaker father looking stern. His right hand rested on the shoulder of his wife, sitting on an ornately carved chair in front of him. Agnes's mother looked meek and submissive. Her hair was parted in the middle. Her eyes were downcast. Her hands were folded in the centre of her lap. A fine aspidistra at the side of the couple seemed to display far more vitality than the photographer's sitters.

But it was the second photograph which engaged Nelly's attention. It was framed in silver, and showed the likeness of a fair young man in army uniform. He was smiling, showing excellent teeth, and he wore his hair *en brosse*. Could he be a sweetheart, Nelly wondered? Could colourless, shabby little Miss Fogerty ever have inspired love in someone so obviously lively? You never knew, of course. Still waters ran deep ... She looked from the photograph to her reluctant hostess, who was now seated in an uncomfortable chair which she had turned round from the dressing table.

'I expect you are wondering why I've come,' began Nelly, removing her scarf.

'Naturally,' replied Miss Fogerty with truth, and just a touch of hauteur. She disliked Nelly, and had never been happy about her appointment as cleaner at the school. She accepted the fact that Nelly was excellent at her job, but she thought her a vulgar creature and not a suitable person to be among young children. She had deplored the fact that it was Miss Watson who had taken on Nelly, and could only put it down to her headmistress's kind heart, and the paucity of applicants for the post at that time.

'Well, I was hoping that my old job might be going still. Always enjoyed it, I did, and I know Miss Watson was satisfied. Pity she's away. Is she going on all right?'

'Yes, thank you,' said Agnes shortly. She did not propose to discuss dear Dorothy's condition with this woman. 'And the post is already filled, Mrs Piggott. Betty Bell is with us now, so that I'm afraid I can't help you.'

'She suit you all right? That Betty Bell?'

'Perfectly,' said Agnes firmly. She rose to indicate that the meeting was ended, but Nelly remained firmly wedged in the armchair.

'I hear she works at Mr Shoosmith's too,' she remarked. 'I wonder she finds time to do two jobs. *Properly*, that is!'

The implications of this snide observation were not lost upon Agnes. Really, the woman was insufferable, and there were all those essays waiting to be marked, and her hair to wash, and the hem of her skirt to be repaired where she had caught it as she had tidied the bottom of the handwork cupboard. What a nuisance Nelly Piggott was, to be sure!

'She is a very hard-working girl,' said Miss Fogerty sharply, 'and manages her various jobs excellently. Not only does she go to Mr Shoosmith, I think you'll find she helps Miss Harmer as well, and we are all quite satisfied with her work.'

Agnes remained standing, and Nelly, facing defeat, struggled from the armchair.

'Wouldn't take much to satisfy Miss Harmer from what I hear,' said Nelly, 'but there it is. If there's nothing I can do at the school, I'll have to look elsewhere.'

She began to arrange the scarf around her fourth chin.

'Don't know of anyone, I suppose, as needs help?'

'I'm afraid not,' replied Agnes, a trifle less frostily now that she saw her visitor departing. She opened the door to the landing and ushered Nelly through it.

'Well, if you do hear of anything you know where I live,' said Nelly, descending the stairs heavily.

'I will bear it in mind,' promised Agnes, now opening the front door.

'Ta ever so, dearie,' said Nelly, sailing down the path.

Shuddering, Miss Fogerty returned to her interrupted peace.

## 14. Comings and Goings

It was Charles Henstock who first told Harold Shoosmith that Phil was accompanying Frank on his trip to the United States.

'I knew Frank was off, and said I'd keep an eye on the garden for him, but I didn't realize that Phil could go too. Do them both good to have a change, and Jeremy will enjoy being off school.'

'They come back early in September, so the boy won't miss much,' replied Charles. 'It will be strange to see Tullivers empty.'

'Empty!' echoed Harold, a splendid idea burgeoning. He decided to visit Frank and Phil Hurst that very evening, and found them in the garden when he did so.

June had come in with what the Irish call 'soft weather'. Skies were overcast, but the air was mild and the wind gentle. Frank's roses were beginning to make a fine show, and both he and Phil were hoeing round the bushes.

They put down their tools to greet Harold.

'Don't let me stop you,' he said.

'Thank God you've come, and given us an excuse to have a break,' replied Frank feelingly. 'I'll get drinks.'

He vanished into the house, and Harold and Phil seated themselves on the grass. A robin, matchstick legs askew, watched them with his head on one side.

'I suppose you realize that you are doing that poor chap out of his worm supper, now that you've stopped hoeing?'

'He's had enough already,' said Phil. 'It's a wonder he doesn't pop.'

Frank arrived with the drinks.

'Heard that Phil and Jeremy are coming with me?' asked Frank, smiling.

'I have indeed. Wonderful news. Charles told me.'

'So we'll be even more glad than before to know you are keeping an eye on things,' said Frank. 'I don't like leaving the place empty, but there it is. Luckily, we've got good neighbours, like you and Winnie to look out for any baddies around.'

Harold put down his drink carefully.

'It's that really which brings me over this evening.'

'How do you mean? Are you going away too?'

'No. I shall be here. I just wondered if you would consider Isobel Fletcher having the house for part of the time. She intends to come back towards the end of June, I gather, unless she's fixed up beforehand.'

'Sounds splendid,' said Phil enthusiastically. 'But would she want to be bothered?'

'Frankly, I've no idea,' confessed Harold. 'It was just a thought. I know she doesn't want to impose on Ella any further, and doesn't particularly relish staying at an hotel. Anyway, perhaps it's cheek of me to suggest it.'

'Not at all,' said Frank heartily. 'I should feel much happier if someone were staying in the place, and I can't think of anyone more suitable. Shall we let you know definitely tomorrow? Then you can get in touch with Isobel, or we will, if you'd rather we did.'

'That's fine,' agreed Harold. He picked up his glass with a satisfied sigh. 'Of course, she may have found something already, but I doubt it. It would be marvellous to have her here, right on the spot.'

Phil looked at his blissful expression with sudden awareness.

'So convenient for the house-hunting,' explained Harold hastily, 'and I'm sure she would be a most careful tenant while you are away.'

'It was a very good idea of yours,' said Frank, 'and now come and have a look at the jasmine you gave us. It's nearly reached the roof.'

Phil collected the glasses and carried them indoors.

'So that's how the land lies,' she said to herself. 'Now who would have thought it?'


Later that evening, when Jeremy was safely asleep upstairs, Phil told Frank about her suspicions. Predictably, he was scornful.

'Old Harold? And Isobel? Rubbish, my dear, you're imagining things! Why, I've known Harold for donkey's years, and he's always been the happiest of confirmed bachelors. He's not likely to change now. Why should he?'

'I don't suppose there's any particular *reason* why he should want to give up his bachelordom, but I'm sure I'm right about this. After all, you were getting on perfectly well on your own when we first met, but you embarked upon matrimony without a qualm.'

'That's different. You are a most attractive woman.'

'So is Isobel. I can quite understand Harold's change of heart.'

'You're incurably romantic, my darling. It comes of writing for all those women's magazines, I expect. So you are all in favour of enticing Isobel here to further the course of true love?'

'I am indeed. To be honest, that's only the secondary consideration. I'd like someone to be in the house basically.'

'And you've no scruples about leaving defenceless Isobel to Harold's amorous bombardment?'

It was Phil's turn to snort.

'I should think Harold's ardour has subsided to manageable levels in his sixties. And Isobel must have had plenty of experience in warding off unwanted suitors in her time.'

'So you think Harold will be unwanted? Poor old Harold!'

Phil reflected.

'I can't speak for Isobel, of course. She may not want to marry again. She has no family to consider now, and she has lots of friends and a comfortable income. She may well turn down any offer from Harold. That's the pity. I'm afraid he would be very upset.'

'I expect he's taken harder knocks than that in his time,' commented Frank.

'Maybe,' agreed his wife, 'but you know what Jane Austen said?' "It is always incomprehensible to a man that a woman should ever refuse an offer of marriage."'

Frank laughed.

'I'll let you, or rather, Jane Austen, have the last word. One thing I've learnt in life is that a man is no match for a woman in affairs of this sort. So, we invite Isobel?'

'We invite Isobel,' agreed Phil.

The sun was slowly dispersing the clouds as Frank walked across to Harold's the next morning.

The chestnut avenue was now in full leaf, and the white and pink candles were in flower. Outside the Two Pheasants Bob Jones's hanging baskets made a brave show, the geraniums quite untouched by those frosts which Albert Piggott had forecast earlier.

A yellow Mermaid rose was in full bloom on the sunny side of Harold's house, and the borders on each side of his path glowed with violas, pinks and double daisies. It all looked remarkably spruce, thought Frank. Surely, Harold could want no more than this for happiness? He had made a perfect life for himself in the place of his choice. Was it likely that he would embark on the complications of married life?

He had no need to knock at the door, for Betty Bell, with Brasso and duster in hand, burst out as he approached.

'Lor!' she said, clutching the Brasso to her heart. 'You fair frit me, you did!'

'Sorry, Mrs Bell,' said Frank. 'Is Mr Shoosmith in?'

'Down the garden, by the bonfire. Shall I give him a holler for you?'

'No, no. I'll go and see him.'

Sure enough, Harold was tending a small bonfire, whose smoke was drifting in the leisurely breeze towards Lulling Woods. Looking at him, with his wife's surmises in mind, Frank had to admit that Harold was wearing very well, and was still remarkably good-looking.

And tidy too, thought Frank, a little enviously. Harold always looked immaculate, even when tackling a messy job, as he was doing now. He himself, Frank knew, would be crumpled and smeared with smuts, his hands black, and his gardening clothes deplorable. Phil despaired of him at times. She had often told him so.

Harold turned to replenish his fire and saw his old friend.

'Hallo, there! What's the news?'

'Unanimous approval of your bright idea! Will you get in touch with Isobel? Or shall we?'

Harold looked a trifle discomfited.

'I think you should deal with her directly, Frank. By all means say I thought of it, if you like, but I'm sure it's best to have a word with her yourselves.'

'Very well. I'll write today, and perhaps she can ring me when she's studied the suggestion, and we can fix up things then.'

'Fine, fine!' replied Harold. He looked as though he might say more, thought better of it, and changed the subject.

'And when do you fly? Do you want a lift to the airport? I'm a free man, you know, and only too pleased to take you.'

'In just over a fortnight, and it would be marvellous if you can take us to Heathrow. You're sure about this?'

'Positive – or nearly so. Come inside, and we'll have a look at the diary.

In any case, it will only be one or other of these dam' committees I seem to have dropped into. I shouldn't be missed.'

Betty Bell was busy setting out cups upon a tray as they went through the kitchen.

'I'm getting you two gents a nice cup of coffee,' she said. 'Here, or in the study?'

'In the study, Betty,' said Harold hastily. 'We've something to look up.'

When alone, Harold usually took his elevenses with Betty, allowing her incessant chatter to flow over him. Today he felt that it would not be fair to inflict all the local gossip on his old friend.

'Okey-doke,' said Betty, to their retreating backs.

The diary for the week in question read: Monday, Vestry meeting 7.0. Wednesday, Dentist 10.30. Scouts' Concert 7.30. Thursday, Remember B and B, Friday and Saturday were clear.

'I wonder what "Remember B and B" means?' pondered Harold.

'What's B and B? Bed and Breakfast?'

'Hardly,' said Harold, his brow puckering with concentration.

'Betty and Someone Else beginning with B?' hazarded Frank.

Harold shook his head.

'If you were Irish,' went on Frank conversationally, 'I should suggest "Remember the Battle of the Boyne", but I suppose that's no help?'

'None,' said Harold. 'However, to get back to our muttons. You said Friday, June 23rd, I believe? Well, that's completely free, so count on me as a willing taxi-man.'

At that moment, Betty came in, bearing the tray with two steaming cups and a plate with gingernuts on it.

'Ah, Betty!' cried Harold. 'Put it here, my dear, and tell me something. Why have I got to remember "B and B" on June 22nd?'

'Coffee morning at the rectory,' said Betty promptly. 'Bring and Buy stall. You promised something to Mr Henstock when he came last week.'

Harold smiled his relief.

'I don't know what I'd do without you,' he told her, as she turned towards the door. 'Every home should have a Betty Bell.'

'Or a wife,' commented Frank. But Harold made no response, except to pass the coffee cup.


A day or two after this meeting, little Miss Fogerty paid another visit to the hospital.

Miss Watson was propped up on a bank of snowy pillows, surrounded by flowers and 'Get Well' cards. She was wearing a pale pink bed jacket, knitted by Agnes as a Christmas present a year or two earlier, that lady was pleased to see. That feather-and-shell pattern had been remarkably difficult to master, she remembered, but it certainly looked most attractive.

'It's so light and warm, Agnes dear,' said Dorothy, stroking the garment. 'And much admired by the nurses.'

Miss Fogerty grew pink with pleasure.

'I'm so glad. But, tell me, how are you getting on? And when will you be able to come home?'

'I *could* come out on Sunday next, but I think I shall stay a few days longer.'

She began to pleat the top of the sheet, and looked very near to tears, Agnes was horrified to see.

'You see, Ray came yesterday. Poor Kathleen was in bed with one of her migraine attacks.'

And very convenient those migraine attacks could be, thought Agnes tartly.

'So that she couldn't come, of course,' went on Dorothy. 'And it seems that they had arranged a holiday for the next two weeks, so that they can't have me there.'

'Come home,' urged Agnes. 'You know that I can help, and the district nurse would call daily. I'm sure we could manage.'

Miss Watson sniffed, and then blew her nose energetically.

'I do hope I'm not getting a cold,' she said, muffled in the handkerchief. Miss Fogerty was not deceived.

'You are the kindest soul on earth,' said Dorothy, recovering her composure. 'I've done quite a lot of thinking since Ray came, and if I stay here for another few days, gaining strength, I think I really will be able to manage at home. Perhaps someone could slip in at midday and get me a light lunch?'

Agnes thought at once of Nelly Piggott, but decided not to mention her just yet.

'If you would let me stay at the schoolhouse,' said Agnes diffidently, 'I could be with you at night, and bring you breakfast before going over to the school.'

'Oh, Agnes dear,' cried Miss Watson, the tears returning and now rolling down her cheeks unchecked. 'Oh, Agnes dear, *could* you? Would you mind? There's nothing I should like more.'

'I should love it,' said Agnes truthfully. 'We'll have a word with Sister and arrange a day next week.'

'And get the taxi from Lulling,' said Dorothy, already becoming more like her efficient, headmistress self. 'And we'll go back together. What a wonderful day it will be!'

She sighed happily, and wiped away the tears without subterfuge.

'It's only the relief, Agnes dear, and being so wobbly, you know. I can't begin to tell you how grateful I am to you, my dear. It's at times like this that one realizes who one's true friends are.'

'Then that's settled,' said Agnes, 'and as soon as the doctor says you may leave, we'll go back to Thrush Green.'

'I can't wait! And now, Agnes dear, tell me how it's all going at school? Are the children behaving well? Is that wash-basin mended yet? Have those Cooke boys really got the mumps? Are there many forms from the office? How's the supply teacher managing? And has the piano-tuner been this term?'

Miss Fogerty was still answering questions when the nurse arrived to take Miss Watson's temperature.

'It's up a bit,' she commented as she shook the thermometer.

'I'm not surprised,' said her patient. 'It's excitement, of the nicest kind, that's done it.'


## 15. Early Summer

The quiet mild weather which had ushered in June, now turned to a spell of gloriously hot sunshine.

Miss Fogerty looked out her sensible cotton frocks and Clark's sandals. Dotty Harmer spread sacks over the chicken run to provide her charges with extra shade. The rector took his lightweight clerical grey from the wardrobe, and Dimity hung it on the line to remove the faint smell of moth-balls. Winnie Bailey and Jenny erected the swing seat, and agreed that although the cretonne was shabby it 'would do another year'.

And, across the green, Nelly Piggott embarked on a mammoth washing spree, hauling down curtains, whisking off blankets and bedspreads, and even snatching up rugs from the floor to thrust into the soap suds.

Albert loathed it all, but recognizing an irresistible force when he met it, resigned himself to the tornado of energy which whirled about him, and took advantage of the sunshine to do a little light tidying of the churchyard. Here, at least, there was peace.

He was engaged in picking a few weeds from the top of the stub wall which surrounded the graveyard when Dotty Harmer stopped to speak to him.

She was an arresting sight at the best of times, but today's summer outfit appeared to consist of a straight low-waisted frock, style circa 1920, made, it seemed, of deck-chair material, and ending just above the knees. A conical straw hat, like a coolie's, surmounted her thatch of grey hair, and lisle stockings, heavily wrinkled, led the eye down to a pair of grass-stained tennis shoes. She was accompanied by the faithful Flossie, now the picture of canine good health.

'I heard,' said Dotty, coming straight to the point, 'that your wife is looking for work. I wonder if she has heard that the Miss Lovelocks need temporary help?'

'Well, no, miss,' said Albert. He took off his greasy cap and scratched his lank hair. 'She ain't said nothin'. Maybe you'd like to tell her? She be washin'.'

'I can't stop now, I'm afraid. I have to meet the bus, at the bottom of the hill, but perhaps you would pass on the message?'

'Very well, miss,' said Albert, unusually respectful. She might look a proper clown, but she was a lady for all that. Got a touch of her old Dad about her, that made you mind your manners, he thought.

He watched her figure receding into the distance, and turned back to the wall again. Yes, he'd tell Nelly when he went into dinner. Nice bit of cold fat bacon he had seen in the larder. A slice or two of that with pickled onions was something to relish, whatever the doctor said. It was a comforting thought.

The sun warmed his back as he pottered about his leisurely activities. He dwelt, with pleasure, upon the possibility of Nelly bringing in more money to the household. But best of all was the thought that he would be free of her company for a few hours. He only hoped that they would occur during opening time.


Edward Young had been busy with plans for converting the stable block into a roomy bungalow, and also for altering the top floor of their house into a self-contained flat.

The latter was a fairly straightforward job, for the attics had been divided into three good-sized bedrooms just before the 1914–1918 war. Old Mr Bassett remembered that his nurse had slept in one and, in those spacious days, the cook had had another, while two housemaids shared the third.

There was water already there, and the large dormer windows looked out upon splendid views. It could provide a lovely home for a single person, or perhaps a young couple. It was a conversion which Edward had had in mind for some time, and he submitted both plans together to the local planning committee.

The Bassetts preferred the stable block. For one thing, it was a ground floor abode, and for another, they were at a short distance from Joan and Edward, and both households could be independent, although close enough in an emergency to help each other.

Doctor Lovell's surmise that his patient would be stimulated by the plans now afoot, was fully justified. Robert took on a new lease of life, and pottered out to the stables with his footrule, planning where favourite pieces of furniture could be placed, how wide the windowsills could be, and other pleasurable activities. He now took a little exercise, or dozed in the sunny garden. His appetite improved and Milly and the family watched his return to health with the greatest satisfaction.

As soon as he was really fit, he and Milly proposed to return to Ealing to settle their affairs and to dispose of the business and the house.

Meanwhile, it was enough to enjoy the sunshine of Thrush Green, and to know that the future looked bright with hope.

Isobel Fletcher had replied with gratitude to the Hursts' letter, and said that she would not be free to accept their kind offer until early July, as prospective buyers seemed to be numerous, and there were several matters to arrange with her solicitor and the bank manager.

Williams and Frobisher had sent only one possibility, and it so happened that it was a house in which an old friend of her mother's had once lived. It had a long drive and far too much ground, and Isobel had turned it down as its upkeep would be too expensive. She hoped that she would have better luck while she was staying at Tullivers.

It was arranged that Winnie Bailey would keep the key, until Isobel was free to come, and that she would order milk, bread and groceries for her temporary next-door-neighbour.

Isobel rang Harold, as well as the Hursts, when she had made her decision.

'It was such a kind thing to think of,' said Isobel. 'What put it into your head?'

Harold could hardly say: 'The strongest desire to have you nearby,' but said that Frank had expressed some doubts about leaving the house empty, and knowing that she intended to return to her house-hunting, the two thoughts had gone together, and he hoped sincerely that it had not been a liberty.

'Far from it,' said Isobel warmly. 'I am terribly grateful to you, and I shall look forward to seeing you again before long.'

'And so shall I,' responded Harold, from the heart.


Nelly Piggott lost no time in calling upon the Misses Lovelock in Lulling High Street.

The sun was still warmly bathing Thrush Green in golden light when she set out from her home. It was half past six, and Albert was already next door at the Two Pheasants, despite Nelly's protestations.

From berating him, Nelly had turned to more womanly tactics, and on this particular evening, dressed in her finery for the forthcoming interview, and fragrant with attar of roses, she bestowed a rare kiss upon Albert's forehead.

'Just to please me, Albert dear,' she said, in her most seductive tones.

But Albert was not to be wooed.

'That soft soap,' he told her, shaking her off, 'don't cut any ice with me.'

With this splendid mixed metaphor as farewell, he then departed next door, leaving Nelly to collect her handbag and go off in the opposite direction.

She was not particularly upset by her failure to wean Albert from his beer. Nelly took a philosophical view of marriage. All men had their little weaknesses. If Albert's had not been liquor, it might have been wife-beating, or even infidelity, although Nelly was the first to admit that, with Albert's looks, a chance would be a fine thing.

She sailed down the hill and along Lulling High Street, relishing the evening sunshine and her own aura of attar of roses.

The three Misses Lovelock lived in a beautiful Georgian house halfway along the main street. Here they had been born, and the outside and the inside of their home had altered very little, except that there were far more *objets d'art* crowded inside than in their childhood days.

The Misses Lovelock were inveterate collectors, and rarely paid much for their pieces of porcelain, glass and silver. Older inhabitants of Lulling and Thrush Green knew this and were always on their guard when the sisters called.

Nelly pulled lustily at the old-fashioned iron bell pull at the side of the door, and Bertha opened it.

'I've come about the place, miss,' said Nelly politely.

Bertha's mind, somewhat bewildered, turned to fish. Had they ordered plaice? Perhaps Violet . . .

'I heard you was needing help in the house,' continued Nelly. 'But perhaps you're already suited?'

'Oh, *that* place!' exclaimed Bertha, light dawning. 'No, not yet. Do come in.'

She led the way into the dining-room which, despite the heat of the glorious day, struck cold and dark.

'If you'll sit down, Mrs Er?'

'Mrs Piggott,' said Nelly, sitting heavily on a delicate Sheraton chair. It creaked ominously, and Bertha felt some anxiety, not only for the chair's safety, but also at her visitor's identity. For, surely, this was the sexton's wife whose conduct had been so scandalous? Hadn't she run away with another man? Oh dear! What would Ada say?

'I will just go and tell my sisters that you are here. You do undertake housework, I suppose?'

'Yes'm. And cooking. I fairly loves cooking.'

'Yes, well – I won't be a moment.'

She fluttered off, leaving Nelly to cast a disparaging eye on the gloomy oil paintings, the heavy velvet curtains and the mammoth sideboard laden with half a hundred-weight of assorted silverware. The work the gentry made for themselves!

Bertha, breaking in upon Ada's crochet work and Violet's tussle with *The Times* crossword puzzle, gave a breathless account of their visitor.

Her two sisters lowered their work slowly, and surveyed her with disapproval.

'But why invite such a person into the house?' asked Ada.

'But can she undertake housework?' asked Violet, more practically.

'Because I didn't know who she was,' cried Bertha, answering Ada, 'and she can certainly do housework. I remember Winnie Bailey telling me what a marvellous job she made of Thrush Green School,' she went on, turning to Violet.

The three sisters exchanged glances of doubt and indecision.

'And another thing,' continued Bertha, 'I've just remembered that she is a first-class cook. It was Winnie who told me that too.'

Ada sighed.

'Well, I suppose we'd better see this person now that she's here.'

She rolled up her crochet work in an exquisite silk scarf, and put it on one side. Violet placed *The Times* on the sofa.

Together the three sisters advanced upon the dining-room. Nelly struggled to her feet as they entered, the chair creaking with relief.

'Do sit down,' said Ada graciously. The three sisters took seats on the other side of the table, and Nelly lowered herself again into the long-suffering chair, and faced them.

'Let me tell you what we require,' said Ada. 'Our present helper is looking after her daughter who is just about to be confined. She will probably be home again in six weeks or so.'

'Yes'm,' said Nelly, surveying the three wrinkled faces before her. Never seen three such scarecrows all together before, she was thinking. Why, they couldn't weigh twenty stone between 'em!

'Two mornings a week, one of them a Friday, but any other morning which would be convenient for you would be quite in order with us.'

She glanced at her sisters who nodded in agreement.

'Tuesday would suit me best,' said Nelly, thinking of washing day on Monday.

'And I hear that you are an excellent cook, Mrs Piggott.'

Nelly smiled in acknowledgement.

'Perhaps, very occasionally, you might prepare luncheon for us?'

'I'd be pleased to,' said Nelly. She waited to hear about payment.

'Have you brought any references?' inquired Ada.

'Well, no,' confessed Nelly. 'But Miss Watson would speak for me, and the Allens at The Drover's Arms.

There was a whispered conversation between the three sisters, and much nodding of trembling heads.

'Very well,' said Ada. 'As this will only be a temporary arrangement we will waive the references. When can you start?'

Nelly decided that she must take a firm stand.

'I should like to know the wages, ma'am, before saying "Yes" or "No".'

'We pay fifty pence an hour, Mrs Piggott, and should like three hours each morning. You would receive three pounds a week.'

Fifty pence! thought Nelly. It was the least she had ever been offered, but it would be useful, and the job looked like being one after her own heart.

Ada, seeing the hesitation, added swiftly: 'You would be paid extra, of course, if you prepared a meal while you were here. Another fifty pence, Violet? Bertha?'

'Oh, yes, indeed,' they quavered obediently.

Nelly rose.

'Then I'll come next Tuesday,' she said. 'Nine o'clock?'

'I think nine-thirty,' said Ada. 'We breakfast a little late, now that we are approaching middle age.'

She rose too, and the three sisters ushered Nelly out of the front door into Lulling High Street.

'Approaching middle age,' repeated Nelly to herself, as she set off for Thrush Green. 'That's a laugh! They must be over eighty, every one of them! Well, I shan't make a fortune there, but it'll be a nice change from cleaning Albert's place.'


It was on one of these cloudless June days that the Hursts flew to America.

Harold, as promised, drove them to Heathrow airport. The sun was hot through the glass and all were in high spirits. Neither Frank nor his wife were anxious travellers, Harold was glad to see. Much travelled himself, he had always felt slightly irritated by his fellow companions who were constantly leafing through their wallets to check that they had passports, licences, tickets and all the other paraphernalia of travelling, or turning to each other with agitated queries, such as: 'Did you turn off the electricity? The water? Did we leave a key with Florrie? Did you remember to tell the police we would be away? Do you think Rover will *like* those new kennels?'

Frank seemed to have everything in hand, and was looking forward to visiting the United States again, and to introducing Phil to his friends there. He loved the warmth and generosity of American hospitality, and the enthusiasm of his audiences. It made one feel young again. He hoped that Jeremy would pay many visits there as he grew older.

That young man was full of excited chatter. Harold let the boy's commentary on the passing scene flow in one ear and out at the other. He was remembering another trip he had taken to Heathrow, with Phil, some years before.

Then she had sat, white and silent, beside him, for the news had just come through of her first husband's death in a car crash in France, and Harold had driven her straight to the airport.

How bleak the outlook had seemed then! Harold's heart had been sore for her, so young and defenceless, with the added responsibility of bringing up a young child on her own. Thank God she had met Frank, and this second marriage had turned out so well.

His mind turned to Charles again and his happy marriage. And then, naturally enough, to the pleasant thought of Isobel coming to stay at Tullivers before long. Would the future hold marriage for him, he wondered?

He turned into the lane leading to the airport.

'Here we are! Here we are!' carolled Jeremy. 'And there are thousands of planes! Look, look! Don't you wish you were coming too, Uncle Harold?'

'In some ways,' replied Harold circumspectly, 'but I think I'd just as soon stay at Thrush Green for a while.'

## 16. Problems for the Piggotts

Miss Watson came home from hospital on a Saturday, which meant that Agnes Fogerty could collect her in the taxi, as arranged, and see her settled at the schoolhouse.

Apart from looking pale and rather shaken, Dorothy Watson had come through her ordeal very well. She leant heavily on two sticks, but managed to get into the taxi without much trouble, and was in fine spirits.

'To be out again, Agnes dear,' she cried. 'To feel fresh air on one's face, and to see children *running*! I can't tell you how lovely it is!'

Agnes had put some early roses in Dorothy's bedroom, and everything that could be done by loving hands awaited the invalid. The bed was turned down, a hot bottle was swathed in a fresh nightgown, and that day's newspaper and letters awaited reading on the bedside table.

Miss Watson, who had been looking forward to having lunch downstairs, saw that she must give way graciously to Agnes's ministrations. Nevertheless, she insisted on limping round downstairs, admiring the care which had been lavished on all her possessions.

'And Betty Bell has made you a sponge cake,' said Agnes. 'It's from Mr Shoosmith, with his love.'

'His love?' echoed Dorothy. 'How kind! He's such a reserved man, I should have been more than gratified with "kind regards". A sponge cake, and *love* as well, really touches me.'

'He's a very thoughtful person,' said Agnes. 'Yesterday he sent Piggott round to tidy the garden here instead of his own, and he has inquired many times about you.'

Miss Watson made her way slowly to the kitchen window at the rear of the house, and gazed with pleasure at the garden. Her roses were beginning to break and the violas edging the beds were gay with blue, white and yellow blooms. A harassed blackbird, followed by four babies larger then itself, scurried to and fro across the newly-mown lawn, snatching up any morsel available and returning to thrust it down the clamorous throats.

She opened the window and leant across the sill. All the scents of summer drifted in upon the warm air, the mingled potpourri of the jasmine on the wall, the old-fashioned crimson peonies nearby, the freshly-cut grass, and the hay field beyond which stretched to the distant greenery of Lulling Woods.

There, in the distance, was Dotty Harmer's cottage, sitting as snugly as a golden cat in the fold of the meadow. Near at hand, glowing just as effulgently in the sunshine, was the bulk of kind Harold Shoosmith's home, and her own beloved little school.

She drew in her breath, overcome by the bliss of being at Thrush Green again, and suddenly realized how tired she was.

She turned to Agnes.

'Wonderful to be back, my dear. And now I'm going to that lovely bed, if you will help me with my shoes and stockings.'

She mounted the stairs slowly, attended anxiously by little Miss Fogerty, and as soon as she entered the bedroom went to gaze upon Thrush Green from the front windows.

There were the chestnut trees in pride of leaf. There were the homes of her friends and neighbours, sturdy, warm and welcoming. Nathaniel Patten gleamed upon his plinth, and gazed benevolently upon the children playing on the swings and see-saw nearby. A pale blue cloudless sky arched over all, and somewhere, close at hand, a blackbird trilled.

Miss Watson turned back into the room.

'What a perfect day, in all ways!' she commented. 'But, best of all, Agnes, to have you here with me. I am a very lucky woman!'

One sunny afternoon, soon after Miss Watson's return to her home, although not yet to her school duties, she noticed a familiar figure entering the gate of the Youngs' house.

'Now what can Molly Piggott – I mean Molly Curdle – be doing in Thrush Green?' she wondered. She had always been fond of the girl. She had been a rewarding pupil, keen to learn and polite in manner, despite her deplorable old father.

Miss Watson had watched her progress as mother's help at the Youngs', with the greatest interest and approval, and her marriage to young Ben Curdle had won everyone's blessing at Thrush Green.

Joan Young was as surprised to see Molly as Miss Watson had been, but welcomed her warmly.

She led her visitor into the garden and they sat in the shade of the ancient apple tree which Molly knew so well. Young Paul's swing had hung there, and she had spent many hours pushing her charge to and fro beneath spring blossom, summer leaf, and autumn fruit.

In the heat of the day the dappled shade was welcome, and Molly pushed her damp hair from her forehead.

'That hill gets steeper,' she smiled. 'Or I'm getting older.'

Her eyes roamed to the stable block. Preliminary clearing had begun, in the hope of planning permission being granted, and a stack of assorted and cumbersome objects, ranging from derelict deck-chairs to an equally decrepit cupboard, leant against the wall.

'That's a heavy job,' commented Molly. 'You planning to use the place as a garage?'

'Not a garage,' said Joan. 'Something more ambitious than that.'

She told the girl about her parents' retirement, and the conversions that they hoped to make. Molly nodded enthusiastically.

'I'm glad they're coming back at last to Thrush Green,' she said. 'It's only right that Mr Bassett should be here. Are they here now?'

'At the moment they are at the Henstocks having tea. Which reminds me, Molly, I've offered you nothing – which is shameful. What can I get you?'

'Nothing, thank you. Well, perhaps a glass of water?'

'I'll bring you some home-made lemonade. The same recipe you used to make up when you were here, remember?'

'Indeed I do. I'll come and help.'

They went back into the cool kitchen to fetch their drinks, and Joan wondered what had brought the girl to Thrush Green.

As if guessing her thoughts, Molly spoke.

'Friends of ours had a bit of business to do today over here, and offered me a lift. Ben's minding George, so I thought I'd look in and see Dad, and you, and anybody else as remembered me.'

'We all remember you,' cried Joan, leading the way with the tray, back to the garden seat.

They sipped their lemonade, the ice clinking against the glass. Above them a starling chattered, his dark plumage iridescent in the sunlight. A fat thrush ran about the lawn, stopping every now and again, head cocked sideways, to listen for a worm beneath the surface.

'I wondered,' said Molly, breaking the silence, 'if you'd heard of anything for Ben to do?'

Joan felt a pang of guilt. She had certainly made inquiries, and mentioned the matter to several friends, but the advent of her parents, and the anxiety over her father's health had limited her search.

'I haven't done as much as I had hoped to do,' she confessed. She outlined her efforts, and promised to make amends.

'The thing is,' said Molly, 'Dick Hasler has offered us a good sum for the fair, and Ben thinks he'll have to accept. There's no end of expense that we can't face. I left him patching up two swingboats. The timber alone cost a mint of money, and there's a limit to the time Ben can spare for repairs. We've faced it now. We'll have to give up, and although it grieves my Ben, we know the fair's day's done - at least, as we ran it. Dick's got plenty behind him, and if he loses on one thing he can make it up on another.'

'In fact, what he loses on the swings, he gains on the roundabouts?' smiled Joan.

'That's it exactly. And this is where we'd like to be for the future, as you know.'

'You're quite right. There's your father to consider too, although I expect you know that Nelly's back?'

'Yes, indeed. One look at that place showed me that. I can't say I take to Nelly,' she went on, in a burst of confidence. 'She's too bold for my liking, but she do keep a house clean.'

'And keeps Albert well fed.'

'But for how long? D'you think she'll stay? In some ways, I hope she will. It would be a relief to us to know Dad was being looked after. But they're not happy together, as you know. I can't see it lasting.'

'Frankly, neither can I,' agreed Joan.

St Andrew's church clock chimed four, and Molly put down her glass hastily.

'I'd best be getting down to the crossroads. I'm being picked up at a quarter past, and I must drop into Dad's again to say goodbye.'

'Now, I promise to do my best to find something for Ben,' said Joan, taking the girl's hands in hers. 'When would he be free to start?'

'Any time,' said Molly. 'We could stay with Dad until we found a place of our own. Anything to get back to Thrush Green, and to start afresh. It's been a sad time for us lately, particularly for Ben. The fair's always been his life, as you know.'

'Something will turn up, I'm positive,' Joan assured her. 'I will write to you very soon.'

She watched Molly cross the grass to go to Albert's cottage. The children were streaming out from school, and Joan thought how lovely it would be when Molly and Ben were back, and George himself would be coming home from Thrush Green school.


Nelly Piggott missed seeing Molly by a mere half hour, as Albert pointed out.

Nelly had been shopping after her bout of housework, and her first attempt to cook lunch for the three sisters.

She was hot, tired and cross. Her corsets were too tight, and so were her shoes. She took scant notice of Albert's remarks, as she filled the kettle at the sink, and Albert resented it.

'I said that our Molly'd called,' he repeated loudly.

'*Your* Molly, not ours,' replied Nelly. 'She's nothing to me.'

'No need to be so white and spiteful,' grumbled Albert. 'Specially as she said how nice the place looked.'

'No thanks to her,' rejoined Nelly, struggling to take off her shoes. 'Fat lot she does for her old Dad, I must say.'

'They sends me money, don't they?' demanded Albert. 'Regular.'

'And where does that go? Down your throat, the bulk of it. I tell you straight, Albert, I shan't be stopping here long if you don't give me more housekeeping.'

'Well, you've left here before, and I shan't stop you clearing off again. When you gets into these tantrums I'd sooner see the back of you, and that's that!'

Nelly reached for the teapot. Things were going a little too fast for her.

'Want a cup?' she asked, more gently.

'May as well.'

'Don't strain yourself,' said Nelly, spooning tea into the pot. She set out cups upon a tray, and poured the tea. They sipped in silence.

Albert was weighing up the pros and cons of life with Nelly, an exercise which he undertook frequently.

Nelly was reviewing the situation which she had taken on at the Lovelocks'. Could she, she asked herself, continue for six whole weeks, albeit only twice a week, in the present frustrating circumstances?

It was the *meanness* of the three ladies which infuriated Nelly. It was one thing to find that the dusters provided consisted of squares cut from much-worn undergarments, but quite another to be denied the tin of furniture polish.

Miss Violet had undone the lid, selected one of the deplorable squares, and scooped out about a teaspoonful of the polish upon it.

'That,' she told Nelly, 'should be *quite* enough for the dining-room.'

Seeing Nelly's amazed countenance, she had added swiftly: 'Come to me again, Nelly, if you need more, although I hardly think you will find it necessary.'

She had swept from the room, tin in hand, leaving Nelly speechless.

All the cleaning equipment was handed out in the same parsimonious style. A small puddle of Brasso in a cracked saucer was supposed to cope with the many brass objects in the house. Vim was handled as though it were gold-dust. Washing-up liquid was measured by the thimbleful. It was more than Nelly could stand, and she said so.

Her complaints brought very little improvement, and Nelly retaliated by cleaning all that she could, and leaving the rest as soon as the rations for the day ran out. But she resented it bitterly. She *liked* to see things clean, and never stinted cleaning agents in her own home.

However, she comforted herself with the thought that it was only for six weeks, maybe less. Surely, she could stick it out for that time, especially as nothing else had cropped up to give her alternative employment?

The memory of the lunch she had been obliged to cook made her shudder. Nelly respected food, and always chose the best when shopping. It was no good being a first-class cook, as she knew she was, if the materials were poor. You might just as well try to paint a portrait with creosote.

When Miss Bertha had fluttered into the kitchen that morning, and had asked her to cook that day's luncheon, Nelly's spirits had risen. She had visions of rolling out the lightest of pastry, of whipping eggs and cream, of tenderising steak or skinning some delicate fish cooked in butter.

'And you will stay to have some too, Nelly, I hope.'

'Thank you, ma'am,' said Nelly, envisaging herself at the kitchen table with a heaped plate of her own excellent cooking. Albert had been left with a cold pork-pie, some home-made brawn, strong cheese and pickled shallots, so Nelly had no qualms on his behalf. She had told him that she intended to shop in the afternoon. Really, things had worked out very well, she told herself, and this would save her going to the Fuchsia Bush for a cup of coffee and a sandwich, as she had planned.

Miss Bertha vanished into the larder and appeared with a small piece of smoked fillet of cod. It was the tail end, very thin, and weighed about six ounces. To Nelly's experienced eye it might provide one rather inferior helping, if eked out with, say, a poached egg on top.

'Well, here we are,' said Bertha happily. 'If you could poach this and share it between three, I mean, *four*, of course.'

'Is this all?' inquired Nelly flabbergasted. 'Why, our cat would polish that off and look for more!'

Miss Bertha appeared not to hear, as she made her way back to the larder, leaving Nelly gazing at the fish with dismay.

'You'd like poached eggs with this, I take it?' said Nelly.

Bertha put two small eggs carefully beside the fish.

'We prefer scrambled eggs, Nelly. These two, well beaten, should be ample for us all.'

'There won't be enough,' said Nelly flatly.

'We add a little milk.'

'Horrible!' protested Nelly. 'Should never be done with scrambled eggs. Butter's all you need, and a little pepper and salt.'

'Not *butter*!' gasped Bertha. 'We always use margarine in cooking. *Butter* would be *most* extravagant!'

Nelly began to see that she would certainly need to visit the Fuchsia Bush to supplement the starvation diet being planned.

'Vegetables?' she managed to ask.

'Plenty of spinach, Nelly, in the garden, and I thought some rhubarb for pudding. There is still some growing by the cold frame. I will leave out the sugar for you.'

'Very well, ma'am,' she said as politely as her outraged sensibilities would allow.

She finished drying the breakfast things, and went, basket in hand to fetch the spinach and rhubarb. On her return, she found half a cupful of granulated sugar awaiting its union with the rhubarb, and about half an ounce of margarine.

Nelly left the spinach to soak, and wiped the thin sticks of rhubarb. They were well past their best, and showed rusty marks when she chopped them.

For the rest of the morning Nelly seethed over the appalling ingredients which were to make a lunch for four people.

'Not enough for a sparrow,' she muttered to herself, as she went about her chores. 'And all windy stuff too. If those old scarecrows is doubled up this afternoon, it won't be my fault, and that's flat!'

She cooked the food as best she could. It grieved her to be using margarine instead of butter, but there was nothing else to use, and mighty little of that.

Miss Violet had set the table. The heavy Georgian silver gleamed, the glasses sparkled, and handmade lace mats lay like snowflakes on the polished mahogany.

Nelly carried in the dish of fish and scrambled egg and placed it before Miss Ada at the head of the table. Her face expressed scorn.

'I took the liberty, ma'am,' said Nelly, 'of picking a sprig of parsley to garnish it.'

Miss Ada inclined her head graciously.

'You did quite rightly,' she said. 'It all looks delicious.'

Nelly returned to the kitchen and surveyed the teaspoonful of food upon her plate. At that moment, the cat leapt through the window.

'Here,' said Nelly, handing down the plate, 'try your luck with that.'

Delicately, with infinite caution, the cat sniffed at the food. A rose petal tongue emerged to lick the fish tentatively, then the cat shuddered slightly, and turned away.

'And I don't blame you,' said Nelly. She threw the scraps out of the window, and watched a gaggle of sparrows descend upon them.

'What I could do to a nice fillet steak!' mourned Nelly, preparing to carry in the dish of sour rhubarb, unadorned by any such rich accompaniment as cream or custard.

Later, when Nelly had washed up and had been complimented upon her cooking by the three old ladies, Nelly tried to forget the whole shocking experience. Never again, she told herself, never again! Not if they went down on their brittle old bended knees would she be party to such a travesty of cooking! It was more than flesh and blood could stand.

It was hardly surprising that Albert found her exceptionally snappy that evening. Nelly had suffered much.

# Part Three
## Safe Arrival

### 17. Living Alone

Miss Watson's enforced rest gave her plenty of time to think. Not that she did not think in her normal state, but this was thinking at a different level.

She was a healthy busy woman, who ran her school and her home with competence. Her mind was always occupied with such diverse matters as ordering fresh stock, arranging a parents' evening, supervising the new probationer-teacher, as well as remembering to order an extra pint of milk because the Henstocks were coming to coffee, to send the spare-room bedspread to the laundry, and to ring the hairdresser to see if she could fit in a permanent wave on a Saturday morning.

These day to day activities left little time for such things as general reading, although she conscientiously tried to keep abreast with present-day writings on education. She rarely visited the theatre in term time, and her travels had been limited to less expensive areas in Europe. She kept up with a few old friends, and saw Ray and Kathleen several times a year, but this was the first occasion when she had been thrown upon her own resources and had experienced solitude, without activity, for hours at a time.

In this present vague post-operation daze, she found reading irksome, and radio and television equally tiring. She was content to lie back and let her mind dwell upon a great many aspects of life which, until now, she had largely ignored.

It was something of a shock to realize that one was not completely self supporting. So far in her life, she had managed her affairs without needing to ask for any help, other than such specialized aid necessary for coping with tax affairs and other money matters, or the occasional legal problem which dear old Justin Venables in Lulling managed with easy experience.

She had never before suffered such physical weakness as now engulfed her, and it was unnerving to find that she needed help to cope with such everyday matters as bathing, dressing and moving about the house. She felt confident that she would be back to normal in a few weeks, but then how could one be sure that other similar accidents might not occur, as one grew older? It was a sobering thought. If the present mishap had occurred when the school had closed, and she had been alone, how long, she wondered, could she have lain there unattended?

Thank heaven for dear Agnes! It would have been impossible to return to her own home without Agnes's help. She dwelt now upon the sterling qualities of her staunch assistant. Her presence in the house, particularly at night, when she felt at her most vulnerable, was wonderfully consoling, and although she had been careful not to disturb Agnes's much needed slumber, it was a great comfort to know that she was there if the emergency arose.

Soon, of course, she must face the fact that Agnes would return to Mrs White's. But need she?

Miss Watson toyed with the idea of inviting dear Agnes to share her home permanently. It would be to their mutual advantage, she felt sure. The only thing was the uncomfortable fact that Agnes might not want to give up the independence she so much enjoyed.

Miss Watson turned over the problem in her mind, with unusual humility. What right had she to expect Agnes to want to live with her? She had been more than fortunate to find a friend so unselfish that she was prepared to look after her for these few weeks. It was asking too much of her to expect that she would want to remain.

And yet Agnes would be the perfect companion! She grew fonder of her as the years passed. She was a fine person, loyal and kind, much more noble, in every way, than her headmistress, thought Dorothy sadly.

No, it would not be fair to ask her, she decided, with a sigh. Agnes might well agree simply because she felt that she was needed to help, ignoring her own feelings.

She was so unselfish. It was very uplifting to live with a saint, but it had its problems.


Next door, Harold Shoosmith was also in a state of turmoil. Isobel would soon be arriving, and he hoped that he would be able to greet her without showing the real depths of his feelings. It was quite alarming to find how often his thoughts turned to her, and he was beginning to fear that the observant residents of Thrush Green might guess the cause of his preoccupation.

He was about to cross the green one morning, to mow the grass at

Tullivers, when Dotty Harmer appeared, looking even more agitated than usual.

'You haven't seen Flossie, by any chance?' she called, hastening towards him.

'Flossie?' queried Harold.

'My dog. My little spaniel. She's run off, you see.'

'No, I'm sorry. I will keep an eye open for her.'

'It's so upsetting,' continued Dotty, hitching up a stocking with a claw-like hand. 'I fear she must be on heat, and I hadn't realized it.'

She peered at Harold sharply.

'I don't embarrass you, I trust?'

'Not in the least,' responded Harold. 'I have been aware of the facts of life for some years now.'

Any gentle sarcasm intended was lost upon Dotty, in her present state of perturbation.

'Of course, of course! But it is so annoying. She may have gone along to Nidden. There is a collie dog there, at the farm, to whom she is rather partial. The results of such a liaison would not be acceptable to the Kennel Club, I fear, but there it is.'

'Well, I'll certainly keep a look out, but it might be as well to call at the rector's, or Miss Bembridge's. They might catch her before she gets into the traffic at Lulling. Would you care to use my telephone?'

'You are most kind! Most kind! But I think I will walk across while I'm here. Besides, I am disturbing your activities.'

'I was only going to cut the grass at Tullivers,' said Harold.

Dotty's wrinkled countenance lit up with pleasure.

'All ready for Isobel? She will be grateful, I'm sure.'

She fluttered off in the direction of Ella's house, leaving Harold to his thoughts.

Betty Bell, always exuberant, seemed to bring Isobel Fletcher's name into the conversation more frequently than Harold could have wished, but he had the sense to hold his tongue on these occasions. There was no point in adding fuel to the fire, he told himself.

But, one morning, Betty arrived in a rare state of indignation.

'D'you know what?' she demanded. 'That fat Nelly Piggott's been trying to get my job off of me!'

'What, here?' asked Harold, alarmed.

'No, no! I'd see you was looked after,' said Betty, as though indulging a backward child. 'No need for you to worry. No, that besom – excuse my

French – has been crawling round Miss Fogerty, I hear, and would have gone in to see Miss Watson too, if Miss Fogerty hadn't put her foot down. The very idea!'

'She wasn't successful, I take it,' ventured Harold.

'I should hope not!' snorted Betty. 'Why, I keeps that place *beautiful*! *Beautiful*, I tell you! Toffee papers, squashed chalk, bubble gum and all. You could eat your dinner off of the floor when I've done with it.'

'I'm sure you could,' Harold agreed, wondering why anyone should be expected to want to eat dinners from floors or, for that matter, why it should occur to anyone to *serve* dinners in such a peculiarly uncomfortable position.

'And if I sees her about,' went on Betty wrathfully, 'I shall give her a piece of my mind!'

'I shouldn't bother,' said Harold, alarmed at the prospect of a noisy row on Thrush Green.

'Or the flat of my hand,' added Betty, and flung out of the room.


There was sudden activity at the Youngs' house. Edward's plans had been passed with unusual rapidity, and the builders, whom he had alerted earlier, were beginning to move in with all their paraphernalia.

Milly and Robert decided that they would make their way back to Ealing.

'I've no excuse for lingering,' said Mr Bassett. 'Thrush Green has put me on my feet again, and we shall only be in your way with the building going on. It's time we went back and put our affairs in order.'

'We shall miss you,' said Joan, 'but you'll be back for good before long. What a marvellous thought!'

'For us too,' said Milly. 'We've been blessed with two wonderful daughters. This would have been a terrible time for us without you to help.'

A week later, Edward drove them to Ealing in their own car, with Joan following behind. They settled the parents in the house, and were relieved to find that Frank had taken an hour or two off work to welcome them home, and to give Robert the latest news of the business.

'I shall be relieved to have them near us,' said Joan, as they drove back to Thrush Green together. 'How long do you think it will be before the stable block is ready?'

'Quicker than builders usually are!' promised Edward. 'I'll see to that!'

It was mid-July before Isobel was freed from her affairs in Sussex.

She arrived on a sunny afternoon, and spent an hour with her new next-door neighbour, Winnie Bailey, before unlocking the door of Tullivers.

Isobel looked tired, Winnie thought, as she poured tea for them both, but then she had had a long journey and probably a good deal of worry in the last few weeks.

'No, still nothing definitely settled,' said Isobel, in reply to her query. 'You know how it is with selling a house. If my present would-be buyers can sell their own, all's well. But they're waiting to see if *their* buyer can sell *his*. How far back the queue stretches, heaven alone knows.'

'And it only needs one to default, I suppose, for the whole chain to collapse?'

'Exactly. Never mind, here I am, and Williams and Frobisher have sent me four possibilities, so I shall go ahead and enjoy looking at them. Better still, it's lovely to think I have so much more time to spend in Thrush Green. Tell me how everyone is.'

Winnie told her about the Young's plans.

'Lucky Bassetts! I envy them the stable conversion. If I didn't want a small house and garden, I think I'd rush across and plead for the top floor flat! Someone's going to have a nice home there.'

Winnie went on to tell her about Ben and Molly Curdle, the Henstocks, Ella, and finally, Harold.

'He's worked so hard in the garden,' said Winnie. 'The lawn looks immaculate, and the roses at Tullivers are the best at Thrush Green.'

'Let's go and see it,' cried Isobel jumping up. 'I feel a new woman after that tea. Once I've unpacked, I shall go to see Harold. He must have been working so hard.'

'I'm sure it was a labour of love,' said Winnie.

But Isobel, leading the way, did not appear to hear.


Now that Isobel had arrived, Harold's happiness grew daily, but he was anxious not to call too frequently at Tullivers, and so lay open the unsuspecting Isobel to the wagging tongues of Thrush Green.

Isobel, as it happened, was not so unsuspecting as Harold imagined. She was used to the admiration of men, and liked their company. An exceptionally happy marriage and a wide circle of friends had given her ease of manner with the opposite sex, and Harold's feelings, although carefully concealed, were guessed by the sympathetic Isobel.

In such a small community it was inevitable that they saw each other frequently, and they enjoyed each other's company more and more.

Isobel took Harold to see some of the places which she had known well in her girlhood around Stow, north of Thrush Green, and he accompanied her to look at one or two of the houses which Williams and Frobisher had recommended.

On the whole, it was a dispiriting job. The houses which were large enough to house the furniture which Isobel wanted to keep, were usually much too large, with endless corridors, high ceilings, and a formidable number of stairs. Those which were of manageable proportions were sometimes thatched, which Isobel disliked, or the rooms were small and stuffy.

'What I want is something in between,' sighed Isobel, as they emerged from one such cottage, Harold almost bent double to miss striking his head on the porch. 'I'm beginning to wonder if I shall ever find what I want.'

'Cheer up,' said Harold. 'I went through all this too when I was looking. It's disheartening for you, but I must confess I'm thoroughly enjoying myself.'

Isobel laughed. 'Well, I should have given up long ago if you hadn't been such a support. It's made all the difference to have some company.'

Harold seemed about to speak, thought better of it, and opened the door of the Alfa Romeo for her.

'Are you feeling strong enough to face "a bijou residence set like a gem amidst panoramic views"?' asked Isobel, consulting her papers.

'I can face any amount of them,' replied Harold bravely.

'Right,' said Isobel, letting in the clutch. 'It's about three miles from here.'

'And after that,' said Harold, 'I'm taking you to lunch at the Fleece. You need to keep up your strength when house-hunting.'

Little Miss Fogerty was as delighted as Harold to have Isobel at Thrush Green, and visited Tullivers frequently.

Miss Watson was now back at school, limping about her duties with a stick, and thankful to be of some use again. Agnes was very anxious about her, and insisted that she returned to her bed for a rest after school dinner and this Miss Watson agreed to do, with surprising meekness.

Now that she was back, the supply teacher departed, much to the relief of all.

'I'm quite sure she did her best,' Agnes told Dorothy earnestly. 'She was very *sincere* and *conscientious*, and most diligent in reading reports, and the leaders in *The Times Educational Supplement*, but I think she found the children rather a nuisance.'

'A case of putting the cart before the horse,' agreed Dorothy.

'It's good to be back on our own.'

It also meant that Agnes had more time to see Isobel, and the two old friends had much to talk about. It was clear to Isobel that Agnes still worried about Miss Watson being alone in the house.

'She's still very unsteady,' she told Isobel. 'One stumble, and she'd be quite helpless, you know.'

'You must let her do as she wishes,' comforted Isobel. 'After all, it could happen anyway, whether you were in the house or not. I'm sure she will be sensible. Lots of women have to live alone. Look at me!'

'But do you *like* living alone? I mean, I'm quite glad to know that the Whites are under the same roof as I am when I go up to bed. It makes me feel safer.'

'No, I can't say that I like living alone,' said Isobel thoughtfully. 'But then I'm not used to it yet.'

'Perhaps,' ventured Agnes, 'you might, in time, of course, marry again.'

'I can't imagine it,' said Isobel. 'At our age, Agnes dear, one doesn't think about it. No, I think I shall be quite happy if I can find a little house here, and know that I'm safely among friends. One really can't ask for more.'

The hot weather continued, one blazing day following the other. Harold Shoosmith reverted to his practice of taking a siesta, as he had throughout his working life overseas, and most of Thrush Green did the same.

The nights seemed to be as hot as the days, and when the full moon shone through Harold's window, he flung off the sheet which was his only covering, and wandered about the house.

A field of corn stretched towards Nidden, and ran hard by his boundary hedge. He leant from the window, relishing a faint breeze that ruffled his hair refreshingly.

In the moonlight the corn was silvered, glowing with an unearthly sheen. In the heat of the day, he had heard the ripe ears cracking under the fierce sun. The harvest would be early this year, although the farmers were already predicting a light yield. What would be in the field next, he wondered? And would Isobel be here by then to see it?

An owl's cry trembled upon the air, and soon he saw the bird swoop silently from a lone oak, sailing downwind upon its rounded wings. What a vast number of lovely things one could see at night, normally missed by having one's head on the pillow! A restless night had its compensations, he decided.

He crossed the landing, and went to see Thrush Green from the window of the front bedroom. The moonlight was so bright that he could see all the houses clearly. It gleamed upon Nathaniel Patten's bald bronze pate, and edged the folds of his frock-coat with silver. A cat was sitting on the plinth at his feet, washing its face.

Harold's eye travelled from Ella's cottage on his far right across the grass, along to Winnie Bailey's, and then next door to Tullivers where, he hoped, Isobel was having a less wakeful night. She had been to see yet another house that afternoon, although on this occasion she had gone alone.

Harold felt deeply sorry for her in this fruitless search, and his mind turned, once again, to the problem that concerned him. How much simpler it would be if she would marry him and live here! But would she want to? And could he ask her, so soon after her husband's death?

He had no doubts now about his own feelings. More than anything in the world he wanted to marry Isobel, and he could think of nothing else.

Harold sighed, and returned to his restless pacing about the house. He knew his own feelings well enough, but what were Isobel's?

# 18. Hope for the Curdles

Joan Young, mindful of her promise to Molly about looking out for an opening for Ben, now set about the task with extra zeal.

With her parents back in Ealing, she had more time to devote to her own affairs. She heard of several jobs, but somehow none seemed quite right for Ben. She was beginning to despair, and told Edward so.

'I'm seeing Tim Collet this afternoon,' he said. 'I'll have a word with him.'

Collets was a family firm of agricultural engineers in Lulling. It had been in existence for over a hundred years. Originally a blacksmith's, such simple tools as scythes, bill-hooks, horse ploughs and pig troughs figured largely in the early years of the firm. More sophisticated equipment such as threshing machines and harvesters soon came along, giving way eventually to the complicated monsters, costing thousands of pounds, which modern farming demanded.

The business was now run by two Collet brothers, Tim and Bob. They were shrewd and hard-working, and employed a dozen or so skilled men. It was the sort of work which Ben would enjoy and would be capable of carrying out. Joan only hoped that there might be a vacancy.

Luck was with them. Tim Collet told Edward that the man in charge of the yard was leaving at Michaelmas, and he was promoting another elderly employee to take his place, so that there would be a job available.

'I was going to advertise it,' said Tim, 'but if young Curdle wants to apply tell him to come and see me as soon as possible. I knew the old lady pretty well, and Ben too. You could trust him anywhere, which is more than you can say for some of 'em these days.'

When Edward told Joan this news, she broached another subject which had been in her mind for some days.

'Edward,' she began, 'if Ben gets this job –'

'Could they have the top flat?' finished Edward for her, and then laughed.

'You're too clever by half,' said Joan.

'Not really. I thought of it when I was talking to Tim. It would be a great help to us if Molly were here to give you a hand. There's bound to be more to do when the parents live here, and I'm sure she would want to have a little job too.'

'I'll write tonight and tell them the position. We certainly couldn't have better tenants,' agreed Joan. 'But will the flat be ready by September?'

'Pretty well, I think. If not, we can put them up, I'm sure. Unless Ben insists on sleeping at Albert's, of course!'

'Poor Ben! We'll make sure that doesn't have to happen. And in any case, I expect Nelly's in the spare bed.'

'She'd be a fool if she wasn't,' said Edward.


As it happened, at that moment Nelly was a long way from the spare bed, but busy in the Misses Lovelock's kitchen washing up greasy plates.

The end of her six weeks' sojourn was in sight, and Nelly had heard, with considerable relief, that the usual help was returning to her duties before long.

She had sworn privately never to cook another meal in that house. However, she had been prevailed upon to cook 'a nice little piece of lamb', which turned out to be an extremely fatty breast of that animal, with peas and new potatoes from the garden.

It was apparent from the infrequent entertaining that was done, that this would be the last occasion when Nelly would be called upon to demonstrate her art, so she swallowed her pride and set about making the best of a cut of meat which she despised.

Winnie Bailey, Ella Bembridge and Dotty Harmer were coming to lunch, and the amount of meat available, in Nelly's opinion, would just about feed two, rather than six. She herself had said swiftly that she was obliged to have something light, and would prefer a dry biscuit and a small piece of cheese if that was all right?

Miss Ada graciously gave her consent, and with her own hands put two water biscuits and about a quarter of an ounce of desiccated Cheddar cheese on a plate, and put it in the larder for Nelly's repast.

Nelly contrived to make a substantial stuffing of onions, bread crumbs and herbs, and rolled the breast of lamb, hoping that the guests had had large breakfasts.

'And welcome they are to *that*,' said Nelly, to the attentive cat, as she thrust the meat tin into the oven, and then set about making a bread pudding, sparsely furnished with a few sultanas which Miss Ada had counted out earlier.

As she handed round the vegetables at lunch time, she listened to the conversation with much interest. Dotty Harmer's dog, Flossie, was the subject of much questioning.

'I'm afraid so,' said Dotty. 'The vet said she could be aborted, but I don't like the idea.'

'Of what?' asked Miss Violet, who was slightly deaf.

'Of *abortion*,' shouted Dotty.

'*Pas devant la bonne*,' murmured Miss Ada, but Dotty was in no mood for such niceties.

'Why not?' she demanded. 'Abortion is a perfectly normal medical fact. Not, as I said before, that I approve of it. I told the vet that Flossie must just go ahead and have them. I am quite capable of looking after her, and her offspring, and I'm sure I shall find good homes for them.'

She cast speculative glances upon her fellow guests, who quailed. Dotty, with animals to place, was rightly feared by all Lulling and Thrush Green.

'I'm quite sure you will,' said Miss Bertha soothingly. 'If we weren't so near the road, and were more capable of giving a puppy exercise, I'm sure we might have offered to have one.'

'But as it is,' chimed in Miss Ada, 'it is quite out of the question.'

'Indeed it is,' agreed Miss Violet.

'The pudding, Nelly. Would you see if it is ready?' requested Miss Ada, and Nelly was obliged to leave this fascinating conversation and return to the kitchen.

'It's like a mad house in there,' she confided to the cat. 'Well-bred they might be – all six of 'em – but they sound half-barmy to me, the things they talk about!'

At the village school, unconfined joy reigned. It was the last day of term.

In Miss Fogerty's new classroom the cupboards were packed to bursting point with books, folders and boxes belonging to the children. Other, less obliging shapes, such as hanks of raffia, snarls of cane and balls of wet clay swathed in damp dishcloths, were also tidied away, with considerable difficulty, into their allotted place.

As always, just as Miss Fogerty, breathless with lodging the last object into the last space, was about to congratulate herself on finishing an awkward and arduous job, one of the children drew her attention to half a dozen large flower vases which should be stowed away.

'They will have to stay on the windowsill,' decreed Agnes. 'Stand them by the fish tank, dear, and you, Jimmy Todd, may go early with the goldfish so that your bucket isn't jogged by anyone on the way home.'

Jimmy Todd, the envy of the class, had a fish tank of his own, and was to look after Freeman, Hardy and Willis for the entire holiday.

'I *hope*,' little Miss Fogerty had confided to Miss Watson, 'I *sincerely hope* that the boy is trustworthy. He is inclined to be a trifle irresponsible at times.'

'He is only seven,' pointed out her headmistress. 'But there's no need to think that he is not perfectly capable of caring for the fish. He has sensible parents, and a little responsibility may work wonders for him.'

Miss Fogerty had her doubts. Secretly, she deplored handing out responsible jobs, such as fish minding and blackboard cleaning, to those who had not earned the honour by worthy and decorous behaviour, but as Jimmy Todd was the only child with a spare fish tank she bowed to the inevitable.

He was sent on his way ten minutes before the others, plastic bucket in hand and fervent protestations of concern for his charges on his lips. Miss Fogerty's last glimpse of him was at the school gates where he had stopped to peer anxiously through the butter muslin which Miss Fogerty had tied over the top of the pail.

She gave a sigh of relief.

'I'm sure they will be quite safe with Jimmy,' she said aloud.

'Jimmy Todd,' said a child in the front row, 'has got three cats as likes fish.'

Miss Fogerty quelled her with a glance.

'All stand. Hands together. Close your eyes. *Close* them, I said, Billy Bates, not *cross* them! Any silly nonsense like that, and you stay in, last day of term or not!'

Fortunately, Miss Fogerty's discipline held, and prayers were said reverently. It was as well, she thought, bidding the children goodbye, as she was due to go to tea with Isobel in five minutes' time.

The hot weather continued, day after day, week after week. The heat was almost overpowering as Agnes made her way to Tullivers, thankful for the deep shade of the chestnut avenue.

'One could really do with a parasol,' she said to Isobel, when they were seated in the shade with the tea-tray before them. 'My grandmother had a beautiful cream one, with lace and frills, I remember. Those Victorians had some excellent ideas.'

'My grandmother,' said Isobel, 'had a dove-grey silk one, and the knob on the handle was of pink china, with a tiny picture of Brighton Pier at the top. I wonder where that went eventually?'

'To a jumble sale, no doubt,' responded Agnes, accepting a teacup.

'And now tell me what you are doing this holiday,' said Isobel. 'I know you have been invited to go to the sea with Miss Watson. Is that soon?'

'She goes next Saturday. Her brother and his wife are taking her down, and staying for a week in this nice quiet hotel that Dorothy likes at Barton-on-Sea. Then I'm going down for the next week, while Ray goes with Kathleen to her sister's, and then they are bringing us both back here.'

'It will do you good to have some sea air, especially if the weather holds.'

'It will do Dorothy good too. There are some nice flat cliff top walks which she can manage now, and easy paths down to the sands.'

'And after that?'

'I shall have a week or so here catching up with all sorts of things I've been meaning to do, and then I shall spend a few days at my cousin's at Cheltenham.'

'And I hope a few days with me if you can spare the time,' said Isobel. 'As far as I can see, I shall be going back before long, and this may be the last time I can offer you hospitality in Sussex. With any luck, I shall have found something near here very soon, and it will be a joy to be near you permanently.'

'I should love to come,' said Agnes, and meant it. Isobel's home was as luxurious as her own bed-sitting-room was spartan. Not that she was discontented with her lot. She had been with the Whites now for a number of years, and appreciated their high standards of cleanliness and responsibility, and their kindness on the rare occasions when she had been obliged to stay in bed because of ill-health.

But it was good to exchange her skimpy bedclothes for Isobel's fluffy blankets and fat eiderdown. It was bliss to have a soft bath towel large enough to envelope her whole body, and wonderful to have exquisite meals served on Isobel's pretty china, instead of on the thick white plates from Mrs White's kitchen.

And then there was the warmth of Isobel's company to enliven her. There had never been anyone quite so dear to her as Isobel, and she enjoyed every minute of her company. Indeed, it had crossed her mind once, when Isobel had first mentioned that she wanted to live near Thrush Green, that she might be invited to share Isobel's home. But, on the whole, she was glad that the matter had not arisen.

Isobel had so many friends already at Thrush Green, and would soon make many more. Agnes did not want her to feel obliged to invite her to meet them, as no doubt Isobel would do. It would be a *strain*, thought Agnes, to have to be sociable when one arrived home, jaded from school, longing simply for a rest with one's feet up, and a quiet cup of tea. Besides, it had to be faced, Isobel's circle of friends was not quite her own. No, it was far better as it was – to visit Isobel in her own home, when she had found it, and to remain in her own modest lodgings which suited her very well. Of course, she was lonely at times, she admitted, but then one simply had to get used to it. There were plenty of single women in the same circumstances and, on the whole, they were certainly better off than those poor unfortunate women who had made unhappy marriages, she told herself stoutly.

But then she was more fortunate than most. The future looked bright. Dear Dorothy was fast returning to health and mobility, and she would always be grateful to her for giving her this lovely week's holiday which lay ahead. 'A small return, Agnes dear, for more kindness than I can ever repay,' is how she had put it.

And then, beyond that, lay the happy prospect of having Isobel actually living at Thrush Green!

Little Miss Fogerty lay back in her deck-chair, and gazed at Tulliver's flowers shimmering in the heat. She was at peace with the world.

Joan Young soon had a reply to her letter. There was nothing they would love more, wrote Molly, than to live in the top flat of the house which had always seemed like home to her.

Ben could not believe in such luck, and was now waiting to hear from the Collets which day they would like to interview him. Reading between the lines, Joan gathered that he was in a high state of tension, poor fellow, and hoped that his ordeal would soon be over. So much depended upon it, he was bound to be nervous.

He did not have to wait long. About ten days later, Molly, Ben and young George arrived at Lulling. Molly and George went to Albert Piggott's gloomy cottage while Ben, dressed in his best blue serge suit, and his dark hair brushed flat against his head, went to see Tim Collet, his heart beating nineteen to the dozen.

Nelly was at her Lulling job, and Molly prepared midday dinner for the three of them, her mind engrossed with what was happening at Lulling. As soon as they had eaten, and she had washed up, she took George out of the way, before Nelly returned, and sat on one of the many seats on Thrush Green.

The excessive heat had scorched the grass, and even the fully-grown trees were beginning to look parched and dusty. But there were a few daisies about, and a friendly collie dog, and these kept young George happily engaged, leaving Molly free to ponder on the jobs that might be ahead.

From where she sat, she had a clear view of the top of the hill, and longed to see their old van arrive with Ben at the wheel.

To her left lay the golden bulk of the Youngs' house, beyond the chestnut trees and the railings which ran along the front of the house. She could hear the noise of the builders at work, the chink of metal on stone, the rumble of a wheelbarrow, and an occasional voice as one workman shouted to another.

If only they could live there! If only Ben had landed this job! She began to tremble at the thought of failure. It would be like getting to the gate of heaven and being turned back. There was nowhere in the world that she wanted to be more. This was home. This was her element, as necessary to her as air to a bird, or water to a fish. Without it she would be nothing, simply an adjunct to Ben's life, going where he went, and making the best of any of the places in which he settled.

But here, at Thrush Green, life would be rich and vital. She and Ben would flourish like plants in a sheltered garden, and George would grow up in perfect surroundings, heir to all the joys of Thrush Green.

The sound of the van chugging up the hill sent her flying across the grass, followed by young George.

There was no need to say anything. Ben's glowing face said it all.

'Oh Ben!' cried Molly, clinging to him, and struggling to control tears of relief.

Ben patted her shoulder.

'There! Let's go straight across to Mrs Young, Moll, and tell her the good news.'

## 19. Miss Fogerty has a Shock

Nelly Piggott faced her last day's work at the Lovelock's with mingled relief and apprehension.

The job had been a frustrating one. It was not only poorly paid, but the parsimony of her employers had tried Nelly's patience to breaking point. It had been a considerable effort to hold her tongue under such extreme provocation, and only the thought of the comparatively short time she needed to endure it, had kept her from outspoken rebellion. No, she would not be sorry to leave this post.

On the other hand, the outlook for any other work seemed bleak. This puzzled Nelly. She was known as a good worker and an exceptionally fine cook. Why was it that she was unable to land another job?

She had haunted the Job Centre. She had asked a dozen or more Thrush Green and Lulling folk if they knew of a job, but always there was some difficulty. One of the reasons, Nelly felt sure, was her past flightiness. Lulling did not approve of wives leaving their husbands, even such unpleasant ones as Albert Piggott, to run off with oil men as glossy and dashing as the one who had persuaded Nelly to throw in her lot with his.

There were other reasons too. Most of the people who were lucky enough to have domestic aid, had employed their helpers for years, as Winnie Bailey had her Jenny, and Dotty Harmer and Harold Shoosmith their energetic Betty Bell. Others, who might have looked for help in the past, had long ago come to terms with doing everything for themselves and had found the result far more satisfactory, and far less expensive. One way and another, it was plain that there were no jobs waiting for Nelly.

As she returned to her house on Thrush Green, on the last afternoon of her employment, Nelly took stock of her position. Financially, she was a little better off than when she had arrived at Thrush Green. Prudently, she had put aside the money she had earned in her Post Office account. By diligent methods, she had been able to abstract some money from Albert, ostensibly for housekeeping, but a certain amount had been added to her own nest egg.

She owned an ancient gold watch, and a gold locket of hideous Victorian design, and these she knew would bring in a pound or two, if she were really hard pressed. The point was, could she afford to break with Albert?

She had long ceased to feel for him any affection or loyalty, but he did provide a roof over her head and enough to feed them both. But he grew daily more cantankerous, and Nelly knew that, before long, just such another row as that which had sent her into the arms of the oil man would blow up.

Crossing the green, Nelly decided that she would give Albert a week's trial. Who knows? Work might turn up to take her out of the house for a few hours a day. Albert might become a reformed character, though that chance was infinitesimal.

She would bide her time for a little longer, and then make her decision.

Albert was emerging from The Two Pheasants as Nelly opened the cottage door. For once, she did not start nagging at him.

Albert was rightly suspicious. What was up, he wondered?

On the appointed Saturday, Miss Watson was collected by her brother and his wife, and departed to the seaside.

Little Miss Fogerty had made her farewells the evening before as she helped Dorothy with her last-minute packing. Watching her assistant's deftness in folding garments and spreading tissue paper, Dorothy thought, once more, how invaluable dear Agnes was, and how dearly she would like to invite her to share the schoolhouse. Perhaps an opportunity would occur during their week together, but, on the other hand, there was always this difficulty of Agnes's unselfishness. If only the suggestion could come from her!

Well, it was no good worrying about it, thought Miss Watson, limping towards the car on that bright morning. Time alone could unravel that problem, and meanwhile she intended to enjoy her much-needed change of air.

Meanwhile, Miss Fogerty set about a number of jobs which she had been unable to tackle during term time.

The position of temporary headmistress, in which Miss Watson's sad accident had placed her, had meant putting aside a great many day-to-day activities which she normally tackled methodically.

Her mending, for instance, which was usually done after ironing, when she studied her sensible underwear and blouses for splitting seams, holes, ladders or missing buttons, had been neglected. The filling of innumerable forms had taken first place, and there had been parents, representatives from educational publishers, and other visitors to the school, who seriously impeded the steady progress of the work which Agnes so much enjoyed.

Now was the time to catch up with her own affairs, and she spent the next day or two replying to letters from friends, doing some shopping, taking shoes to the repairer's, and all the other little chores which she wanted to see finished before embarking on the longed-for week with Dorothy.

But two days before the great day, poor Miss Fogerty received the shock of her life. St Andrew's clock had just chimed four o'clock, and Miss Fogerty was about to switch on her kettle and make a cup of tea, when Mrs White called from below to say that she had just made a pot of tea, and would she like to join her?

It was while they were sipping the refreshing beverage in Mrs White's immaculate sitting-room, that the blow fell.

'I've been trying to summon up courage to tell you all the week,' confessed Mrs White. 'Arthur's got promotion, and we're moving to Scotland.'

Her face turned pink with the anxiety of imparting this news. Poor Miss Fogerty's turned white at hearing it.

She put down her cup with a clatter.

'Oh no!' she breathed at last. 'I can't believe it! You mean – ?'

'I'm afraid so,' nodded Mrs White, beginning to look tearful. 'I can't tell you how sorry I am about it. You've been a wonderful lodger, and a real good friend too, but Arthur can't afford to turn down this chance. It'll make a deal of difference to his pension, you see.'

'Of course,' said Agnes. She felt numbed with the shock. What a terrible thing to happen! How soon, she wondered, would she need to go?

As if reading her thoughts, Mrs White resumed her tale.

'There's no need for you to worry about leaving just yet. We don't go until the end of August, and Arthur's job starts on the first of September. There's a house that goes with it, and with the extra he'll get we hope to be able to buy our own house, ready for retirement one day.'

Agnes did her best to collect her scattered wits.

'I'm very glad for you both,' she said sincerely. 'The future certainly looks bright. It's just that I'm a little taken aback, you know, and at a loss to know where to find other lodgings. I doubt if I shall ever be so happy elsewhere as I have been with you.'

Mrs White sighed with relief.

'You've taken it wonderfully. I can't tell you how I've dreaded breaking the news.'

She turned briskly to her duties as hostess.

'Now let me give you a fresh cup of tea. That must be stone cold by now.'

Like my heart, thought poor Agnes, doing her best to hide her feelings. What on earth would she do now?

Later that evening, she went along the road to Thrush Green and called to see Isobel at Tullivers.

Her old friend was alone, and Agnes poured out all her troubles. Isobel was almost as upset as she was herself.

'If only I had found a place here,' was her first comment, 'you could have taken refuge with me. The awful thing is, Agnes dear, I shall probably be back in Sussex by the time you need another home. Does Mrs White know of other digs?'

'She didn't say anything.'

'Could you stay at the schoolhouse?'

'I'm sure Dorothy would let me stay there temporarily, if need be, but I really must find something permanent.'

'If I were you,' said Isobel, 'I should go and enjoy your holiday, and then come back to face this problem. The best thing to do, I think, would be to put an advertisement in the local paper, as soon as you return.'

'I thought I might tell the rector. He's so kind. He helped with finding a place for you with Miss Bembridge, you remember, and he would know the sort of place I wanted.'

'An excellent idea! I'm positive something will turn up before the end of August. Meanwhile, Agnes, you are going to stay to supper with me, I hope.'

'I can think of nothing nicer,' said little Miss Fogerty, much comforted.


The intense heat ended, as expected, with a crashing thunderstorm which began at seven in the evening and continued for most of the night.

The people of Lulling and Thrush Green waited eagerly for the rain to fall. Water-butts stood empty, flowers wilted, the summer pea pods were shrivelled on their stems, and even the farmers, now that the harvest was largely gathered in, looked forward to a downpour.

For some hours it looked as though nothing would fall. Crash followed crash, angry rumblings echoed round the sky, and sheet lightning lit the scene with eerie flashes, but still the rain held off. It was almost midnight before the welcome sound of pattering drops cheered the waiting inhabitants.

The relief was wonderful. The delicious smell of rain water cooling hot stones and earth was then more appreciated than the most expensive scent. Rain splashed on the parched grass of Thrush Green, and pattered on the great dusty leaves of the chestnut trees. It gurgled down the gutters to Lulling, and formed wide puddles across the road outside St Andrew's church. It sent the local cats, out upon their nightly forays, scampering for home, and encouraged the thirsty wild creatures to venture forth for their first satisfying drink for many a long day.

The air grew blessedly cool and fresh. The wakeful ones sought those blankets which had been unused for weeks, and snuggled into their beds with thankful hearts.


The morning after the storm dawned clear and fresh. The world of Thrush Green sparkled in the sunshine, and everyone relished the slight coolness in the air, and the rejuvenation of all living things.

Even Albert Piggott gave the green a grudging smile as he walked across to St Andrew's. Here he proposed to spend a leisurely hour or two surveying his domain, safe from Nelly's gaze.

Nelly had finished at the Lovelock's, and mightily relieved she was to be able to set to and do her own chores without one eye on the clock. The Misses Lovelock had been sticklers for punctuality, and would not have been above docking Nelly's wages if she had arrived late. Knowing this, Nelly had been very particular in arriving promptly.

She had been paid in full, and wished goodbye by all three ladies. Miss Ada had been gracious enough to say that she would be willing to supply a reference if Nelly required it at any time. Nelly thanked her civilly.

The snag was that there was still no work available, and the thought of being at close quarters with Albert, day in and day out, was a daunting one.

She thought about her future as she dismantled the stove and prepared to scour each part in strong soda water. Albert had been at his grumpiest for the past week. The truth was that he disliked the heat, and that Nelly's cooking was again playing havoc with his digestion. He enjoyed venting his ill-humour upon Nelly, and during the thunderstorm whilst they were hoping for rain, he had been particularly unpleasant about Nelly's chances of employment.

'Can't expect decent folks to take on a trollop like you,' was the phrase that hurt most. It still rankled as Nelly attacked the cooker. The thing was, it was near the truth, and Nelly knew it.

She began to think of Charlie, the oil man. With all his faults, he had never been unkind to her, or insulted her as Albert did. Looking back now, she forgot his meanness, his dishonesty with money, and the long evenings she had spent alone, trying to keep his supper hot without it spoiling.

She thought of his attractions, his glossy black hair, the music hall ditties he was so fond of singing, and the good times they had enjoyed together at local pubs. True to her principles, Nelly had stuck to bitter lemon or orange juice while Charlie swigged his whisky, but she had enjoyed meeting his rowdy friends and joining in the songs around the bar piano.

She paused in her scrubbing and gazed out of the steamy window towards Thrush Green. Not much life here, that was for sure! And what would it be like in the winter, when the curtains were drawn at four o'clock, and Albert had left her for The Two Pheasants next door? A living death, decided Nelly, just a living death!

She would have done better to have looked for a place where she was. There was far more scope for her talents in Brighton than ever there would be at Thrush Green. She pondered the matter for a full hour, by which time the cooker had been reassembled, and the frying-pan filled with bacon, liver and sausages for the midday meal.

'Fatty stuff again, I see,' grunted Albert, when his plate was put before him later. 'You knows what Doctor Lovell said. You trying to kill me?'

'Chance'd be a fine thing,' retorted Nelly. 'The devil looks after his own, as far as I can see.'

Albert snorted.

'You'd be a far sight fitter,' went on Nelly, 'if you laid off the beer. All that acid fair eats away the lining of your stummick. I was reading about it in my women's paper.'

'You wants to change the record,' snarled Albert, with heavy sarcasm. 'And if you looked for a job instead of wastin' your time with women's papers you'd be a bit better off.'

Nelly rose from the table with as much dignity as a sixteen-stone woman could manage, and went to the dresser drawer. From it she abstracted a cheap packet of stationery and a ballpoint pen, and made her way upstairs.

Sitting on the side of the spare bed she composed a letter to Charlie. It was not an easy letter to write, and how it would be received was anybody's guess. It took Nelly nearly an hour to get her thoughts on paper, and when at last she had sealed the envelope and stuck on the stamp, she descended the stairs.

Albert was fast asleep in the armchair. His mouth was open, and he snored loudly, making a maddening little whining sound as he did so. The dirty dishes still littered the table, and the newly-cleaned stove bore fresh splashes of fat.

Nelly opened the door, and marched straight across the grass to the post-box on the corner of Thrush Green. She was oblivious of the fresh beauty about her, and the bright new world which the rain had created.

She dropped the letter in the box, and heard its satisfying plop as it reached the bottom.

Well, she'd done it! She'd burnt her boats, thought Nelly, and now she must face the future!

## 20. A Proposal

Miss Fogerty travelled by coach from Thrush Green to Bournemouth where she was being met. She determined to take Isobel's advice and postpone all thoughts of finding new accommodation until she returned, but she had called on Charles Henstock, before she left for her week's holiday, and told him of her predicament.

'My dear Miss Fogerty,' said that kind man, his chubby face creased with concern, 'I shall do my very best to find somewhere for you. Try not to let it worry you when you are away. You need a break after all the troubles of last term. Something will turn up, I feel convinced.'

He had told his wife about the encounter, and Dimity at once thought of Ella.

'The only thing is she has said so little about taking a lodger recently, that I'm beginning to wonder if she really wants one.'

'We can only ask,' said Charles. 'Perhaps you could broach the subject?'

Dimity did, that very afternoon, and as she had surmised, Ella did not appear at all keen.

'The point is, Dim, I've been thinking it over, and I've got quite used to being alone here, and I'm not all that hard up. I mean, look at my clothes!'

Dimity looked, and was secretly appalled.

'I've had these trousers five years, and this shirt much the same length of time, and I can't see myself bothering to buy much in that line. And then I don't go out as much as I used to, nor do the same amount of entertaining as we did when you were here. One way and another, I think I'd sooner scratch along on my own.'

'But you thoroughly enjoyed having Isobel,' Dimity pointed out.

'Isobel's one in a thousand and in any case it was only for a week. I just don't want anyone permanently.'

'In a way,' said Dimity, 'I'm relieved to hear it.'

'Not that I'd see little Agnes homeless,' continued Ella. 'If she hasn't found anywhere before term starts, I'm very willing to put her up for a bit while she's looking round. I'm fond of that funny little soul.'

'We all are,' replied Dimity.


It was soon after this, that Harold walked across to Tullivers to tell Isobel that he had ordered an Alfa Romeo very like her own, and was now bracing himself to part with the ancient Daimler which had played an important part in his life.

The day was cool and cloudy. In fact, the violent thunderstorm had brought the hot summer weather to an end, and there were to be very few sunny days until the autumn.

He found Isobel busy writing letters. She gave him her usual warm smile which affected his heart in such a delightful way, but he thought that she appeared somewhat worried.

'Anything wrong?' he asked, seating himself at the table where her writing things were littered.

Isobel put her hands flat on the table with a gesture of despair.

'A lot, I'm afraid. I was coming to tell you. I shall have to drive home again. There's a muddle about the sale of the house.'

'Can't the estate agent cope with that? Must you go today?'

'Either today, or tomorrow morning. The sale's fallen through again.'

She sighed, and looked so desperately unhappy, that Harold could not bear it. He had never seen her cast down. In all their fruitless searchings for a house she had always managed to maintain a certain buoyancy of spirit which was one of the reasons why he loved her.

He put a hand over one of hers, and spoke urgently.

'Isobel, let me help with this. I can't bear to see you so unhappy, and it's all so unnecessary.'

'Unnecessary?' queried Isobel.

'I've wanted to say something for weeks now, but it has never seemed the right moment. I don't know if this is – but hear me out, Isobel, I beg of you.'

He tightened his grip on her hand, and began his plea. Isobel sat very still, her eyes downcast upon their linked hands, and heard him out as he had asked.

'And will you?' he ended. 'Could you, Isobel?'

She smiled at him, and at last regained her hand.

'Thank you, Harold dear. You must let me think for a day or so. My mind is so confused with all that's happened, I shall need time. But I do thank you, from the bottom of my heart. It is the loveliest thing that has happened to me for a long, long time.'

'You dear girl!' exclaimed Harold. 'And please don't keep me waiting too long! I warn you, I've been in a state of near-dementia for the past months.'

Isobel laughed. 'I promise you an answer before the end of the week, but I must get back and sort out some of this muddle. Oh, the misery of selling and buying houses!'

'You know the way out now,' Harold pointed out.

'You would never know,' replied Isobel, 'if I'd married you or the house.'

'I'll take that risk,' Harold assured her.


As always, the building activity at the Youngs' took considerably longer than had at first been imagined, despite Edward's daily exhortations.

To be fair, the builders worked well, but there were interminable delays in getting materials from the suppliers which held up the proceedings.

It was plain that the top flat was going to be ready before the stable block conversion, but even so it did not look as though the second bedroom would be ready in time for the Curdles' arrival in September.

Joan wrote to let them know how things were, and was glad to hear that the negotiations for the sale of the fair to Dick Hasler were now almost completed. They would be selling their caravan home when they came to Thrush Green, wrote Molly, and the money would help them to furnish the flat.

But, asked Molly, Ben could not bear to part with his grandmother's wooden gipsy caravan, and could they bring it with them? Would there be somewhere out of the way where it could stand? It might be quite a useful spare-room, and Ben would be very pleased if they would like to use it as such at any time in the future.

Joan felt a surge of happiness when she read this. What could be better? Mrs Curdle's much-loved caravan had always been an important part of Thrush Green's life. May the first had been the highlight of the year, and it was only fitting that the caravan should return to its old haunt forever, and to stand close to the last resting place of its famous owner.

'There's plenty of room in the orchard,' Edward said, when he heard about the proposal. He was as delighted as Joan to think of having the caravan at Thrush Green.

So were their neighbours and friends. Winnie Bailey, in particular, welcomed the idea, remembering how old Mrs Curdle had visited her regularly every year.

'It's so much part of Thrush Green history,' said the rector, summing up general opinion, 'that it's the *only* place for it. We shall all treasure it.'

Nelly Piggott awaited an answer to her letter with some anxiety. For one thing, she wanted to take it from the postman as soon as it arrived. No one could accuse Albert of undue interest in the meagre correspondence which was slipped under the door, but he might well open a letter which was written by hand thinking it might be from Molly, who was about the only person who did write to him.

Manilla envelopes, with typed addresses, were beneath his notice. They would either contain bills, or some other objectionable enclosures, which would be stowed, often unopened, behind the clock on the kitchen mantel shelf, for later perusal.

Nelly was usually up first, and downstairs by the time Willie Bond delivered the post. If Willie Bond was on duty, he arrived whilst Nelly was on her own in the kitchen.

But if the second postman, Willie Marchant, delivered the mail then he arrived a good half-hour later, and by then Albert was at large in the kitchen with her.

A fortnight had passed and still there was no response from the oil man. Of course, Nelly told herself, he might be away. He might even have moved house, but in that case, surely he would have left an address at the Post Office, and his letters would have been forwarded.

It was more likely, Nelly was bound to admit, that he did not consider a reply necessary, and did not intend to waste good money on a stamp for one who had upped and left him comparatively recently.

'Can't blame him, I suppose,' said Nelly to Albert's cat, when Willie Bond had departed after leaving a seed catalogue addressed to Albert, the only item of mail.

But it was worrying. It would be better to know the worst. It would be *far* better, Nelly told herself, to have a rude letter telling her what he thought of her, than this horrible silence.

During this waiting period she had cleaned the house from top to bottom. Any object which could be assaulted with strong soda water, yellow soap and a stiff scrubbing-brush, had been so treated. Anything which could be polished, whether it were of metal, wood or glass, had been attacked mercilessly. Even the cat, once so thin, had been fattened with Nelly's good food, and was given a brisk brushing, and its ears cleaned out with oily cotton wool twisted into a serviceable radish shape.

In between these frenzied spells of cleaning, Nelly took short walks. Sometimes, in order to get away from Albert, she took herself to Lulling and surveyed the shops, or called at the Job Centre, in case she would need to earn again. Sometimes, she strolled towards Lulling Woods, and once went as far as The Drovers' Arms and called on the Allens, secretly hoping that there might be work for her there, if the oil man did not come up to scratch. But there was nothing there, as the Allens made clear, softening the blow by giving her a cup of tea and Garibaldi biscuits, before she made the return journey.

Albert was more melancholy than ever, and Nelly was beginning to wonder how much longer she could stand the suspense of waiting, and the tedium of her husband's nagging.

When, one happy morning, Willie Marchant handed in the letter she had been waiting for, she was able to put it quickly into her overall pocket before Albert realized what was going on.

When he had departed to his duties at St Andrew's, she opened the envelope. The letter was short and to the point:

Dear Nelly,
    Come on back, you old faggot.
Forgiven and forgotten.
                    Love,
                    Charlie

Nelly could have wept with relief. There was a man for you! Big-hearted, took life as it came, willing to forget and forgive! She wouldn't leave him again in a hurry, that was sure! Why, he'd even put 'Love' at the end! No doubt about it, Charlie was one in a million!

She sat down at the kitchen table and wrote back. Her letter was even more brief than Charlie's:

Darling Charlie,
    Coming Wednesday,

Best love,
Your Nelly

She had to walk down the hill to Lulling to buy a stamp, but she was too happy to mind. Normally, she found the return journey, up the steep hill, distinctly daunting, but on this occasion she sailed up it as blithely as a Lakeland fell climber.

Life was about to start again for Nelly Piggott.

At Barton-on-Sea Agnes and Dorothy sat on the veranda of the small hotel, and admired the sea.

It was still difficult for Dorothy to negotiate the steps nearest to the hotel, leading to the beach and the weather was not as reliable as one could wish for a seaside holiday. The veranda gave them shelter from the wind, and all the sunshine that was available.

'Besides, dear,' Miss Watson pointed out, 'here we are handy for our library books and knitting, or a cup of coffee, if we want it. And sand can be rather *pervasive*. Into everything, isn't it? But don't let me stop you, Agnes, if you want to have a walk along the beach. I'm quite happy here.'

Agnes assured her that she was perfectly contented.

'We'll have a little stroll along the cliff top later,' said Dorothy. 'Grass is so much pleasanter to walk on than sand.'

Miss Fogerty agreed automatically. It was wonderful to be here, taking in the fresh salt-laden air, feeling the warmth of the sun, and the comfort of Dorothy's presence. But her mind still fluttered round her problem, despite her determination to shelve it, as advised by dear Isobel and Charles Henstock. It was easier said than done.

For two days now she had fought against the temptation to confide in her headmistress. Agnes had always found it difficult to keep anything from her. By nature she was not a secretive person, although she could be discreet with other people's confidences.

She gazed out to the sparkling sea, watching the gulls swoop and scream, as they swerved for food being thrown to them by someone hidden from her sight below the cliff. Involuntarily, she sighed.

Miss Watson was quick to notice.

'Agnes dear, are you *sure* you want to sit here? Do say if you feel like doing anything else. I want this little holiday to be *exactly* as you want it. I shall feel *most unhappy* if I am holding you back.'

'Indeed, Dorothy, I am doing just what I want,' cried Agnes.

'But you don't seem quite yourself,' replied Dorothy solicitously. 'Are you quite well? Are you worried about anything? Surely you can tell an old friend any troubles?'

Her kind face, peering so anxiously into that of her companion's, was Agnes Fogerty's undoing.

The floodgates opened, and the whole pitiful story poured forth. Mr White's promotion, his pension, his savings, Mrs White's reluctance to tell her lodger, her tact in doing so, her past kindnesses, all flowed from Agnes in a stream of words, to which Dorothy listened with mingled pity and hope.

'And so,' concluded Agnes, having recourse to one of her best Swiss handkerchiefs, 'I must look for something else. I didn't mean to tell you, you know. It isn't fair to unload my troubles on you when you are still convalescent.'

Miss Watson took a deep breath of good sea air.

'I don't consider myself *convalescent* any longer,' she said robustly. 'And you have taken a great weight off my mind.'

'I have?' quavered Agnes.

'You see, I dearly wanted to ask you if you would consider living permanently at the schoolhouse. There's nothing I should like more, but I feared you might feel I was in need and your unselfishness would prompt you to do something which perhaps you did not really want to do.'

'Not really want to do?' echoed Agnes.

'You must think it over,' went on Dorothy. 'I shall quite understand if you refuse. I know that your independence means a lot to you, and I respect that. I respect it very much.'

Little Miss Fogerty returned her handkerchief to her pocket, and sat up very straight.

'I don't need any time, Dorothy, to think it over. To live at the schoolhouse would please me more than anything in the world, if you're *really sure*.'

'I've been *really sure* for months,' said Dorothy. 'And now I think we might celebrate with that cup of coffee, Agnes dear, if you can reach the bell.'


At Thrush Green, Harold Shoosmith awaited Isobel's answer with anxious impatience. She had been gone for three days now, and he was sure that she would keep her promise and let him know within the week. But what a ghastly length of time that seemed!

Neither Willie Bond, nor Willie Marchant, had ever seen him so swift to take in the letters. The telephone receiver was snatched from the cradle before it had time to ring twice, and Harold was remarkably short with those who rang up. After all, it might be the very moment that Isobel was trying to get through.

Betty Bell noted his agitation with some sympathy and amusement.

'I bet you miss Mrs Fletcher,' she remarked conversationally, over elevenses.

Harold ignored the remark.

'A real nice lady,' continued Betty, crunching a ginger biscuit. 'Miss Harmer was only saying yesterday as how it would be lovely to have her living here.'

'Here?' interjected Harold. Was it so obvious?

'In Thrush Green,' explained Betty. 'Or nearby. Everyone wants her back.'

Not as much as I do, thought Harold, pushing back his chair.

'Well, I must get on with my hedge-cutting,' said Harold, making his escape.

It was Betty Bell who answered the telephone half an hour later.

'Hang on,' she shouted cheerfully. 'I'll get him.'

She hung out of the kitchen window.

'Mrs Fletcher on the phone,' she yelled, and admired the speed with which her employer abandoned the shears and sprinted up the path.

She would dearly have loved to listen to the conversation on the bedroom extension, but decided to retreat to the landing where, with any luck, she would be out of sight, and might hear at least one side of the proceedings.

She had to wait some time, for there seemed to be a great deal said at the Sussex end, but at last her vigil was rewarded.

'Oh, Isobel!' cried her employer. 'You darling! Yes, I'll be with you at twelve tomorrow, with a bottle of champagne.'

There was another break, and then: 'I can't say all I want to, but I'll say it tomorrow. Yes, Betty's here, and listening too, I've no doubt. But who cares?'

When a minute later he put down the telephone, Betty sauntered down the stairs with as convincing an air of innocence as she could muster.

'Betty,' said Harold, his face radiant. 'I'm going to get married.'

'Really, sir?'

'To Mrs Fletcher,' said Harold.

'We all said you would,' said Betty, picking up her duster.

# Epilogue

One golden October morning, Robert and Milly Bassett at last arrived at Thrush Green.

The air was crisp and clear, and the sky that pellucid blue which only early autumn brings. The chestnut leaves were turning colour, and some had already fallen, spreading a glowing, crackling carpet beneath the trees.

Over lunch, Joan had plenty to tell her parents. There were still several things to finish at their new home, and Joan insisted that they slept in the old house until she was satisfied that the new plaster had dried out.

Otherwise, the stable block had become a charming one-storey house, sheltered by the Cotswold stone garden wall, and shaded by mature trees. Robert and Milly were delighted with it.

'And how about Ben and Molly?' asked Milly. 'How's the new job going?'

'Splendidly. He's so happy, and Tim Collet told Edward that he'll probably put him into a more responsible job when one of the older men leaves after Christmas.'

'And Molly?'

'As helpful as ever, and relieved to be near her father, of course, especially now that Nelly's left him.'

'It's little George I want to see,' said Milly.

'He's at school now, with Miss Fogerty. He was promoted to filling in the weather chart this week, so you can see he's happy enough!'

The Hursts were back, Joan told them, and Frank had evidently made a great hit with his lecture tour, and had been invited to go again the following year.

'But our most exciting news,' said Joan, when she poured the coffee, 'is of Harold Shoosmith. He's on his honeymoon at the moment, and you can guess the flutter his marriage made here.'

'Better late than never,' pronounced Robert. 'And he couldn't have chosen more wisely.'

Obedient to the directions of his wife and daughter, Robert went to lie down for an hour and, to his surprise, had a short nap. The journey must have tired him more than he realized.

Much refreshed, he rose and made his way into the garden, and wandered among the falling leaves, admiring the Michaelmas daisies, the golden rod, and the velvet brilliance of the dahlias. It was a lovely time of year to come home, he thought, and sighed with pleasure.

He turned into the orchard and caught his breath with delight. There, beneath a gnarled apple tree, stood dear Mrs Curdle's caravan. Joan had not mentioned this, and he went to investigate.

It was in excellent trim. The paint was fresh, the brass polished, the minute windows sparkling.

The top half of the door was open, and Robert could see that it looked just as he remembered it in Mrs Curdle's day. There was the shining stove, the framed text above it, and the gaudy counterpane smoothed over the bunk bed.

It gave Robert enormous joy to see the little home again, and he was smiling as he retraced his steps.

He went out of the open front gate and surveyed the scene.

On his right was the village school. The younger children were already emerging from the new classroom at the back of the playground, George, no doubt, among them. In the distance, he could see little Agnes Fogerty, and waved to her.

She waved back, and he thought what a splendid thing it was that she and Miss Watson had joined forces. Nothing like a little companionship as you grew older!

Beside the school, Harold's house stood with its windows closed, awaiting the return of its master and new mistress from the Greek islands.

'And if Harold isn't showing his slides at a Women's Institute meeting next season, I'll eat my hat!' thought Robert, knowing his Thrush Green.

His eyes wandered to The Two Pheasants where the hanging baskets still made a brave splash of colour. Across the expanse of grass, someone was moving among the stones in the graveyard at St Andrew's, where so many of Robert's old friends, including Mrs Curdle, rested forever.

It looked like the rector, Robert thought, shading his eyes against the sinking sun, and he was about to walk across to greet him, when he heard the front door open behind him, and the sound of voices.

Joan was accompanying Dotty Harmer to the gate, and he turned to greet his old friend, who looked, if anything, even more tattered than usual.

She interrupted her flow of conversation just long enough to say how lovely it was to see him in his own surroundings, and then returned to her discourse.

'Now, I can thoroughly recommend either of the two spaniels. Well, spaniel-types, I'd better say. Their tails leave much to be desired, but of course they may fill out as they grow. Both bitches, and a beautiful pale gold.

'I wouldn't suggest the collie. He's going to be enormous, judging by his paws, and I'm trying Percy Hodge for him. I hear he wants another dog, and after all, it was his present collie that was the father. Or *one* of them,' added Dotty, strictly honest.

'That leaves the black and tan terrier-type dog, and the shaggy little bitch. She's going to be *most unusual*, and highly intelligent too. So just think it over, Joan dear. I know whichever you choose will have a marvellous home.'

'Can I bring Paul down to see them when he's home from school? It will really be his puppy. He misses his old dog terribly since she died last winter.'

'Of course, of course.'

She suddenly became conscious of Robert listening with quiet pleasure to the conversation.

'Would you like a puppy, Robert? You'll have all the time in the world now, to train it.'

Robert shook his head.

'I'm too long in the tooth for puppies,' he told her. 'I'll take a share in bringing up Paul's.'

'Very well,' said Dotty, bending to adjust a suspender against her skinny thigh. 'I'll be getting back. Flossie tends to get a little agitated if I'm away for long. Post-natal emotion, of course. Otherwise, she's a wonderful little mother.'

She nodded briskly, and set off across the grass to Lulling Woods, her stockings in imminent danger of collapsing, and one claw-like hand holding on to her disreputable straw hat.

Joan and her father turned back towards their home.

'D'you know,' said Robert, putting an arm round his daughter's shoulders. 'I've thought so often about coming back here. I've thought about the house, and the garden, and the chestnut avenue, and St Andrew's church, and Nathaniel Patten's statue, and all my dear friends here. But the fact is –'

Here he stopped, and drew in his breath.

'The real joy of the place didn't hit me until I saw Mrs Curdle's caravan, and dear old Dotty finding homes, as always, for puppies.

'Now I *know* that I really have returned to Thrush Green.'

# Gossip from Thrush Green

*To*

*Janet*

*With Love and Thanks*

# Contents

# 1. Afternoon Tea

In far too many places in England today, the agreeable habit of taking afternoon tea has vanished.

'Such a shocking waste of time,' says one.

'Much too fattening a meal with all that dreadful starch,' says another.

'Quite unnecessary, if one has had lunch or proposes to eat in the evening,' says a third.

All very true, no doubt, but what a lot of innocent pleasure these strong-minded people are missing! The very ritual of tea-making, warming the pot, making sure that the water is just boiling, inhaling the fragrant steam, arranging the tea-cosy to fit snugly around the precious container, all the preliminaries lead up to the exquisite pleasure of sipping the brew from thin porcelain, and helping oneself to hot buttered scones and strawberry jam, a slice of feather-light sponge cake or home-made shortbread.

Taking tea is a highly civilized pastime, and fortunately is still in favour at Thrush Green, where it has been brought to a fine art. It is common practice in that pleasant village to invite friends to tea rather than lunch or dinner. As Winnie Bailey, the doctor's widow, pointed out one day to her old friend Ella Bembridge, people could set off from their homes in the light, and return before dark, except for the really miserable weeks of mid-winter when one would probably prefer to stay at home anyway.

'Besides,' said Ella, who was fond of her food, 'when else can you eat home-made gingerbread, all squishy with black treacle? Or dip into the pounds of jam on the larder shelves?'

'I suppose one could make a sponge pudding with jam at the bottom,' replied Winnie thoughtfully, 'but Jenny and I prefer fresh fruit.'

'Jenny looks as though a sponge pudding might do her good,' said Ella, naming Winnie's maid and friend. 'She seems to have lost a lot of weight recently. She's not *dieting*, I hope?'

Winnie proffered the dish of shortbread, and Ella, who was certainly not dieting, took a piece.

'I've noticed it myself,' confessed Winnie. 'I do hope she's not doing too much in the house. As you know, we've offered to look after Tullivers when Frank and Phil are away, and Jeremy will stay with us. So I'm determined that Jenny shall not overwork then.'

Tullivers was the attractive house next door to Winnie Bailey's. Built of the local Cotswold stone, it faced south, standing at right angles to her own home, and their gardens adjoined. Since the death of her doctor husband, Donald, she had been more thankful than ever for her good neighbours, the Hursts.

Frank Hurst was an editor, and his wife Phyllida a freelance writer. They had met when Phil was busy submitting work some years earlier. Her first husband had been killed in a motoring accident, and she had been left to bring up her young son Jeremy with very little money.

This second marriage had turned out to be a very happy one, and the inhabitants of Thrush Green thoroughly approved of the Hursts, who played their part in village life, supplying prizes for raffles, jumble for the many rummage sales, and consenting, with apparent cheerfulness, to sit on at least half a dozen local committees. Jeremy was a happy child, now in Miss Watson's class at Thrush Green village school, and due to start at his new school, in nearby Lulling, next September.

In April, Frank and his wife were off to America where he was to spend six weeks lecturing. It was too long a period to keep Jeremy from school, and Winnie had offered at once to look after him.

'It would give me enormous pleasure,' she assured the Hursts, 'and the boy is never any bother. Just the reverse in fact. It would be such a comfort to have a man about the place again.'

And so it was arranged.

On this particular February afternoon, when Winnie and Ella were enjoying their modest tea-party, the weather was as bleak and dreary as any that that wretched month can produce.

A few brave snowdrops had emerged under the shelter of Winnie's front hedge, and the winter jasmine on the wall still made a gallant show, but the trees remained gaunt and bare, and the prevailing colour everywhere, from heavy clouds above to the misty fields below, was a uniform grey.

'The winters get longer,' commented Ella, craning her neck to look out of the window, 'and the summers shorter. Dimity and Charles don't agree, but I'm going to keep a weather diary next year to prove my point.'

Charles Henstock was the rector of Thrush Green, and had married Dimity, Ella's lifelong friend, a few years earlier. They lived contentedly in the most hideous house on the green, a tall, badly proportioned Victorian horror, covered in peeling stucco, whose ugliness was made more noticeable by the mellow beauty of the surrounding Cotswold architecture.

Most of the Thrush Green residents were resigned to this monstrosity, but Edward Young, the local architect, who lived in the most splendid of Thrush Green's houses, always maintained that a glimpse of the Henstocks' rectory gave him acute pains in the stomach. His wife Joan, a cheerful down-to-earth person, dismissed this as quite unnecessary chi-chi, and hoped that he was not going to grow into one of those tiresome people who affect hyper-sensitivity in order to impress others.

This trenchant remark had the effect of restoring Edward's good humour, but he still stuck to his guns and was the first to attack the unknown and long-dead architect of Thrush Green's great mistake.

'Dimity,' went on Ella, 'was wondering if she could persuade Charles to move his study upstairs. It's so cold and dark at the moment, and they could easily turn that little bedroom over the kitchen into a nice snug place for the writing of sermons. Heaven alone knows, there are only about two rooms in the house which get any sun.'

'I gather he doesn't like the idea,' commented Winnie.

'Well, he's not being *too* obstinate, but suggests that they wait until after their holiday.'

'That should put it off nicely,' agreed Winnie, pouring her guest a second cup of Darjeeling tea. 'Now tell me the rest of the news.'

Ella frowned with concentration.

'Dotty is toying with the idea of adopting a little girl.'

Winnie put down the tea pot with a crash.

'She can't be! The way she lives? No adoption society would countenance it!'

Dotty Harmer, an elderly eccentric friend, beloved of both, lived some half a mile away in a dilapidated cottage, surrounded by a garden full of chickens, ducks, geese, goats and any stray animals in need of succour. Indoors lived several cats, kittens, dogs and puppies. Occasionally, a wounded bird convalesced in a large cage in the kitchen, and once an ailing stoat had occupied the hospital accommodation.

'He is rather smelly,' Dotty had admitted, 'but it's handy for giving him scraps when I'm cooking.' Even her closest friends had found hasty excuses for declining invitations to meals whilst the stoat was in residence. At the best of times Dotty's food was suspect, and a local ailment, known as 'Dotty's Collywobbles', was quite common.

'I don't think Dotty has thought about that side of it. She told me that now that she was getting on it might be a good idea to train someone to take over from her, and look after the animals and the house.'

'The mind boggles,' said Winnie, 'at the thought of dear Dotty training *anyone*.'

'Well, she said it seemed a shame that she had no one to leave things to when she died, and it really could provide a very nice life for someone.'

'I am shocked to the core,' confessed Winnie. 'But there, we all know Dotty. She's probably forgotten about it by now, and is full of some other hare-brained scheme.'

'Let's hope so,' said Ella beginning to collect her bag and gloves. 'And that reminds me that I must get back to collect my goat's milk from her. She promised to call in about five-thirty with it, and I want her to choose some wool for a scarf. I've dug out my old hand loom, and I warn you now, Winnie dear, that all my friends will be getting a handwoven scarf next Christmas.'

'You are so kind,' said Winnie faintly, trying to remember how many lumpy scratchy scarves, of Ella's making, still remained unworn upstairs. Sometimes she wondered if fragments of heather and thistle remained in the wool. It was impossible to pass them on to the local jumble sales for Ella would soon come across them again in such a small community, and Winnie was too kind-hearted to inflict them upon such distant organizations as Chest and Heart Societies. The members had quite enough to put up with already, she felt.

'By the way,' said Ella, turning at the front door, 'are you going to Violet's coffee morning? It's in aid of Distressed Gentlefolk.'

'I should think those three Lovelock sisters would qualify for that themselves,' observed Winnie.

'Don't you believe it,' said Ella forthrightly. 'With that treasure house around them? One day they'll be burgled, and then they really will be *distressed*, though no doubt they're well insured. Justin Venables will have seen to that.'

She set off down the wet path, a square stumpy figure, planting her sensible brogues heavily, her handwoven scarf swinging over her ample chest.

Winnie watched her departing figure affectionately.

'Yes, I'll be there,' she called, and closed the door upon the bleak world outside.


The Misses Lovelock, Violet, Ada and Bertha, lived in a fine old house in Lulling High Street, less than a mile downhill from Thrush Green.

Here the three maiden ladies had been born at the beginning of the century, and here, presumably, they would one day die, unless some particularly forceful doctor could persuade them to end their days in one of the local hospitals.

They had been left comfortably off by their father, which was as well, as the house was large and needed a great deal of heating and maintenance. Not that they spent much on these last two items, and prudent visitors went warmly clothed when invited to the house, and could not help noticing that walls and woodwork were much in need of fresh paint.

The amount spent on food was even more meagre. The sisters seemed able to survive on thin bread and butter, lettuce when in season, and the occasional egg. Guests were lucky indeed if meat appeared on the table, not that the Lovelocks were vegetarians, but simply because meat was expensive and needed fuel and time to cook it. Most of their friends consumed a substantial sandwich before dining with the Lovelocks, or faced an evening of stomach rumblings whilst sipping weak coffee.

The extraordinary thing was that the house was crammed with valuable furniture, and with glass cabinets stuffed with antique silver and priceless porcelain. All three sisters had an eye for such things, and were shrewd bargainers. They were also quite shameless in asking for any attractive object which caught their eye in other people's houses, and this effrontery had stood them in good stead as a number of exquisite pieces in their collection proved. There were several people in Thrush Green and Lulling who cursed their momentary weakness in giving way to a wheedling Miss

Ada or Miss Violet as they fingered some treasure which had taken their fancy.

On this particular afternoon, while Winnie was tidying away the tea things and Ella was unlocking her front door, the three sisters were sorting out an assortment of articles already delivered for the bring and buy stall at the coming coffee morning.

'I wonder,' said Violet pensively, 'if we should buy this in, dear?'

'Buying things in' was another well-known way of acquiring some desirable object. It really meant having first pick, as it were, at the preview, and many a donor had looked in vain for some pretty knick-knack on the stall when one or more of the Misses Lovelock had had a hand in the preparations.

Violet now held up a small silver-plated butter dish in the form of a shell.

Ada scrutinized it shrewdly.

'I think Joan Young sent it. Better not. It's only plate anyway.'

Violet replaced it reluctantly.

'Would you say fifty pence for these dreadful tea-cosies?' asked Bertha.

'Mrs Venables crocheted those,' said Ada reprovingly, 'and you know how her poor hands are crippled with arthritis. At least seventy pence, Bertha, in the circumstances.'

Bertha wrote three tickets for that amount. Ada always knew best.

A circular biscuit tin bearing portraits of King George V and Queen Mary proved to be a treasure chest of buttons, buckles, beads and other trifles.

The three white heads met over the box. Six skinny claws rattled the contents. Six eyes grew bright with desire.

'And who sent this?' inquired Bertha, anxious not to offend again.

'Miss Watson from the school,' replied Violet. She withdrew a long piece of narrow black ribbon studded with jet. 'How pretty this would look as an edging to my black blouse!'

'It would look better as a trimming on my evening bag,' said Bertha. She took hold of the other end.

'Miss Watson,' said Ada dreamily, 'will not be able to come to the coffee morning. These things were left her among a lot of other trifles, she told me, by her aunt in Birmingham.'

'Well, then –' said Violet.

'In that case –' said Bertha. Both ladies were a little pink in the face.

'Put it on one side,' said Ada, 'and we'll think about buying it in later.'

I see there are some charming jet buttons here too. They may have come from the same garment. A pity to part them, don't you think?'

Scrabbling happily, the three sisters continued their search, while outside the lamps came on in the High Street of Lulling, throwing pools of light upon the wet pavements, and the damp figures of those homeward bound.

One of the figures, head bent, and moving slowly towards the hill which led to Thrush Green, was that of St Andrew's Sexton, Albert Piggott, who lived alone in a cottage facing the church and conveniently next door to The Two Pheasants, Thrush Green's only public house.

Albert was always morose, but this evening his gloom was deeper than ever. Cursed with habitual indigestion which his diet of alcohol, meat pie and pickles did nothing to help, he had just been to collect a packet of pills from Lulling's chemist.

Doctor Lovell of Thrush Green, who had married Joan Young's sister and had served as a junior partner to Donald Bailey, was now the senior partner in the practice, and Albert Piggott was one of his oldest and most persistent patients. It was vain to try to get the irritable old man to change his ways. All that he could do was to vary his prescription now and again in the hope that Albert's tormented digestive tract would respond, at least temporarily, to new treatment.

'Plain bicarb again, I don't doubt,' muttered Albert, slouching homeward. 'What I really needs is good hot meals.'

He thought wistfully of Nelly's cooking. Nelly, his wife, had left him – twice, to make it worse – and both times to share life with the oil man whose flashy good looks and honeyed words had attracted her on his weekly rounds.

Nelly now lived with her new partner on the south coast, and it was he who now enjoyed her superb steak-and-kidney puddings, succulent roasts, and well-spiced casseroles. The very thought of that chap's luck brought on Albert's indigestion.

Not that Albert lacked attention. In many ways, he was better off.

Nelly's cooking had tended to be rich, even by normal standards. She excelled with cheese sauces, fried potatoes, and creamy puddings. Her cakes were dark and moist with fruit, her sponge cakes were filled with butter icing, and more icing decorated the top. Doctor Lovell's pleas to her to provide plainer fare for her husband fell on deaf ears. Nelly was an artist. Butter, sugar and the best quality meat and dairy foods were her materials. She cooked, and Albert ate. Doctor Lovell hadn't a chance.

But since Nelly's departure, presumably for good this time, his daughter Molly had done her best to look after the old man.

She was married to a fine young fellow called Ben Curdle, and the couple lived nearby with their little boy George in a flat at the top of the Youngs' house. Ben was employed in Lulling, and Molly helped Joan in the house. The arrangement worked well, for Molly had been known to the Youngs for all their lives. They had rejoiced when Molly had finally succeeded in escaping, through marriage, from the clutches of her selfish old father. Now that she was back in Thrush Green they only hoped that she would not be so kind-hearted as to fall into the trap again.

Molly, wiser than Nelly, cooked with prudence for her father, leaving him light dishes of fish or eggs as recommended by the doctor. More often than not these offerings were given to the cat by Albert, in Molly's absence. He dismissed them as 'pappy stuff' and either went next door for his pie and beer, or used the unwashed frying pan to cook himself another meal of bacon and eggs.

At times Molly despaired. Ben took a realistic attitude to the problem.

'Lord knows he's old enough to know what's good for him. Let him go his own way. Don't upset yourself on his account. He never put himself out for you, did he?'

There was truth in this. Molly had enough to do with looking after Ben and George, and the housework. She loved being back in Thrush Green. The only snag was her obstinate old father. At times she wished that Nelly would return to look after him. Although she disliked her blowsy stepmother, at least Albert's cottage had been kept clean and he had been looked after.

Albert trudged up the hill, the rain slanting into his face from the north. Lights glowed from the cottage windows. A car swished by, splashing the old man's legs.

The bulk of St Andrew's church stood massively against the night sky.

'Best lock up while I'm on me feet,' thought Albert, changing course towards the building. The door was ajar, but no one was inside.

Albert stood in the dark aisle looking towards the three shadowy windows behind the altar. The familiar church smell compounded of damp and brass polish met his nostrils. Somewhere a scuffling and squeaking broke the silence.

'Dratted mice!' exclaimed Albert, kicking a pew end.

Silence fell again.

Albert withdrew, clanging the heavy door behind him. From beneath the door mat he extracted an enormous key. He locked the door, and stuffed the key into his pocket to take across to the house for the night.

Standing in the shelter of the porch he surveyed the view through the rain. His own cottage, directly opposite, was in darkness. The Two Pheasants was not yet open, although he could see the landlord moving about in the bar.

Beside the pub stood the village school, the playground now deserted and swept by gusts of rain. A light was on in the main schoolroom which meant that Betty Bell was busy clearing up the day's mess. There was a light, too, downstairs in the school house where Miss Watson, the headmistress, and Miss Fogerty, her assistant, were sitting snugly by the fire discussing school matters in the home they shared.

Almost hidden from Albert's view by the angle of the porch was the fine house which stood next door to the school. Here lived Harold Shoosmith, a bachelor until his sixties, but now newly married, and very content. There were lights upstairs and down, and the porch light too was on.

Albert grunted disapprovingly.

'Waste of electric,' he said aloud. 'Money to burn, no doubt.'

He hauled his large watch from his pocket and squinted at the illuminated dial. Still a quarter of an hour to go before old Jones opened up. Might as well go home and hang up the key, and take a couple of these dratted pills.

Clutching his coat around him, Albert set off through the downpour.

## 2. Friends and Relations

An hour or two later, as Albert Piggott sipped his beer and warmed his legs by the fire at The Two Pheasants, his daughter Molly tucked up young George, and then went to the window to look out upon Thrush Green.

Rain spattered the glass. The sash window rattled in its frame against the onslaught of the wind. The lights of the pub were reflected in long puddles in the roadway, and the leafless trees scattered drops as their branches were tossed this way and that.

It was a beast of a night, thought Molly, but she loved Thrush Green, whatever the weather. For the first few years of her marriage she had accompanied Ben on his tour of towns and villages with the small travelling fair which had once been owned by his grandmother, the redoubtable

Mrs Curdle, who had also brought up the boy. She now lay in St Andrew's churchyard, her grave lovingly tended by her grandson.

It grieved Ben to part with the famous fair, but it was the only thing to do. Customs and fashions change. A small family fair could not compete with bingo halls and television, and in the end Ben had sold it, and had taken a job with a firm of agricultural engineers. Molly's happiness was a joy to see, and Ben was content.

Or was he? Molly pondered upon this question as she gazed upon the dark wet world. Never by word or sign had he shown any regret for the life he had given up, but Molly sometimes wondered if he missed the travelling, the change of scene, the renewing of friendships in the towns where the fair rested.

After all, he had known nothing else. His home, as a child, had been the small horse-drawn caravan which now stood, a permanent reminder of Mrs Curdle and that way of life, in the orchard of their present home. He had played his part in the running of the fair, willing to do whatever was necessary at any time of the day or night.

Surely, thought Molly, he must sometimes find his new mode of living irksome. To leave home at the same time, to learn to watch the clock, to put down his tools when a whistle blew and to return to Thrush Green at a regular hour. Did he find it dull? Did he ever hanker for the freedom he once had? Did he feel tied by so much routine? Was he truly happy?

A particularly vicious squall flung a sharp shower against the glass by her face, making the girl recoil.

Well, no point in worrying about it, she told herself. She was lucky to have such a good-tempered husband, and maybe he was just as happy as she was.

She left the window, looked at her sleeping son, and went to cook Ben's supper.

Over the way, at Tullivers, Frank and Phil Hurst also had a problem on that stormy night.

Robert, Frank's son by his first marriage, was farming in Wales. He rarely rang up, and still more rarely wrote a letter, although father and son were fond of each other, and Frank was proud of the way in which the youngster had tackled life in Wales, a tough hill farm and four boisterous children.

'I've got a proposition for you, Dad,' said the cheerful voice on the telephone. 'When do you set off on the lecture trip?'

Frank told him.

'And you'll be away all through May?'

'That's right. Back the first week in June, if all goes well.'

'It's like this. A friend of mine, just married, is coming up to his new job in an estate agent's, somewhere in your area, near Oxford. He's got to be out of his house in April, and I just wondered if you'd feel like letting him have Tullivers for a few weeks.'

'Hasn't he got anywhere to go this end?'

'Their place isn't ready, and won't be until the summer. I wouldn't ask, Dad, if it weren't for the fact he's been good to me in the past, and there's a baby on the way as well. He's a nice chap. Very musical . You'd like him.'

'I can't say yes or no until I've talked it over with Phil. In any case, I'd need some sort of references. And I really don't know if I'd like a stranger in the house – or have any idea what to charge him.'

'Well, he hasn't much cash, that I do know, but he'd want to pay his whack obviously.'

There was silence for a moment, broken at last by Frank.

'I'll have a word with Phil, and ring you tomorrow.'

'Oh good! It would help him enormously if he knew there was somewhere to go when he leaves here. Give him time to look around, and chivvy the workmen your end.'

There was a crackling sound and Frank replaced the receiver.

Phil looked at him inquiringly.

'What's the problem?'

Frank told her.

'I'm not keen on the idea,' she said eventually. 'We don't know him from Adam, and I don't want to have someone here who might turn out to be a nuisance to the neighbours.'

'I should turn it down flat,' agreed Frank 'if it weren't for Robert. He speaks well of him, says he's musical, known him for some time evidently, and he's been a good friend to him in the past. I must say it is all rather complicated.'

'Well, say we must know more and would like to meet him and his wife,' suggested Phil. 'And if we have any doubts, we harden our hearts.'

And on this sensible note the problem was shelved for twenty-four hours.

The storm blew itself out during the night, and Thrush Green woke to a morning so sweet and pearly that spirits rose at once.

Even Willie Marchant, the gloomy postman, noticed the sunshine as he tacked purposefully on his bicycle back and forth across the hill from Lulling.

'Lovely morning, Willie,' said Ella, meeting him at her gate.

'Ah!' agreed the postman. As usual, a cigarette end was clamped to his lower lip. Was it pulling the skin, or did he essay a rare smile? Ella could not be certain.

The Reverend Charles Henstock met Willie as he returned from early service, and collected his post from him.

'This makes one think of Spring,' commented the rector, sniffing the air appreciatively.

'Long way to go yet,' said Willie, as he pedalled away on his rounds. He was never one to rouse false hopes, and whatever his secret pleasure in the change in the weather, he intended to show his usual dour countenance to those he met.

General optimism greeted him.

Joan Young pointed out the bulbs poking through in her shrubbery. Little Miss Fogerty, who took in the letters at the school house, said that a blackbird had begun to build in the hedge. Harold Shoosmith next door could be heard singing in a fine resonant baritone voice, and his new wife gave Willie such a ravishing smile when she opened the door that he almost forgot himself and smiled back.

The Thrush Green post delivered, Willie set off in a leisurely way along the narrow lane which led westward to Lulling Woods. Once out of sight of Thrush Green eyes, Willie propped his bicycle against a stone wall, put his canvas mail bag on the grass to keep out any dampness, and sat himself upon it, leaning back comfortably in the lee of the wall. Here the sun was warm, a lark soared above him, greeting the morning with the same rapture as his clients, and Willie took out a fresh cigarette.

It was a good spot, Willie admitted, looking at the distant smudge of Lulling Woods against the sky line. Definitely a smell of new grass growing, and that was a fresh mole hill over there, he noted. Tiny buds like beads studded the hawthorn twigs nearby, and an early bemused bumble bee staggered drunkenly at the edge of the track.

Willie blew a cloud of smoke, and stretched luxuriously. Not a bad life, he told himself, especially with the summer ahead. Could do a lot worse than be a postman on a fine morning.

The barking of a dog reminded him of his duties. Dotty Harmer's cottage, a quarter of a mile distant, was his next call. Obviously, she was up and about, as the barking dog proved. No doubt the old girl was feeding the hens and goats and all the rest of the menagerie she kept in that ramshackle place. Nutty as a fruit cake, thought Willie, rising stiffly from the crushed mail bag, but got some guts. You couldn't help liking the old trout, and when you think of what she put up with when her wicked old Dad was alive – well, you had to hand it to her.

Willie himself had been a pupil for a short time under the redoubtable Mr George Harmer, headmaster of Lulling Grammar School. The memory of that martinet, his rigid rules, and ferocious punishment if they were broken, was still fresh in the minds of those who had suffered at his hands, although the old man had lain in the churchyard for many years now, leaving his daughter to enjoy the company of all those animals which had been forbidden whilst he lived.

Good luck to her, thought Willie, clambering on to his bicycle again. She deserved a bit of pleasure in her old age.

As he had guessed, Dotty was in the chicken run. She was trying to throw a rope over a stout bough of the plum tree which leant over the run. For one moment of alarm, Willie wondered if she were contemplating suicide, but Dotty would be the last person to take an easy way out of anything.

'Ah, Willie! How you startled me! I'm having such a job with these Brussels sprouts.'

She pointed to five or six leggy plants which were attached to one end of the rope. All became plain.

'You want 'em hauled up? Give it here,' said Willie. With one deft throw he cast the other end over the plum branch and pulled. Up went the plants.

'How high?' asked Willie, his head level with the dangling sprouts.

Dotty surveyed them, frowning with concentration.

'Not *quite* as high as that, I think, Willie. You see, I want the hens to get some exercise in leaping up to reach the greenstuff. They lead rather a sedentary life, and I'm sure their circulation and general good health would be improved by a little more exercise.'

'Ah,' agreed Willie, lowering the plants a trifle.

'On the other hand,' went on Dotty, 'I don't want them *too low* –'

Willie gave a slight hitch. The plants rose three inches.

'Or, of course, that defeats the object. But I don't want them so high that they lose heart and *don't try* to jump. Or, of course, too high for them to jump in *safety*. I don't want any *injuries*. Hens have funny little ways.'

Not the only ones, thought Willie, patiently lowering and raising the sprouts before Dotty's penetrating gaze.

'Right!' shouted Dotty suddenly, hand raised as if about to stop traffic. 'I think that will do splendidly. What do you think?'

'That's about it, I reckon,' said Willie, tying a knot.

Dotty beamed upon him.

'Most kind of you, Willie dear. Now if you'll just come in the kitchen I'll let you have two letters I wrote last night.'

He followed her towards the back door, stepping over three kittens who jumped out at him from the currant bushes and dodging a goat which was tethered to a clothes post on the way.

The kitchen was in its usual state of chaos. Willie was quite familiar with its muddle of bowls, saucepans, boxes, string bags, piles of newspapers and a hundred assorted objects overflowing from the table, shelves and chairs. A vast fish kettle, black with age, simmered on the stove, and from it, to Willie's surprise, came quite a pleasant odour of food cooking.

'Now where did I put them?' inquired Dotty, standing stock still among the muddle. 'Somewhere safe, I know.'

She shifted a pile of newspapers hopefully. Willie's eyes raked the dresser.

'They'd be on top, most like,' he suggested, 'seeing as you only wrote them last night.'

'Very astute of you,' said Dotty. She lifted the lid of a vegetable dish on the table, and there were the letters.

'Safe and sound,' said Dotty happily, pressing them into Willie's hand. 'And now I mustn't keep you from the Queen's business. A thousand thanks for your help with the hens. I'm sure they will be much invigorated after a few jumping sessions.'

She picked up a slice of cake which was lying on the table beside a small brown puddle of unidentified liquid. Coffee perhaps, thought Willie, or tea? Or worse?

'What about a little snack?' suggested Dotty. 'You could eat it on your way.'

'I'd best not, much as I'd like to,' replied Willie gallantly. 'It'd take the edge off my appetite for breakfast, you see. Thank you all the same.'

'Quite, quite!' said Dotty, dropping it down again. This time it was right in the puddle, Willie noticed.

He escaped before Dotty could offer him anything else, and moved briskly down the path towards his bicycle.

The hens, as far as he could see, were ignoring the sprouts completely. You'd have thought they would have done the decent thing and had a look at them anyway, thought Willie resentfully, after all the trouble they had gone to.

He went on his way, in the golden sunshine, suitably depressed.


Little Miss Fogerty and her headmistress, Miss Watson, were break-fasting in the sunny kitchen of the school house. Each had a boiled egg, one slice of toast, and another of Ryvita and marmalade.

It was their standard breakfast on schooldays, light but nourishing, and leaving no greasy frying pan to be washed. On Saturdays and Sundays, when time was less limited, they occasionally cooked bacon and egg or bacon and tomato, and now and again a kipper apiece.

Dorothy Watson loved her food but had to be careful of gaining too much weight. Agnes Fogerty, who had lived in lodgings nearby for many years, had discovered an equal interest in cooking since coming to live with her friend, and enjoyed watching her eat the dishes which she made. Agnes's weight never varied, whatever she ate, and had remained about eight stone for years.

Miss Fogerty had never been so happy as she was now, living with Dorothy and next door to another old friend, Isobel Shoosmith, who had been at college with her years before. Although she had not realized it at the time, looking back she could see that her life at Mrs White's had been quite lonely. True, she had had a pleasant bed-sitting-room, and Mrs White had cooked for her and had always been welcoming, but on some cold summer evenings, sitting in her Lloyd loom armchair by a gas fire, turned low for reasons of economy, Agnes had experienced some bleakness.

It was such a pleasure now to wake each morning in the knowledge that she was near to her friends, and had no need to make a journey, in all weathers, to the school. She was usually down first in the kitchen, happy to see to the kettle and the eggs and toast in readiness for Dorothy, who was still rather slow in her movements since breaking a hip.

It was that accident which had led to Agnes being asked to share the school house, and she looked forward to several years together before retirement age. What happened then, Miss Fogerty sometimes wondered? But time enough when that day loomed nearer, she decided, and meanwhile life was perfect.

Willie Marchant had brought two letters, one from the office obviously and one which looked as though it were from Dorothy's brother Ray. Miss Fogerty sipped her tea whilst her headmistress read her correspondence.

'Ray and Kathleen are proposing to have a week or ten days touring the Cotswolds next month,' she told Agnes, as she stuffed his letter back into the envelope.

'How nice,' said Agnes. 'Are they likely to call here?'

'A call I should like,' said Dorothy, with some emphasis, 'but Ray seems to be inviting himself and Kathleen to stay here for a night or two.'

'Oh!' said Agnes, somewhat taken aback. The school house had only two bedrooms. The one which had once been the spare room she now occupied permanently. Before then, she knew, Ray had sometimes spent the night there on his travels as a commercial salesman. Since Dorothy's accident however things had been a little strained. She had confidently expected to convalesce with her brother and his wife, but they had made no offer, indeed nothing but excuses. If it had not been for Agnes's willingness to help, poor Miss Watson would have been unaided in her weakness. It was quite plain to Miss Fogerty that she had not forgiven or forgotten.

'I could easily make up a bed in the sitting room,' offered Agnes, 'if you would like to have mine. Then they could have the twin beds in your room.'

'It won't be necessary, Agnes dear,' said Dorothy, in the firm tones of a headmistress. 'We are not going to put ourselves out for them. They have quite enough money to afford a hotel. They can try The Fleece if they must come and stay here. Frankly, it won't break my heart if we don't see them at all.'

'Oh Dorothy!' begged gentle little Miss Fogerty, 'don't talk like that! He is your own flesh and blood – your own brother!'

'No fault of mine,' said Dorothy, briskly, rolling up her napkin. 'I didn't choose him, you know, but I do choose my *friends*!'

She glanced at the clock.

'Better clear up, I suppose, or we shall be late for school. I really ought to look out some pictures for my history lesson this morning.'

'Then you go over to school, dear,' said Miss Fogerty, 'and I'll see to the breakfast things.'

'You spoil me,' said Miss Watson, limping towards the door.

And how pleasant it was to have someone to spoil, thought Agnes, running the tap. More often than not she did stay behind to do this little chore, but never did she resent it. Looking after others, children or adults, was little Miss Fogerty's chief source of pleasure.

Miss Watson, making her way carefully across the playground, thought fondly of her assistant. She was the soul of unselfishness, as her ready offer to vacate her bedroom had shown yet again. But Miss Watson was determined that Agnes should now come first. She had been a loyal colleague for many years, respected by parents and children alike, and since the accident had proved a trusted friend and companion.

All that stuff about blood being thicker than water, thought Miss Watson robustly, was a lot of eyewash! She had had more help and affection from her dear old Agnes than ever Ray and Kathleen had shown her. It had to be faced, they were a selfish pair, and she had no intention of upsetting Agnes's comfort, or her own, to save them a few pennies.

'You can come and help me to carry some pictures, George dear,' she said to young Curdle who was skipping about the playground. It was by way of being a royal command.

She swept ahead to enter her domain, followed by one of her willing subjects.

## 3. Jenny Falls Ill

That halcyon spell of weather lasted exactly two days, and then bitter winds lashed the area and continued into March.

During this bleak period the problem of letting Tullivers to Robert's friend was resolved. Frank discovered that he knew the young man's father. He and Dick Thomas had worked together on a west country newspaper for some time. He had an idea he had even met this son, Jack, when he was a babe in arms.

Robert had got the local vicar to send a letter to his father vouching for the young man, which Frank found rather touching. Obviously, Robert wanted everything to go smoothly. Frank was impressed too by a letter from Jack Thomas, and by the fact that he had managed to get his landlord to extend his stay until the end of April, which would mean just one month at Tullivers if Frank were willing to let.

The young couple came to lunch at Tullivers one boisterous March day and seemed enchanted by all that they saw. They discussed dates and terms, and Frank promised an agreement in writing. He was obviously much taken with them.

Phil was more cautious.

'They seem a sensible pair,' was Frank's comment as the Thomases drove away.

'I hope so,' said Phil. 'She didn't seem to know much about cooking, I thought.'

'Never mind! She'll soon learn,' replied Frank indulgently.

'That's what I'm afraid of! With my kitchen equipment!' retorted Phil. 'Anyway, they both looked clean, and were polite. We forgot to ask him about his music, by the way. Does he play an instrument?'

'A guitar,' said Frank.

'Well, that sounds reasonably quiet,' conceded Phil. 'I shouldn't like dear Winnie and Jenny disturbed with drums and cymbals.'

'Oh, I'm sure they wouldn't be so thoughtless as to upset the neighbours,' said Frank reassuringly, 'but I will mention that when I write.'

'It might be as well,' agreed Phil. 'After all we don't really know them, and they may not realize that most of us go to bed around ten at Thrush Green.'

And so the matter was left.

Across the green, at the rectory, Ella was visiting Charles and Dimity

Henstock. The question of the rector's holiday was being discussed, and Dimity, always anxious for the health and happiness of her husband, was doing her best to get him to make a decision.

Ella, forthright as ever, was giving vociferous support.

'Don't be such an ass, Charles. Of course, you need a holiday. Everyone does. You'll come back full of beans, and with some new ideas for sermons.'

Charles looked wounded.

'My dear Ella, you speak as though you hear the same sermon time and time again. I assure you –'

'Oh yes, yes!' said Ella testily, fishing out a battered tobacco tin and beginning to roll herself a cigarette. 'I know it sounded like that, but I didn't mean anything so rude. You manage very well,' she continued kindly.

She licked the cigarette paper noisily.

'And I can truthfully say,' she continued, 'that I have only heard that one about the Good Samaritan three times, and the one about arrogance twice. Mind you, as you well know, I don't go *every* Sunday, but still, it's not a bad record on your part, Charles dear.'

The rector's chubby face was creased with distress, but he remained silent. Dimity flew to his support.

'Those sermons, Ella, were *quite different*. Charles approached the subject from a fresh way each time, and in any case, those themes are universal, and can stand being repeated. But you have a point, dear, about returning refreshed from holiday, and I wish Charles would see it.'

'If it's money you need,' said Ella bluntly, 'I can let you have some.'

'We're quite accustomed to being short of money,' said Charles, with a smile. 'But thank you, Ella, for a kind offer. The difficulty is to find the time.'

'Well, what's wrong with nipping away for a week or so between Easter and Whitsun? I can quite see that you've got to fix a holiday in a slack period. Like farmers.'

'Like farmers?' echoed Charles, bemused.

'They have to go away after hay-making or after harvest, you surely know that? And they usually get married in October when the harvest's in, and they have some corn money for a honeymoon.'

'What a grasp you have of agricultural economy,' commented Charles, 'but now I come to think of it, I do seem to marry young farmers in the autumn.'

'I think Ella's suggestion of a May break is very good,' said Dimity, bringing the subject to heel again. 'Why not write to Edgar? Better still, ring him up one evening. Yorkshire would be lovely then, if he could spare the house.'

Charles looked from one determined woman to the other. He knew when he was beaten.

'I'll do something this week,' he promised. 'In any case, I have neglected Edgar sadly for the last few months. That living of his in Yorkshire keeps him very busy, and I really should be the one who writes. But where do the weeks go, Ella? Do you know?'

'They turn into months far too quickly,' said Ella, 'and that's because we're all getting old and can't pack as much into a month as we used to. I'm sure Edgar will understand. What do you propose to do? To have a straight swap of livings for a week or two?'

'Probably. I must say, we both love the dales, and Edgar and Hilda seem to enjoy the Cotswolds. It's just a case of arranging dates.'

'Which is where I came in,' said Ella, heaving herself to her feet. She ground out her cigarette end in the earth surrounding Dimity's choicest geranium plant on the window sill. Dimity caught her breath in dismay, but, as a true Christian, forbore to comment.

'And of course I'll feed the cat,' continued Ella, making for the door. 'Does she still live on pig's liver?'

'I'm afraid so,' replied Dimity. 'Such dreadful stuff to chop up.'

'No worse than tripe,' said Ella, and vanished.

It was towards the end of March that Winnie Bailey crossed from her house into the surgery which had been her husband's, and was now occupied by John Lovell, the senior partner in the practice, since Donald's death.

He was a quiet conscientious young man who had learnt a great deal from Winnie's husband, and was liked by his Thrush Green patients.

He glanced up from his papers as Winnie entered, and went to fetch a chair.

'I saw that the waiting room was empty,' said Winnie. 'Are you just off on the rounds?'

'In a few minutes, but no great hurry. Any trouble, Winnie?'

'It's Jenny. She's been off her food for a week or so, and has a horrible cough. But you know Jenny. She won't give up, and says it's nothing. Do come and have a look at her, John dear.'

'I'll come now,' said the young man, picking up his stethoscope. 'There's a particularly vicious flu bug about. It may be that.'

Together they returned to the hall, and thence to the kitchen, where Jenny stood at the sink peeling potatoes. She was unusually pale, John Lovell noticed, but her eyes were inflamed, and her forehead, when he felt it with the palm of his hand, was very hot.

'Sit down,' he directed. Jenny obeyed, but cast an accusing look at Winnie.

'Mrs Bailey,' she croaked. 'There wasn't no need to bother the doctor.'

'Unbutton your blouse,' he directed, arranging his stethoscope, 'and open your mouth.'

Gagged with a thermometer, and immobilized with the stethoscope dabbed here and there on her chest, poor Jenny submitted to a thorough examination.

When it was over John Lovell pronounced sentence.

'Bed for you, and lots to drink. You've a fine old temperature and your lungs are congested.'

'But I'm doing the potatoes!' protested Jenny.

'I can finish those,' said Winnie. 'You must do as Doctor Lovell tells you. Up you go, and I'll bring you a hot water bottle and some lemon barley water.'

'I'll go back to the surgery,' John told Winnie, 'and let you have some inhalant and pills.'

Jenny departed reluctantly, and Winnie looked at John.

'I don't think it's much more than an infection of the lungs, but it could be the first stage of something catching. I suppose she's had all the childish ailments?'

'I'm not sure. She was brought up in an orphanage, you know, until she came to her foster-parents here. She was about ten or twelve, I think. No doubt she had all the catching things at the orphanage, but I'll find out from her.'

John went to fetch the medicine, and Winnie put on the kettle for Jenny's bottle.

Later, with two pills inside her, a hot bottle at her feet, and the jug of inhalant steaming on the bedside table Jenny tried to remember if and when she had had whooping cough, scarlet fever, measles, chicken pox, and all the other horrid excitements of childhood.

'I can't honestly recall all of them,' she confessed. 'There was always something going the rounds at the orphanage with so many of us. I know I didn't get ringworm,' she added, with some pride.

'Anyway, don't worry,' said Winnie. 'Let me drape this towel over your head, and you get busy with the Friar's Balsam.'

'Is that what it is?' said Jenny, from beneath her tent. 'I thought it was some new mixture of Doctor Lovell's.'

'It's probably got a long and different name,' agreed Winnie, 'but I wouldn't mind betting it's basically dear old Friar's Balsam.'

'Well, *that* can't harm me,' agreed Jenny with relief, and bent to her task.


The next day was one of those windy blue and white March beauties when great clouds scudded eastward, and the sunshine lifted everyone's spirits at Thrush Green.

Everyone, except Albert Piggott.

He was wandering morosely round the churchyard, billhook in hand. If challenged, he would have said that he was busy cutting away the long grass which grew near the tombstones and the surrounding low wall. In fact, he was killing time until ten o'clock when the pub opened.

A small van drew up near him on the other side of the wall, and Percy Hodge, a local farmer, clambered out.

'Ah, Albert!' he began. 'D'you want a little job in the garden?' Occasionally, Albert 'obliged' locally with odd jobs, but latterly he had preferred his leisure to this extra drinking money. Still, Percy was an old friend ...

'What sort of job?' he inquired cautiously. 'I don't mind telling you, Perce, I ain't the man I was since my operation.'

'Nothing too heavy,' Percy assured him. 'But I've been given a sack of seed potatoes, and I ought to get 'em in. My dear Gertie always put the spuds in. I miss her, that I do.'

Albert was embarrassed to see tears in the eyes of the widower. Mind you, he could sympathize. By and large, wives were kittle-kattle, more trouble than they were worth, but when it came to cooking or gardening they had their uses.

'I suppose I could give you a hand,' said Albert grudgingly. 'But I don't reckon I'm up to digging trenches for a hundredweight of spuds.'

'Oh, I'd be with you,' said Percy, blowing his nose, 'and of course there'd be a few for your garden, Albert. Or don't you bother to cook spuds, now your Nelly's gone?'

'Molly does some for me, now and again,' replied Albert, secretly nettled by this reference to his truant wife. 'I don't go hungry, and that's a fact.'

'Your Nelly was a good cook, that I did know. Same as my dear Gertie. A lovely hand she had with puff pastry. I miss her sorely, you know.'

Albert grunted. Who would have thought old Perce would have been so sorry for himself? Other men had to make do without a wife to look after them. He began to move slowly away from the wall. With Perce at a loose end like this he'd have him there gossiping all day.

'When d'you want me to come up?' he asked, slashing at a dock.

'Tomorrow night suit you? About six, say? Or earlier.'

'Say five,' said Albert. 'Gets dark early still.'

A welcome sound fell upon his ears. It was the landlord of The Two Pheasants opening his doors.

Percy Hodge turned to see what was happening. Albert put down his hook on a handy tombstone and looked more alert than he had since he awoke.

'Come and have a pint, Albert,' invited Percy.

And Albert needed no second bidding.


Hard by, at the village school, little Miss Fogerty was enjoying the exhilarating morning.

The view from the large window of her terrapin classroom in the playground never failed to give her exquisite pleasure. For years she had taught in the north-east-facing infants' room in the old building, and had pined for sunlight.

Now, transposed to this modern addition, she looked across the valley towards Lulling Woods and relished the warmth of the morning sun through her sensible fawn cardigan.

How lucky she was to have such an understanding headmistress, she thought. Headmistress and good friend, she amended. Life had never been so rich as it was now, living at the school house, and teaching in this delightful room.

She glanced at the large wall clock, and returned to her duties. Time for the class lesson on money, she told herself. There was a great deal to be said for the old-fashioned method of teaching the class as a whole, now and again, and some of these young children seemed to find great difficulty in recognizing coins of the realm.

She bent to extract a pile of small boxes from the low cupboard. Each contained what Miss Fogerty still thought of as the new decimal money in cardboard. Time was, when she taught for so many years in the old building, that those same tough little boxes held cardboard farthings, halfpennies, pennies, sixpences and shillings. There was still the ancient wall chart, rolled up at the back of the cupboard, which showed:

| 4 farthings make | 1 penny |
| 12 pennies make | 1 shilling |
| 20 shillings make | 1 pound |

Miss Fogerty remembered very clearly how difficult it had been to trace the real coins and cut them out of coloured paper to fix on to the chart. But it had lasted for years, and these children's parents had chanted the table hundreds of times. She felt a pang of nostalgia for times past.

There had been something so solidly *English* about farthings and shillings! And feet and inches, come to that. She hoped that she was progressive enough to face the fact that with the world shrinking so rapidly with all this air travel, and instant communication methods, a common monetary unit was bound to come some day. But really, thought Miss Fogerty, putting a box briskly on each low table, it seemed so *alien* to be dealing in tens when twelve pence to the shilling still haunted the back of one's mind.

'My granny,' said young Peter in the front row, 'learnt me a new song last night.'

'Taught, dear,' replied Miss Fogerty automatically.

'Called "Sing a song of sixpence". Shall I sing it?'

'Later, dear. Now, all sit up straight, and listen to me.'

'What is *sixpence*?' asked Peter.

High time we got on with the lesson, thought Agnes Fogerty, and directed her class to open the boxes.

Next door, Harold Shoosmith and his wife Isobel were admiring some early daffodils in their garden. From the house came the whirr of the vacuum cleaner as Betty Bell, their helper, crashed happily about her work.

'One thing about our Betty,' observed Harold, 'she tackles everything with a will. Lord alone knows how many glasses she's smashed since she's worked here.'

'Not many since I came;' replied Isobel. 'You haven't noticed but I do the glasses now.'

'Ah! That accounts for the fact that I haven't had to buy any more for eighteen months! Marrying you was the best day's work I ever did.'

'Of course it was,' agreed Isobel matter-of-factly. 'How lucky for you that I took you on.'

A window opened above them and Betty's voice hailed them.

'*Telephone!*' she roared.

While Harold was engaged with his caller, Betty caught at her mistress's arm.

'Is it all right if I go a couple of minutes early? Dotty – I mean Miss Harmer – wants me to give her a hand moving out her dresser. Lost some letter or other down the back as ought to be answered today.'

'Of course you can go,' said Isobel. Betty Bell was in great demand, she well knew. Dotty Harmer had employed her long before Isobel, or even Harold when a bachelor, had appeared on the scene. As well as these duties, Betty also kept the village school clean. Isobel was wise enough to recognize that a certain amount of flexibility in Betty's employment was inevitable.

'I must say,' went on Betty, attacking a side table with a flailing duster, 'it's a sight easier working here than at Miss Harmer's. I mean it's clean to start with. And tidy. Always was, even when Mr Shoosmith lived here alone. You don't expect a man to keep himself decent really, let alone a house, but he was always nicely washed and that, and the house always smelt fresh.'

Isobel said gravely that she was pleased to hear it.

'But down Miss Harmer's it's a fair old pig's breakfast, I can tell you. Can't never find nothing, and the dusters is old bloomers of hers like as not. Washed, of course, but you can't get the same gloss on things with 'em like this nice one.'

Isobel felt unequal to coping with this conversation, and said she would go and see to lunch.

An hour later, Betty entered Dotty's kitchen to find her other employer sitting at the cluttered table studying a form.

'Oh, how nice of you to come, Betty! As a matter of fact I managed to reach this wretched letter by inserting a long knitting needle in the crack. It fell down, and I was able to get it by lying on the floor, and wriggling it out with a poker.'

Her wrinkled old face glowed with pride.

'Well, you won't want me then,' said Betty, swatting a fly on the table. 'Filthy things, flies.'

'Oh, do wait while I just fill it in,' said Dotty, 'and perhaps you would be kind enough to post it as you go past the box.'

'Sure I will,' said Betty, lunging with a handy newspaper at another fly. 'You've got some real nasty flies in here.'

'Poor things,' said Miss Harmer, putting down her pen. 'So persecuted. I often wonder if they are as dangerous to health as modern pundits suggest. My grandmother used to sing a charming little song to my baby brother when flies were *quite accepted*.'

She began to sing in a small cracked voice, while Betty watched her with mingled exasperation and amusement.

> 'Baby bye, there's a fly,
> Let us watch it you and I,
> There it crawls, up the walls,
> Yet it never falls.
>
> I believe with those six legs
> You and I could walk on eggs.
> There he goes, on his toes,
> Tickling baby's nose.'

'Well,' said Betty, 'fancy letting it! Downright insanitary!'
Dotty tapped the neglected form with her pen.
'Now, how did it go on?

> Round and round, on the ground,
> On the ceiling he is found.
> Catch him? No, let him go,
> Do not hurt him so.

Now you see his wings of silk
Dabbling in the baby's milk
Fie, oh fie, you foolish fly!
How will you get dry?'

'Did you ever?' exclaimed Betty. 'I mean, flies in the *milk*!'

'Well, it only goes to show how kind-hearted the Victorians were. And really so much more sensible about disease. My brother grew into a splendid specimen of manhood, despite flies.'

Betty looked at the clock.

'Tell you what, Miss Harmer, I'll come back for that form this afternoon. It'll give you time to work it out, and anyway Willie don't collect till five o'clock.'

Besides that, she thought privately, there was her shopping to do, and heaven alone knew when that would get done if she stayed listening to old Dotty.

'Perhaps that would be best,' agreed Dotty, turning again to her task, while Betty made her escape.


## 4. Dimity Gets Her Way


As the Hursts' departure for America drew nearer there was much speculation about the temporary residents who were going to stay at Tullivers.

'Well, for your sake, Winnie,' said Ella Bembridge, 'I hope they're a quiet lot. Don't want a posse of hippies, or a commune, or whatever the "in-thing" is.'

'Good heavens,' said Winnie reassuringly, 'Frank and Phil would never let the place to people like that! I have every confidence in their judgement. They both liked the young couple, I know, and Frank knew his father years ago.'

'That's not saying much,' said Ella, lighting a ragged cigarette. 'I know a lot of respectable people of my age with the most *extraordinary* children.'

'Jenny says Phil is putting away her best glass and china, which is only prudent, but she seems quite happy to leave everything else as it is. And if she's content, I don't think we need to worry.'

'And how is our Jenny now?'

'She's still got this wretched cough, but won't stay in bed. She's up in her room now, in her dressing gown, dusting the place. I'm getting John to look at her again today. She's still so flushed, I feel sure she's running a temperature.'

'Will she need to do anything at Tullivers?' asked Ella.

'Phil won't hear of it,' replied Winnie. 'She offered, you know, but now that these young people are coming, they can cope, and I intend to dust and tidy up before they arrive, to save Jenny's efforts.'

'You'll be lucky! You know Jenny. A glutton for work!'

She was about to go when Dimity and Charles entered.

'We did knock,' said the rector, 'but I expect you had something noisy working.'

Winnie looked blank.

'Like the vacuum cleaner, or the fridge, or the washing machine,' enlarged Charles.

'Or the mighty wurlitzer,' added Ella.

'No need to knock anyway,' said Winnie, returning to normal. 'Do sit down. We were just discussing our new neighbours-to-be.'

'I shall call as soon as they have settled in,' said Charles. 'It will be so nice if they turn out to be regular churchgoers.'

'He plays the guitar,' said Ella.

'I trust that does not preclude him from Christian worship,' commented Charles.

'I heard that they met at Oxford, but didn't finish their courses,' contributed Dimity.

'Perhaps they preferred to get out into the world and earn their livings,' was Ella's suggestion. 'Bully for them, I'd say.'

'Well, he's an estate agent now,' said Winnie. 'Or at least, he will be. He's joining a firm somewhere near Bicester, I believe, so Robert said. Frank mentioned it.'

'Dotty intends to supply them with goat's milk,' said Dimity.

'Do they like it?' asked Winnie.

'They will after Dotty's called on them,' forecast Dimity.

'Well, I'm sure they will be very welcome here,' said the rector. 'We must see that they have an enjoyable stay at Thrush Green.'


Later in the day, Doctor Lovell mounted the stairs to see Jenny. She had insisted on dressing, but lay on her bed, trying to read. Her flushed face, and hot forehead, bespoke a high temperature.

'Let's have a look at your chest,' said John Lovell, after studying the thermometer.

Jenny cautiously undid the top button of her blouse.

'I shall need more than that, Jenny,' observed the doctor. 'You needn't be shy with me.'

Jenny undid two more buttons with reluctance, and John studied the exposed flesh.

'Ever had chicken-pox?'

'I can't remember,' said Jenny. 'We had all sorts up at the orphanage.'

'Well, you've got it now,' said John. 'So no stirring from this bed until I tell you. Keep on with the tablets, and I'll see you have a cooling lotion to dab on the spots.'

'But what about Mrs Bailey?' cried poor Jenny. 'Won't she catch it?'

'If she had any sense,' replied the doctor, 'she caught it years ago, and is immune. Now, into bed with you.'

Jenny's illness made a pleasurable source of discussion at The Two Pheasants that night.

'No joke getting them childish ailments when you're grown up,' said the landlord, twirling a glass cloth inside a tumbler. 'My old uncle caught the measles when he was nigh on seventy, and we all reckoned it carried him off.'

'Affects the eyes, measles does,' agreed Albert Piggott knowledgeably. 'Got to keep the light low, and lay off the reading. I met a chap in hospital when they whipped out my appendix –'

Meaning glances, and a few groans, were exchanged among the regular patrons. Were they going to go through that lot again from old Albert?

'And he'd had measles a few months before and had to have his spectacles changed after that. Proper weak, his eyes was. Watered horrible.'

'Mumps is worse,' contributed Willie Marchant. 'Can upset all your natural functions. Rob you of your manhood, they say.'

'Well, we don't want to hear about it in here,' said the landlord briskly. 'There's two ladies over there, so watch what you're saying.'

Willie Marchant did not appear abashed, and continued.

'But chicken-pox is nasty too. Mixed up with shingles, and that's a real killer, I'm told.'

'Only if it meets round your ribs,' Albert assured him. 'You can have spots all over, but if they meets round your middle you're a goner.'

At this moment, Percy Hodge entered, and was informed of Jenny's illness.

'Poor old girl,' commented Percy, looking genuinely upset. 'I got it when I was about twenty. Got proper fed up with people telling me not to scratch. As though you could stop! Well, she's got my sympathy, that's a fact.'

'One thing,' said one of the regulars, 'she's in the right place. Got the doctor on the premises, as you might say, and you couldn't have anyone better than Mrs Bailey to look after you.'

And with that, all agreed.


The next morning Winnie was surprised to open the front door to Percy Hodge. He was holding a basket with a dozen of the largest, brownest eggs that she had ever encountered.

'Thought Jenny might be able to manage an egg,' said Percy.

'Won't you come in?'

'Well, that's nice of you. How is she?' he asked, following Winnie down the hall and into the kitchen.

'She seems a little easier now that the rash has come out,' replied Winnie, unpacking the basket and placing the superb eggs carefully in a blue and white basin. 'Percy, I've never seen such beauties as these! I shall take them upstairs to show her later on. I'm sure she will be so grateful. What a kind thought of yours.'

Percy suddenly looked shy.

'Well, I've known Jenny since we was at Sunday School together. She's a good girl. I was sorry to hear she was poorly. Give her my regards, won't you?'

He accepted the empty basket, and retraced his steps to the front door.

'Of course, I will,' promised Winnie, and watched Percy cross the green towards the lane leading to his farm.

What a very kind gesture, thought Winnie, toiling upstairs with the eggs, and Percy's message, for the invalid.

She suddenly remembered that Percy was a recent widower. Could it be ...?

But no, she chided herself, of course not. She must not put two and two together and make five.

'Just look what someone's sent you,' she said to the invalid, holding out the blue and white bowl.

'Good heavens!' cried Jenny. 'We'd best have an omelette for lunch!'


It was a sparkling April morning when the Hursts drove off from Tullivers to Heathrow.

Harold Shoosmith had offered to drive them there, and Jeremy and Winnie Bailey accompanied them in the car to see them off.

Much to everyone's relief, Jeremy was cheerful and excited. Winnie Bailey was quite prepared to cope with some tears at parting, but was pleasantly surprised when the final kisses were exchanged without too much emotion all round.

'Not very long before we're back,' promised Phil, producing a small parcel for her son. 'Don't open it until you get back to Aunt Winnie's, darling.'

Jeremy waved vigorously to his departing parents and was quite willing to return to Harold's car, clutching the present.

It had been arranged beforehand that there would be no waiting about at the airport to see the aeroplane leave the ground.

'God knows how long it will be before we finally get away,' Frank had said to Winnie. 'You know how it is these days: "Regret to say there is a mechanical fault". That's a two-hour job while they solder on the wing. Then the tannoy goes again: "Regret there is an electrical fault", and off you go for your forty-third cup of coffee while they unravel the wires for another hour. No, Winnie dear, you and Harold make tracks back to Thrush Green with the boy, and then we shall be able to ring you to ask if you would mind fetching us back until the next day.'

Luckily, Frank's prognostications were proved wrong, and their flight actually departed on the right day, and only a quarter of an hour behind schedule.

'What do you think it can be?' asked Jeremy shaking the parcel vigorously, when they were on their return journey. 'It doesn't rattle.'

'Try smelling it,' suggested Harold. 'Might be bath cubes.'

'*Bath cubes?*' said Jeremy with disgust. 'Why *bath cubes?*'

'Right shaped box. Long and thin.'

'It might be sweets,' said Winnie. 'Some rather gorgeous nougat comes in boxes that shape.'

Jeremy's small fingers pressed round the edge of the wrapping paper.

'Anyway, I'm not to open it until we get home,' he said at last, 'so put your foot down, Uncle Harold. I'm *busting* to see what's inside.'

He sat in the front passenger seat, parcel held against his stomach, and babbled happily to Harold about car engines, motor boats, his kitten, what Miss Fogerty said about tadpoles and a host of other interesting topics upon which Harold commented briefly as he drove.

In the back, Winnie Bailey, much relieved at the good spirits of her charge, dozed gently, and did not wake until the car stopped at Thrush Green.

'Now I can open it, can't I?' begged Jeremy.

'Of course,' said Winnie and Harold together.

The child ripped away the paper, and disclosed a long red box. Inside, lying upon a cream velvet bed lay a beautiful wrist watch.

Jeremy's eyes opened wide with amazement.

'Look!' he whispered. 'And it's mine! Shall I put it on?'

'Why not?' replied Harold.

He helped the child to slide the expanding bracelet over his wrist. The three sat in silence while the child savoured his good fortune.

At length, he gave a great sigh of supreme satisfaction.

'I can't believe it's really mine,' he said to Winnie. 'I'm so glad I've had chicken-pox.'

'Chicken-pox?' said Winnie, bemused.

'I can go straight up to Jenny and show her,' said the boy, getting out of the car, and making for the Bailey's gate without a backward glance.

'I must thank you on behalf of us both,' said Winnie to Harold with a smile.


Over at the rectory Charles and Dimity were poring over a letter from their old friend Edgar. There was nothing that he and Hilda would enjoy more than two weeks at Thrush Green in the near future.

He had already made tentative arrangements with obliging neighbouring clergymen who would undertake his duties while he was away, so that Charles and Dimity would be quite free. He suggested the first two weeks in May, with Easter behind them and Whitsun well ahead.

Charles thought of Ella's remark about farmers taking their break between haytime and harvest. How well it would fit in, these two weeks between the great church festivals!

'I must get in touch with Anthony Bull at Lulling, and see if dear old Jocelyn feels up to coming out of retirement at Nidden,' he told Dimity, naming the Lulling vicar, and a saintly eighty-year-old who occasionally held the fort for local clergymen in times of emergency.

'Of course they'll help,' said Dimity, 'and they know full well that you will be happy to do the same for them at any time.'

'I'll go and see them both today,' replied Charles, 'and we'll ring Edgar about tea time.'

'Make it after six, dear,' said Dimity. 'Yorkshire is a long way off, and the phone call will be so much cheaper.'

'How right you are,' agreed the rector. With his modest stipend, it was a blessing to have Dimity to remind him of the need for frugality.

He looked round his study when his wife had departed to the kitchen.

Since his marriage, Dimity had done her best to mitigate the austerity of this sunless room where so much of his work was done.

She had put a rug down by the desk, to keep his feet from the inhospitable cold linoleum which covered the floor of the room. She had bought some shabby but thick curtains from a village jumble sale, to take the place of the cotton ones which had draped the study windows ever since he had taken up residence years ago.

There was always a small vase of flowers on the side table, at the moment complete with pheasant's eye narcissi and sprigs of young greenery from the garden. An electric fire had been installed, and although Charles himself never thought to switch it on, used as he was to a monastic chill in the room, Dimity would tiptoe in and rectify matters on icy mornings.

He was a fortunate man, he told himself, to have such a wonderfully unselfish wife, and one who had the gift of making a home in the straitened circumstances in which they lived.

He thought of her suggestion about transferring his things from his present room to the upstairs one above the kitchen. Frankly, he disliked the idea. The very thought of carrying all his books up the steep stairs, of getting new shelves built, of sorting out his archaic filing system, and of asking someone to help him to manhandle his desk and armchair and all the other heavy furniture which was needed in his work, appalled him.

And yet Dimity was quite right, of course. That room was certainly much lighter and warmer. They would not need the electric fire as they did here. In the end, he supposed, they would save money. But what an upheaval! Could he face it?

He looked again at the results of Dimity's labours on his behalf. How it would please her to have him safely ensconced in that pleasant back room! Surely, it was the least that one could do, to give way to one who was so unselfish and loving!

Charles leapt to his feet on impulse, and traversed the dark wind tunnel of a corridor to find Dimity in the comparative warmth of the kitchen at its end.

'My dear,' he cried, 'I've decided that your idea of moving the study upstairs is a wonderful one! As soon as we get back from Yorkshire we'll transfer everything, and meanwhile I'll think of someone to ask to make some shelves while we're away.'

Dimity left the onion she was chopping on the draining board and came to hug her husband.

'What a relief, Charles dear! It will be so much better for you, I know. You really are a good man.'

Her face was radiant.

'I ought to be a lot better,' replied Charles. 'One can only go on trying, I suppose.'

That afternoon, when Charles had mounted his bicycle to go down the hill to Lulling to visit the vicar, Dimity went across the road to see Ella at the cottage which she had shared for many years with her redoubtable friend.

She found her threading her ancient handloom on the table in the sitting room window.

'Hello, Dim,' she greeted her friend. 'Look at this for organization! I'm getting ahead with my scarves for Christmas. Any particular colour you fancy?'

Dimity swiftly went over the plentiful supply of Ella's scarves which were already stocked in a drawer. Pink, fawn, yellow, grey – now, what *hadn't* she got?

'I think a pale blue would be lovely,' she said bravely. 'It goes with so many colours, doesn't it? Thank you, Ella.'

She sat herself on the well-worn sofa, and watched Ella's hands moving deftly at her task.

'I've brought some good news,' she began.

'Won the pools?'

'Alas, no. But Charles has agreed to move his study upstairs.'

'Well, it's about time too. I wonder he hasn't had double pneumonia working in that morgue of his. Want a hand shifting stuff?'

'Well, not at the moment, Ella dear. But perhaps later. We don't propose to do anything until we come back from our holiday.'

'Tell me more,' demanded Ella.

Dimity explained about Edgar and Hilda, and the hoped-for help of Lulling's vicar and old Jocelyn.

'Thrush Green will be empty for most of May then,' said Ella. 'What with the Hursts away, and you two gallivanting in Yorkshire.'

'Oh come!' protested Dimity, 'that's only four of us. And in any case, the new couple will be at Tullivers then. Think how nice it will be to have some fresh faces here.'

'Depends on the faces,' replied Ella. 'Frankly, I prefer old friends. For all we know, these two outsiders are going to cause more trouble than Thrush Green bargains for.'

And as it happened, Ella was to be proved right.

## 5. The Henstocks Set Off

The last day of April closed in golden tranquillity. Warm and calm, from dawn until sunset, there had been promise of the summer to come.

The daffodils and early blossom in the Thrush Green gardens scarcely stirred all day, and the bees were already busy, their legs powdered with yellow pollen.

Joan Young, wandering about their small orchard, thought that she had never seen such drifts of daffodils there before. They surged around the wheels of Mrs Curdle's ancient caravan, and she remembered, with a sudden pang, that this would be the first year without Curdles' Fair to enliven May the first.

What must Ben be thinking? He never mentioned the fair in her presence, but she knew that Molly wondered if he grieved over the loss.

For that matter, all Thrush Green mourned the passing of their much-loved fair. Now old Mrs Curdle lay at rest across the green she knew so well, and this reminded Joan of something else.

She returned to the house and called upstairs to Molly.

'Help yourself to daffodils. There are masses just now, and if Ben wants some for his grandmother's grave, tell him to pick all he wants.'

Later that evening she saw Ben carrying a fine bouquet across to the churchyard. He had paid his tribute to his grandmother every May day since the old lady's death, and Joan liked to think that his loyal affection was shared by all Mrs Curdle's friends at Thrush Green.

Much to the consternation of everyone, the question of Dotty adopting a child cropped up once more.

She broached the subject herself one morning when she called at the rectory.

'You know it's weeks now since I wrote to four or five reputable adoption societies, and still no result. Isn't it dilatory? Here I am, hale and hearty, and all prepared to share a good home with some child in need – male or female – and all I've had have been acknowledgements of my letters.'

'But, Dotty dear,' began Dimity, 'these things always take time.'

Charles, more bravely, spoke his mind.

'I think you should reconsider the whole question of adoption, Dotty. You may be hale and hearty, but you are getting on, and I don't think any adoption society would allow a child to settle with you. And naturally, a home that can offer *two* parents is going to be preferred.'

Dotty snorted impatiently.

'I have filled in a form or two, come to think of it, and of course I had to put my age and status on them. And a rather strange fellow came to see me.'

That, thought Dimity, would be enough to put anyone off. Dotty's kitchen alone would strike horror into the heart of anyone trying to find a home for a stray cat, let along a young human being.

'Are you sure he was from one of the societies?' asked Charles. 'Some very odd people call at houses these days to see if they are worth burgling later.'

Dotty dismissed this alarmist suggestion.

'Oh, he showed me some papers and a card which guaranteed his claims. I rather forget which society he represented, but I gave him a cup of coffee. He left most of it,' she added. 'Rather a waste of Dulcie's good goat's milk, I thought, but dear old Flossie finished it up when he had gone.'

She patted the cocker spaniel at her feet with affection. Flossie's tail thumped appreciatively on the rectory floor.

'I feel obliged to say this,' said Charles. 'I am positive that this idea of yours – though well-meant, and typical of your generosity, Dotty my dear – is quite wrong, and I can't help feeling that no adoption society would find you a suitable person to bring up a child.'

'And why not?' demanded Dotty, turning pink with wrath. 'I should put the child's interest first every time. There is plenty of room in my cottage, and all those lovely animals to enjoy. And of course I intend to leave my possessions, such as they are, to the child when I die.'

The kind rector sighed, but stuck to his guns. As Dimity, and all his parishioners knew well, his gentle manner cloaked an inflexible will when it came to doing his duty.

'Give up the idea, Dotty. Why not invite a younger relative or friend to share the cottage and to help you with your charges. What about Connie? You enjoy her company.'

Connie was Dotty's niece, a cheerful single woman in her forties, who lived some sixty miles west of Thrush Green and occasionally called on her aunt.

'Connie has quite enough to do with her own smallholding,' replied Dotty. 'And now she has taken up breeding Shetland ponies, and could not possibly find time to move in with me – even if she had the inclination.'

She reflected for a moment.

'Of course, if I could buy that small paddock of Percy Hodge's, there might be an incentive for Connie to bring the ponies there. I must say I should enjoy their company.'

'And Connie's too, I trust.'

Dotty shrugged her thin shoulders.

'Oh, Connie's quite a reasonable gel. David brought her up very sensibly without too much money to spend, but I don't want *Connie*. And I'm quite sure Connie doesn't want *me*!'

She rose to her feet, hitched up her wrinkled stockings, and set off for the door, followed by the faithful Flossie.

'I'm quite sure all your advice is for the best, Charles,' she told him. 'But I know what I want, and I don't intend to give up my plans just yet. Have a good holiday in Yorkshire. I shall call on Edgar and Hilda when they have settled in, and bring them a goat's cheese which is already maturing nicely in the larder.'

And on this gruesome note she left them.

The possibility of some poor unfortunate child finding itself adopted by Dotty was an absorbing topic of conversation for the residents of Thrush Green and Lulling.

All agreed that the idea was typical of Dotty – generous but outrageous. However, the general feeling was summed up by Willie Bond, Willie Marchant's fellow postman.

'No one in his right mind's going to let the old girl have a child living in that pig sty. Stands to reason, these adoption people know what they're up to. She doesn't stand a snowball's chance in hell.'

It gave his listeners some comfort.

Equally absorbing was the strange behaviour of Percy Hodge during the indisposition of Winnie Bailey's Jenny.

The present of eggs was followed by some lamb chops, a box of soap, a large tray of pansy seedlings which Winnie felt obliged to bed out in pouring rain, and several bunches of flowers.

Jenny was bewildered by these attentions, and somewhat scornful.

'What will people think? Silly old man! Making me look a fool.'

'Not at all,' replied Winnie. 'It's most thoughtful of him. I'm sure it's all done in a purely friendly spirit.'

'Well, I'm not so sure he isn't missing his Gertie's cooking,' said Jenny bluntly. 'Looking around for a housekeeper, I'd say. I've half a mind to snub him soundly, cheeky old thing! As if I'd ever leave you!'

'Don't worry about it,' begged Winnie. 'Just accept the situation, and be polite to him. Time enough to worry if he pops the question.'

But despite her calm exterior, Winnie herself was a little perturbed. Jenny, she suspected, had summed up the position very neatly. If, of course, her feelings changed, marriage to Percy might be a very good thing for dear unselfish Jenny. He was a kindly fellow, affectionate and thoughtful. He had a sizeable farm and a pleasantly situated farmhouse which Jenny would enjoy cherishing. No, thought Winnie, of course she would not stand in Jenny's way if that was what she wanted one day in the future, but how she would miss her if that situation arose!

Comment at The Two Pheasants was less polite.

'No fool like an old fool,' quoted one of the customers.

'You'd think old Perce would count his blessings being a peaceful old widower,' said another sourly. It was well-known that his own marriage was fraught with acidity, acrimony and the results of too much alcohol.

Albert Piggott grunted his agreement. He knew about wives too.

'Not that Jenny wouldn't do well for herself,' he conceded. 'Percy's a warm man. Got a bit in the building society, and some in the post office.

He told me so himself one day. And then his Gertie was a rare one for managing. I bet she left a nice little nest-egg. No, if Jenny's got any sense she could do worse than plump for old Percy.'

'What Jenny does is one thing,' announced the local dustman, pushing across his glass for a refill. 'What I hates to see is a chap of Percy's age making sheep's eyes at a gal. Looks a right fool he does, mincin' along with a ruddy bunch of flowers in his hand. Don't seem to care what people say, neither. I told him straight: "You be a bigger fool than you look, Perce Hodge, and that's sayin' something!" But he only smirked. Hopeless, that's what he is! Absolutely hopeless!'

'Ah! He's got it bad,' agreed Mr Jones, the landlord. 'But there, that's love. Takes you unawares like. Now drink up, please gentlemen! You can all see the clock!'

And the affair of Percy and Jenny had to be discussed later in the night air of Thrush Green.


Jeremy, naturally, was an interested observer of Percy's attentions, and frequently inquired about them.

Winnie did her best to evade his questions, but he was a persistent young man, and sometimes caught her off guard.

'What will you do if Jenny goes to live at the farm?' he asked one evening, looking up from an ancient jigsaw puzzle which Winnie had unearthed for his pleasure.

'I don't suppose she will go,' answered Winnie equably. 'Jenny seems very happy here.'

'But it may be the last chance she gets of getting married,' pursued Jeremy. 'I mean, she's quite *old*. Do you think she'll have any babies?'

'Was that the door bell?' asked Winnie, playing for time.

'No. You see, you have to be pretty young to have babies. Paul told me all about having them last holiday.'

He searched among the box of pieces and held up a bit of blue sky triumphantly.

And how much, wondered Winnie, did Paul Young impart to his friend of this particular subject? And had Phil been informed?

'Do you think Jenny knows about babies?'

'I'm quite sure she does,' said Winnie hastily.

'Well, it all sounded pretty odd to me when Paul told me, but I was jolly glad to know what that button in your stomach was for at last.'

'Really?' said Winnie, much intrigued.

'Didn't you know? It blows up like a balloon, and when it pops, a baby is there.'

'Indeed?' observed Winnie politely.

'I'm surprised you didn't know,' said Jeremy severely. 'I should have thought Uncle Donald would have told you, him being a doctor. He must have seen it happen.'

'Probably,' said Winnie, 'but he was always very careful not to discuss his patients with me.'

'Ah! That's it, of course! But you will let Jenny know what happens, won't you? She might not be sure.'

'I am positive that Jenny knows all that is necessary,' said Winnie, 'and in any case, arrangements between Mr Hodge and Jenny are entirely their affair. It's something we should not discuss.'

Jeremy looked at her in mild surprise.

'But *everyone*, absolutely *everyone* is talking about it in Thrush Green!' he told her.

And that, thought Winnie, could well be believed.

'Time for supper,' she said briskly, and made her escape to the kitchen.


The day of the Henstocks' departure for Yorkshire dawned bright and windy. Great clouds scudded across the sky before an exhilarating south-wester.

Dimity and Charles packed their luggage into the car in high spirits. The ancient Ford had been polished the day before, and gleamed with unusual spendour.

Before they set off, Dimity called at Ella's to give her the key and a number of agitated last-minute directions.

'There are six tins of evaporated milk in the larder, for the cat, but there is one opened in the fridge which should be finished up. And there's *plenty* of pig's liver in the freezer, Ella dear, if you don't mind taking out a *small* packet the night before you need it. I've left scissors as well as a knife and fork with her plates, and perhaps –'

'My dear Dim,' said Ella, 'calm down! I know where everything is, and that cat won't starve, believe me. Now, you two go and have a real break, and forget all the duties here. They'll be waiting for you when you get back – you know that.'

'We really will relax,' promised Dimity. 'You can't imagine how we've been looking forward to it. You know the house will be empty until Wednesday? Hilda and Edgar are breaking their journey at Coventry to see a cousin in hospital.'

'I'll keep my eye on things,' Ella assured her, ushering her firmly down the garden path. 'Now off you go, and I'll see you the minute you get back. Have a lovely time.'

She watched Dimity flutter across the road and enter the gloomy portal of the Victorian rectory, then turned back to tackle the daily crossword.

'Poor old Dim,' she said aloud, as she searched for a pencil. 'Do her a world of good to see the back of that dreary house.'

She little thought that her words would prove to be a prophecy.

The bright breezy weather continued in the early days of May, much to the satisfaction of Thrush Green gardeners, zealous housewives who rushed to wash blankets, and Miss Fogerty and Miss Watson who had the inestimable relief of seeing their charges running off steam in the open air at playtimes.

'I think I really must find some new toys for the wet day cupboard,' observed Agnes to her headmistress. They were enjoying their morning coffee in Agnes's new classroom, and the infant mistress was surveying a pile of torn comics and incomplete jigsaw puzzles which were due to be deposited in the dustbin.

'They've done very well,' conceded Miss Watson, scrutinizing the top comic. 'I see this one is dated 1965. Pity dear old "Rainbow" is now defunct. Did you have it as a child, Agnes?'

'Alas, no! My father thought comics an unnecessary indulgence, but I sometimes saw "Rainbow" at a little friend's house. I particularly enjoyed Marzipan the Magician, and a little girl with two dogs.'

'Bluebell,' said Miss Watson. 'At least, I think it was. It's some time since I read the paper, but how I *loved* Mrs Bruin! I wonder why she always wore a white cap, and that same frock with a poached-egg pattern?'

'Easy to draw, perhaps,' suggested Agnes practically. 'Do you think I could transfer some of the boxes of beads to the wet day box?'

'An excellent idea,' said Miss Watson. 'And remind me to look out some old "Geographical" magazines when we go home. Plenty there to amuse them. Such beautiful pictures – and if you like they could cut some out and start scrap books.'

'That's most generous of you,' said little Miss Fogerty, pink with pleasure at the thought of such riches. With such small joys are good infants' teachers made happy, which may explain why so many remain ever youthful.

Later that evening, Miss Watson routed out the magazines from the landing cupboard, and the two ladies were busy leafing through them when the telephone rang.

Miss Watson retired to the hall and was there for some time. Agnes was just wondering whether a splendid picture of an African family wearing only long ear-rings and a spike through the nose was quite suitable for infants, when her headmistress returned. She was breathing rather heavily.

'That was Ray,' she said. 'They are just about to set off on this Cotswold tour they had to postpone because of that wretched dog of theirs.'

'Is it better?' asked Agnes.

'Unfortunately, yes! They propose to bring it with them – which I consider a mistake, and told Ray so – but, as you know, they are quite besotted with the animal and fear that it might pine in kennels.'

'Won't it be difficult to find hotels willing to take a labrador? I mean, it's such a large dog.'

'It is indeed, and this one is completely untrained, as you know. That is why Ray asked if they could stay here for two or three nights.'

'Oh! Can we manage?'

'We *cannot*!' said Dorothy Watson firmly. 'I told him so last time he mooted the question, and I suppose he thinks that I may have changed my mind. Well, I haven't. I have invited them to tea on the day they arrive in Lulling, and the dog can stay in the car while they eat it.'

'But, Dorothy, it may be a cold afternoon,' pleaded Agnes. 'Perhaps it could stay in the kitchen?'

'Well, we'll see,' said Dorothy, relenting a little, in the face of her friend's agitation. 'But I make no rash promises.'

And with that little Miss Fogerty had to be content.

She spent the night comforting herself with the thought that dear Dorothy's bark was always worse than her bite, and with another thought, equally cheering, that blood was thicker than water, and even if The Fleece forbade animals, The Fuchsia Bush always allowed pets to accompany their owners at lunch or tea.

The last of Agnes Fogerty's hopes was somewhat dashed the next morning by Willie Bond, the fat postman who shared the Thrush Green post round with gaunt Willie Marchant.

'Heard the latest?' he inquired, passing over three manilla envelopes obviously from the Education Office, and a postcard from America which, no doubt, was from the Hursts.

'No, Willie. What is it?'

Agnes could hear the kettle boiling, and was anxious to return to her duties.

'They say the old Fuchsia Bush is packing up.'

'Never!' gasped Agnes. 'I can't believe it! It always seems so busy.'

'Well, there it is. Can't make it pay, seemingly, and them girls wants the earth for wages, no doubt, so it'll have to put up its shutters.'

'We shall all miss it,' said Agnes.

'Your kettle's boiling from the sound of things,' said Willie, making slowly for the gate. 'Be all over the floor by the time you gets there.'

'Yes, of course, of course!'

Agnes hurried down the hall and met Dorothy entering the kitchen. She told her the dread news.

Miss Watson took the blow with her usual calm demeanour.

'I've no doubt that the story is greatly exaggerated, Agnes, and I shan't waste my time believing it until I have heard officially. Willie Bond was always a scaremonger, and I remember that he was always given to tell tales, even as a child.'

'But I wonder how he came by the story?' wondered Agnes, tapping her boiled egg.

'Time alone will tell,' responded her headmistress. 'Could you pass the butter, dear?'

## 6. A Turbulent Tea Party

As Miss Watson had surmised, Willie Bond's tidings were grossly exaggerated, although, even in the modified version, the truth was quite upsetting enough to the inhabitants of Lulling and Thrush Green.

The Fuchsia Bush, it seemed, was going to be open from 10 a.m. until 2.30 p.m., catering as usual for exhausted shoppers needing morning coffee, and local businessmen and women needing a modest lunch. The premises would then close until 6.30 p.m. when it would offer dinner to those who required it. The time-honoured afternoon tea was now a thing of the past, and regret and acrimony were widely expressed.

'Never heard such nonsense,' said Ella Bembridge to Winnie Bailey. 'The Fuchsia Bush was always busiest at tea time, and they've got that marvellous girl in the kitchen who knocks up the best scones in the Cotswolds. Why, those alone bring in dozens of travellers between four and five every afternoon.'

'They say it's a staffing problem,' replied Winnie. 'Evidently they can get part-timers to come in the morning and to cope with the lunches, and more to appear in the evenings, when the husbands are home to look after the children.'

'Well, it's a scandal,' replied Ella, blowing out a cloud of acrid smoke. 'It was just the place to meet after shopping or the dentist, and I must say their Darjeeling tea took some beating. As for trying to compete with The Fleece and The Crown and Anchor for dinners, it's plain idiotic.'

'Well, Jenny tells me that she knows two women who are going to do the evening stint there, and everyone feels it might work, so we must just wait and see.'

Miss Watson, proved right yet again, was inclined to be indulgent about the lost tea time at The Fuchsia Bush. In any case, teachers were usually buttoning children's coats, and exhorting them to keep out of trouble on their homeward journeys, at the relevant opening time. As she remarked to little Miss Fogerty:

'It won't affect us greatly, dear, but I think it is very foolish of these tea shops to close at such a time. American tourists alone must miss experiencing a truly English tea with attentive waitresses in those pretty flowered smocks to serve them.'

Miss Fogerty, whose purse had seldom allowed her to indulge in even such a modest repast as tea at The Fuchsia Bush, agreed wholeheartedly. She disliked change.

The Misses Lovelock, whose Georgian house stood close to the premises, were the only ones who seemed to favour the project.

'We shall have a little peace on summer afternoons now,' said Bertha. 'Why, I've even seen coaches stop there and drop *hordes* of people – some of them *not* quite out of the top drawer – and of course quite a few wandered about while they waited to go in, and one day a most dreadful man, with a squint, pressed his face to our window and very much frightened us all.'

'Good job it was downstairs,' Ella had remarked. 'Upstairs you might have been in your corsets, or less.'

Bertha chose to ignore such coarseness. Really, at times one wondered about Ella's upbringing!

'No,' said Violet, hastening to Bertha's support, 'we shan't mind The Fuchsia Bush closing for teas, whatever the rest of Lulling is saying.'

'You'll just get the racket later in the day,' observed Ella, stubbing out a cigarette in a priceless Meissen bon-bon dish at her side. 'Be plenty of cars parking, I expect, when they open in the evening.'

And, happy to have the last word for once, Ella departed.

The visit of Miss Watson's brother Ray and his wife occurred about this time. Although little Miss Fogerty was glad to see that Dorothy's sisterly feelings had prompted her to invite Ray and Kathleen to tea after school, nevertheless she had inner forebodings about their reception.

There was no doubt about it. The unfortunate coolness which had arisen dated from Dorothy's enforced stay in hospital with a broken hip some time before. Agnes, who had been a devoted visitor, realized that Dorothy's assumption that she would be invited to convalesce at Ray's was misplaced, to say the least of it. Luckily, she had been in a position to offer immediate help, and took up residence at the school house to look after the invalid. Dorothy, ever grateful, had reciprocated by asking her old colleague to make her stay a permanent one, and very happily the arrangement had turned out.

But Ray and Kathleen would never, it seemed, be quite as dear to her headmistress. Agnes could only hope that the proposed tea party would pass off pleasantly, and that bygones would remain bygones.

It was a perfect early May afternoon. Agnes had taken her little brood for a walk along the track to Lulling Woods, passing Dotty Harmer's house, and waving to that lady as she tended a large and smoky bonfire of garden rubbish near the hedge.

The grass was dry enough for the children to sit on before they returned, and Agnes leant back against a dry stone wall out of the light wind and admired some early coltsfoot across the track, and some young ferns, curled like sea horses, against the Cotswold stone. The children seemed content to lie on their backs, chewing grass, and gazing at the sky above. It was a well-known fact that little Miss Fogerty had the happy knack of keeping children quiet and contented. The present scene would have proved this to any onlooker.

Agnes allowed her mind to dwell on the approaching confrontation. Dorothy had made a superb three-tier sponge cake, using five eggs and the best butter, and Agnes herself had cut cucumber sandwiches during the lunch break, and carefully wrapped them to keep fresh. Home-made scones with plum jam, and some delicious chocolate biscuits filled with marshmallow completed the meal provided. It was particularly unselfish of dear Dorothy to add the last ingredient to their afternoon tea, thought Agnes, as she adored marshmallows but was obliged to resist such temptation in the interest of watching her weight.

Agnes looked at her watch.

'Time to be going!' she called, and shepherded her charges back to Thrush Green.

The two ladies were back in the school house by a quarter to four. Dorothy had changed into a becoming blue jersey two-piece, and Agnes had put on her best silk blouse with her mother's cameo brooch at the neck.

The tea tray waited in the sitting room, and on a side table were all the festive dishes. Some golden daffodils scented the air, and the ladies waited expectantly. The visitors were due at four o'clock, but at ten past they had not appeared.

Dorothy began to get restive, wandering to the window to look down the road, and then back to the kitchen to make sure that the kettle was ready. Agnes viewed her growing impatience with some apprehension. Dear Dorothy was a stickler for punctuality.

'Isn't it extraordinary,' exclaimed her headmistress, 'how people never arrive on time? I mean, if I say between seven and seven-thirty, it's usually a quarter to eight before the bell rings. Why not seven-fifteen? Why not seven, for that matter?'

Agnes assumed that this was a rhetorical question and forbore to answer.

The little clock on the mantel piece struck a quarter past four, and Dorothy plumped up a cushion with unnecessary force.

'Of course, Ray never had any idea of time, nor Kathleen, come to that. Ray was even late for his own wedding, I remember. The whole congregation waiting for the bridegroom! You can imagine! One expects some delay before the bride appears but –'

She broke off suddenly.

'Here they are at last! And about time too. Would you switch on the kettle, Agnes dear, while I let them in?'

Polite kisses were exchanged in the hall, and Miss Watson led the way into the sitting room. No apologies were made for their late arrival, she noticed, although it was now twenty-five minutes past the hour, but she decided to ignore the omission. As she had remarked to Agnes, time meant nothing to this pair.

'And how are you finding The Fleece?' she inquired.

'Rather run down,' said Ray. 'Under new management, I gather, and not very competent.'

At that moment, a ferocious barking broke out, and Agnes, coming in with the tea pot, very nearly dropped it in her alarm.

The two visitors had rushed to the window, so that Agnes put down the tea pot without being greeted.

'Oh, *poor* Harrison!' cried Kathleen. 'He's seen a horrid cat. So upsetting. We'd better bring him in, Ray.'

Ray began to make for the door.

'By all means go and calm the dog,' said Dorothy, with a touch of hauteur, 'but I think it would be wise to leave him outside while we enjoy our tea.'

'He always has tea with us,' said Ray. 'He usually has a saucer on the hearth rug. With plenty of milk, of course.'

'But not today,' replied Dorothy firmly, the complete headmistress. 'Now do say hello to dear Agnes who has been looking forward to seeing you so much.'

Reminded of their manners, Ray and Kathleen greeted her warmly, and did their best to ignore the persistent whining and yelping issuing from their car. But clearly their minds were elsewhere, and conversation had to be carried on at a high pitch to overcome the appalling din made by the unhappy animal.

'I take it that the management at The Fleece welcomes animals?' ventured little Miss Fogerty.

'I wouldn't say *welcomes*,' said Ray. 'Harrison is being allowed to sleep in his basket in one of the stables. No dogs in the hotel. That's the rule, we were told the minute we arrived.'

'Why "Harrison"?' asked Dorothy, passing the cucumber sandwiches. Kathleen looked momentarily pleased.

'Well, you see he is the image of the butcher who used to come round when we were first married. Isn't he, Ray?'

'Exactly. Same brown eyes, same expression –'

'Same black coat?' murmured Dorothy.

The visitors laughed politely.

'Almost,' agreed Kathleen, 'and certainly interested in *meat*.'

Agnes, who began to feel that the dog would be better ignored, if such a happy situation should ever be possible with the earsplitting cacophony engulfing them, asked after Kathleen's health. At once, Ray's wife assumed a melancholy expression.

'I'm having some new treatment for my migraine attacks,' she told them, accepting a second cup of tea.

'It's terribly expensive, and I have to make two trips a week, but I think it may be doing me good.'

'I am so glad,' said kind Agnes.

'And I've been having attacks of vertigo,' volunteered Ray, with a hint of pride. 'Something to do with the middle ear. Very disconcerting.'

Agnes wondered if the dog's powerful voice could contribute to this discomfort, but thought it wiser to remain silent. Not once, she noticed, with rare warmth, had they inquired after poor Dorothy's broken hip – a much more serious business, surely!

'But there,' continued Kathleen, with sad recognition, 'I suppose we can't expect to be as spry as we were twenty years ago.'

'Indeed no!' agreed Dorothy, rising to cut the splendid sponge. She walked across to Kathleen, plate in hand. Was her limp rather more pronounced than usual, Agnes wondered? A little stiff from sitting perhaps, she decided.

'And how is the leg?' inquired Ray, somewhat tardily.

'I do my best to ignore it,' replied Dorothy. 'No one wants to hear about the troubles of the elderly.'

Kathleen greeted this pointed remark with a swiftly indrawn breath, and a meaning glance at her husband. He, man-like, pretended to be engrossed with his tea cup.

'And where are you proposing to go tomorrow?' asked Agnes hastily.

Before Ray could answer, Kathleen spoke.

'It's amazing how quickly people get over these hip operations these days. Why, a young curate we know was actually *dancing* six months after he fell from his bicycle.'

'He was fortunate,' said Dorothy.

'Oh, I don't know,' said Kathleen, shouting above the racket from the imprisoned dog. 'I'm sure it's a matter of attitude of mind. He *intended* to get better, just as quickly as possible. I think some people enjoy being invalids.'

Agnes noted with alarm that a pink flush was suffusing Dorothy's face, a sure sign of temper, and really, thought her loyal assistant, she had every right to be cross under the circumstances.

'I don't,' said Dorothy shortly.

'Of course not,' agreed Ray. 'It was exactly what I said to Kathleen when she was so worried about you in hospital.'

'Indeed?' replied his sister icily.

'Kathleen was a martyr to her migraine at the time, as you know, otherwise we should have invited you to stay with us when you were discharged. But we knew you wanted to get home and pick up your normal life again. I said so at the time, didn't I, Kathleen?'

'You did indeed, dear,' said Kathleen, dabbing her mouth with a spotless linen napkin and leaving lipstick as well as jam upon it.

Before any civilized reply could be made, there was a rapping at the front door. Agnes, glad to escape, hurried to open it, and was confronted by Dotty Harmer with Flossie on a lead. A battered metal milk can dangled from the other hand.

Without being invited, Dotty pushed past Agnes and entered the sitting room. She was in a state of considerable agitation, and burst into speech.

'Oh, Dorothy my dear, there is a poor dog *absolutely stifling to death* in a car outside. No window left open, and it is in a terrible state of anxiety. Aren't people thoughtless? Really they need a horse-whipping, and my father would have administered it, I assure you, if he had come across such fiends! Someone calling at The Two Pheasants, I suppose, or at the Shoosmiths.'

'The dog belongs to my brother here,' said Dorothy, with a hint of smugness in her tone. 'I'm sorry it upset you so, Dotty dear. I'm afraid it must have upset a great many people at Thrush Green during the past hour.'

Dotty was not the slightest bit abashed.

'I don't think I have had the pleasure of meeting you before,' she said, transferring Flossie's lead to her left hand and entangling it dangerously with the milk can, whilst proffering her right.

'My sister-in-law Kathleen. My brother Ray. My friend Miss Harmer,' intoned Dorothy.

Ray bowed slightly, Kathleen gave a frosty smile, and Dorothy waved at the tea tray.

'Let me give you some tea, Dotty. Do sit down.'

Outside, the barking changed to a high-pitched squealing, even more agitating than before. Ray began to make for the door.

'Excuse me, I'd better bring Harrison in,' he said. He was through the door before anyone could stop him.

'So kind of you, Dorothy, but I'm on my way to Ella's and mustn't delay.'

She began to make her way to the door. Flossie's lead was now hopelessly tangled around Dotty's wrinkled stockings.

At that moment, Ray's labrador, slavering at the mouth, burst into the room, gave a demented yelp, and rushed at Flossie.

The noise was indescribable. Flossie, the meekest of animals, screamed with alarm. Harrison charged into the table, knocking the sponge cake, chocolate biscuits, two tea cups, milk jug and a flurry of knives and teaspoons to the floor.

Dotty, pulled off balance, fell across Agnes's chair, driving her mother's cameo brooch painfully into her throat. Dorothy, ever quick-witted, sat down abruptly before her own precarious balance added to the confusion, and Kathleen, cowering in her chair, gave way to hysterics.

This scene of chaos confronted Ray when at last he regained the sitting room. With commendable promptitude he caught Harrison by the collar, and held him firmly, while Agnes and Dotty recovered their balance. The milk can had rolled under Agnes's armchair and was dispersing a rivulet of goat's milk over the carpet.

'I apologize for this mess,' said Dotty. 'You must let me pay for any cleaning you have to have done. Goat's milk can be so very *pervasive*. I'd better return home and fetch some more for Ella. Luckily, Dulcie is giving a splendidly heavy yield, at the moment.'

Quite in command of herself, she smiled politely in the direction of the hysterical Kathleen, now throwing herself about alarmingly in her chair, waved to Ray, and took the shaken, but now well-behaved, Flossie into the hall. Agnes accompanied her, hoping that the blood on her throat from the brooch's wound would not stain her best silk blouse.

'Are you *sure* you would not like to rest for a little?' inquired Agnes. 'The dining room has a most comfortable armchair, if you would like a few minutes' peace.'

'Thank you, my dear, but I am quite all right. The air will refresh me.'

Agnes watched her walk to the gate, as spry as a sparrow, and none the worse it seemed for her tumble. She returned, full of foreboding, to the scene of battle.

'Who *is* that interfering old busybody?' Ray was asking, as she returned.

'A dear friend of mine,' replied Dorothy, 'and a true animal lover. I absolutely agree with her that it was *monstrous* of you to leave that dog shut in the car.'

Kathleen's hysterics were now slightly muted, but had turned to shattering hiccups.

'If you remember,' she began, and gave a mighty hiccup, 'you yourself refused to have poor Harrison indoors.'

'I should have thought that *even you* knew better than to leave the car hermetically sealed. Calling yourselves animal lovers,' said Dorothy, with withering scorn. 'And the poor thing so badly trained that it cannot be brought into a Christian household.'

She bent down to retrieve the best china from the floor, whilst Ray picked up teaspoons with one hand and dabbed at the goat's milk with the other holding his handkerchief.

'*Please*, Ray,' said Dorothy, 'leave the mess to Agnes and me. We don't want it made worse by the use of your handkerchief.'

Agnes felt that, provoked though she might well be, such a slur on the cleanliness of her brother's personal linen was carrying things rather far.

'I will fetch some clean water and a cloth,' she said hastily, and made her escape.

A wild wailing noise followed her. Obviously, Kathleen was off again!

'I think,' Ray was saying, when she returned with her cleaning materials, 'that we had better be going.'

'I wholeheartedly agree,' said Dorothy, standing facing him.

'You have thoroughly upset poor Kathleen,' he went on, 'and you know how she suffers with migraine.'

'When it suits her,' responded Dorothy.

'Are you implying,' cried her incensed brother, 'that Kathleen *pretends* to have these dreadful attacks?'

A terrible hiccup arrested Kathleen's wailing. She was now on her feet, eyes blazing.

'How dare you say such things? You know I'm a martyr to migraine! Not that I've ever had the slightest sympathy from you. You are the wickedest, most callous, unfeeling –'

Another hiccup rendered her temporarily speechless. Ray took the opportunity to put his arm about his wife, and to shepherd her and the panting Harrison to the door.

'Come along, my dear. We'll go straight back to The Fleece, and you must lie down with one of your tablets.'

'But poor Harrison hasn't had his tea,' wailed Kathleen. 'You know he likes it on the hearth rug!'

'There is plenty for him,' observed Dorothy, 'wherever he looks on the carpet.'

It was Agnes who saw them to the door, and then into their car.

'I shall never come here again,' cried Kathleen, still hiccuping violently.

'We are deeply wounded,' said Ray. 'I don't think I shall want to see Dorothy – sister though she is – for a very long time!'

They drove towards Lulling, Harrison still barking, and Agnes returned to break the dreadful news that Dorothy might never see the pair again.

'What a relief!' said her headmistress, with infinite satisfaction. 'Now, we'll just get this place to rights, and have a quiet evening with our knitting, Agnes dear.'

## 7. *The Fire*

After such a devastating experience it was hardly surprising that little Miss Fogerty slept badly. Usually, she read for half an hour, and then was more than ready to plump up her pillows, put out the bedside light, and welcome deep sleep within ten minutes.

But on this occasion sleep evaded her. She went over, in her mind, all the terrible details of that catastrophic tea party. The noise of Kathleen's hysterical wailing still sounded in her ears. Ray's furious face, and Dorothy's tart retorts tormented her memory.

St Andrew's clock struck midnight, and she tossed back the bedclothes and went to survey Thrush Green by moonlight.

It was still and beautiful. No lights shone from the houses around the green, but the moonlight silvered the windows and dappled the young leaves of the chestnut avenue. Far away, along the lane to Nidden, an owl gave his wavering cry, and from the other direction came the distant sound of one of Lulling's rare goods trains chugging through the deserted station.

The air was cool from the open window and scented with the pheasant-eye narcissi which grew against the wall. Agnes took deep breaths, relishing the silence and the peaceful scene. Below her, and to her right, the empty playground stretched. In twelve hours' time it would be astir and strident with children running and shouting.

The thought made Agnes return to her bed. She must be fit to attend her duties in the morning. At this rate she would have seven hours' sleep at the most. She must compose herself.

She smoothed her sheets, straightened her winceyette nightgown, and put her head, with its wispy grey plait, down to the welcoming pillow.

The party must be forgotten. She owed it to the children.

Within ten minutes she was asleep.

At about the same time, a little farther along the road, Albert Piggott sat up in bed and rubbed his rumbling stomach.

Should he, or should he not, go downstairs, take one of his indigestion tablets and make a cup of tea? It was on occasions like this that he missed a wife. It would have been the simplest thing to have aroused Nelly with a sharp dig of the elbow and to recount to her the overwhelming pain which he was suffering – pain which could only be assuaged by recourse to medicine and a hot drink – and which was too severe to allow him to fetch those ameliorations himself.

However, Nelly was not in bed, but presumably in that of the oil man who had supplanted him in his fickle wife's affections. If he wanted medical attention he would have to supply it himself.

Muttering to himself, he climbed out of bed, a thin unsavoury figure clad in pants and vest, for Albert scorned such effete practices as changing from dayclothes into night attire, and stumbled down the stairs. His little cat, as thin, but far cleaner, than his master, greeted him with a mew, and was pleasantly surprised to be given a saucer of milk when Albert took the bottle from the cupboard.

The kettle seemed to take an unconscionable time to boil, and Albert gazed out of the kitchen window to the bulk of the church across the way.

It was as bright as day now that the moon was high and nearly full. It shone upon the rows of tomb stones which now lined the stubby walls of the churchyard, and lit up the Gothic windows facing towards Lulling.

Sharp black shadows fell across the dewy grass, and even Albert's meagre appreciation of natural beauty was stirred by the sight.

He made the tea, poured out a mugful and took it back to bed with the bottle of tablets.

Propped up against the greasy pillow he sipped noisily, relishing the comfort of the hot liquid flowing into his tormented stomach. Two tablets were washed down, as he surveyed the moonlit bedroom.

He became conscious of the smell of smoke. It was very faint, and he dismissed it as coming from the embers of the bonfire he had seen Harold Shoosmith making that morning. Nothing to do with him, anyway, thought Albert, depositing his empty mug on the linoleum.

The pain was now lulled into submission. Albert belched comfortably, turned over, and fell asleep.

Below, in the kitchen, the cat licked the last delicious drops of Albert's bounty, washed his face, and then set out, through the open kitchen window, upon the business of the night.

An hour later, Harold Shoosmith smelt the smoke. Could his bonfire be responsible? Surely, it had been out by tea time when he had conscientiously stirred the remnants? Nevertheless, bonfires occasionally had the disconcerting habit of resuscitating themselves and, apart from the danger, it was a pity if the beauty of such a night was being fouled by smoke of his making.

In the adjoining bed, his wife Isobel slept peacefully. He slipped quietly from his own, and made his way to the bathroom which overlooked the garden where the rogue bonfire had been lit.

All was peaceful. He could see the empty incinerator quite clearly in the light of the moon. Not even a wisp of smoke curled from it, he noted with relief.

But where then was the fire? Had Miss Watson or the landlord of The Two Pheasants been burning garden rubbish? As far as he could see, their gardens were as clear as his own, although some smoke began to drift across from some conflagration farther along the green towards the south, even as he watched.

He ran, now seriously alarmed, into the spare bedroom whose side window looked across to the church and rectory.

To his horror, he saw that the smoke was pouring from the roof of the Henstocks' house, and before he could close the window a cracking report rent the air, the ridge of the vicarage roof dipped suddenly, and a great flame leapt into the air illuminating billowing clouds of thick smoke.

He ran downstairs, and Isobel woke to hear him crying:

'The fire brigade! And quickly! Thrush Green rectory is well ablaze!'

She heard the receiver slammed down, and within two seconds Harold was dragging trousers over his pyjamas and fighting his way into a pullover.

'I'll come and help,' said Isobel, reaching for her clothes.

Within five minutes a little knot of helpers was gathered at the blaze. The sight was awe-inspiring. The collapse of part of the roof had let in air which intensified the conflagration. Flames were now shooting skyward, and the upstairs windows showed a red glow. Smoke poured from the main bedroom window, and there were terrifying reports as the glass cracked in the heat.

Mr Jones, the landlord of The Two Pheasants, was organizing a chain of water carriers from the tap in his bar, and Albert Piggott, stomach pains forgotten, had trundled out an archaic fire-fighting contraption which had been kept in the vestry since the Second World War and had never been used since the time when a small incendiary bomb had set light to the tassels of the bell ropes, and an adjacent pile of copies of Stainer's 'Crucifixion', in 1942.

This relic, when attached to a nearby hydrant well-hidden in nettles in the churchyard, spouted water at a dozen spots along its perished length and saturated several onlookers.

'Get the dam' thing out of the way!' yelled Harold Shoosmith. 'We'll have someone falling over it!'

He and several other men, including Edward Young, the architect, and Ben Curdle, were busy removing furniture, books and papers, and anything they could grab downstairs, before the inevitable happened and the whole top floor collapsed. These were being piled, well away from danger, by willing hands. Ella Bembridge, for once without a cigarette in her mouth, worked as stoutly as the men, and would have forced her way into the building to collect some of Dimity's treasures, if she had not been forbidden to do so by Harold, who had taken charge with all the ready authority of one who had spent his life organizing others.

The welcome sound of the fire brigade's siren sent people scattering to allow its access across the grass to the blazing house. It was a joy to see the speed and economy of effort with which the hoses were turned on.

'This started some hours ago, by the look of things,' said the captain to Harold. 'I can't think how it went undetected for so long.'

Harold explained that the house was empty, and at that moment a

second fire engine arrived from Nidden, and started work at the side of
the building where the flames seemed thickest.

A terrible roaring sound began to emanate from the doomed building,
and the bystanders were ordered to get well away. With a thunderous
rumbling the top floor of the rectory now collapsed. Sparks, smoke and
flames poured into the air, and the heat became intense. People began to
cough in the acrid air, and to rub eyes reddened with smoke and tears.

Now, it was quite obvious, nothing more could be rescued. The rector's
modest possessions which were still inside the house must be consumed
by the fire. It was a tragedy that few could bear to witness, and Winnie
Bailey, in dressing gown and wellingtons, led the redoubtable Ella away
to her own house across the green. It was the only time she had seen her
old friend in tears.

At first light, the people of Thrush Green gazed appalled at the havoc
left by the events of the past twelve hours. Blackened stones and the gaunt
charred remains of beams smoked in the morning air. Dirty rivulets of

water moved sluggishly towards the gutters at the roadside, and puddles surrounded the remains of the Henstocks' home.

A tarpaulin had been thrown over the pathetic remnants which had been snatched from the blaze, and Harold had arranged for them to be stored in his garage and garden shed out of the weather's harm.

'I think Ella has Charles's telephone number,' he told Edward as the two begrimed and exhausted men were returning to their homes. 'But what about Hilda and Edgar? Aren't they due today?'

'Good Lord! I believe they are,' agreed Edward. 'I'll see if Joan knows anything about them. But first things first, old man. Bath and then coffee. Then a couple of hours' sleep for me – and you too, I recommend.'

'You're right. No point in ringing Charles and Dimity until about eight or nine. It's a tragic business, and particularly wretched when they are having one of their few breaks. Shall I ring or will you?'

'Do you mind tackling it? I'm supposed to be on the 9.30 train to London tomorrow – I mean, this morning – for a meeting.'

'Of course, I'll do it. Poor old Charles, it will break his heart, I fear.'

Four hours later, he sat in his study and rang the Yorkshire number. As he listened to the bell ringing so far away he wondered how on earth one could break such appalling news to a friend.

He was amazed to find how tired he was after the night's activities. Muscles he had never noticed before seemed to have sprung into painful evidence. His eyes were still sore, and the hairs on his arms were singed. As for his finger nails, despite energetic use of the nail brush, he had not seen them so grimy and broken since his schooldays.

Luckily, it was Charles who answered the telephone, Harold had already rehearsed what he should do if Dimity had lifted the receiver. Charles would have to be summoned. This was the sort of thing the men must cope with, thought Harold, true to his Victorian principles.

'Nice to hear you,' was the rector's opening remark. 'You're up early. Everything all right at your end?'

'I'm afraid not. Charles, I have to tell you some bad news. Are you sitting down?'

'Sitting down?' came the bewildered reply.

'Because this is going to be a shock,' continued Harold doggedly. 'There was a bad accident here last night.'

'No! Not anyone hurt! Not *killed*, Harold, don't say that!'

'Nothing like that. Perhaps *accident* was the wrong word. The fact is, your house has been badly damaged by fire.'

There was a brief silence.

'Hello!' shouted Harold. 'You there, Charles?'

'Yes, yes. But I can't have heard right. The house damaged by fire? How badly?'

'I hate to tell you – but it is completely gutted. I think it is quite beyond repair, Charles, as you will see.'

'I can't take it in. I really can't,' said the poor rector. 'How could it have happened? We switched off everything, I'm sure, and we hadn't had a fire in the grate for days. Surely, no one would be so wicked as to set fire to the place?'

'I'm sure it wasn't that,' said Harold. 'I just felt you should know that our spare room is waiting for you and Dimity when you return, and could you tell us where to get in touch with Hilda and Edgar?'

'Oh dear, oh dear,' wailed Charles. 'How perfectly dreadful! Of course, they were due to arrive today, and I've no idea how we can get in touch. They were breaking their journey down to have a day or two in the midlands. Wait now, they were going to visit a cousin in hospital. In Coventry, I think Edgar said. Beyond that, I know nothing, but we shall start for home –'

The rector's voice broke, and Harold distinctly heard a sniff before he resumed.

'We'll be back during the day, Harold, and our deepest thanks for offering us shelter tonight. What a terrible affair. I must go and break it to dear Dimity, and then we must clear up things here, and set off for Thrush Green without delay.'

'We shall look forward to seeing you,' said Harold.

'And Harold,' said Charles in a firmer tone, 'I very much appreciate your telling me the news so kindly. It couldn't have been easy. You have prepared us to face whatever awaits us there, quite wonderfully.'

He rang off, and Harold went to tell Isobel how well he had taken it, and to make another assault upon his finger nails.

Joan Young came over to the Shoosmiths' house as soon as Edward had departed for London.

'I thought I'd offer to track down Hilda and Edgar,' she said. 'In any case, they can stop with us until things get sorted out. If only we knew how to get hold of them!'

'I thought of ringing hospitals in Coventry and asking if Mr and Mrs Maddox were expected,' said Harold.

'Well, yes,' agreed Joan doubtfully, 'but do hospitals usually ask the names of visitors? It's such a shot in the dark.'

'Perhaps they could relay a message to the wards asking if anyone was expecting a visit from them. Is that possible, do you think?'

'It sounds highly unlikely,' said Joan, 'but I'll go back and put out a few feelers.'

The voice from the first hospital was brisk and rather impatient. Joan envisaged its owner as rushing, bedpan in hand, upon an urgent errand.

She embarked upon her message.

'Yes, yes!' said the voice. 'But if you could tell me the *patient's* name, I can get a message back to you.'

Joan said weakly that she did not know who the Maddoxes were visiting.

'In that case, I don't think I can help you. Visitors come at two o'clock until four here. I could get them to give their names at the reception desk, but as we have two hundred beds in this building alone, it would be rather a task.'

Joan said that she quite understood, thanked her and rang off. Obviously, this was going to be the pattern of any further investigations she might make. She decided that the project was impossible, and went to find Molly Curdle to help her with the beds for the unsuspecting Maddoxes, now, presumably, making their way to Thrush Green in expectation of a few carefree days in the rectory, poor dears.

Most of the inhabitants of Thrush Green went about their daily affairs in a state of shock that morning. Very few had slept throughout the night, and most had been helping to rescue the Henstocks' property until dawn arose and the firemen had departed.

Only the children, it seemed, viewed the wreckage with excitement. Little Miss Fogerty and Miss Watson had been far too upset to face their usual boiled egg at breakfast, and had nibbled Ryvita and marmalade simply to fuel their energies to get through their school duties.

Dorothy had given a short talk to the school at morning prayers, and told them how necessary it was to be of exceptionally good behaviour as so many people had been upset by the truly dreadful events of the night.

She then composed a suitable prayer asking for comfort to be given to the rector and his wife, and offering thanks for the bravery of the firemen and helpers, and for the merciful lack of injury to any person involved.

Agnes was full of admiration for Dorothy's powers of extempore prayer, and led her infants across the playground still pondering upon this facet of her headmistress's varied ability.

It was young George Curdle who spoke first.

'But why did God let the fire happen?' he asked.

For once in her life, Agnes felt unable to answer.

As it happened, Dimity and Charles arrived first on the scene, having driven non-stop from Yorkshire. Hastily prepared sandwiches had sustained them as they drove, and they chugged up the hill from Lulling as St Andrew's clock struck three.

No one saw them arrive, and for that they were grateful. They halted the car on the edge of the battered and rutted grass which was still sprinkled with the ash and trodden cinders of last night's activities.

Dimity covered her face with her hands and her thin shoulders shook. Charles's face was stony as he gazed unwinking at the scene. He put his arm round his grieving wife, but was quite unable to speak. They sat there, silent in their distress, for five terrible minutes.

Then, sighing, Charles opened the door and stepped into the desolation of what had once been Thrush Green rectory.

He stirred the damp black ashes of the study floor with his foot. He could scarcely see for the blur of tears behind his spectacles, but he bent to investigate a glint of metal among the dust.

Turning it over in his hand, he recognized it. It was the silver figure of Christ which had been mounted on the ivory cross behind his desk. It was distorted and blackened by the heat, but Charles knew immediately what it was. He slipped it into his pocket, and turned to help Dimity over a low sooty wall which was all that was left of her kitchen.

And it was at that moment that Ella came from her cottage, and Harold and Isobel from their house, to give them what comfort they could.

That evening, when Edward Young arrived home, he found Hilda and Edgar, as well as Dimity and Charles, in his sitting room, still trying to get over the shock of the disaster.

It was as well that Joan had not continued with her efforts to trace them through Coventry hospitals and nursing homes, for their cousin, as it happened, had been sent home at the weekend and they had visited him in his own bedroom, finding him well on the way to recovery.

There was so much to discuss between all the old friends that it was beginning to get dark before the Maddoxes retired to an early bed. They proposed to leave after lunch the next day.

Joan and Edward walked back with the Henstocks to Harold's house, and hoped that they would be able to sleep, and so be released from their unhappiness for a few hours' oblivion.

They walked on together, past the silent school and the public house, until they rounded the bulk of St Andrew's church and stood facing the ruins.

The acrid stench which had hung over Thrush Green all day was almost unbearable here.

Joan looked with pity and distaste at the mess which had once been the rectory.

She caught a glimpse of Edward's face in the dying light.

'Edward!' she said accusingly. 'You're *pleased*! How can you be so *heartless*!'

Edward hastened to explain himself.

'My darling, three-quarters of me grieves for dear old Charles and Dim, just as much as you do. But the other quarter – the professional bit – is so relieved to see the end of that ghastly place that it can't help rejoicing in a perverse sort of way.'

Joan gazed at him with disgust, and then began to smile.

She took his arm, and they turned their backs upon the wreckage, and set off towards their home.

'I suppose you are already planning a new house, monster that you are,' she observed.

'How did you guess?' asked Edward.


## 8. *At Young Mr Venables'*


It was hardly surprising that, with all this excitement at Thrush Green, the advent of Tullivers' temporary residents passed with very little comment.

They had arrived in a battered van. Young Jack Thomas and his wife Mary appeared to have only two suitcases, but a vast array of cardboard boxes which seemed to be full of electrical equipment of some sort. Winnie Bailey, watching shamelessly from her bedroom window, surveyed the writhing tangles of flex and plugs and supposed that they might have brought their own television set, or portable electric fires with them.

As she watched, a noisy motorcycle roared up and parked alongside the van. Two figures, clad in black leather, dismounted and took off their helmets. Both shook out long blonde hair, but Winnie thought that one might possibly be a male.

All four vanished into the house, and Winnie decided to let them remain undisturbed for an hour or so before calling to see if she could be of any help. Jeremy was due soon from school, and after tea he could accompany her.

The boy was excited at the idea of seeing the new occupants of his home.

'Do you think they'll mind some of the cupboards being locked? I mean, mummy said my toys would be safer if I left them in the landing cupboard locked away, but they might need it for clothes and things, mightn't they?'

'I'm sure there's plenty of cupboard space for their needs,' Winnie assured him, thinking of the paucity of their travelling cases.

She lifted the heavy knocker which old Admiral Trigg had fixed to the front door of Tullivers years ago. It was in the form of a dolphin, a suitably nautical object for the old sea-farer to approve, and weighed several pounds. The door itself shuddered as the knocker thudded back into place.

Jack Thomas opened the door and gave Winnie such a dazzling smile that she was won over at once. She had handed the key earlier to his wife Mary, so that this was her first encounter with the new householder.

'Hello, you must be Jeremy,' said Jack, 'and of course you are Mrs Bailey. Do come in.'

They stepped into the sitting room where Winnie was surprised to see that several chairs had vanished and the remaining furniture was pushed back against the walls. The centre of the room was bare except for a number of the large cardboard boxes which Winnie had observed.

'Where are the chairs?' asked Jeremy.

'Oh, we've put 'em in the dining room. We'll probably live in there while we're here. You see, we need this space for the gear.'

He waved vaguely towards the tangle of wires in the boxes.

'Now, is there anything you need?' asked Winnie, returning to firmer ground. 'Bread, milk, eggs? Have you found out how to work the cooker and the lights? Do let me know if I can help.'

'Very sweet of you,' he said, with another heart-melting smile. 'I think we've all we need. We're going down to Lulling for a meal tonight.'

'I hear The Fuchsia Bush and The Fleece put on quite a good dinner,' replied Winnie.

'Oh, we'll fetch fish and chips,' said Jack. 'Much cheaper and less fag anyway than a meal out. And no washing up when you eat them straight from the paper.'

'Very true,' agreed Winnie.

'Shall I call the others?'

'No, no, don't trouble them. I'm sure you've all got enough to do moving in. But do come over if you want anything. I'm in most of the time. I hope you'll enjoy your stay with us,' she added politely, making for the door.

'I wish we could have fish and chips for supper,' said Jeremy wistfully as they walked home. 'But they'll have to wash up their plates, won't they? They won't really eat it all out of the paper with their fingers, will they? Won't they make dirty marks on the furniture?'

'Oh, I shouldn't think so,' said Winnie untruthfully. The same thought had gone through her mind, she had to admit.

But greasy fingers or not, thought Winnie, entering her own immaculate home, that smile of Jack Thomas's would forgive him anything.

The next few days were sad and busy ones for Charles and Dimity. The salvaged articles from the fire were pitifully small, and every hour brought a new loss to light. Luckily, they had the clothes which they had packed for their Yorkshire holiday, and Harold and Isobel were able to lend them some immediate necessities, but there was the bewildering business of insurance and other matters to see to, and these things worried poor Charles very much.

Harold was a tower of strength, but so many necessary papers and documents had been consumed in the fire, and the fact that the property belonged to the Church with all sorts of legal and technical complications, made him advise Charles to see his friend Justin Venables, the Lulling solicitor.

Charles decided to walk down the hill to Twitter and Venables' office at the end of the town. His appointment was for four o'clock, and the May sunshine was at its warmest as he set off past the school and across the green.

He averted his eyes from the empty spot where once his beloved rectory had stood. As it happened, two large lorries were on the site loading the remains of the rubble. Once they departed there would only be the scorched grass and the blackened soil to mark the place of the rector's home. The Church officials had been kind and sympathetic. He would be taken care of, supplied with a resting place very shortly, and would be kept informed, at every step, of the decisions of his ecclesiastical masters.

He had been severely upset to find that the investigation into the cause of the fire proved conclusively that faulty wiring in the airing cupboard was to blame.

The immersion heater was housed in the lower part of this cupboard, and Charles could not forgive himself for not switching it off before they left the house. He said so to Harold.

'But, you see, Dimity said we must leave on the hot water because Betty Bell's cousin from Lulling Woods was coming in to do some spring-cleaning before Edgar and Hilda arrived. I fear I was greatly to blame. Of course, I confessed at once to the man who came about it.'

'Forget it,' advised Harold. 'That wiring should have been renewed years ago, and the Church is jolly lucky you two weren't burnt to cinders in your beds. Why, some of it is two-plug stuff, and some three, and you've got lead-covered wiring in your study and rubber stuff in the kitchen, and what looked like naked copper to me in that back kitchen of yours.'

'It is rather a hotch-potch,' agreed the rector. '*Was*, I mean. But then, you see, bits were added over the years, and I suppose they used whatever was in fashion. I know we had some trouble when we put in the refrigerator. All the lights blew out once when we opened the door. And the kettle used to snap on a red light sometimes, which frightened me very much, though Dimity assured me that it was a safety device. I'm afraid,' concluded the rector sadly, 'that I don't really understand electricity.'

'You'd have needed Faraday himself to sort out the system in your house,' said Harold. 'Just be thankful you weren't there when it finally blew up.'

'It wasn't so much *blowing up* as *smouldering*, they tell me,' replied Charles. 'You see the heat caught the lining paper on the shelves and that set light to the linen, and then the wooden slats, and then the roof timbers. And once the air got in everything became so much fiercer. I really can't bear to think of it. But, as you say, Harold, we must thank God that no one was hurt.'

He tried to put his anxieties out of his mind as he went down the hill to Lulling. The town was looking beautiful in its spring finery. The Cotswold stone garden walls were hung with bright mats of mauve aubretia and yellow alyssum. Daisies starred the lawns, and everywhere the heady scent of hyacinths and narcissi hung in the warm air.

The lime trees lining Lulling High Street fluttered their young green leaves, and the ancient japonica which fanned across the Misses Lovelock's Georgian house was already bright with scarlet flowers. Outside The Fuchsia Bush two tubs of splendid pink tulips flanked the door, and every window in the street, it seemed, held a vase of fresh spring flowers.

The rector's spirits rose as he strode along relishing the beauty around him. As expected, he was stopped several times by friends who commiserated with him and cheered him with their concern and sympathy.

He felt almost jaunty by the time he reached the solicitors' office, but the gloom of the entrance hall, a study in ginger-coloured grained paintwork, had a sobering effect upon the good man.

A plump middle-aged lady showed him into Justin's office on the left-hand side of the hall, and he was greeted affectionately.

'Just let me set you a chair, padre,' said Justin. 'Not that one. Take this, it has a padded seat.'

He levered up a heavy chair with a high Jacobean-type back and a seat upholstered in leather which was so old and rubbed that it resembled suede. It was, as Charles found, surprisingly comfortable.

'Tea now, I think, Muriel,' said Justin to the plump lady.

'Yes, sir,' she said, so humbly that Charles would not have been surprised to see her genuflect, or at least pull her forelock had she had such a thing. Obviously, Justin was the master in this establishment.

'Well now, just tell me the trouble,' began Justin, when the door had closed.

Charles gave a remarkably concise account of his actions before and after the fire, and explained his position as a tenant of Church property.

Justin listened carefully, his fingertips pressed together. He watched his client over his half-glasses and thought how rare and pleasant it was to be face to face with an absolutely honest man.

A discreet knock at the door heralded the arrival of Muriel with the tea tray. It was lowered reverently upon a vacant space on Justin's desk.

The good rector, had he given any thought to the matter, would have been grateful for a mug of ready poured out tea with perhaps a bowl of granulated sugar with a well-worn teaspoon stuck in it. He was much impressed with the elegant apparatus now before Justin.

Two delicate china cups stood upon a snowy linen tray cloth. An embroidered satin tea-cosy covered a silver tea pot, and small cubes of sugar, accompanied by silver clawed sugar-tongs, rested in a matching bowl. Some excellent shortbread fingers were ranged alongside.

'Well!' exclaimed Charles happily, 'I really didn't expect such a beautiful tea! And what a handsome tea cosy!'

'It is rather nice, isn't it?' agreed Justin, surveying it as though he had just noticed it. 'One of the girls in the office ran it up one Christmas. And the tray cloth too, I believe. Very good with her fingers obviously. A slice of lemon, Charles, or milk?'

'Milk, please. Do you usually have time for tea? I hope you haven't gone to all this trouble on my behalf.'

'From four to four-thirty is tea time,' replied Justin firmly. 'I only see old friends then whom I like to invite to share my tea tray. Try the shortbread. Muriel makes it for me weekly.'

The rector could not help thinking in what a civilized way Justin seemed to conduct his business. He had no doubt that just as much work got done in the leisurely framework of Justin's day as was accomplished by so many feverish young men rushing from one thing to another.

'Of course, we have always stayed open until six o'clock,' said Justin, submerging his lemon slice gently with his teaspoon. 'So many of our clients appreciate being able to call here after their work is over. One needs a cup of tea to refresh one towards the end of the day.'

'Very sensible,' agreed Charles, dusting shortbread crumbs as unobtrusively as possible from his clerical grey trousers.

Over the tea tray Justin dealt with the rector's anxieties, and assured him that all would be satisfactorily arranged with the insurance people, the Church authorities, and all other interested parties in this sad affair.

It was exactly twenty-eight minutes past four when he rose and shook his old friend's hand in farewell.

'By the way,' he said, on his way to open the door, 'I am retiring at the end of this year.'

'You can't be!' exclaimed Charles. 'Why, you know you are always referred to as "young Mr Venables"! Who will take over?'

'Young Mr Venables will be seventy next birthday,' smiled Justin, 'and the boys here are in their forties and fifties. Plenty of good fellows to carry on at Twitter and Venables, believe me.'

'I can't take it in,' confessed Charles. 'Of course, I shan't mention this until you give me permission to do so.'

'You have it now, my dear fellow. There's no secret about it. Now, I mustn't keep you.'

He opened the office door, and saw Charles out into the sunshine.

The rector retraced his steps in thoughtful mood, pondering on Justin's decision to retire. Seventy next birthday, he had said. Well, perhaps he was right to leave the somewhat gloomy office and to feel free to enjoy his fishing and his golf when the sun shone. Certainly, Justin had served the little town well, as had his father before him. No doubt the middle-aged boys would carry on the good work, but it wouldn't please his old clients.

A car drew alongside the kerb just as Charles was approaching the Misses Lovelock's house. It was driven by the vicar of Lulling, the Reverend Anthony Bull, and his mellifluous voice floated across the warm air.

'Get in, Charles, if you are making for home. I'm off to Nidden.'

Charles was rather looking forward to walking home in the spring sunshine, but it would have been churlish to turn down this offer, and in any case, he always enjoyed Anthony Bull's company.

He was a tall handsome man with a fine head and expressive hands. As a single man he had fluttered many maiden hearts, and even now, happily married as he was to a rich wife, a steady supply of embroidered slippers, hand-knitted socks, and useful memo pads decorated with last year's Christmas cards, flowed into the vicarage from adoring members of his congregation.

'We only got back from a few days in Devon yesterday,' said the vicar, 'and were appalled to hear about your house. I gather you are at Harold's for the time being, but if you want to come to us, Charles, the vicarage has plenty of room, and we should both be delighted to put you up.'

Charles thanked him sincerely. The vicarage was an elegant Queen Anne house, overlooking Lulling's extensive green. It was common knowledge that Mrs Bull's wealth had contributed to the comfort of their establishment. The beautiful old house had flourished under her cosseting, and Charles could not think of anywhere more lovely to shelter, if the need arose. He tried to say as much to the generous vicar.

'You've heard the rumour, I expect,' said Anthony Bull, 'about the re-organization of the parishes around here? It's a case of spreading us rather more thinly on the ground, I gather. Nothing definite yet, but I shouldn't be surprised to hear that we are all going to play General Post before long.'

'Do you know,' said Charles, 'I haven't heard the game of General Post mentioned since I was a child! Nor Turn the Trencher, for that matter, nor Postman's Knock. Do you think people still play those party games?'

'I should like to think so,' responded the vicar, drawing up outside Harold's house on Thrush Green, 'but I fear they play rather more sophisticated games these days, with perhaps rather less innocent enjoyment.'

At that moment, Charles saw Dotty Harmer emerging from Ella's, milk can in one hand, and Flossie's lead in the other. He did not feel equal to coping with that lady, much as he admired and respected her.

He hurriedly got out from the car.

'Thank you again, Anthony, for the lift, and your very kind offer of help.'

The vicar waved and drove off towards Nidden. What a beautiful glossy car it was, thought Charles, without a trace of envy. It was fitting that such a fine fellow as dear Anthony should travel in such style, and live in such a splendid house.

He opened Harold's gate, and walked with a thankful heart into his own temporary abode.

## 9. *Trouble at Tullivers*

It was soon apparent to the inhabitants of Thrush Green that young Jack Thomas departed from Tullivers each morning at eight o'clock. The shabby van took the road north towards Woodstock, and presumably from there he went to the estate office where he was employed.

His wife Mary and the other two residents were not seen until much later in the morning. The more censorious of Thrush Green's housewives deplored the fact that only once had Mary been seen to shake the mats, and that was at eleven-thirty in the morning. As for the nameless pair with the motorcycle, they seemed to be invisible most of the time, although

Ella reported that she had seen them having coffee one morning in The Fuchsia Bush, and later had noticed their vehicle propped outside the Job Centre in Lulling High Street. Were they proposing to settle locally, people wondered?

About a week after the fire, the peace of Thrush Green was shattered between eleven and twelve one starlit night, by the raucous sound of pop music and the throbbing of drums. Occasionally an ear-splitting shriek broke the rhythm, and above it all was the wailing of a nasal voice which might have been a woman's or a banshee's.

The downstairs lights at Tullivers were still ablaze at that time, and the noise certainly came from that house. Ella Bembridge, some hundred yards or more away, was wakened by the din, and so were Isobel and Harold Shoosmith, equally far away.

'What the hell goes on?' muttered Harold, leaning out of his bedroom window. 'Thoughtless louts! They'll wake everyone at the Youngs' place, and I should think poor old Robert Bassett will be blown out of his bed at this rate.'

Robert Bassett and his wife were the elderly parents of Joan Young. Their home, converted from stables in the Youngs' garden, was one of the nearest houses to Tullivers. He had been very ill, and it was natural that Harold should be concerned first with his old friend's position so close to this shocking noise.

'I shall go and ring them,' said Harold firmly. Isobel heard him padding downstairs to the telephone.

There was a long wait, and then he returned.

'So much dam' racket going on they can't hear the bell,' he fumed. 'I've a good mind to ring the police.'

'Wait a bit,' urged his wife. 'It will only make more-to-do if the police come. It may stop soon.'

'I doubt it,' said Harold grimly, but he shut the window, and got back into bed.

He was not the only one to telephone to Tullivers. Edward Young, outraged on his father-in-law's behalf, also failed to get through, and as he was just out of a hot bath, he did not feel inclined to traipse across to Tullivers to remonstrate in person.

Joan had been along to see her parents, and had found them quite cheerful and in bed. Philosophically, they had inserted the ear plugs which they always took with them when travelling, and they appeared less perturbed than their children.

Winnie Bailey had contented herself with viewing Jeremy's sleeping form and postponing complaints until morning. The cacophony ended about half past one. The lights went out at Tullivers. The residents at Thrush Green heaved sighs of relief, swore retribution at some more reasonable hour, and fell thankfully asleep.

Only Winnie Bailey's Jenny remained wakeful, and she was seriously considering the geographical advantages of Percy Hodge's farm house, should she ever be invited to live there. There was now no doubt that Percy was seeking a second wife, and was being uncommonly attentive to her.

Jenny, brought up in an orphanage and later a drudge – though a grateful one – to the two old people who had taken her in, could not help feeling touched by Percy's devotion. On the other hand, did she really want to marry at all?

Life at Thrush Green with kind Winnie Bailey held all the happiness that she needed. Never had she enjoyed such luxury as her own small flat overlooking the green. Winnie's companionship was doubly precious because she had never known such warmth and generosity of spirit. And how good she had been to her in this last illness! And then she loved the house they shared. It was a joy to polish the lovely old furniture, to set the kitchen to rights, to shine the windows, the silver, the brass. The thought of leaving Winnie and the fine old home which they shared was insupportable.

And yet – poor Percy! He certainly missed his Gertie, and he was a fine old fellow still. She would be cared for if she threw in her lot with his, and did he not perhaps need her more desperately than Winnie did? Jenny's warm heart was smitten when she recalled the buttons missing from his jacket, and the worn shirt collar that needed turning. What a problem!

St Andrew's church clock chimed four, and Jenny heaved a sigh. Best leave it all until later! She'd be fit for nothing if she didn't get a few hours' sleep, and tomorrow she had planned to turn out the larder.

She pulled up the bedclothes, punched her feather pillow into shape and was asleep in five minutes.

Harold Shoosmith rang Tullivers at seven-thirty next morning to remonstrate with young Jack Thomas before he left for work. The young man was as profuse in his apologies as can be expected from someone at that hour, only partially dressed, and attempting to get his own breakfast. It wouldn't happen again. They would make sure that all the windows were shut, and the volume kept down, during future rehearsals.

Before Harold had time to inquire further, the telephone went dead. Other residents rang later in the day but did not get quite as civil a response as Harold had received.

Winnie Bailey decided to call in person during the evening when, she supposed, young Jack Thomas would be home and would have had a meal after his day's work.

She found him sitting in the kitchen with Mary. As the motorcycle was not propped up near the front door, its usual resting-place, she imagined that the other couple were out.

The Thomases looked very tired and young, and Winnie wondered if she were being unkind in complaining. But the thought of further troubled nights, the disturbance of her charge Jeremy, and all the other neighbours nearby, hardened her heart.

They listened somewhat listlessly to her complaint. Even Jack's usual dazzling smile seemed dimmed, and he passed a hand over his hair as if bemused. As well he might be, thought Winnie tartly, after such a late night!

'The fact is,' he said, when Winnie had finished speaking, 'Bill and Lottie are going through a bad patch, and we offered them shelter while we're here. I used to run this band, and Lottie was our vocalist. Bill's the drummer – well, tympanist altogether really. Cymbals, triangle, the lot. Quite handy.'

'But can't he take it over? I mean, you seem to have a job of your own which must be quite demanding. I should have thought you needed your sleep as much as the rest of us.'

'Well, the job doesn't bring in much bread, you know.'

'Bread?'

'Dough. Money,' translated Mary. 'If we can get an engagement now and again, it would help all four of us.'

'I can quite see that,' said Winnie, 'and I am all in favour of earning extra money if you can. But not at the expense of your neighbours' well-being.'

'Well, we have to practise,' said Mary. 'No one's going to take us on, unless we're competent.'

'We honestly had no idea we were making so much noise,' protested Jack. 'I promise you we'll take more care in future. I can't say we'll stop entirely. We need the money, and Bill and Lottie are even more hard up than we are. At least, I've got a steady wage coming in. They're skint.'

'They seem to have money for what they want,' commented Mary to her husband. She sounded very bitter, and Winnie suspected that she at least would be glad to see the back of her two fellow residents.

'Well, I'll say no more,' said Winnie, rising. 'But for pity's sake spare Thrush Green any more nights like the last one. We're used to peace and quiet here after ten o'clock at night.'

The four young people at Tullivers were definitely in their neighbours' bad books. Apart from those who had accosted them openly with their complaints, there were plenty who stopped to tell each other how severely they had been disturbed, and how reprehensible such thoughtless conduct was.

'But there you are,' said Ella to Dotty as they shared a pot of coffee. 'Young things these days do exactly as they like. No respect for the older generation. No discipline, as we had.'

'Well, I certainly got enough,' admitted Dotty. 'As you know, Father was a trifle strict with his family.'

Ella privately considered this gentle censure as the understatement of the year. Tales of old Mr Harmer's punishments towards refractory pupils and his own children were enough to make even Ella blanch. The boys of his family had left home as soon as they could. Only Dotty had remained to look after her widower father in his old age, and a pretty thin time she had had, according to local gossip.

'One thing, they won't be here much longer,' said Dotty comfortably.

It was echoed, with some relief, by Miss Watson to her assistant.

'A *temporary* nuisance,' was her comment. 'I hear Mr Shoosmith and Mrs Bailey both complained the next morning, so I shall not bother to tell them how we feel about such behaviour. But if it happens again –' Here Dorothy stopped, with such a fierce headmistressy look, that even little Miss Fogerty trembled for anyone at Tullivers transgressing again.

Mr Jones at The Two Pheasants gave his opinion that that lot at Tullivers must have been dragged up in the back streets of some modern Sodom or Gomorrah to behave so badly, and he didn't know what the Hursts would find – or wouldn't find – when they returned. Which, he added, couldn't be too soon for him, and his audience at the bar agreed heartily.

Albert Piggott, nursing his half-pint of beer in the corner, gave a highly-coloured account of how he was awakened by the din, and a further discourse, with repellent details, of what it had done to his stomach in the middle of the night.

One listener, more squeamish than the rest, hastily changed the subject to the report of young Mr Venables' retirement, and this new topic engaged the attention of Mr Jones's clients until closing time.

'Never be the same without him,' asserted Percy Hodge. 'Had a lovely way with him in court. Look how he got old Dotty off the hook when she run down that Cooke boy!'

'*Miss Harmer*,' said the landlord reprovingly, 'never done it. That's why.'

'That's as maybe,' replied Percy, undeterred by Mr Jones's rebuke. 'The point is a young chap like Mr Venables is going to be missed in Lulling. He spoke up for me something wonderful when the cows got out and some fool fellow came off his motorbike among 'em. Luckily they wasn't hurt.'

'What about the fellow?' inquired a stranger from Nidden.

'Oh, he broke a thigh and something in his back, I believe,' said Percy vaguely. 'Nothing much. They took him off to hospital, so he was all right. But my poor cows was upset for days.'


The rector of Thrush Green had no hard feelings towards the young newcomers. Harold Shoosmith would have said, if asked, that Charles

Henstock had no hard feelings against any one, which made him the unique and saintly creature that he was.

As it happened, the affairs of the noisy night had not disturbed him, or Dimity, at all. They had both been deep in the sleep of the thoroughly exhausted, having had few good nights since their own tragedy.

So the rector's first pastoral visit to Tullivers was undertaken in happy mood. He felt rather ashamed, as he walked across the springy turf, that he had not called before, but so many pressing things in connection with the fire had engaged him, that he had found little time for his duties.

As he crossed the grass, he admired the rooks, swirling and dipping around the tall trees towards Nod. Perhaps they were 'winding up the water' as the old country folk said, and there would be rain in the night after this calm and sunny evening.

He purposely kept his eyes averted from the empty space where once his house had stood. He could not bear to look upon the gap. Would the church build him another house there? The ground belonged to it, of course. Or would that plot be sold, perhaps, and another home found for him?

It was worrying not to know what might happen. Harold and Isobel were kindness itself, but he and Dimity could not stay indefinitely. As it happened, they were going tomorrow to see dear old Mrs Jenner along the Nidden road. He had heard that she had a flat to let. It would be conveniently placed for church and parish, and he felt sure that it would be approved as temporary accommodation.

By now he was at Tullivers' front door, and even the unobservant rector could not help noticing that the late Admiral Trigg's massive brass knocker, in the shape of a dolphin, was tarnished as though it had been weeks since its last polishing.

Jack Thomas opened the door and looked a little startled when he saw the parson's collar.

'Oh, do come in,' he said, hastily remembering his manners. 'Mr Hendrick, isn't it?'

'Henstock. Charles Henstock,' answered the rector. 'And I must apologize for being so tardy in making your acquaintance, but you know we've had a little trouble lately.'

'We heard. Jolly tough luck. Did you lose much?'

He opened the door of the sitting room and ushered in his visitor. Charles could not help wondering what had happened to the chintz-covered armchairs and sofa which normally furnished the room. Now only three or four upright dining chairs stood against the wall, whilst a collection of wires, a microphone, and various instruments littered the centre of the carpet.

Charles perched on one of the chairs to which he was waved. Jack Thomas reversed another and sat facing him, with his arms folded along the back. Charles felt a flurry of panic, as though he were about to be cross-examined. He took a grip on himself.

'My wife and I wondered if we could be of any help while you are with us,' he began.

'As a matter of fact, Mrs Bailey has been very – er – *motherly*, and helped us quite a bit.'

'Oh, I'm sure of that! We are with the Shoosmiths at the moment. So handy for the church.'

There was a pause.

'Perhaps you are church goers?' he went on gently. There was a curious smell in the house. Some herbs perhaps, used in cooking? He found it rather disquieting.

'Would you like to meet the others?' asked Jack abruptly. 'They're a bit tied up at the moment, but I could fetch them.'

'Dear me, no!' replied the rector. Tied up? What an odd expression! 'But perhaps you would tell them that I called and hope they would like to attend any of our church services. I took the liberty of bringing a list of the times.'

He put a slip of paper on a small table beside him. There were marks of wet glasses upon its once glossy surface, and Charles was perturbed to see that one corner of his list turned darkly damp.

'Thank you,' said Jack, turning upon the rector the smile which had so dazzled Winnie Bailey. 'I don't know about Bill and Lottie, but Mary and I used to go to church once. We were both christened, I know, and I was confirmed at school, the same week that I was vaccinated during a smallpox scare.'

Really, thought the rector, getting to his feet, he speaks as though he were doubly insured in the space of a few days!

However, he found himself smiling kindly upon the young man. There certainly was something very fresh and attractive about him, and he was remarkably frank about being a lapsed church goer.

'Well give my regards to your wife and friends,' he said, opening the front door, 'and we'll hope to see you all again before long.'

Jack walked with him to the gate, gazing about him and breathing deeply.

'One thing, we're enjoying Thrush Green,' he told the rector. 'It really is a marvellous place to live.'

'We think that too,' replied Charles simply, and allowed his eyes to stray to the ravaged plot which he had once called home.

For the first time since the dreadful event, he found he could look at it with less pain. Was it a case of Time-the-great-healer? Or simply that he was getting accustomed to that sad gap in the sky line? Or was it that he felt that one day a house would rise again where his own had fallen?

Whatever the reason, the good rector was grateful for this small blessing of relief, and hurried back to the Shoosmiths' with a lightened heart.

Much to the relief of Thrush Green's inhabitants, the cacophony from Tullivers was not repeated. True, rehearsals went on, but Jack Thomas had kept his word. Windows were closed, and the lights went out around midnight – quite late enough for the early-to-bed neighbours, but certainly an improvement on the first night's prolonged din until the small hours.

Occasionally, the musical equipment was packed into the van when Jack returned from his work at the estate office, and all four would drive off for the evening. Presumably, some engagements had been secured, and rumour was rife at The Two Pheasants about how much they would be paid.

'I'd pay to get *out* of the room if that Lottie girl got screeching,' commented one.

'Some likes that sort of racket,' said his neighbour. 'My two kids has it on all the time on the telly.'

'More fool you to let 'em.'

'They wouldn't get no more than twenty quid between 'em,' surmised another. 'Wouldn't go far between four, would it?'

'The landlord at The Star over Lulling Woods way, gave 'em ten quid apiece, I heard, for an evening there.'

'Then he wants his head seen to,' said Mr Jones firmly, and changed the subject.

But there was a change of feeling towards the young people now that some improvement had been made in their behaviour. Bill and Lottie were seen but rarely, but Mary and Jack were about the green and in the local shops at Lulling, and were much more sociable.

Winnie Bailey, who knew that the girl was pregnant, invited her to coffee one morning and renewed her offers of help. She had the feeling that Mary did most of the house-work, and the shopping and cooking.

She suspected too that the girl resented the other couple's presence. They certainly did not seem to pull their weight in the running of the household, and the girl appeared tired, as well she might be, as her pregnancy advanced.

Winnie asked how Jack's house-hunting plans were progressing, and Mary showed signs of enthusiasm for the first time.

'There's a small house near the office – the end one of a terrace, which I think we'll be able to have in a month's time. It will mean staying at a hotel for a few days after the Hursts come back here, but we shan't mind that.'

'And Bill and Lottie?'

'With any luck, they will have found somewhere in the next week or two. Not that they're searching very hard,' she added.

'Can they go back to their parents?'

'They *can*, but they don't want to. The first thing is to get a job. They're always hard up. Well, who isn't? I know I'm always staggered at the amount of money we seem to get through each week. I hope we'll be able to budget more satisfactorily when we get our own place. At least we shan't have Bill and Lottie scrounging for a loan.'

'Things will certainly be simpler,' agreed Winnie diplomatically, refilling her guest's cup. 'There's nothing so exciting as one's first home.'

She looked about the familiar sitting room, crowded with the personal treasures of many years.

'This was my first home,' she told the girl, 'and my last, I hope.'

'If I'm a quarter as happy,' said Mary, 'I shall be quite content.'

## 10. *A Golden May*

Mrs Jenner, who had a sizeable old farmhouse a mile along the road to Nidden from Thrush Green, was a cousin of Percy Hodge's.

Like Dotty Harmer, her contemporary, she had been the only daughter, and when her mother died she kept house, and occasionally did a little nursing for neighbours.

She had trained at one of the London teaching hospitals and had worked in the capital until her mother fell ill. She was a large strong woman, eminently kind and practical, and well thought of in Lulling and Thrush Green.

On the death of her father she had refurbished the empty bedrooms, and had two or three paying guests who were in need of home nursing.

The service she gave was outstanding, and many a local family blessed Mrs Jenner for the help she gave with elderly or invalid relatives.

But when Mrs Jenner's seventieth birthday had come and gone, she took stock of her situation. She now found it increasingly difficult to care for her patients as she wished. Carrying heavy trays upstairs, turning mattresses as well as elderly bodies, and facing disturbed nights all took their toll, and though Mrs Jenner's heart was as willing as ever, her ageing limbs were beginning to protest. Reluctantly, she decided that she must give up her nursing.

The next step was to provide a small income for herself. The old farmhouse was her main asset, and after considerable planning she decided to turn the top floor into one good-sized flat to let, and to live on the ground floor.

Her last patient had left her in February, and the alterations to the house were virtually complete by the time the fire had ravaged Thrush Green rectory. After she had heard that Charles and Dimity were settled temporarily at Harold's she wrote to the rector and offered them the flat if it would be of any help to them. They welcomed the suggestion. No one could have a better landlady than Mrs Jenner, and the accommodation was conveniently placed for all the rector's parish duties.

The top floor was light and spacious, the furniture was of good solid country-made workmanship, but Mrs Jenner obligingly offered to move some elsewhere if the rector preferred some of his own pieces.

In truth, the farmhouse was infinitely more comfortable than the rectory had ever been. Large windows overlooked the sunny garden with fields beyond.

'Perce has those now,' said Mrs Jenner, naming Jenny's admirer. 'His father and mine farmed this place together, and it was split up when they died. I only need this garden, and I let my few acres to Percy who can do with them. He's a good help to me when it's needed. Keeps me in vegetables and milk, and can turn his hand to anything to do with wood or metal.'

'He's a very skilled fellow, I know,' agreed the rector.

'Great shame about Gertie. He misses her sorely,' went on their landlady. 'But there, you know all about that. Come and see the kitchen.'

As she led them from one room to the next, Dimity realized that she was going to be more comfortable in these quarters than she had been anywhere in her married life. The carpets and curtains were well-worn, but beautifully clean. The armchairs were deep and snug, the windows gleamed, the furniture was glossy with years of polishing. Above all, it was warm.

Whatever the future held for her, Dimity became more and more certain as she followed Mrs Jenner about the old thick-walled house, that her new home, whenever it materialized, was going to be as similar in light, warmth and comfort as it could possibly be to Mrs Jenner's house. It would be smaller, she supposed. Some of the new church houses were even bungalows, she believed. How wonderful to have a home which would be easy to keep warm and clean! She recalled, with an inward shudder, the bleak Victorian rectory – its wind-tunnel of a passage, leading from the north-facing front door to the back one, its vast Gothic windows which rattled in the wind, its high ceilings, its wintry bedrooms and the ever-damp cellars. She knew that Charles grieved for its loss. She did too, for that matter, for it had been her first home as a bride. Nevertheless, she realized, as never before, that the place had been ugly, cold, impractical and hideously expensive to run.

She gazed about Mrs Jenner's neat kitchen. A small stove gave out a steady warmth. A kettle purred upon it. The saucepans winked from the walls, and a row of fine geraniums basked in the sunshine on the window sill.

'You won't want to make up your minds just yet, I feel sure,' said Mrs Jenner. 'But let me know when you decide.'

Dimity's eyes met those of Charles.

'I think we've decided already,' said the rector, with a smile.

'Then we'll have a cup of tea,' said their new landlady, lifting the kettle.

The next morning Dimity crossed the green to visit her old friend Ella Bembridge and to tell her about their new temporary home.

She found her engrossed in the morning post. Willie Marchant was wheeling his bicycle from one gate to another, and had acknowledged her presence with a casual wave as she passed.

'Anything exciting?' asked Dimity.

'Two bills, a catalogue about Shetland woollies and a very vulgar leaflet about some hideous pottery with an order form headed: PLEASE RUSH ME THE FOLLOWING. That's enough to put you off for a start, isn't it?'

Dimity agreed.

'Besides this awful pottery they do jewellery based on Viking designs. Cashing in on those telly programmes, I suppose, though anyone less lovable than the Vikings it would be hard to find, I imagine.'

'Well, I suppose you could call them *brave*,' said Dimity tentatively.

'Don't you start,' growled Ella. 'The more I saw and heard about them, the greater grew my admiration for dear old King Alfred. *Great* he certainly was, coping with those dreadful chaps with names like throat-clearings.'

'I've got some good news,' said Dimity, feeling it was about time to leave the inflammable subject of the Vikings. She told her about Mrs Jenner's flat, and Ella grew equally enthusiastic.

'Well, you couldn't do better. I should settle there permanently if I were you.'

'That would be blissful, wouldn't it? But I daresay the church people have other plans for us.'

At that moment there was a knock at the door, and Winnie Bailey entered.

After greetings, she unfolded a snowy linen napkin to display a minute piece of knitting.

'Do you, by any chance, have a spare number twelve needle, Ella dear? Mine has vanished. Jenny and I have turned everything upside down, and it's nowhere to be seen, and I want to give these bootees to Mary Thomas before they go.'

'Do babies wear bootees now?' asked Ella. 'I thought they were brought up in grow-bags.'

'I think the term is something like "growies",' said Winnie vaguely, 'but I always imagined they had bootees on inside those things.'

'My little brother,' said Dimity, 'had a long flannel which was folded over his feet and secured with two enormous safety pins.'

'Well, these grow-bags are simply the modern equivalent,' explained Ella, 'and I'm sure I have another twelve needle somewhere, unless I used it to stake a drooping indoor hyacinth last winter.'

She set about rummaging in the drawer of a side table, scattering knitting needles, crochet hooks, carpet needles, bodkins, safety pins, stitch-holders and a mixed assortment of other metal tools for handicrafts.

While she was thus engaged, Dimity told Winnie about their new plans.

'Yes, I did know,' admitted Winnie. 'Percy Hodge told me last night when he came to see Jenny.'

'I might have guessed,' said Dimity, 'that everyone in Thrush Green knows the news now.'

'Well, I didn't know, did I?' said Ella comfortingly, advancing with a bristling handful of knitting needles.

'There you are, Winnie. All twelves, and ranging from my Aunt Milly's bone ones to pseudo tortoiseshell via steel and modern plastic. Take your pick.'

Winnie studied the needles.

'And how is Jenny? Is she likely to marry Percy, do you think?'

'I'll take the steel ones, if I may, Ella. And about Jenny – well, I really don't know. She still looks washed-out to me, I'd like her to have a few days away. To my mind, she's worried over Percy too. I hardly like to dissuade her – she might think my motives were a trifle self-centred – and I don't feel like doing the opposite. She must make up her own mind. I'm strictly neutral. All I want is Jenny's well-being.'

'But she might find that with Percy,' cried Dimity earnestly, thinking of her own late marriage to her beloved Charles. 'I mean it really seems so *cruel* to turn down the love of a good man like kind Percy. Especially when he misses Gertie so much.'

Her two companions gazed upon her with mingled affection, amusement and exasperation.

' "When in doubt, don't", is my motto,' said Ella forthrightly. 'And as for *love*, well, you know what the Provincial Lady maintained. She reckoned that a sound bank balance and good teeth far outweighed it in value.'

'I can hardly put that forward to Jenny,' said Winnie, rolling the needles with the bootees into a white bundle.

'Well, just tell her to look before she leaps,' advised Ella, accompanying Winnie to the door.

'I can only speak from personal experience,' said Dimity, 'but I have never for one moment had regrets about my marriage.'

'Naturally,' agreed Ella, 'but then Charles is in a class of his own.'

'You are particularly fortunate,' said Winnie.

'As though I didn't know!' exclaimed Dimity.

One golden May day succeeded another. In the growing warmth of early summer Thrush Green shook out its leaves and flowers, to the delight of its inhabitants.

The school children spent every playtime out in the sunshine, much to the relief of Miss Watson and Miss Fogerty, and even Albert Piggott looked less morose, and had taken off two of his winter waistcoats and his disreputable muffler.

Farmers surveyed their promising hay fields, gardeners plied hoes and gardening forks and bustled about with packets of seeds, twine and knives sticking out of their pockets. Birds flashed to and fro, feeding young, or scrapping with others who approached too near their own particular territory. Activity was everywhere apparent.

Except, it seemed, at Tullivers.

There the garden grew more neglected. Harold Shoosmith, surveying it worriedly whenever he passed, wondered if he should offer to mow the grass and clip the hedges. It was Frank and Phyllida he was thinking about, not the present occupants whose laziness appalled him. As it happened, Jack Thomas emerged one evening with the Hursts' mower, and cut the lawns, and one Sunday he snipped away the longest of the sprouting twigs in the hedge.

Obviously, Mary was in no condition to garden, and the other pair were seldom seen. Winnie began to wonder if they were still living there, and asked Mary one day over the dividing hedge between their gardens.

To her surprise, the girl's face flushed with anger.

'We've sent them packing,' she said shortly.

'I'm sorry. I shouldn't have asked. I didn't mean to upset you.'

'You haven't. Actually I'm so relieved, I can't tell you. They never fitted in, you know.'

'It looked rather that way.'

'Jack's too kind-hearted. They told him this sob story just before we came here, and he was sorry for them and offered them shelter until they found a job.'

'And have they?'

Mary gave a snort of disgust.

'They haven't exactly tried. They made a great thing of going down to Lulling to the Job Centre, but as far as I could see, they had no intention of taking anything offered them. I think they thought that the group would make a bomb. But of course it hasn't. Anyway, it was agreed that we should split any fee four ways, so that no one had very much.'

She paused for a moment.

'Especially if you're on pot,' she added.

'Pot? Drugs, do you mean?'

'Cannabis, and a bit of cocaine. I don't think they've got to the hard stuff yet, but I bet they will pretty soon. The stink of the stuff made me so ill. That's what finally decided Jack to send them packing.'

'So I should hope,' said Winnie.

'The final straw,' said Mary, 'was pinching the housekeeping money last week. I thought it had been vanishing for some time, a fiver here and there. You know how easy it is, especially when four people use the purse.'

'What was your system?'

'Oh, whoever went shopping for meat or eggs or groceries just took the purse. We all put in a fiver at the beginning, and then had a share out at the end of each week, and refurbished the funds again.'

'It sounds a good idea.'

'In theory, yes. In practice, particularly with half paying out for drugs, it was hopeless. My gold bangle's gone too. I may have lost it – the catch was loose – but I can't help feeling they pinched it. Jack refused to believe me – he's much more high-minded than I am. Anyway, I got some of that powder you can scatter in cash boxes and so on. It stains a thief's hand bright red. It certainly worked with Bill and Lottie last Thursday. We caught them literally red-handed. I've never seen Jack so furious. They were out within an hour.'

'Where have they gone?'

'I don't know. They can go back to their parents, but of course they don't want to. We had our last share out and they pushed off with about three pounds apiece. The motor bike's in good order. It's up to them now. Frankly, I hope I never clap eyes on them again. They've thoroughly spoiled our time here.'

'Put them out of your mind,' advised Winnie. 'It's over and done with, and now you must look ahead to the baby and take care of yourself and Jack.'

'You are quite right. We should be able to move into the new house next week, and we're both looking forward to making a fresh start.'

She looked about her at the sunny garden, murmurous with bees among the wallflowers.

'We shall miss Thrush Green. It would have been perfect if only we had been alone.'

'You won't be far away,' said Winnie cheerfully. 'You'll be able to visit us, I hope, and see Thrush Green in a more favourable light.'

'See Eden without its serpent? I'll look forward to that.'

That same day, after the school children had raced home, Miss Watson and Miss Fogerty enjoyed a well-deserved rest in the school-house garden.

In common with the majority of Thrush Green residents, a modest tea was before them.

A tray with two cups and saucers, milk jug, tea pot and a plate bearing half a dozen delicious lemon curd tartlets, made a brave sight.

The two friends were content to bask in the sun in silent companionship. An inquisitive blackbird made forays from the hedge, its bright eyes focused on the tea tray. Apart from its pattering claws upon the dead leaves, and the distant shouts of tardily departing children across the green, a blissful somnolence enwrapped them.

Agnes allowed her mind to drift from school matters to the more personal needs of her modest wardrobe. Should she buy another cotton frock, suitable for school, or should she get Miss Crookshank to make up the length of blue checked gingham she had prudently bought before material became so expensive?

The difficulty was that Miss Crookshank would probably need quite a month to get the frock made, pleading pressure of business, her mother's illness and other excuses, all probably quite genuine, Miss Fogerty told herself, but the result would be that the fine spell would probably be over by the time the garment was completed.

And, of course, she must get a new pattern. That princess-style, button-through one which had done so well for so many years, had its drawbacks. Far too often the bottom button had burst off when showing the children how to be a really energetic galloping horse in the playground. And, on occasions, she had discovered that the bodice gaped, which was immodest to say the least. Perhaps something with a yoke? No zip, of course, and certainly not at the back. Far too difficult to reach.

There was a lot to be said for buying a frock readymade. She had seen some attractive ones in two of the Lulling shops, but the prices had been excessive, and it was really a shocking waste not to have the gingham made up. On the other hand, was the gingham perhaps too light in colour for school wear? One must remember how quickly clothes grew grubby in contact with such things as coloured chalks, modelling clay, charcoal sticks, paste and poster paints, not to mention innumerable infants' fingers clutching at one's raiment.

Agnes, juggling gently with this problem, was brought to earth by a squeak from her companion.

'Oh dear, I didn't mean to wake you,' began Dorothy.

'I wasn't asleep, dear, I assure you. Did something sting you?'

'No, no. I was about to get up to carry in the tray, and my leg gave a twinge. All over now. I think I must have been sitting awkwardly.'

'Should you see the doctor again?' asked Agnes, full of solicitude.

'No, I'm really quite fit. Well, as fit as I'm going to be, I suspect.'

'But surely,' protested Agnes, 'you will go on getting stronger? It isn't all that long ago –'

'It's well over a year,' said Dorothy. 'It may improve, of course, but I seem to have been at this stage for months now. It doesn't worry me, Agnes dear, because I just face the fact that I'm slower and can't walk as far as I did. On the whole, I can do all I want to do.'

'I sometimes think you do too much,' said Agnes loyally. 'You should let me help you more.'

Dorothy laughed.

'You spoil me as it is. Besides, you are quite a few years older than I am.'

Agnes nodded, and silence engulfed them again. A bold robin now came to reconnoitre, and the blackbird rushed at it, scolding furiously. The robin stood its ground.

'Agnes,' said Dorothy at last. 'Have you ever thought of retiring?'

'*Retiring?*' cried Agnes. 'Why, do you think I should? I mean, am I working as you would wish? Do I do my duties satisfactorily –?'

Dorothy broke in upon this panic.

'Of course, you do *everything* quite beautifully, Agnes. I've yet to meet a better teacher, as you should know. No, I only passed the remark because retirement is rather in my mind at the moment.'

'You don't mean it!' gasped Agnes. 'Why, you are still in your fifties – and don't look it, I assure you! I thought you would want to stay at Thrush Green until you were sixty-five.'

Dorothy nodded absently, her eyes upon the robin.

'So did I. But since this fall, I've been thinking about things. Everything is much more of an effort. I'm beginning to wonder if I should go at sixty.

I could give a year's notice when I get to fifty-nine next birthday. That should be ample time for a new head to be found.'

Agnes's mind, so recently swinging indolently from readymade frocks to Miss Crookshank's versions, was now in a state of violent agitation. To think that dear Dorothy was even contemplating such a step! She had always looked upon her as so much younger and stronger than herself. After all, her own birthday would bring her to sixty-two, and she had quite resigned herself to the idea of staying until she was sixty-five. In any case, she hoped to put a little more in her Building Society account before she drew her pension. She had thought about returning to modest lodgings when the time came for Dorothy to give up the school house or even earlier. It was not a very exciting prospect, she knew, but she could hardly expect Dorothy to want her for the rest of her days, when the job they did together was over.

In her bewilderment, she scarcely took in all that Dorothy was saying.

'I should have thought about it long ago,' Dorothy was saying. 'Something really modest, a bungalow perhaps with a small garden and a view of the sea, of course. What do you think, Agnes?'

'I don't quite follow you, Dorothy,' said little Miss Fogerty unhappily. Everything was awhirl in her mind.

'If I decided to retire at sixty,' said her headmistress patiently, 'I should have to have a house. I was thinking aloud really – wondering about dear old Barton-on-Sea. What do you think?'

'You've always loved it there,' said Agnes carefully.

'But would you love it too?'

Agnes turned bemused eyes upon her.

'Would I be there too?' she quavered.

Miss Watson gave one of her famous snorts.

'*Of course* you'd be there too! I hope you don't intend to desert me when we've both retired.'

'Oh, Dorothy!' began Agnes, appalled at the idea of treachery.

'Unless,' said Dorothy, suddenly and surprisingly unsure, 'you would rather not?'

'Rather not?' echoed Agnes. 'Just do let me get my breath, Dorothy dear, and I'll try to tell you how I feel.'

'I'll pour us both another cup while you're pondering,' said Miss Watson, lifting the tea pot.

## 11. *A Sea-Side Interlude*

June arrived, and Tullivers stood empty again awaiting the return of Phil and Frank Hurst.

Jeremy grew more and more excited as the time drew nearer, and Winnie shared his joy. She admitted to herself that she was relieved at the departure of the young people next door, and she and Jeremy were glad to be putting things to rights after their slapdash housekeeping.

It did not take long to get Tullivers looking ship-shape, although there were one or two things which would need more specialized attention than Winnie and Jenny could give.

A coffee table was badly stained, and someone appeared to have trodden tar or some equally viscous material into the sitting room carpet. The latter defied all their combined attempts to clean it. Obviously, the whole thing would need to go to professional cleaners.

Upstairs, there was a cracked hand basin and a peculiar stain down one wall in the back bedroom. But, at first sight, Tullivers gave its usual peaceful sunny welcome.

'Well, we've done all we can,' said Winnie, shutting the front door. 'I'll put some flowers inside on the day they arrive. How good it will be to see them back!'

They went next door, and Jenny filled the kettle for Winnie's tea tray. The children were already coming out of school, and Jeremy would be looking forward to a slice of her gingerbread.

'Leave that for a minute, Jenny,' said Winnie, 'and come and sit down.'

She led the way into the sitting room and she and Jenny sighed with pleasure at being at rest after all their activities next door.

'Now, Jenny,' began Winnie, 'I've something to put to you. Are you happy here?'

'Happy?' exclaimed Jenny. 'You know I am! Never been happier. It's like a dream come true.'

'Good,' said Winnie. 'And I'm equally happy, except for one thing.'

She looked across at Jenny's bewildered expression.

'And that's your health, Jenny. You have never really picked up after that wretched illness, and I'm going to see that you have a little holiday.'

'But I don't *need* a little holiday!' wailed Jenny. 'I shouldn't know what to do! Honest, I wouldn't.'

'Well, I should like a little break myself as soon as Jeremy's back at Tullivers, and I have made inquiries at a very quiet hotel in Torquay where I propose we go together. I shall stay for the weekend and leave you there for another week. The sea air will do you a world of good.'

'But what –' began Jenny, when Jeremy burst in.

'I'm *starving*!' he cried.

'Hear that?' said Winnie rising. 'We'll talk about this later on, Jenny, but meanwhile we must get the tea ready. We can't have the Hursts coming back to a boy skeleton.'

And Jenny, her head awhirl with these holiday proposals, went to cut up the gingerbread.

On the same afternoon, at the Youngs' splendid house, Joan and Molly were busy taking down the long and heavy velvet curtains which had kept out the bleak winter draughts of Thrush Green, and were replacing them with light chintz ones for the summer.

'Do you know,' said Joan, 'that these windows are almost fifteen feet in height? I hope to goodness all these curtains last out our time. We should never be able to afford more.'

Molly, perched on a kitchen chair, was doing her best to reach the hooks at the top, and deciding that she must fetch the step ladder after all.

'How many metres would you need, I wonder?'

'Heaven alone knows, and I don't intend to try and work it out at my age. I'd have to tell the shop people in yards, and let them do the sums.'

At that moment, Molly gave a little cry, swayed on her precarious chair and was caught by her alarmed mistress.

She helped the fainting girl to an armchair, and pressed her head down upon her knees. She was much agitated. Molly never ailed.

Should she send for her brother-in-law Doctor John Lovell? But then he would probably be out on his rounds at this time.

She crouched on the floor gazing anxiously at her patient. To her relief, she saw the colour returning to Molly's cheeks, and the girl sat up.

'Lean back,' advised Joan, 'and I'll get you a drink.'

She hastened into the kitchen and collected a glass of water and some brandy. What could be the matter?

'Only the water,' whispered Molly, 'that other stuff makes me sick.'

Joan watched her as she sipped.

'Have you felt faint before?'

'Once or twice. Nothing much. Let's get on with the curtains.'

'Not on your life! They can wait. You're going upstairs to lie down. I shan't be able to look Ben in the eye if he finds you ill.'

'You know what I reckon it is?' said Molly.

'Tell me.'

'A baby on the way. To tell the truth, I thought it might be, and this seems to settle it.'

'Well, I'm glad to hear it, Molly dear, and you're going to see Doctor Lovell first thing tomorrow. When do you think it's due?'

'If I've reckoned aright, it should be late in December.'

'A Christmas baby!' cried Joan. 'Now, isn't that good news? You were very naughty to clamber about on that chair. If only I'd known!'

'No harm done,' said Molly cheerfully, getting up. 'You know, I'd much rather carry on here than go upstairs.'

'You'll do as you're told for once,' said Joan firmly. 'Edward will give me a hand with these curtains when he comes home. What are husbands for, I'd like to know?'

The Hursts returned to an ecstatic welcome from Jeremy and a heartfelt one from all their old friends at Thrush Green.

At first, they forbore to tell them of the shortcomings of Tullivers' temporary residents, but as Harold Shoosmith told Isobel: 'It is only a matter of time before all is revealed – and that much embellished, I have no doubt.' He was to be proved right within a week.

But before these unwelcome comments were made, Winnie and Jenny had packed their bags and taken the train to Torquay.

Jenny's agitation at first hearing of the plan had gradually changed to pleasurable anticipation. This was increased when she recalled that an old childhood friend, another inmate of the orphanage, had married a draper in the town. It was true that they only wrote to each other at Christmas time, exchanging handkerchiefs or bath salts, but they shared potent memories of their early home and had a strong affection for each other.

Winnie was delighted to hear of this link, and an invitation to Harry and Bessie to have tea with them at the hotel on the Sunday was warmly accepted.

The hotel itself gave Jenny confidence at once. She had secretly feared that everything would be over-poweringly grand. Certainly all in sight was harmonious and beautifully kept, a virtue which appealed to house-proud Jenny immediately. But besides this, the hotel staff were welcoming, the service unobtrusive and efficient, and the windows overlooked a well-kept garden with the sparkling sea beyond. Jenny's spirits rose as she unpacked in the bedroom next to Winnie's, stopping to gaze at the view on each trip to the wardrobe. Who would have thought she would ever be in such a lovely place? And so far from Thrush Green too?

To her surprise she felt relief rather than sadness at the thought of the distance between her present bedroom and the one at home. Somehow it was good to get away from the old familiar view, the chestnut avenue, the children running to school, Mr Jones watering the hanging baskets outside The Two Pheasants.

Above all, she had to admit, it was a relief to get away from Percy Hodge. Perhaps now she could see things more clearly without his presence to upset her.

Ah well! Tomorrow she would see Bessie again, and her husband for the first time. It was good to be looking forward to new interests. She would forget Thrush Green for a while, and really make the most of this wonderful holiday.

The sunshine which enhanced Jenny's first view of Torquay bathed the entire country.

At Thrush Green, early roses graced the window sills of Miss Fogerty's classroom. Mr Jones's geraniums burst into exuberant bloom, and the sound of the lawn mower was heard in the land.

The meadow leading to Lulling Woods was ablaze with buttercups. Daisies starred Thrush Green itself, and mothers watched their toddlers clutching bunches in their fat hands. The wooden seats were warm to sit upon, and young and old, eyes closed against the dazzling light, dreamt and dozed in perfect bliss.

Even Albert Piggott appeared less malevolent and, billhook in hand to show that he was mindful of his duties, sunned himself upon a flat tombstone by the churchyard wall.

Along the lane to Nod and Nidden the cow parsley frothed and shed its lacy flowers in the breeze. Dotty Harmer admired its fragile beauty as she took Flossie for her afternoon walk. To tell the truth, the spaniel would have much preferred to spend the afternoon lying in the plum tree's shade in Dotty's garden but, obliging as ever, accompanied her beloved mistress with every appearance of pleasure. She was grateful to her owner, and had not forgotten how she had been rescued by her and given such a loving home. What if the melting tar did squeeze between her claws in this unpleasant way? It was a small price to pay for the pleasure of sharing a walk with Dotty and making her happy.

The elder flowers were beginning to open, turning their creamy faces to the sun, and Dotty turned her mind to making elderflower champagne if only she could remember where she put the recipe. Behind the kitchen clock? In the Coalport vegetable dish? In mother's secretaire? She would have a good look round when she returned home.

She came within sight of Thrush Green, shimmering in the heat. Perhaps it would be a good idea to call at Ella's. The recipe had come from her in the first place.

She crossed the green, a scraggy shabby figure topped by a frayed coolie straw hat, the object of mirth to two young mothers lolling on one of the seats. Flossie panted obediently behind her.

Ella was in her garden, sitting in a deck chair. Across her lap was draped a small sack, and across that lay some strands of raffia in gaudy colours. A large needle threaded with a piece of scarlet raffia was in Ella's hand, but it was not being used.

Ella was asleep, her mouth ajar, her head lodged sideways. Dotty surveyed her for a few moments, trying to decide if she should tiptoe away. However, the recipe was needed immediately if she wanted to pick really fresh elder flowers.

She coughed discreetly, and Ella awoke.

'Golly!' exclaimed Ella, reverting in her bemused state to the ejaculations of her childhood. 'You made me jump!'

'I'm sorry about that, but the front door was wide open, so I just came through.'

'And quite right too,' said Ella. 'Pull up that other chair and relax. What weather! That's why I opened the front door. You get a nice breeze right through the house that way, though I don't suppose the police would approve.'

'Was that young officer a good speaker? I couldn't come to the W.I. last Wednesday. One of the hens was indisposed, and I felt I should be at hand, you know.'

'Quite,' said Ella, envisaging Dotty crouched in the hen run holding a flaccid claw in her own skinny hand. 'How is she now?'

'Oh, quite recovered, thank you. I was sorry to miss the talk. About safety precautions, wasn't it? Not that I ever think of locking the house, though I suppose one should.'

'He seemed to think that *opening* the door to strangers was even worse.'

'But why? After all, one is obliged to open the door to see if they really are strangers.'

'Evidently, they are inclined to knock you on the head,' replied Ella, 'and then take anything of value before you come round.'

'How very unpleasant! I can't say I get many strangers, do you?'

'The odd tramp now and again. I always fill their billycans with hot water as requested, and give 'em a slice of bread and cheese.'

'I must admit that I do too. My father was quite outspoken about tramps, and said some very *wounding* things to them, I thought. You know, about Satan finding mischief for idle hands to do, and able-bodied men always being able to find work if they really looked for it. They seldom called twice.'

'I must say, I try to protect myself from an inundation of tramps by warning them not to leave any of their cryptic signs on the gate post.'

'Do they do that?'

'So I'm told. You know – a circle means: "Here's a soft touch", or a cross means: "Look out! The old cat chucks water over you!" Something of the sort.'

'I must look out for those things. By the way, Ella, what are you making with that sack?'

Ella held up her handiwork.

'Peg bags. Always sell well at sales of work, and the raffia brightens them up, doesn't it?'

'Yes, indeed,' agreed Dotty doubtfully. 'But won't the colours run if the bag gets wet?'

'Why should it get wet?' protested Ella. 'You don't leave your peg bag out in the rain, do you?'

'Yes,' said Dotty.

Dotty would, thought Ella.

'But as it's a good stout bag made out of father's old Burberry years ago, it doesn't come to any harm, you see.'

Here Flossie, who had taken advantage of some shade under a lilac bush, yawned noisily and thumped her tail upon some defenceless forget-me-nots.

Dotty took the hint.

'Time we were off, Ella dear.'

'Won't you stay to tea?'

'No, thank you. Dulcie must be picketed elsewhere for the rest of the day. She's eating voraciously now she's pregnant, and I thought a short spell by the hazel bushes would enliven her diet. Goats really do appreciate variety. That's why I never get cross when I find that the dear thing has pulled something off the line for a snack. She's obviously short of some particular mineral or vitamin.'

Flossie struggled to her feet and lumbered over to her mistress.

'She feels the heat,' commented Ella, charitably ignoring the havoc caused by the spaniel's progress through the flower bed.

'Perfect weather,' she went on, 'to be on holiday. It will do Winnie and Jenny a power of good by the sea.'

Ella accompanied Dotty through the cool hall and out into the blaze of Thrush Green. She watched her old friend cross the grass and turn into the walled lane of golden Cotswold stone on her way to Lulling Woods and the most pampered goat in the locality. It was not until next morning that Dotty realized she had forgotten to ask for the recipe.

At Torquay, the Sunday tea party was a great success, and Winnie departed for home on the Monday morning feeling relieved that Jenny had such good friends in the neighbourhood.

Bessie and Harry lived over the shop, not far from the harbour, and from their upstairs sitting room there was a view of the sea which delighted Jenny.

She was invited to lunch on the Tuesday, and when Harry had returned to his duties below, the two old friends settled down to compare the course of their lives since leaving the orphanage.

They sat comfortably on a little balcony overlooking the steep street and the distant sea, their feet lodged in the decorative ironwork and their heads in the shade of the canopy above them.

Jenny sighed contentedly.

'Who'd have thought we should find ourselves so comfortable when we were at the orphanage?'

'We've both been lucky,' agreed Bessie. 'And Harry's the perfect husband. I wonder you didn't marry, Jenny. You were always a pretty girl.'

'Never had much chance,' replied Jenny. 'Ma and Pa took up all my time. Not that I grudged it, mark you. They was good to me, and I was glad to pay 'em back, but I didn't get out and about much.'

'But now they're gone,' persisted Bessie. 'Don't you ever think of it?'

In the silence that followed only the distant sea gulls cried. Jenny wondered if she should unburden herself to her old friend, and perhaps get her advice. On the other hand, her natural shyness made her reluctant.

But the sun warmed her legs. The sea air was exhilarating. Thrush

Green and its gossipers were far away, and for once Jenny threw aside her caution.

'Well, as a matter of fact, Bessie, there is someone at the moment,' she confessed, and the tale of Percy's attentions, her own embarrassment and uncertainty, Winnie Bailey's kindness and her needs, all came tumbling out.

Bessie, eyes closed against the brilliance of the afternoon, listened attentively. In common with the rest of mankind, Bessie loved a story, and here was a romantic drama of real life – its heroine lying close beside her and, better still, asking for her advice.

'So there it is,' finished Jenny, feeling mightily relieved after such an outpouring, 'and I hope I'll know what to do by the time I get back. It's my belief Mrs Bailey got me away to give me a chance to sort out my feelings rather than improve my health.'

'It's a bit difficult to know where one ends and the other begins,' said Bessie sagaciously. 'I had stye after stye on my eyelids when Harry was courting me, but as soon as I said "Yes" they vanished.'

'But what do you think? He's such a good chap and he does miss his Gertie terribly. She was a wonderful manager, and the best cook in Thrush Green some said. He's lost without her, and his clothes are getting something dreadful – buttons off, cuffs frayed – you know how men get their things.'

Bessie sat forward and propped her chin on her fist. She gazed out to sea as she spoke slowly.

'It's like this, Jenny. I don't doubt he's in need of a wife, and I don't doubt he'll find one pretty soon, if he's the nice fellow you say. But it's *you* I'm thinking of. Do *you* want to live with this Percy for the rest of your days? Do *you* want to give up the life you've just found simply because Percy's clothes need mending? You've always been unselfish. I can remember that from when we were little kids, and you've spent all your time till now looking after Ma and Pa. I don't say Percy wouldn't be grateful, and would treat you right. I'm sure he would. But is it what you want?'

'If you put it like that,' said Jenny, 'I suppose I should never have thought of Percy in that way, if he hadn't come – well, I suppose you could say – *courting*.'

'I'll tell you something else, Jenny, which always helped me when I was trying to decide about a man. I was no flibbertigibbet, mind you, but I did have quite a few lads in my time, before I met Harry, and I used to say to myself when they started to get serious: "Now, would it break my heart to see him with someone else?" And, d'you know, half the time I used to think it would be a relief if they *did* find someone! Then I knew my own feelings!'

Jenny laughed.

'What a sensible way of looking at it! I can't tell you how you've helped, Bessie, and I think I'll know my own mind before I go back to Thrush Green. It's just that I hate to think of Percy being hurt.'

'Nice men aren't hurt for long,' said Bessie robustly. 'They find someone else quite easily, believe me. Mark my words, if you turn down your Percy he'll be married within the year! I've seen it happen time and time again, and no hearts broken either.'

And then the subject of Percy was shelved, and for the next few hours the talk was of what happened to Mary Carter, and to Joan King, and to the two sisters who ran away and incurred the wrath of the Principal.

Later, Jenny walked back to the hotel through a rose and lavender sunset, and loitered in the garden before going to her room.

The air was fragrant with night-scented stock, mignonette, and the aromatic spiciness of the cypress trees.

For the first time for months, Jenny felt at peace. The old saying about a trouble shared being a trouble halved was perfectly true, she reminded herself as she went thankfully up to bed.

## *12. Bessie's Advice*

Winnie returned to her empty house and, much to her surprise, found that she quite enjoyed having it to herself.

Jenny's presence was always a comfort to her, particularly after dark, and she certainly missed the chatter of Jeremy after his few weeks' stay. But now that high summer was here, and the scents and sounds of Thrush Green floated through the open windows, Winnie felt no hint of loneliness and found a certain quiet pleasure in having no interruptions to her train of thought as she moved about the house she had lived in for so long.

Perhaps, after all, she would not miss Jenny so desperately if Percy's suit were successful. It was a surprising thought, and one which gave Winnie some pleasure. It must mean that she was over the worst of the shock of her dear Donald's death. Time, it seemed, as everyone had kept telling her, did heal wounds. She had not really believed it, but now she wondered. At least, this new-found confidence was welcome, and if Jenny were to leave her then she could bear it with greater fortitude than she had thought possible.

Her happiness continued through the week. Jenny was due to come home at tea time on the Saturday, and Winnie had instructed her to take a taxi from Lulling Station, despite Jenny's protests about the expense.

'I'm not having you walk over a mile, and uphill at that, struggling with a suitcase and all the rest of the luggage. And suppose it rains? No, you must do as I say, Jenny.'

And Jenny had agreed.

But on Friday afternoon Percy Hodge had appeared on the doorstep with a bunch of Mrs Sinkin pinks as big as a cauliflower and had announced that he would be meeting the 4.10 train.

'But we've arranged for Jenny to come up by taxi,' explained Winnie, somewhat taken aback.

'I know that. But I'd particularly like to have a word with Jenny, and it's a pleasure to meet her off the train. No need for a taxi when I've got the car.'

Winnie could do no more than thank him, but the expression 'like to have a word with Jenny' sounded ominous. Was he going to propose marriage between Lulling Station and Thrush Green? And what would Jenny think when she found Percy waiting at the station? And suppose that Percy was a little late and Jenny had already taken the taxi? Oh dear, what a muddle!

By the time seven o'clock came Winnie was decidedly agitated, although she realized that Percy and Jenny's affairs were their own business. In the end, she decided to ring Jenny at Torquay, and to let her know that Percy was meeting the train, and to leave it at that. At least, the girl would be prepared.

As it happened, Jenny had spent her last evening with Bessie and Harry, but Winnie left a message with the girl at the switchboard and could only hope that Jenny would get it when she returned. In a way, it was a relief not to have to speak directly to Jenny. She might have wanted lengthy explanations.

Winnie went to bed, telling herself that she had had quite enough for one day, and the morrow must take care of itself.

The morrow, as it happened, brought Ella Bembridge to the door at ten o'clock in the morning.

Winnie had been in her garden picking roses and inspecting the raspberry canes. It looked as though there would be a fine crop this year, but rain would be needed to plump up the berries. The sky was cloudless, as it had been now for a week or more, and despite the needs of the raspberry canes, Winnie could not find it in her heart to pray for a change in the weather.

'Another glorious day!' she greeted Ella.

'Not for the Lovelock girls!' replied Ella. As none of the three sisters would ever see seventy-five again Winnie could not help feeling that *girls* was not the exact word for her three aged friends.

'Not ill?' exclaimed Winnie.

'Burgled!' said Ella, sitting down heavily on a delicate Sheraton chair which creaked a protest.

'No! When? How? What have they lost?'

'The answers are: Yes. Yesterday. By a person or persons unknown. And they're not sure yet what has gone, but it's nearly all old silver.'

'Poor old darlings! It will break their hearts. They loved their bits of silver.'

'Well, they were told often enough to keep it in a cupboard or a bank, but you know them! They said they enjoyed seeing it about them.'

'And why not? What's the fun of having lovely things if you don't enjoy them? My mother was left a diamond bracelet by her grandmother, and it was so wickedly valuable that it never saw the light of day but was in the bank's vault. My mother often grieved for it, I know.'

'Best place for it,' said Ella sturdily. 'You remember what that police officer told us about keeping valuables out of sight?'

'Of course I remember. And as a matter of fact, I've even locked the front door when I've been shopping in Lulling recently. What's more, I forgot where I'd hidden the key, and had to wait for Jenny to let me in. I'm sure people weren't so dishonest in our young days. It does make life very difficult for everyone.'

'Well, I thought I'd let you know in case you were seeing the girls some time soon.'

'I'll ring them to see if I can help,' said Winnie, 'but quite what to do is the question, isn't it? Their silver must have been worth a fortune. I suppose they were insured?'

'Lord knows!' replied Ella, heaving herself from the protesting chair. 'By the way, d'you want gooseberries? Bumper crop I've got, so come and help yourself. The Lovelock girls were picking theirs when the thief got in evidently.'

'What a bold fellow! And yes, please, I'd love some gooseberries to bottle. Nothing nicer than hot gooseberry tart on a bleak December day. Can I come one day next week when Jenny's back?'

'Any time you like,' said Ella, and stumped out into the morning blaze.

It was Miss Violet Lovelock who spoke to Winnie on the telephone, and although she sounded upset, her account of the burglary was remarkably clear and detailed.

'It's the *effrontery* of the crime that has so shaken us,' she cried, in her high quivering voice. 'We were only in the garden, you know, all busy picking our beautiful golden gooseberries for bottling. The wretched fellow must have pushed open the front door and seen us at it through the hall window. It gives a clear view of the garden as you know.'

'But why should he open the door?'

'Well, dear, the milkman normally leaves our bottles in that rather fine cache-pot by the doorstep, but in this hot weather Bertha said it might be wiser for him to put it just inside the front door, and she left a note to that effect in the cache-pot. The thief must have seen it.'

'Very likely.'

'The milkman has been so unpunctual lately. We never know when he will appear. He's courting May Miller at the draper's, and his van stands outside for *hours*. I wonder he's not had up for loitering with intent.'

'You can't have a van charged with loitering, Violet dear.'

'Well, anyway,' went on Miss Lovelock, 'this wretched fellow lifted a carrier bag from the hall stand, went into the dining room and put *everything* – simply *everything* – from the sideboard into it. He also took everything from the hall table too.'

'And no one saw him?'

'Well, dear, a man on the bus saw him, we gather. The thief must have stepped into a bus as soon as he emerged. Extremely fortunate for him when you consider the paucity of public transport these days. This man – who saw him, I mean – has given a description to the police. He noticed that the carrier bag *clanked*, but as it was a Debenham's bag – such a *respectable* firm – he simply supposed that he had been buying kitchenware of some description, saucepans and fish kettles and so on.'

'Do Debenham's sell kitchenware?'

'I'm not sure. Shops sell such odd things these days, though never what you want. Bertha is having such a job buying double satin baby ribbon to thread through her best nightgown. It seems to have vanished from the market.'

'What's the next move, Violet? Are the police being helpful?'

'Oh, very! Most sympathetic. The only thing is that we are having such difficulty in providing a correct list. I wake in the night and think: "Now, did I mention the pseudo-Lamerie posset cup which although made in Birmingham in 1905 was solid silver and quite charming?" The young officer who is dealing with us is patience itself, and always ready for a cup of Earl Grey tea. Luckily, he doesn't take sugar.'

There speaks a true Lovelock, thought Winnie, frugal even in adversity.

She put down the telephone after further expressions of sympathy, and went about her domestic duties.

The news about Molly's coming baby was soon general knowledge at Thrush Green. Everyone, with the exception of the baby's grandfather-to-be, Albert Piggott, was delighted.

'Lot of fuss about nothing,' growled Albert when congratulated by his fellow-drinkers at The Two Pheasants. 'If you ask me there's too many people in the world already, without adding to 'em.'

'You'll have to look after yourself a bit more, Albert me boy,' said one sagely. 'Can't expect Molly to do as she usually does for you, with another on the way.'

'D'you think I ain't thought of that meself?' snapped Albert, and gazed gloomily into his empty glass.

Little Miss Fogerty decided to put aside the cardigan she was knitting for next winter and to buy some baby wool at once for a jacket for the new child.

She was somewhat agitated about the choice of colour for the finished garment.

'I like pink myself,' she told Miss Watson, as they cracked their boiled eggs, 'and I've no doubt Molly is hoping for a girl this time. But if it is another boy, pink looks so *effeminate*, doesn't it? Perhaps blue would be safer. Girls look just as pretty in blue, don't you think?'

Miss Watson agreed somewhat absent-mindedly, and Agnes was instantly alert.

'Tell me, Dorothy, is your leg paining you?' Her own problems were forgotten at once.

Miss Watson sighed.

'To tell you the truth, Agnes, I had a most disturbed night with it.'

'Then we'll call in Doctor Lovell immediately.'

'No, no. I saw him not long ago, you remember, and he told me then that it was nothing to worry about. It was only *referred pain*, he said.'

'So what!' remarked little Miss Fogerty, quite militant on her friend's behalf. 'If it's pain, it's pain, and hurts! What's the difference between *legitimate* pain and this *referred* variety?'

'I quite agree,' confessed Miss Watson, wincing as she moved her chair. 'All very unsatisfactory, but is one in a position to argue? I think we'll wait a day or two, and see how it goes on. I may have slept in an awkward position, and put my pelvic girdle out a little.'

'Maybe,' agreed Agnes. 'That's the worst of bones. They're all joined on and, I must admit, in the most careless fashion at times. But I warn you, Dorothy, I shall have no hesitation in summoning the doctor if I see you are suffering.'

Miss Watson smiled at her good friend. On the rare occasions when she was roused she looked, as she did now, like a ferocious mouse.

'I've no doubt I shall be as fit as a flea tomorrow,' she assured Agnes.

But even fleas, she reminded herself, as she rose painfully from the table, must have their off days.


Dimity and Charles Henstock, now happily installed at Mrs Jenner's, met Dotty Harmer in the lane leading from Thrush Green to Nidden. They told her the news of Molly's expectations.

Dotty stood stock-still, looking bemused, while Flossie snuffled happily at Charles Henstock's legs, her plume of tail greatly agitated in her pleasure.

'Due in December? What a long time. Are you sure that's correct, Charles? I've forgotten the gestation period for humans. Goats, rabbits and cats I am perfectly sound on, but *babies* now . . .'

'I can assure you, Dotty, that December is correct,' said Dimity. 'Nine months, you know, is the time needed, and now it's June, so in six months's time the baby will arrive.'

'Yes, yes, I'm quite sure Molly would know. Such a competent little mother as she is. It's just that I had forgotten for the moment.'

'Come and have some tea in our new home,' suggested Charles. 'You've thought no more, by the way, about adopting a child of your own?'

'I can't say I've had any encouragement,' retorted Dotty. 'From the adoption societies – or from you, for that matter, if you recall, Charles dear. I've decided to give up the plan. With much regret, I may say.'

Charles heaved a sigh of relief.

'And, yes please, I should love a cup of tea with you at Mrs Jenner's.'

They began to retrace their steps, Flossie bounding ahead.

'Of course,' said Dotty conversationally, as they entered Mrs Jenner's gate, 'elephants carry their young for two years. I think that is what was confusing me. Poor things!' she added pityingly.

Charles and Dimity, following Dotty's scarecrow figure up the path, exchanged glances of shared joy.

What would they do without Dotty?

As Jenny's train rushed eastward from Torquay through the June countryside, she looked back upon her holiday with great contentment.

To have been by the sea would have been happiness enough. So seldom had she seen it that the wonder of its immensity and its changing moods, even viewed from the serenity of Meadfoot Beach, filled her with awe and excitement.

She remembered the thrill of paddling at the edge of the waves, watching them frilling round her ankles. She had not ventured to bathe, paddling was as much as she dared to do, but the sight of her feet, grotesquely distorted beneath the green water, filled her with joyous amusement.

The sea itself and the soft salty air had worked wonders for her spirits. Jenny began to realize how very run down she must have been, and would always be grateful to Winnie Bailey for recognizing the state of affairs, and for dealing so briskly and generously with it.

Swaying gently to the rhythm of the train, Jenny watched the telegraph poles flicker past against the background of green woods and fields. She would never be able to repay Winnie's kindness. The holiday had been wonderful, and an added bonus had been the joy of meeting Bessie again. The warm contentment which now engulfed her was due as much to Bessie's friendship and advice as to the healing properties of Torquay's sea and air.

Yesterday evening Bessie had raised again the subject of Percy Hodge, guessing that Jenny must be feeling some tremors again at the thought of returning to Thrush Green and to facing her admirer once more.

She did not know, of course, that Percy was to meet Jenny's train. Winnie Bailey's guarded message still awaited Jenny's return to the hotel. But she thought it would do no harm to see if her old friend were more settled in her mind. She raised the matter delicately, and Jenny sighed.

'I remember what you told me about imagining someone else with your young man,' she said, 'and it worked, you know. If only some nice woman would take on Percy I think I'd be truly relieved. He does *need* someone so.'

'I'm glad to hear you say that,' replied Bessie. 'But it needn't be you who supplies it. After all, Jenny, if his lost buttons and frayed collars worry you, then you could always offer to do some mending for him, as an old friend. You don't have to *marry* the fellow, now do you?'

And Jenny had laughed and agreed.

How sensible Bessie was! Of course, that was the right way to deal with Percy's ardours. Perhaps if she had had as many admirers as Bessie had in her young days, she would not have worried so much about dear old Percy's attentions. It was the sheer unexpectedness of being wanted by someone which had so agitated her. Bessie was probably quite right to say that Percy would find someone else within the year. She hoped he would. He was a good man and deserved some comfort and companionship.

As for her own feelings, well – it was nice to have been courted. She would always be grateful to Percy for singling her out. But what a relief it would be to be freed from the necessity and embarrassment of thanking him for flowers, eggs, soap, plants and all the other kind presents which Percy had brought to the door!

She closed her eyes against the Wiltshire meadows flashing past, and gave a sigh of contentment. Now she knew what to do. Now she could face Percy at the station. Probably he would say very little and just pick up her case, and talk about the weather. Then there would be no need to say anything much, except to tell him about Torquay. That should last beautifully until they reached Thrush Green. There really would not be much time to discuss feelings, thought Jenny with relief, and in any case, Percy was not a demonstrative man. And who knows, with any luck, his passion – such as it was – might have cooled in her absence, and meeting the train might simply be the gesture of an old friend.

As would be her offer to do his mending, thought Jenny, if the occasion arose. Well, at least she was in command of her own affairs now, and could cope with whatever Percy offered.

She dozed a little as the sunlight roamed around the carriage. The train's brakes squealed and the rhythm altered. Jenny awoke to see familiar fields running alongside.

She lifted down her case and stood by the window, swaying in the movement of the rattling carriage. In the distance she could see a little knot of people, and one figure standing alone. It was Percy.

He ran along by the side of the train and wrenched open the door. Jenny smiled and handed down the case as the train squealed to a halt.

Perfectly in command of her feelings, she began to step down, but before her foot had reached the platform, she was lifted bodily by Percy and enveloped in a great bear hug.

'How I've missed you, my girl!' cried Percy.
And Jenny's heart sank.

## *13. Jenny Decides*

Winnie Bailey awaited Jenny's arrival eagerly, but with a certain amount of anxiety. Had she received her message about Percy? How would Percy greet her? Would she have come to any firm decisions about her future whilst at Torquay?

The train was due at Lulling Station soon after four o'clock. Winnie prepared a tea tray. Jenny would need some refreshment after her journey, and over it perhaps she would hear something of Jenny's plans, as well as an account of the holiday.

By a quarter to five Winnie was beginning to feel slightly worried. If Percy had driven Jenny straight through Lulling High Street and up the sharp hill to Thrush Green, they would have arrived by half past four at the latest. Of course, she told herself, the train might have been behind time, but the more disturbing possibility was that Percy had made a detour to find a quiet spot to make a proposal.

She surveyed the tea tray. There were two cups and saucers, some tomato sandwiches and home-made biscuits. It might be as well to put out another cup in case Percy was now a fiancé. Trying to control her agitation, Winnie went to find a third cup, and to check the kettle.

At that moment, she heard a car stop, and hurried to the window.

Jenny alighted, and Percy lifted out her case from the back seat. They held a short conversation, and Winnie thought that Jenny seemed rather put out. Percy's face expressed his habitual happy bemusement when in Jenny's company, and he seemed to want to carry the case to the door.

Jenny lifted it herself, said farewell to her suitor, and strode determinedly up the path. Percy waved, and got back into the driver's seat, as Winnie hurried to open the front door.

'Won't Percy come in?' she asked.

'He's got to get back,' said Jenny shortly, watching the car pull away from the kerb.

'Well, my dear, it's lovely to have you home, and I'm just making some tea, so come and sit down.'

'I can do with a cup,' said Jenny thankfully. 'Percy can be a bit of a trial at times.'

And Winnie, pouring boiling water in the tea pot, felt a pang of blessed relief.

Over the tea-cups, Jenny gave an account of her surprising welcome at the station.

'I was fair taken aback, as you can imagine, and I told him pretty straight not to behave so silly. But, bless you, he don't seem to take much notice when he's set on something, and he drove round the back way – he *said* to dodge the traffic, but that was all my eye and Betty Martin – which is why I'm so late. He would stop in the old avenue, and there he went on about how he'd missed me, and now I was back we could think about getting married, until I could have hit him.'

'And what did *you* say, Jenny?'

'When I could get a word in edgeways, I said I was sorry but I wasn't planning to get married to anyone, and certainly not to him. But you might just as well talk to a brick wall as Percy Hodge. He didn't seem to take it in. In the end I got quite wild, and begged to be put down so as I could walk home to get a bit calmer. But he wouldn't have it.'

'A persistent fellow,' agreed Winnie, feeling more cheerful every minute.

'More tea, Jenny dear?'

Jenny passed her cup.

'It's thirsty work turning down chaps, I can tell you,' she said, 'especially when they're as pig-headed as Percy. Well, in the end he said he was off to Wales tomorrow morning to get some cattle, and he'd be away two or three days, so I could get used to the idea of being engaged, and he'd call when he got back.'

'Oh dear, Jenny! Are you sure what you want to do?'

'Mrs Bailey,' said Jenny earnestly, 'I've thought of all this ever since I've left here, and I'm positive I don't want to marry Percy. What's more, I don't want to leave you.'

Winnie felt tears of relief pricking her eyes.

'Well, it's wonderful news for me, of course, and I'm glad you know your own mind. But I shouldn't like you to throw away your future happiness out of loyalty to me. Percy's a good fellow, and would make a kind husband, I'm sure, and he's obviously devoted to you. It's a good thing you have these few days to think things over.'

'I don't need a few days,' said Jenny robustly. 'I know now, and I feel all the better for coming to a decision. When Percy comes back I'll make it quite clear to him.'

'But do be *kind*!' pleaded Winnie. 'He'll be so disappointed.'

'Bessie says she wouldn't mind betting he's happily married within a year,' said Jenny shrewdly. 'But it won't be to me! I'll just go and rinse the tea things.' She jumped to her feet.

'You won't,' said Winnie. 'You've had enough to cope with in the past hour. Tea things can wait.'


There was no doubt about it. Jenny's holiday had set her up again, and she attacked her work with renewed vigour. Winnie rejoiced in her return to health and good spirits.

She said nothing more to Jenny about Percy, nor did she breathe a word to anyone else in Thrush Green, but somehow or other it seemed to be general knowledge, by the end of a week, that Percy Hodge had received his marching orders from Jenny.

Comment at The Two Pheasants was now completely contrary to earlier views expressed. Far from thinking that Jenny might have done very well for herself as Percy's second wife, the general opinion seemed to be that she had shown very good sense in repelling his advances.

Some went even further.

'Take my word for it,' said one worthy, 'she found something better down in Devon. You can tell by the look of her. Fair come to life since going to Torquay. There's a man at the bottom of it, I shouldn't wonder.'

'Can't blame her. After all, old Perce has been no more'n a thin string of misery since his Gertie went. Jenny's got herself to think of, and she's well enough off as she is in Doctor Bailey's place.'

'Talk about a lot of women clacking,' cried the landlord, 'you chaps is worse than the lot! Putting two and two together and making half a dozen! Maybe Perce hasn't asked her yet.'

'He ain't been near the place since he called after he got back from Wales. Why, he was everlasting mincing along with ruddy great bunches of flowers and that before she went away. Now look at him! Ain't I right?' he appealed to his fellow drinkers.

There were confirmatory grunts of agreement. Albert Piggott had the last word.

'It's my belief they've both seen the light, mates. This marrying and giving in marriage, what is cracked up so, can be a terrible let-down. And I'll have another half-pint of bitter, please, seeing I'm a free man without a wife to nag me.'

It was soon after this that Harold and Isobel Shoosmith had a little party. Encouraged by the blissful spell of June weather, when the roses and pinks were at their most beguiling, and the sun was still above the horizon at nine at night, they invited some two dozen old friends to have a drink with them.

The Henstocks and the Hursts arrived together. Frank Hurst had known Harold for many years and had been introduced to Phyllida by him when she was trying desperately to earn her living as a freelance writer and had first come to live at Thrush Green.

Agnes Fogerty was one of Isobel's oldest friends. They had met as girls at college, and it was a shared joy now to live next door to each other. Dorothy Watson, chic in navy-blue silk, accompanied her assistant. The Youngs, the Bassetts, Winnie Bailey, Ella Bembridge and Dotty Harmer were all at the party, as well as several Lulling friends, including Anthony Bull, Lulling's handsome vicar.

The evening was warm and windless, and the guests wandered about in the garden congratulating Harold and Isobel on their superbly mown lawns and weedless garden beds.

'All Harold's doing,' Isobel told them. 'I'm just the deadheader of roses and pansies – a very lowly assistant gardener.'

'Any news about your new home?' inquired Anthony Bull of Charles, as they stood together under a copper beech tree.

'I gather there is some debate about building a smaller place on the old site, or finding a readymade establishment and selling the existing plot. I suppose that the land might command a good price, although I know very little about these things.'

'It is not very big,' observed Anthony. 'I wonder if it would fetch a good price. Doubtful, I should think. But tell me, are you comfortable at Mrs Jenner's?'

Charles's chubby face was lit with a smile.

'Incredibly comfortable! Dimity and I had no idea one could be so warm and happy. The windows face south, you know, and the light is wonderful. I never need to put on my desk light when I am writing. I can't get over the joy of it.'

'It's a house I've always admired,' said Anthony. 'Much the same age as our vicarage. Those eighteenth-century builders knew what they were doing, didn't they?'

'Without a doubt,' agreed Charles. 'Without a doubt. Although I grieve for our poor departed home, I'm just beginning to realize that it was badly designed, and dear Dimity must have put up with most uncomfortable surroundings, without a word of complaint.'

'Ah! You married an angel, Charles, and I did too. We are fortunate fellows.'

Phyllida Hurst came up to them.

'Good news! The Thomases' baby arrived yesterday. A boy, and Jack sounded so pleased on the telephone. Wasn't it sweet of him to ring?'

'A charming young man, I thought,' said Charles. 'And of course he would let you know. After all, they were greatly obliged to you for letting them have Tullivers.'

Anthony Bull had walked away to have a word with Miss Watson and Miss Fogerty. Phil spoke rapidly.

'I've only just discovered that the other young couple must have been a sore disappointment to you all.'

'Really?' replied Charles, his face puckered with bewilderment. 'I hardly saw them, I must confess.'

'They were on drugs, you know.'

'The sort you smoke?'

'I gather so.'

'That must have been the peculiar smell I noticed when I called. I thought it was something cooking – herbs, I imagined, of some sort.'

'Well, that's one way of looking at it!'

'How did you find out? Did Jack Thomas tell you?'

'No. Jeremy did.'

'*Jeremy!*' exclaimed the rector, 'but how on earth – ?'

'One of the boys at school has an older sister who has been on the stuff. She knew that the Thomases' friends bought it, and told her brothers who told Jeremy evidently. I gather she's given it up now, thank God. Foolish girl to start, of course.'

'Well, you have surprised me,' said Charles. 'I can only hope that the other two will follow her example. And I am delighted to hear about the baby. Do congratulate the Thomases for us, if you are in touch.'

His eye alighted on the three Lovelock sisters who were admiring two small silver dishes containing nuts.

'Ah, do excuse me, Phyllida. I must have a word with the Lovelock girls. I haven't seen them since the burglary.'

He hastened away. Phil noted the predatory gleam in Miss Violet's eye as she put back the little dish on the table.

Was she already replacing their lost collection, wondered Phil? She hastily quashed the unworthy thought, and went to talk to Joan Young.

Later that evening Dorothy Watson and Agnes Fogerty rested in their sitting room and discussed the excitement of the party.

'I thought that Joan Young looked very well in that bottle green frock. A very pretty neckline.'

Dorothy had a great eye for dress, as Agnes knew, and took enormous interest in the clothes of others. Agnes herself was content to be clean and respectable, but ever enthralled to hear her friend's comments on others' appearance.

'And did you notice,' continued Dorothy, 'that Ada Lovelock's evening bag was freshly adorned with some jet edging which looked to me remarkably like the stuff I sent to be sold at her recent coffee morning? I have never known such greed as those Lovelock sisters show when it comes to gewgaws.'

'You can't call all their lovely things *gewgaws*,' protested Agnes. 'And in any case, you can't be sure that the trimming was the material you sent.'

'Agnes dear, I am quite sure,' said Dorothy firmly. 'I am the first to admire your fair-mindedness, but you must not deceive yourself. That trimming was undoubtedly *appropriated*, one might say *purloined*, by the Lovelocks, well before the coffee morning.'

'That's as maybe,' agreed Agnes, 'but the poor souls have suffered terribly from the loss of all their beautiful things, and I do think that they might be forgiven for buying in that jet edging. They might easily be in a state of shock.'

'They've been in that particular state of shock ever since I've known them,' said Dorothy. 'However, they're much too old to change their ways now, so we won't waste time in censuring them. Agnes dear, after all that sherry I'm uncommonly thirsty. Do you think a glass of fresh orange juice would be a good idea for us?'

'Of course it would,' said Agnes, getting up at once. 'Keep your legs up, my dear, you have been standing quite long enough, while I get us both a drink.'

One day, thought Dorothy, watching her friend bustling towards the kitchen, I hope I shall be able to repay the kindness of that completely selfless soul. But will it ever be possible?

A few mornings later, Charles Henstock sat at his desk and gazed out at the sunlit garden. He was attempting to write next Sunday's sermon, always a difficult task, and not made any easier on this gorgeous June day by all the happy distractions outside the window.

A blue tit, with a mimosa yellow breast, clung to the coconut half which swung from a branch of the old plum tree. His antics were as delightful as they were graceful. A bullyboy of a blackbird bustled below, chasing all the other groundlings away from the crumbs which fell from the tit's energetic assault on the coconut.

Above, a tiny silver aeroplane ruled a fast-fading line across the blue sky, and over in Percy Hodge's field a red and white cow sat chewing the cud with the same vague bliss in its surroundings which now enveloped the good rector. And curled up in the chair beside him was their cat, which had settled down at Mrs Jenner's as happily as they had themselves.

Dimity had gone to Lulling to shop and Charles found his new abode very quiet. Dimity's parting words had been to the effect that he would have peace in which to compose his sermon.

He certainly had that, he thought, putting down his pen and propping his head on his hand. How pretty the young leaves looked on the plum tree! How beautifully fashioned was the wing of the fluttering tit! How vivid the beak of the blackbird!

This was a very pleasant place to live, and he thanked God humbly for leading him to such a haven after the tragedy of the fire. Where, eventually, would his home be, he wondered yet again? It was surely time that he heard something from the Church. Anthony Bull, who always seemed to be so much better informed about things, had said that the new rearrangements of the parishes may have held up Charles's particular problem, but it was all rather unsettling. One would like to know one's future.

The good rector sighed, and picked up his pen again. He must make a start at least before Dimity returned. A great black rook now alighted on the grass and began to sidle timidly towards a crust thrown out by Mrs Jenner. The small birds took no notice of this formidable figure in their midst.

The rector decided suddenly to turn his observant idling to good account. His sermon should be about the joy of living in the present, and of looking at the wonders around. Did not Our Lord Himself tell his followers not to worry about the morrow, what they should eat, what they should put on?

Now inspired, Charles began to settle down to his writing and to sharing his own happiness with his beloved parishioners.

While he was busy scribbling, Molly Curdle was being driven in the local taxi to the County Hospital for an ante-natal examination. Doctor Lovell felt certain that all was well, but decided that a check on his own findings would be a sensible precaution at the splendid new maternity wing.

Joan Young would have taken her but had promised to go to a Women's Institute meeting in the neighbouring county. This involved lunching with the as-yet-unknown president, delivering her talk, judging the monthly competition – almost as hazardous and thankless a task as judging a baby show – and then driving back some twenty-five miles. Arthur Tranter was taking her place.

He was a cheerful man, some years older than Molly, but they had both attended Thrush Green School, and knew each other fairly well.

She sat beside him in the taxi, and they chatted amicably of this and that. Molly was careful not to mention her condition and congratulated herself on her still trim figure. However, she need not have troubled to hide anything from the percipient Mr Tranter.

'Havin' the baby up the County then?' he remarked conversationally.

'Possibly,' said Molly.

'I'll take you up if you want me to,' offered he.

'I gets no end of young mums to take there from Lulling. Bit far though, I always think. Too far sometimes for some of 'em. I've brought three into this world in my time, so you don't need to worry.'

Molly remained silent.

'I always say they can name 'em after the old taxi. Maurice, say, or Austin – both good names. I had a Cadillac once, bought off of an American chap up the air base, but none of the mums would name their kids after that. Might be called Cad for short, see?'

He roared with laughter at his own joke, unaffected by Molly's disapproval. She was glad when they began to run through the suburbs of the country town. It was quite bad enough having to face a strange doctor without Arthur's coarse remarks.

'You'll want the ante-natal, love, won't you? I'll be waiting. I've got a flask of coffee and today's paper so don't worry if you're held up. You never can tell with hospitals, can you?'

'No, indeed,' agreed Molly tremulously. Now that they had actually stopped outside the door, fear gripped her, and distasteful as she found

Arthur Tranter at least he was an old acquaintance and a link with all that was familiar at distant Thrush Green.

As if he guessed her thoughts, he leant out and patted her arm.

'Cheer up, duck. All be over in next to no time, and we'll step on it and get you home before you have time to turn round.'

She gave him a grateful smile, and went in to face the trial ahead.

## 14. *After the Storm*

The beautiful spell of June weather broke with a violent thunderstorm one torrid night. Lightning flickered eerily for several hours before the thunder asserted itself, and the rain began to rattle on the parched earth. Gutters gurgled, rivulets rippled down the hill to Lulling, and water butts, which had stood empty for weeks, filled rapidly.

So violent was the storm about three o'clock that Harold and Isobel decided that a cup of tea would be a very good thing, and Harold went down to make it. As he waited for the kettle to boil, he surveyed the wet world of Thrush Green through the window.

Other people were awake too, it seemed. There was a dim light at Tullivers, and Harold guessed correctly that it had been put on to allay young Jeremy's fears. There was another light at Ella Bembridge's. No doubt, thought Harold, she is brewing tea, as I am.

No lights showed otherwise. Presumably the Youngs, the Bassetts, Winnie Bailey, Jenny and all the other good folk of Thrush Green, were either deep in slumber or riding out the storm in the darkness of their bedrooms.

Harold thought, not for the first time, how fortunate he had been to settle at Thrush Green. Thousands of miles away when he was in business, he had first heard of this tiny English village, the birthplace of Nathaniel Patten, a zealous missionary, whose work Harold admired deeply. It was Harold who had been instrumental in raising funds to buy the fine statue of Thrush Green's most distinguished son. He could see it now, glinting as the lightning lit the view. It was good to think that such a good fellow was properly honoured, and Harold was proud of his part in the affair.

He had not bargained though for the generous welcome he had received from the inhabitants of his chosen village. That was a bonus. He had found several people, much of his own age and interests, in this little community who had now become firm friends. He thought with affection and gratitude of the Henstocks, the Baileys, the Hursts, and many others who had made his path here so pleasant. He was lucky to have such good neighbours and Betty Bell to minister to his domestic comfort.

But luckiest of all, he told himself, as he attended to the boiling kettle, was the stroke of good fortune which had come unwittingly through little Agnes Fogerty next door. Her friendship with Isobel, her old college connection, had given him his wife, and a happiness he had never dared to hope for at his age.

Balancing the tray with great care, Harold mounted the stairs, ignoring a crash of thunder which rattled all the window panes.

Isobel, as beautiful as ever, was sitting up in bed, serenely ignoring the violence which raged outside.

'A quarter past three,' she exclaimed, catching sight of the bedside clock. 'What a time to be drinking tea!'

'Anytime,' Harold told her, 'is time to be drinking tea.'

Some half mile to the west, out of sight of Thrush Green, Dotty Harmer was awakened by the din and lay worrying about her animal charges.

Would Dulcie, the goat, be alarmed by the storm? She was of a nervous disposition, and goats were generally acknowledged to be sensitive to climatic conditions. The chickens and ducks were much more phlegmatic by nature, and were no doubt quite unperturbed in their roosts. As for the many cats, they always took events very philosophically, and dear old Flossie, apart from flinching at any particularly ferocious roll of thunder, seemed quite calm at the end of Dotty's bed.

No, it was dear Dulcie that was her chief worry. Possessed of enormous strength and sleeping in a somewhat battered shed, even by Dotty's standards, she might well crash her way out and do extensive damage to her own and her neighbours' gardens.

There was no help for it, Dotty told herself, but to get up and investigate. The rain lashed against the cottage windows, the wind howled, and the lightning was alarming, but Dotty knew where her duty lay, and clambered out of bed.

She went as she was, barefoot and in her nightgown, down the stairs, followed by the faithful Flossie. In the kitchen she thrust her feet into wellingtons and dragged on her old mackintosh.

As a token concession to the elements she also tied a scarf over her skimpy grey locks, took a torch, and set off to Dulcie's shed.

The onslaught of the rain quite took her breath away, but she battled down the path beneath the flailing branches of the old fruit trees, which scattered showers of water and leaves with every gust of wind.

She looked into the hens' house and, apart from some squawks from her disturbed charges, all seemed well. No sound came from the ducks' shelter, and Dotty decided to leave well alone.

She struggled on, and was suddenly aware of what hard work it was. Her legs seemed leaden. Her heart raced. Water ran down her face from the already sodden scarf, but she pressed on.

By the light of the torch she saw that Dulcie was sitting down. Her chain was slack and in good order, and she was licking a lump of rock salt with evident enjoyment.

'Dear thing,' said Dotty. 'Good Dulcie! Just ignore this dreadful noise, my dear. It will all be over by morning.'

Much relieved, she shut the door again. She trundled the glistening garden roller against it, for good measure, and decided that all would be safe until morning.

It was easier going back with the wind behind her, but Dotty was glad to get to the porch where Flossie, who had taken one look at the weather, had prudently waited for her mistress.

The kitchen was a haven, and Dotty was thankful to rest on the kitchen chair before taking off her wet clothes. Five cats looked at her from their various resting places, ranging from a stack of newspapers to a pile of Dotty's underclothes which were awaiting ironing.

When she could breathe again more easily, Dotty struggled out of her coat and boots. The hem of her nightgown was drenched, but she could not be bothered to change it.

She wondered if it would be worthwhile making a hot drink. She felt uncommonly exhausted. Perhaps she needed a tonic? Perhaps she should see Doctor Lovell? She had not felt her heart behaving in that odd jumpy way before.

She sat for a few more moments, savouring the warmth of the kitchen, the cats' presence, and pondering upon the possibility of visiting Doctor Lovell.

'Oh, drat doctors!' exclaimed Dotty at last, and wearily climbed the stairs.

Most of Thrush Green's inhabitants had been disturbed in the night, but the morning dawned still and grey.

A light mist veiled the distance, and the warm earth, thoroughly drenched by the night's heavy rain, caused a humidity which reminded Harold of his days in the tropics.

Betty Bell, arriving like a whirlwind from Lulling Woods, gave a vivid account of the devastation caused in that usually comatose hamlet.

'And my neighbour's nappies – well her *baby's* nappies, of course, but you know what I mean – was wrenched off of her line and went all which-ways. Why, one of 'em blew into the pig sty! Think of that!'

Harold, who was trying to read his post in the study, made suitable noises. Despite the fact that his wife now ran their house, Betty still sought him out as soon as she arrived, to keep him up to date with local affairs. It could be rather trying.

'And they do say that one of them poplars up the rec was struck. Felled to the ground, Willie Marchant told me, and all frizzled round the edges. When you think – it might have been you or me!'

'I doubt if we should have been standing in the recreation ground at two in the morning,' commented Harold, slitting open an unpleasant looking envelope with O H M S on the corner.

'I was going to pop in to see if Miss Harmer was O K, but I was a bit behindhand after collecting some flowerpots and a bucket and that what had been blown into our hedge. Still, I'll look in on the way home.'

'That would be kind,' agreed Harold.

'Well, I'm glad nothing happened here,' said Betty. 'No tiles off, nor trees broken and that. I'd best get on. Anything particular you want done? Windows, say, or silver?'

'You'd better have a word with my wife,' said Harold.

'I'll do that,' replied Betty, and vanished.

Next door, Miss Fogerty found her charges unusually heavy-eyed. She had planned to teach them a charming little poem of Humbert Wolfe's, but gave up when she found them bemused from lack of sleep and a prey to sighs and yawns.

Always a realist, she faced the fact that such a delightful poem deserved full attention, and at the moment something less intellectually demanding was called for.

'Give out the modelling clay, George dear,' she told young Curdle. 'You can choose which you want to make. Either a basket full of different sorts of fruit, or a tea tray with cups and saucers, and something nice to eat on a big plate.'

'And sugar lumps in a bowl?' asked Anne Cooke.

'Of course. And don't forget the teaspoons.'

There was a marked improvement in interest as the boards and glisten-ing wet balls of clay were distributed.

Miss Fogerty watched them attack their work, and smiled upon them.

Baskets of fruit and tea trays were always good for twenty minutes at least, thought Agnes with satisfaction.

Albert Piggott, not many yards from Thrush Green School, felt as lazy and out-of-sorts as the children. To his disgust, the storm had blown leaves and twigs into the church porch, ripped one or two notices to shreds, and soaked the heavy mat which was bad enough to shift when it was dry, let alone sodden with rain.

He set about his duties dourly, one eye on the door of The Two Pheasants.

His indigestion was even worse than usual this morning. Perhaps fried food was not good for him, but what could a chap cook when his lawful wedded wife had took off with the oil man? He could not fiddle about with pastry and vegetables and mixing gravy and all the other nonsenses his Nelly had mucked about with.

He plied his broom lethargically. Waste of time, all this cleaning. Come tomorrow it would be as bad again.

There was a welcome rattle from the door of the public house. Jones was unlocking, and about time too! Maybe half a pint, and a slab of cold pork pie, would settle his stomach.

Albert propped his broom against a Zenana Mission poster which had escaped the full fury of the storm, and set off with more vigour than had been apparent all the morning.

'Well, Albert, what a night, eh?' the landlord greeted him. 'I feel a bit washed out this morning, and that's the truth.'

He spoke for all Thrush Green.


A few mornings later, Ella Bembridge was surprised to see Dotty Harmer approaching, carrying the milk can which she usually brought about tea time with Ella's regular order of goat's milk.

Her old friend looked wispier and greyer than ever, she thought, as she ushered her into the sitting room. Flossie followed like Dotty's shadow.

'You're early today,' she said, taking the milk can from Dotty's bony hand. 'My word, you're jolly cold. Dotty! Are you all right?'

'Perfectly,' replied Dotty, looking about her vaguely. 'I've just milked Dulcie, so I thought I would come straight up with your milk while it was fresh.'

'And very nice to see you,' replied Ella. 'But you usually give me the afternoon milk.'

Dotty did not answer. Ella thought that she looked more than usually dishevelled and extremely tired.

'Let me get you a drink,' she urged. 'Coffee? Tea? Orange squash?'

'Could I have a small whisky? Father calls it a sundowner.'

'Of course you can have a small whisky, but it's not exactly sundown, you know. It's hardly ten o'clock.'

'Such light evenings,' agreed Dotty. 'I shall shut up the hens when I get back. Which reminds me, I can't stay very long. Father had one of his tantrums this morning, and didn't want me to come out.'

She sat nodding to herself, oblivious of Ella's shocked silence.

What on earth had hit poor Dotty? Her dreadful old father had been dead for twenty years! 'One of his little tantrums', as Dotty euphemistically described it, would have struck fear into the stoutest heart when he lived, but he was now resting with other Thrush Green worthies under Albert Piggott's sketchy care.

'Dotty,' began Ella, 'you are not well. It's only ten o'clock *in the morning,* and you know you haven't had a living parent for years! I'm giving you coffee. I'm not sure if whisky would be the right thing for you just now.'

'I certainly don't want *whisky*,' responded Dotty. 'If Father smelt strong liquor on my breath he would be most upset.'

She looked down at Flossie.

'What's this dog doing here?' she inquired. 'You didn't tell me you were getting one.'

By now, Ella was seriously alarmed. The poor soul's mind was wandering, and what on earth did you do with such a patient? John Lovell would be in his surgery now, but she could not leave her. She decided to get to the telephone in the hall where she would have a clear view of the front door if Dotty attempted to escape.

'I'm going to put on the kettle, Dotty, so lean back and have a rest. I must ring the butcher too, so don't worry if I'm a minute or two.'

'Pray take your time,' said Dotty graciously. 'It stays light until almost eleven o'clock, you know, so there's no hurry.'

She leant back obediently in the armchair, and closed her eyes.

Ella, much agitated, hurried to summon help.


John Lovell came himself before starting his rounds.

He was greeted by Ella with almost incoherent gratitude, and by Dotty with considerable hauteur.

When Ella had taken in the coffee she had found Dotty fast asleep, and snoring in an eminently genteel fashion. Ella, much relieved, hoped that she would stay in this state until the doctor called. She awoke as Ella went to the front door.

'I'd like to examine her on a bed, Ella,' he said. 'All right?'

'Of course,' she replied. 'Dotty dear, you don't mind if Doctor Lovell has a look at you?'

'I mind very much,' cried Dotty, her papery old cheeks flushing pink, 'but as he has been called – *not* at my request, I hope he understands – I shall let him examine me, but I trust that you will be present.' She seemed to be more her old self since her nap.

Ella and John Lovell exchanged glances.

'Of course Ella can stay,' said the doctor. 'Let's go up.'

He was wonderfully gentle with their old friend, Ella noticed. She could not help noticing too, with considerable alarm, how pathetically frail Dotty was. Her legs and arms were like sticks. Her rib bones could be clearly seen as well as the bones of her neck and shoulders.

Ella turned to look out of the window as the examination went on.

Dotty bore all in silence, but sighed with relief when he said that she could get dressed again.

They left her to do so and descended the stairs.

'What is it?' asked Ella.

'You can have it in one word. Malnutrition. She's in a pretty bad way, Ella, and I'm getting her into the Cottage Hospital right away. Can I use your phone?'

'Carry on. I'm shattered, but not surprised. She eats next to nothing, and works far too hard with that menagerie of hers.'

She stopped suddenly, hand to mouth.

'We'll have to get someone to look after them. I'll take on the cats and the poultry, and dear old Flossie can stay here – but that damn' goat is beyond me, I don't mind confessing.'

'Don't worry. We'll get something sorted out. But she must get some attention immediately.'

He went into the hall, and Ella slumped inelegantly on the sofa, feeling as if she had been sand-bagged.

Flossie lumbered across the room and put her heavy head on Ella's knee. Ella fondled her long golden ears.

'Flossie, my girl,' she told her, 'we're in a fine old pickle this morning.'


Surprisingly enough, Dotty submitted to all the plans made for her with unaccustomed docility. John Lovell gave the two friends and Flossie a lift back to Lulling Woods and left them there to pack a bag for Dotty while he continued on his rounds.

Ella had expected a spate of instructions about food for the animals, and her own domestic arrangements, but Dotty scarcely said a word. She gave Ella directions about where to find clean nightgowns, a sponge bag, soap and so on in a weak voice, but seemed content to let her do the work.

It was as if she had had quite enough of present problems and was already drifting into oblivion. Ella had never seen anyone in such a state of exhaustion, and was very much alarmed. It was a great relief when a car from the hospital arrived and she could get into it with the patient.

A cheerful nurse, whose face seemed vaguely familiar to Ella, took charge of Dotty, and said that Ella could see her at any time. This sounded ominous to Ella, who knew little about modern hospital methods. She had a confused idea that only those at the point of death were allowed visitors. Surely, one had to come between two and four, or six or seven, and then only with one other person at the bedside?

She kissed Dotty goodbye, and wandered out into Lulling High Street. Where on earth had she seen that nurse before?

It was odd to be at large in the town at almost twelve o'clock. She felt shaky, and the thought of the hill up to Thrush Green was a little daunting. She made her way to The Fuchsia Bush to get a cup of coffee, and to rest.

She had not been inside since the new arrangements had been made. It had been redecorated in a hideous shade of plum red which clashed appallingly with the old mauve curtains and made the interior unpleasantly gloomy.

Two waitresses, who had been busy painting their nails, now broke off their conversation, and the taller one advanced reluctantly to Ella's table.

'Just a cup of coffee, please.'

'We don't do coffee after twelve.'

'It isn't twelve yet,' Ella pointed out.

'But it will be by the time I get the coffee,' replied the girl, huffing on her nails to dry the varnish.

Honest wrath began to give Ella back her usual strength.

'If I don't get coffee within three minutes,' she said flatly, 'I shall see the manager immediately.'

'Oh well!' replied the girl, flouncing off, and casting her eyes to heaven as she passed her friend.

The cheek, thought Ella, taking out her tobacco tin and beginning to roll a cigarette with shaking fingers! Bad enough closing this place at tea time and making it look like a third-rate brothel – whatever they looked like – without having chits of girls making a song and dance about fetching a cup of instant when requested.

In the old days there had been some very pleasant waitresses here, thought Ella, blowing out a cloud of acrid smoke.

Ah, that was it, of course! That nice nurse had worked here years ago. No wonder her face was familiar. Some relation of dear old Mrs Jenner's, if she remembered rightly.

The coffee arrived, with only a small amount slopped in the saucer. It was hot and refreshing, and by the time Ella had drunk half of it, she was feeling more herself.

She must buy some meat for Flossie on the way back, and go and collect her at Dotty's and see that the rest of the animals were safe until the evening. As for Dulcie, she must find someone to milk that wretched animal, but at the moment she could not think of anyone brave enough to tackle the brute.

She stubbed out her cigarette, left the exact money on the bill slip – no tip for that young woman today – and went out into the sunshine.

As much refreshed by her little skirmish as by the coffee, Ella set off briskly to tackle the hill, and all that lay before her at Thrush Green.

## *15. Dotty Faces Facts*

While Dotty Harmer lay, unusually quiescent, in her bed in the women's ward of Lulling Cottage Hospital, and Ella puffed up the hill to Thrush Green trying to decide if it were better to collect Flossie immediately or after she had eaten an early lunch, her old friend Dimity Henstock was busy discussing household matters with Charles.

'We really must buy more bed linen, Charles. Everything in that line went, as you know, and the July sales will be starting quite soon. I could save quite a lot of money.'

'Well, my dear, you know best, of course, but the insurance people haven't paid out yet, and our bank account is as slender as ever, I fear.'

'I do know that. The thing is that we shall have so much to buy with it. Beds, for instance. I think it would be sensible to have two single beds in the spare room. We've only had the double one there which means larger sheets which are expensive to launder.'

'But only *two* sheets,' pointed out Charles, 'instead of four.'

'Now I come to think of it,' said Dimity, 'Ella has some of my single sheets that I used when I lived there. I left them with her, but I don't think she has used them. Perhaps I could find out.'

'But we can't take Ella's sheets!' protested Charles.

'Strictly speaking, they are mine. Of course, if they are in use I shall leave them for Ella, but it would save me buying quite so many new ones. We shall need new blankets and covers too, of course.'

'Can you get all you want with fifty pounds?' asked Charles, his chubby face puckered with anxiety.

'No, Charles, I'm afraid I couldn't. But I shall spend fifty pounds to the very best advantage, believe me.'

'I know that.'

'If only the insurance people would pay up! Couldn't you write to them, or get Justin Venables to prod them?'

'I really don't like to do that.'

'Well, it's getting rather desperate, you know, Charles. I know we are very happy and comfortable here with Mrs Jenner's things, but we must look ahead to when we have a place of our own.'

The rector sighed.

'We have indeed been blessed. If only we could have a house as warm and light as this, Dimity.'

'And as old and beautiful,' agreed his wife. 'Well, whatever it is it will be lovely to settle in again. I'll call on Ella this afternoon, and find out about the sheets.'

'You won't rob her of them, will you?' pleaded Charles.

'Good heavens! I knew dear old Ella long before I met you, Charles, and you can rest assured that neither of us is going to fall out over a few rather shabby sheets!'

And with that the good rector had to be content.

Dimity set off to walk the half mile or so from Mrs Jenner's to Thrush Green. It was a calm day – 'soft weather' as the Irish call it – and there were very few people about.

Dimity enjoyed the peace of it all. She walked slowly, relishing the sounds of the countryside heard so clearly in the still air. A cow lowed in one of Percy Hodge's distant fields on her left. In the high branches of a walnut tree on her right she heard the excited squeaking of what she guessed were some long-tailed tits searching busily for insects, and she stopped by a farm gate to listen to the rare summer sound of a cricket in the grass.

It was all so very soothing, and Dimity's anxieties grew less pressing now that she was in the fresh air and able to enjoy the slower tempo of life about her. She wished that their plans were more definite. Surely they should know by now if a house were planned for the old site, although she was beginning to hope that somewhere else might be found for them. It would be good to make a fresh start. Not that she would ever want to go far from her friends at Thrush Green, but she felt that she could not face the effort needed to supervise the plans for a new abode, nor the delays which were bound to arise.

If only some pleasant place, like Mrs Jenner's, within a mile or so, say, from their old home could be found, how perfect it would be! Both she and Charles were now getting over the first numbing shock of their loss, and were beginning to long for a place of their own. Dimity knew Charles too well to expect him to take any positive action in asserting his needs. He would be content to wait humbly for what the Church provided, secure in his belief that all would be for the best. Dimity, a little less quiescent, was beginning to wonder if some pressure might not be a good thing.

She strolled on, and soon came in sight of Thrush Green. A sturdy figure, leading a spaniel, emerged from the lane which led to Lulling Woods, and Dimity recognized her old friend.

She caught up with her as she crossed the grass towards the home they had once shared.

'I was just coming to see you,' she cried, bending down to pat Flossie. 'How's Dotty?'

And Ella told her the sorry tale.

'Well,' declared Dimity, with unusual firmness, 'it's a blessing in disguise, Ella. She's looked really ill for months now, and won't take any advice. I'm quite relieved to hear that she's being properly looked after for a change.'

'But that's only temporary, Dim, that's what worries me. I think, in a way, this trying to adopt a child was her muddle-headed way of having companionship and a bit of help with the work. Honestly, I'm pretty tough, but after clearing up the worst of that kitchen of hers, I was whacked. It wants a complete turnout from top to bottom, that house of Dotty's, but who is going to take on the responsibility?'

'Do you think the niece might come for a bit when Dotty comes out of hospital?'

'Connie? She might. But she's got a small-holding of her own, I believe. Mind you, they get on pretty well, and Connie's got a good head on her shoulders. I don't think she'd stand any of Dotty's bullying. By the way, did you come for anything special?'

Dimity explained about the bed linen.

'I shall be glad to know they're in use,' replied Ella. 'They've been stored on the top shelf of the airing cupboard ever since you got married. Do them good to see the light of day.'

'And you're sure you have enough? Charles is most anxious that we don't take anything away which might be useful.'

'My dear old Dim, I've all my own stuff, and when mother died I inherited hers, including some lovely heavy linen sheets with lace insertion. Perishing cold in the winter, but bliss on a hot summer's night, so have no fear on that score. And incidentally, I have a pair of her rugs up in the loft which I shall never use. Say if you want them when you move into the new place. Heard any more yet?'

Dimity told her how things stood, and how she was beginning to worry about the delay.

'It'll sort itself out,' said Ella, rising. 'Let's get those sheets down before we forget them. And do you want some blackcurrants? The bushes at the end of the garden are laden.'

'Yes, please. It's Charles's favourite fruit. Nothing so good as blackcurrant tart in the winter.'

'Unless it's dear old rhubarb,' said Ella. 'Can't think why people turn up their noses at rhubarb. Good for you all the way through, I reckon.'

They were upstairs retrieving Dimity's sheets when Ella looked at her watch.

'It's Dulcie I'm worried about. She's due to be milked before evening and I haven't found anyone to do it. I'm damned if I'm going to. Any ideas?'

Arms clutching sheets, Dimity turned her mind to Ella's problem.

'Percy Hodge might do it, I suppose, but he's pretty busy. Let's ring Charles. He might know of someone. He comes across all sorts of interesting bits of knowledge on his parish visiting.'

'And tell him to come down to tea,' said Ella, as her friend dialled. 'You'll need the car to get the sheets home, let alone the blackcurrants.'

Dimity relayed the message and then broached the subject of Dulcie.

'But Albert Piggott once had goats,' said Charles immediately. 'I'm sure I could persuade him to take on a little task like that. He would be delighted to help Dotty, I'm sure.'

Dimity could not feel quite as positive about Albert's delight as her warm-hearted husband, but passed on the good news to Ella.

'God bless Charles!' cried Ella. 'If anyone can persuade Albert to take on extra work then he's the man to do it.'


Charles was as good as his word. He left the car outside Ella's house and walked by the church to Albert's cottage.

He found his sexton standing at the sink, washing up some crockery in water so murky and afloat with unsavoury flotsam that Charles wondered if it would really be more sanitary to leave the china unwashed.

Charles explained the purpose of his visit while Albert prodded morosely at the congealed food in a pie dish. His expression brightened considerably when goats were mentioned.

'Now, they're animals with a bit of character,' said Albert. 'It was my dad, not me, sir, as kept goats. We had two nannies and a billy. We was brought up on goats' milk, all the lot of us. My old mum swore you could get the tubercular from cows' milk. Lor' bless you, I can milk old Dotty's – I mean Miss Harmer's – Dulcie, with one hand tied behind me.'

He waved the dripping dish mop confidently.

'It's uncommonly good of you, Albert,' said the rector. 'I shall pay you myself while the arrangements last, of course. And I'm quite sure that Miss Harmer would want you to have any surplus milk. It would do your indigestion good, I'm sure.'

'I always enjoyed a mug of goats' milk,' said Albert. 'And my cat'd help out.'

'Then that's settled then,' said Charles, getting to his feet. He gazed thoughtfully at the bowl of filthy water in the sink.

'Is there any hot water in the kettle?' he asked.

'Plenty. Want a cup of tea?'

'No, thank you, Albert. I'm having tea with Miss Bembridge who will be so grateful to you for coping night and morning with Dulcie's bounty. No, I just thought that some fresh hot water might make your present task easier. I fear I interrupted your work.'

'They're clean enough by now, I reckon,' said Albert, casting a perfunctory glance at his handiwork. 'They'll soon be dirty again time I've used 'em. Housework's a thankless job at the best of times. Fit only for women, I always say.'

Charles, thankful that no woman was present to take up the cudgels, hastened out into the fresh air of Thrush Green.


The summer term proceeded with increasing activity, as Sports Day, Open Day, a Leavers' Service and end of term examinations all took place during the last few weeks.

Dorothy and Agnes coped with their usual efficiency, but both confessed to being inordinately tired one summer evening.

'You have every excuse,' Agnes told her friend. 'After all, the responsibility of the school's running falls largely upon your shoulders, and you have to be ready at any time to meet parents and managers and people from the office whenever any problem crops up. As well as coping with your poor leg,' she added.

'I greatly fear,' replied Miss Watson, 'that it's old age as well. So often I have told friends that they can't expect to get through as much work as they did when they were twenty years younger. Now I realize that I ought to take my own advice, but somehow, Agnes, one never thinks of oneself as old.'

There was a note of dejection in her voice which aroused Agnes's immediate sympathy.

'You do too much, you know. I hesitate to put myself forward, Dorothy, but I would willingly take on some of your less important duties if it would help.'

'I know you would. You are a great support and comfort, but I really think that the time has come to make a decision about retirement. I'm fifty-nine in a fortnight's time, and I intend to let the office know unofficially, early next term, that I propose to go at the end of the next school year.'

'Whatever you decide to do will be right, I am sure,' said loyal little Miss Fogerty, 'but won't it be a terrible wrench?'

'It will be *whenever* I go,' said Dorothy. 'But I shall feel much happier if I can see the end in sight. Can you remember how much in advance one's official resignation has to go in?'

'Three months, I think.'

'Then I shall put mine in at the end of the spring term. Plenty of time for advertisements to go in. Thrush Green School should draw many applicants. It's a pleasant spot to live in, and an efficient school, although perhaps it's not my place to say so.'

'You are quite the right person to say so. And whoever takes on the job will have you to thank for a splendidly working and happy school.'

'Thank you, Agnes, but I don't forget my staff too. The one big problem now is where we shall live. Do you still favour Barton-on-Sea, or somewhere close by?'

'It sounds perfect.'

'Well, I propose that we both spend a few days there when we break up, and have a look at some of the properties the agents have sent. We can stay at that nice little boarding house, and take our time over things. Agreed?'

'Yes, indeed, Dorothy. I shall look forward to it.'

Miss Watson gave a sigh.

'It will be a comfort to start moving towards retirement. And best of all, Agnes dear, to know that you feel you can be happy there with me. We must go into ways and means one evening when we feel more energetic, but I think my savings should be enough to find us somewhere modestly comfortable.'

'I hope you will use mine too,' said Agnes. 'Now, can I get you anything? Something to drink? Something to read? Your knitting?'

'What about a game of "Scrabble"? Always so soothing, I think.'

And little Miss Fogerty hastened to get out the board.


To the surprise of all Thrush Green, Albert Piggott approached his new duties with comparative zest.

He was observed setting off soon after eight in the morning towards Dotty's and again about six in the evening. Ella's milk was delivered as usual, on his return at night, and Betty Bell's left in the cool larder at

Dotty's for her to collect on her way home from her many duties at Thrush Green.

Dulcie, always a generous nanny with her milk, seemed to take to Albert, and he carried home a plentiful supply for himself and his cat. Both appeared to flourish on it, and although Albert was teased by his usual colleagues at The Two Pheasants because he took to asking for a half a pint of bitter instead of a pint, he put up with their joking with unusual good temper.

'It's a durn sight better dealing with animals than that church and graveyard,' he told them. 'That Dulcie's got more sense than any of you lot here. We gets on a treat. Goats is intelligent animals. And that's more'n you can say for men.'

'You'll be getting fat,' someone said, 'swigging down milk.'

'It's my belief it's doin' me good,' declared Albert. 'Wonderful soothing to the stummick. I reckon I'll buy some regular from Miss Harmer when she gets back. Saves me cooking too. Doctor Lovell said himself as milk's a *whole food*, and he's nobody's fool.'

To Ella's delight, he also offered to feed the hens and ducks in the mornings to save her making two trips a day. Such a change of heart in such a curmudgeonly character made a fascinating topic for the inhabitants of Thrush Green, and all agreed that Charles Henstock never did a better day's work than calling on Albert for help.

Meanwhile, Dotty remained in hospital. Her recovery was being very slow so that she had plenty of time to think things over.

She was a surprisingly good patient. When some of the nursing staff had discovered that Dotty was in the women's ward there had been misgivings. Dotty's eccentricity was only exceeded by her obstinacy, as was well known in Lulling. The reputation of her fearsome father was still remembered, and in fact one of the doctors attached to the hospital was a former pupil of his, and could tell blood-curdling accounts of his late headmaster's disciplinary methods.

But, in truth, Dotty was a realist, and quite prepared to endure cheerfully what had to be. She saw now, as she rested against her pillows, that she had been foolish to think that she could cope with her energetic way of life without properly fuelling the machine which was her ageing body.

She accepted the nurses' ministrations with grace and gratitude. She believed the doctor, who remembered her father, when he told her gravely of the risks she ran by neglecting herself. He made it clear to her why she had been suffering from dizziness, why her back had a perpetual ache, why her legs throbbed and her heart palpitated so alarmingly. She would have to alter her way of life, he told her. If she intended to keep so many animals then she must have help. There really should be somebody living in the house with her. Had she thought of giving up altogether, and going to live in an old people's home? He could recommend several, very comfortable places, and with a warden to keep an eye on things.

To Dotty, the prospect appeared bleak in the extreme. Not that she had anything against homes for old people, and in fact her regular visits to local alms houses had always been enjoyable, during her father's lifetime, when she was younger and took on such duties. And several of her friends lived in just such places as Doctor Stokes mentioned, and seemed remarkably happy with their little coffee parties and handiwork, and visits to the hairdresser and chiropodist obligingly laid on by more mobile friends.

But Dotty knew quite well that such a way of life would never do for her.

For one thing, she would be *tidied up*. The haphazard clutter of objects, beneath her own thatched roof, which constituted home for Dotty, would have to be sorted out, given away or just put on the bonfire. She did not think that she could face such upheaval.

And then the thought of living without any animals was quite insupportable. To Dotty, her animal friends were far more dear than her human ones. Like Walt Whitman she could easily 'turn and live with the animals, so placid and self-contained'. They demanded so little and gave so much in return. She appreciated, with the poet, that:

> They do not sweat and whine about their condition,
> They do not lie awake in the dark and weep for their sins

and that they faced life with the same robustness as she herself faced it. The idea of living in a home, no matter how warm, clean and cared for she might be, but without even one animal for company, could not be borne.

She came in the end to a compromise. As the animals died, she would not replace them. She could not betray them by giving them away unless it were possible to place them in as perfect a setting as their present one. Perhaps young Jeremy Hurst might like two of the rabbits? Or Joan Young's Paul? They would be well cared for there, she knew.

The chickens and ducks were elderly, and Mr Jones from The Two Pheasants would dispatch them humanely when their time came, as he usually did. And she must resist the temptation to buy more pullets, or to put twelve lovely pearly eggs under a broody hen. How she would miss yellow chicks running around!

The cats had been spayed, luckily, so that there would be no more kittens, sad though the thought was. As for Dulcie and Flossie they must stay on, and for a very long time too, Dotty hoped. She had been amazed to hear how willingly Albert Piggott had coped with the milking. With luck, he might be persuaded to continue, and of course, once Dulcie was dry, there must be no more mating.

Well, it was all very sad, thought Dotty, and gave a great sigh. A little fair-haired probationer nurse hurried to her side.

'All right, Miss Harmer?'

'Yes, thank you, nurse. I was only making a few plans for the future. Rather exhausting.'

'Like a cup of tea?' asked the girl, offering the panacea for all ills.

'Do you know,' said Dotty, sitting up and straightening her bed jacket, 'that would be most acceptable. Only a little milk and no sugar, please.'

She was feeling better already.

## 16. Sunday Lunch at the Misses Lovelock's

One Sunday morning the Misses Lovelock fluttered along Lulling High Street to St John's church. This large and beautiful building stood in an open space south of the town, and its tall spire was a landmark for many miles around.

It was three times the size of St Andrew's at Thrush Green and was noted for its stained glass windows, dating from the sixteenth century. Throughout the summer, coach loads of tourists came to see the church and to take photographs, particularly of the fine east window above the altar.

In their younger days, the Misses Lovelock had taken their turn in manning the modest stall near the vestry where books and pamphlets, bookmarks and slides of the outstanding features of St John's were on sale. Invariably, after their visit, the tourists wandered across the green into the High Street and sought tea at The Fuchsia Bush.

It was this recollection which formed the theme of their conversation as they proceeded towards morning service.

'I really can't think that The Fuchsia Bush is any better off for closing at tea time. Why, only yesterday, Violet, I saw a coach stop, and the driver banging on the door. There were quite thirty people on board, and I'm sure they all looked the sort who would want sandwiches, scones and home-made cakes.'

'Some,' said Miss Violet, with a sniff, 'looked as though they would want fish and chips as well.'

'What I'm trying to say, dear,' pointed out Miss Ada, 'is that The Fuchsia Bush is turning away good money.'

'Well, they get it at night, I suppose, at dinner time.'

'I think not. I was talking to one of the staff at the fishmonger's and she says they are never more than half full. People are finding it too expensive, she said, and prefer to eat at home.'

'And very sensible too,' put in Miss Bertha. 'I only hope that The Fuchsia Bush will see the folly of its ways, and remember that it is there to *serve* people. And people want *tea* from four o'clock onward. And if they desire to partake of fish and chips then, why shouldn't they find it provided?'

She gave a stern look at Miss Violet who pretended not to see, but rearranged a dove-grey glove.

'Winnie Bailey was wondering if a petition might be a good idea, with lots of signatures, you know, to persuade the management to open again at tea time.'

Bertha bridled.

'I shall certainly not append my signature. I do not intend to kow-tow for the sake of a cup of tea which I can brew for myself rather better next door.'

'I was thinking of the visitors, Bertha,' ventured Violet.

At that moment, the chiming of the church bells changed to one steady tolling of the tenor bell.

'We must step lively,' said Bertha, quickening her pace. 'It looks as though our hall clock must be running slow.'

During the sermon, Violet allowed her gaze to dwell on the glowing glass of the famous window. To be sure, she had never been able to see with absolute clarity just what the pictures showed. She knew that the incidents depicted were the draught of fishes, Jairus's daughter, and the miracle of water turning into wine. The illustrated pamphlet told her so. The colours were really magnificent, but there were so many pieces of glass in each picture, and all so intricately interposed, with those squiggly worms of lead everywhere, that she had often wondered if that really was a net full of fishes (Herring, perhaps? Surely not in the Sea of Galilee?) or simply the lower part of the fishermen's robes. Not perhaps the most *practical* garment for a fisherman, when one came to consider it.

Thus musing, she let her eyes pass from the mystery of the windows to the frank and handsome face of dear Anthony Bull as he stood declaiming in his beautiful voice.

What an actor he would have made, thought Violet! Such a presence, such manly beauty, such clarity of diction! And he really gave very sound sermons, nothing too highbrow and yet not patronizingly simple, as though his congregation was composed of non-intellectuals. This morning's subject, for instance, on the theme of good fellowship and the need to consider the feelings of others in everyday life, was being very well expressed.

She only hoped that Bertha, who could be rather unnecessarily tart at times, was listening attentively. How lucky they were in Lulling to have such a fine vicar! He really deserved a larger and more knowledgeable congregation than this quarter-filled church. A *better house*, thought Violet, was how it would be put in theatrical circles. Certainly, such a star performer, she decided, admiring a graceful gesture of his hands, deserved a truly discriminating audience, and no doubt he would have one some day.

Meanwhile, it was to be hoped that he would remain the vicar of Lulling for many a long day, delighting them all with his outstanding looks, his kindly manner and the genuine goodness of his way of life.

Sunday lunch at the Lovelocks' was always cold. Violet had set the table before going to church. Starched linen, heavy silver and Waterford glass dressed the table with splendour. It was a pity that the meal set upon it was so sparse.

Six thin slices of corned beef were flanked on one side by a Coalport dish containing sliced cold potatoes, and on the other by equally gelid carrots. A beautiful little cut glass bowl contained beetroot in vinegar. Liquid refreshment to accompany this inspired course consisted of lemon barley water in a glass jug covered with a lace cloth beaded round the edge.

'A very good sermon this morning,' commented Bertha, chewing her corned beef carefully with her few remaining teeth.

'Such a pity there were not more to hear it,' agreed Violet. 'I was thinking so in church.'

'Well, we appreciate dear Anthony even if we are only a few,' said Ada. 'I think we can pride ourselves on being discriminating here in Lulling. We are very lucky to have him.'

Bertha cut a ring of beetroot carefully in half.

'But for how long, I wonder?' she said.

Her two elderly sisters gazed at her with curiosity. Had Bertha heard a rumour? And if so, from whom? And why had they not been told?

Bertha attempted to assume an air of nonchalance under their scrutiny. She was not very successful.

'Oh, it was just a chance remark of Mrs Bull's when I saw her at the draper's yesterday. She was buying some hat elastic.'

'Bertha, people don't buy *hat* elastic these days!' cried Violet.

'Well, no, but I imagine she needed it for her undergarments, and one wouldn't want to ask for *knicker* elastic in a public place.'

'*Knicker* or *hat*,' pronounced Ada, 'is beside the point. What did she say?'

'Oh, something about changes in the air, and Anthony much perturbed about decisions to be made.'

The two sisters looked disappointed.

'That could be anything from altering the site of the compost heap in the churchyard, to replacing those dreadfully shabby hassocks in the Lady Chapel,' said Ada.

'Or some little matter of church ritual,' added Violet, putting her knife and fork neatly across her empty plate.

'Maybe, maybe!' agreed Bertha airily. 'Well, time alone will tell.'

She rose and collected the plates. When she returned she was bearing a full dish full of glossy black cherries.

'A present from dear Colonel Fisher yesterday evening,' she said, 'when you were both in the garden. I thought I would keep them as a surprise for dessert today.'

'Do you remember how we used to hang them over our ears?' said Violet, picking up a pair. 'We used to pretend the black ones were jet earrings and the red ones were ruby.'

The three old faces glowed at the memory, Anthony Bull's affairs forgotten in the excitement of this delicious surprise.

'I remember it as if it were yesterday,' declared Ada. 'You were always the pretty one, Violet, with your fair hair. The red cherries suited you best.'

'We were all pretty children,' said Bertha firmly, 'though no one would think so to see us now. Still, we are clean and healthy, and I suppose that is something at our age.'

They enjoyed their cherries, removing the stones politely from their mouths, behind delicately curved bony hands.

Later they stacked the china and silver in the kitchen to attend to later, and went into the sunshine to rest.

The sun warmed their old bones and Bertha yawned.

Violet began to giggle.

'Do you know, Bertha dear, your tongue is as purple as a chow's!'

'Really? No doubt yours is too after eating black cherries.'

The three old ladies put out their tongues and surveyed each other's. Laughter shook their thin frames, and for a brief moment they reverted to the three little girls who had played in this same sunlit garden, wearing starched pinafores and cherry ear-rings, over seventy years earlier.


A week or two later, the problem of Dotty Harmer's convalescence arose. Ella Bembridge had offered to have her at her cottage, but Winnie Bailey, secretly fearing that Ella's home might not provide the peace which Dotty would need for a week or two, suggested to her old friend that the invalid might stay with her.

'The spare room is empty, as you know, Ella dear, and Jenny is longing to do a bit of spoiling. We are both in the rudest of health now, and it would be a real pleasure to have Dotty. You've done more than your share with Flossie and the other animals.'

Ella gave in with good grace.

'Well, to tell you the truth, I am rather behind with my weaving, and the garden's been neglected. Not that I mind much, first things first, you know, but if you're quite sure, I'm happy about it.'

It was arranged that Harold Shoosmith and Isobel would collect Dotty, and Flossie would be transferred to Winnie's to be reunited with her mistress.

And so, one August afternoon, Harold and Isobel set off in the car, which had been polished for the occasion, to fetch their old friend.

She still looked remarkably frail and her steps were faltering as she made her way to the car on the arm of matron – a high honour not lightly bestowed. But Dotty's spirit was unquenched, and she chatted cheerfully all the way along Lulling High Street, up the hill, and past Ella's cottage, the gap left by the destroyed rectory, and the grass of Thrush Green.

Winnie welcomed her with a kiss and Flossie with ecstatic barking. Harold and Isobel promised to call the next morning, and then withdrew, leaving Winnie and Dotty alone in the sitting room.

Dotty's thin hands were caressing Flossie's long ears as she gazed happily about her.

'I can't tell you how good it is to be here. They were so *very* kind to me at the hospital, but I pray that I may never need to go there again.'

'Well, I hope you will stop with me for as long as you like,' said Winnie. 'You must get your strength back, you know.'

'My strength?' exclaimed Dotty in amazement. 'But I am quite strong now, Winnie. I shall thoroughly enjoy staying overnight here, but of course I must get back to the animals tomorrow morning.'

'We'll talk about that later,' said Winnie diplomatically. 'But now I am going to ask Jenny to make the tea.'

'How is she?' asked Jenny when Winnie appeared in the kitchen.

'The same old Miss Harmer,' Winnie told her, with a smile.

'Oh dear!' cried Jenny. 'That means we might have trouble!'


Dotty's niece, Connie Harmer, had kept in touch with her aunt's Thrush Green friends throughout Dotty's illness, and had driven some fifty miles from her home at Friarscombe to see the old lady in hospital.

She was a sturdy woman in her forties, with auburn hair now streaked with grey, and a square weatherbeaten face. She was as much attached to the animals as was her aunt, and perhaps this was why she had never married, finding the human race, and particularly the male of the species, very much inferior to her own charges.

The Henstocks, Ella Bembridge and Winnie Bailey were old friends of hers, and were glad to see her when she came to see Dotty in her hospital bed. She was frank with them all.

'It's like this. I'm quite willing to have dear old Aunt Dot to live with me, but will she come? If she's too groggy to cope alone at Lulling Woods, I'd certainly consider selling up and making my home with her, if that seems the right thing to do, but I don't relish the prospect, and that's the truth. In any case, I'd need a month or two to make arrangements for some of the animals, and selling the house would take time.'

'Let's see how things go,' said Winnie, at whose house this conversation took place. 'It's best that she convalesces here, near Doctor Lovell, and we'll all keep in touch. But somehow, Connie, I can't see any of us persuading Dotty to leave that cottage of hers.'

'Nor me. Ah well, she's lucky to have such noble friends around her, and you know I'm willing to take on any permanent responsibility when the time comes. I've always been very fond of Aunt Dot, crazy though she is at times.'

'That goes for us all,' Winnie told her.

Luckily, Dotty was soon persuaded to continue to stay at Winnie's for at least another week, and appeared to have forgotten her resolve to rush back to the animals by the next morning.

It was one of the disconcerting things about the invalid at this time. She was vague about time. 'Let's say more than usually vague,' amended Charles Henstock, and although Doctor Lovell was optimistic about the full recovery of his patient, even he admitted that Dotty would be better in the permanent company of someone like her reliable niece.

It was while she was still recuperating that Lulling was agog to learn that the Misses Lovelock had been summoned to the local police station to view some pieces of silverware which had come into the hands of the police.

Full of hope, the three sisters tottered along one bright morning, stopping only by the Exchange to read some extraordinary messages, written in chalk, on the walls of that building. The words were not familiar to the three ladies, but the content of the slogans was. The writer presumably did not approve of the Prime Minister nor of the country's police force.

'But, Violet,' said Ada in bewilderment, 'does one spell that word like that?'

'Ada dear,' said Violet, with some hauteur, 'it is not a word that I find myself needing to spell.'

Bertha, as usual, took charge.

'We must draw the attention of the officer on duty to this defacement, when we call in. I'm sure he will deal quite competently with the matter, correct spelling or not. It is not the sort of matter for ladies to concern themselves with.'

'Should you end your sentence with a proposition, Bertha?' asked Violet innocently.

But she was ignored, and the three mounted the steps of the police station.


Sadly, there was only one of the Lovelocks' lost objects among the display set out on the trestle table in a back room with Police Constable Darwin on guard.

'Father's rose bowl!' cried Ada.

'What a miracle!' cried Violet.

'Given to him on his retirement!' cried Bertha. 'How wonderful of you to recover it.'

They walked slowly round and round the table, gloating over the beautiful objects before them.

'And where did you find all these lovely things, officer? So clever of you.'

'Well, miss,' said Police Constable Darwin, 'I'm not at liberty to say, but it wasn't us chaps at Lulling as came across this lot. But several people, besides you ladies, have lost stuff around here, so it's our turn to show it.'

'And have the other people found theirs here?'

'You was the first to be asked,' the constable told them.

'Well, that is most gratifying. Most kind. We feel quite honoured, I assure you. Now, are we allowed to take home Father's rose bowl?'

'I'm afraid not, miss. It'll have to be exhibited in court, see, when we've picked up the thieves. There's still a lot missing. If you notice, miss, all this is the big stuff, salvers and bowls and that.'

With commendable delicacy he ignored a seventeenth century toilet set, with a pair of silver chamber pots to match, and directed the Misses Lovelock's attention to trays, tea pots and other tableware, including the rose bowl, which stood at the farther end of the table.

'We reckon this is only about a quarter of what's missing. The smaller stuff's probably been passed on. Melted down already, I don't doubt.'

There were horrified gasps from the ladies, and Police Constable Darwin hastily tried to make amends for his gaffe.

'But let's hope not. After all, this lot's turned up. Keep your fingers crossed, ladies. Anyway, I'll mark this rose bowl down in the book as belonging to you. Want another look round to make sure?'

'No, thank you, officer. You have been most helpful. There was just one other little matter,' added Bertha, the natural spokesman of all three.

'Yes, miss?'

'Have you been on outside duty this morning? On your beat, I believe is the correct expression?'

'Well, no, miss. I was detailed by Sergeant Brown to stand by this lot this morning. Very valuable stuff here. But I'll pass on any message.'

Bertha wondered if this fresh-faced young man would really be experienced enough to deal with the unpleasant matter of the Corn Exchange's graffiti, but she decided swiftly that he had probably been adequately trained and was quite used to seeing – and perhaps even hearing – the phrases written on the wall.

'We just wanted to direct your attention, officer, to some quite dreadful messages written with some prominence on a public building near by.'

'Oh, them scribbles on the Corn Exchange,' replied the constable, with relief. He had begun to wonder just what else these old tabbies were going to disclose. 'Don't you worry about them. One of the Cooke boys, no doubt. Anyway, young Armstrong's been told off to clean it up, so everything's under control.'

'I'm delighted to hear it,' said Bertha graciously.

'In very bad taste to deface a building with such words,' added Ada in support.

'And not even correctly spelt,' said Violet, adding her mite.

'I think,' said Bertha ominously, 'it is time we returned home.'


## 17. Housing Plans

The first two weeks of the summer holidays were spent by Miss Watson and Miss Fogerty in recuperating from the rigours of the term.

They also managed to fit in a number of personal arrangements which had been postponed during term time. Miss Watson had her hair permanently waved, one troublesome tooth extracted and two filled, and several shopping expeditions for new corsets and other underwear.

Miss Fogerty, whose hair was straight 'as a yard of pump water', as she said, dressed it in a neat bun, and washed it herself. She did, however, need to visit the dentist who luckily only found one filling which needed attention. Her modest shopping resulted in a new flowered overall for school use, a pair of light sandals, and a petticoat. She was sorely tempted to buy a navy blue jersey suit, reduced in the summer sales, but with the possibility of helping with the purchase of a shared home she decided it would be imprudent to spend too lavishly.

The friends had reserved rooms at their favourite Barton guest house on the front for two weeks from the middle of August, and both ladies looked forward to the break eagerly. The discussion of money affairs about the buying of a permanent home there did not take place until a day or two before their departure. Dorothy Watson had obviously given the matter much thought.

'Now, I know just how independent you are, Agnes dear, and I very much appreciate your offer to help in buying a place to share, but I've decided against it.'

'But, Dorothy –' protested Agnes, but was cut short. Miss Watson was at her most decisive, a schoolteacher at her firmest and fairest.

'It's like this. I should like to buy the house so that I can alter my will and leave it, with any other little things of value I might have, to be shared between my three nephews. I do not intend to leave anything to Ray and Kathleen apart from my mother's tea service which I know Ray would like. They have quite enough as it is, and I consider that they have forfeited any claim on my property after their dreadful behaviour. But I like the three boys, and I think they are making their way in the world quite splendidly, despite their parents.'

'Yes, I do see that, Dorothy, but nevertheless –'

Miss Watson drove on relentlessly.

'Of course, I shan't see you left without a roof over your head, Agnes dear, should I go first. The house will be left so that you can stay there for as long as you wish, and when you have done with it, then the three boys shall have it.'

'Oh, Dorothy, you are too good! But I pray that I may go first.'

'First or second, Agnes, hear me out. I've given a great deal of thought to this matter. Now, if you *insist* on putting something towards this venture –'

'I do. I do indeed!'

'Then I suggest that you could contribute to the furnishings which we are bound to need. No carpet or curtain ever seems to fit a new home, and I'm sure we shall need various extras, and possibly redecoration, although I think we should share that expense.'

'I agree wholeheartedly with anything you suggest, Dorothy, but it really isn't enough from me. At least I can pay rent, surely?'

'I was coming to that. If you feel that you can pay the same amount as you do here, Agnes, it would be a very great help, believe me. Now, what do you think?'

'I think you are being uncommonly generous, as always, Dorothy.'

'Well, it seems the simplest and most straightforward way of arranging things. I thought I might go and put the matter to Justin Venables. He will deal with things if we do find somewhere, and I should like him to know what we have in mind. Will you come with me? I only hope he won't retire before we've finished with his services. One wonders if those youngsters in the firm have quite the same wisdom as dear Justin.'

'Of course I will come. And I don't think we need to have any doubts about the junior partners, Dorothy. I am sure that Justin has trained them quite beautifully.'

'Let's hope so,' said Dorothy. 'And now that that's over, I think I'll go and look out some of my clothes ready for packing.'

'And so will I,' replied little Miss Fogerty.

The two ladies retired to their bedrooms, one congratulating herself on a difficult matter successfully dealt with, and the other to think, yet again, about the boundless generosity of her friend.

The abrupt conclusion of Percy Hodge's courtship of Jenny had occasioned plenty of comment at the time, but as the weeks had gone by other topics had taken its place until Percy's suit had almost been forgotten, if not by Jenny, at least by the majority of Thrush Green's inhabitants.

It was some surprise then to Harold Shoosmith when Betty Bell, crashing about in his study with the vacuum cleaner, shouted the information that Percy was looking elsewhere for a wife.

To tell the truth, Harold had not heard clearly for the racket around him, and was on the point of fleeing to more peaceful pastures.

Betty, seeing that she might be baulked of her prey, switched off the machine and began to wind up the cord.

'Percy! You know, Percy Hodge as was hanging up his hat to Jenny at Mrs Bailey's,' she explained.

'What about him?'

'I just told you. He's courting someone else now.'

'Well, good luck to him. No harm in angling elsewhere if he hasn't succeeded in landing his first fish.'

'I don't know as Jenny'd care to be called a fish,' said Betty, bending down to wind the cord carefully into figures of eight on the cleaner's handle.

Harold watched this manoeuvre with resignation. If he had asked Betty once to desist from this practice which cracked the cord's covering he had beseeched her twenty times. It made no difference. At some point in her career, Betty had decided to wind cords in a figure of eight style, and stuck to it.

'Well, who is it, Betty? Come on now. You know you're dying to tell me. Someone we know?'

'You might, and you might not. Ever been up The Drovers' Arms?'

'Beyond Lulling Woods? No, I can't say I have. Does the lady live there?'

'Works there. Name of Doris. She cleans up, and helps behind the bar of a Saturday. She's from foreign parts, they say.'

'Really? What, Spain, France, or further afield?'

Betty looked shocked.

'Oh, not *that* foreign! I mean she speaks English and goes to our church. No, she's from Devon, I think, or maybe Cornwall. A long way off, I know, but speaks very civil really.'

'And you think Percy calls there? It may be that they keep the sort of beer he prefers.'

'Percy Hodge,' said Betty, setting her arms akimbo and speaking with emphasis, 'was always content to have his half-pint at The Two Pheasants. What call has he got to traipse all the way to The Drovers' Arms, unless he's courting? Besides, he's always carrying a great bunch of flowers, and he gives 'em to this Doris.'

'Ah!' agreed Harold, 'that certainly sounds as though he means business. I hope you all approve at Lulling Woods?'

'Well, he could do a lot worse. She's a hefty lump, and can turn her hand to helping on the farm, I'm sure. Clean too, and cooks quite nice. Not as good as Percy's Gertie, I don't suppose. She was famous for her pastry and sponges. But still, this Doris can do a plain roast, they tell me, and is a dab hand at jam making. She should do very nicely, we reckon.'

'I'm glad she's approved,' said Harold gravely, 'and I hope that Percy will soon be made happy.'

He nodded towards the cleaner.

'Finished in here?'

'I wondered if you'd like your windows done. They look pretty grimy from your tobacco smoke.'

'Better leave them,' said Harold, deciding to ignore the side swipe at his pipe. 'No doubt Mrs Shoosmith will tell you the most urgent jobs.'

'Come to think of it,' said Betty, trundling the cleaner towards the door, 'she's waiting for me to help turn the beds. It flew right out of my head with you chatting away to me.'

She vanished before Harold could think of a suitable retort.

That same afternoon, Ella Bembridge left her cottage to post a letter at the box on the wall at the corner of Thrush Green.

It was warm and still, and she was just wondering if she would take a walk along the lane to Nidden to call on Dimity and Charles when she saw her old friend approaching along the avenue of chestnut trees.

Dimity was on the same errand with a half a dozen letters in her hand.

'Coming back with me?' inquired Ella, after their greetings.

'I mustn't, Ella. I've a nice joint of bacon simmering away, so I can't be long. Charles has gone sick visiting at Nidden.'

'Well, let's sit down for a minute or two here,' replied Ella, making her way to one of the public seats generously provided for exhausted wayfarers at Thrush Green. 'Heard any more about your housing plans?'

Dimity looked perturbed.

'Not really, but Charles had a letter this morning confirming these rumours about amalgamating the parishes.'

'First I've heard of it,' announced Ella. 'What's it all about?'

'Well, Anthony Bull's two parishes of Lulling and Lulling Woods are to be merged with Charles's Thrush Green and Nidden.'

'Good heavens! Anthony will have a massive parish to work, won't he?'

'It looks like it.'

Ella suddenly became conscious of Dimity's agitation.

'And what happens to Charles?'

'Nobody knows. All the letter gave was the news that the four parishes would be merged.'

'Do you think this is the reason for not hearing about rebuilding the rectory?'

'It looks very much like it. I simply can't get Charles to do anything about it, although I've done my best to press him to make inquiries. We really ought to know where we stand. It is all most worrying. I'm so afraid he will now be moved. If it is too far from Lulling and Thrush Green, as it might well be, I shall be so lost without all our old friends.'

Dimity sounded tearful, and Ella patted her thin hand comfortingly.

'Cheer up, Dim! Worse troubles at sea! You'll probably hear in a day or two that building's beginning on the old spot over there, and you'll have a spanking new place to live in.'

'Somehow I don't think so. I'm afraid any spanking new place we have to live in will be miles away.'

She blew her nose forcefully, and jumped to her feet.

'Well, it's been a comfort to talk to you, Ella, as always, but I must get back to the bacon. You shall be the first to know if we hear anything definite.'

She hurried away across the green, and Ella returned more slowly and thoughtfully to her own house.

As it happened, it was Edward Young, the architect, who heard more about the empty site at Thrush Green.

The rumour reached him by way of an acquaintance who was on one of the planning committees.

'About eighteenth hand,' Edward told Joan, 'so one takes it with a pinch of salt, but I think there's something brewing all right. Evidently, the Church is putting it on the market and the local council would like to buy it.'

'But what for?'

'Well, it's only a small area, but this chap seemed to think that a neat little one-storey unit of, say, four or six houses for old people might be put there. Actually, he said there were plenty of tottering old bods at Thrush Green that could do with them.'

'He's not far wrong,' commented Joan.

'Or perhaps a health clinic. I think that's a better idea myself. The one at Lulling's had its day, and it's a long way to walk there. Particularly if you are pregnant like our Molly.'

'It would certainly be useful,' said Joan. 'Which do you think it will be?'

'My dear good girl, don't ask me! You know what these rumours are. But I'm pretty sure he's right about the site being sold. And we'll keep a sharp eye on what gets put up on it, believe me. We've had our years of penance with that eyesore of a Victorian rectory. I hope our children will see something less horrific in its place one day.'

The day of Dorothy and Agnes's departure to Barton dawned bright and clear. The taxi had been ordered for ten o'clock to take them to Lulling Station, and the pair were up early.

Harold and Isobel called to collect the key and to get last minute directions as they had offered to keep an eye on their next-door neighbours' property.

They had been told about the proposed house-hunting and were full of good advice. Both Isobel and Harold had gone through this exhausting experience within the last few years, and did not envy the two ladies. But they heartily endorsed Miss Watson's desire to retire at the age of sixty, although they wondered if her successor would be quite so good a neighbour. Time would tell.

Meanwhile, they urged them to enjoy their break, promised to look after the premises, and waved them on their way.

'I shall miss Agnes dreadfully,' said Isobel, as they returned to their garden. 'She means a lot to me.'

'It only takes an hour or so to drive to Barton,' replied Harold. 'We'll make a point of visiting them as often as you like.'

Naturally, the Shoosmiths said nothing about Miss Watson's future plans, but nevertheless it was soon common knowledge in Thrush Green that she was going to retire and planned to live elsewhere.

'We shall miss them both,' Winnie Bailey said to Frank and Phil Hurst. 'Miss Watson's been a marvellous headmistress, and dear little Agnes is a real institution. It won't be easy to replace two such dedicated women.'

'Well,' said Frank, 'they're doing the right thing to get away while they still have their health and strength.'

'And sanity!' quipped Phil. 'At times Jeremy alone drives me mad. How they can cope with dozens of them round them all day beats me.'

'They finish at four,' said Frank. 'And look at the holidays they get!'

'They certainly do not finish at four,' said Winnie firmly. 'I've often seen the light on at the school and I know those two have been getting something prepared for next day. I wouldn't want their job for all the tea in China.'

Comment at The Two Pheasants was less complimentary.

'Time old Aggie packed it in,' said one. 'Why, she taught my mum as well as me! Must be nearly seventy.'

'But Miss Watson don't look that age! Mind you, she's no beauty, but she've kept the colour of her hair, and still hobbles about quite brisk with that bad leg of hers.'

'Living at Bournemouth, I hear.'

'I heard it was Barton.'

'Well, somewhere where all the old dears go. Bet that'll cost 'em something to find a house in those parts.'

And this gloomy prognosis gave them a pleasurable topic for the rest of the evening.

Meanwhile, the two holiday-makers were finding the property was indeed expensive, especially of the type they had in mind.

The house agents who attended to them all pointed out, with depressing unanimity, the fact that most retiring people wanted just such a place as they were seeking, small, easily-run, with a view, but not too much garden.

'Of course, people come from all over England, and particularly from the north, to enjoy our milder climate,' said one exquisitely dressed young man. 'There are always plenty of clients – usually elderly – who are waiting for something suitable. It won't be easy to find you exactly what you want.'

This was the fifth estate agent's they had visited that day. Dorothy's feet hurt, and her temper was getting short.

'I imagine that these elderly clients of yours die fairly frequently,' she said tartly.

The young man looked startled.

'Well, of course, in the fullness of time they er – pass on.'

'In which case there must be vacancies cropping up,' pointed out Miss Watson. 'You know what we are seeking. Please keep us informed.'

She swept out before the young man could reply, followed by her equally exhausted friend.

'No more today, Agnes,' she said. 'Let's go back to the hotel for a cup of tea, and I will write a few postcards when we've had a rest. Isobel and Harold were absolutely right. House-hunting needs a great deal of stamina.'

After tea, the two sat on the veranda with their tired legs resting on footstools. Agnes was busy knitting a frock for Molly Curdle's expected baby and Dorothy busily filled in her postcards.

'I shall send one to Ray and Kathleen,' she said, sorting through half a dozen on her lap. 'So much easier than writing them a letter which, in any case, they don't deserve. Still, I should like them to know our plans. What about this one of the sunset? Or do you think they would like this clump of pine trees?'

Agnes, sucking the end of her knitting needle, gave both pictures her earnest attention.

'I think the sunset,' she decided.

Dorothy nodded, and set to work, as Agnes returned to counting her stitches. She wrote:

Very much enjoying a few days here. Good weather and comfortable hotel.

Also looking for a house, as I am planning to retire next year. Agnes joins me in sending

Love,<br>Dorothy

'There,' said she, thumping on a stamp, 'that should give them something to think about. I've two more to do, and then perhaps we might walk along to the pillar box if you are not too tired.'

'I should like to,' said Agnes, obliging as ever. 'I have only to finish my decreasing and I shall be ready.'

The two ladies bent again to their tasks, while overhead the gulls wheeled and cried, and a refreshing breeze from the sea lifted their spirits.

## 18. Help Needed

Dotty Harmer returned to her cottage after ten days with Winnie Bailey. To everyone's relief, Connie came to Lulling Woods each week, staying overnight and seeing that the larder was stocked, the laundry done and that Dotty was taking her pills.

Albert Piggott, of his own volition, offered to continue to milk Dulcie. The two had become very fond of each other, and whether the free milk, enjoyed by Albert and his fast-fattening cat, had anything to do with the arrangement, no one could say, but everything worked out well for everybody.

Betty Bell called in each morning on her way to work, and often on her return, and Ella and the Henstocks called frequently.

It was not the ideal arrangement, for it was quite apparent that Dotty needed a constant companion, but it was the best that the community could devise for someone as independent and headstrong as Dotty. They were aware that Connie was keeping a sharp eye on things, and knew that she would come to the rescue if need be.

Meanwhile, Dotty began to put into practice some of the good resolutions she had made in the hospital. Within a month of her return, the ducks had been dispatched and their remains rested in the deep freezer of the Lulling butcher. Jeremy was the doting owner of two rabbits: ('Of the same sex, *please*,' Phyllida had begged), and although Paul Young could not take on any more pets as he was now away at school during term time, he knew someone in Lulling who would give two more rabbits a kind home. Some of the more elderly chickens ended their lives humanely and became boiling fowls for Dotty's friends, and very soon the animal population at Dotty's home was halved.

She was philosophical about these changes, and also did her best to feed herself more adequately. She had promised Doctor Lovell that she would sit down at midday to eat a meal.

'Even if it is only a boiled egg and some milky coffee,' he told her.

'You'll be back in hospital if you neglect yourself. And after the meal, you are to lie down on the bed for a full hour. Understand?'

The threat of hospital kept Dotty obedient to his demands, although she found it a terrible waste of time. But gone were the days, she realized, when she chewed an apple for lunch as she stood by the stove stirring the chicken's mash.

Lying down on her bed seemed even worse – positively sinful to be so slothful. However, she found that she frequently fell asleep during her enforced rest, and so grudgingly admitted that young Doctor Lovell must be speaking the truth when he said that she would be bound to tire easily for some time.

Still, she told herself, with every day that passed she must be getting stronger, and with Albert to manage Dulcie, and kind friends rallying to her support, she told herself that everything would be back to normal in no time.

Albert Piggott's daughter, Molly Curdle, was particularly pleased to see the improvement in her father's health.

'You know,' she said to Ben one evening, 'it's not just the milk that's setting him up. It's having a job that he likes.'

'Well, it certainly seems to suit the old boy,' agreed Ben. 'And I've a feeling he'd be better off helping out with animals round here somewhere, than trying to keep the church going.'

'It'd be ideal. I know he don't really pull his weight as sexton, and never has, to tell the truth. But these days some of the work's too heavy for the old chap. I wondered if we might have a word about it with Mr Henstock. What d'you think?'

Ben looked thoughtful.

'Best have a talk to your Dad first in case he cuts up rough. Might think you're interfering. But if he don't mind, I'll speak to the rector. I reckon he might be pleased to get someone to take proper care of the church and graveyard. At the moment they're both a shocking sight. Coke crunching underfoot whenever you walk in church, and weeds up to your knees round the graves. It must vex the rector, and plenty'd complain, but you know Mr Henstock! Too good by half!'

'I'll speak to Dad this week,' promised Molly.

To her relief, Albert agreed with uncommon docility that the work was too much for him, and that he would welcome some help. He was not quite so keen to accede to Molly's suggestion that more work with animals might be found, if he liked the idea.

'Depends what sort of animals,' he said. 'I ain't going to Percy Hodge's, for instance, to muck out his cow shed. That'd be jumpin' from the frying pan into the fire. But I don't mind helping out with pets like Miss Harmer's.'

'Well, I'm sure Mr Henstock will have some ideas,' said Molly hastily. 'Ben might mention it when he sees him.'

Charles Henstock was as pleased as Molly at the turn of events. For a long time he had realized that his curmudgeonly sexton and caretaker was not doing the job satisfactorily. He had hesitated to call him to account for two reasons. First, was there anyone else willing to take on the work, and second, would Albert be hurt to be thought incapable of carrying on?

With Ben's disclosures it was plain that the second difficulty was overcome. If Albert were given the lighter duties, such as sweeping, dusting and cleaning the silver and brass-work, then the outside duties in the graveyard, and the heavy work of keeping the boiler filled with coke, could be offered to a younger and more energetic man.

'The snag is,' said Ben, voicing the rector's fears, 'there don't seem to be many suitable chaps available. Of course, Bobby Cooke has given our Dad a hand now and again in the past – but them Cookes –' His voice trailed away.

The rector replied cheerfully.

'Well, I know that the Cookes as a family do tend to be a little *feckless*, but Bobby as the eldest child was always more *reliable* Poor Mrs Cooke had so many children, and so fast, you know, that I think the later arrivals were somewhat neglected.'

No one, thought Ben, could have put the Cookes' case so kindly as the rector. On the whole, the tribe was dismissed as dirty, dishonest and a disgrace to Nidden and Thrush Green.

'And I happen to know,' went on the good rector, 'that poor Bobby Cooke was made redundant – if that is the correct expression – last week, from the corn merchant's. He may be glad to take on some of Albert's duties. I could certainly find out.'

'I'm sure you'll do what's right, sir,' said Ben. 'It would be a great weight off our shoulders if we could see the old man settled.'

'I shall do my best,' said Charles. 'And how is Molly keeping? When is the baby due?'

'Around Christmas,' Ben said.

'Ah! Then I shall look forward to a christening in the New Year.

Another little Curdle to greet! We still remember your wonderful grand-mother here, Ben.'

'I never forget her. Never for a day,' replied Ben soberly.

And Charles Henstock knew that this serious young fellow was speaking the truth.

After a remarkably dry summer, the latter part of August turned cold and wet.

Luckily, the bulk of the corn crop was gathered in, and although strongly denied by the local farmers it had been a good year.

Not, of course, that this made the farmers happy. A good harvest meant that prices would be low, and that ruin faced them. A poor harvest meant that they had little to sell and so, equally, ruin faced them. Farmers have always had hard lives.

'No good trying to please 'em,' declared Albert in The Two Pheasants. 'If the weather's right for the turnips, it's all wrong for the wheat. And if the sun shines for hay-making, it's too dry for the kale to grow. Farmers is kittle-cattle, to my way of thinking. Always on the moan.'

'He can talk,' observed one to his neighbour, but he said it behind his hand. 'Is that what Percy Hodge does?' he inquired more loudly. 'Moan, I mean?'

There was general laughter.

'Percy's too taken up with that Doris up The Drovers' Arms to worry over much about harvest this year. Come October I'll bet he's getting wed, with all the other young farming chaps.'

'But his Gertie's not cold in her grave,' cried one.

'She's been gone over a year,' said his drinking companion. 'I bet that house of Percy's could do with a spring clean by now.'

'His sister, Mrs Jenner, goes in now and again, they tell me. She'll see him right. Pity Jenny wouldn't take him on, but then why should she?'

'If you ask me,' said Albert, although nobody had, 'girls is too choosy by half these days. Comes of learning 'em the same as boys. They wants a good wage, see, and forgets they ought to be glad to look after a good husband for the love of it.'

There was a short silence after Albert's little speech. Most of them were thinking privately of Albert's wife Nelly. She certainly hadn't had a good husband, and one could hardly blame her for leaving Albert's abode to take up residence with that oil man chap who, though markedly unpopular with the males in Thrush Green, seemed to have had a way with the women.

And that, both sexes would agree, was a quality singularly lacking in Albert Piggott.

'Well,' said one at last, putting his tankard down, 'I'd best get back to work.'

He opened the door, and a squall of wind and rain blew in.

'Looks like summer's gone,' he commented, as he went out into the wet.

Rain streamed down the windows of the local school-house as Miss Watson and Miss Fogerty unpacked after their holiday.

They had returned much refreshed, although little progress had been made with their plans for buying a house. However, they had met several house agents who promised to keep them informed about suitable properties as they became available, and from what the two ladies had seen they were even more sure that Barton and its immediate neighbourhood would suit them both very well. Their efforts had not been wasted.

'How lucky we were to have such a fine spell,' remarked Agnes, gazing out at the driving rain veiling the houses on the farther side of Thrush Green. 'Somehow I don't mind a bit if we get rain now. It's quite restful, isn't it?'

'It is while we're still on holiday, Agnes dear. But quite a different kettle of fish if it continues into the beginning of term next week. You know how fractious infants get if they are cooped up indoors.'

'I do indeed,' said little Miss Fogerty, with feeling. 'By the way, I've sorted out the post, and your letters are on the dresser. Not much for me, I'm thankful to say, but a pretty card from Isobel's daughter on holiday in Ceylon. Always so thoughtful.'

'You mean Sri Lanka,' corrected Dorothy, turning her attention to the pile of letters.

'I shall always think of it as Ceylon,' said Agnes, with gentle dignity. 'Fancy asking one's friends if they would like China or Sri Lanka tea!'

It was an hour or so later, when the two ladies were enjoying a cup of the latter, that Dorothy opened the letter from her brother Ray.

'Well!' she exclaimed, putting down her cup with a crash. 'Of all the effrontery! Really, Agnes, Ray and Kathleen would try the patience of a saint! Do you know what Ray is asking?'

She tapped the letter with her teaspoon.

'Listen to this: "If you are getting rid of any of your furniture when you move, would you please let us have first refusal of the following." And then, my dear, he gives a list of about *twenty* of my best pieces of furniture! What a cheek! What a nerve! I've a good mind to ring him – after six, of course – and tell him what I think of his grasping ways.'

Agnes, recognizing the flushed cheeks and heaving cardigan as danger signals, assumed her most soothing air.

'Don't upset yourself over such a thing. I should ignore the letter, and if he writes again, or telephones, you can answer him then.'

'I expect you are right,' conceded Miss Watson, stuffing the objectionable message into the envelope. 'And in any case, now that the telephone charges have gone up again, it would be a most expensive call.'

'Have another cup of tea,' said Miss Fogerty diplomatically, and refilled the cup.

Across the green, Phyllida Hurst was also drinking tea, with Winnie Bailey. She had called to deliver the parish magazine, and had been divested of her dripping mackintosh and persuaded to stop for a while.

'Have you heard this rumour about Albert getting some help with the church?' asked Phil.

'Dimity said it's pretty certain that Bobby Cooke is going to do the heavy stuff. Albert seems to be past digging graves and humping coke about.'

'Wasn't he always?'

Winnie laughed.

'Well, he hasn't exactly strained himself over any of his duties, all the time I've known him, but I think he really does need some help now. The Cooke boy is as strong as an ox.'

'And about as bright, I'm told.'

'At least he's honest,' responded Winnie, 'and you can't say that about the rest of the family.'

'And speaking of church matters, is there anything in this tale about Anthony Bull leaving St John's?'

'I've heard nothing except from Bertha Lovelock, and it's my belief she's got hold of the wrong end of the stick. Not that one would be surprised to hear of his advancement. He's much too decorative and ambitious to stay long here, I fear. He always reminds me of dear Owen Nares.'

'I never came across him,' confessed Phil.

Winnie sighed.

'It's at times like this that I realize how old I'm getting,' she said. 'But what's your news? Any more lecture tours?'

'Yes indeed. They want us to go again next year. I'm not sure if I shall accompany Frank though. In any case, we don't intend to let the house again. That was rather a disaster I feel.'

'No harm done,' Winnie assured her. 'And don't forget, I will caretake very willingly. And Jenny will help too. It's a great relief to me that she is still with me.'

'And likely to remain here, I imagine,' said Phil, getting up. 'I must be on my way, rain or no rain. We see Percy sometimes ploughing along with a nice bunch of roses for Jenny's successor. Does she mind, do you think?'

'Frankly, I believe she's relieved. It was an embarrassment to her to have the poor fellow calling here so often, and she's quite sincere, I'm sure, in saying that she's happier as she is.'

'It's all worked out well then,' replied Phil. 'Better to be single than unhappily married,' she added as she went into the porch.

Winnie watched her splash down the path.

'Poor Phil,' she thought. 'She knows all about an unhappy marriage. Thank goodness this second one has turned out so satisfactorily.'

The rain grew heavier as darkness fell, and by ten o'clock a strong wind added to the unpleasantness of the night.

It tore the leaves from the horsechestnut trees on Thrush Green, and buffeted Nathaniel Patten as he stood on his plinth, gazing with sightless eyes upon his windswept birthplace. It howled round the gravestones in St Andrew's churchyard and screamed down the alleyway by Albert Piggott's cottage.

The signboard at The Two Pheasants creaked as it swung, and very few inhabitants of Thrush Green dared to open a window more than a slit in the face of such violence.

Charles Henstock, lying awake at Nidden, listened to the tapping of the plum tree's branch against the window pane. The old house creaked now and again, and occasionally gave a shudder as the full force of the gale caught it, but it stood as sturdily four-square as it had done for centuries, and it was a comfort to be in such a solidly constructed building.

There was no doubt about it, Charles told himself, he had grown uncommonly fond of this ancient farmhouse and would miss its mellow beauty when they had to leave. Of course, a new house would have advantages, but there was something about an old loved house, where generations had lived, which gave one a comforting sense of continuity.

He realized now that his old rectory had never provided such a consolation to the spirit. It was not only the bleakness of its position and its poorly planned interior. This earlier house, where now he awaited sleep beside his slumbering wife, had an indefinable feeling of happiness. Perhaps builders in Georgian times enjoyed their work more than their Victorian successors? Perhaps the families who had lived here were contented with their lot, and their happiness had left its mark? Whatever the cause, Charles thanked God for giving him this pleasant place in which to recover from the shock of that disastrous fire.

He hoped for, but was too modest to pray for, as pleasant a home in the future, but was confident that by putting his fate in God's hands all would be for the best. He was sorry that Dimity worried about the delay. He knew that most men in his position would press for information about any proposed plans, and would make demands about their rights.

Charles knew, as Dimity knew, that he was incapable of behaving in such a way. Before long, he would hear something. God would never desert him.

He remembered the story of the falling sparrow, turned his face into the pillow and, ignoring the storm raging outside, was comforted.

The next morning, the garden was littered with wet leaves and twigs.

Willie Marchant splashed up Mrs Jenner's path, and put a letter through the box.

The rector opened it carefully at the breakfast table. It was a beautiful thick cream-coloured envelope and bore a crest on the back.

The letter was short, and Dimity, watching its effect on her husband, felt some alarm.

'My dear,' said Charles, 'the Bishop wants to see me next Thursday afternoon. He doesn't say much, but I expect it is to do with the rearrangement of the parishes.'

'What time?' asked Dimity.

'Two-thirty, he says.'

'Well, I'll come too and you can drop me in the market square. I've so much shopping to do it will keep me busy while you are gallivanting with the Bishop.'

'I don't suppose we'll be *gallivanting*,' said Charles, smiling. 'But I've no doubt you will be able to get in two hours' shopping quite comfortably.'

And so the matter was left.

## *19. Charles Meets His Bishop*

The start of the new school year fell on the following Tuesday and, as the two friends feared, the wet weather still shrouded Thrush Green with veils of windswept rain.

Miss Fogerty's new arrivals were unusually tearful, and there were one or two trying mothers who wanted to stay with their offspring until they had cheered up. Little Miss Fogerty, who had been coping with the reception class for more years than she cared to remember, had great difficulty in shooing them away. She knew perfectly well that once their mothers had vanished the howlers would desist from their lamenting and would resign themselves, after vigorous nose-blowing organized by Miss Fogerty, to threading beads, making plasticine crumpets, or having a ride on the rocking horse.

But within an hour, peace reigned in the infants' room and Miss Fogerty had pinned up the weather chart, found two clean Virol jars to receive the bunches of asters and marigolds brought by the children, and decided to appoint George Curdle as blackboard monitor.

Dear George, for whom Miss Fogerty had a very soft spot, was becoming rather boastful about the new sister he was hoping for at the end of term, and a little energetic board cleaning might channel his energies usefully, thought his teacher. Besides, he would have the inestimable privilege of going outside with the board rubber now and again to free it of excessive chalk dust by banging it briskly against the school wall. To be appointed board monitor was recognized as an honour. George Curdle, she felt sure, would perform his duties with proper zeal.

Next door, Miss Watson's older children were busy writing their names on the covers of their new exercise books, exhorted by their teacher to be neat and clear in their calligraphy.

While they were thus seriously engaged, Miss Watson surveyed the rain-drenched view through the window and wondered if she would write or telephone to the office when informing them of her decision to retire. Of course, the formal resignation would be written, well in advance of the specified three months' notice required, but as her mind was now made up it would be helpful, no doubt, to the office to know her plans well ahead.

She turned to look at the bent heads, the carefully guided pens and the odd tongue protruding with the effort involved. Her last class! After all these years, her very last class!

Well, they looked a nice little lot, and she would do her level best by them. But a warm glow suffused her when she thought that this time next year she would probably be looking through the window of some charming little place at Barton, and admiring the sea in the distance.

Thrush Green had been a happy place to work in, and had brought her the ineffable good fortune of meeting dear Agnes, but she would not be sorry to go. A complete change of scene would do them both good, and Thrush Green, after all, would still be waiting for them whenever they wished to pay a visit to their old friends.

'I can see some *beautiful* writing,' said Miss Watson, limping down the aisle towards her desk. 'I think we are going to do some good work in here this year.'

Molly Curdle, dusting her flat at the top of the Youngs' lovely house, wondered if the rain would stop in time for George and the other children to have their break in the playground.

He had run off on his own to school this morning, looking forward to seeing his friends and Miss Fogerty again. No doubt, he'd be blabbing to all and sundry about the new baby, thought Molly resignedly. Not that she worried unduly. Most people knew now, anyway, that a second child was coming. She only hoped that it would be as amenable and happy as George.

Strange to think that in five years' time another little Curdle would be running to Thrush Green School! Who would be there to teach them then? Not Miss Watson and Miss Fogerty from all she had heard.

But of one thing she felt certain. She and Ben would still be at Thrush Green whatever occurred. In all his years of wandering with his grandmother's fair, this place was the nearest he had had as a settled home. Now old Mrs Curdle lay in the churchyard, and her grandson and great-grandson lived close by. Molly prayed that they might never have to move again.

She stooped, with some difficulty now that her pregnancy was advancing, and attended to the legs of the chairs. This afternoon, rain or no rain, she must go across to see her father and collect his washing, and hear his news.

Sometimes she wished that Nelly, trollop though she was, would return to look after her husband, but there was small chance of that, thought Molly, and one could hardly expect it.

Well, things could be a lot worse. She had her health and strength, and Ben was happy in his work.

If this new baby was a boy she was determined to call him Benjamin after his father. Ben had said it would be muddling to have two of the same name, but Molly was adamant.

'You can't have too much of a good thing,' she had told him. 'He'll be Ben – another Ben.'

'With any luck,' he had replied, 'it'll be a girl.'

Albert was newly returned from The Two Pheasants when his daughter called early that afternoon.

'Was just about to have a nap,' he grumbled. 'Come for the washin'?'

'That's right dad. How's the job? Seen young Cooke yet?'

Albert grunted.

'Ah! He's coming down one evenin' this week, so he says, to see what needs doing. Rector's coming too, and we're goin' to sort things out then.'

'What about wages? Will you have to share now with Bob Cooke?'

'Seems I'll be havin' a bit less, but that's only fair if I'm not doin' the work. Anyway, old Dotty's paying me well for the milking, and the rector wanted to know if I'd take on odd jobs like feeding people's hens and cats and that when they're on holiday. I've said I'll see to young Jeremy's rabbits when they go to Wales at Christmas – that sort of thing. Suit me fine, that will. Probably make as much like that as digging the dratted graves in this 'ere clay.'

Molly doubted it but kept her counsel. In any case, the old man's temper was better than it had been for many a long year which was all that really mattered.

'And Jones next door said he could always do with a hand with the empty beer crates at closing time, so I shall have plenty to do.'

'Will you get paid for that?' asked Molly suspiciously.

'Well, not in hard cash, like,' admitted Albert. 'More in kind.'

'I was afraid of that,' said Molly, picking up the bundle of washing.


After tea, the rain ceased. The clouds scudded from the west, leaving a strip of clear sky on the horizon. Lulling Woods stood out clearly, navy blue against the golden strip, and Jenny, looking from her window, guessed that tomorrow would bring a fine day. Perhaps she could take down the landing curtains? It would soon be the end of summer, she thought sadly, and time to put up the velvet curtains again to keep out the bitter winds of a Cotswold winter.

As she stood surveying the scene, a well-known figure trudged into sight from the lane to Nidden.

In earlier times, Jenny's heart would have sunk, for without doubt the man would have turned left along the chestnut avenue to approach her house.

Now, to her relief, she saw that Percy Hodge was plodding straight ahead, past The Two Pheasants, no doubt on his way to see his new love, Doris.

He was carrying a basket this evening. What delectable present was in it this time, Jenny wondered. A chicken, perhaps? A dozen pearly eggs? Some early plums? Whatever it was, Doris was more than welcome, thought Jenny cheerfully. She only hoped that Percy's second attempt at wooing would end successfully.

She remembered with amusement what Bessie had forecast. 'He'll soon find someone else,' she had said, 'if he's as nice a man as you say he is.'

Well, thank goodness he had found someone, decided Jenny. Whether he would be married again before the year was out, as her old friend had surmised, was in the lap of the gods, but at least she would be relieved to know that dear old Percy was settled.

She watched him turn down the lane by Albert Piggott's on his way to Lulling Woods and Doris.

And with a sigh of relief, and no regrets at all, Jenny turned back to her happy solitude.

Jenny's weather forecast was correct. The rain had gone, leaving a sodden countryside and dripping trees and gutters, but above the sky was clear and blue and there was a freshness in the air that made one think of autumn.

'Bit parky coming along,' cried Betty Bell, bursting in upon Harold and Isobel Shoosmith still at the kitchen breakfast table. 'Are you late or am I?'

'We've been taking our time,' replied Isobel. 'Lots of letters this morning. But we've finished now, and we'll get out of your way.'

'No hurry,' said Betty. 'I called to see Miss Harmer as I came by. Actually, I popped in last night after I'd done the school. She don't look right to me.'

'Oh dear! Is she eating properly?'

'Seems to be. I mean, she'd got a bowl of cornflakes this morning with some brown sugar on it, and Dulcie's milk. Nourishing, I should think, if you can face goat's milk and brown sugar. Which I can't, and that's a fact.'

'Shall I go down there, Betty?'

'I don't think I would today. She'd think I'd been telling tales, see? Anyway, Miss Connie comes this afternoon, and stays there tonight, so she'll have company.'

Betty tugged off her coat and hung it on a peg on the back of the kitchen door.

'If you haven't got any particular plans for me,' she said, 'I thought I'd have a bash at the china ornaments in the drawing room. They look a bit grubby.'

As the china ornaments were Chinese porcelain, very old, beautiful and valuable, it was hardly surprising that Harold winced. 'Having a bash' was exactly how Betty attacked her work.

Isobel, with habitual aplomb, coped beautifully with this kind offer.

'I'd rather hoped to turn out the spare room today, Betty. I'll come up and help you turn the mattress and we'll make up the bed.'

'Right,' said Betty, rummaging in the cupboard for the carpet sweeper, handbrush, dustpan, polish, dusters and other equipment for the on-slaught. 'See you pronto.'

She lugged the paraphernalia into the hall, and then returned.

'You know them two next door are going to leave next year?'

'Yes,' said Harold, folding his newspaper.

'And Albert Piggott's givin' up half his job?'

'Yes,' said Harold.

'And the Hursts are going to America again?'

Harold nodded.

'And they're not going to put up another house for poor Mr Henstock? Ain't it *mean*? There's going to be an ugly great clinic place there. Heard anything about that?'

'Not a word,' said Harold, rising from the breakfast table. 'And you don't want to believe all you hear, Betty.'

'Sorry I spoke!' said Betty, flouncing from the room.

Husband and wife exchanged rueful glances.


Charles Henstock polished his old car during the morning, ready to visit the Bishop promptly at two-thirty.

The Bishop detested unpunctuality and was not above saying so. Charles respected the great man's principles, and was determined not to offend.

'Let me just see how you look, dear,' Dimity said, before they set off.

She scrutinized her husband from his pink and shiny bald head to his old but gleaming shoes.

'Very nice, Charles, but do remember to pull up your socks before you go in. The Bishop is always so beautifully turned out. He's as immaculate as Anthony Bull, and that's saying something.'

'Anthony has a great advantage. He is a fine-looking fellow. Anything would look well on him. The last time I saw him he was tending his bonfire, and he still looked as though he had just emerged from a band box.'

Dimity privately thought that Anthony Bull's stipend allowed him to buy expensive suits made by his tailor, while dear Charles was obliged to purchase his off the peg. However, she did not voice this unworthy thought.

'Well, you look very well yourself,' she told Charles comfortingly, 'and now we must be off.'

The rain had freshened the countryside, and the shabby hedgerows of late summer were now sparkling with moisture. Already the ploughs were out, turning over the bright stubble into long wet chocolate furrows.

Dimity noted the yellowing leaves already showing on the beech and wild plum trees. Soon autumn would be upon them, and although she loved the mellowness, the rich colouring and the joys of bringing in the harvest fruit and vegetables, she felt a little shiver of apprehension about the cold weather to come.

The rectory had always been so bleak. Surely, wherever they went would be more comfortable than their last domain! Perhaps the Bishop would give Charles some firm idea of his plans for their new home. It was certainly most disconcerting to be kept in such suspense.

However, Charles knew her views well enough on this matter, and it was useless to try to make him assert himself. Charles was Charles – sweet, far too humble and a living saint. She would not have him changed one iota!

'If you drop me at the back of Debenham's,' she said, 'I can go through their bed-linen department, and you won't hold up the traffic by trying to stop at their main entrance.'

Charles did as he was told, promised to pick her up again at four o'clock, and set off, feeling a little nervous, to his appointment.


The Bishop lived in a fine red-brick house at the end of a long drive bordered with lime trees.

Charles parked his car in as unobtrusive a spot as possible beside a flourishing prunus tree, and tugged at the wrought-iron bell pull by the white front door.

A very spruce maid welcomed him and showed him into the Bishop's drawing room.

'I'll tell the Bishop you are here,' said the girl. 'At the moment he is telephoning.'

She departed, leaving Charles to admire the silver cups on a side table, and the oar hanging above the fireplace. The Bishop was a great oarsman, Charles remembered, a true muscular Christian. Perhaps that contributed to his good looks, thought Charles, and bent to pull up his wrinkled socks as Dimity had told him.

The solemnly ticking grandfather clock by the door said two minutes to the half hour when Charles heard the Bishop approaching.

He stood up as the door swung open.

'My dear fellow! I hope I haven't kept you waiting. You are wonderfully punctual. Come into my study. We'll be unmolested there.'

He strode through the hall, followed by the good rector who admired the clerical grey suit which clothed those broad shoulders and neat waist.

He certainly was a handsome fellow.

But at least, thought Charles, I remembered to pull up my socks.


Connie Harmer arrived at much the same time as the Bishop invited Charles to take a seat in the study.

She found her aunt resting obediently on her bed, kissed her affection-ately and inquired after her progress.

Connie's expression was as calm and competent as ever, but inwardly she was much alarmed. Dotty looked old and haggard. Her lips and cheeks wore a purplish tinge. She was definitely vaguer in manner than at her last visit.

'I'm dying for a cup of coffee,' said Connie, pulling off her driving gloves. 'I'll bring you one too.'

Dotty nodded dreamily in agreement, and Connie went downstairs.

Her first job was to ring Doctor Lovell. His receptionist promised to tell him the minute he returned from his rounds. Then she put on the kettle, and thought hard while it came to the boil.

Well, the time had come. She had made her plans, and friends had offered a good price for her house and land. Aunt Dot had always been good to her, and she could live very happily here in her cottage, bringing only a few of her most cherished animals to share the rest of their lives with Dotty's.

She carried the tray upstairs and put it down on the bedside table.

'There we are, Aunt Dot. And when you've finished it, we're going to have a little talk about the future.'

\*

At four o'clock Dimity waited in the vestibule at the rear entrance of Debenham's, surrounded by parcels.

Charles arrived soon after and they piled everything into the back of the car in great haste, as a van man drew up, practically touching Charles's back bumper with his own, and putting his head out of the window to address the rector.

From his accent he would appear to be a Glaswegian, thought Charles, and so – perhaps fortunately – his message was entirely incomprehensible to southern-English ears. His demeanour, however, was threatening and abusive, and Charles and Dimity were relieved to drive off.

'I was going to suggest that we had a cup of tea at Debenham's,' said Charles, 'but it wasn't a good place to park evidently. We'll stop at the Oak Tearooms instead. Anyway, they have quite the best toasted tea cake in the district.'

Dimity knew better than to question her husband while he was driving in traffic, and it was not until they were safely ensconced among the oak panelling and chintz curtaining of the renowned tearooms that she began.

'And how did you find the dear Bishop?'

'As upstanding as ever. He inquired most kindly after you. Ah! Here comes the girl!'

The girl was approximately the same age as the rector, must have weighed thirteen stone, and was dressed in a rather tight flowered coat overall.

'Could we have some of your delicious toasted tea cake? And a pot of China tea for two?'

The waitress wrote busily on a little pad.

'Any jam, honey or other preserve? We have our home-made apricot, mulberry and quince.'

'How lovely that sounds!' cried Dimity. 'Like a list of jams from Culpeper!'

'We only keep our own, madam,' said the girl with some hauteur.

'Then shall we try mulberry, dear?' asked Dimity. 'I don't think I've ever had it.'

The waitress added MJ to her pad and departed.

'And now tell me, what happened, Charles?'

The rector began to look quite shy.

'Did you know that Anthony Bull is leaving Lulling?'

'Really? Now you come to mention it, I believe Bertha Lovelock said something about it.'

The rector's look of shyness was replaced by one of startled exasperation.

'But how on earth could she know? It isn't general knowledge yet!'

'Well, you know how things get about in a small community,' said Dimity soothingly. 'Anyway, where's he going? Not retiring surely?'

'Far from it. He's been appointed to a splendid living in one of the Kensington parishes. Rather High Church, I gather, and a most beautiful building. Anthony will be just the man for it, the Bishop said. I'm so glad he has got preferment. I always felt that Lulling was only a stepping stone to greater things for Anthony.'

The waitress reappeared with the tray and set out the tea pot, milk jug, hot water container and a large dish covered with a silver lid.

A small bowl containing a wine-coloured confection aroused Dimity's interest.

'And this is the mulberry jam? What a beautiful colour.'

'We make it on the premises,' replied the waitress, thawing in the face of Dimity's enthusiasm. 'We have a tree in the garden. It is reputed to be a hundred and fifty years old.'

'How wonderful!'

The waitress made off again, and Dimity applied herself to pouring out the tea.

'But what about us, darling? Did he mention anything about our new house?'

'He did indeed. I think two of those sugar lumps. They seem rather small.'

'They're called *fairy* lumps, I believe,' said Dimity. 'Well, go on.'

'I'm afraid there won't be a new house, my dear.'

Dimity dropped the sugar lumps in her dismay.

'Not a new house? Then where on earth are we to go?'

Her husband had now bent down to retrieve the tongs from beneath the table. When he reappeared his face was very pink.

'To an old one, Dimity. I have been offered the living of the four merged parishes, and we should live at Lulling Vicarage.'

Dimity gazed at him open-mouthed.

'Charles!' she croaked at last. 'I can't believe it! That lovely, lovely house!'

'Don't cry, Dimity! Please don't cry,' begged Charles. 'Aren't you pleased?'

Dimity unfolded a snowy handkerchief and wiped her eyes.

'Of course I'm pleased. I'm just completely overwhelmed, that's all.

Oh, Charles dear, this is an honour you so richly deserve. Won't it be wonderful to have our own home at last?'

'I'm glad you are pleased. It means we shall still be among our friends, and I shall still be able to take services at St Andrew's.'

'And when do you take over?'

'Probably before Christmas. Anthony expects to be inducted in October or November.'

'And then we shall be able to move in,' said Dimity happily. She spread mulberry jam in reckless bounty upon a slice of tea cake. 'What a blessing I didn't fall for some curtaining remnants this afternoon. They would never have done for the vicarage windows.'

She looked with surprise at the jam dish.

'Oh dear, Charles! I seem to have taken all the mulberry preserve.'

'I think we might be able to afford some quince as well,' said Charles. 'By way of celebration, you know.'

And he raised a plump hand to summon the girl.

## 20. *Looking Ahead*

After the long dry summer, autumn came early to Thrush Green.

The great leaves of the chestnut avenue turned golden and soon the boys from the village school would be collecting conkers.

In the cottage gardens, Michaelmas daisies and goldenrod flourished, and Mr Jones began to wonder if his hanging baskets would last out their time before the first frosts came.

Ploughing and sowing was done, and the fields lay brown and bare. Busy housewives bottled the last of the fruit, the blackberries, the bramley apple slices, and the quartered pears, and added them to the richness of the earlier summer fruits in their store cupboards.

Ella Bembridge added two more handwoven scarves to her Christmas collection, and decided that she must buy a replacement for the tweed suit she had had for ten years, not to mention a stout pair of brogues ready for the winter.

Miss Fogerty and Miss Watson decided to go to their favourite guest house at Barton for half term at the end of October. At least three houses sounded hopeful, judging from the estate agents' information. Naturally, one expected them to over-egg the pudding a little, as Dorothy pointed out to her more trusting partner, but even so, things looked promising. It would be lovely to clinch a deal, and thank heaven they had no house of their own to dispose of, added Dorothy. With any luck, they should have a place of their own before the winter had passed.

The news of Charles's new appointment gave enormous pleasure to everyone.

'The ideal man!' said Harold. 'The Bishop's done the right thing.'

'And we shan't really lose you,' as Ella said to them both. 'I mean, you'll be nipping up to take early service just as usual, and Dimity can still get the crib ready for Christmas at St Andrew's.'

Connie Harmer arrived to take up residence with her aunt during November. The old lady appeared to be delighted at the arrangement, and her doctor and friends who had feared that she might suddenly dig in her heels and refuse to countenance any change in her way of life, breathed sighs of relief and welcomed Connie in their midst. Dotty herself was so absorbed in the half a dozen new animals of Connie's that her health seemed to be much improved, though, no doubt, as Betty Bell pointed out, Connie's cooking, which was first-class, had a hand in the old lady's improvement.

Doris, at The Drovers' Arms, displayed a pretty engagement ring, and Percy Hodge put up the banns at the end of November.

'And thank heaven for that!' said Jenny to Winnie. 'I must write and tell Bessie she was dead right!'

Albert Piggott continued to help at Dotty's and elsewhere when needed, and also found time to supervise Bobby Cooke's church duties. The young man received rather more kicks than ha'pence, but his upbringing had inured him to such discomforts and he seemed happy enough.

The most encouraging news for Thrush Green and Lulling came one afternoon at the beginning of December when a notice appeared on the door of The Fuchsia Bush in Lulling High Street.

THIS ESTABLISHMENT WILL BE OPEN FROM 9.30 A.M. UNTIL 6.00 P.M. IN FUTURE read the astonished passers-by.

'I hear they hope to get the Christmas shoppers in,' said Miss Bertha.

'And I heard that those evening meals never really caught on,' added Miss Violet.

'About time they realized that it is *tea* people want,' said Miss Ada, voicing the view of all.

It was during the last few frenzied days of Christmas shopping, when The Fuchsia Bush was certainly doing a roaring trade from four o'clock onwards, that Molly Curdle's baby was born.

'Just think,' said Winnie Bailey to Jenny. 'It weighed nine pounds!'

'Poor thing!' said Jenny. 'But at least it's a girl. I know Ben hoped it would be. I wonder what they'll call it? It was going to be another Ben, if it had been a boy.'

'I have a shrewd idea that it will be "Anne" after Ben's dear old grandma,' said Winnie. 'If she grows up as splendid as her namesake she won't hurt.'

One mild January afternoon a small entourage walked out from the Youngs' gate.

Skipping ahead was young George Curdle, unnaturally clean and tidy, from his watered-down hair to his well-polished shoes.

Behind him walked his mother, holding the new baby well-wrapped in the beautiful old shawl which had first enveloped Ben himself. Beyond his parents came Joan and Edward Young and Mrs Bassett, Joan's mother. Her father had promised to come to the christening tea, but did not feel equal to standing at the ceremony.

The air was soft and mild. It had a hint of springtime in it, and some early snowdrops and aconites, near the churchyard gate, made an encouraging sight. Against the church wall a shower of winter flowering jasmine spilled its yellow flowers.

As Ben passed his grandmother's tombstone he patted it approvingly, noting the name and date anew.

'Pity she can't be here to see this one named for her,' he said to his wife.

'Maybe she knows anyway,' was her reply, as they passed into the church porch.

# READ MORE IN PENGUIN

In every corner of the world, on every subject under the sun, Penguin represents quality and variety – the very best in publishing today.

For complete information about books available from Penguin – including Puffins, Penguin Classics and Arkana – and how to order them, write to us at the appropriate address below. Please note that for copyright reasons the selection of books varies from country to country.

**In the United Kingdom**: Please write to *Dept. EP, Penguin Books Ltd, Bath Road, Harmondsworth, West Drayton, Middlesex UB7 ODA*

**In the United States**: Please write to *Consumer Sales, Penguin USA, P.O. Box 999, Dept. 17109, Bergenfield, New Jersey 07621-0120.* VISA and MasterCard holders call 1-800-253-6476 to order Penguin titles

**In Canada**: Please write to *Penguin Books Canada Ltd, 10 Alcorn Avenue, Suite 300, Toronto, Ontario M4V 3B2*

**In Australia**: Please write to *Penguin Books Australia Ltd, P.O. Box 257, Ringwood, Victoria 3134*

**In New Zealand**: Please write to *Penguin Books (NZ) Ltd, Private Bag 102902, North Shore Mail Centre, Auckland 10*

**In India**: Please write to *Penguin Books India Pvt Ltd, 706 Eros Apartments, 56 Nehru Place, New Delhi 110 019*

**In the Netherlands**: Please write to *Penguin Books Netherlands bv, Postbus 3507, NL-1001 AH Amsterdam*

**In Germany**: Please write to *Penguin Books Deutschland GmbH, Metzlerstrasse 26, 60594 Frankfurt am Main*

**In Spain**: Please write to *Penguin Books S. A., Bravo Murillo 19, 1º B, 28015 Madrid*

**In Italy**: Please write to *Penguin Italia s.r.l., Via Felice Casati 20, I–20124 Milano*

**In France**: Please write to *Penguin France S. A., 17 rue Lejeune, F–31000 Toulouse*

**In Japan**: Please write to *Penguin Books Japan, Ishikiribashi Building, 2–5–4, Suido, Bunkyo-ku, Tokyo 112*

**In Greece**: Please write to *Penguin Hellas Ltd, Dimocritou 3, GR–106 71 Athens*

**In South Africa**: Please write to *Longman Penguin Southern Africa (Pty) Ltd, Private Bag X08, Bertsham 2013*

# BY THE SAME AUTHOR

'Miss Read, as a country dweller, has been blessed with a love of nature, a taste for every one of the dramas with which rural life is fraught, and a sense of humour' – Elizabeth Bowen in the *Tatler*

Miss Read's books about village life are written with charm, humour and charity to delight readers everywhere.

*Published in Penguin are:*

*Novels*

*Non-Fiction*

The Year at Thrush Green, A Peaceful Retirement *and* Farewell to Fairacre, *all read by June Whitfield, are available or forthcoming as Penguin Audiobooks.*

# BY THE SAME AUTHOR

*Miss Read omnibus editions in Penguin*

**Chronicles of Fairacre**

Humour, charm – and charity – blend in these three novels, *Village School*, *Village Diary* and *Storm in the Village*, to make up a refreshingly acute and astringent view of life in the country.

**Life at Thrush Green**

Bubbling with drama, quarrels, gossip and romance, life at Thrush Green is never dull ... This attractive omnibus edition contains *Thrush Green*, *Winter at Thrush Green* and *News from Thrush Green*.

**Further Chronicles of Fairacre**

Four much-loved books – *Miss Clare Remembers*, *Over the Gate*, *The Fairacre Festival* and *Emily Davis* – are collected in this volume.

**Fairacre Roundabout**

Life in Fairacre ebbs and flows with the seasons. Every face is familiar and each home reverberates with local news. And at the heart of the community is Miss Read, caught up in its joyful festivities – and its minor irritations. This delightful omnibus contains *Tyler's Row*, *Farther Afield* and *Village Affairs*.

**Christmas at Fairacre**

In this charming anthology of Christmas tales, past and present, some of the most memorable events ever to occur in and around Fairacre are recalled by Miss Read in the novels *Village Christmas*, *The Christmas Mouse* and *No Holly for Miss Quinn* and in additional short stories.

**Tales from Thrush Green**

Two of Miss Read's delightful novels of rural life, *Affairs at Thrush Green* and *At Home in Thrush Green*, have been brought together for this hugely enjoyable omnibus.